Antietam Affairs

Dennis Roumm

Nestor, with warmest regards

Copyright © 2024
All rights reserved. No part of this book may be reproduced or transmitted in any form or by any means, electronic or mechanical, including photocopying, recording or by any information storage and retrieval system without permission in writing from the publisher.

Rocinante Press—Marietta, Georgia
ISBN: 979-8-9914181-0-2
Hardcover ISBN: 979-8-9914181-2-6
eBook ISBN: 979-8991418119
Library of Congress Control Number: 2024919647
Title: *Antietam Affairs*
Author: Dennis Roumm
Digital distribution | 2024
Paperback | 2024

This is a work of fiction. The characters, names, incidents, places, and dialogue are products of the author's imagination, and are not to be construed as real.

Published in the United States by New Book Authors Publishing

Dedication

To my wife, Teresa, whose companionship and help has been my guiding star in bringing this book to print.

A special thanks to my friend, Gail McCauley: A true renaissance woman. It was her enthusiasm and encouragement that inspired me to stay the course and bring this work to fruition.

Epigraph

Those who have been under fire are moved to a greater sadness for those of all wars who lie in the ground as casualties of the conflict. Life ends for all reasons and at all ages, and the dying is the same whether young or old, in peace or war, in bed or in the street. But, for those who have sipped the bitter wine that pours from the cup of war and have died so violently as in the clash of two armies, their deaths are grieved more tragically by those who have drunk from the same cup and lived.

Chapter One

July 15, 1988

The stars seemed incredibly close to earth and the moon shone so brightly for being in its third quarter. Dave Cooper stood on a step stool and fastened the third bike onto the overhead rack on the van, then paused a moment to gaze at the night sky. There was something almost mystical about the evening, he thought; something unusual about this celestial display of heavenly bodies that served to lend a comfortable feeling for the beginning of his three-day vacation. He convinced himself it was a good omen, and hoped for a relaxing, long weekend.

Staring spellbound at the astral brilliance, he was interrupted by his nine-year-old son, Jeff, who stood on the steps of the porch and watched his father for a while. "Dad," Jeff finally asked. "Are there any big hills at—where are we going again?"

"Antietam," Dave answered him. "I'm not sure. I don't remember really well. It's been years since I was there. Why?" he asked, stepping down off the stool.

"Well, remember that big hill at Gettysburg?"

"Yeah. That was a lot of fun coasting down it, huh?"

"Yeah. It was. Are there any hills at Antietam?"

"I think so," Dave said. "I don't remember how they've laid the roads out, though. There's one big hill that I'm sure has to have a road up to it. It's right on the other side of this stone bridge that's there. "Burnside's Bridge," it's called. The Confederate army was on the other side of it—up on a hill. There weren't a whole lot of them, but General Burnside, a Union general, threw thousands of men against that bridge trying to cross Antietam Creek. Thousands of men streaming forward—and everybody trying to get across that one bridge not even two lanes wide—all bottle-necked up and being cut to pieces by the Confederates."

"Oh," Jeff said as he stood listening, fascinated.

"And you know what the tragedy is about the whole thing? Nobody checked how deep the water was. Hell! They could have waded across and not been any more wet then to their chests."

"Huh?" Jeff exclaimed in amazement.

"Yeah! It's true. Something like 14,000 men trying to get across to the west side of the stream, most of them over that bridge, and they could have just waded over."

Dave took the last bike and wheeled it into position to be lifted onto the overhead rack.

"Need any help?" Jeff asked as he came off the steps and closer to the van.

"No. I don't think so. This is the last one," Dave said as he gripped the blue ten-speed bike and raised it over his head.

Jeff watched his dad with admiration as the man carefully climbed first one, then the second step of the stool, then eased the bike into the tire rail.

"Whew!" Dave gasped as the bike was quickly secured to the uprights. "I don't want to do this all day long. Glad that's done."

The strain was not as great on him as David Cooper led his son to believe. At five foot nine inches tall and one hundred seventy-five pounds he was in great shape for his thirty-eight years. At thirty-five, he had started taking karate classes and earned a black belt a year later. Though he finally had to give up formal instructions because of a lack of time, he still kept fit by working out regularly or getting up early in the morning to jog with Carol, his wife of fourteen years.

"Tim Johnson wouldn't need a ladder to do that," Jeff said, grinning at his dad.

"Tim Johnson is six foot four. It's not often he needs a ladder for anything," Dave chuckled.

"I know. He's tall!" Jeff exclaimed. "How long will it take us to get there?"

"Where? Antietam? I don't know. Four hours, maybe. Not sure. I've got to check the map again. We're going to get up early, though. You can sleep in the seat."

"I know. Mom says Sarah and I are responsible for remembering our own pillows."

"Good. Try and remember them."

"I will."

"Okay," Dave said as he stepped down from the stool after securing the bike. "I guess I'm ready to bring out the camping gear. You gonna' help?"

"Yeah. Mom wants me to get the bike bags first," Jeff answered.

"Good. We'll need them on the bike trip."

Dave turned to head into the house but Jeff stood there a moment, a quizzical look on his young face. "Dad. Remember that picture of that dead soldier at Gettysburg? The one in Devil's Den."

"Yeah. That's a famous picture. 'Course, it was posed, you know. Remember I told you that? He didn't really die right there like that. Mathew

Brady, the guy that took the picture, pulled him into that position. He figured to sell more pictures, I guess. And it worked. Why?"

"Well...I was going to ask you, 'how do you suppose he died'?"

"What do you mean, 'how'?"

"Well, do you think he got hit in the stomach, or what? Where did he get hit? There weren't any holes in his head or anything."

"I don't know," Dave said as he put his arm around the boy. He paused a moment in thought. "Maybe he got hit with shrapnel. A shell could have burst nearby and a piece bounced against his head. It's hard to tell."

"Do you think he got hit in the stomach?" Jeff asked, not wanting to drop the subject.

"Could be. That was a terrible way to die back then. That's called 'gut shot,' and there was nothing to do for it but lie there and wait for death."

"How would you die from that?" Jeff asked.

"I'm not certain. Bleed to death, if you were lucky. Probably peritonitis, though. That's when your stomach contents enter your system and poison you slowly and painfully. Some soldiers would pay their buddies, or plead with them, anyway, to shoot them dead so they wouldn't have to suffer in agony."

"Eww..." Jeff shuddered as his mind quickly envisioned that. "That'd be terrible."

"Which, to die that way or to have to have somebody shoot you so you'd die quick?"

"All of it," Jeff said, looking saddened now that he'd listened to this.

"I know. Wars are terrible to have...and everyone knows it. But we keep on having them," Dave said. He, too, was now a bit downcast. Experience had been his teacher.

Jeff looked up at his dad, his head cocked in curiosity. "Why do we have them, then?"

"Humph! Politics." Dave replied emphatically, a touch of anger in his voice. "Politics and greed."

"Huh?"

"Someone, or some group, wants to have control over another group...and, of course, the other side doesn't want that. Or, one group wants to have the land claimed by another group—so they fight. Oh, there are all sorts of reasons people go to war, and it all comes down to greed." Dave looked up into the night sky as if in search of a better answer that might suddenly appear written across the heavens. When nothing was revealed, he shrugged and hugged his son to him. "C'mon. We better get packing so we can go tomorrow."

"Okay," Jeff said a bit uneasy. He moved sluggishly as he trailed his father to the door.

Dave noticed and stopped on the porch till Jeff caught up with him. "Listen. Don't think about any of that right now. I went through that whole death and destruction scene years ago and I try not to think about it. It really sends me down when I do. Just be happy. We're going on vacation tomorrow! Camping; biking; fishing. Hey! We're gonna have fun. Save the sorrow and the reverence for the battlefield. That's why they're preserved. You're to think about things like suffering and death and the cruelties of war when you stand on the field. Don't let that drag you down right now."

He hugged the boy to him. "It's good you have a deep feeling for the people that have died in wars; the agony and the suffering people can go through. Hold those feelings forever and do whatever you can to avoid or end a war you feel is unjust. Remember what Lincoln said: 'that those men shall not have died in vain.' That's real important," Dave said, trying to reassure the boy, yet not to sound too depressing. "C'mon. Help me carry out the camping gear."

"Okay," Jeff said, trying to sound a bit more 'up.'

As they entered the modest ranch-style house, they both went to the stairway off the kitchen that led down to the basement. Jeff headed for a closet in the remodeled game room section of the cellar to search for the bike packs. Dave went to the unfinished, dimly lit side, one entire wall of which was lined with shelving.

Arranged somewhat in order, at least to the eye of the one whose job it was of arranging them—Dave's—were canned goods, fishing and camping gear, old toys, paint cans and brushes, and other miscellaneous items commonly stored from sight of visitors. Dave looked at the pile of camping gear on the floor before the shelves. He'd been laying out the familiar items necessary for the expedition during the last week, checking off each against a list that seemed to grow longer every year.

As he began to lug the first armful of equipment up the stairs, he mused over how they seemed to have expanded on the "bare necessities" for camping and surviving in the "wilds" of a KOA campground. "The older I get the more comforts I need," he said to himself. And though he still enjoyed doing most of the cooking over an open fire, the camp stove always came along...as did the air mattresses, bed pillows, shower flip-flops, blow dryer, and anything else that could be stuffed and squeezed into every nook in the van.

Outside, with the first load of gear delivered, Dave raised the neatly rolled tent over his head and set it into place on the roof rack. He grabbed a sleeping bag in each hand and climbed the three steps of the stool, placing them next to the tent, then turned and jumped off the stool onto the hard surface of the driveway. He paused for just a second and, like a flash of lightening, a veiled memory burst through from his subconscious to reveal itself as vividly as when he'd actually experienced it. He was dressed in camouflage fatigues, a .45

automatic in his hand, standing in a field. "Oh, God! No!" he murmured aloud. He blinked his eyes several times and shook his head in an effort to will away any of the recurring, chilling thoughts of that dark period in his life. He tried to move his legs in the hope that he could walk away from the memory, but it was upon him. He gave in and stood motionless in the driveway wondering why, after so many years, one of the old ghosts had again crept back as they sometimes used to at the most unexpected moments, triggered by even so simple an act as jumping off a stool.

In a dreamlike haze he could see the choppers setting down quickly in a clearing about a half mile behind the skirmish lines. The sounds of the battle that raged up ahead sent shivers through his spine—the quick whistle and sudden explosion of mortar shells; the rattle of machine gun fire; intermittent spatterings of automatic weapons being fired by nervous and excited men.

"Go! Go! Go!" shouted the chopper door gunner, and a dozen men hurriedly exited the machine, spreading out, staying low, their instincts keeping them alert and aware.

As the wave of helicopters took off, more came in behind. A big fight was building. The men just delivered began to push forward, making their way toward the woodline. Hurrying. Glancing to their sergeant or lieutenant for directions. As they moved on, others came behind; the scene repeated over again many times.

Dave Cooper came with 2nd Platoon of A Company on the third wave in. Jumping out onto the grassy field he looked quickly for directions from his captain and spied the man talking to the battalion colonel. The captain signaled to him, directing him forward and to the left, and as Dave repeated the signal to his men a runner scurried over to him from the captain:

"Lieutenant, the 'old man' wants you to take the platoons in alongside B Company. There's a ridge about two klicks over to the left. Set up along there," the man shouted over the din of confusion.

"What's the situation, Sergeant?" Dave asked as the man had already started to turn to leave.

"All hell's broke loose, Sir. Whole brigade will be in here before this is over and done." And with that the man headed off, running back to join the colonel and the captain who were huddled over a map with a radioman.

Two of Dave's platoon sergeants came hurrying over. He told them what he'd learned and what it was he wanted them to do. As they hurried to take the men forward, Dave felt a slap on the back.

"'bout time you got your company out here with us. The whole fuckin' V.C. army is coming down on us," the man grinned in greeting.

It was Sam Baker, First Lieutenant, B Company. Sam was a Chicago University computer science graduate who, like Dave, had been in ROTC.

Unlike Dave, Sam had graduated with honors and was now paying back the government with four years of his life for helping to put him through school.

Dave, on the other hand, had partied more than he'd studied. When he'd flunked out at the end of his junior year and his 2-s deferment had expired he was drafted into the army. He'd managed to enter O.C.S. and now, a lieutenant of A Company, six months "in country," he and Sam had grown to become close friends in an occupation where your friends often weren't around long—especially lieutenants.

Sam was in his ninth month in Vietnam. Twenty-one years old, he was married to a strikingly beautiful but very overweight woman. Three years his senior, she taught history to tenth graders somewhere in suburban Chicago.

Dave had seen her picture, for Sam always carried it in his helmet. Just before entering a fire fight, he'd pop the steel pot off his head, glance at the picture and mumble something unintelligible, then replace it. This done, an odd change would come over him. His fighting blood would get up and he'd become another person. From the kind, reserved, six-foot-one inch gentleman that he most often was, he'd turn into some blood-chilling, frightening battle machine that seemed to thrive on this type of dangerous action. He carried a .45 automatic in one hand and a machete in the other, waving the long, razor-sharp weapon so dramatically and fiercely as he shouted orders that even his own men would shudder as they fought with him.

Only a month ago they had been together in a jeep returning from a staff meeting at battalion headquarters. Captain John Fails and Chief Warrant Officer Tom Smith had accompanied them, the four drinking whiskey as they raced along the dirt roads in the jungle. As they raised a trail of dust down a narrow cut that served as a road for transports between base camps they could see a disabled truck up ahead, the hood raised as if mechanical trouble had caused it to stop dead in the center of the narrow road.

Dave pulled to a stop well back from the stalled vehicle.

The four officers armed themselves with their .45's—Sam drawing out his machete, as well—and slowly, cautiously approached the truck.

A fatigue-clad soldier stood on the fender, leaning into the engine compartment, seeming to ignore the approaching party. When they had neared to within thirty yards of the truck Sam halted them. He looked at the man a moment, studying him, then raised his pistol and took aim at the man's back. "Ambush!" Sam hollered, and fired a bullet into the soldier's head.

Instantly Dave and Sam jumped to one side of the road and took refuge behind a fallen log. The other two dove behind a pushed-up mound of dirt created in the excavation of the road.

Muzzle flashes and flying lead from the woods before them proved Sam was correct, they had walked into an ambush.

"Fuck!" Dave yelled above the rattle of automatic weapons. "How the fuck did you know?"

"Grunts don't wear sandals," Sam said. He quickly stuck the barrel of his .45 over the tree and squeezed off a few rounds in the direction of the bullets that came thumping into their protective log.

Dave did likewise, holding his pistol just at the edge of the log and emptying a clip into the trees ahead. As he reloaded from his cartridge belt he glanced quickly at his friend—then looked again in amazement. Sam's breath was short and deep, almost snorting. His nostrils flared; face reddened; his chest huffed up—he seemed taller and broader than his usual one hundred eighty-pound frame.

"Can't be...more 'n...six or eight of 'em...," Sam hissed through clenched teeth. "C'mon! Let's rush 'em!"

"What?" Dave said, astonished. "Are you fucking crazy?"

"Come on! What choice do we have?" he said, his blood boiling now.

"Fuck you!" Dave shot back. "We can turn and get the fuck out of here!"

Dave looked across the road where Captain Fails and CWO Smith were huddled down in the safety of the excavated ditch. "He wants to rush them," he hollered over.

Both men started to laugh, even with dirt spraying over their heads from the bullets slamming into the mounded earth.

"Hey! John Wayne! You lead the charge," Fails laughed.

"No! He's serious," Dave yelled.

"Yeah, okay," Smith shouted. "Let's surround them."

"No. Wait!" Fails said. "I'll call 'Arty.' We'll smoke their asses." He grinned and pretended to make a radio call for artillery support.

Sam wasn't listening. He'd fired the last few rounds of his clip into the shadow of the trees and was reloading.

"Ready?" he asked as he picked up his machete with his left hand.

"Ready? Ready for what?" Dave asked, his eyes wide in amazement that his friend actually intended to do this.

"C'mon!" Sam yelled, his face a deep crimson.

"C'mon, your ass! You're too drunk and so am I. You're fuckin' nuts, Sam," Dave said, hardly able to believe his ears.

Sam was getting ready! He rolled on the ground to a nearby tree and stood, back tight against it. He cocked his arm, holding the pistol at nose level, barrel pointed up, machete tightly grasped. Suddenly, he yelled a blood curdling cry from deep in his throat, the sound of which reverberated through the trees and would cause even the bravest man's knees to quiver—and he was gone! Charging through the trees alongside the road like a madman he fired rapidly, waving the machete over his head. Sam was attacking!

Either from an instinctive reaction to protect a buddy or the whiskey giving them added courage, Dave and the other two soldiers began to give a covering fire, squeezing off rounds as rapidly as they could. Then, as if on cue, they were up...charging and running after Sam. They all three started yelling, trying to affect the same bone-numbing, stomach-wrenching holler that Sam kept eliciting, but falling short of its actual reproduction.

As they got closer, they could see the dark figures turning to flee, running into the shadows of the jungle—and Sam was right behind them. He was chasing them on, deeper into the undergrowth, pursuing them frightfully and mercilessly as he kept up that chilling wail and flailing his machete above his head.

Dave and the others stopped their chase, coming together from either side of the road to meet at the abandoned truck.

"Do you fucking believe we did that?" asked Fails, breathless and a bit paled from the shock of the experience. "We must be really crazy...or really drunk."

"He's crazy," said Smith. "We're drunk."

A silence followed. Each man began to search the eyes of the others as the realization of what they had just been through began to sink in. They had acted together in a way that none of them could believe they singly would have behaved, and it frightened them. They had physically hurled their bodies at death, but it did not claim them—not this time. It had passed them over, delaying its dark summons for some future meeting.

Their minds were a tumult of confusion as they looked to each other for some explanation of their actions. No one could speak. Their breathing was heavy and their hearts pounded. Each man wanted to say something...anything; to express how they felt at the moment but no one could form the words.

Then, as the shock of the event began to slowly ebb, a smile formed on the captain's lips. The other two noticed this and looked at him, wondering. "That was real stupid, wasn't it?" he said with a sheepish grin.

Dave smiled now, also, shaking his head in disbelief at the utter foolishness of their attacking automatic weapons with hand guns. "Heh! Real stupid!" he replied.

Smith now started to chuckle about the episode, then burst into laughter. "Did you...did you see Sam...go after those...other three over there?" he managed between fits of laughter. "Machete swinging...and that yell! Ha! Where did...where did that come from?"

Dave and Captain Fails began to join in the laughter, the incident becoming comical now that the danger had passed and they had survived it.

"Oh, gawd," Dave laughed, holding himself up by the grill on the truck as he was in hysterics. "Those gooks...must have...shit their pants...when he came…charging at 'em." He mimicked Sam by gesturing with his hand over his head.

They were all bent double with laughter, leaning against the truck or holding onto the grill to keep from falling over.

"They gotta be…halfway…to China…by now," Fails burst out. "And Sam's probably…still chasing them!"

Their laughter ended quickly, though, when they looked over and saw Sam returning from the woods. He was limping slightly and his trousers were wet around his left front and lower groin area.

"Sam, you're hit!" Dave exclaimed in alarm. He started for him to help but Sam waved him back.

"Yeah, I'm hit," he said with more annoyance than pain. As he came closer, he re-sheathed his machete to its canvas scabbard, then reached down to bunch up some trouser material and wring it out. It wasn't blood. The other men were relieved.

Dave chuckled as he watched Sam disgustedly wring a few more drops from his clothing. "What'd you do, piss your pants?"

"Ha! I wish I had," Sam replied. He reached into his trouser pocket and retrieved a silver pint flask. "They got me where it really hurts. Glenfiddich: really good scotch," he said as he held the flask up to show them. There was a large dent across the center of the silver container. Sam tipped the flask slightly to reveal a small hole that allowed the precious contents to escape.

"Well, I'll be damned. Ricochet," Dave said.

"I'll be damned. Good scotch!" Fails said with some enthusiasm. He took the flask from Sam and inhaled the fragrance. "Ahhhh…" he sighed upon exhaling. "You've been holding out on us, ol' buddy."

"Naw," Sam said, watching the captain take a good swig, swirling it and savoring the taste. "It was a present from my brother. He said he found the flask in an antique shop, had it reconditioned, filled it with my favorite, and sent it to me. I was saving it. I'd have shared it with you guys later. That's sipping liquor, there. The other stuff's for chugging. Damn. Now the flask is ruined and the scotch is all but gone."

Dave smiled, amused at Sam's concern. "Yeah, well…you've still got your balls, at least. Hadn't been for that flask you might have lost them…and more!"

For a soldier in Vietnam, time is measured only in days left to serve "in country." Each day is torn from the calendar with a sigh of relief for having survived the last and always there is the fear for what the next day might hold. By Dave's recollection it had been a month since that jeep ride. His company had fought mostly in small fire-fights of platoon-sized engagements, setting up an ambush or out on search-and-destroy missions. Now that they were heading into a larger battle, he was glad to have Sam's company protecting his flank. His was an aggressive, hard-hitting group of men that could be counted on when things got hot.

The sound of gunfire began to increase up on the line as Dave's company began to add their weight to the foray. All the time, more choppers were landing, depositing their riders, then hurrying to lift off for the next wave to land. The wounded began to filter back to the aid stations and medivacs were shuttling in and out for the more seriously hurt. Jets screamed in from overhead, flying low to survey their strike zone in preparation for releasing their deadly cargo on the next pass.

Still in a crouch from his talk with his sergeants, Dave smiled up at Sam. "Hey, guy! Good to see you. What's going on up there?"

Sam began to speak, but, though his lips moved, no sounds were emitted. Instead, his words were over-ridden by the faint sound of a familiar female voice. Sam's form, as well as the entire scene around him, began to blur, receding into some dark corner of Dave's memory from where it arose. He found himself back in his driveway in Homer City. The faint voice that was calling out belonged to Carol.

"Dave! Dave! Would you answer me!" she called from the porch.

He shook off the lingering trail of dark memories, glad to be back in the present again.

"What are you doing?" she hollered out to him.

"Oh…um…trying to fit this stuff all on the roof rack. I got the bikes up. Now I'm working on the gear," he answered.

"Well, come get the phone. It's Sam."

Dave smiled. "Yeah? I was just thinking about him. Figured he'd be calling tonight. Is he there yet?"

"Where? Antietam? Yeah. He said he got there late this morning. C'mon. You talk to him," she said, sounding tired.

Dave came to the porch and followed his wife into the house. "Almost ready," he said as they went toward the kitchen for the phone. "I'll pack the rest of the gear tomorrow. I'm just going to throw a few more things on top and tie it down."

"Good. Come help me finish getting Jeff and Sarah organized. I'm about exhausted and I've still got a load of laundry to do. I'll be up half the night."

"Yeah. I know, I'll give you a hand in a little bit," he said as he kissed her forehead. He put the phone to his ear. "Sam, you old dog, you…"

Carol walked out the back door, hoping the fresh summer air might rejuvenate her. She could hear Dave talking to Sam on the phone but couldn't make clear what they were discussing. Sometimes he laughed heartily, sometimes his voice was low.

When his tone changed to one of concern, Carol became curious about the conversation but knew Dave would tell her when he hung up.

She walked out to the flower beds and inhaled the sweet fragrance of the blooming phlox, her favorite. A certain calmness came over her as she gazed at the flower gardens in the dim illumination of the patio lights. She always felt calm and relaxed when she worked with her flowers; nurturing them, weeding them, watching them grow and bloom.

As a light summer breeze shifted the scents, she caught the bolder less sweetened fragrance of the marigolds bordering the vegetable garden. Planted mostly for repelling certain little, unwanted insects, their scent was not as pleasant as the many other varieties surrounding her. Another shift in the breeze brought a smile to her face as she inhaled the distinct, pleasant aroma of the roses that bloomed all down the split-rail fence on the north side of the yard. Dave had brought home the original, single cutting from a trip down the lower Shenandoah Valley as they re-traced one of 'Stonewall' Jackson's routes. They'd found it growing wild on the site of a long-abandoned farm where only a keen eye and a bit of imagination could reveal where the house once stood.

The original owners must surely have stood on their front porch and cheered as the tattered, gray clad soldiers tramped by on their way to confront the invading blue columns. Canteens had most probably been filled from the old spring nearby to quench the thirst of the weary, dusty men of both armies. All that remained of the spring were a few large, cut stones at its source from under a towering oak, itself now showing the strain of having stood its sentinel post these many years as most of its limbs stretched wide but leafless under the June sun.

Carol walked along the red brick paths her husband had so meticulously laid to serve as dividers between the beds and let her mind wander to Dave and how deeply she loved him.

They had met in college, about a year after Dave had returned from the war. He told her he was glad they hadn't known one another his first year as a civilian for it had taken him that long to find any positive perspective of life after what he'd been through. Now, however, with a newly acquired self-discipline—compliments of the United States Army—and a knowledge of the various characters he could expect to associate with should he not succeed, Dave returned to Penn State University and finished his undergraduate studies. Completing a master's degree had then netted him a job as production supervisor in a plant that produced nothing but track pins for army tanks. Thousands upon thousands of special alloys, cut, ground and polished pins. It was a medium sized production facility in the town of Homer City, Pennsylvania.

He and Carol had married right after graduate school and found a quaint little house to rent just a few miles from Dave's work. It was not a year later that they purchased the house, knowing its potential; some landscaping and a little proper maintenance could turn it into a very comfortable abode.

Shortly after they had moved to Homer City, Carol had found work as an assistant purchasing agent at the D.F. Smathers and Sons Fabrication Company. The company's intent was to hire a woman to meet Federal regulations on female quotas and enable it to land some lucrative government contracts. Carol had proven so proficient at her job, though, that she soon headed the purchasing department.

After several years of scrimping and saving, Dave opened the first of his three auto parts stores. He had grown weary of answering to supervisors less competent than himself at the Gails Corporation. Also, he felt somewhat guilty about supporting the military industrial complex, believing he was contributing, in an indirect way, "to the suffering and misery of others." He had experienced enough of that directly during his tour in Vietnam and believed the only positive gain he had to show for his army adventure was his friend Sam Baker.

Carol smiled affectionately as she sat on the garden bench and thought of Sam. Dave and Sam had corresponded often after their return from the war. Countless letters passed between them and several phone calls each month kept the phone bill a major expense in their budget. Several times a year one of them would spend a weekend visiting the other. Carol certainly had no objections to this. She liked Sam. He was tall and sturdy, handsome and rugged.

His frame was built in square-like proportions with strong shoulders and a broad chest, giving one the impression that this man could not be moved unless he so consented. His jaw, like the rest of his body below it, was square, yet above that his face was soft and gentle. His eyes, a misty blue, were restless and dreamy, and if you looked real close they revealed a wondering spirit. It was as if, Carol believed, he was searching for something he had lost or left unfinished. He could entertain her and Dave for hours with his funny, witty stories and he appeared to be secure and content with his life. But there was a certain emptiness or loneliness about him which could only be detected in the quieter moments of the weekends when they talked of more personal, heartfelt subjects and concerns.

Dave was Sam's best friend. A rather pitiful fact considering that at any given time they were separated by at least three hundred miles. The closest Sam had come to living near Homer City were the ten months he'd lived in Pittsburgh—a fifty-mile drive from Dave's house. It had been a fun time for the two men as they were able to see each other often. Working for a private company, Sam had helped develop a computer system for a joint venture between the Pentagon and Carnegie-Mellon University.

When Washington then offered him the job of supervising its installation and programming, he'd jumped at the opportunity, knowing it would mean locating closer to Dave and Carol, if even for a short time. The work was mostly classified so Dave learned little of its purpose, and so was careful to remain silent on his political sentiments concerning Sam's involvement with the military.

Sam was a drifter, a brilliant drifter, but a drifter nonetheless. His skills and ability with all aspects of computers made him marketable anywhere in the country he wished to reside. He had designed whole systems and written the programs for large institutions. He had helped design and build several leading home computers for IBM. He was a genius, known to every personnel director of every major computer company in America and Japan (though he refused to work for the Japanese).

"Still," Carol sighed as she thought of him sympathetically, "for all of his talents and good looks there was that loneliness." She knew well that it stemmed from his homecoming from the war. Arriving back in Chicago he'd found his wife, Barbara, had, for the past eleven months, joined a health spa, dieted, and was back to the 115-pound figure Sam had adored back in high school.

After she kissed him "hello" at their doorstep, she handed him his bags and some other personal belongings—and then gave him a copy of the divorce papers. Seems she'd also been "working out" with the young judo instructor from the health spa—a fellow five years her junior. Now she was taking judo lessons for free—the boy had moved in with her. Sam hadn't settled in one city for longer than a three-year period since. And as far as Carol knew he hadn't had a serious, steady relationship with a woman longer than one night, either.

Every time Carol asked if he was seeing anyone special, he would become evasive or try to change the subject. When she'd suggested she might invite one of her single girlfriends along on one of their camping trips in the hope she and Sam might grow interested in one another he smacked her rump and threatened to "burp and make fart noises" to embarrass them all if she did.

"Honey...whatcha doing?" Dave called, coming out to the gardens from the house.

"Ohh...just relaxing. Taking a break. What'd Sam have to say?"

"Well, he's getting the campsite organized. Getting the wood in, stealing a picnic table from another site. You know," Dave said as he sat beside her.

"Yeah. Going to get us in trouble before we even get there. He's not stealing firewood, is he? Remember that trip to Fredericksburg?"

"Yeah...I know," Dave replied, lowering his head in shame.

"I was so embarrassed!"

"Well, hell, Hon, even I thought the guy had packed it in and left. Who closes up a camper like that just for the day?"

"Who cuts a half cord of wood if they're leaving?" she countered.

"Yeah, well...we paid him for it," Dave said.

"Ha! After he threatened to call the ranger and have us all thrown out!"

"Hrrumph."

"So, what else did Sam say?" Carol asked, snickering over her husband's obvious discomfort at her bringing up that old memory.

Dave ceased blushing and a look of concern showed on his face. "Well, apparently there's some trouble brewing at the battlefield," he said.

"That's why they're called battlefields," she chortled, then straightened when she saw Dave was not amused. "Like what?"

"I guess some developer bought some ground out from under the park service or something. They got hold of some old farm that's right up against the battlefield and are planning to build condos or housing units."

"What? Oh, no!" Carol exclaimed.

"Yeah. I read a little about it before. I didn't know it was this serious, though. Apparently, they've got the sewage permits and are going after the building permits. Sam's not sure. He's going to ask around some tomorrow to find out more about it."

"Jeez! Why can't people leave anything alone!" Carol said.

Carol looked at Dave tenderly. He was staring down at the ground, lost in thought. She knew this would affect him and Sam. That was one of the peculiarities of the two men's relationship; they both shared an inexplicable, inexhaustible fascination for the Civil War. Countless vacations were spent touring various battlefields and Carol had been dragged along on them all.

Everywhere!

From Fort Sumter to Appomattox. They had retraced the movements of Stonewall Jackson up and down the Shenandoah Valley; walked and studied the troop movements at Fredericksburg, Drewry's Bluff, Harpers Ferry (three times), Petersburg, Gettysburg (four times—she absolutely refused to go back there again), and so many others. She would always try to listen attentively to all the names and events—who the generals were, the dates and times, which side won and why. In fact, Carol knew far more than she'd ever wanted to know. She cared, yes, but only as much as the average tourist might.

This was Dave's and Sam's hobby; their interest, not hers. Carol enjoyed reading, quilting, gardening, lying on the beach, visiting amusement parks. She didn't mind that both men read countless books on the subject, called one another on the phone to argue tactics or discuss troop movements—fine! But she would go on these trips only if Dave would promise to take her on a separate vacation of her choice, later. And, though Dave always kept his promises, the battlefield tours were far outnumbering the beach trips.

Dave and Sam did, at least, try to make the trips entertaining by telling stories of incidents that occurred during the battle; startling accounts of heroism performed by individual soldiers, perhaps, or a story of a company mascot that barked its warning of impending doom for its company on the eve before they were all cut down in front of a stone wall; stories of young drummer boys who grew old from the horrors of war before they were even of shaving age; women who put on uniforms, cut their hair and bound their bosoms to fight beside their husbands. So many stories they knew, uncovered by the extensive research that would precede each trip. And, too, they most always took the bikes, riding along the narrow park roads, stopping to picnic, maybe toss the frisbee or football awhile. That helped to make the trips more enjoyable.

But then, there were always the times of eerie silences. They might all be walking along talking and laughing or telling some interesting highlight...and then they'd pause. One or the other, but most often both together, would stop, gaze out over the fields, and be silent—a long, reverent, doleful silence; as though they were remembering something...something held deep in the psyche that would begin to stir and to struggle upward. Perhaps they were reliving some forgotten calamitous event from a former life, or relating their own past violent experiences through some subliminal, spiritual communication with the ghosts of the men that fell on that field.

Carol didn't know; neither did Dave or Sam. All they knew was that some feeling or passion would envelop them and they would suddenly pause, their minds would close off to the present moment and drift to the sounds of battle—cannons booming, small arms crackling, men screaming in agony, officers shouting orders, the confusion, the smell of gun powder...the stench of death. Their senses would be overwhelmed by it. It was eerie, that was for certain. And it would usually end by whoever was in this strange delirium shuddering suddenly, as though a chilling, dark wind had blown across their body to penetrate to their very soul. Then, when they would turn around, their face displaying some puzzlement and discomfort, Carol would put her arm around them and hug them and it would take a few moments for them to shrug off the feelings and rejoin the living.

They would all, then, continue on their way, or begin telling another story, as if the momentary lapse into this curious sub consciousness was not to be noted with any more weight than a coughing spell or a sudden, temporary gastrointestinal disorder. On some occasions, when these transcendental experiences were particularly sensational, as they were on some fields as opposed to others, they would try to talk about them. Always, it was speculative at best; theories spoken around an evening campfire.

Neither of the men had courage enough to inquire of other veterans or Civil War buffs if they had had similar experiences. They sensed the nature of it as seeming to require that it remain private and personal. So, they were content to let it remain a mystery and simply accept it as something of a curiosity.

Carol watched Dave stand and begin wandering along the brick pathway. He seemed troubled. "Sam pretty worked up about this?" she asked.

"Yeah...a little," he replied, his back to her as he examined a loose brick with his feet, rocking it back and forth under the soles of his shoes. He turned to look at her. "It's just irritating, you know. It's not enough they take the best farmland. They've got to swallow up our history, now, too! Damn governments don't care. 'This hallowed ground'. Hell, it's only 'hallowed' till somebody with enough money decides it's worth more in condos. 'We must desecrate; we must develop this ground,'" Dave said, satirizing Lincoln's famous speech.

"There ought to be some way of working these things out; some legislation that can be drafted that'll help out the landowners through a tax break on historical land and keep it from being sold for development. I mean, you can't really blame the farmers for wanting to get something out of their years of hard work. But we're talking about our nation's heritage; our history. Men gave up their lives on those fields. They deserve more than to have a Volvo parked over their graves. They've earned at least the right to have the fields they fell on left undisturbed. Hell, Carol, those are battlefields, not amusement parks. Let them build their damn houses somewhere else."

Carol watched as her husband had become so agitated, pacing up and down the garden path as he spoke. "Oh, I can see this is going to be a fun vacation," she sighed. "We're supposed to be going away to relax." Then she showed a cute, inviting smile and stood to move over near him. Dave stopped pacing and watched her with some suspicion as she approached. He knew that look she was casting him; that cool, sexy, enticing smile she was wearing—and he loved it!

She used it whenever she wanted to talk him into doing something he might not ordinarily wish. "You know," she said as she so-o-o seductively slid her arms around his neck and cuddled in close, "we could always go to the shore," she purred as she looked up at him. "Rent a little efficiency...late night strolls along the beach"...she began to tease his ear with her finger. "Remember...under the pier last summer," she cooed into his ear with her soft voice.

Dave remembered! The stirring in his loins was proof both of how well he remembered and how persuasive Carol was at influencing a change in their vacation plans. She began to move against him, purring, "So, sailor, whady'a say? Interested in the sea...and me?"

"Ohhh! You devil, you," Dave said, returning the hug by wrapping his strong arms about her, "Hmm...I remember when we did it in the Johnny-Jump-ups," he said with some suggestion in his voice.

"Mmmm...I remember that. Ooh, Dave," she gasped excitedly at the thought.

"Ready for a repeat performance?" he asked, kissing her neck hotly.

"Mmmm..." she cooed as their lips met passionately.

"Mom! Can I take my yellow jacket? You didn't pack it," their eleven-year-old daughter, Sarah, yelled from the doorway. She was trying to peer out into the dimly lit garden where her parents were embracing.

"I was content with just a dog, remember," Dave smirked to his wife.

Carol laughed but called out, "We're coming!" Then, "So much for a romantic interlude."

"Keep the motor running. Bedtime is coming soon. And after..."

"And after, we'll both be too pooped from packing. C'mon, sailor. Other duties call."

As they turned and headed to the house Dave reached down to squeeze Carol's cute behind. "Heh! We'll see who's too tired. Ol' Dave has a few revitalization techniques he's learned over the years," he chortled.

Carol put an arm around him and gave him a quick hug. "C'mon, old man. I'll help you up the steps."

Chapter Two

July 18, 1861 Manasses Junction, Va.

Under a hot July sun, along a six mile stretch of the Bull Run Creek in northern Virginia, two opposing armies clashed for the first time over issues that were to determine the very destiny of a young nation now divided in two. They had been pounding away at each other all day in an effort to secure the field in each other's favor and to crush, or drive away in route, the forces of the other.

In the late afternoon, around Sudley Springs, a ford in the creek on the extreme west of the field of battle, the Union forces were attempting a flanking movement. In the center and east of the line, Northern forces had managed to fight well against the gray-clad Southerners and this movement was meant to turn the flank, roll up the length of the Rebel forces and crush them vigorously.

All had started well enough, but upon meeting stiff resistance, the blue line faltered, then stopped. The Union soldiers could see fresh reserve troops filing in to support and reinforce the Confederate ranks, and soon, as the gray army began a counter-attack, the blue line began retreating; orderly, at first; but then panic followed.

Coming down on Sudley Springs from the west was a small contingent of Federal Cavalry—Companies "A" and "B" of the "4th" Cavalry, "64th" Regiment—that had been patrolling the extreme western flank of the field. Drawing up behind a little knoll about a half mile before the ford, a scout came galloping back to report to the young lieutenant of Company "A." He pulled his horse up quickly and saluted the blond officer. "Sir, I'm afraid it looks as though the army is in retreat," he exclaimed.

"What? Are you sure of this? How can that be?" the lieutenant asked in astonishment.

"I don't know, Lieutenant, but they're falling back on the ford. Looks pretty bad for us. We may get cut off on this side of the creek. We better hurry and skedaddle," the man said. His horse, sensing the fright of its rider, began to dance about uneasily, and while the soldier fought to control the beast, the Lieutenant of "B" Company rode over to hear the report. As he pulled his horse up, he could see the look of concern on the two men's faces. Before he could speak, the Company "A" commander exclaimed, "We better go have a look. Private Rome, here, says the army is in full retreat; falling back over the ford."

The scout, still trying to control his unwieldy mount, continued with his report even as he pulled the rein to move the horse in small circles. "Looks like one brigade is trying to fall back in some order, Lieutenant. Trying to keep the Rebs off everyone else's backs. They're sure taking a pounding, though."

Without a word the two young lieutenants spurred their mounts for the hilltop, Private Rome following quickly, his mount more than eager for a run.

As the three men galloped to the crest of the little hill that overlooked the scene of violence below, they pulled up instantly and were horrified by what they saw. There, below them, they could see the entire right wing of the Union Army had given way and was in full retreat. The scene was one of pandemonium. A gray wave of ten thousand glistening bayonets was surging forward, pursuing the fleeing, fragmented forces of the blue army.

On the near end, not far from the little knoll on which the three men observed the terrible destruction unfolding before them, a lone brigade of brave Union soldiers stood firm, trying to fend off the attackers until the Federal army could get safely back across the ford.

They kept up accurate, heavy volleys, firing as they drew back, but their casualties were mounting rapidly as a battery of Rebel artillery tore huge gaps in the line. It would be only a matter of time before they, too, would break under the pressure from the overwhelming odds and the murderous fire from the cannon and begin to flee, only to add to the number of those killed or captured.

The two young lieutenants looked aghast at the havoc on the field below.

Private Rome, his horse again becoming unmanageable, said fitfully, "C'mon, Lieutenant, we better get across before we're cut off!"

The young officer of Company "A" shot the scout a reproachful glare at hearing this. "We'll go, all right. But it'll be through those guns, first!"

"What?" exclaimed the scout in disbelief, his mount now rearing and prancing about nervously. "But that's near suicide!"

"No," said the officer confidently. "We'll be coming up on their flank. They won't even notice us 'till we're upon them. Once we've silenced those guns we'll ride right up through the Rebs and cut our way out. It's our only chance. Go tell Sergeant Parker to bring up the troops.

We'll form line of battle here. It's perfect!" he said excitedly, enthused at the prospect of finally being able to join in the fighting. He glanced to his companion, the lieutenant of "B" Company, and the man nodded in agreement with the plans set forth. He smiled wryly and said, "Well, if we live, we both may gain a Captain's promotion out of this."

"But, Sirs..." the private began to protest, struggling to control his horse.

"Go!" shouted the blond lieutenant to the man.

"Yes, Sir!" Private Rome answered, and he dashed off to the awaiting companies, muttering something about how he 'should have joined the navy.'"

When the troops were brought up and in line of battle, the two lieutenants took their respective places in front of their troops. Company "A" was to lead the attack while "B" Company would follow close behind. The handsome, blond lieutenant drew a magnificently hand-crafted sword from its polished, decorative scabbard and rode the length of his line, trying to instill his own confidence and bravery into his men. "Right! You men of Pennsylvania. Let's show those Virginians what we're made of!" he shouted. He took his place before his troops and, holding the gleaming sword high, shouted, "Draw sabers!" and the sound of two hundred or better swords being pulled from their metal scabbards resounded upon the little knoll.

"Bugler...stand ready! At the gallop!...Charge!" he cried out. The blue lines swept forward, down off the rise and over the field to the unsuspecting cannoneers.

In a matter of moments, the blue troops swarmed over the gray-clad soldiers who were servicing the guns. Slashing and hacking, they struck down many. Those who could, fled in fear, leaving their guns to the victorious and jubilant Federal troopers.

The men began to cheer as they rode among the captured pieces of which they had so easily, but so violently, taken possession.

"Silence, men!" shouted the lieutenant. "No time for that. Limber up a few to take with us. Spike the rest! These guns have taken their last toll of Union Men! Hurry, Men!... Be about it!" he cried out, for he could see a gray line of Confederate infantry forming not a hundred yards behind. Once they started firing, counter-attacking to retrieve their stolen guns—it would alert the Rebel line in their front and the small force of blue cavalry would be trapped and annihilated.

When three of the guns were limbered to their drafts, the lieutenant quickly shouted the orders, "By column of fours! Fall in at the gallop!" He waved his sword overhead as a rallying point and for the attention of his men.

When some semblance of a formation was obtained, he took the column on a bold dash up to the main line of the clashing armies. The attacking Confederate line, their backs to the hard-riding blue cavalry column, was caught completely off guard. As the brave young officer encountered the gray line, he cut a swath with his saber to open a passageway for the column to follow. They poured through as the Rebel infantry recoiled in surprise at this attack from their rear. By the time the Southerners were able to rally themselves and realize it was but a small party of cavalry, the blue riders were well within the safety of their rear-guard, splashing across the ford, the captured guns in tow.

The lone, defiant brigade, fighting so determinedly to keep the humiliating defeat from becoming a complete catastrophe, sent up a resounding cheer as the valiant cavalry came racing into their line. The courage of this little band of Union horsemen added a fresh resolve to the too few defenders who, before this event, were beginning to lose their confidence almost as fast as their numbers.

Now, with a new spiritedness, the tattered and worn brigade managed an orderly and protracted rear-guard defense, covering the flight to safety of much of the routed Union army.

Inevitably, the sheer weight of numbers won out over courage and the thinned ranks of the bold defenders finally began to crumble. As the first of the parched, exhausted soldiers began to give way, the gray warriors began to surge toward the weakened positions. "Lady Luck" was to cast her smile upon those tired men, however, for just as the line faltered, the pursuit ended; the musketry diminished. Night had fallen on the field and the Confederate command had ordered a respite to reorganize their disoriented lines.

This fortunate repose allowed the shattered Union forces to slip back into the refuge of the fortified defenses of Washington. There, for the next several months, they would lick their wounds and reorganize their demoralized forces.

March 1, 1862 Eight months later: North bank of the Potomac River, near Washington

Theodore Sandfeld Duncan made his way down the darkened aisle of the National Theater with his friend Thomas Edwards. They were late by fifteen minutes—a rather good showing considering their regiment had been delayed returning from a reconnaissance mission due to the swollen fords along the Potomac River.

It had been raining for three days—a constant, steady drizzle that a soldier detests probably more than anyone else. They had slept under canvasses, but the ground was so saturated that it quickly soaked through any bedding of leaves or branches. After three days in this misery—sloshing through knee deep, shoe-sucking mud in which the horses constantly stumbled and the two field pieces were more often mired to their axles—they had returned with nothing to report in the way of Rebel activity.

When Theodore ('Sandie,' as he was affectionately called in the officer's mess) was able to clean up and get into his dry clothes, he made his way to

Thomas's tent at Company "B" headquarters. The rain was pounding steadily, now, as he entered Thomas's tent, his slicker dripping with an icy slush that was neither rain nor snow.

"Hey, old boy," Thomas greeted him with a cheerful smile. "Are you certain you still want to go to this tonight? There will be other nights."

"Oh, we must!" Sandie replied, pulling off his rubber slicker and warming his hands over the heat of the little stove. "It's not often a fellow from Pittsburgh gets a chance to watch a professional play with famous actors in it."

Thomas chuckled, "You're not from Pittsburgh; it's raining horribly out there; and I read where a lot of the actors have come down sick. Half the cast will be stand-ins. Sandie, we'll be covered in mud by the time we get there. You'll hardly impress anyone, particularly Congressman Covode, by looking like we just got in."

"But we did just get in. Besides, I've planned for all of that. We'll wear our slickers tucked tight, carry our dress boots in our sacks, wear our field pants while riding. When we get to the city, we can change at Mrs. Bordlinger's. It's just around the corner from the theater. Then we can swagger in all dressed as if for parade and we'll look our finest."

"Mrs. Bordlinger's! Sandie, that's a house of...of...Well, you know. It has a reputation," Thomas laughed.

"So, it does. But that's not to worry about. I've heard a lot of the upper-brass have frequented the house on many occasions. They go to the city under the pretense of procuring supplies. They're procuring, all right. But I'll wager it's not salt pork or hard tack they're procuring there. Besides, it'll only be for the night. We'll be in after dark and out early. No one will recognize two lone captains amongst all the blue uniforms about. Our reputations will remain untarnished."

"So, you've got it all schemed, aye? All right. We'll go. Let's to it!" Thomas said as he stood from his chair to finish dressing.

On through the mud and rain Sandie and Thomas rode, sometimes at a canter when the road was straight and the footing was sure, but mostly at a walk. The movements of thousands of troops and hundreds of wagons, cannons and caissons had pretty well torn up the roads in the last year.

Sandie's reason for hurrying to attend tonight's performance was both his excitement at having secured a two-day pass—the first in six months—and the fact that he would see a professional production of a play in a real theater, and with professional actors. He had not been exposed to any cultural events until he had attended the college in Pittsburgh, and then he'd had little money for such luxuries. His father owned a dry goods store and grist mill in Hannastown which did well enough to keep them all comfortable, but room and board at the college had taken all he could afford.

Sandie had been in his last year of study when he heard the bugle call. An engineering student who excelled in his discipline, he devoted all of his energies to study, knowing the financial strain it placed on his family. His only relaxation was his reading of philosophies and religions and attending an occasional concert or play. The plays were usually a production by townsfolk and performed in a theater that was viewed as 'disgustingly primitive' by any touring professional troupes.

Tonight, however, was to be a special occasion. As they slogged through the mud and rain, Sandie slipped his hand under his slicker and into his waistcoat pocket to grasp again the tickets that had been handed to him personally by Congressman Covode. The congressman had come out to the cavalry camp from Washington to greet and inspect the four companies from his home district, two of which had distinguished themselves valiantly in the previous campaign at Bull Run.

At once, the congressman had taken to the lad of twenty-two. At five feet nine, Sandie's one hundred seventy-five-pound frame was solid and square, built by years of heavy lifting at the grist mill. His blond hair, cut neat and straight was combed to one side and, try as he might to keep it back, one lock would inevitably fall across his forehead.

He was handsome in feature and in speech, and looked the very image of a dashing cavalryman. He had had the fancy of all the young girls in his district, though he never courted or showed much of an interest in any of them. His attention was always either at the mill, or store, or to his studies of mathematics and philosophy. When asked by anyone why he had never chosen a favorite from among the beauties of Westmoreland County his reply had always been that "the young lady who will catch my eye has not been introduced to me yet" and that "there will be time for that after college." In truth, he found the darlings of his area too overbearing; always seeming to want to throw their favors to him; always trying too hard to impress him.

He was content to await the arrival of the one lady that would someday draw his interest and fascination. Certainly, there had been a few weekends at school when a classmate might arrange for Sandie to escort a young lady to some social event. But generally, he declined most invitations in favor of using the time for study.

Now, as the rain pelted against their slickers, Sandie thought it a special delight that he and his friend would be the guest of the congressman. He would be sitting among powerful, famous people; people with the influence to shape the very destiny of this young nation. Sandie was in awe of such people. He followed their statements and actions in the papers that circulated in the camps and always cheered them on when they spoke of putting down the

Rebellion; of how it was "the duty of all young men to follow the flag and join the ranks to restore the unity of the nation."

In fact, it was a speech delivered by Congressman Covode at a Union support rally at the Colony Hotel in Pittsburgh that so inspired Sandie to put his last year of college on hold and join the 4th Pennsylvania Cavalry that very evening.

His mother, typically, had cried at the news. His father, being a strong Union man himself, was elated at his son's opportunity to demonstrate his loyalties to the flag. So elated, in fact, that he provided him with the finest horse to be had in the county (the finest a miller and dry goods merchant could afford, anyway).

He offered to equip his son with all of the most modern equipment necessary and it was only through the assurances of the regimental commander that he need not go to such expense—that the army would issue the needed equipment—that his father had relented. In the end, he satisfied himself with presenting to his son a fine cavalryman's sword, hand-forged by Harold Clawson, a blacksmith and toolmaker who, by way of being an old friend of the family, took special care in its forging. Its blade was of the finest quality iron, heated and folded repeatedly to withstand the hardest of impacts. Then, it was sharpened to an edge so keen it could halve a silk scarf that floated down to it when dropped from a few feet above.

The pommel and hilt were cast in a precise ribbon over oak leaves design and the handle then wrapped in sharkskin held with twisted gilt wire. It was then taken to Paul Cashdollar, the artisan potter, tinsmith and silversmith who carefully engraved the long blade with scrollwork and etchings of scenic views and familiar buildings of Hannastown, including the Duncan home, storefront, and mill, that whenever Sandie might find himself pining for home, he might draw the sword and look upon it and feel comforted. Below the channeling, toward the pointed end of the blade, were etched the words "The Union Forever May God Protect the Right."

It was probably as fine a sword as any general could wear for dress parade or presentation. Even its metal sheath was fashioned in like manner, its scrolling inlaid with copper, polished to a brilliance that caused it to gleam above all other ceremonial scabbards.

Yet, this was a weapon—made for killing—and its creators took care in its fashioning that all of its beautiful artwork was tapered and leveled for easy cleaning and the wiping of the blood it was destined to draw.

The creation of this instrument had been undertaken in complete secrecy from Sandie. He was aware only that his father was acting suspiciously pleasant these last few weeks prior to Sandie's having to report for service. Sandie wondered how a man, whose son was soon to leave the security and comfort of home for the harsh uncertainties of battle, could behave as if his son were merely preparing for an afternoon of social picnic. This perplexed Sandie, as his father and he had always been very close, he being the only male child among four younger sisters.

Then came that Sunday afternoon. In three days, Sandie was to report to camp. As they left the church steps his father suggested they take a stroll about the village, mumbling something about how Sandie should take a long, thoughtful look around the village since he would not be seeing it for some time.

As they walked, they talked mostly about the weather, about how busy his father would be at harvest without Sandie's help, though he guessed he'd hire the young Bonnett boy to help for awhile. He would manage to get the work done. Only when they had reached the town square did Sandie notice that the entire congregation seemed to be ambling along behind them some twenty yards back, or so.

Also, there was a crowd of familiar faces gathered around the bandstand in the center of the park. Sandie wondered what was going on. Then his father grasped his arm and escorted him directly to the crowd of about fifteen people gathered there. They all turned as if only now noticing the two men approaching. They stopped talking and parted to either side of the steps that led up to the platform.

"Father?" Sandie asked, puzzled, though now he began to suspect something was about—something that had to do with him and the fact that he was to be the first of his community to enlist for the war.

Now, all the congregation that had been seeming to just be ambling along behind, gathered below the platform. They looked up at the boy admiringly, respectfully, silent; waiting for something, or someone.

On the platform with the two Duncans was the mayor, Grover Campbell, a portly man in his early fifties who wore a pencil thin moustache and combed his thinning hair from one side of his head to the other to cover his balding dome. At every public occasion he always amazed the audience by seeming to surpass his previous appearance in windiness of speech and in his ability to outrace his wife in expanding his coat seams to match his stomach. Flanking him to either side stood Harold Clawson, a broad-shouldered giant with hands the size of mountains; and Paul Cashdollar, a small, thin, elfish-looking fellow with a pleasant, affectionate smile for Sandie.

"What is this about, Pa? What have you gone and done?" Sandie asked with a bemused smile. He used the word "Pa" only during affectionate talks with the man and almost never in public, most often addressing him as "father" or more formally as "Sir."

Now Sandie took his father's arm as they approached the trio on the bandstand. A sidewards glance revealed a proud, beaming father who seemed to almost strut beside his son.

"Be patient. You'll see," he said in almost a reverent tone.

Grover Campbell stepped forward from between the two men flanking him, reached into his coat pocket to retrieve some papers and unfolded them. He cleared his throat with a loud "Ahem!," and began to speak.

As the crowd stood listening, Grover began telling about the proud history of Hannastown; how "some of its men had fought in the Revolutionary War, and others in the war of 1812." He spoke of how "the loyalty of its citizens was never in question" and that "her sons and daughters always responded to the call of the stars and stripes." He spoke on...and on...and on...until people began to shift their feet; began to fidget and whisper; began to yawn and stretch.

Forty-five minutes he rambled, seeming not to notice how many people were now sitting on the lawn, pulling blades of grass or picking up pebbles to flick off with their thumb. They were used to Grover's speeches, and though they were respectful of him since he was a neighbor and a driving force in the community, still, they had little patience with his blustering speeches.

Now, as he began to wind down his remarks, people began to stand again, listening as he congratulated Sandie on his courage and patriotism; on his carrying forth the proud tradition of the boys that went before him in other wars, etc...etc...etcetera. And when he had finished, people began to applaud—as much that the speech had finally ended as for the gallant lad to whom it had been addressed.

Grover shook hands with the boy and murmured to him to "take care" of himself and "the best of luck" to him and "you do us proud" and more, shaking the boy's hand over and over while the audience of friends clapped and cheered. Grover smiled widely as he grasped the boy's hand, thinking the ovation was over the "inspiring" remarks he had just orated.

As the applause died away, Sandie's father put his arm about him, hugging him close, saying, "Son, I can't express what I'm feeling about you; about your leaving us, and all." He looked into the boy's eyes and both father and son were just a bit watery-eyed, but choking back an emotional display in public. "I wish it was me that was going—going down there to show those people what's right; to put down this rebellion and all. I'm just too old. So, you'll have to do my fighting for me. I'm gonna miss you, son," he stammered.

Quickly the proud man wiped a tear from his cheek with the back of his hand and turned his head a moment to regain his composure. When he had control of his emotions, he gazed upon his son again. "To, uh, to help you out if the fighting gets tough...and to help you remember better us folks back home, some of us have made you a little goin' away present. It isn't much, but we think it'll help," he said to the boy.

A box was brought up onto the platform—a long, skinny box made of thin white pine. It had dove-tailed corners and fitted lid with polished brass hinges and latch, and stained in a light color to off-set the darker, highlighted engraving. This was the handiwork of Henry Repine, the cabinet-maker who now carried the box onto the stage.

"Oh! It's lovely. What a beautiful box!" Sandie exclaimed as it was held before him.

"Go on, son! Open it!" his father urged him excitedly.

As the lid was lifted, the eyes of everyone on the stage opened wide in awe. "Oh! Oh, my heavens!" Sandie gasped in amazement. He carefully reached and lifted the beautiful sword from its bed of blue satin that lined the box. He raised it slowly, admiringly, for this was a piece of art! Not just a blade for cutting flesh, but an adornment to be worn in fashion the way a woman might wear ear-bobs or a bracelet and necklace; the way a man will wear a gold chain across his vest pockets. This sword was even more. It shone brightly from hilt to tip of scabbard as Sandie held it high for all to see. 'Ohhs' and 'Ahhs' were exclaimed by the crowd as they gazed at it. When he pulled it from its sheath an applause rang out from the on-lookers as he held it high over his head, whirling it about.

"Oh, Father! It's beautiful!" he exclaimed.

"Ha! Ha! So you like it, huh?" his father asked, exuberant at his son's reaction.

"Like it? I love it! It's wonderful! I'll be the envy of the regiment. I doubt if any general carries a saber this elegant," he said. Then, slowly lowering the sword, he looked at his father through watery eyes, and in a softer voice he said, "I love you, Pa."

"Aw, Sandie," his father blushed, and before everyone, they embraced. Then they wept. Openly, and unashamed, they hugged and released their tears for all to see.

"Three cheers for Sandie Duncan!" someone yelled, and the gathered friends cheered "Huzza!...Huzza!...Huzzah!"

****

That had been one year, two major battles and a few light skirmishes ago—if being shot at at any time can be called a light skirmish. Sandie's regiment was always in the thick of the fighting, and always, they were licked by Jeb Stuart and his horsemen whenever the two armies clashed. Sandie, at least, was able to save honor by always withdrawing his company only under orders, and then only at the last moment when they were about to be overwhelmed. He'd won praise repeatedly from his superiors, though too often his rewards were only to be called upon for more arduous and dangerous assignments and, as yet, only a captain's promotion.

All of this was to be put out of mind for the next two days, however. For, being granted a two- day leave, he and Thomas were going to make the most of their stay in Washington. They would find suitable lodging when they could. All that mattered now was that they get to the theater as quickly as possible.

As planned, they arrived at Mrs. Bordlinger's in early evening. A young colored servant greeted them with a big, wide smile. "See to ya' hossez, Suhs?" he asked as he gathered their reins. "I takes real fine care ub dem. Groom dem un feeds dem un all, Suhs."

Thomas grinned widely. He'd never actually spoken to a negro before, nor even heard them speak. "Thanks, boy. Be sure to give them some oats, not just hay. Cover them with a blanket to keep the chill off. They're on leave same as us."

"I knows all 'bout hossez, Suh. I was de head ub massah's stables till da gum boats dun chase off da massah un hid whole fably. Yes, Suh! I knows all 'bout hossez," the young man said proudly.

"Fine. That's a fine lad. Here! Here's a quarter. Give them your special attention," Thomas said as he flipped the young man a coin.

"Yes, Suh! I sho will," he gleamed as he caught the silver piece in the air and slid it into his pocket. He held the reins as the two captains unstrapped their haversacks from the saddles. "Oh! I is tah tell you dat Miss Kitty un Miss Bawba, dey is not in t'nite. Dey is ailwin wit de fevuh o' sumpin. But Miss Flo'ence un Miss Lilly, dey jes got back t'day fuhm Philedefia un is all rested un re-freshed." Then he paused as he watched Sandie and Thomas look at one another and blush some at hearing this. Then, still with a broad smile, he went on. "'couse, der is otha' gals, but dey is de fav-o-its ub most ub de gents."

Sandie and Thomas both smiled and nodded to the fellow. As they began to walk toward the porch Sandie said, "Thanks for the message. We'll, uh, keep that in mind."

As the servant began to lead the horses away the two men looked at one another and laughed heartily, shaking their heads in disbelief over this exchange with the young man.

When they opened the front door and entered the large house, they stopped at the doorway to gaze about. "Whoa!" Thomas said in surprise as his senses reeled from the dramatic change in the air. Heavy cigar smoke, mixed with an overpowering scent of various perfumes left little room in the lungs for oxygen. A large parlor to the left of the foyer seemed to be where everyone was gathered.

The two young men started timidly into the room but stopped suddenly as they caught the eye of a strikingly beautiful woman seated on a sofa across the room with a young lieutenant. She smiled to them, said something to the young man with her, then rose to greet the new visitors. As she started toward them the soldier reached out for her but she thwarted his feeble attempt by brushing his arm away. He was very obviously drunk.

"Well, hello, boys. First time here?" she asked, smiling warmly to them as she came closer.

"Uh, yes, actually," Sandie answered.

"Well, then, we'll just have to make you boys feel especially welcomed," she said. "This is my home. I'm Mrs. Bordlinger. But, please, call me Sal. All my friends do."

"Uh, yes. Fine. Pleased to, um, meet you, Sal. Um,..I'm Sandie...and, uh, this is, uh, is Thomas," he stammered.

"You're nervous. Please. Relax. You're not in camp, and I'm certainly not a general. Can I fix you boys a drink? It's compliments of the house. It'll help you relax; take your mind off the war. There's cigars if you'd like," she said, motioning to a box on the fireplace mantle.

No...uh,..no thanks. Well, yes! Maybe a drink...a small one. Um, scotch, I guess," Sandie said. He wasn't used to liquor and had only some experience with it at regimental headquarters where some of the officers seemed to favor this drink. On this occasion he decided a drink just might help relax him.

"C'mon in, boys," Sal said, turning to lead them into the parlor. They followed her across the room toward a small table by a window. On the way, the young lieutenant roused from his stupor long enough to make a reach toward the well-proportioned woman.

"Sal," he murmured as he reached dizzily for her, but the woman casually brushed his arm aside and continued on. The young man fell back, slouching into the cushions.

The two young cavalrymen looked nervously about the room as they followed the woman. There were half a dozen men sitting on chairs and sofas around the dimly lit room. Some read the papers and smoked cigars while others just sat and fidgeted uneasily while they sipped their drinks. Four of the men wore uniforms, officers of various ranks—the highest being a colonel, his distinctive hat proving him to be from the stout "Iron Brigade" from Michigan.

The other two men wore suits and appeared to be calm; probably they were regular visitors to this establishment. Everyone gave a quick glance at the newcomers, then averted their eyes lest they be recognized or remembered at some later encounter. A piano player over in the corner was playing something soft and soothing and never gave notice that anyone else had joined the group.

"I suppose Liberty gave you all the particulars of the evening concerning the girls," Sal said to them as she poured two glasses and handed them to the men.

"Um...uh...sort of," Sandie replied awkwardly. "Actually...you see...um,.. we...we sort of just need a place to, um, change clothing and...to clean up. We're due at the theater and...just getting in and all...we...only heard of your...hospitality from some of the officers at camp." And with that said, Sandie took a big sip of the scotch, fighting hard not to choke from the burning sensation that flamed in his mouth and spread clear down into his stomach.

"Oh, I see," replied Sal, sounding a bit disappointed at the loss of the prospective income. "Well, fine. I'll have Julia show you to a spare room in the back where you may freshen up. You understand, of course, that the charges will still hold the same. Ten dollars."

"Phuffft!" Thomas choked in mid-sip at hearing this. "Ten dollars?"

"Did you gentlemen ride?" she asked.

"Yes," Sandie answered.

"Well, I'm assuming Liberty is stabling your horses. And what with the war having caused the price of quality hay and grain to be so high and all. Boys, it's only fair. These services are generally compliments of the house for...shall we say other business," she said politely, but pointedly.

"Other business," Thomas muttered under his breath.

"Tell you what, boys. Since you'll be staying the night, and I assume you'll be passing on having one of the girls accompanying you, I'll have Julia make you a fine breakfast in the morning." Sal told them.

Sandie and Thomas looked at one another and shrugged. Both knew that on such short notice and as crowded as Washington was, they had no choice. Sandie reached into his pocket, withdrew his purse, and counted out the money into the lady's hand. She took it, smiling cheerfully, and turned to Thomas. "Apiece," she said holding that same smile.

"Phuffft!" Thomas choked again in mid-swallow on the scotch. "Apiece?"

Mrs. Bordlinger stood with her hand extended, palm up, waiting patiently.

"Okay. Okay. You're quite a businesswoman, Sal," Thomas said as he fished into his coat pocket for his purse.

"One has to be when one is left on their own in this town," she said, and her tone was a bit less pleasant; her smile gone. "My husband was killed by a rebel marksman at Bull Run. I was left penniless and alone." She picked up a little bell from the liquor table and jingled it, saying, "Hard times make for hard bargains, gentlemen."

A negro girl entered the room. She was slender and pretty and could easily have been one of Sals "girls" save for the fact that she wore the dress of a servant. She, also, had an unusually large and inviting bosom that stood high and firm, and for an instant, tempted both men to reach out for them in curiosity. "Yezz'em?" she asked in a low voice, looking toward the floor, as if she were addressing her former owner.

"Julia, dear. These men need a room to freshen up. Please show them to the spare room off the kitchen where they might change and wash."

"Yezz'em," the girl bowed slightly.

"This way, please, Suhs."

The two men bowed politely and thanked Sal for her hospitality, excused themselves, and turned to follow the curvaceous young girl as she led them back to the foyer. As they turned left into the hallway and passed the long stairway leading to the chambers above, they glanced up to see a young woman descending the stairs, arm-in-arm with a gray-haired cavalry officer. The men nodded to one another in passing, the older man trying to hide his face by looking down at the stairs. With no further acknowledgements, Sandie and Thomas both continued on with the girl into the kitchen.

She led them through a large pantry containing shelves of canned goods. Cured hams and bacon, herbs and spices hung from the ceiling.

"Phewww," Thomas whistled. "'Hard times make for hard bargains,' indeed! She could feed our entire regiment for a fortnight with these provisions."

The pantry led into a small room, and here, again, they found more supplies of meats and vegetables of all kinds lining the walls and hanging from the ceiling. Amid all this was a small cot in the center of the room against one wall. Above it was a mirror of sufficient size for dressing. A basin and pitcher were placed on a small, battered stand next to the bed. A straight-backed, cane chair stood to the other side.

The girl lit an oil lamp by the basin and turned to the men. "Ya'll can freshin up in heah. Th'ar be fresh water in the bowl. I'll fetch yah s'mo' towels."

"Thank you, Julia. We'll be fine," Thomas said. Neither man moved until the girl had departed and was well out of hearing. Then they both guffawed simultaneously over the whole situation.

"Twenty dollars!" Sandie laughed and threw himself onto the cot.

"Well, at least we won't go hungry," Thomas chuckled, shaking his head.

"True. And it's dry and warm," Sandie added.

"Hear! Hear! That's a comfort," Thomas agreed.

"Comfort? That Julia's bust would be a comfort," Sandie chortled.

"See here. Mind yourself. You're an officer and a gentleman," Thomas laughed.

"Uh...field grade; and only of volunteers. I don't think I have to behave myself unless I'm regular army," he mused.

"Ha! Ha!" Thomas laughed. "This place is full of regulars. That colonel coming down the stairs is regular. I believe he was just finished 'minding himself'."

"Well, we'd better hurry and change. We'll soon be late if we don't get a hawk on it," Sandie said. "We can discuss our getting twenty dollars worth later."

The two young captains began to hurry and dress for the different sort of entertainment that awaited them that evening.

****

The theater was but a few blocks from Mrs. Bordlinger's home which helped to account for the house catering to officers as well as the more "well-heeled" of the city. The common soldier could find the comforts of open and willing arms at further reaches in the city and at somewhat lower prices.

The muddy roads, lack of convenient sidewalks and the over-crowding with both soldiers and civilians all prevented Sandie and Thomas from arriving on time. As the usher escorted the two men down the aisle to their seats, they found, however, that they were but a few moments late. The opening act having only just started.

"Congressman Covode," Sandie greeted the man as he took one of the two empty seats beside him. "Sorry we're late. We only just got in."

"That's quite all right. Though I was beginning to think you might not show," the older man said, extending his hand in greeting.

"Well," Sandie said, grasping the man's hand, "fortunately, the Rebels delayed us no longer than necessary."

"Oh, I see." replied the congressman. Then, "Oh, this is Mrs. Covode," he said as he introduced the gray-haired lady seated next to him.

"Pleased to meet you, Ma'am." Sandie smiled to the woman and gave a slight bow of his head. The woman nodded in return.

"Dear, this is the boy I was telling you about, Theodore Duncan. Hannastown."

"Yes. My pleasure, Mr. Duncan."

"No. The pleasure is mine, Ma'am," Sandie said, sounding very formal and courteous. The Covodes were a respected and honored family in Westmoreland County and Sandie hoped to make a positive, lasting impression on them.

"Ahem!" Thomas nudged his friend in the side, waiting impatiently for an introduction.

"Oh. Sorry." he said to Thomas, and though it was a bit awkward in the cramped theater seats, Sandie managed an introduction of his friend. "Sir, this is my friend, Captain Thomas Edwards, "B" Company. Thomas...Congressman and Mrs. Covode."

"Pleasure, Sir," Thomas said enthusiastically, reaching across Sandie's front to shake the man's hand.

"Indeed it is," answered the congressman. "Where are you from, my boy?" he asked as if he were truly interested, but also in the practiced manner of a politician.

"Harrisburg, Sir," Thomas replied, glad the man had inquired.

"Hmmm...not my district. Pity. How did you come to be in the 64th Regiment?"

"Well,.." he started to explain, but then came a "Shshshsh..." from two seats over from Thomas's right. The three men looked to see who it was that was shushing them. As they were in the front row the lights from the stage illuminated their forms well enough, and they could see, also, a young woman of about twenty years of age leaning forward and looking at them. Her shoulder-length, light brown hair was worn with the front pulled back and fastened with a long, blue, satin ribbon. Her gown was elegant; white, with blue satin trimmings and a matching choker around her neck with a cameo pin in the center.

She was smiling politely and, as she spoke in a soft, friendly voice, it sounded to Sandie like the ringing of the nightingale on a warm summer's eve back home. "I've read this play. You'll not want to miss these following lines or you'll not understand the story," she said to them.

The others nodded politely, sat back in their chairs and were quiet. But Sandie found he was frozen in his forward-leaning position staring at the girl, drinking in her features. Her face was round and soft, with a delicate chin below thin lips that curved into a beautiful, pleasant smile. Her skin was just slightly tanned, suggesting a healthy, robust enjoyment of the outdoors. Her nose, small and delicate. But what really seemed to captivate Sandie's attention was her eyes. They were a deep, warm blue; very bright and alive. Perhaps it was the glow of the gas lanterns of the stage, but those eyes seemed to sparkle and glow with a brilliance all their own.

"Sir. The play?" she said, widening her smile at the young man who was gazing at her so intently.

"Oh! Oh! S-Sorry," Sandie stammered, awakening from his marveling stare and embarrassed that he had been seeming to gape at the girl as they were both, yet, leaning forward in their seats.

Her smile for him was warm and friendly, and her eyes wondered over the features of his face. "Quite all right," she replied. Then slowly, her gaze lingering a moment more, she moved back in her seat.

Sandie shifted in his seat. His heart was racing, his breath shortened. In fact, he could hardly breathe at all. His face, he knew, was flushed, for he could feel the blood coursing through his veins. "What was happening?" he wondered, as he felt the perspiration on his brow. He pulled his kerchief from his pocket and dabbed at his brow and cheeks. "Whew! It's warm in here. Don't you think?" he whispered to Thomas, turning his head slightly under the guise of addressing his friend, but, really, trying to steal another look at the comely girl sitting but three seats away.

"Hm?...What's that?...No. No, I'm quite comfortable, actually," Thomas replied, breaking, for an instant, his avid attention to the production on the stage.

"Damn him," thought Sandie as he realized how intensely interested everyone else was in what was taking place on the stage. "Didn't anyone notice that he was taken ill?" He wondered who the man was seated between Thomas and the girl. A beau, perhaps; her husband, maybe? "Gawd! He's much too old for her. Perhaps she's with that woman to her right. That could be her mother...Yes! That's it! She's accompanied by her mother and father—of course!" Sandie thought as he tried to carefully steal a look her way.

"Oh! Move your head, you old fool!" his mind hollered at the older man seated there blocking his view of the girl. All Sandie could see of her was her nose. "Ah-h,..but what a beautiful nose it is," he sighed inwardly. He ever so carefully leaned just a little forward—just an inch or so..."Oh!" he jerked back quickly, for suddenly the young woman had leaned just slightly forward, shifting in her seat, and had turned her head, her eyes catching Sandie's gaze. He was so embarrassed. He felt like a young schoolboy with a crush on one of his classmates; not the strong, brave, fearsome cavalryman he had become over the last year.

"Was she still looking at him? Dare he try to steal a glance? How humiliating if she caught him again. Hadn't he made a big enough fool of himself already?" he thought. But he couldn't resist. He found her beauty too overwhelming. Slowly...carefully...he turned his head; ever so slightly. He was hidden by Thomas's head—"Good," he thought. "Now, lean forward...like you're just shifting your weight in your seat," he commanded himself. "Just getting comfortable"...he played in his mind. "That's it...just a little more forward...Damn it!" he yelled inwardly. The older man seated between Thomas and the girl was glaring at him, catching him in his attempt to steal a glimpse of her. The man had a mean, stern expression on his face; a look that went firing toward Sandie with greater fierceness and more danger than any mini-ball Sandie had avoided in battle. This look said "STAY AWAY!" and there was no ducking it. It was aimed at Sandie like a full charge of canister and it hit him squarely in the chest—in the heart, to be more precise.

Sandie sat back and slumped in his seat, depressed; discouraged. "How," he thought to himself, "how could such a beautiful young thing as she be in any way associated with such a scowling old ogre as that?"

The curtain closed for intermission and the house lights were brought up. Sandie couldn't believe he had sat through two acts and not been aware of any of the action or dialogue from the stage. He found it equally difficult to believe that anyone else in the audience would have noticed the play, either, when such a lovely girl as she sat among them. "She should be up on the stage," he thought. "She need only stand there and the audience would cheer and applaud her beauty."

"Well, boys. Care to join me for a drink?" asked the congressman.

"Sir?" Sandie asked of the request.

"Brandy. Over intermission. There's a room upstairs. They provide it for, um, certain friends. Come join me for a glass. We can talk," explained the elder statesman.

"Oh, yes. Thank you. We'd enjoy that. Wouldn't we, Thomas?"

"By all means. Yes!" Thomas replied.

A large portion of the audience was now standing, stretching their legs and moving about in the aisles. Sandie, Thomas and Congressman Covode rose, bid their leave from Mrs. Covode, and turned to depart for a hurried dram in the private rooms above. Just as Sandie turned to join the other fellows, who had but a few footsteps on him, he wheeled quickly and, "Oh!" he exclaimed. He'd bumped right into that incredibly beautiful young lady! "I'm sorry." he stammered as he realized who it was he'd run into. He was instantly and completely mortified.

She had been standing, talking to the older man and woman who had been seated on either side of her. She turned, now, to see Sandie standing there so deeply red with embarrassment, and she smiled to him.

"That's quite all right, young man," the older woman answered first in a friendly, courteous reply. "No harm done."

The older man only scowled at him.

Sandie couldn't move. He was frozen. That dazzling, beautiful young lady was smiling at him, saying something about him "being excused," and "not to mind," but he couldn't hear it all clearly. Birds were chirping and singing all around him; strange bells rang out all over the theater in soft, sweet, varying tonations. His knees started to weaken. He found himself drawn into her deep, brilliant, blue eyes; drowning in those two sapphire pools.

Then, from somewhere amid all these splendid sensations he was experiencing, there came an annoying buzz. He felt himself being drawn away; pulled back from the blissful, serene calm of those jewel-like eyes by a harsh, perturbing whine.

"Ex-cuse me?" he heard himself ask in faint response, for he was now able to identify the agitating distraction as being the voice of the older man.

"I asked if you were all right!" came the rather jarring voice again. This time it registered fully with Sandie for the man was practically in his face. "You don't look well! Are you ill? Do you have a fever?" he asked contemptibly.

"Now, Milrose," said the older woman in a more patronizing voice, "don't be so angry with the young man. If he is ill it'll do him no good for you to get him excited."

"Ill?...me?...uh, no...uh"...Sandie stammered, distracted. He tried to tear his gaze from the girl to respond to their comments but found he was repeatedly drawn back by her beauty.

"You ought to see a doctor! You're perspiring! And it's not even hot in here!" the man snapped. "What right have you to come in here and infect all of us with some camp malady? Could be smallpox!"

"But...Uncle...I'm...sure that..." came a voice soft as velvet and sweet as the scent of heather on a summer breeze. It was the lovely young lady speaking. Sandie knew, for he could see her lips moving, though her words came more to him as music. She was attempting to come to the defense of this handsome young soldier. But, like he, was unable to form a complete sentence, her eyes wandering dreamily over the features of the daring cavalryman.

"Sandie! Sandie! Are you coming?" came a more familiar voice, now penetrating the young men's blissful but confused enchantment. It was Thomas, returned to see what had delayed his friend. "I thought you were right behind us. I looked back and you weren't there."

"Say! Are you with him? Listen. Its bad enough you people pollute our city with your foul language, improper manners and creeping parasites...It's getting so respectable people can't go out anymore!" came the gruff voice of the older, balding man.

Thomas looked stunned at hearing this from the stranger. Taken completely by surprise at these biting comments, he just looked at the man questionably.

"Uh...yeah...Sure," Sandie replied to Thomas as his friend now tugged anxiously on his arm. This served, finally, to pull him from the enraptured captivation he'd been drawn into over the lovely young girl. He bowed politely to her. "Ma'am," he said, excusing himself, and he let Thomas drag him off.

"...and you'd better get your friend there to a doctor!" came a last, growling comment from the older man as the two captains moved off.

"Who was that?" Thomas asked with a bemused grin as they moved up the aisle.

"I don't know," Sandie replied pensively. "But I sure wish I did. Isn't she the most gorgeous person you've ever seen?"

"Who? The girl? Yes. She's pretty, all right. I'm talking about that man. What was he ranting on about?" Thomas asked.

"Hmm? I don't know. I, uh...I wasn't listening to him. I don't know," Sandie said, his thoughts distracted by the lingering memory of the girl.

"Are you all right? You seem kind of...I don't know...strange; distant, maybe. Are you coming down with something?" Thomas asked, puzzled over his friend's behavior.

"Lord only knows, Thomas. Lord only knows."

Chapter Three

Another Fine Project By
"MARCO DEVELOPMENTS"
Specialists in Design and Construction
Shopping Malls
Condominiums
Housing
Restaurants
Hotels.

The S-76 Sikorsky helicopter roared in low over the short, green stalks of the cornfields. Following the contours of the low rolling hills, it swooped across the highway, just missing the project sign that stood at the entrance to the yet unfinished luxury condominium site. Whirling along just a few feet off the ground, it traced the asphalt driveway the half mile distance to where a dozen office and supply trailers were parked, climbing only at the last instant to avoid a collision.

It stationed itself above them for a bit, hovering for a few moments and then, zooming off, it began to circle the entire 120-acre construction site, skirting by inches the heavy electric transmission lines and nearly nipping the top of the boom on the hydraulic crane that was swinging around to lower a roof truss into position.

"Fuckin' crazy Bastard!" the crane operator yelled in fright as he jerked hard in reverse on the swing control lever. The dangling wooden structure began swinging wildly, nearly toppling the two workers holding firmly to the guide ropes to it. They, too, had a few choice words to shout as they fought both to control the swinging truss and to keep their footing atop the narrow boards of the end walls.

The craneman set the brake and quickly stood out on the gantry to watch the helicopter finally swing back around to the office trailers. It hovered over a clearing between the trailers and a building complex. A hundred or more carpenters stopped nailing in mid-swing, or stood with arms full of boards to watch the 'copter slowly, and gently, set down.

Two men in white shirts came out quickly from an office trailer and stood on the portable metal porch at its doorway. They, too, watched as the whirling blades began to slow their beating rhythm.

"Oh, fuck! It's him," muttered Frank Walters, the project supervisor, a husky, graying man in his late fifties. He spoke in a gravelly voice, the result of countless Camel cigarettes lit one from the other. The rather large paunch and heavy bags under his bleary eyes indicated years of relieving stress at the serious end of the bar and bottle. Frank wished he had a drink right now, for he knew it was "his ass in the fire" for the project being behind schedule. His, and Tom Charles', the younger, slim, bespectacled architect standing beside him.

"Damn!" I was rather hoping he'd send out Bill or Johnny," sighed Tom as he, too, watched with some apprehension as the chopping rotors slowed even more, the swirling dust beginning to settle now.

Tom had designed the buildings and the entire plan. He had only been with "Marco Development" a little over two years. His first project for them, a two-hundred acre, moderately priced, suburban housing plan outside Richmond, Virginia, had won him promotion in the company and the approving eye of his superiors. That project had gone perfect. This project was anything but! Cost overruns in the site sewage facility and miscalculations in the design of the structural supports had added thousands of dollars to correct having the sewers back up, as well as to prevent the second floors from falling into the first floor.

Not so bad. Tom had, of course, provided for some cost overruns in his estimate. What he hadn't expected, and what now caused both his and Frank's stomachs to knot a little, was the arrival of the corporate helicopter from the Bethesda, Maryland, offices. They knew, all too well, who was at its controls.

Most of the work crew cocked their heads and watched with some irritation to see who would step out of the luxurious company helicopter. The word "Marco" emblazoned along its underbelly and sides, as well as the recklessly ostentatious display of flying gave clue to the importance of its pilot.

"Damn! Charlie, I love flying these things."

"Yes, sir. I know," replied the pilot as he busily shut the engine down. Concealed behind his dark flight glasses, he gave a side-long look of disgust at the young man in the co-pilots seat. "But flying like that is going to get us both killed one of these days—if I don't get my license revoked first."

"Ahhh! Don't worry about it, Charlie," said the young man. "I've got friends in the F.A.A. I'll take care of that."

"Hmmm," sighed the pilot as the blond, thirty-six-year-old man opened the door of the machine and stepped out. Staying low, he lifted his briefcase from behind the seat and hurried out from under the slowly rotating blades. The blue-collar men all watched as the impeccably dressed businessman walked the seventy yards or so to the office trailer. The two men in white shirts came off the steps to greet him, smiling, their hands extended as he drew close.

"Morning, Mr. Brody," said Frank, awkwardly pulling his hand back when it was ignored.

"Morning, James," Tom greeted him, his smile diminishing as he, too, withdrew his empty hand.

The young man they called James Brody ignored both pleasantries. He stood before them but looked over at the project area as the echo of pounding hammers and the roar of heavy equipment began resounding from the construction site. He seemed to be thinking; analyzing. The look on his face, the squint in his eye, both served to give the impression he was calculating, most likely, progress in relation to dollars. Whatever it was, he did not seem pleased.

Both men waited for him to speak, trying not to show their nervousness, but anxious to know what was going through the mind of the young man.

After a couple of moments, he spoke, still gazing at the work site. "Running a bit behind schedule, aren't we Thomas." It was a statement, not a question, and it was directed at the dark-haired architect. Frank seemed to relax a little as the blame now fell not on him, but on the man beside him.

"Well...uh...not really. That is...it'll be easy to get back on track once the floor joist problem is corrected; he said, a little breathlessly, though he tried to sound reassuring to his boss.

"This little mistake of yours is going to cost me about 150,000 dollars, you know." James said matter-of-factly, and with just a touch of irritation in his voice.

"Yeah, James. But...but...look at it like this, you'll still get the benefit of the initial savings we'd figured on by using the 'Denning' floor plan over the 'Lazor'. It'll cost us a little more, initially, but you're still saving money," the architect explained, trying his best to sound convincing.

James now turned his head to the architect and gazed at the shorter fellow. Although he said nothing, the slight frown on his boss's face showed Tom the man was not comforted by the explanation. He looked at Tom a long moment, as if he were studying the man's mind. Then, drawing a breath to finally begin a reply he was suddenly interrupted when the office door opened. A thin, balding man leaned out looking rather embarrassed and timid. "Uh...excuse me. Mr. Brody?"

"Yess," he replied, drawing out the "s" to show his displeasure at the interruption.

The man turned a deep crimson. "Uh, sir, there's a...uh...call for you. It's your office."

"Inside, gentlemen," he said giving a nod toward the door. "Let's see how you've solved keeping my floors from falling in—economically." He moved deliberately between them, forcing the two subordinates to step back for him to pass. As he entered the trailer, the two men rolled their eyes at each other despondently and followed him in.

The young man responsible for the growing anxiousness and aggravation both the architect and the supervisor were feeling was James Marcus Brody. At thirty-six years of age, he was president and major stockholder of "Marco Development Corporation," as well as a number of its subsidiary companies. Armed with a Harvard law degree and a Wharton M.B.A., he had taken over control of his grandfather's construction business at twenty-eight. Investing in private student housing at various state-owned universities, then into condominiums and small shopping malls, his business had burgeoned into a major corporation in just a few years. Then came larger development projects, one after the other, the collateral of one providing the capital for the next. Bankers and financiers began to stumble over one another to offer him money.

The really big move came when he began to purchase large tracts of abandoned waterfront properties for pennies, then rebuilding with federal loans to turn them into fashionably expensive apartments and shopping districts. Money, power and influence seemed to snowball toward him, engulfing him so completely at such a young age that he grew tremendously fond of having all three—and he learned how to use them to his advantage.

He was a modern-age "Midas" and he reveled in it. Every project he invested in succeeded even to the bewilderment of his financial backers. He would buy farm land or large tracts of unusable acreage in areas few people would travel or visit, causing his "backers" to balk or worry. Then, before the development plans were even announced, he would use his influence with government people to have a major highway constructed nearby under the guise of connecting major urban areas for economic reasons.

Having already purchased the land on either side of the highway, housing and condominium projects would start to flourish and shopping malls would begin dotting intersections—all with the familiar "Marco Development Corp." sign out front.

Handsome and resolute, he stood six foot two, well proportioned, slim, but not skinny, with a milky-white complexion. He wore his hair in neat, golden locks that curled just at his shoulders as if to purposely defy the staid "Wall Streeters," and lived a flamboyant lifestyle much as the new "Texas oilmen." Talk-show appearances and magazine articles all added to the fame and celebrity status of the wealthy young man.

Women, he had aplenty. Starlets and models lined up at his door hoping to audition for a part in his life—and he loved it! Dating one after the other, he enjoyed the flattery and pampering to his every fantasy and whim. He was careful, though, never to allow romance to interfere with business. Most often he would feign a romantic interest in a wealthy starlet, gaining her trust and confidence with subtle hints of matrimony. He would talk them into helping finance a new business venture—on his terms, of course. Then, after the deal was closed and the monies received, he would drop them quickly and move on to the next wealthy prospect. The only tangible asset the woman would lose was James, and perhaps a percentage point on her investment.

The long term would show a profit, however, for not only did she receive a return on her money, but notoriety always followed any relationship with this young man, boosting her popularity and demand.

Inside the office trailer, two disconsolate men stood leaning over one of the drafting tables pretending to be studying blueprints. Actually, they were straining their ears to eavesdrop on the conversation James was having with his office. Both men were soon to hear the young man's ire directed at them, but what they were listening for now was a glimpse into the "mind of the master" at work, for James was an artist in his field. His manner of confidence and assuredness in crafting a deal virtually guaranteed him the ear of his listener—and then their checkbooks—for any endeavor he wished to pursue.

They were disappointed this time, however, for all they overheard was some routine discussion of appointments and meetings; nothing of the backroom deal-making they had hoped to listen in on. Not yet, anyway. As he placed the phone in its cradle he turned to them. "Sit down, guys. Let's talk," he said.

Tom and Frank took chairs by the drafting table. James stood leaning against a file cabinet, his arms akimbo, with all the demeanor of a father about to reprimand his sons. "Now, relax, Frank. I can tell you're nervous. But, it's okay. Don't worry. I've taken care of that little problem with the boundary line," James said, a slight grin on his face.

Frank blew a long, relieved exhale of smoke from his cigarette. James was referring to that "not so little" problem of the property lines having been staked incorrectly. For some reason the young, recently-hired company surveyor had begun his calculations on northern, adjacent farmland instead of using the long-abandoned railroad siding running nearby to the east from which all other existing boundaries had been referenced. This threw the entire project thirty feet onto a county-owned right-of-way; land which was earmarked for a community park. Frank, believing the company surveyor's interpretation of the calculations was correct, decided to continue construction. The ensuing court battle and adverse publicity finally revealed his misjudgment. The county supervisors had balked at selling off this ground to Marco Development and the costly alternative was for the company to re-dig the footers and rebuild the foundation walls where they should have been.

The surveyor was let go immediately and Frank had worried for his own position. Though James said no more about it, that feigned smile told Frank quite enough. He was aware of how subtly vindictive and unforgiving James could be in matters of money regardless of what he might express verbally. Frank's only relief was that he still had a job, probably owing to the many years he'd been with the company. He believed more would be heard of this later, probably resulting in his being assigned to smaller, less costly projects when this one was completed.

"How'd you manage that, James?" Frank asked, and as soon as the words escaped his lips he gasped inwardly with regret that he'd asked it. He couldn't believe he'd asked. He knew it was none of his business and he didn't believe the young man would tell him, anyway. It just seemed to slip out of his mouth as the next natural sentence to this conversation. He was stunned with the reply.

"Well, let's just say it's dealt with." James said, holding up his hand and rubbing his thumb against his first two fingers—a sure indication that money, again, could solve many problems.

"No shit! You bought off the supervisors," Frank said in astonishment. "I didn't think anyone could get to those bastards. Imagine, stalling millions of dollars over thirty lousy feet. Well, that's Virginia's politics for ya'," he muttered, lighting a cigarette from the smoldering stub of the last one.

Tom sat listening attentively, his arms folded across his chest. He was amazed and impressed with the behind the scenes magic that money could work. He was also awaiting his turn under the gun. Frank had been with the company for years, working his way up through promotions with old man "Jim" Brody, James' grandfather and namesake, the founder of the original company. Tom was new and could handily be used as the "scape-goat" for this whole mess.

"Well, it wasn't just the thirty feet," James explained. "Reilly King just doesn't like change. He grew up just over the hill there and didn't like the idea of the land being developed. He used to hunt pheasants here. Thought we cheated old man Colston out of his farm...didn't pay 'im enough for what it was worth. You know. Sooo...I had him up to the house the other night for dinner—flew him in on the chopper, put on a big spread and all. We talked about it awhile, you know, about progress, how things had to change and grow. You know my spiel. You've heard it before."

"Yeah. Ha!Ha!" Frank laughed hoarsely. He turned slightly and slapped Tom's knee as though he was letting him in on a private, company joke, that James' "spiel" was a euphemism. Exhaling smoke from a long drag on the cigarette, Frank started to cough as he chuckled. Too many years of smoking. Tom just smiled back, a little confused, very much interested.

"Ha!Ha!"...*cough*...*cough*... "What's this...*cough*...little spiel...cost us...this time!" Frank asked as he tried to clear his lungs and catch his wind, making disgusting choking noises.

"Mmm...couple weeks in Hawaii for his whole family, an access road into the park area...some other incentives," Marc shrugged, as though this was all typical in the course of doing business.

"Who else's vote did you swing around?" Frank asked excitedly, his face quite crimson and his eyes a bit watery from coughing. He was caught up in the thrill of this "behind the scenes" maneuvering. "You needed two ta' bring it our way."

"Clarence," James said coolly, though a haughty air of triumph was glimmering in his eye.

"Yeah! What'd that take? He's a weird one, that guy. Down on this whole project from the start," Frank said, shaking his head and frowning at the very thought of the man. He remembered having met Clarence Wilmer and recalled the hostility between them at that meeting. Clarence, a man usually favorable toward growth and development, particularly if it meant jobs for the locals, had tried to bid on the excavation work at the site. He became angry and bitter when be learned the company would not be using any local labor. All supplies and labor would be furnished from headquarters since the project was within the "economic" proximity of their Bethesda resources. Frank had been short with the man when they had met; even, perhaps, a bit too arrogant. But that had been before the boundary dispute. He was afraid he'd soured the supervisor too greatly to ever hope to repair the damage and turn the man's vote. He was glad to hear his boss had been able to come to terms with the man.

"Well...nothing, actually," James said. He moved to the window and gazed out at the work in progress on the buildings. With his back to the two men, he casually glanced over his shoulder, smiling. "Uhhh...by the way, Clarence's company will be doing the excavation work at both the Frederick Mall and the Sharpsburg project."

"Uh, huh," came Frank's acknowledgement with a grin and a nod. The bids were just coming in for both projects, making it rather easy for Clarence Wilmer's company to enter the winning numbers.

Frank and Tom were both surprised that they were being made privy to what most certainly should have been secretive information. Tom could only surmise that they were being informed out of James' need for boasting. He'd only closed his "negotiations" this morning and seemed to need to strut once more over his business savvy.

James turned around to face the two men. His grin now dropped to a straight face as he looked—firmly at the architect. "Tom. You, on the other hand, should be shot. You should have caught both your mistakes on paper before we even dug a hole. You cost me a lot of money, ya' know. But I like your design. I like your layout. I had your plans reviewed by Little and Singer before we even came out here. They caught it and drafted a revised print."

"What?" Tom about gasped in astonishment at hearing this. To have sent his plans to two senior architects without his knowledge of it was objectionable enough in itself. But not to tell him of the problems uncovered and to let him proceed ignorantly was both an embarrassment and an insult.

"You are good, Tom. You've got a lot of potential. You're really an asset to my company with your imagination and talents in design. But you're weak in structurals and careless in coordinating details. That's why I had your plans reviewed without your knowing it. That's also why I let you start construction, hoping you'd catch your mistakes. And you did. I allowed for the cost overruns. I know you'll be more careful in the future," James said to him, emphasizing the last statement with a bit of condescension in his voice.

"Mmm...I will," Tom mutters. He really didn't care for the patronizing tone in which he was being reprimanded. James was younger than he and though there was considerably more money behind James and he was talented in business, Tom felt he was every bit the equal of his boss, though in other areas.

A silence fell between the three men. Frank puffed away on his cigarette, trying not to be in the room as he faded into studying a blueprint. James had his gaze fixed on Tom, watching as the man seemed to be thinking remorse—fully of his errors now that his boss had confronted him with them.

Tom, though, was inwardly steaming. His mind raced with thoughts, once again, of quitting Marco Development. He could take his wife, Connie, and their two sons, and move to most any area of the country. He would set out his shingle and open "Charles' Architectural Services." The dream would live!

Then he thought of how much he would be giving up. The years of struggling to build his own company could never match what James was paying him now. Hired away from "Drexel, Shuman and White" two years ago, his present employment had brought him more prosperity than he could have imagined.

The salary, the benefits...Oh, the benefits!—company limos, vacation houses in exotic places, company aircraft to carry him anywhere he wanted to go. Connie had told him he was talented. "Marco only hires the best," she had said. But they both knew it was his lack of confidence in himself as the reason he hadn't started his own company.

Staring at the floor, his mind filled with contempt for the young man he knew was still staring at him and waiting for a reaction, Tom let his mind drift toward the building design in which "his" company would be housed. He'd drawn it over and over again, blueprinted down to the last receptacle; decorated and arranged its furniture to include even the pencil sharpeners—then he'd tear it up. In periods of depression, when things weren't going well, he'd draft it all over again.

No changes. It was perfect. Every time he'd come close to gaining the courage to resign—would start, even, to draft his resignation—some recurring, unidentifiable feeling would cause him to lose nerve and to tear it all up. "Some things we can act on by our own selves," his wife would comfort him in saying "other things must come in their own time. If it is meant to be, it will happen. Just be patient and wait till you know inside that the time is right for a move. James compensates you quite well financially, even if he is hard to work for. We'll let events lead us where they may and be satisfied with whatever we're to have. You're a kind, gentle and talented man, Tom, and you've got a good heart. You can do so much. Wait to move when your heart really tells you," she would say.

Tom was building nerve again now. He knew this side of James, the side that always had to point out the mistakes or weaknesses of others. Always it was done in some humiliating, embarrassing way that would leave James to shine as the one who had uncovered or caught the mistake. Only last month Tom had been present at a meeting where James had rebuked a purchasing agent for inclining more favorably toward the purchase of several specific models of earth-moving equipment.

James presented several charts and brochures to demonstrate to the man why he should favor a different model. Displays such as this were constant with James. He kept a close, watchful eye over every aspect of his business, and it made Tom, and almost everyone else in the company, uneasy.

James finally broke the silence, believing Tom had had enough time to feel foolish and embarrassed over this "little mistake." "Well, enough about that. How's the work on the Antietam complex coming?"

Tom snapped out of his mind drift, and so, too, his growing nerve to resign. He realized James was asking about the other project he'd been assigned to design, the Antietam Luxury Condominium and Housing Complex—one hundred fifty acres of lush farmland that was smack up against the Civil War battlefield. In fact, the ground had seen a part of the fighting only in a more minor way considering the enormity of the blood shed on other parts of the field of battle. The park system had never purchased this property and it had come up for sale by the private owner who'd grown too old and too tired of trying to scratch a living from its soil. Tom was to design the complex to enjoy the most advantage of the scenic fields of battle.

Out of some guilt or reverence, or something he just couldn't pinpoint, Tom had designed the buildings in low profile to "blend in" with the natural settings. The roof lines, the colors, even the driveways were designed to fade into the background to have as little distorting impact on the topography as was possible. Tom had been pleased with his work. It was one of his most brilliant creations considering what he was attempting to accomplish—hiding an entire housing complex from visiting tourists. It was rejected flatly!

James wanted something bold and pretentious; something loud; something that would stand out to everyone. "Thousands of visitors tour that place every year. The people buying our homes want to show off. They want to be looked at and held in wonder," James had told him. "You buy luxuries for status as well as comfort. You spend fifty K for a car and you want people to notice. Hell, man, thousands of people are going to notice who's driving away from those homes. I want the tourists to look at those homes and wonder, 'Wow! That fella must have money!' You design me something that says 'I'm a success. I have power!' That'll be what sells my units."

"Uh…well…it's coming along," Tom lied to his boss. "I've got some ideas I'm playing with." In truth, he'd come to the first "designer's block" he'd ever experienced. He hadn't been able to put a blasted idea onto paper yet.

"Good. Good. I'll be expecting to see something concrete in the next month or so. Uhh…you're not having a problem with this are you?" James asked suspiciously.

"No…no. I…uh…I'll have something for you in a month. Why?"

"Well…I just wondered. I've heard there are some objections to this project getting accepted. You know; protestors, rabble-rousers; people against progress or anybody trying to make a buck. There are a couple groups forming, trying to get the local government to withhold the building permits. They think my buildings will detract from the appearance of the fields. Hell, they're not even on the battlefields—least not right on them. It's like that tower in Gettysburg. A lot of people tried to shut that project off when it was proposed. Hell, I've been there. It's hardly noticeable. Shit! If I'd have done that project, you'd have noticed! Protestors be damned! That guy's got a gold mine if he'd use his head and make it into something bigger, more attractive." James paused a second. He seemed to be thinking; plotting. His eyes glazed over a bit as if he were inspired suddenly with an idea. Then he snapped from it. "Just thought you might be against it, too," he said.

"Me? Hey. Doesn't matter what I think. You play the tune. I just dance." Tom said with a shrug.

"Okay. Good. I just wondered. After that last proposal of yours…eh…just curious."

"No. I'll have something for you!" Tom said, a bit of indignation in his voice.

"Good. Now, let's get on these figures for the supporting beams and where the materials are coming from," James said.

Tom and Frank began to rifle through their papers. It was going to be a long, trying day for both of them.

Chapter Four

Sandie, Thomas and Congressman Covode followed the crowd down the aisle, slowly filtering back to their seats. Sandie felt he was floating on air! Over drinks with the congressman in the private rooms above, he and Thomas had been invited to a party at Stewart House. "Not a big deal" the congressman had told them, "Just a little reception for the arrival of the British ambassador. We've got to make him comfortable and welcomed, you know. Don't want those damned English siding with the Rebels."

"Not a big deal!" Sandie gasped inwardly. "For the congressman, perhaps—a man used to the lavish parties of the Washington monied." But for Sandie it was a chance to participate, if even momentarily, in a life-style he had only heard stories of and could only ever have dreamed about. As they turned from the aisle to move toward their seats Sandie felt a lump rise in his throat. He had spied that lovely blue-eyed girl sitting patiently for the curtain to rise.

He was following Thomas and Congressman Covode and had to glance down to watch the movements of their legs as he seemed to have forgotten how to move his own. His knees became stiff and unbendable; the muscles of his thighs and calves seemed no longer to cooperate in working rhythmically or naturally. He had to force the movements in his limbs lest they seize up altogether and leave him frozen and paralyzed there in front of the entire theater crowd.

At once she looked up and caught his gaze! She smiled to him. Such a smile! She hadn't smiled at the congressman or at Thomas. She was smiling at him! A warm, uplifting, gentle and friendly smile. And those eyes! Wide, attentive, glimmering; shining so brilliantly.

Sandie tried to smile back to her but felt himself a failure at matching such an angelic expression. He had confidence enough in his handsomeness—his thoughts confirmed over and again by the many lovelies that had pursued his attentions back home. But that was in Hannastown, Westmoreland County. This was Washington. Tens of thousands of young men were encamped about the city. Plenty enough there were of men with not only good looks, but of higher social standing and rank than he to catch the glance of a girl with her charms. But it was he, Sandie Duncan, that she was smiling at and gracing with her gaze at this moment.

"Hello. Did you have a pleasant intermission?"

She spoke to him! Sandie's heart pounded in his chest. He wondered if he would be able to reply. Had his mouth become as frozen and as stiffened as his legs? He somehow choked out the words. "Y-yes. I did. Thank you."

"Good. The third act is a rather long one. It may seem to 'drag on' in parts but I think you'll enjoy it."

"Th-thank you," he said, and was relieved that he managed a reply without stammering too badly. Their smiles lingered upon each other as Sandie paused near her momentarily. He wanted to say more. He wanted to speak to her and ask her all about herself; what was her name? How old was she? What's it like in heaven? Was she an earth-bound angel? He wanted to hear her voice again; to hear the music escape from those inviting lips. No aria sung in any music hall in Pittsburgh that Sandie had attended could match the sweet tones emitted from those lips when she spoke.

Then, he became aware of the gruff, balding man sitting next to her. He was staring daggers at Sandie. "Excuse me, young man. You're blocking my view and the play is about to begin. Care to take your seat!" It was a statement, not a question, and Sandie got the message.

"Sorry, Sir," he said in apology and bowed to the man, believing it would be best to show politeness should this prove to be the girl's father. Then, with a deeper bow and a nod to the young lady he excused himself and moved to his seat.

"Harrumph! Cavalrymen! You've got to be wary of cavalrymen, Katie," he heard the man grump in a not too low aside to the girl.

Sandie reeled upon hearing this. He'd only just taken his seat and all but exploded out of it with excitement. "Katie! That was her name! Katie! Katie! Katie!" he sang out in his mind, and he did all he could do to control himself from standing and shouting it before the entire audience. "Katie. What a fitting name," he thought. It echoed through the corridors of his mind, over and over—"Katie...Katie...Catherine...Cathleen..." He chanced to steal a quick glance at her while everyone was engrossed in the play. No one noticed him. How long it had been since the curtain opened he hadn't really noticed. "Cathleen...Sure. That was it. She's a Cathleen," he mused. "No. That's her Christian name. She's definitely a 'Katie'."

It was not long, or so it seemed to Sandie, that the house lamps were lit and people were standing to cheer the performers. Sandie stood with everyone else and applauded appreciatively. Only, his applause was inclined more toward the young lady he'd heard called 'Katie.' He continued stealing glances her way from the corner of his eye and noticed, much to his delight, that she, too, was often diverting her eyes from the stage toward him.

When the crowd finally began to exit the theater, Sandie was obliged to remain and talk awhile to Congressman Covode. He watched as Katie moved along the aisle accompanied by the older woman and that growly, balding man.

His heart sank lower the further she moved away. He would never see her again; he knew that. He fixed the memory of her smiling face and flashing blue eyes securely in his mind, hoping to recall it on cold, wet nights as he lay in the fields awaiting the next day's dangers. Surely, just the remembrance of that beautiful smile would warm him some as the Virginia rains pelted his blanket.

****

As the sun began to fade in the west there cast an orange hew to the sky. A heavy rain earlier that morning had added to the sloppiness of the sidewalks and streets, causing difficulties negotiating through the crowded city of Washington. This, however, did little to deter Sandie and Thomas from exploring the sites of the now divided nation's capital. After a hearty breakfast, prepared for them by Julia, the two had set off on a day's trek around the town.

They inspected the extensive defenses of the city, visited the hospitals to chat with convalescing members of the regiment, viewed the unfinished dome of the Capitol building and toured other public buildings of interest to newcomers. They finished the afternoon with a supper at the Willard Hotel, dining with several staff officers of the 2nd Pennsylvania Volunteers. The fare had been plentiful and delicious with turkey and potatoes, stuffing, desserts, and a fine wine to wash it all down. A splendid meal considering that they had subsisted these last few months mostly on boiled beef, hardtack, and coffee.

With their stomachs full but their purses nearly empty, they had returned to Mrs. Bordlinger's to bathe and dress for their evening finale; the reception and dance at Stewart House. They polished their brass buttons, buckles and other hardware, shined their shoes and whisked their uniforms. When they had dressed, they both made a handsome pair, certain to turn the heads of a few of the Washington lovelies, as they had been assured by the congressman that there would be plenty of them in attendance. They were fine figures of dashing cavalrymen, standing tall, proud and manly.

"Miss Sally says ta' tell ya'll yo' hossez is ready out front," came a voice through the hanging hams and herbs.

"Thank you, Julia. We're about ready," Thomas yelled back through the door to her. "Ready, old boy?" he asked of Sandie, standing to look and admire himself in the small mirror attached to the wall.

"Ready!" Sandie snapped excitedly as he stood from the bed where he'd put a last shine to his boots. He nudged Thomas aside from the mirror while buckling his sword over the yellow sash. He ached for a peek at how he would appear to others, especially the fair maidens. "Ahh...dashing!" he quipped roguishly as he admired himself.

"Come on. We don't want to be late. The ladies are waiting. Let's see if we can't stir a few hearts tonight," Thomas chimed as he gathered his overcoat.

"Mm..." Sandie replied, pausing a moment. He thought of the beautiful 'Katie', the lovely young lass he'd seen last night. "Oh," he thought wistfully, "if only I could gaze upon that comely face again." A faint smile from the memory of her drew a certain sadness from his heart as he resigned himself to the improbabilities of ever meeting her again. Washington was such a large city and was literally bursting with people.

****

The dapple-gray mare and the big bay came to a halt by the two brightly lit lamp posts at the end of the curved carriage path. Music from the orchestra filtered down from the gaily-lighted mansion—a lively quickstep with a military air, vaguely familiar to the two captains as one played by the regimental band during grand reviews of the Cavalry Corps. Many carriages were pulling up to unload their passengers and were greeted by colored servants who politely helped the visitors down, then escorted them by lantern up the short walk to the large oak doors.

Sandie and Thomas quickly scanned what they could see of the huge, gray, cut-stone building. Built in the style of the southern plantation houses they had passed in their course of invasion into Virginia, it sat only some forty paces from the street behind an ornate wrought iron fence that appeared to surround the entire property.

The cobblestone carriage path arced to a short walkway, then back again to the road. A narrow alley leading to the rear out-buildings separated the house from the dwelling to its left. On the north side, tall, dense evergreens were grown to screen the inquisitive eyes of neighbors not thirty paces from the long trellis festooned porch. The front of the house lacked the usually popular front portico but was adorned with a pair of enormously oversized oak doors with ornate carvings. On either side of the three marble steps leading up to the doors, small sculptured cherubs greeted visitors with silent blasts of their long, stone trumpets.

Thomas gave a low whistle of admiring awe at the enormity of the mansion. "It's big," he noted, as though one could choose from so many adjectives but that the simple one, he chose said enough. He squeezed the horse's flanks and headed up the path toward the greeters.

"It is that," Sandie replied, following his friend's lead and moving his horse along.

"Welcome, Suhs! Welcome to de' Stu'ut huss. We is ruht pleast ya'll cuhd jine us t'nite," drawled a colored servant as he took the reins of both horses and held them as the two officers dismounted. Another servant came out from around the alley and over to the horses, gathering the reins from the first man. "Lucas, heah, will tend to de' hossez. Go ruht on in n' enjih y'seves," he said as he smiled cheerfully to them and motioned with his hand toward the door. He bowed low as they passed before him.

"Thank you. We hope to," Sandie said as he and Thomas could barely hide their exuberance.

As they all but bounded the few steps to the massive doors the one on the right side seemed to swing open magically to allow them entry. After passing through the doorway, they came to stand on a long, wide, raised foyer of polished oak planking. Their excitement was stifled some, then, as they sheepishly beheld the interior of the house. Just off the few steps of the foyer was a cavernous room filled with finely dressed men and women.

Sandie and Thomas exchanged nervous glances for each other's reaction for, truly, neither man had ever experienced such an extravaganza. The expensively decorated room served to accent the wealth and power of the people gathered. A hasty sweep of the room revealed handsomely attired gentlemen in their finest suits. The many military figures present wore tailored uniforms that showed no wear save perhaps from reviews on the parade grounds. The women wore lovely, long gowns of the finest silks and the newest cottons, proving that, even with the blockade against the southern ports, contraband was still permeating north to the textile mills of New England. No deprivations caused by the war were in evidence here. In fact, the greater part of the wealthy present were the direct recipients of the fortunes to be made supplying the necessities for waging war.

"Welcome, gentlemen. May I take your wraps?" asked the doorman as he stepped up behind them. He had gently closed the massive doors, surprising them as he approached from his hidden silence.

"Uh, yes. Thank you," answered Sandie as he and Thomas began to remove their coats. When they turned to hand them to the man, they noted his rough, weathered face. He was a big man, with broad shoulders—not at all what one would expect of a doorman's appearance. They also noted he extended only his right hand; the left one being gone at the elbow.

"A mini-ball at Bull Run, Captains," the man explained proudly when he saw them both looking at the empty sleeve. "I was with the First Corp at Blackburn's Ford."

"Oh. I'm sorry," Sandie replied.

"Mrs. Stewart was kind enough to give me employment as her butler and coachman. Not much a smith can do with only one arm."

"No. You were fortunate to find employment," Thomas said.

"Mrs. Stewart is very kind. May I announce your presence, Sirs?"

As they laid their coats over his arm and set their hats in the clasp of his hand Sandie said, "Well, uh, I'd rather you wouldn't, actually. See, um, we're guests, sort of, of Congressman Covode."

"Oh. Very good, Sirs. You'll find the congressman right over there," the man said, pointing with the arm over which the coats were draped.

"I see," Sandie replied as he spied the congressman standing with a group of men, two of whom wore the Union blue with Brigadier General insignias. "Thank you. We'll go over at once."

The man made no reply but handed the wraps to a young colored servant girl and turned to greet the next arrivals. Thomas and Sandie both watched the girl as she went to the cloakroom just off the foyer. "Do you suppose all negro women have such large bosoms?" Thomas chortled to his friend.

"Thomas!"

"Well...everyone I've seen seems to be overly endowed in that respect."

"Tttt! Mind yourself," Sandie chided him good naturedly. "Besides, you've probably not seen but half a dozen ever."

"Mmm...and they've every one of them been, shall we say, 'ample.'"

"Ha! Ha! You're incorrigible."

Congressman Covode caught sight of the two men approaching and greeted them with enthusiasm. "Ah!...Well, boys. Welcome!...Welcome!," he said as he shook their hands.

"Congressman...," they both replied in greeting as they exchanged handshakes.

"Glad you could make it. Any trouble finding the place?"

"Not at all. Everyone we asked knew exactly where to direct us," Thomas answered.

"Yes. I suppose anyone who's been in the city a spell has learned of it. Nice place, huh?"

"Indeed," Sandie beamed. "Thank you for inviting us."

"No problem. My pleasure. Always glad to show my hometown boys a good time when I can. The Mrs. doesn't go out much for parties these days. She tires easily. So, that left one opening, anyway. Besides, a gathering this big, who's going to notice another face among all these folks? Say! Let me introduce you all. Boys, this is General McPherson and General Wheatly. I'm sure you're both familiar with those names."

"Oh, yes indeed," replied Sandie, exchanging handshakes with the two senior officers.

"Certainly," Thomas said as he, too, shook hands with them. "We covered General Wheatly's flank at Bull Run."

"Indeed?" responded the General with a certain enthused interest. "Then you must be with the 64th Regiment!"

Thomas smiled, "Yes, sir. The very same. Companies "A" and "B." In fact, it was Sandie, here who commanded the lead in charging the batteries that were pounding your withdrawal."

"Well, then. I'm indebted to you, Captain. You saved the lives of many good men by your bravery."

Sandie blushed and bowed slightly but made no reply.

The congressman beamed delightedly. "Yes. Well. That's the stuff the "64th" is made of. Lots of fine, brave lads in my district. Why, only last month I..."

"Excuse me," interrupted the blond young man in the dark suit. He had been standing silently, listening to the conversation and waiting for his introduction. As he could tell the congressman was about to begin a political oration for the benefit of a potentially influential vote from his district, he broke in. "I'm John Hay. Pleased to meet you both," he smiled earnestly.

As they shook hands Sandie asked, "John Hay, secretary to President Lincoln?"

"Yes," John answered, blushing a bit. He still was not completely comfortable with his rise to a position of such notoriety. "I'm sorry. We didn't catch the names," he injected, for the congressman had forgotten to introduce the two captains.

"Theodore Sandfeld Duncan," Sandie said with a bow. "Folks call me Sandie, if you please. My friend, here, is Thomas Edwards."

Thomas, smiling slyly, mocked Sandie in jest by bowing politely and saying, "My friends call me...Thomas, if you please."

John Hay laughed at this but bowed respectfully in return. "Pleasure, gentleman. Have you had refreshment, yet?"

"No. Not yet," Sandie replied to the young man of about his own age. "We've only just arrived."

Thomas and the other men had fallen into conversation and John Hay interrupted once more. "Excuse me, gentlemen. I'm going to show our new acquaintances to the refreshment table. They must have something to drink to chase away the evening chill."

"Certainly. Certainly. I'm forgetting myself," said the congressman, mindful that a possible vote must be shown a grand time. They must return to camp with good stories to tell of the generosity and thoughtfulness of their Congressional representative to his home district boys. They, in turn, would thank him with their votes.

55

"Thanks. But I'm fine," Thomas replied, deciding he would rather stay and discuss matters with the two generals. To have high-ranking friends could prove beneficial if the war were to last longer than expected.

Sandie and John Hay made their way through the crowd in the direction of the refreshment tables across the room. They moved along the outer perimeter as couples were dancing to a lively quickstep while others stood watching and conversing.

"So, Mr. Hay. What's it like?"

"Please. Call me John. What's what like?"

"You know. Working for Mr. Lincoln."

"Oh. Well...it's fascinating. He's a remarkable man. But don't be too awfully impressed. I'll likely ask you the same."

"Pardon?"

"What's it like, Sandie? What's it like to draw your saber and lead a charge into cannon and musketry?"

Sandie thought a moment, then smiled. "Oh. It's fascinating. It's a remarkable experience." The two men laughed together at this.

At once, Sandie stopped him, halting John with a quick pull at his arm. The secretary looked back at his friend, curiously noting a change had come over him. His face was flushed and his mouth was agape. He seemed frozen; rigid; still clinging tightly to John's arm.

"What is it, Captain? Are you all right? You're not ill, are you?"

"No...no...I'm...fine," Sandie replied, obviously distracted. Then, "John. Do you know that young lady?"

John Hay looked in the direction of the refreshment tables at which Sandie's gaze seemed fixed. There, at the far end of the tables, stood a group of four young ladies and an elderly, gray-haired woman. "Which one?" the secretary asked.

"The one in the green satin."

John Hay smiled. "Whoa! Sandie, my friend. You cavalrymen are brave and daring. That's Cathleen Wheatly. General Wheatly's daughter. You've certainly set your sights high. A wonderful girl, I'm told. Intelligent, pretty. An accomplished pianist, too. But rather independent, or so I'm led to believe. Many a good horseman has tried to bridle that filly, if you'll excuse the expression. All have failed. Now, you take Miss Mary Hurd, there. She's a sweetheart. That girl can..."

"Do you know her?" Sandie cut him short.

"Who? Cathleen? I've met her. She's accompanied the General to see Mr. Lincoln on several occasions."

"Will you introduce me?'

"Oh, Sandie..."

"Please?"

"Oh, very well. But I feel you'll avail yourself to no end. She's a charming person, but not the kind of woman you'll be likely to..." John dropped his thought in mid-sentence. He could tell from the expression on Sandie's face that nothing he could say would deter the young officer's interest in the girl. "Come on. I'll introduce you."

"Thank you, John. Thank you," Sandie beamed in delight.

"Hmmm..." John Hay smiled as he led the young man to the small party of women.

Sandie stood back some, waiting anxiously. A hundred thoughts swirled through his mind as he wondered what he might say to her when they were finally and formally introduced. He watched as his new friend leaned into the group and whispered something in the young lady's ear. She said something to the other girls and turned, departing their company to follow the young secretary. When she saw Sandie standing there and recognized him as the 'young officer' to whom she was to be introduced she stopped short. A smile came over her face—that same, sweet, gentle and friendly smile she had shown to Sandie just the night before.

John Hay had continued over to Sandie and only now realized the girl was not with him but had halted a few paces away. He glanced from one to the other, quizzically. Then he noticed the warm smiles they had for each other.

"Uh...Miss Cathleen Wheatly," John began awkwardly. "May I introduce Captain Theodore Duncan? Uh, 'Sandie' as he is known to his friends," John said, trying to be light, but not at all sure of what to make of this situation.

"You certainly may, Mr. Hay," the girl said, her eyes and smile fixed on the young cavalryman.

John was beginning to feel a bit uncomfortable. It appeared to him these two had met before, yet Sandie had asked for an introduction. Though puzzled, he continued. "Ahem! Uh...Captain Duncan. I'm pleased to introduce Miss Cathleen Wheatly. 'Katie,' to her friends, as most of us know her by." Then John Hay paused—watching; waiting.

Neither Sandie or Katie spoke as they stood gazing at one another until, after what seemed an interminably long time—at least for the Secretary—Katie finally spoke. "Well, Captain, did you enjoy the performance last night?"

Sandie managed to pull himself from his seemingly intoxicated state of paralytic bliss to answer her, though he could not pull his gaze from the comely girl's deep blue eyes that were as equally affixed to his. "Yes. Very much so. Though I found myself much more impressed with the beautiful scenery," he said, his voice inflection implying he meant more than the stage sets.

"Yes," she replied, blushing slightly. "I believe I know what you mean. I, too, found myself...drawn somewhat...to the scenery."

"Tell me. If you are General Wheatly's daughter, who were those people accompanying you? The older gentleman seemed not to take kindly to me."

"Oh, ho!" Katie laughed. "That was Uncle Milrose and Aunt Lin Sheffield. I stay with them while father is at camp. I'm from Philadelphia originally. They're really rather harmless. Uncle Milrose doesn't like soldiers—particularly cavalrymen. He fancies me marrying a lawyer or banker. He's very protective and tries to guard me from any gentlemen whose parent's name he hasn't recognized."

"Oh, I see," Sandie laughed gaily. "Well, I'll remember that and try to keep my distance of him then."

John Hay had stood listening and decided his presence was no longer required. Delighted that the two seemed to be managing well enough without him, he excused himself. "Well...uh...If you both will excuse me. I must circulate. Politics, you know. Mrs. Lincoln has taken ill this afternoon with one of her headaches.

So, unfortunately, the President couldn't attend tonight. I've got to pull the Ambassador from our friend Mr. Seward, there, or we'll be at war with England before the night is through. It was wonderful meeting you, Captain. Please, let's have a dram together before the night is over."

Sandie wrestled his eyes from the girl to acknowledge the young man's departure. "It's been a pleasure, Mr. Secretary," he bowed, and with an aside wink to him he added, "And thank you."

"Hmm...I hope so," John Hay said earnestly. He clapped a warm, friendly hand on Sandie's shoulder and looked at him thoughtfully, repeating, "I hope so." Then he turned to Katie and bowed politely. "Miss Wheatly," he said to excuse himself.

"Mr. Hay," she replied with a curtsy, and as John Hay departed, melting into the crowd, Katie looked admiringly at the young man before her. "So, Captain, you're friends with Mr. Hay?"

"Please. It's 'Sandie.' Yes, I suppose so, though I've only just met him. Delightful fellow."

"Yes. We all think so," Katie replied. Then she blushed slightly as she realized she had been obviously studying Sandie's face so intently. She averted her eyes but found herself quickly drawn back to meet his again. "So, um, Sandie...from where do you hail...originally?" she asked awkwardly, believing her face must surely be showing its flush.

"Oh, uh, a little town just east of Pittsburgh. Hannastown."

"Oh. I've never been to Pittsburgh. I've never been...further west than...Harrisburg. We have...relatives there," she said, seeming to have to force the words out.

"Oh...I see..," Sandie replied.

They spoke haltingly, searching for words, as though conversation was really not appropriate to their being together. There seemed so much to absorb just visually admiring each other that speech was unimportant—almost a hinderance. There came an awkward moment in which they both realized they had just been gazing fancifully at one another.

Their short silence was interrupted, however, as the orchestra began an introduction to a waltz and Katie's eyes perked as the music began to fill the room. "Oh! It's a piece by Strauss. I know this number. It's lovely. One of my favorites," she smiled, her attention turned to the music.

Sandie raised his eyes upward, listening to the gentle rhythm of the introduction. "Yes. I've heard it before, too. Though only in the square back home. There's a small group of musicians who play on holidays and festivals. It sounds quite different with an orchestra," he said. Then he brought his gaze back to the young girl and looked warmly into her eyes. "May I have this dance, Miss Wheatly?"

"You certainly may, Captain Duncan," she replied, all but trembling with delight.

They moved out onto the dance floor among the other couples, and as he took her hand in his and laid his other to her waist he could feel the warmth emanating from her. Their hands seemed to fit so comfortably together, as though they had been molded by design, and though Sandie trembled every bit as much as she did, the feeling of holding her like this seemed strangely familiar. He ached to pull her closer; to feel her lithe, supple figure against his.

They smiled to each other as they listened to the introduction to the piece, and when they began to dance their bodies moved so effortlessly and rhythmically across the floor. They turned and twirled with such ease and grace that one would have thought them teamed for years. They were a splendid sight, the beautiful young lady and the handsome officer.

"You waltz very well, Captain," Katie beamed, enjoying both the embrace and the assured movements of her partner. "You've obviously had much experience. Do they dance quite often in Pittsburgh?"

"You flatter me, Miss Wheatly. But I confess I've only had several occasions to practice...and only with my younger sisters. My mother has a belief that to appreciate life you must appreciate music and dance, for that is the outward expression of the soul's thankfulness to God. If you've ever been to a village festival after the fall harvest, you'll know of what I'm talking."

"Mm..," Katie replied dreamily, for at this moment her soul was more appreciative of the young man in whose arms she was being swept so easily across the dance floor.

"And so, Miss Wheatly, how does one account for your resplendent abilities at dance? Though I detect you have a certain natural grace that complements your beauty."

Katie gave no reply to the young man, but her sudden blush and a tighter squeeze of his hand by hers told him more than her words ever could. For the first time in his life Sandie felt passions he had only ever read about in books or had heard talked about by others. His heart beat rapidly and his mind became dazed.

He felt he was floating above the dance floor as his body moved to a rhythm matched by the lovely girl in his arms. Neither spoke again as they glided and whirled about the floor, completely oblivious to the other couples around them. Occasionally, they would glance at one another, their eyes meeting. Then, they would blush and look away, neither of them able to vocalize the thoughts and feelings swirling about in their minds.

The waltz ended, and Sandie and Katie stood in the center of the floor, still embraced, as if to await the continuation of the music. Neither was willing to release the other, as though to do so would be to let go of the magic they had both just experienced. They looked deeply at one another, their minds failing in the blurred, hazy search to recognize any words or expressions that would even begin to capture the emotions developing within them.

Sandie became aware that they were the only couple still out on the dance floor and that they were still holding one another tightly. "Um...shall we get some air?" he stammered. He could feel the heat between them, created from both the exhaustive movements of the dance and from their increasing passions.

"Yes. That would be nice. I'll...I'll get my shawl," she replied as they both slowly, reluctantly, lowered their arms and uncoupled from their embrace.

"I'll accompany you," he said, not wanting to leave her presence lest he find this was but a dream and escorting her would keep him from awakening too soon.

She smiled and blushed at his eagerness. "Thank you, Captain. You are a gentleman."

"Please. You must call me 'Sandie.' I hear 'Captain' all too often at camp and I'd dearly love to hear my name come from your lips."

She looked at him with that gentle, endearing smile. "Well...Sandie, only if you'll return the favor by addressing me as Katie."

"That would be my deepest pleasure...Katie."

"Katie," he repeated again to the air, enjoying the sound of hearing himself say her name. He offered his arm for escort and was overjoyed as she slid hers so comfortably through his to make their way to the cloakroom.

From inside, the soft refrains of the orchestra wafted gently on the cool March breeze. The dim glow of the oil lamps posted along the garden path added a dramatically romantic setting as Sandie and Katie strolled about the gardens talking and laughing, sharing stories of each other's lives. They told of their pasts and of their dreams for the future. They walked aimlessly, arm-in-arm, strolling about the bordering boxwoods and arborvitae, making uncounted repetitions along the extensive brick paths.

They nodded in greeting to the occasional other wandering couples but were otherwise oblivious to all else save their own increasing infatuation with one another. Gone from them both were any thoughts or worries about the war. Tonight, they were but two young, innocent people learning about each other and falling in love.

After an enchanting while along their walk, Sandie noticed Katie shiver as the chill air had finally penetrated her shawl. "You're freezing," he said, taking her hands and warming them in his own.

"I...hardly noticed," she replied. "But I think I am."

"Come. Let's go in and beg the orchestra for another waltz," he said. Then he embraced her in the proper manner and began to waltz her gaily along the garden path. "I want to dance all night with the beautiful Cathleen Wheatly," he declared.

"Oh-ho! Sandie!" she laughed following his flowing step. "Oh, let's do!" she urged him eagerly.

The conductor was more than willing to oblige the young couple and played several selections to which the pair danced and whirled so delightedly. John Hay stood with the English Ambassador and watched the two glide gracefully around the dance floor. He was close enough to where young Thomas stood with the group of union officers to lean toward the gathering. "Well, Thomas, it would appear your friend has made a very beautiful acquaintance here tonight. And your daughter a rather dashing and handsome new suitor, General."

Thomas laughed heartily, "Ha! Ha! Good for Sandie. He deserves so beautiful a companion tonight after the action he's seen this past year. Uh, with all due respect, General."

"Hmm..," General Wheatly mused as one corner of his mouth turned up in a slight smile. He was glad to see his daughter enjoying the evening so. He hadn't known her to be so sprightly and vibrant since before her mother was stricken with consumption eighteen months ago. It had been a very depressing and sorrowful experience for them both, watching his wife wear away before them. Though they had determined to put on a good front, the tragedy of her illness and death had affected them both greatly. They had only just started to become closer in their relationship with each other when the war pulled him away from his daughter, deepening the emotional scars for them both.

Now his Katie had a prospective suitor and was appearing to emerge from the melancholia she'd been languishing in these many months. The General was not entirely pleased that the man to re-awaken those vibrant feelings wore a uniform, for, surely, if he fell in battle, it would have a devastating effect on her.

But he was agreeable to the relationship, at present, as he could see the positive affects the young man was having upon his fine, lovely Katie. "Well," he said with a wide, pleasant grin, "if he can match her energy and enthusiasm, he's well suited for her."

When the evening was drawing to a close and the guests began to depart, Katie brought young Sandie over to her father. She was a bit breathless, but her face was aglow with an excited radiance matched only by that of the young captain's whose hand she held in tow. "Father, I believe you've already met Captain Duncan. Isn't he a marvelous dancer?"

"Yes," the older man replied, giving a nod of salutation to the junior officer. "The two of you managed to draw quite an amount of gossip and conjecture."

"Oh? By whom?" Katie asked, for she really hadn't noticed that anyone had been discussing her interest in the young man.

The General laughed, as did Thomas beside him. "Oh, Katie. I think every young man in attendance tonight managed to stop by and inquire as to who the young officer is that has drawn your attention so. I believe, Captain Duncan, you had the envy of all the male guests here. And you, my dear daughter, have a lot of gossiping to do with more than a few jealous girlfriends."

Katie smiled and held to the young captain's arm. "Well, I'll let them all call on me later. Let them stew for a few days and wonder about Sandie. I had the pleasure of dancing with the most dashing officer in Washington...next to you, of course, father," she added with a laugh.

Sandie blushed. He could find no words to express his feelings of joy and delight at what he had experienced tonight. Never could he have imagined he would have encountered such an enchanting person as Katie—and fall in love with her. At least he assumed he was in love. All the feelings and desires and emotions he was experiencing told him that this must surely be love. He was so captivated by her charm and beauty, and it felt so natural and comfortable to be with her. "When you find the right girl, you'll know," his mother had often assured him. "If the Good Lord has a mate for you, He will lead you to her, and no amount of searching on your own will find her. Just be patient and she'll come by—so unexpectedly it will knock you over," she had said. Truly, this is what has happened, Sandie thought as he stood proudly beside the girl as she spoke so ecstatically with her father.

"I've invited Sandie to breakfast with us tomorrow, Father. And your friend is welcomed as well, Sandie."

"Thank you," Thomas bowed appreciatively. "Thomas Edwards, at your service, Miss," he said to introduce himself.

"Excellent," General Wheatly remarked. "Breakfast is at eight. I rejoin my brigade tomorrow and must be on the road before noon." He pulled a gold time-piece from his coat pocket and opened it, a little jingle playing as he observed the hands. Snapping it closed, he said politely, "And now, gentlemen, I must call for my carriage. I'm sorry to have to pull my daughter away from you, Captain, but it is late and I've a few matters to attend to before retiring."

While Sandie and Katie exchanged saddened glances that their evening together was drawing to an end, General Wheatly expressed his farewells to those around him, knowing, sadly, it would be a last goodbye to a few of those to whom he was speaking.

Sandie escorted Katie and her father to the cloakroom and, when the carriage was led around, he helped the girl up into the seat beside the General.

"Till tomorrow, then," he beamed, kissing her hand as it just seemed a natural and proper action, and he thrilled at the sight of her wide, excited, blue eyes sparkling in the reflective light of the lanterns that lined the pathway.

"Till tomorrow," she replied, moving her free hand over his to press it gently.

Sandie pulled back and bowed a good evening to the two. The coachman then gave a flick of the reins to start the team of matched bays onward. As the carriage pulled away Sandie watched it until it disappeared into the night.

****

Though the reception had lasted late, Sandie and Thomas, being accustomed to having only a few hours sleep, had awakened early and arrived at the Sheffield home by 7:45. It was a modest home, of colonial vintage, and but a fifteen-minute ride from Mrs. Bordlinger's. A dense, six-foot high boxwood hedge ran the length of the yard in front, broken only by a short wooden gate leading to the porch.

Their horses tied to the rail in front, Sandie and Thomas entered the gate and approached the house. They had but reached the first step of the porch when the door swung open and they were greeted by the bright smile and glimmering eyes of Katie Wheatly. "Well, good morning, gentlemen. Please, come in. I hope you brought your appetites. Aunt Lin and I have been cooking up a storm for all you men. At least you'll all have full stomachs on your return to the camps."

"Morning, Katie," the two men greeted her, removing their hats. Thomas ascended the four wooden steps to the porch and proceeded to the door, halting only when he realized his companion was not following. Sandie had stopped at the bottom step, hat in hand, while Katie stood leaning against the white support post, one arm draped leisurely around it.

The two stood gazing at each other, their eyes telling of their excitement at being together again; as though the dream of last night were continuing. The few hours of separation had seemed interminable for them both and they now stood silent, looking admiringly and thoughtfully at one another.

Thomas watched them for a moment as he stood in awkward silence. Then, when his rumbling stomach reminded him these two might stand there for eternity just gazing at each other he said, "Well, I don't know about you two, but I'm starved."

"Oh," Katie blushed and managed to pull her eyes from the handsome boy to smile to his friend. "I promised you both a delicious, hearty meal. Please, follow me in," she said as she turned to lead them into the house. As they followed her to the dining room Katie explained, "Father's already at the table. Colonel Selkirk has also joined us. He's with one of Father's regiments."

Sandie slowed his pace and asked timidly, "Is, uh, is your…"

"…Uncle Milrose joining us?" Katie finished for him, anticipating the question from the hesitant stammer in his voice. "No," she laughed. "I think he's too embarrassed over his rough treatment of you the other night and is feigning drowsiness. He said he was going to sleep in awhile and we were not to hold off breakfast waiting for him."

"Good. I can relax and enjoy this better knowing that," Sandie laughed.

"Sandie, you weren't fretting about Uncle Milrose, surely?" she asked.

"Mm…a little, perhaps. I believe I'd feel more comfortable charging double canister. At least I know what's coming and have a chance of not being hit by it."

Katie didn't laugh at this—She winced at the talk of war and did not want to hear of it. Sandie sensed her mood change and said no more, following her into the dining room where General Wheatly and Colonel Selkirk sat at the table sipping coffee from large mugs.

Greetings were exchanged and introductions to Colonel Selkirk were made once the two captains were seated. Katie poured coffee for them, then hurried to the kitchen. Aunt Lin Sheffield popped her head out of the kitchen door to greet the new arrivals and pleasantries were exchanged with her. She was a warm, friendly, cheerful woman which led Sandie to wonder how she ever managed with such an impudent husband.

While the men were alone, General Wheatly looked earnestly at Sandie with the same deep, blue, reflective eyes that Katie had been given and Sandie immediately felt relaxed and comfortable in his presence. There was an air of sincerity and self-assuredness about the man that gave the impression whatever he stated could be believed and relied upon; that he could be trusted. Integrity and capability were his motivations, rather than political ambitions, and joined to serve him well in gaining the respect and appreciation of both his army subordinates and superior officers.

"Well, Captain Duncan," he said to the boy. "I believe I'm indebted to you twice over."

"How's that, Sir?" Sandie asked as he swallowed a sip of the fresh, hot coffee.

"First, for covering my retreat at Manasses and saving what could have otherwise become a terrible number of casualties in my command," he said. Sandie was about to comment, but the General continued. "And second, for bringing my Katie out of the melancholia she has been in this last year or so. I haven't seen her so vibrant and spunky in a long time. It gladdens my heart to see her like this."

Sandie blushed some at listening to the General speak to him of this. He looked into his coffee cup to gather his thoughts for a reply, but before he could speak Colonel Selkirk said, "Indeed, young man. General Wheatly informed me earlier that I was to breakfast with the bold fellow that led that charge. I am equally indebted to you—that was my regiment taking most of the pounding from those guns."

"Well, I could see that," Sandie began. "Actually, I had the advantage. We came up on them suddenly and knew we had surprised them. By the time they managed to wheel their guns around they had only discharged a few rounds when we were upon them. The rest was rather easy work," he said modestly. "We did capture several pieces in the affair. I was really proud of my men. They fought courageously," he explained. Then he paused a moment in thought, and when he began to speak again his voice had a softer, more reflective tone, "In regards to your second gratitude, please, don't thank me!" he said, blushing a bit boyishly. "I guess it's pretty obvious I'm enthralled with Katie's charms. You have a wonderful daughter, Sir, and I find it difficult to believe she could ever have been melancholy. The night I first spied her at the theater—that velvety hair, glowing complexion, her pretty smile, those deep, blue eyes; oh! those eyes! I just knew I...oh, uh...sorry," he mumbled as he caught himself. He could see the others exchanging smirks at his expense from his having prattled on. Then, boldly, he professed, "It is my pleasure, Sir," and he sank into his chair, hiding behind his cup.

Thomas, seated next to him, chuckled and lightly elbowed Sandie in jest.

"Well," said General Wheatly, "You strike me as a fine young man. And though I know little of your background, other than you are not afraid of cannon or musketry, you have my permission to call on my daughter if it pleases her...and it would appear that it does."

"Well said!" intoned Colonel Selkirk. "You would have my blessings as well, Captain, if she were my daughter." Then the Colonel sat back in his chair and sighed reflectively. He chuckled some and looked at General Wheatly. "Of course, even if you withheld your blessings, it wouldn't stop Katie. That girl of yours will go after and get whatever she's made up her mind about," he said.

"Humph! She got that from her mother," the General said emphatically.

Colonel Selkirk laughed. "Ha! Ha! I know better. I've known you all for too long. Let me tell you boys. Once last month..." he began, but was interrupted by Katie and Aunt Lin appearing from the kitchen carrying trays of eggs, ham slices, bacon, potatoes, and more.

"Well, here we are, gentlemen. A hearty breakfast to fatten you all up a little," Lin said cheerfully.

"I know they don't feed you this well in camp," Katie said as she and Lin set the trays before them. "Eat heartily. There's plenty more in the kitchen and we've even prepared enough to fill your sacks for the road back to camp."

The men "ahhhed" in delight and appreciation at the meal set before them. Katie took a seat across from Sandie, beside Colonel Selkirk while Aunt Lin sat at the end of the table, opposite General Wheatly.

After the blessing, plates were filled and fresh coffee poured. The conversation was light and informal, the men carefully avoiding talk of war lest it upset the ladies. At some point the conversation turned to the discussion of railroads and the General made mention of his pre-war occupation as a railroad engineer.

On hearing this, Thomas, eager to capture the man's favor, as well as simply continue the flow of the conversation, foolishly and mistakenly exclaimed how fascinating it must be to pilot a large locomotive down the tracks, going through different towns and cities, hauling gondolas of freight and cars of people!

The General showed an amused smile while Katie and Colonel Selkirk both exchanged slightly embarrassed glances. "Well...actually, Thomas, I didn't run them. I designed and built them," the man informed him.

"Oh.., uh.., sorry," Thomas squeaked with a flushed face as he shrank in his chair. There was an awkward silence for a moment, until Sandie started to chuckle some, which caused smiles to appear on the faces of the others around the table as well. Sandie then burst into laughter and slapped his crimson-faced friend good-naturedly on the back. The others could contain themselves no longer and they, too, began to laugh uproariously at Thomas's mistake.

"Fah! Go ahead. Laugh all you want," Thomas grumbled, shaking his head in mock annoyance. "I can take it," he said as he sat there with such an expression of pretended impatience, waiting for them to finish their laughter. Unfortunately for Thomas, the harder they tried to stifle their laughter, the more they would laugh. When finally it seemed they were in control of themselves, someone would give a little chortle and they would all burst into laughter again.

When they at last managed to control themselves the General suggested that Thomas tell them all a little of his background as propitiation for his unwitting remark.

Thomas lowered his head some and looked at them all from under his brow. "Well, I guess you all know I'm not an engineer, anyway," he said, making light of his embarrassment and drawing chortles from them all. "Actually, I was born and raised in Harrisburg, or near there. My father farmed for a spell but didn't like it much. He went into dry goods and harness sales; traveled away from home a lot. I've attended some private academies and had some home tutoring but there wasn't ever enough money for college. The last couple of years my two brothers and I have been having a go at a hardware and implement store. It's going rather well, too; or it was. Two of us are serving and left the business in the care of our younger brother. I'm sure he's at wits end by now and wishing he were in the army. Father took ill this year and can't get around much to do anything. Poor little brother must care for the whole family. It's really straining him, I'm sure. He's only seventeen. A lot of responsibility for a boy so young."

"Well, he's to be admired, certainly," Katie said sympathetically.

"Yes. Especially as his nature is that of being rather wild and reckless. Oh, that boy would make a cavalryman, that's for sure! I'd wager he'd feel right at home on a good horse and clashing with Johnny Reb."

"Uh, that's not to say all cavalrymen are wild and reckless. Is it, Thomas!" Sandie said as he deliberately kicked his friend under the table and nodded toward Katie.

"Huh? Oh! No! No! Not at all! Why, um, only last month our, um...our entire regiment charged, er, I mean trotted against a...um...a Rebel position while...while reading poetry." Thomas said with a straight face. "Walked our horses real friendly like right up to Johnny's line and the whole regiment recited a poem in unison. Set those Rebs to fleeing wildly! Bored them senseless, we did."

Everyone groaned over this, and Colonel Selkirk, highly amused, said, "Interesting. Uh, take any prisoners?"

"Mm...two! They were college professors. Stayed behind to correct a passage. Said we had a bad copy and they couldn't take hearing Longfellow read so corruptly."

Again, everyone groaned at Thomas's story. They were all, now, quite relaxed and as the hours passed, they exchanged stories and incidents from their lives of days more happily remembered than the last year had been. Sandie noticed that Katie seemed to listen so intently whenever he spoke of his past, absorbing every detail. This was flattering to him for he enjoyed sharing information about himself with her. He found he was doing likewise whenever she spoke. But further, he was committing her face and voice to memory, knowing that he would fall asleep at night picturing her as she was now, sitting there smiling at him, and his ears would echo the sweet tones of her melodic voice.

When the clock in the parlor sounded eleven chimes the General lowered his head and was silent for a moment, as if in prayer. He gave a long, dispirited sigh of resignation as he raised his head to speak to them all. "Well, gentlemen, and ladies, this has been most enjoyable. Not only was the meal superb, but the company was excellent, as well. Were these other times we might continue sitting here enjoying one another's stories till supper. However, it is time. We must be on the road."

"Oh, Father, must you leave now? Can't you wait till after noon meal?" Katie pleaded, hoping to stay their departure a while longer. The man just looked at her, his eyes telling the sorrow of the forced parting.

"Ahh...your father's right, Katie." said Colonel Selkirk. "We must be going. It's a long ride back to camp and we all have duties to perform."

Katie knew this to be true, and while she had asked it she had been looking mostly at Sandie. Her eyes began to cloud just a bit as she was saddened that the young man was about to leave.

"Come, John," the General said, addressing the Colonel by his Christian name. "Let's see to the horses."

"I'll...gather your pack, Father," Katie said as she rose with the four men.

Aunt Lin, who had been bustling between the kitchen and the table the entire time, remained seated as the men stood and stretched. When they began to move toward the door she stood. "I'll...fix you all...a sack...for the road," she said tearfully. Then, raising her apron to wipe her eye she turned for the kitchen. Lin feared for her brother, knowing that his courage and bravery would find him always where the danger was the more extreme. Now she feared for Sandie, as well. This new relationship between the young captain and the niece of whom she was so fond would surely be impacted by the dangers of the war. So many gallant young men were returning from the battles crippled or maimed—if they returned at all!

The men moved silently out to the porch and stood awhile. The General and Colonel Selkirk both lit cigars and puffed reflectively on them, gazing out at the street or up at the sky.

"Well, maybe we'll finally have a sunny day," the General remarked as he watched the clouds beginning to break apart.

"Mm, it'd be nice after the last week or so of rain," the Colonel answered. "The roads dry out we can get the spring campaign underway and end this damned war the sooner!"

The two men stepped down off the porch unhurried, and somewhat reluctantly. Sandie leaned against one of the wooden posts as Thomas sat on the top step. Their eyes followed the two older men meandering casually to the corner of the house, heading for the stables behind. A trail of bluish cigar smoke drifted lazily upward.

Aunt Lin came to the door and looked out onto the porch, forcing a smile from behind reddened eyes. "If you boys bring me your packs I'll fill them for the road," she said, her voice trembling.

"Wonderful!" Thomas exclaimed and stood promptly. "I'll go and get them."

As Thomas proceeded down the walk and out to the street where the horses were tied, Aunt Lin came out to join Sandie. She stood beside him awhile, peering down the quiet Sunday morning street, visible over the tops of the hedge from the porch. Sandie sensed she wanted to say something but was finding it difficult to either verbalize it or to muster the courage.

"What is it, Lin? You seem troubled." he inquired, standing straight to address the gentle woman.

"It's just...Oh, I don't know how to put this," she stammered, obviously upset and seemingly angry at herself for not being able to vocalize her concerns.

Sandie was patient and sympathetic as be looked at her. "It's okay. Parting is always difficult. Watching a family member going off to the uncertainties of war is..."

"No!" she blurted. "It's not my brother, Miles, I'm worried about, at least not totally. I'm used to seeing him off, though I dare say it never gets any easier. It's...it's you I'm concerned about this time," she explained, the tears welling in her eyes.

"Me?" he asked, somewhat perplexed.

"Yes!" Lin continued, staring off the porch in an effort to say her mind without letting the tears fall. "It's obvious Katie has taken quite a fancy to you. Quite deeply, I would say, if the way she sits there staring all starry-eyed at you is telling anything. I've never seen her so excited over any boy before. I just...I'm worried about you. That's all. It would tear me up to see Katie's heart broken."

"Well, now, Miss Lin. I don't know how to relieve you of your concern except to tell you that this is no mere trifle on my part. I don't know how or why or for what reason, but the feelings that Katie has developed for me I assure you are returned in kind. Maybe even more so! I've never experienced these feelings for anyone before and, believe me, my intentions are completely honorable concerning her. For you, or anyone, to think anything to the contrary is to do harm to my honor!" he said emphatically, showing the hurt he was feeling at the mere suggestion.

Lin flushed at hearing him say this. Her expression was, at first, of confusion, then of anger. Then, slowly a bemused smile began to form and she looked at him fondly. "Dear boy," she said, "You've mistaken my meaning. Any fool can tell you two have fallen head-over-heals for each other. I know what you feel for her. Your eyes show it every time you look at her. What I fear is for your safety. Oh, Sandie, you two are both so young, so impetuous! You have so much to learn about each other; so much ahead of you. It would just break Katie's heart if you—." She stopped herself; unable to finish the sentence. As though to say it might somehow bring it about. "You...will take...care of yourself, won't you?" she asked looking directly and pleading into his eyes.

"Of course I will, Lin. I'm not going to let anything happen to me. I promise you I'll not do anything foolish that might put me in jeopardy," he assured her. "It really isn't as dangerous as everyone makes it out to be. Really! Oh, a few fellows get hurt, but they're mostly infantry. The cavalry usually only escort generals around or guard crossings," he lied. "We almost never get fired upon, and when we do we usually always skedaddle. Most of our work is done in the rear, guarding the wagons and depots. Pretty dull stuff, actually."

Lin gave him a look that told she wasn't really believing his story. But she decided to drop it, her point being made. "I've known Katie since she was a little girl," she continued. "She used to spend summers here with Milrose and me; used to climb up on Milrose's lap and have him read stories to her. Learned to ride here at the stables in Georgetown. She's an accomplished rider. Did you know that?"

"She told me she loved horses," Sandie replied.

"Oh, she's a talented one, that girl. Very smart, besides pretty."

"Yes. I'm sure," said Sandie. "She certainly knows her literature and music."

"Yes, she does. She's been to several ladies' academies. She could teach piano, you know. Other subjects, too."

"She'd make an excellent teacher," he concurred.

"I just...I just don't want to see her hurt. She and her father both took Lydia's illness so hard. I'd just be sick to see her have to endure that suffering again," she said.

"And you won't," Sandie said, trying to sound reassuring. "Trust me. Nothing's going to happen to me."

Lin was about to comment further when Thomas returned, bounding up the walk and onto the porch with his packs.

"I crammed all my clothing into your bags, Sandie," he said, handing the empty satchels to Lin. "We'll divide it up back at camp."

"Fine," Sandie replied.

Lin took the leather bags and went into the house as Katie came out carrying her father's packs. The two older men now appeared, leading their tacked horses into the street. She paused by Sandie and Thomas, smiling to them.

"Katie," her father called from the street, "Is that my bag?"

"Yes, Father. I'll bring it to you," she called back.

She went down the walk to the hitching post on the street. Sandie and Thomas waited on the porch, knowing she would want a few moments alone with the man to say their goodbyes. When they believed enough time had passed, the two younger men started down the path to the gate but Katie came through and stopped in front of Sandie, smiling up to him. She took his arm, tugging at him to follow her.

"Tighten Thistle's girth and bridle, will you, Thomas?" he asked over his shoulder as Katie led him toward the side of the house, out of sight and hearing from the others.

When they arrived at the side of the house she turned to face him, her eyes beginning to moisten. She glanced into his eyes, then quickly lowered them to his chest. Sandie watched her, concerned. She glanced up at him again and her tear-filled eyes displayed the anguished struggle to verbalize what she so wanted him to know.

Anticipating her thoughts and emotions he took her hands and pressed them tenderly together in his. "Katie, my dear. I think I know what it is you're wanting to say. We've only just met and have known one another for so short a time. But, Oh! these last two days have been the most precious and cherished I have ever experienced. From the moment I first saw you something inside told me our spirits were to be connected in some special way. I've never had feelings for anyone, nor anything, that seemed so right or so strong. It's almost as if we had met and loved one another before, in some other time or place, and this is but a continuation of that romance. Do you feel it? Am I wrong? Tell me it isn't just me but that you share those same feelings."

Her face flushed with emotions, she fought to restrain her tears of joy at having found him and, now, the sadness at his leaving. She looked deeply and lovingly into his eyes as she absorbed what he had said to her. He could feel her trembling as she moved her hands along his coat sleeves to cup his arms as she bit her lower lip to control a quivering chin. At last, unable to contain herself any longer, and finding words failing her, she cried," Oh, Sandie!" and threw herself into his arms. She began weeping into his shoulder, hugging him tightly.

Sandie held her securely. Though this all was so new to him it felt very natural to be holding her like this as he stroked the back of her hair tenderly and waited as she wept against him. In a few moments he released her and pulled back some. He took the yellow scarf from around his neck and offered it to her to dry her tear-streaked face. As she gained a modicum of composure, dabbing at her face, she looked up at him. "You must...think me...awful...

to have broken down like this," she stammered.

"No. Not at all," he said affectionately. "I'm mad with joy that someone as wonderful as you cares this much for me."

"Oh, Sandie! But I do care about you. And you're right, it is as if we'd been together before. That night in the theater, when I shushed you all for talking too loudly and I saw you looking at me with that amazed...Hannastown expression on your face I just knew there would be something to happen between us."

"You did?" he asked in surprise. "You certainly seemed cool about it. I felt like I was bumbling and stumbling all about. I was, in fact. I thought you hardly noticed me except for maybe wondering how that stooge in the blue uniform was allowed in the theater."

"Well...I was cool about it," she smiled. "It was like, well, something touched my heart and I knew we were to meet again. As though it was pre-ordained. Oh, Sandie, I've never felt like this before, either. Not in this life. It's as though all my life there has been this strange emptiness, and the moment we first danced together and we held each other I felt the void no longer there," she said as she dabbed at her eyes once more with the scarf. "And now that we've met...you're leaving again," she said in so saddened a voice.

"Oh, Katie, Katie, Katie," he sighed as he embraced her warmly again. As they held each other he murmured softly into her ear, "Please don't weep at our parting. Now that we've found each other there is nothing that can pull us apart. Our hearts have been touched by one another's and we'll carry that feeling together whatever the distance or time. We'll be together again soon, and we'll make it a cause for a great celebration! Don't fear for me. I'll be fine. The good Lord protects those who truly believe. He brought us together in His time and I know he'll join us together again," he assured her. Then he drew back to look into her eyes.

"Oh, I do wish to believe that, Sandie. I couldn't bear it should anything happen to you."

With no other words spoken they gazed passionately at one another. Then, drawn together as if by some inner spiritual force experienced only by those who have ever felt the deep, magical forces of love for another, they pressed their lips together in a long, passionate kiss. Their hearts beat rapidly as they held each other as though this embrace must last them both a lifetime. When at last they released their kiss they smiled to each other, knowing, truly, their fates were now to be forever intertwined.

"Come. Walk me to the front. I want to look back when I'm down the street and see you watching and know that you'll be waiting for me to return," he said as he took her arm in his.

"Oh, of course I'll be waiting for you," she said as they slowly strolled toward the front of the house. "I'll come out to the street every morning and look for you, and I'll write you every day."

"I'd like that," he replied happily as they turned the corner of the house. Then he paused, halting them both and looked at her quizzically. "'Amazed Hannastown expression.' What the devil is that?"

Katie blushed some at this and turned her head to him. She showed that same beautiful, perky smile as the night in the theater when he'd just spied her. "Well-l-l... actually...it's a...um...a farm boy look. You know, country boy comes to the big city."

"What?" he laughed at hearing this.

"Well," she chortled. "I didn't want to hurt your feelings by phrasing it that way, but you just had this look on your face..."

Sandie nudged her playfully and she drew back, laughing. This was the Katie he liked to see; a laughing, light-hearted girl with such a warm, endearing smile. "Hannastown expression," he grumbled whimsically as they continued on. Katie's smile broadened as she crowded against him.

"Well, there you two are," General Wheatly said as he and the other two men were sitting their mounts waiting for Sandie.

"Right there, Sir," Sandie called to the older man. He turned to Katie and took the yellow scarf from her hand. Holding it stretched between both hands he kissed it, then hung it around her neck. He took both her hands together in his. "I'll be back soon," he whispered to her, and he kissed her cheek tenderly. Then he turned and went through the gate to his horse.

The others were silent as they turned their steeds to head down the road. Aunt Lin came down to the gate to wave them goodbye with Katie, and even Milrose Sheffield ambled out now, appearing at the gate with a cigar in his mouth and a coffee mug in his hand. Miles Wheatly saw him come out through the gate and gave him a nod and Milrose nodded back. Sandie and Milrose only looked at one another momentarily, neither acknowledging the other. Then Sandie turned his horse with the others and the party began to move out, heading down the muddy road.

Sandie gave a glance backward as the sun broke from behind a cloud. There was Katie, standing in the middle of the street. He raised his hand in a last wave and saw her stretch her arm in reply. The horsemen turned left at the next road—heading south.

"My daughter certainly has taken a fancy to you, Captain Duncan," said the General. His voice had taken a marshal tone to it as they were no longer in the 'house setting' and must now begin to bring their military bearing back into focus.

Sandie had been trailing a length behind the others and now, at hearing the General address him in a tone that rang with more of a tactical nature to it, he nudged his horse alongside the three men. "Yes, she has, Sir. And I, to her," he replied, a bit indignant over the sound of the man's voice.

"Indeed. I've noticed," the General continued. "Now, uh, in view of these recent developments in your new...'relationship' with my daughter, I trust you will perform your military duties with...how shall I say this...a bit less reckless bravado."

"Sir?" Sandie asked, not sure he was interpreting the General's meaning correctly. Was he asking him to stay behind his men when the action became heavy?

"You must restrain yourself a bit, Captain; not place yourself in...certain desperate situations," he said, trying to choose the words carefully.

"General Wheatly," Sandie said, a bit nettled at the suggestion. "I am aware of my responsibilities both socially and militarily. I shall conduct myself in the field with the same exercise of caution that I believe you, yourself, would demonstrate."

That said, he squeezed his horse to a trot and rode ahead a distance from the others. He wished to be alone for awhile to think over the events of the past weekend.

Chapter Five

July 16, 1988

"There, you hold the pole, Jeff," David Cooper said to his son. Jeff came over and gripped the dining fly corner pole while his father hammered a steel peg into the ground. "There," the man said as he lashed the nylon cord to the peg, securing the last corner upright of the plastic shelter.

"Mom! Dad's got the dining tarp up," Sarah yelled from the corner pole she had been entrusted to hold straight so the others could be set.

Carol was in the tent huffing and puffing into the little red valve stem of an air mattress. "Good," she hollered back as she peeked out through the nylon mosquito netting. "Daavve" she wailed in pretended misery. "Do this for meee..."

"Ha, ha! What's that, honey?" he asked as he approached the tent to see what it was she was agonizing over. When he looked, he exclaimed, "Oh, no! Not the dreaded air mattresses! Ahhhh!" he cried out in mock terror.

"C'mon, Dave. You're more of a blowhard then I am," she laughed.

"Blowhard, am I? I'll show you blowhard," he laughed as he started to tickle her devilishly all over. Carol wriggled and squirmed wildly, frolicking with him over the pile of bedding.

"You are a blowhard! ...Ahhhh!... You are a ...ahhhh, ha! ha! David! Stop that!" she gasped between laughter as they continued wrestling.

"Free for all!" Jeff yelled as he charged into the tent joining the melee on the floor. Sarah rushed in right behind him, whooping loudly in excitement as she, too, leaped into the pile of squirming, tickling bodies. She landed on her father's back so that now the whole family was rollicking in the pile of down bags and foam pillows.

"Hey! You crazy people in there!" came a voice from outside the tent. They all stopped and looked to the tent flap to see Sam Baker peering in.

"Sam!" they shouted in unison.

"Hi, guys," he smiled to them. The Coopers began to untangle themselves from each other, raising up and filing out of the tent as Sam held the netting aside for them. "When did you all get here?"

"About an hour and a half ago," Dave replied. "See you got the wood in," he smirked, giving Sam a sidelong glance.

"Yeah. Legitimately, too," he laughed, recollecting their last experience at firewood accumulation.

Carol smirked, "you two better not get us into trouble this time. It doesn't leave a good impression on the kids to see their father handcuffed and hauled off to jail, you know."

"Hey. We'll be good. Trust us," Sam said as he raised his right hand as if swearing an oath.

"So, where were you? Out biking?" Dave asked his friend.

"Yeah. Getting some exercise. I got a new tent, thank you for noticing," Sam said.

"Yeah. We did notice. It's nice. We looked it over when we pulled in," David said. "I like the pole lantern, too. That'll help," he said in reference to the lantern hanging on an aluminum pole near the picnic tables.

"I'm glad you got us a spot near the bathrooms," Carol said appreciatively. "I can rough it with the best of 'em, but give me a hot shower and a clean bathroom"

"My wife. A real trooper, huh?" Dave said as they all chortled.

They spent the remainder of the afternoon getting the campsite in order. Sam built a fire to get the coals ready for cooking supper while the Coopers finished work inside the tent and around the kitchen area. When the site was in good order and the logs were burning down, they all joined together for a stroll around the private campground.

As they walked, commenting on the other tents and RVs at the various sites around the loop, they tossed a football to each other. They mocked the play-by-play television announcers as they took turns at quarterback and receiver. Sam walked with Carol and Sarah while Dave and Jeff traded off at receiver and defender about thirty yards in front. "Montana back to pass...he's being rushed out of the pocket!...He looks down field for a receiver...He sees Cooper open! He throws long-!" and as Dave went for the ball, allowing Jeff to cover him closely, Jeff knocked the ball away. "Ohhh...he blows it!" Sam announced. "Yes, folks. It's amazing. I guess Cooper's just too old for this game. A 'has been' who's just hung around too long."

"Hey, Sam," Jeff hollered back to him. "Be Terry Bradshaw this time."

"Why? I like Montana. He was always my favorite."

"Yeah. But I like Terry Bradshaw," Jeff said.

Dave picked up the ball and immediately went into quarterback role. "He can't be. I'm Bradshaw," he said. "...Bradshaw back to pass, he sees Swan open! ...He pumps once...No!...A fake!...He throws to his wide-out!...Carol Cooper!" he hollered as he tossed the ball at her.

"Ahhh!" she screamed, surprised by the ball coming at her. But her instinctive reaction caused her to open her arms and catch the ball.

"Hey. Pretty good," Sam said, and he bent low, rushed in at her and picked her up over his shoulder. "Baker tackles her on the fifty," he shouted. "No! Wait! ...That's her age!" he exclaimed as he ran her back a few yards, then set her gently down.

"Fifty?" she shouted at him. "I'll give you fifty!" She drew back the ball as if to wail it at him and Sam ducked back. Carol quickly turned and threw the ball to Jeff. "Yeahhh! Touchdown!" she cheered with a laugh.

"Tricked!" Sam said in feigned discouragement. "That's why women aren't allowed in the game, you know. Men could never anticipate their moves."

Jeff tossed the ball to his dad, who then tossed it to Sam. "So, Sam. What else did you learn about this housing development they're planning on putting in?" Dave hollered back to him.

"I don't know. Nothing really. We'll have to go into town or else ask a park ranger," Sam shrugged.

"Damn. They can't leave anything alone, can they?" Dave said disgustedly.

When their walk delivered them back to their campsite they began to prepare supper. The coals were perfect for cooking now, and Dave laid out the stainless-steel grate he'd always brought along for this purpose, placing it across one half of the fire ring. It served as a perfect working surface on which to fry the steaks and potatoes. Everyone pitched in to prepare the meal and, while devouring everything that had been placed on the table, they talked at length, catching up on what was happening in their lives.

"So, you're about to open store number three, Dave? Wow! You're really becoming king of the auto parts business," Sam said, pleased to know his friend was doing well.

"Mmm, yeah. It's pretty neat. We went computerized last year and it's proved a significant savings in paperwork and efficiency. I can triple my stock and keep track of all my inventory. What one store is low on can be shuttled from another within minutes. I can see who has the item and how many there are of them. Oh, it's fantastic! It keeps track of all my inventories, does my book work, everything."

"I told you years ago to computerize. But did you listen to your best friend? No-o-o-o. I should have taken a leave and come written your program for you."

"Yeah. I thought of that," Dave replied, "But I didn't feel right in asking. Besides, the program was part of the package."

"Mmm...Keeps you busy having three stores, huh?" Sam asked, assuming that the growth of Dave's business was due to the long hours of work devoted to it.

"Yeah...well, you know what? No. Not really. You know, for years I practically lived at the store, but lately that's all changed. I'm staffed well enough with the right, energetic people that the place pretty well runs itself. All the day-to-day activities are handled by Alan who's trustworthy as anybody. I'm only needed for the really important decisions. It's all rather done automatically. It's great! I can usually work regular hours, now."

"Way to go, Dave," Sam said, happy for his friend. "Now all you have to do is sit around figuring out how to invest all that cash flowing in."

"Heh! It's not that easy. I deal in volume. I keep prices low and rely on turnover," he said. Then he smiled a little in afterthought. "We're doing okay, though. Just bought a new van. Paid cash for it. It's a year old, but you know how I feel about buying new," he said.

"Mm. I do. I'm not sure I agree with you, but you're the one making the big bucks," Sam said matter-of-factly.

"So, how 'bout you, Sam," Carol asked. "Tell us what's been happening in your life."

"Ehh...later. Let's dig into some of that fresh apple pie you baked. It looks delicious," Sam said to her.

"Ah-h-h..," Dave sighed contentedly as he reached over to get the pie for slicing. He smiled widely as he picked up the pie knife. "Carol's the best pie maker in Indiana County."

"I hear that!" Sam grinned and put his arm around her. "Pretty, and can bake! What more does a man need in a woman? Ohh, if only I had met you first," he sighed dramatically.

"Harrumph!" Dave grumbled jestingly as he sliced the pie into sections. "You haven't been around when her temper flares. Oouiee!!"

"Careful there, mister," she said, shooting him a stern look as she played along. "You may find yourself sleeping in the tent when we get back home."

Dave looked up into the air and sighed resignedly to the winds. "Oh, we men who are slaves to our women."

Carol just smiled and shook her head amused.

The pie was quickly consumed and did prove to be as delicious as the men had anticipated. Then came the not-so-pleasant task of cleaning up. The dishes had to be washed under a pump spigot—Dave and the kids taking turns on the handle. Carol and Sam took care of the rest of the chores—storing the food, wiping the table and refilling the water bottles. Then they rebuilt the fire in preparation for toasting marshmallows. As dusk settled in and the sinking sun cast an orange glow about the sky, everyone found a comfortable spot around the fire for an evening of rest and conversation.

While the children toasted marshmallows on pointed sticks Dave entertained them with ghost stories from supposed incidents from his boy scouting days. As the dancing flames caused eerie shadows in the darkness of the surrounding woods, lending a haunting affect to the stories Dave told with such sincerity, the children kept edging their chairs closer to their mother. When he'd finished his fifth tale, a truly frightening but wholly unbelievable incident, everyone made groaning comments and critiqued it as being one of his poorer.

"Hey," Dave said in his own defense. "What can I say. You guys have heard all the other ones and I'm running out of ideas. It's not easy making up all those on the spur-of-the-moment."

"Ah, ha!" Sarah said accusingly. "Then you admit you're just making them up. I thought you said they were all true. Dad! Lying to your children. Honestly! Jeff and I will be scarred for life over this."

"Oh...um...uh...Did I say 'made up'? I meant, um, remembered. Yeah. That's what I said. Remembered. It's tough remembering all those incidents."

"Yeah. Right, dad. It's too late. We caught you," she said as everyone laughed.

There came a lull in the conversation and all eyes stared silently into the fire for a long while, watching the flames leap and dance, listening to the crackle of the dried hemlock logs.

"There's just something about a good campfire," Dave said as he watched the sparks ascending into the darkened sky.

"Ugh! Uh." Sam grunted in caveman mimicry.

"No. Really. There's like this basic instinctive feeling about huddling close to a fire; even on a warm night."

"Mm...I know what you mean," Sam nodded. "It's almost a spiritual experience; like there's a humbling effect or something. Makes you realize mankind's advances since discovering how to use fire."

"I think it's neat," Jeff said, throwing small twigs into the snapping flames to watch them ignite and burn away quickly.

"Yeah, well...it's also time for you kids to hit-the-hay," Carol said with a long stretch. "Go brush your teeth and I'll come tuck you in."

It was with no small amount of protest and arguing that Jeff and Sarah were finally in their bags and Carol was able to rejoin the men as they sat talking quietly around the fire.

Sam looked up at Carol and smiled, his eyes following her as she sank into the low camp chair. She caught the apparent smirk on his face and knew he was bursting to tell them something.

"Okay, Sam. What is it?" she asked.

"I'm moving to Pittsburgh," he announced, a broad smile rounding his face as he waited for their reaction.

Dave was quick to respond, and it was with joy and enthusiasm. "What? That's great! When? How? What's going on," he asked, practically coming out of his chair. "Did you take a new job?"

Sam was still waiting for Carol's reaction. She smiled with one corner of her mouth and leaned forward to toss a twig into the fire. "Sam...Sam...Sam..." she sighed. "What are we going to do with you?"

Sam dropped his smile and looked at her, puzzled over her comment. He sucked on his lower lip and watched as she poked at the fire with another, longer twig. "Jeez, Carol. Don't fall over from excitement."

She looked up at him pointedly for that remark.

"What? I thought you'd both be happy. I mean, we're friends and all, aren't we?"

"Oh, I am happy, Sam. I think it's terrific. We'll all be able to get together more often. Jeez, we'll even be able to get you to one of our big barbecues," she said. Then she leaned closer to him and put a hand on his knee. "But, Sam, when are you going to settle down? You've got to put in roots somewhere," she told him, her voice sounding both concerned and exasperated. "You move around so much. You've got to find a home sometime."

"Oh. I get it," he said. "We're back to that again. Now, c'mon, Carol. Listen. I've been out with girls. I've tried dating. It's no good. They all have something weird about them. It's really tough playing the dating scene. All the good ones are married. There's nobody out there. At least, none that I've found."

"Well, where are you looking? In bars?" she asked curiously. "I mean, do you go to night clubs or...I don't know, dating services or something?"

Sam smiled as he thought of that. "Heh. You know, I could never bring myself to do the dating service thing. It's sort of in the same category with bar hunting. That just seems too desperate to me. You know where I always went? Markets."

"What?" Dave asked, surprised.

"Yeah. Really. Look. Girls in bars are out to find men in bars. Everybody's playing this whole 'cool' game. They're all dressed to-the-tooth, looking real pretty, all made-up, and all. You don't know what they really look like without the make-up. They're putting on their 'cool' attitudes and they're well on their guards. Now, a woman in a supermarket; she's shopping for food, not men. She's in her casual clothes, little make-up, and no defenses up. She's being pretty much her natural self. Right?"

Carol squinted an eye as she thought of that, then replied, "Well, okay. Go on," she smiled. "This is interesting."

"Right. Okay. So, we've got this woman being all natural and friendly—women are always friendly in markets. I mean, they're there for food; it's brightly lit; they can feel safe. So, I grab a cart—men look more stable with a cart rather than carrying one of those baskets. It looks too breezy, too...I don't know—not permanent; sort of a "just passing through" kind of thing to carry a basket.

So, I grab a cart and I start throwing in some obvious 'singles' type foods; a small head of lettuce, a couple fresh carrots—stuff that's obviously for only one person. It's all got to be organic, too. You don't want to put any fast-food stuff in there. It scares them off. Women like health-conscious guys."

"Ha, ha, ha! Sam! You're too much," Carol laughed at hearing this.

"No. Wait. Listen, now. So, I go up and down the aisles looking for a woman whose got the same sort of cart; food for one person, mostly healthy, organic foods, etcetera. Then, I real casually and nonchalantly start studying the same thing she's looking at on the shelf. You know, like chicken tetrazzini-for-one, or something. Then, I act puzzled and go 'hmm. I've never tried this. Is it any good? Well, that's the opener. The rest is easy. You start talking, comparing foods, talk about how difficult it is cooking for one and stuff like that. Pretty soon you're exchanging phone numbers and making a dinner date."

By now Dave and Carol were shaking their heads over Sam's explanation.

"What?" ...Sam asked as he saw the reaction of his two friends by the glow of the crackling fire.

"Nothing. No. No. This is good," Carol tittered. "Go on."

Sam looked at her suspiciously, then at Dave, who was sitting there with an amused smile on his face as he listened. Sam chuckled a little himself, over his story, but continued. "Okay. I know it sounds crazy. But it works. It really does!" Then he looked at them from under his brow. "I also go to laundromats," he said sheepishly.

"Tee hee," Carol chortled barely able to restrain her laughter. "Tell me this one."

"Well. You've got to find the right laundry; where all the good-looking, educated girls go. You, sort of, very discreetly, check out their laundry—to be sure there are no men's clothes in the basket."

"Yeah," Dave chuckled. "I'll bet you're discreet."

"Okay. Okay. Anyway, then I play dumb about doing some wash—whether this new sweater, or that new shirt, or something, can go in with something else. Well, you start talking and, again, you're exchanging phone numbers."

Carol and Dave were exchanging smirks.

"Well, Sam," Carol asked. "If your system works so well—where are all these ladies at?"

"Eh," Sam sighed resignedly. "They usually turn into a fizzle. I don't know, maybe it's me. I just can't seem to get interested in any one girl."

"Well, it's not you, Sam," Carol assured him. You're a warm, generous, handsome and intelligent man. You'll find the right girl someday."

"I hope so," he sighed.

"Tell me about your new job," Dave interrupted. "What's it about?"

"Well, I'm doing some work for the Pentagon, again. It's all kind of secretive and hush-hush. Remember when I helped set up the venture between the military and Carnegie Mellon?"

"Vaguely," Dave replied. "You said they just wanted to do some research on C.M.U.'s machine. You didn't tell us much."

"No, I still can't. It's all classified. Well, I got everything rolling for them and, you know me, grass doesn't grow long under me, and I left after a while. So, they've got a problem, now, and they think only 'ole Sam here can straighten it out. I'll be doing a lot of traveling back and forth between D.C. and Pittsburgh."

"They called 'you'?" Carol asked.

Sam snickered. "Yeah. Funny, isn't it? Those Pentagon fellas' and I didn't get along very well. They're so damn stuffy and serious all the time. But they called and asked if I'd come down and help change over to a new program they want to run. I think it has to do with the 'star-wars' stuff. I told them I wouldn't work on salary. I'd only do it on consulting. Hell, man. You wouldn't believe the big bucks I'm gonna' make. Your tax dollars at work. They must be desperate."

"Yeah," Dave said. "But you're one of the best, Sam."

"Sam, you've only been in Cleveland six months!" Carol said.

Sam looked down at the fire and threw a stick into the orange and yellow flames. "Yeah. Well...it's lonely there," he said.

There was a long silence as the three studied the glowing embers of the slowly diminishing fire. Sam took a stick and stirred the coals, releasing sparks that rushed upward into the black sky.

"I had a weird dream last night," he said in a serious and troubled voice.

"Yeah? What was it?" Dave asked.

"I don't know. It was weird. Maybe a 'Nam' flashback. I don't know."

"Mm. I still have daydreams about it sometimes, but it hasn't haunted my sleep in years. Think I'm done with that. I hope so, anyway," Dave said.

"Thought I was, too," Sam said, poking reflectively at the fire. "Listen to this, though. Tell me what you think. I saw myself...well, it was me, but it wasn't me; at least, not how I look now. Anyway, I was lying back on the cold ground...I could see the bright sun shining down. Big guns were booming and banging away and the rattle of, I don't know, muskets, maybe, or automatic weapons sounded around me. Men were shouting and yelling. I could hear guys screaming. Then it grew quiet...and darker. The sun seemed to have gone down really quick; real early. It was pitch dark, which was strange because I remember thinking that the moon was full just the night before…and I lay there thinking, 'this is strange; even the pickets aren't firing. I'm cold…so cold…so thirsty'…" Sam paused and poked at the fire with a stick. A shudder ran through his body as he dwelled on the memory of the dream. "Weird, huh?"

Carol and Dave both sat absorbing this, neither of them moving, wanting to hear more. "Then what happened?" Dave asked, fascinated.

"I don't know. I woke up and it was morning. What do you think?" Sam asked, looking at them for their interpretations.

"Hm…I've never had one like that. Not that I remember, anyway," Dave shrugged.

"Mm…I don't know, Sam," Carol said. "It's certainly strange sounding. But, you know, there's so much that goes on that we can only guess about; speculate over. You know, the "forces of the universe" and all. It sounds like it's something reaching from your past, your Vietnam days. Something you did you inwardly regret maybe, or something you should have done but didn't do," she explained, her voice soft and understanding. "Everything is cyclical. You've heard the expression "what goes around, comes around." Scientists call it a "law of the universe: for every action there is an equal and opposite reaction." That's the principle of how we get rockets into space. Eastern religions call it Karma. Same thing. I believe that you're always given a second chance at things, and if a person is wise enough to perceive that some things come around again they can act accordingly. That's if they did it wrong the first time."

"Give me a 'for instance'," Sam said, mulling over what she'd been saying.

"Well…hmmm…okay. Like the soldier who flees from danger during battle; or someone who runs from a bully instead of standing their ground. Eventually the situation will come up again, in some form, and the person will have a chance to prove their courage. If they choose to flee again, they're bigger cowards than they were before and will have to live with the results of their actions. If they act bravely, they'll get to live with the rewards of their courage."

"Yeah. I see that," Sam replied. "But it's not a question of bravery. Hell, I proved that over and again enough in Nam."

"Yes. But my point is this; there may be something you have to face again. I don't know. It might, also, be something life wants to give you, Sam, that you didn't get in the past. Some little reward for a past action. And life is just preparing you for it, showing you in advance, trying to reach your conscious level from deep in your spirit. Dreams often alert us to something that we're not aware of when we're awake. There are so many mysteries in life. You can only be patient and let what will happen, happen."

"Que será, será," Dave mumbled to add what he could to Carol's otherwise lengthy and involved philosophical interpretation of Sam's dream.

"Something like that," she went on, trying to tie it all together for the two men. "Oh, you can control some things, like where you live, what investments you make, how you treat people...you know, everyday decisions. But I really feel some of the major decisions and events are made from the results of our past actions; our 'Karma'."

"So, you think something is going to happen to me?" Sam asked. "Some major catastrophe?"

Carol shrugged. "I don't know. Why a catastrophe? You're a good-hearted person, Sam. It could be something terrific is going to happen to you. Maybe life owes you something positive and you're being prepared to receive a wonderful present or experience. I do know you're troubled by that dream. It must have touched something in your soul. When a dream affects you that greatly it's for a reason, and the wise person at least takes a second look at it."

"How do you know all this? I've never heard you talk this deeply before," Sam asked.

"Oh, she's always going on like this," Dave answered. "She's our resident sage. I give her credit, Sam. She usually knows what she's talking about. Carol has a lot of perception of the spiritual world. Sometimes it's almost scary."

Carol smiled over the words of confidence from her husband and patted his knee in appreciation. Then they all were silent awhile, their thoughts turned inward as they watched the logs melt away into coals.

Dave finally broke the solemn quiet as he shrugged, "'course, it could have been something you ate, too," he said, and they all chortled over this.

Sam gave a big stretch and a wide yawn, "Well, my karma is leading me to my tent," he said. He slowly struggled up from the low camp chair and gave an even bigger stretch and wider yawn. A chain reaction started as Dave, then Carol, each followed with their own long, outward stretch and sleepy yawns.

"Stop that!" Carol laughed at the end of her second yawn. "It's contagious!"

"Yeah," Dave said as he began to move his tired body up out of the low chair. "I guess it's time to turn in. I'm bushed."

He helped Carol up from her chair and the three began to move to their tents, saying good night as they dragged off.

When Dave and Carol had crawled into their sleeping bags and Carol had snuggled up against Dave, he hugged her tenderly, saying quietly, "You know, I really hope you're right about this, that something good does happen to Sam. He's good people. I wish only the best for him."

"Me too, Honey," she said, patting his hand that laid across her breast. "Good night."

"Mm...night, Hon," Dave mumbled as he closed his eyes for sleep.

Chapter Six

July 17, 1988 9:00 A.M.

The thermometer was already at eighty-four degrees when the van pulled into the parking lot of the Antietam National Battlefield. Sam's bike carrier—a bumper-mounted system—had been adapted to fit the van so they could all ride together in one vehicle. As they stepped from the air-conditioned van onto the black asphalt a wave of heat rolled over their senses.

"Oh, man! Are we ever going to boil today," Dave said.

"Well, make sure we take both water jugs," Carol reminded him.

"What's the matter?" Sam chuckled. "You get too used to an air-conditioned office? Going soft in your old age?"

"Yeah," Dave replied. "The older I get the less I can take the extremes in temperatures. Think I'd like to retire to Maryland. It's not too bad in this area most of the year." He gave a good long stretch...which Carol interrupted with a surprised, playful poke to his ribs.

"Oh, listen to you," she said. "You sound like an old man."

"Harrumph...Some days I feel like one," Dave said, moving away from his wife to resume his stretch in safety.

"Let's go," Sam said as Carol began to lock the van. "We may as well start at the visitor's center."

"When are we going to ride the bikes?" Sarah complained as Carol moved her out of the way of the door. "I'd rather ride the bikes."

"Later." Carol said. "We're going to tour the visitor's center first. Then we'll ride. You've got to know what went on here, first, right? You've got to know what you're looking at."

"Well, Dad and Sam can tell us all that," Jeff said. "I'd rather start riding, too."

"Hush, you two," their mother said. "There's all kinds of interesting things in there. Just listen and pay attention inside so you'll have a better understanding of it all."

An hour and a half was spent in the visitor's center by the small party. They viewed an informative film explaining the battle, toured the small museum in the lower level and purchased some books and souvenirs from the gift shop.

Dave and Sam inquired of a park ranger for information concerning the tract of land in dispute between the citizens' group and the development corporation. The ranger had but a few quick moments to lend as charter buses were arriving out in the parking lot, delivering groups of various ages.

Presently, a troop of wildly cheerful and yelling Boy Scouts was overtaking a group of senior citizens making their slow ascension of the sloped walkway. As the three men turned to see the screaming horde of youngsters descending upon the glass door front the ranger chuckled, saying, "Oh my. Here we go." He managed to suggest that Dave and Sam stop by and look over the old Schiels farm—a site at which one of the Union Corps had been headquartered.

Also, interestingly enough, just a year ago the remains of several Federal cavalrymen had been unearthed by a farmer leasing the fields as he was turning the sod in a new section. It was not within the park boundaries, but it was worth a look, he told them, as this was the one-hundred-and-fifty-acre farm that was up for sale.

"Why would there be Union cavalry buried there?" Dave asked. "I don't remember reading about any clash that far back of the lines."

"No. Not during the battle of Antietam," the ranger said. "Around mid-July, 1864, a small skirmish had been fought there by several units attached to Early when he was retreating from his attack around Washington..." But before the man could finish his explanation the scouts were vaulting through the door, surrounding the information desk and bombarding him with questions from all directions at once. He hurriedly scribbled something onto a scrap of paper and handed it to Sam.

"Thanks for your help," Sam voiced to him above the chattering, olive-clad youths.

"Anytime! Enjoy your visit!" the ranger hollered back, then he turned to the youths to try to answer those questions he could clearly discern from their barrage of inquiries.

As they stepped away from the information desk Sam examined the message hastily scrawled on the paper. "Historic Antietam Foundation, Inc.," it read, then listed the address as a post office box in Sharpsburg. He shared it with Dave, then folded it neatly and tucked it into his pocket.

"We should try to get in touch with them while we're here to see if there's anything we can do to help," Dave said.

"Mm...that's what I was thinking," Sam replied. "I'd like to do more than just send money. 'Course, I'm sure they need that, especially."

The two men joined Carol and the kids out in the parking lot and began making preparations for the bike trip. Water bottles, an emergency repair kit, food and snacks, first aid kit, picnic blanket, frisbee, and some other miscellaneous items were all packed into the baskets and panniers, everyone sharing in burdening some portion of the load.

By late morning they were well on their way along the paved park roads, exploring the points made famous by the horrendous amounts of blood spilled and lives lost in attempting to attack or defend them: the Dunker Church, the West Woods, the Cornfield, the North Woods, the Mumma Farm. At each stop Dave and Sam would explain to Carol and the kids what action had taken place in that area. Then, the two men would discuss, though only between themselves, various aspects of the fighting or certain tactical maneuvers until, unable to stand it longer, Carol would interrupt them by dragging them to their bikes to move on to the next stop.

By mid-afternoon, with Jeff and Sarah all but screaming about how hungry they were, they arrived at the picnic area along the Boonsboro Pike. There, they took time to devour the sandwiches, fruits, and other nourishments they had prepared back at camp, and with the temperature nearing 98 degrees, they rested under the shade of the trees, relaxing and enjoying the day.

When it was time to move on, Sam suggested they divert from their trip for a visit to the Pry House, the site of General McClellen's headquarters and visited by Lincoln when he came out from Washington to urge the General to pursue Lee's retreating army. This was agreeable with Carol, but Jeff and Sarah protested that it was too hot, they were too tired, and they should all return to camp to rest and go swimming. The tour could be resumed tomorrow.

Being the youngest, they were, of course, out-voted, though a compromise was worked out with them. After a visit to the Pry House, they would return to the van by way of a direct road through Sharpsburg. Carol schemed this route believing that, if she could only get the two men to postpone until tomorrow, a stop at the National Cemetery that lay along this route, they were practically home free. Any other route would lead them past too many points of interest and the temptation to stop would be too great for the men to resist.

When this was explained to everyone Sarah and Jeff agreed to the plan, grudgingly, and Dave and Sam grumbled that, yeah, it was acceptable to them as long as they could get there earlier the next day to resume the tour. Carol rolled her eyes, exasperated at having to be the mediator between the two kids and the older men.

As they peddled off down the Boonsboro Pike Sam led them all onto a diverging road he believed would be less heavily traveled. They were no longer within the National Park boundaries and, typical of motorists the world over, no one was obeying the speed limit, particularly the heavy delivery trucks. This narrower country lane would be a safer route to the Pry House, if not a shorter one.

The party coasted down a little hill and around a slight curve, shaded this last half mile by trees on either side of the road. Coming out of the curve the road then ran straight and level for a quarter mile distance, flanked by open sun-drenched fields till it curved again into a section of woods. To the right of this level section was a broad field of waist-high corn. On the left there grew a second cutting of timothy and clover, the field sloping gently upward for about ten acres, then rising more quickly to crest the hill for another twenty acres or so.

When they rode out of the woods and onto the level Sam, a good fifty yards in the lead, turned his bike to the side of the hay field and dismounted. The Coopers pulled over beside him as they caught up in turn and began to look around curiously for a monument or marker to explain Sam's reason for stopping under the hot sun.

"What? Why are we stopping," Sarah asked, standing astride her pedals.

"I don't know," Dave shrugged. "Why are we stopping, Sam?" he asked his friend.

Sam didn't answer. He seemed to be strangely distracted by something out in the field, his attention turned toward listening for something or looking for something as yet unseen.

"Sam?" Dave asked.

Sam turned and looked at Dave with a perplexed expression. He didn't answer right away and appeared confused.

"Sam? Are you all right?" Carol asked.

"Phew!" Sam exclaimed with a shake of his head as if clearing it of an uncomfortable thought. "That was weird! Talk about déjà vu."

"Really? Did you just experience it?" Dave asked.

"Oh, I get them," Sarah said, smiling over this. "That's neat when that happens. It's a real weird feeling."

"Yeah. Me too," Jeff said. "I've had those."

"I don't know. At least I think it was déjà vu," Sam explained, the look on his face showing he was still trying to analyze the experience. "As soon as we hit the flats, here, it was like I was suddenly half out-of-body or something. Like...I was here, but I was also, I don't know...not here." He put his hand over his heart. "You should feel my heart. It's beating a mile-a-minute."

No one replied to this—there was nothing, really, anyone could say. They just waited patiently as Sam slowly shook off the experience, trying to let it pass.

"Man!" he said. "I've never experienced anything like that before. Whew!" Then he turned to his bike and flipped the kickstand up, anxious to move away from the feeling by out-pedaling it.

"There's a sign up ahead, there," Dave said. "Let's go up and read it."

"Yeah...sure...Let's go," Sam replied, turning his bike onto the road. As the others pedaled off, Sam gave a last gaze into the field and, shaking his head, vexed, he mumbled, "Weird...," then rode off to join the others.

A hundred yards from where they had stopped for Sam they pulled over to the left again. Off where the field began to rise more steeply stood a large plywood sign supported by two wooden posts. "Help Save This Land From Development" it read, then gave the same name and address written on the paper in Sam's pocket.

"This must be the farm the ranger was talking about," Dave said.

"Yeah. You're right. It has to be," Sam replied as they all gazed out over the fields, surveying the landscape.

"What?" Sarah asked. "Is this the place they want to put the houses on?"

"Mm...yeah," Dave answered her. "Try to imagine houses all over here. This whole hay field and way up over the rise. A hundred and fifty acres is a lot of ground."

Jeff was not wholly certain what they were talking about. He'd only half listened when his father had told them about it on the drive down, being preoccupied with sorting baseball cards from his collection. "Who wants to do this?"

"I don't know for sure," his father said. "Apparently some development company bought all this ground, or is in the process of buying it, and wants to build luxury houses here. It'll spoil the natural beauty of the whole area, to say nothing about the atmosphere of the battlefield. How can anyone visit this battlefield and have any conception of the violence and fury that happened here while they're in the middle of a housing development? How can you stand in somebody's asphalt driveway and feel reverence for the men that died here? It's just not right!"

"Can't anybody stop them?" Sarah asked as she looked out over the gently rolling fields.

"Well, this group, that foundation, there, is trying," Dave said, nodding toward the sign. "I don't know. I hope so. I'd say that if the sign is still up there must be some hope, yet. I can't imagine the developers letting it stay up if they already own it."

Sam had set his kickstand and was out about twenty yards in the field. He turned around to the group and shrugged in exasperation. "It's not just here, you know. It's happening all over. South Mountain's another example. They want to build houses around Turner's Gap, right where Gibbon's "Iron Brigade" made its famous advance against the Rebels—and it's all for money! Anything to turn a buck!" he exclaimed, shaking his head in disgust. "What was it Lincoln said: 'A nation with no regard for its past will do little worth remembering in the future.' That's what's happening all over. We're tearing down our heritage in the guise of progress and development—and it's all just greed."

"Hell, the governments aren't doing much to stop it, either. They could pass zoning restrictions, land use restrictions. But they don't. Houses bring in revenue, tax dollars. Hell, there's no money in vacant fields. Plow up the bones and blood and let's put parking lots and condos there!" Sam raged.

"And here's what's so damn funny about it; after awhile, it's not even scenic anymore. It's all houses! The very reason people bought the houses in the first place—to live in a scenic, historic setting that's different from other developments—becomes just that—just another housing development! So, they move onto another site and develop it, and the whole cycle starts all over again.

"Look at Key West. I was down there last year. Remember? Well, it'd been about seven, eight years, maybe, since I'd been there last. They've got it so built-up that the reason people go there—its charm—is about all gone! The whole place is concrete and condos. What's the point of going there anymore? You can visit any city on the coast and see the same thing. Hell, it's no wonder foreigners are taking over the country. We're willing to sell off anything—even our heritage—to the highest bidder."

Dave was standing astride his bike, one elbow propped against the handlebars and resting his chin on his hand as he listened to his friend rant and rage. "You finished?" he asked calmly.

Sam rolled his eyes and blushed some, realizing he'd been caught up in venting his frustrations and anger. He smiled and said, "Yeah. I guess."

"Good. C'mon. Let's go."

Sam walked back to his bike and the others smiled to him in sympathy as they steered theirs out onto the road. With no words spoken, they pedaled down the lane into the shade of the trees where the road began to curve again.

Sam lagged behind the others by a good sixty yards, or so. He pedaled along leisurely, his eyes glued to the brown soil between the rows of growing corn on the right, scanning the ground for any hint of metal that might have been plowed up by the farmer and washed clean by the spring rains.

He had found various relics this way on visits to other battlefields—exploded shell fragments, mini-balls, a shattered bayonet tip, a Confederate belt buckle—and hoped he might chance to spy a souvenir from the violent clash that occurred on this field, buried far more than a century and now exposed to the eye of the careful observer.

That explained why he crashed into the little white Honda parked along the berm of the road.

Coming out of the shadows of the grove of trees the road straightened again, rejoining the cornfield that had swept around behind the small patch of woods. Riding, now, at a brisk pace to catch up with the Coopers, his eyes still sweeping the fields to the right, Sam noticed a young lady standing about forty yards out in the green field. Her arms were crossed over her front as she had her back to the road. He watched her, curious, as she seemed to be standing in silent meditation. She was fashionably dressed in a knee-length white skirt and blue printed blouse, her blonde hair neatly sweeping her shoulders.

There seemed something mysterious about her to Sam. She wasn't the landowner for she displayed no air of concern for the crop. There appeared nothing of spectacular or especial interest to the topography other than the usual beauty of the low rolling hills common throughout this area. She stood as if in contemplation or observation, sometimes looking skyward or to the horizon, then gazing to either side. Sam thought perhaps she was searching for something. He couldn't tell.

He watched her with intrigued interest while he pedaled along at the edge of the road. She turned her head, suddenly, to look at him and they watched each other momentarily. Then, oddly, she moved her hands to clasp her cheeks and yelled, "Watch out!"

Sam hadn't a second to react, for, suddenly, he found himself flying head-over-heels onto the trunk of a late model Honda Accord. He landed on his back with an "Oof!" then tumbled over the right rear fender with a deep, guttural "Ah-h-h-h..." and onto the grassy berm with a low, winded, agonizing "Uh-h-h-h...."

Barely able to comprehend what had happened to him, Sam lay on the ground trying to determine if he was hurt, certain only that he was quite disheveled and disoriented. He'd once been thrown into the air by the concussion of a close exploding mortar shell and the feeling now was not dissimilar. Then, he had looked up to see the sweaty, dirt-streaked face of an army medic standing over him asking, "Are you hurt?" Now, as he looked up he viewed the pleasant sight of a beautiful, soft, round face looking down at him. Though dark sunglasses covered the eyes of this woman in her early thirties he could tell her face had a look of grave concern. "Are you all right?" she asked, leaning over his prostrate form.

Sam lay there, not moving. Though he was bruised in several places he was not badly injured. In fact, he found it amusing that, as this beautiful face had come into his view, partially eclipsing the sun shining directly above her, it created a halo effect around her head. He chuckled over this corona-like simulation as he shaded his eyes to better see her. "Ha! I knew heaven would be like this—full of pretty girls!"

A smile encircled the woman's lips at hearing this. "You took quite a tumble," she said. "Are you okay? Are you hurt?"

Sam groaned as he sat up. The young woman awkwardly extended a hand to help him but he waved it off. "Ug-h-h...no. I'm okay," he told her. "At least...I think so."

Dave, Carol and the children had ridden back and were now beginning to surround him as he sat on the ground.

"Sam. Are you okay?" Dave asked, approaching and kneeling at his friend's side. "What happened?"

The young lady answered first, turning her head to Dave. "I don't know. I was out in the field, your friend called to me, and when I looked back, he crashed into my car. I don't think he saw it."

Sam looked up at the girl, a bit piqued. "I wouldn't have hit it if I'd have seen it...and I didn't call out to you."

"Yes, you did."

"No, I didn't. I was just watching you out there wondering what you were doing. You looked back and started watching me and, well...I, uh...wasn't watching where I was going, I guess," he explained, lowering his voice to an embarrassed mumble about the last part.

Dave extended a hand to his friend to help him up. "Are you hurt at all?" he asked as he gave a pull to bring him onto his feet.

"Hurt! Dave, I just did a back-flip onto a Honda with a half-twist onto the ground," he said, rolling his back to test for broken or bruised vertebrae. He walked around some to be certain both legs functioned as they should. Everyone watched with some concern and were relieved when he appeared to be all right. A bit shaken and bruised, perhaps, but not so very hurt.

"You, uh, you folks are tourists?" the girl asked as they watched Sam adjust his clothing and brush himself off.

"Yes. From around Pittsburgh," Carol replied. "And you?"

"Pittsburgh? Really? Well, that is interesting," the girl said. "I'm going to be teaching in a Monroeville school this fall."

"Really?" Carol said. "That's just down the road from us. What subject?"

"Music. Elementary music...and some chorus, I understand, though I'm not as proficient in that as I should be. It's just a temporary. I'll be substituting for a woman going on maternity leave for the year. These days you take whatever you can, wherever you can."

"You're right about that," Dave said. "Especially in western Pennsylvania."

"Actually, my hometown is Philadelphia. Mainline, if you know it. I've only ever been to Pittsburgh once. I toured it when I went up for my interview. It seems like a nice city."

Sam looked up from brushing his knees off. "Harrumph! There's nothing there anymore. Pittsburgh died in '81 when the mills all closed."

"Oh, that's not true!" Carol chided him. "There's still a lot of industry and commerce."

"Ha!" Sam snorted. "The only people left there are frail, white-skinned jerks who sit inside all day and punch computer keyboards and I'm about to become one of them! The 'real' people have all gone looking for productive jobs that add some real value to the country."

"Sam! Stop that!" Carol reprimanded him. "Don't listen to him. He's not usually like this. I think taking a spill rattled his brain—and his manners."

Sam stood upright and glared at Carol, chafed by her comment. Then, slowly, he calmed down, realizing neither Carol nor this young lady were deserving of such petulant behavior. He didn't understand, himself, why he had said what he did unless it was from the embarrassment of having looked so clumsy by tumbling in front of such a beautiful woman. As he regained his composure he shrugged. "You're right. I'm sorry," he said to Carol. Then he turned to the woman and spoke to her in a calmer and friendlier tone. "Actually, Pittsburgh has a lot of character. There are a lot of wonderful people living both in and around the city. I think you'll enjoy your time there."

"Well, I'm certainly glad to hear that," the woman said. Then she looked curiously at Sam, cocking her head slightly as if to study his face. "Excuse me. I'm sorry to sound so bold, but...have we met before? You seem rather...familiar to me."

Sam smiled, amused, and fixed his attention on the woman with greater scrutiny. She was beautiful; a supple five foot, six inches with an ample bosom and well-proportioned hips and legs, her complexion was clear, fresh and healthy. She had a delicate nose and a small, gentle chin and lips that were soft, sensuous and inviting. She wore her honey-blonde hair stylishly turned under at her shoulders, lending an air of sophistication about her.

Her eyes were hidden by dark sunglasses which served to add a mysterious, enchanting quality to her. Sam hoped he had met her before. But, looking at her, studying her features, he drew a blank. "Hm. I only wish we had. But I'm sorry. I know I'd remember having met you before," he said in a most complimentary tone.

This drew a blushing smile from the girl. "Thank you," she said genially, flattered by the comment. "It was...just a feeling. I'm sorry."

"Heh! So am I," Sam replied.

She gave him another curious glance, then said, "Well, I must be getting back to work. I've taken enough time off already." She removed her sunglasses and deliberately eyed Sam up and down to be certain there were no serious cuts or bruises. "So, you're all right, then?"

Sam drew a surprised inward breath as their eyes met. Those eyes! He thought to himself, they looked so familiar, somehow. They were a beautiful deep, sensitive blue; alert; attentive; gleaming! He had seen her somewhere before. But where? From somewhere deep in his soul there sparked a faint glimmer of familiarity, but it was nothing he could kindle bright enough for recollection. "Uh...yeah. Sure," he answered her. "I'm okay."

"Fine. I'm glad," she replied. Then forcing a hesitant step from a leg that seemed unwilling to move away from him she turned to Dave and Carol, reluctantly tearing her eyes from Sam. "Well, I...I hope you enjoy your stay here at Antietam," she said to them.

"Thanks," Carol answered cheerfully. "It's been fun, so far."

"Good," the girl replied. Then, turning to Sam once more she said, "You know, you really should wear a helmet."

"Mm. I know," he said, nodding in agreement. He watched her walk around to her car, admiring how well she carried herself. "See ya' around," he said with a slight wave of his hand.

She paused at the car door before getting in and gave Sam a warm, friendly smile. "I hope so. That'd be nice." Then, as an afterthought she added, "I'm not sure what you meant by it, but you're certainly not frail, nor a jerk."

Sam turned the corner of his mouth in a reluctant smile. He certainly felt like both after having sprawled out in front of her with such indignity.

As they watched the Honda drive away the two men glanced at one another. Dave released a long, low whistle and stammered, "Ahem. Yes...Well..." as he and Sam communicated, by way of glances, thoughts that Carol would not have appreciated hearing verbalized.

It didn't matter. She intercepted the message between the two anyway. "Okay, guys. Cool down," she said.

"Pretty girl," Dave commented, trying to sound casual and matter-of-fact.

"Yeah. She is," Sam replied, a bit distracted. He was still watching down the now empty lane, his mind swirling as he tried to place her from somewhere in his past. When the others turned to their bikes Sam shrugged and mumbled, "Oh, well..." The mystery of who she was would linger but a short while, though for the moment it left him with an unsettled feeling.

After a tour of the Pry House—and the rather lengthy discussion between the two men concerning it—the little party headed back toward Sharpsburg, traveling now by way of the more heavily used Boonsboro Pike. Sam had wished to avoid the other route under the pretense of having already toured it, saying, "perhaps new monuments and statues could be viewed along the Pike." In truth, though Sam did not inform the Coopers of this, he feared a recurrence of the haunting sensations he'd experienced when passing the Schiels farm earlier.

They entered the little town of Sharpsburg from the east, Sam in front and leading the group past the turn that would have set them back on to the road to the visitor center at the battlefield.

"Where are we going?" Sarah shouted to any adult who might enlighten her as to why they had not made the turn at the intersection. She was tired, parched and seat-sore, and wished only for the cushiony comforts of the air-conditioned van.

"I thought we might look for a cold drink," Sam hollered back. "All the water's warm and I'm dying for something cold."

This perked her some and she managed a slight smile at the idea, miserable as she felt. "Sounds good to me."

"Me, too," Jeff exclaimed from further back. He was trailing behind the others, having the greater difficulty due to his shorter legs and smaller bike.

They rode down the main street for several blocks, then turned down a side street as Sam was interested in a quick tour of the little town as well as a comfortable restaurant. After a few blocks and several more turns he pulled over to the curb, the Coopers following in turn, pulling alongside and parking their bikes at the edge of the sidewalk. Dave and Carol were quick to realize Sam's reason for stopping in front of the 18th century, dilapidated board and batten log house. The two youngest were not. They surveyed the street expecting to see a sign for "Pepsi" or "Coca Cola."

"What's going on?" Jeff asked. "Why are we stopping here? I don't see anywhere to get a drink."

"No. Not here," Dave said, reaching into his back pocket for his wallet. "See that sign in the window? This is the headquarters of the group that's trying to save the Schiels farm from developers." He handed his son a five-dollar bill. "Here. Go back to that store we passed around the corner. Get us all something to drink. We're going in to talk to these people and find out more about this."

"I thought we were going to get something to drink and head back," Sarah complained. "I'm tired and thirsty and just want to go. If you guys go in there, we'll never get back to camp."

"Oh, quit complaining and go get us a drink," Carol told her. "We won't be that long. Bring them back here...and you can get yourself some ice cream if it'll make you feel better about it."

"Well, it'll help. It's not a very good bribe but I'll take you up on it. C'mon, Jeff," she said to him, motioning for him to follow her.

The three adults stood back by the curb and quickly surveyed the exterior of the small, two-story dwelling. It appeared as though little maintenance had been performed on it in many years. Though badly in need of a coat of paint and some trim boards replaced, it still displayed a structural soundness.

The stone foundation appeared solid, showing little sign of shifting or crumbling. But the wooden porch that had been added in later years sagged terribly and required extensive renovation. The rain gutters, what remained of them, needed to be replaced, but the tin roof, though crying out for a coat of protective paint, was not beyond salvaging.

Paint peeled from old window frames that still held the distorted, silver-blue panes from long ago, adding an authenticity to the age of the log house. For all its defects and shabby appearance, however, there was a certain charm and coziness to the old structure, if only because of its age and endurance.

Sam moved up onto the porch. "C'mon. Let's go in," he said, opening the wooden screen door with the "Please Walk In" sign hanging on it.

When they entered the front room, a quick inspection revealed the primitive pioneer construction of the log house and the later attempts to update its conveniences. The first floor was one large room with a crudely installed partition to halve the living area from the kitchen. Out-dated electrical wiring ran along the bottom logs and was covered by a wooden channel, but where it followed the rough-sawn second floor joists overhead to a simple light fixture it was clearly exposed. A worn, faded carpet covered the floor.

The front room was sparsely furnished with two old, overstuffed chairs and several metal folding chairs surrounding a coffee table that held brochures and pamphlets pertaining to the Foundation and the Antietam battlefield. Female voices could be heard in the next room over the soft refrains of a piece by Handel on the stereo. Dave and Sam each picked up a brochure and began to read. Carol stood and looked around the room, waiting.

"Hi!" came the cheery voice of a woman who appeared in the partition doorway. "How are you all today?" she asked.

"Oh, we're just fine, thank you," Carol replied to the neatly dressed woman of about forty.

"Is this your first visit to Antietam?" she asked, approaching them.

"Yes, actually," Dave replied.

"Fine. I hope you're enjoying your visit. Have you toured the battlefield yet?"

"Part of it," Dave said. "We've been biking it. We did some today. We'll do more of it tomorrow."

"Whew!" the woman exclaimed and fanned herself. "It's certainly hot out for that. You must be exhausted."

"Well, somewhat," Dave said. "But, it's fun."

"Good. I'm glad to hear you're enjoying yourselves," the woman replied. Then, nodding toward the pamphlets the men held she asked, "Do you know about our organization?"

"Just bits and pieces," Sam said. "That's why we stopped in, hoping to learn more about it. We passed the Schiels farm. I guess that's the one being sold off?"

"Yes. It is," the woman replied, dropping her pleasant smile and adopting a more serious voice. "A little over a year ago this house was slated for demolition. You can see some of the holes where bullets passed through and impacted into the logs during the battle here," she explained as she went to a wall and pointed to several holes in the logs. "Well, some concerned citizens believed it would be a shame to demolish a structure so much a part of the history of the town. We formed the "Historic Antietam Foundation" in an effort to raise funds to purchase the house, then to re-sell it with protective covenants in the deed to preserve the exterior appearance to how it looked during the period of the battle. We believe we've found a buyer for it. There's a woman very much interested in purchasing it. That's the good news. The bad news is that the Schiels farm has come up for sale and a developer is looking to purchase it to build homes on it."

"So, we hear," Dave said. "Can they be stopped?"

"Well, the owners have granted us first option to purchase it. We've managed to raise fifty thousand dollars in donations from groups and individuals, so far. The Civil War Heritage Foundation has given us seventy-five thousand, and we're applying to the McPherson Foundation for a grant for the rest of the monies. We have some other options we're looking into, but time is really running out on us. We've got less than two weeks to come up with the money or the developers take over."

"Oh, man! That's awful," Sam exclaimed.

"Mm...yes. If we can close the deal on this house, we'll have a little more to apply toward it, but the McPherson grant may be our only real hope," she explained.

"And the Park Service can be of no help?" Dave asked.

"No. I'm afraid not, other than lending moral support and encouragement. Money is too tight and there's a lot of opposition to increasing the park boundaries. Our lawyer is making an effort to lobby for scenic easements to be established but, so far, that hasn't passed."

Before the woman could continue, she was interrupted by another voice in the next room shouting. "Damn it!" Then they heard a loud 'thud,' followed by an agonized, wailing, Ow-w!... "Ow! Ow!...Ow!...Ow!...The woman turned to the doorway to see what the clamoring was about, the three visitors close behind and peering in around her.

The room was furnished with two old, metal desks—the top of one serving as a computer workstation—several easy chairs, some file cabinets and a small dropleaf table holding a vase of wild flowers. But what attracted everyone's eye was the sight of a young woman leaning against one of the desks. She was bent slightly, coddling her right foot in her left hand.

Sam and the Coopers couldn't help but smile fondly as they spied her. It was the same young lady upon whose car Sam had performed his impromptu acrobatic bicycle dismount.

"My goodness!" the woman in front of them exclaimed. "What happened?"

Without glancing up, but displaying herself to be in agony as she massaged her foot the woman said fitfully. "That damned computer! It ate my work!"

"You've got to watch those computers. They start with simple letters or spreadsheets, then go on to feet when you're not looking," Sam said as he made his presence known to the woman and stepped into the room.

The woman looked up abruptly, realizing visitors were present. "Oh!" she exclaimed, embarrassed. Then, "Oh, hello," she said, managing both to smile and to sound more cheerful as she recognized Sam as the man she'd met earlier.

"I usually keep a club handy when I'm working with a particularly nasty and aggressive computer," Sam joked. "Some of them can have really powerful bytes."

The woman blushed some and smiled at his attempted humor. "No. I...I got mad and kicked the desk a good one. I should have kicked the computer but it'd be too expensive if I broke it. So, I probably broke my toe instead," she said, slipping off her pump to massage her stocking toes.

"That seems to be going around today, "Sam laughed as he pulled a chair from behind one of the desks. "Here. Sit down," he said to her.

The woman complied, taking a seat as the others gathered into the room and around her.

"Oh, this is embarrassing," she said with them all watching her caress her toes.

"Naw-w-w... relax," Sam said. "I've blackened toes more than a couple times, myself, over these machines. Besides, it's no more embarrassing than my back-flip onto your car this afternoon."

She smiled up to him at this. "No. I suppose not. That was unfortunate. How are you feeling?"

"Mm, about the same as your toe probably does—only, over my entire body," he said.

Sam moved around to the desk with the computer and sat before the keyboard. "What's it doing?" he asked, looking the machine over to familiarize himself with it.

Both women were at first startled by his rather extraordinary behavior and they glanced at one another for some clue as to how they should react. The younger woman then looked at Sam questionably, as though his taking a seat behind her desk was highly irregular. She started to stammer a reply in protest but was cut short as Sam began to tap on the keyboard.

"You say it's eating your files, eh?" Sam asked, staring thoughtfully at the screen as he typed.

"W-well...yes. It has a habit of losing, or misplacing, items. I'll store a list, or a letter, and they'll just vanish. I was trying to retrieve a grant proposal I'm working on and it's not where I stored it," she explained. "I spent all day yesterday searching for the mailing list. Lord knows where it was. I just, luckily, happened upon it and I still don't know under what I found it."

"Hmm," Sam said as his fingers tapped around the keyboard. Then he paused and looked up at her. "Uh, you don't mind, do you?"

"Well...I...don't know. I...I guess not," she replied hesitantly. "You're familiar with computers?"

"Oh, a little. I have my own. Of course, it's not like this one," he said and began to type again. His fingers moved quickly and assuredly as he would type for a while, wait for the results, then type again. Everyone watched as he worked at the keyboard with the same agility and confidence as a virtuoso pianist performing his warm-up exercise.

Abruptly, he stopped, looked over to the woman and smiled warmly. "Sam Baker," he said with a bow of his head. "And those are my two best friends and the greatest, most patient and understanding people in the whole world—Carol and Dave Cooper."

"Well," the woman smiled pleasantly, her blue eyes sparkling radiantly as they reflected the late afternoon sun streaming in through the window. "Pleased to meet you, Mr. Sam Baker. Kelly Gracie," she introduced herself, returning his bow with a slight nod of her head. "And this is my friend, Marylou Greggs."

"A pleasure, Kelly; and Marylou," Sam said, his eyes fixed to the woman smiling at him.

"Are you from this area, Marylou?" Carol asked, standing beside the woman.

"Oh, I'm from up in Hagerstown. I teach at the junior high school. I was born and raised here."

"I'm envious," Dave said enthusiastically. "I love this area. I'd like to live anywhere around here if I could."

"Yes. It is a nice area," Marylou said. "I don't think I'd like to live anywhere else."

"I don't blame you," Dave replied.

"Where are you all from?" Marylou asked.

"Actually, from the small town of Homer City. It's just east of Pittsburgh by about fifty miles," Dave answered.

"I've never been in that area," Marylou said.

"It's nice there, too," Carol interjected. "We enjoy living there. Dave would just like to be closer to all the Civil War battlefields. He's drawn to this area. He and Sam both," she said, shaking her head resignedly.

"Well, Kelly will be right up in your area this fall. She's going to be teaching in Pittsburgh."

"Yes. So, we've heard," Carol replied.

"Oh? You people have all met before?"

Sam paused his typing and smiled at Kelly, then looked at Marylou. "We, uh, we sort of had a little 'run in' today. Yes."

Carol explained to Marylou how they had come to meet Kelly earlier that day. While she told the story, Sam continued on with his work at the keyboard and monitor. The front door opened and Sarah and Jeff were soon in appearance carrying large waxed cups of iced tea.

"Okay, we're back," Sarah announced as she and Jeff handed drinks to their parents and Sam. Her eyes swept the room hurriedly, noting the log wall interior. "This is a neat house. Does somebody live here?" she asked.

Kelly smiled to the young girl. "I am; for the summer. But I think you should talk your parents into buying it," she teased.

Sarah did another hurried scan of the room and rolled her eyes. "It's not that neat," she said. "I'd rather keep our own house."

The grown-ups laughed and Carol then introduced the two children to Kelly and Marylou.

Sam finally looked up from the screen and exclaimed, "Ha! I think I may have found your problem here."

"Really?" Kelly asked with a pleased but surprised look on her face.

"Yeah. This is going to take some time to correct, though," he said. Then he looked at Carol and Dave. "What do you want to do? We could go back to camp and eat and I could come back later tonight. This is going to take a while."

Kelly looked a bit perplexed at Sam's suggestion. While Dave seemed to shrug it off as "Okay with him," she was having mixed feelings of both gratitude that the man was offering his help and anxiety over this handsome stranger—a man she knew so little about—tampering with the Foundation's records and equipment.

"Well, uh...this is your vacation. Isn't it?" Kelly asked. "I mean, I'd really hate for you to give up your time for this. I'm sure I can get it working again properly."

"No. I'm afraid you can't," Sam told her. "Your keys are in desperate need of cleaning; I think there's a wire or circuit not making proper contact; and, Lady, this program is a shambles!"

Kelly just sat there looking at Sam. She showed a bewildered expression as she blinked slowly and deliberately, absorbing what the man had just told her. She glanced up at Marylou for suggestions or counsel but the darker-haired woman appeared just as confounded. She only shrugged, signaling she was deferring the decision to Kelly. The two-woman gazed at one another as Kelly seemed to be mulling this all over. The idea of having this fellow in to put the system back into working order did appeal to her but, still, there was much else to consider.

"Will anyone be here tonight?" Sam asked, interrupting her thoughts. "I could always come in tomorrow if you've got other plans."

Kelly looked at him. "Oh, no. Don't do that. You shouldn't give up your time. I'm, uh, I'm staying upstairs for the summer—drab as it is. I stay free while I'm working for the Foundation; at least until the house is sold. Then, who knows?"

"Listen," Sam said, "I really want to do this. I feel just as strongly about preserving the battlefields as any one of you people. This can be a part I can play. I'll give a donation; sure! But this is something more concrete that I can do and really feel good about."

Kelly tilted her head sympathetically. She understood his eagerness and desire, but she was still a bit hesitant in consenting.

"You really ought to let him, Ma'am," Dave said in a matter-of-fact and reassuring voice. "Sam's a whiz with computers; anything with circuits and contacts and little green boards."

"You work with them?" she asked.

"Yeah. I've had experience with them," Sam said casually. "It's what I do."

"Hell," Dave said, "Sam probably helped design that one."

"No. Not this one," he smiled, sitting back in the chair.

Inwardly, Kelly was delighted that this handsome stranger qualified to return later, even though his credentials were referenced only by his best friend. There was something about him that intrigued her and she really wanted to see him again, hoping to be able to pinpoint what it was that so mystified her. "Okay. Tonight, then," she told him. "I've got to go out for a bit, and Marylou will be leaving shortly. But I'll leave the key to the back door under a rock by the door."

"Great!" Sam exclaimed. "I'll go back and get cleaned up, get a few things I'll need and see you back here later, then."

"Fine," Kelly replied, amused at his enthusiasm as he seemed so excited at the prospect of returning later. She carefully slid her foot back into her shoe and stood to test the pressure of her weight upon it. Relieved to find it functioning and only a little sore she saw the visitors to the door, bidding them an "enjoyable visit" and exchanging other pleasantries. When they had departed and she returned to the partitioned room, Marylou's eyes followed her over to her desk. As Kelly rummaged through some papers she could feel her friend's eyes still on her. "What?" she asked, looking up abruptly.

Marylou casually drifted her eyes toward the ceiling. "Oh...nothing," she said, smiling impishly.

"C'mon, Lou. Out with it. What is it?"

"Nothing...Only, you may end up with a bed warmer for those cold nights up in Pittsburgh," she snickered.

"Marylou!"

"He's awfully good looking; and built! Whew!"

"Lou! You're married!"

"Well...?"

"Okay," Kelly laughed. "He is handsome."

"And?"

"And built," she added. "Lou! What you're thinking! I can read your mind and shame on you!"

"Well, he does seem to be pretty eager to return. I have a feeling it's more than the computer's circuits he's interested in."

"Oh, stop that. I don't even know him," Kelly said. Then, in a low voice, added, "At least I don't think I do."

"Hmm?" Lou asked, noticing the puzzled expression that grew over her friend's face.

"Mm...oh, nothing. Nothing," Kelly said, trying to shake herself of the curious feeling she had toward the man. "Just...I don't know, there's something peculiar about him; something almost familiar," she said, still distracted by thoughts of him as she tried to recollect some memory of him from deep in her mind. "I get the strangest feeling that...well, never mind," she said, pushing the thoughts away, finally. "Anyway, he's coming back to help with the machine. That's all."

"If you say so," Lou replied.

"Lou, I'm seeing John. Remember?"

"Oh, him. You should forget about that wimp. Dump him for a real man."

"Lou!" Kelly exclaimed, astonished at her friend's remark. "I know you don't care for him, but what's wrong with John? He's tall, handsome...successful. He's a very good lawyer."

"He's a jerk!" Lou stated bluntly. "C'mon, Kel, he's pale, boring and stiff. He's so...so...I don't know, mechanical, I guess. He dresses straight out of L.L. Bean or Brooks Bros. depending on the occasion. He's a phony; a fake! Talk about a 'yuppie!' That coin was minted with his face on it! What you see in him is beyond me."

102

"Okay, he has his faults. But who doesn't? He's a nice man and he treats me wonderfully."

"He treats you like dirt! He only shows up when it's convenient for him. He's always off fishing somewhere, or working late. I think he only sees you 'cause you look good on his arm. Did you ever notice he usually only takes you to parties or to his rich, yuppie friends' houses. Just don't close yourself off to everyone else."

"Meaning?"

"Date around. There's got to be other men out there better than he. Just don't hide behind him 'cause he's available and pretends to be what you're looking for in a guy. Underneath those clothes and that learned disposition lies a real geek."

"Go home, Lou," Kelly said, wishing to end this conversation.

"Yeah. I'm going," she said as she gathered her purse and a folder of papers. "I'll see you in the morning."

"Oh, I'll be here. If this fellow can straighten out the computer, I'm going to be chained to it trying to finish that grant proposal," she said as she watched Marylou preparing to leave. When they'd said their goodbyes, Kelly started to work at the computer again, attempting to bring to the screen the material she had been compiling. Again, the machine failed to function properly and she smacked the top of the monitor with her open palm. "Damn it!" she exclaimed in frustration. She switched off the machine, deciding to place some hope in the abilities of the handsome fellow who was to return that evening.

****

Everyone was unusually quiet on the trip back to the campsite. The children were exhausted and had collapsed in their seats and Dave and Carol were thankful for the respite from the bickering and complaining that always accompanied Sarah's and Jeff's 'wind-down' when they had exerted themselves. They had listened with straining patience to the youngsters' whining and fighting the whole last mile back to the van from Sharpsburg.

Sam sat quietly in the bench seat with the kids and, though he gazed out the window, his mind was far from the rolling landscape and green pastures the road was taking them through. His thoughts, instead, were focused on the lovely girl with the deep blue eyes back at the log house. He wondered from where in his past he had met her. A warm, pleasing sensation grew in his heart as he pondered her, picturing her lovely face in his mind. But with it there was also growing an underlying mysterious feeling that he could as yet not explain.

It was a feeling as if he "owed" her something or, perhaps, had done her some injustice or wrong in the past. He was certain he had not dated her when he was younger—he'd been out with so few girls in high school and had dated only a select few since his divorce. He had always been fair and honest in his business dealings so he ruled out ever having hurt her in that respect.

All he could be certain of was that the more he thought of her, the more the feelings grew—both feelings -and he was determined to know the answer why. It seemed to beckon him; to pull at him like a magnet and draw him back to her. "We should just cook hot dogs tonight," he heard himself say as he leaned forward toward Carol and Dave.

"Oh, yeah?" Dave replied. "Why so?"

"Eh, I don't really feel like cooking on the fire. Seems like too much work tonight. We're all tired. We should just light the camp stove. It'd be a lot faster," he said, hoping they'd be receptive to the idea.

Carol and Dave glanced at one another and smiled for they knew Sam was anxious to return to Sharpsburg.

"That must be some machine, Sam," Carol teased. "You're pretty anxious to get back to work on her—I mean 'it'."

"Pardon?" Sam asked, his voice inflection such that it told he wished Carol to elaborate on what she was implying.

She looked back at him and snickered. "It's put together rather well, isn't it?"

Dave looked at his friend from in the rear-view mirror," I like the design, myself," he said with a chuckle. "Great component parts from what I could see."

Sam grimaced and shook his head over his friends' teasing. "I get it. I get it. Okay. You two think I'm going back 'cause I might be interested in Kelly Gracie," he said, sounding a bit rankled. "Did it ever occur to either of you that I'm just interested in helping out the Foundation?"

Dave and Carol looked at each other and answered together, "No!"

Sarah perked up some, saying, "I think you should date her, Sam. She's real pretty."

"Ah-h-h...you're just a kid—What do you know about it?"

"Ha! I'm eleven years old and I know a pretty girl when I see one. And she's pretty!"

"Okay. Let's just drop it, you guys. I'm going back to work on the system and that's all."

"Sure," Dave replied. "Whatever you say. Listen, why don't I pull into a restaurant and we'll just eat out. It'll be a lot faster. Besides, you're right. I don't feel like cooking either."

Everyone was agreeable to the idea as they were tired and hungry from the long hot day on the bikes. When they reached Harpers Ferry, the town near where their campsite was located, Dave found a suitable restaurant at which to stop. They were all rather quiet during the meal, everyone interested in replenishing their expended calories more than in conversation.

With their return to the camp Sam hurried over to the showers to clean and dress. The kids went into the tent and collapsed on the bedding, too tired even to help their father kindle the evening campfire—something they loved to do.

Tonight, they were too exhausted even to grab a chair and watch their father build the fire. Carol, at least, kept him company. Sitting in a low comfortable camp chair with lemonade and novel in hand, she had settled in for a relaxing evening after a rather arduous day.

When Sam returned from the bathhouse Carol watched him hang his towel and washcloth over the clothesline strung between two trees outside his tent. "You look nice," she commented cheerfully.

"Yeah?" Sam asked, glancing over his shoulder to her. "Thank you."

Dave looked up from the fire ring where he was crouched trying to coax a small flame into more aggressively licking at some larger dried maple twigs. He saw his friend dressed in casual cotton slacks, pull-over knit shirt and loafers with no socks. It was a simple but handsome outfit and Sam did look good in it. "Hey, partner. You do look nice; not that you're out to impress anyone, of course," he said with a little chuckle.

"Aw-w, c'mon, Dave. Don't start with me."

"Okay. Sorry. Only, tell me you're not at all interested in that girl, Kelly."

Sam turned from the clothesline and moved to the fire where he crouched down beside Dave, his face showing a more serious expression. He sucked on his lower lip as if to fade into deep thought. Then, putting a hand compassionately on Dave's shoulder, he began to nod his head slowly, hesitantly. Dave watched his friend, expecting at any moment for Sam to utter something in the affirmative. "Ya' know," Sam finally said, increasing the pressure of his hold on Dave's shoulder, "You just might be right." Then, catching Dave off guard, he playfully pulled backward and sent Dave sprawling onto his back. Laughing, Sam sprang up and jumped away, expecting some form of retaliation.

Dave just lay there, sprawled on the ground, and looked up at his friend. "Ass-hole," he mumbled. "I'll put a snake in your sleeping bag tonight."

"Eh...it'd be worth it, seeing you laid out so gracefully like that," Sam chuckled. "Wish I had my camera."

Dave sat up and brushed himself off and looked over at Carol as she was laughing at this scene. "What are you laughing at?"

"You...you looked pretty funny going backwards," she said, and flailing her arms backwards and crying out "Ahhhhh..." she mimicked her husband's motions and started to laugh again.

Dave harrumphed.

Sam went into his tent to put away his biking clothes and wash kit. When he reappeared, he headed for his car, carrying a flashlight for when he returned later, in the darkness. Dave followed him and watched as Sam rummaged through a tool bag in his trunk, taking inventory of an assortment of electronic repair tools. "You carry this stuff around with you? Most people carry a socket set and pliers and stuff to work on their cars. What did you think, we might bring a T.V. or toaster along with us?"

"Hey, I have those tools, too. They're in that other bag," Sam said, pointing to a small canvas bag. "I guess I've always carried this stuff around. It started when I was a kid and fixed my friends' transistor radios or their parents' T.V. sets. I just got in the habit of always having them handy."

"Okay. I can buy that," Dave said. "Well, listen. I'll keep the fire burning for you. I suspect you'll be late."

"Mm...yeah. This'll take a few hours," Sam replied. He zipped the bag closed and moved around to lay it gently onto the passenger's seat. "Well, I guess I'm going in," he said.

"Okay," Dave replied, following Sam around to the driver's door. "Good luck on this."

"Thanks," Sam said, and just before he entered the car he hollered to Carol, "Night, Carol. I'll see you in the morning."

"Bye, Sam. I hope it works out. I guess we won't see you till morning."

"No. You'll be in the sacks when I get back."

"Well, drive safe, and good luck with...whatever it is you're going to do," Carol said.

When Sam drove off, Dave returned to add more wood to the flames that had now started to catch and grow higher. As he carefully placed larger sticks on the pile, he noticed his wife was still gazing thoughtfully over to where Sam's car had been parked. "What's on your mind, hon?"

Carol set her book on the ground beside her and leaned forward to hug her knees. "Oh, I don't know. Call it woman's intuition, I guess, but I just have a feeling about Sam. Did you notice the change that's come over him in the last couple of hours?"

"You mean how anxious he was to get back to town? Sure did."

"Mm...yeah. But it was his eyes. They're usually just a cloudy blue; just eyes. Tonight, they really took on a glow. Like he just came alive or something."

"Ha!" I think he's real interested in that girl," Dave said.

"Mm, hm. I'd say so. I saw the way she was looking at him, too. There might be something there."

"I hope. That'd be great," Dave replied, continuing to coax the fire along by adding larger branches. "What's your 'intuition' tell you about how it will go between them? Good or bad?"

Carol smiled, "Too early to tell. But I know Sam's out to impress her and draw her interest."

"Heh!" Dave laughed. "Even I could tell that." He stood up from the fire and drew back to admire his handiwork. "Think I'll go roust the kids. They'll be hungry for marshmallows."

"How do you know?"

"'Cause I'll make them. I'm not going to let this good fire go to waste. This is a perfect marshmallow toasting fire."

****

Sam was working diligently at the computer when Kelly let herself in through the back door. She was carrying a basket of laundry and smiled to Sam as she set the load down.

"Well, hello," he greeted her. "Out doing your laundry?"

"Yes. What a bore. Next to ironing it's probably one of the most lonesome chores a body can do."

"I'll second that," Sam replied as Kelly moved around the desk and peered over his shoulder at the screen.

"So, how's it going? When did you get here?"

"Oh, around seven," he answered, glancing at his watch to see it was now close to nine o'clock. "I found a bad connection on the ribbon cord. That would explain why some of your information wouldn't make it onto the disc. I soldered it and cleaned your keys. At least the mechanical part is done. Somebody's been in and worked on this machine before. When did you have it serviced last? From the looks of things, it's been a while."

"I don't know. It was donated to us by a company from D.C. It was used but the company said it checked out okay."

"Hm. Well, whoever serviced it was careless. The line I soldered looked to have been cut accidently by the fellow's screwdriver.

Anyway, I've just started exploring the program to find out where the problem is and see if we can't straighten it out. This may take a while," he said, trying to prepare her for a long night.

"Great!" Kelly exclaimed. "I mean...great...that you're...doing this, not that...it'll take a long time," she said, blushing some. "It's real nice of you."

"Hey. I'm pleased to do it. I'm glad I can help."

"Well, you are. Immensely! We're all indebted to you if you can make this thing function properly. I'm not very proficient on them. I know enough to get by—if they're working right," she explained. Then she moved away and retrieved her laundry basket. "I'm going to put these away and then I have some work I must look over. Let me know if you stumble upon something that looks like a grant proposal. I've really got to get working on it and pass it on to the board for review. We're coming up on our deadline and I'm so far behind on everything because of that stupid machine."

"Sure. I'll look for it," Sam said. "But, if this has been on the fritz for a good while, now, why didn't you get somebody in to look at it before?"

"Well, we were supposed to. My boyfri— um, our attorney was to send someone out from D.C. He contacted a technician from the same company that gave us the machine and they said they'd be out as soon as they could. I guess they're pretty busy, though. They've been putting us off for several weeks. It's really very frustrating."

"I can imagine," Sam said, watching her carry the basket to the foot of the stairs.

She paused, briefly, to glance back at him and smiled when she saw he'd been trailing her with his eyes. "Well, maybe you'll be the one to change all that frustration for me," she said as she began to climb the steps.

"Yeah. I hope so," Sam replied. "I'm sure going to give it a try."

Sam worked for close to half an hour at the terminal, the room quiet, save for the occasional mechanical rattle of the computer functioning its commands and the creaking of the floor overhead as Kelly moved about upstairs. When the phone rang on the desk Kelly hollered down, "I'll get it!" and hurriedly descended the rickety wooden stairs.

Clad in a long cotton summer dress and sandals and her hair in a neat braid, then twisted into a bun high on her head, she looked cool and comfortable in spite of the hot night as only the slightest air moved through the open windows. Sam inhaled deeply as the gentle fragrance of her freshly applied perfume permeated the room.

Kelly quickly picked up the phone and put it against her ear. "Hello," she answered on the sixth ring. "...I was upstairs, changing. I just got in. Where are you?" she asked of the person on the other end. She turned her back and walked to the end of the cord and began to speak in hushed tones. Sam tried not to listen and to distract himself by turning his attention to the computer, but in such a small room it was difficult not to overhear.

He heard her ask the caller if they couldn't "make it out tomorrow night," and then the sound of disappointment as she asked "When" she would see them again. "...Well, okay," she replied. "If you're that busy I guess we'll just have to wait." Then her voice became troubled as Sam heard her tell the caller, "...I had that dream again last night."

"...Yes. It woke me up and I couldn't go back to sleep. I wish I could understand it. It's so fitfully vivid. I've been having it so often, lately."

"...No, I won't. You know how I feel about pills."

Kelly glanced over her shoulder at Sam as she said "...Just working on some papers. There's a fellow here from up north who's working in the computer."

"...Yes. I know that. But he thinks he can fix it."

"...Well, where is he, then? You keep telling me, 'He'll be out, he'll be out,' but he hasn't shown, yet."

"...Just some tourist; from Pittsburgh."

"...Maybe he will, but he can't harm it any more than it already is."

"...Yes. I'm trying to work on it but it's difficult for me. I told you I've only ever written one, and then I only helped write it. You said you'd help me on it and you haven't, yet. Without the info in the computer, it's impossible to finish. Time is running out, John! We've got to get that McPherson money or we'll lose the ground to Marco."

Kelly turned now, facing Sam, and he could hear, clearly, everything she said as she kept taking slow, unconscious steps toward the desk, following the phone cord back to its cradle. Staring at the wall behind Sam, she talked plainly, seeming oblivious to Sam sitting right in her path. "...Okay. I'll see you this weekend, then?"

"...Call me tomorrow if you get the chance." She said goodbye to the caller and placed the phone onto the receiver, then stood staring at the phone as though considering either the caller or the conversation.

Sam looked up at her as she stood just on the other side of the desk, her hand still on the phone. "Boyfriend?" he asked, interrupting her thoughts.

"Hm? Oh. Sort of. At least, I've been seeing him, anyway. He's a lawyer in D.C. He's acting as legal counsel for the Foundation. Free of charge. Isn't that nice of him?"

"A lawyer who's waived his fee? Heh! Either he has some angle or he likes you very much."

"Oh, he...he does," she said, though with just a slight hesitation. "He's a very nice man."

"I'm sure he must be if he's won your attention," Sam said to her.

Kelly smiled over the compliment. "Well, thank you," she said as she looked at him. Their eyes lingered on one another momentarily, neither of them drawing a breath as they seemed to study each other's face. Then Kelly averted her eyes, blushing some. "Well, I'd...I'd better review some of the material the publicity committee has been putting together," she said, picking up a folder from the desk.

Sam returned to the keyboard, feeling a bit embarrassed himself over their intense exchange of glances. "Okay...uh...I should get back to work, too," he said, positioning himself straight in the chair. He watched her take a seat behind the other desk and begin to sort through the papers from her folder, organizing them around the already cluttered desk top. "Explain something to me, Kelly," he asked quizzically. "What exactly is your job with the Foundation? Are you, like, the office coordinator of all of this; or the secretary, maybe?"

"Yes," she said, continuing to arrange the papers.

"Yes?"

"Yes. All of the above. "I've been coming to Sharpsburg for a lot of summers, ever since my dad brought the family here on a visit a long time ago. I'd spend a few days riding a bike or renting a horse to ride over the battlefield. It's really lovely in this area," she said. "Anyway, the Foundation was formed last year when this house was to be sold for demolition and we all helped raise money to purchase it and, hopefully, to resell it for restoration. The group grew larger and, since it's comprised of all volunteers, someone was needed to work regularly at it. I had the summer free so I said I'd take the post, especially with the Schiels farm up for sale, now. We can't let that fall into the wrong hands. It'd be a disaster! I don't really have a title. I guess 'office manager' would be suitable. I don't get paid for it but I do get free lodging. I feel so very strong about what the Foundation is trying to accomplish that I'm thrilled to be a part of it."

"Yeah. I agree with you there," Sam replied. "So, you're a Civil War enthusiast? I haven't known many women to share that interest."

"I didn't say that," Kelly responded. "I've read some on it; maybe as much as everybody else. But...it's this place. It holds some fascination for me. There's just something about this area that keeps drawing me back to it. I suppose it's the lovely scenery, though I must say it's beautiful all over northern Virginia and Maryland. I don't know why, really. What's even more curious is that whatever it is that draws me here every year has become so much more forceful this past year. That's why I jumped at the chance for an excuse to live here this summer, hoping to discover just what the attraction is. Does that sound a little strange?"

"No. No, it doesn't," Sam replied. "It's not unlike my friend Dave and I. We keep visiting different battlefields every summer. We,..uh...we served together in...uh...in Nam," he said with some reluctance. "Huh! You'd think we both would have had enough of wars and battles after that. But I don't know, it's like you said, we're just drawn to these places. It's almost mystical. We really can't explain it and we quit trying long ago. We just roll with it and let the feelings lead us where we're supposed to go next," he explained. Then he shrugged. "You know, I suppose it sounds really crazy to hear that, except that there are thousands of other guys out there feeling the same thing.

There're all kinds of organizations; Round Tables, and reenactment groups—and everybody feels the same tug, the same mysterious, fascinating pull. It's nothing that can be identified or explained. But it's there."

Kelly's face lighted as she nodded in agreement, delighted over being able to share her peculiar sensations with a sympathetic ear. "I know what you mean. It is something mystical, isn't it? It's as if I'm supposed to be here for some reason. So, I keep coming back, hoping I'll find out why," she said, her eyes fixed on the handsome man. When it occurred to her that she'd been staring just a little too fancifully at Sam she quickly looked away. "Um, would you like a coke or something?" she asked, her face flushed some as she felt a bit embarrassed. She was inwardly amused over how like a little school girl flirting with a classmate she'd become. "I could...brew some coffee? There might be a beer?"

"Herbal tea would be nice, if you have it," Sam replied. "Is there a stove here?" he asked, quickly surveying the room as if he'd missed noticing one.

"No. The house is really rather primitive. There's the one sink over there on the wall," she said, pointing to a small, old, white, cast-iron bowl with individual hot and cold spigots. "The bathroom is upstairs. Well...what there is of one. There's only a commode against the one wall with a little partition; no door, or anything. And a couple of the fellas did install a sort of temporary shower for me. It's one of those free-standing units that's kind of just 'there.' It's functional, at least. I use a hot plate to warm food. The wiring would never handle a range."

"Bet you eat out a lot," Sam chuckled.

Kelly smiled, "Mm....well, I don't eat much anyway. And Marylou is always bringing me care packages from her house. She makes extra portions and brings them in the next day. She's really a terrific cook so I do all right. I'll, uh, I'll go get the hot plate. It won't take but a minute," she said, standing and moving to the stairs.

"Can I help?" Sam asked as he made a move to stand.

"No. I can manage. It's not that heavy," she replied, ascending the open wooden steps. She soon returned with the hot plate and tea kettle which she placed on top of the two file cabinets. When she'd plugged it in and turned the switch on, she made a second trip upstairs, this time for a tray of teas, cups, honey and spoons which she placed on the desk.

Sam had been following her with his eyes the entire time, finding himself fascinated with her every move. "Did you ever work in Albany?" he asked as she leaned over the tray to place a tea bag in each cup.

She looked at him curiously, "No. Why do you ask?"

"Just trying to place you. Remember you said you thought you knew me? Well, you were right. You seem familiar to me, too. It's been bugging me all evening just exactly why, though."

"Well, Sam Baker," she said as she lifted the kettle from the hot plate. "Suppose you tell me a little about yourself and we'll see if we can find the connection."

Sam watched her pour the water into the cups and while she prepared the tea he started. He began with his high school years in Chicago, then his university studies. Kelly set the cup of tea before him as he reluctantly tried to explain his marriage, his army years, and his divorce. Sam watched her sit across from him and sip her drink as he moved on to his post-graduate studies, his friendship with Carol and Dave, and only a few of the larger companies with which he'd been employed. When he mentioned having worked for the government Kelly's ears perked.

"The federal government? Really?" she asked, interrupting him. "Have you ever had experience writing grant proposals when you worked for them?" she asked hopefully.

Sam slumped back in his chair and shook his head. "No...no. Not when I worked for them. I was always hired when the money had already been appropriated for a project."

"Oh. I see," she said, sounding just a bit disappointed.

Kelly confessed to not being able to place herself at any of the locations Sam had yet mentioned. "Tell me some more places you've worked, Sam. Maybe it was some other place we've met. Have you been in the Philadelphia area?"

"No. I've been through Philly, but I never worked there," he replied. Then, sitting back in the chair Sam took a sip of tea and stared reflectively into the cup as he thought of the many places he'd moved in the last two decades. He sucked on his lower lip, his eyes cast down into the cup, and he released a long sigh. When he raised his eyes to meet Kelly's he said, "Well...that's, uh...kind of hard to recall. I've, uh, I've moved around quite a lot. Maybe it'd be easier if you told me where all you've been. You've probably had a lot more stability than I."

"Well...let's see," Kelly said sitting forward in her chair, eager to share her background with him. "I was born in Philly; my father is in engineering and my mother had been a concert pianist until I was born. That's why I was steered in that direction—music, I mean. I went to Temple, then on to Julliard. I performed for a few years but found it too...I don't know...stuffy, maybe? I don't know. I just didn't care for it that much. So, I started teaching music. Nothing permanent; just temporary positions. I did a couple of years teaching piano at East Stroudsburg College in Pennsylvania, different high schools and private schools in, or near, Philly; and, next fall, Pittsburgh."

"Whoa!" Sam chuckled. "And Carol calls me a drifter. Sounds like your resumé is almost as long as mine."

Kelly laughed. "I suppose it does look that way. But it's not from choice. I'd like more than anything to have a permanent home. There just doesn't seem to be much out there. Teaching positions are difficult to find. Besides, I haven't found any one place I really care to stay."

Sam squinted accusingly at her and nodded affirmatively. "A drifter," he proclaimed. "You just stated the first definition."

"Stop that!" Kelly laughed. She reached behind her head to pull the pins holding the bun securely, then began to untwist the braid. "Anyway, I like to think of it more in terms of...well...seeking adventures, or...keeping a fresh perspective. I suppose, in a way, it is drifting, perhaps, but it's not anything that's caused by unhappiness."

"Loneliness," Sam stated. "We do it cause we're lonely. People like us are searching for some fulfillment, some happiness, that may, or may not, exist. And we just haven't found it yet, whatever it is."

Kelly paused from loosening her braid and looked as though she were giving Sam's statement some thought. She smiled and tossed her head to swish her golden hair, sending it flowing gently to her shoulders. "Maybe you're right," she said. "But then, maybe it's just there are no teaching positions for ex-pianists."

Sam retorted by curling his lip in a pretended sneer. Kelly laughed and reached into her purse to retrieve a brush which she used to begin running through her hair in long, sweeping strokes.

Sam watched her, mesmerized; enchanted. He leaned forward to rest his elbows on the desk top and cradled his chin in his hands. "So, you were a concert pianist?" he asked. "Tell me more."

"Oh, ho! That was quite a while ago. I haven't performed professionally in years."

"Will you play something for me sometime?" he asked looking directly and deliberately for her reaction. "Whenever we get where there's a piano handy?"

Kelly paused the brush in mid-stroke. Her eyes widened but she didn't look at him. Her pulse quickened, flushing her face momentarily as she realized what the question implied. She turned her head to gaze at him, the brush still held at its half-sweep through the golden hair and those wide, deep blue eyes betrayed any attempt at restraining her excitement over him.

Sam became aware that his own facial expression deceived his attempt at asking the question in a casual manner. His heart raced to hear her answer, hoping she would not fluff the question off with a casual, polite reply.

"Why, Sam, I'd be pleased to play something for you," she said, her smile beaming warmly as their eyes met. "We'll have to look for some place that has a piano."

Sam's mind screamed in elation and his heart leapt into his throat at hearing this. It took all his effort to remain composed as he looked at her and smiled. "Good. Good. I'd like that." then, when he was finally able to pull his eyes from the woman he said, "Well. I, uh, I'd better get to work on this."

"Yes. I've got a lot to do here, too," Kelly said as she nervously stroked the brush through her hair.

The two began to work at their respective places but the silence in the room, broken only by the low mechanical sounds of the computer functioning or the occasional shuffling of papers, began to seem awkward. Kelly looked over to Sam and asked, "Do you mind if I put some music on? I work better if I have some background music playing."

"No, not at all," he replied.

Kelly stood and went over to the stereo system that sat on a wall shelf. She slid a cassette tape into the receiver and a soft but lively waltz began to sound from the speakers. Sam listened a moment as Kelly returned to her seat. "Strauss," he commented. "The Artists' Life Waltz."

"Very good!" she smiled to him. "You like classical music?"

"Yeah. I'm partial to waltzes. And Strauss is my favorite."

"Really! That's wonderful. He's my favorite, too," she beamed.

They listened awhile, then, turning to their work they resumed their tasks feeling a bit more relaxed as the music filtered softly through the room. The tape played on to its end and was replaced by another, then a third and a fourth. Little conversation passed between them as Sam labored at correcting the problem with the program, his fingers busily tapping the keys and his eyes fixed on the monitor.

Kelly had moved to the overstuffed chair, spreading her papers before her on the coffee table and now, around midnight, she leaned back, set her feet up on the table, and closed her eyes to rest.

Sam glanced over at her when he heard her breathing change. He sat back in his chair to watch her sleep and smiled as he believed she looked as beautiful in her sleep as she did awake—perhaps even more so as she appeared so vulnerable and innocent in the big cushioned chair. He stood and moved around to her to gently nudge her. "Kelly...Kelly," he said softly.

"Hm?...What?" she stirred, slowly opening her eyes.

"Go up and go to bed. I should only be a little while longer," he said as he helped her to her feet.

Kelly roused herself only enough to be helped to the stairs by Sam and to drag herself up the steps. She mumbled goodnight to him and Sam wasn't certain if she heard him tell her he would be by in the morning to show her what he had accomplished.

Returning to the computer Sam worked quite late. Discovering what he believed to be a "virus" in the program he dialed up and logged onto the powerful Carnegie-Mellon University computer, using its specific programs to locate and neutralize the bug that had somehow found its way into the Foundation's discs. After some long, assiduously careful hours of work he sat back and gave a long stretch, satisfied that he'd been able to get the program to function correctly.

He allowed himself only a moment of inward satisfaction, however. Anxious to employ his talents and capabilities to help the Foundation—as well as to impress the now soundly sleeping woman upstairs—he drew a breath, pulled himself back to the machine, and began to search for the grant proposal Kelly had been working on. When he called it to the screen, finding it now in its proper file, he was surprised and gladdened to discover Kelly had already accumulated and assembled all of the pertinent information needed.

All he, Sam, had to do was to put it together and type it in the professionally appropriate style and prose. He began to work immediately, typing rapidly and steadily, filling in the information as requested on the supplied forms. Only occasionally did he need to browse the files for additional information, and then he found the woman had done a remarkable job of organizing the data for quick retrieval.

When, at last, he rolled his chair back from the computer he crossed his arms and sighed contentedly. Reaching out with one hand he placed a finger above the key marked "print." "Done!" he said as he pushed down on the key. As the printer began to function, he stretched wide and long, releasing a yawn that nearly tore at the corners of his mouth. Now he need only wait until the material was printed so he could gather it together and stack it neatly on the desk to await the sleeping Kelly's review the next morning.

The next morning, Sam realized, had already arrived. He glanced at his watch to see it was 4:35 A.M. As he stretched again, he decided there was little sense in returning to the campsite at this hour. He could curl up in the cushioned chair to catch some sleep and return to camp before the Coopers departed for the battlefield later in the morning.

Drawing himself out of the swivel chair behind the desk he went to the little sink beneath the stairway and rinsed out the old, stale tea from his cup and filled it with water. As he began to take a sip, he heard Kelly murmur something from upstairs. "What's that?" Sam asked, thinking she was addressing him.

He moved to the steps and climbed the first two boards but before he could ask again what she'd said to him he heard her speak further. It was a troubled, indiscernible mutter. A plea, perhaps, or a pained comment. He couldn't tell. He knew, only, that she was talking in her sleep. "No..." she groaned aloud, then something else was mumbled in a troubled tone with "no...don't..." as the only identifiable words.

Sam stealthily crept up a few more steps to peer over the landing into the room. There were no interior walls on the second floor except for around the commode. There, painted plywood sheets had been nailed on either side of it with a curtain drawn between them to shield its visitor.

The free-standing fiberglass shower unit had been plumbed in just beside the commode. Several old bureaus and lamp tables, a metal card table with chairs, a large, old comfortable oak rocker and a small, old refrigerator were about all the other furnishings in the room. The floor was of rough planking and bare except for a braided rug in which the large brass bed was positioned against the center of one wall.

The scattering of light up the stairway from below afforded enough illumination for Sam to see Kelly's form on the bed. She slept on her back, restless and murmuring. Quietly, his heart pounding rapidly lest he awaken her, Sam climbed to the top step and into the room. He watched as Kelly now moved her arms outward, either reaching to grasp something—or someone— or to shield herself from the same.

Sam approached the bed and leaned over the restless woman, pulling the sheet up over her from where she had thrashed it to her knees. "Shshsh...It's all right," he whispered to her. "Shshsh..." And either his words had filtered gently through to her subconscious or the dream then ended, for her body relaxed and she turned onto her side. Sam stood a moment and gazed compassionately at the now resting form of the lovely woman, relieved at seeing her discomfort had now passed.

Moving off as silently as he'd approached, Sam slipped back down the stairs to the office area. When he flicked off the overhead light, leaving only the shadowy glow from the computer monitor to light his way, he nestled into the cushioned chair, propped his feet up on the coffee table, and fell fast asleep.

Chapter Seven

Sam released a low groan and shifted in his slumped, curled position in the chair from his right side over to his left. Aware that the morning light was filtering into the room he let his eyelids open just a bit to determine how bright it actually was, hoping to discover it was still very early and he could sleep a while longer.

Though his body yearned for a few hours more his biological clock was informing him he had probably received all the rest he was going to be allowed. He slowly opened his lids to test the daylight and became aware of a form standing by the desk but a few feet away from him.

Rolling his lids wider he saw that it was Kelly, dressed in a sleeveless pink tee shirt and black running shorts. Her hair was pulled back into a pony tail and fastened with pink bands in several places. She stood holding a glass of orange juice in one hand and the papers Sam had prepared only hours ago in the other.

"Mhgh..." Sam mumbled as he tried to stir; his head groggy from the lack of sleep.

"Well, good morning," she smiled cheerfully to him.

"Mmugh," Sam replied from his fetal-like scrunch in the chair.

"You look so uncomfortable. I'm sorry."

"Mm. They say Thomas Jefferson used to sleep sitting up. What time is it?"

"Seven," Kelly answered him, watching as he drew himself up only enough to give a long stretch and yawn. "How late were you up?"

"Mm...I don't know. I don't think I actually went to sleep, yet."

"Aw, poor Sam," she sighed sympathetically.

"Yeah. Poor Sam," he moaned in agreement. He made a first, feeble attempt at lifting himself from the chair, but, finding it too difficult, collapsed back into it.

"Sam, do you want to go up in my bed?" she asked, feeling compassion for how tired he appeared.

Sam glanced over at her and managed a sly grin. "Heh! Now there's an offer I haven't heard very often. Thanks anyway, but Dave and Carol will probably be showing up soon and they'd spoil the whole romance," he said. But when he saw Kelly smile good naturedly, though looking askance at his playful remark he shrugged, "Guess I better get cleaned up."

"Okay," Kelly replied. She watched him struggle to his feet and waved toward the file cabinets with the hand in which she held the sheaf of papers. "I put some coffee on for you."

"Hope it's strong," he mumbled, dragging his body to the coffee maker that sat on top of the file cabinet. He poured a cup from the pot and, while he stirred in some milk, glanced back to see Kelly watching him with a rather peculiar, though endearing smile. "What?" he asked, wondering why the look.

"This," she said, holding up the hand full of papers.

Sam took a swallow of coffee and turned to lean against the file drawers. Running his hand through his hair he looked away in an effort to mask his pride as he could tell she was pleased with his work. "It's okay, isn't it?"

"Okay?" she exclaimed as if in disbelief he should ask that. "Sam, it's...it's fantastic! How long did you work on this? How did you know what to say, how to phrase it?" she asked, all but stumbling over her words.

Sam played it cool, taking another sip of coffee, but a smile encircled his lips as he brought the cup away. "Oh, it didn't take long. You had all the data and info assembled. I just put it in order and did the phrasing."

"Sam, you just saved me hours of work—and hours of untold fretting. Goodness! After reading this even I'm ready to take out a loan and donate the money. It's wonderful!" Then she looked at him with a suspicious smile. "Wait a minute. You told me you never wrote a grant proposal before."

"And I didn't. At least, not when I worked for the government. 'Course, a couple different companies I worked for had government contracts and existed only through Defense Department money. We were always writing for more research money. Then, too, I helped design a program for some medical research. That was a private firm working with both federal and state monies. I liked that better than defense work. I don't get along too well with Pentagon people. But they need me so they pay me well."

Kelly had a look of confusion, but more, one of astonishment as she interrupted him. "Wait a minute. Wait. You actually do design computers? You don't just work with one?"

"Yeah. Why? What'd you think?"

"I-I don't know. I guess I thought you worked in an office just analyzing data or punching stuff into them or something."

"Oh, ho! No," Sam chuckled. "My. Let's see. I've worked for I.B.M., Sperry, Apple, uh...oh, the list goes on. I've either written programs for, or helped design and build everything from small home computers to big mainframes. Sometimes, just for kicks, I'll write a program for some specialty research, like medicine or something."

"Uh huh," Kelly nodded, listening attentively to Sam's explanation.

"I wrote a program once for auto mechanics to use in helping fix engine problems. I don't really know anything about engines, I just pulled together a bunch of repair manuals and made a step-by-step guide for locating and correcting problems on certain engines. G.M. paid me handsomely for it. I even wrote a program for the scrap steel industry for keeping their inventories straight. Whew! What a different breed of dog those people are," he chuckled.

"Jeez, Sam, I'm impressed," Kelly said, feeling a bit embarrassed.

Sam showed a blushing smile and shrugged. "Naw. Don't be. It's just what I do. I've always been good with electronic stuff. It just comes natural to me. I've always been good at math the way some people are just naturally good at art, or music; or the way some mechanics just have a knack for engines. It's just what I do."

"Well, you must do it pretty well."

"I guess," he replied.

"Well, listen. I'm going out for a jog. I'll probably be about an hour, or so. Make yourself at home. I've laid out some clean towels if you want to shower. Marylou may be showing soon. I never know just when to expect her," Kelly said. Then she added, "I'll pick you up some breakfast, if you'd like?"

"Yeah? Great! That'd be real nice. Eggs, scrambled; whole wheat toast; no bacon, unless its slab cut; home fries, if they make their own. I don't care for pre-packaged stuff."

Kelly chuckled, "Fussy, huh?"

"Only about some things."

"Okay," she laughed. "See you in a while." She turned to leave, then paused and turned back to face him. "Oh. By the way; dinner is on me tonight."

"Yeah?" he perked up at hearing this.

"Yes. It's the least I can do to show my appreciation for the work you've done."

Sam smiled in delight. "Thanks. I'd like that."

Kelly winked at him, then turned and departed.

****

Sam freshened his coffee and went to the computer to spend some time on the machine "spot checking" the program to be certain it was functioning correctly. Satisfied with its performance, he went up the stairs to shower, hoping to rejuvenate his tired body. Now, seeing the second floor of the log house by daylight, he was impressed with Kelly's ability at making the rather crude, drab living area more comfortable.

Various handmade crafts adorned the walls, interspersed with some chosen landscape paintings in both oils and water colors. Silk flowers, artfully arranged in baskets and wreaths, were also decoratively displayed on the logs. Freshly cut wild flowers filled vases that were placed on the bureaus and table, their sweet, gentle fragrance managing to penetrate the otherwise musty, stuffy smell so similar to the attics of older homes.

Sam reached into the shower stall and turned on the hot water. After setting the faucets to the proper temperature he stripped down, laying his clothes neatly over a chair by the table. Then, hanging a towel on the chrome peg of the stall, he climbed in and drew the curtain closed.

He took a long, leisurely shower, letting the cool streams of water spraying over his body slowly revitalize him. As he stood under the nozzle, he began to ponder the curious and peculiar incidents that, in the last twenty-four hours, had culminated in his standing naked in the shower of a beautiful woman's apartment. He closed his eyes to develop a picture of Kelly in his mind and smiled as he conjured the vision of how she looked when he'd first opened his eyes this morning to see her standing but a few feet away. "Ahh, he mused inwardly, "she would be a lovely one to wake up and see every morning."

"Kelly, I made lasagna last night and I'm putting some in your fridge for you," came a voice that suddenly shattered Sam's thoughts back to reality. He opened his eyes, startled. "You've got to tell me how it went with that hunk-of-a-fella last night. Gawd! What a gorgeous man."

It was Marylou, and Sam wasn't sure just what to do. He should speak, he thought, to at least let her know it was not Kelly she was addressing. Then he smiled as he decided to wait to hear what else the woman might have to say about him. He wasn't disappointed.

"I hope he turned out to be as great as he looked. You didn't let him get away, did you?"

Sam chuckled. This was too good! "No. She didn't," he answered, barely able to restrain from laughing.

Instantly, the shower curtain was pulled wide and Marylou stood before him.

"Ahh! Hey-y-y" Sam gasped and quickly turned sideways, covering his genitals with his hands.

"Well, well, well," Marylou said as she stood there looking at him, a hand on her hip and a cool smile on her face. "Look what I found."

"Would you...would you pull the curtain, please?" Sam stammered, trying to fade into the corner of the stall.

"I already did," Marylou said with a naughty laugh, finding Sam's embarrassment amusing.

"The other way, please."

"Oh, okay," she pouted as she drew the curtain across the bar. "You shouldn't have let me go on like that though."

Sam turned the water off and reached around the wall for his towel, groping for where it should have been hanging. Unable to locate it, his hand felt for, then found, the hook—empty. Sticking his head out of the cubicle he looked around the corner to see it hadn't fallen to the floor. Marylou was standing by the table, the towel dangling from one hooked finger.

"Looking for this?" she smirked.

"Please?" Sam asked, sighing a bit.

"Not till you say you're sorry."

"I'm sorry. Now can I have the towel?"

"Mm...not good enough. A little more specific, please."

"I'm sorry I let you go on about me," he said, sounding rather rote.

"Come on. Come on," she signaled with her hand for him to continue.

"...And I should have made my presence known. I was in the wrong," he added, then waited for her reaction.

Marylou teased him by pretending to consider whether his apology was sufficient.

"Aw, c'mon, Marylou. Give me the towel. Please?"

She scrunched it into a ball and threw it at his head. Sam caught it and pulled back in to dry off, adding, "But I sure as hell enjoyed hearing it."

"I'll bet you did," she said. "So, you stayed the night?"

"Yeah. Sort of," Sam replied through the curtain.

"Well. Kelly sure surprised me. I didn't take her for one who'd even kiss on the first date, let alone..."

"We didn't," Sam said emphatically. He opened the curtain and stepped out; the towel now wrapped securely around his waist. "Don't change your impression of her. I worked late and slept in the chair downstairs—if you can call it 'slept'. More like, I closed my eyes for a bit."

"Where is she now? Out jogging?"

"Yeah," he replied, slipping his watch onto his wrist, then pulling on his shirt.

Marylou watched him as he dressed, her eyes roving approvingly over his brawny form. When Sam went to take the towel off to pull on his underwear and pants, he glanced at her and asked, "Uhm...do you mind?"

"No. Not at all," she snickered, but complied by turning her back to him.

"I got the program functioning smoothly then finished up writing the grant she was working on," he explained.

"You did? Wow! Kelly was really fretting over that. The ass-hole she's been dating was supposed to take care of all that. But, hell, he's never around."

"Tell me some about Kelly," Sam asked.

Marylou glanced back over her shoulder to see Sam was now dressed and sitting down to put his socks and shoes on. She turned back around to face him. "Well, Kelly can be a very capable, 'take charge' type person when she sets her mind to something. She has her insecurities, like everyone else, but she doesn't always open up and display them like a lot of people do. She moves around a lot."

"Yeah. She told me that. We talked some last night."

"Did you?" Marylou asked excitedly. "Good. I hope you two get to be friends; especially for when she goes up north this fall. Kelly won't admit it but I think she's kind of lonely. I think that's why she's seeing that jerk of a lawyer, just to have somebody to be with. I don't see anything between them. She sees him as a nice guy who's well educated and she overlooks what a real dork he is."

"I gather you don't care for him," Sam chuckled.

"Not really. He's a lawyer with some big firm in D.C. I guess he makes a lot of money. What lawyer doesn't? Anyway, he started coming to the Foundation meetings when the land issue came up and he volunteered his services. I don't think he's done a whole lot for us, though. Most of the really important stuff ends up either written wrong, or he's left something out, or it's submitted too late. Like this grant thing. He's been supposed to help Kelly write it for weeks. He knows how important it is but he always has some excuse why he can't make it out to help her. He shows up at night; he and Kelly go out to dinner, or a movie, then he says he's too tired, or has some case to prepare for and they'll start on it tomorrow night. Same thing all the time. He's just a big phony!"

"Well. I'm glad of that," Sam said. "No one else?"

"No. It's too bad, too. But lucky for you if you're interested," Marylou said with a wink.

Sam smiled. "Oh, I might be. If I thought, for sure, she would be, as well."

"Ha! I wouldn't worry about that. She'd be nuts not to be. And if she isn't, I am."

"You're married, aren't you?"

"Yeah," Marylou smiled. "I'm just kidding around."

"I figured as much," Sam laughed.

"So, you going to see her again?"

"She's coming back, you know. I didn't think she'd jog away and leave all her stuff here."

"Wise-ass. You know what I mean."

"Yeah. Well, I guess she's taking me to dinner tonight."

"Great! That's a start, anyway."

Sam stood and moved to one of the old bureaus that had a large mirror fastened to its top. Then, choosing one of several brushes laying on top of it, he began to run it through his hair. "So, how far does Kelly run? She said she'd be about an hour or so."

"C'mon. I'll pour you a cup of coffee," Marylou said as she started for the stairs.

Sam set the brush down and began to follow her down, listening as the woman explained. "I don't know, really. A couple miles, I guess," Marylou said. "It takes her awhile because she has this weird thing that she does when she's out."

"What's that?" Sam asked as they went to the coffee maker and Marylou poured them both a cup.

"Well, she jogs over the battlefield. Then she'll pick a section of ground—I don't think it's any particular spot, or anything—but she'll just stand there listening, or looking around. She'll stand there for, say, ten or fifteen minutes—maybe more; maybe less. It's kind of eerie-like. Like she's waiting for something to happen. Sometimes she'll be sitting at her desk, or at the computer, and on impulse she'll just pick up and leave, drive out to a spot on the field and walk out into it and just stand there."

"Yeah. That's how I met her yesterday. She was out in a field on the Schiels farm. Maybe she's looking for souvenirs, or something."

"No, I finally asked her one time. She said she doesn't know why. Just that some feeling will come over her and she finds herself doing it. She says there's some sadness attached to it but she can't explain what it is or why. Does that sound odd?"

"Mm...maybe. And maybe not. There's got to be some reason, though. But, hell, a girl as pretty as her is allowed a few idiosyncrasies," Sam laughed.

Marylou smiled fondly. "I guess." Then she turned to the computer. "So, show me what you did."

Sam joined her at the machine and explained what maintenance he'd performed. Then he told her of having discovered a virus and the steps he'd used to neutralize it. "We're seeing these more and more, lately. It's really a despicable thing for someone to do. It's often hard to combat. Yours was a rather simple one, fortunately."

"How did it get in there?"

"Hard to say. It could have come with the program, or it could have been picked up if you were logged on to another computer. I don't know. It's something we're still learning about."

"Could someone have purposely planted it there, someone trying to sabotage the Foundation?"

"Well, we wouldn't rule that out."

"But, that's terrible. Could the developers be that greedy that they'd do something like that?"

"You tell me. I'm new here. This project would have to be pretty important to them."

"I suppose it is," Marylou said. "They're certainly spending a lot of time and money trying to fight us. Of course, there's a lot of opposition to us even from the locals. People are afraid that if we acquire and protect this land we won't stop until we have a protective sphere all around the battlefield—which is actually what we would like to have, too. They're afraid it'll lower their property values."

"You've tried zoning restrictions and land use ordinances?" Sam asked.

"We've been able to get a few things passed. But they're not as restrictive as we'd like and there are legal ways people are getting around them. Some of the government officials would like to see all the ground around here developed. They're viewing it with an eye toward the revenue it can generate."

"They usually do" Sam sighed.

In response to a loud knock at the door Marylou excused herself to answer it. "It might be fresh recruits," she chimed. When she returned, it was with the Coopers in tow.

Sam had taken a seat on the swivel chair at the computer and, now, as he spied his friends entering, he smiled warmly to them. "Hm. We thought it might be paying customers," he joked.

"No. Just us," Dave said, giving a little wave in greeting. "How you doin?"

"Okay, I guess. I expected you guys, but not this early," Sam said. He glanced at his watch and proclaimed, "Wow? It's only 8:45."

"Yeah...well..." Dave stammered, searching for an excuse. "We were worried about you."

"You were nebby. Wondering what ol' Sam was up to."

"Yeah. That, too."

"Well, c'mere and I'll show you," Sam said.

As they gathered closer to the desk, Marylou offered, then poured, coffee for the Coopers while Sam explained why he hadn't returned to camp last night. He showed them what he'd found wrong with the computer and briefly explained how he'd corrected it. Then he told them what he'd learned of both the Foundation and of the Schiels farm from his talks with Kelly and Marylou.

Kelly soon appeared, entering through the back door and carrying several small, brown, paper bags. "Well, hello," she said cheerfully to everyone as she set the bags on the desk. When they had all exchanged pleasantries, she turned to Sam and asked how he was feeling.

"Better. Thanks," he answered. "The shower helped."

"Good. I'm glad," she said at hearing this. "I picked up some breakfast for you. I thought you might enjoy a sampling of the local cuisine—grits and biscuits with gravy."

"Uh...sure. Great!" Sam replied, though he was uncertain just how his system would react to it. He'd never really experienced that combination so early in the morning. Northern diets are not always compatible with what is regularly consumed south of the Mason-Dixon. But, for the sake of a new friendship, especially with one so lovely as the woman before him, Sam decided he'd give it a try and hope there would be no sufferable consequences from it later.

Kelly withdrew the Styrofoam containers from the bags and set them out for Sam. "Did he tell you what he did with the computer?" she asked Dave and Carol.

"Yeah," Dave replied. "Can't ride a bike too well but he's the best with electronics."

"Well, did he also tell you he wrote, in one night, a grant proposal I've been agonizing over for weeks?"

"Mm. Sometimes he's good to have around. Most of the time he's a pain, but we find him useful. Cheap labor, you know."

Holding a fork full of gravy-covered grits, Sam paused and looked up at Dave. "Oh, you are so funny. I've got to find myself a new best friend."

"Well, he saved me quite a burden of work. I'm treating him to dinner tonight as a reward," Kelly said.

Dave and Carol both smiled at this. "Isn't he a great guy?" Carol said to Kelly.

Kelly smiled and nodded.

"Hey. We brought you some clothes, Sam," Dave told him. "We figured you might want to change."

"Thanks. I appreciate that," Sam replied, still struggling to force down another fork full.

Dave asked Jeff to retrieve Sam's bag from the van and Sarah accompanied him, knowing she'd be excluded from the grown-ups' conversation anyway.

"So, are you going to finish the tour with us?" Dave asked his friend who by now was making pained faces with each new mouthful.

Sam forced a swallow, then quickly chased it with coffee. "Well, sure. Why wouldn't I?"

"I didn't know. I mean, you didn't get any sleep last night—not to amount to anything."

"Hey. I'm fine. It's not the first time I've worked late and gone with little sleep." Then Sam looked at Kelly. "You want to go with us? It'd be great having you along."

"Thanks. But I've got some things to do—especially now that I can bring up all my information."

"So, we're still on for dinner, though?" Sam asked.

"For sure! Be here at six. Just casual. Nothing fancy."

"I hope," Sam replied. "I didn't bring along any suits. I'm camping, remember. Supposed to be roughing it."

"Oh, yeah," Kelly laughed.

When the kids returned with Sam's bag, he excused himself and went upstairs to change. The others talked while waiting for him, answering Kelly's questions about Dave's business, about Homer City, life in the coal regions, and about Pittsburgh. When Marylou learned that Carol was a quilter her interest was sparked as she shared the same hobby. The two women began a separate conversation, warming to each other rapidly as they talked of patterns and patches. Jeff and Sarah, bored with both conversations, went outside to pass the time and wait for the adults.

Dressed now in comfortable shorts and a loose-fitting soccer shirt, Sam rejoined the others. They chatted a while longer, then made their way to the front door, saying their goodbyes as Kelly and Marylou escorted them out onto the front porch. The Coopers began to climb into their van but as Sam headed for his car, parked a few spaces behind them, Kelly called out, "Hey, Sam!"

"Yeah?" he asked, stopping in the street and turning around to her.

"Watch out for parked cars," she snickered.

"Yeah…well. Only white Hondas parked on the berms," he replied. "Shouldn't be much of a problem if you stay here." Then, grinning widely, he started for his car, adding, "See you at six."

****

It was well past noon when the party of bikers stopped for lunch under the shade of some spreading oaks on the Federal's side of Burnside's Bridge. Carol spread a blanket under the trees to prepare lunch and, while the two men walked the field and discussed troop movements and tactical decisions of the Union commanders, Sarah and Jeff dropped pebbles from the bridge into Antietam Creek. When Carol called them all together to eat, everyone returned to the blanket—hungry and hot, but in good spirits.

The day was a bit less humid than yesterday, a slight breeze making the sweltering sun's rays more tolerable. While they shared a meal of crackers, French bread, cheese, beef sausage, sliced apples and lemonade, no one spoke much. Mostly, they just gazed around at the scenery, watched other tourists explore the fields and bridge and munched on their snacks, enjoying the day.

When Sarah and Jeff declared they'd had enough they ran off to explore the trail along the creek that led down to Snavely's Ford. Unable to contain herself longer, Carol looked at Sam and demanded, "Okay, Sam. The kids are gone. Let's hear about it."

Taken a bit off guard, Sam had to think for a minute. "Hear about what?" he asked. Then, seeing the attentive expression on Dave's face as he drew closer to listen with a keen interest, Sam realized what it was they wanted to hear. "Oh, ho! You mean about Kelly," he laughed. "Well, there's not much to tell other than she seems like a wonderful person."

"So, you're going to see her again?" Carol asked. "She's taking you to dinner?"

"Yeah," Sam replied, pausing to gaze out into the fields. "It's sort of a reward for helping her."

"Uh huh," Carol laughed. "Sam, this is so neat! You come three hundred miles to fall in love with a woman you haven't even known for two days. There's something magical here."

Sam looked at her in surprise. "Now, wait a minute, Carol. Don't go rushing this. She's a neat girl. But who said anything about love?"

"Ahh, Sam. I see the way you look at her—and she at you. There's a spark there. You just need to fan it some to get it burning."

Sam blushed and shook his head. "Oh, Carol. You're unbelievable."

"Hey, Sam. Somebody's got to give you a push. It may as well be me."

Sam smiled affectionately at her, but whatever he was going to reply was interrupted by Dave. "Well, we better get on with it or Sam'll be late for his big date. We've still got a lot of ground to cover."

"Big date," Sam muttered as he started to stand. "Now I get it in stereo."

It took but a short time to pack the bikes and continue on their way. Sam was distracted and distant for the remainder of the tour, letting Dave explain most of the history at each stop along the route. He did add bits and pieces to Dave's commentary but was less inclined to discuss the minutia of the battle with him. Dave knew the reason for his friend's unusual reserve and made every effort to keep his lecturing short.

When they pedaled into the visitor's center parking lot at 3:30, Carol and the kids were very pleased and relieved—and quite amazed—that they had breezed through the tour so quickly. The bikes were unpacked and placed in their carriers and by 4:30 the group had arrived back at the camp site. The Coopers began to kindle a fire for cooking their dinner while Sam went off to shower and change clothes.

****

At exactly six o'clock Sam Baker stood at the door of the headquarters for the Historic Antietam Foundation. The sign read "Please Walk In" but Sam felt a certain reluctance about simply opening the door and entering. He gave a few tentative wraps with his knuckles but, feeling silly for his shyness, he opened the door and stepped in, changing the sign to read "Closed." He walked through to the back room and, finding no one downstairs, hollered out, "Hello!"

"Up here, Sam," Kelly hollered down to him. "I'll be just a minute, or so."

Sam lingered around, gazing at pictures on the walls and nebbing at papers piled on the desks. The floor above was a scant seven feet high and, being of simple planking laid over two-by-six joists, Sam could hear Kelly's every footstep as she moved around overhead.

In a short while he followed the sound of the creaking floor over to the stairway and watched as Kelly descended. A tanned foot clad in a white leather sandal stepped onto the top stair tread. Then her curvaceous figure came down into view, dressed in white cotton slacks and a blue flower-print blouse.

As her face now appeared from the shadow of the second-floor landing Sam's eyes lit with excitement. She was gorgeous, he thought, seeing her golden hair so delicately grace her shoulders and her eyes sparkling with a brilliance all their own. She wore little make up, but what she had applied served to subtly accent her refined countenance. Button earrings of pearl encircled by gold braid adorned her ear lobes and a beautifully crafted gold locket, suspended by a fine gold chain, hung from her neck. Sam stared in awe.

She caught his stare and smiled pleasantly. "Well, I'm ready," she said.

"So you are," he replied, breathless. "You look stunning."

"Well, thank you," she said, approaching and taking his arm in escort. "I'd better if I'm to be seen with such a handsome man this evening."

Sam smiled at the returned compliment as they left the house and proceeded out to the street. "Let's take my car. It's softer," Sam said as he walked her to the racy little silver car parked across the street. He opened the gull wing door for her and she giggled in surprise as she bent to enter it. Sam moved around to enter and sit behind the wheel.

"This is cute," Kelly laughed again. "Isn't this one of those DeLoreans?"

"Yes. It is. I bought it as one of the last ones built. This one doesn't go back in time, though. Only forward into the future," he chuckled.

"That's fine. Our pasts have a way of catching up to us anyway," she said as Sam started the engine. "Head up toward Hagerstown. There's a quaint little place up the road I was at once. It serves pretty good food."

Sam wheeled the DeLorean into the street and took the highway leading north. As they drove, they talked over a variety of subjects, discussing the Foundation, at length, and all of the issues, obstacles and importance of preserving treasured historical sites. Kelly was curious about Pittsburgh and Sam explained what he'd learned of the city during his stay there, then quizzed Kelly on Philadelphia.

When they reached Hagerstown, Kelly directed him through the streets and into the parking lot of a small, unassuming inn. "The exterior belies the quality of its fare," she told him as he helped her out of the car. "I think you'll enjoy it."

"Well, the company's all I really care about," Sam replied. They walked across the gravel lot to the screen door entrance of the beige painted concrete block building, passing a red neon sign in one of the windows' proclaiming Stroh's was served on tap. A waitress greeted them inside and led them through the dimly lit room, negotiating a maze of some thirty tables arranged in a semi-circle around an oval bar of brilliantly polished maple. Soft music played in accompaniment to the many quietly chatting couples.

The waitress placed menus before them and made recommendations for the chef's specialties. When they had ordered, Kelly looked over to see Sam gazing intently at her. She blushed some and cocked her head in question.

"I'm sorry," Sam said, but continued to gaze directly at her. "It's just that the candlelight is reflecting so brightly in your eyes. They're beautiful. Did you get them from your mother?"

Kelly flushed at the compliment and glanced away momentarily. "Well, thank you. But no, actually, I got them from my father. My mother's are blue but not nearly as deep as my father's."

Sam pulled his eyes from Kelly, fearing he was making her too uncomfortable. He did, however, sense that his growing infatuation of this comely woman was being returned by her interest in him. They were both becoming relaxed, now, as there were no longer any awkward moments of silence—only quiet lulls in which either of them would wait until one or the other felt moved to speak. Their eyes continually returned to linger awhile on each other before wandering off to further explore the room.

Kelly ended one such lull by informing Sam she'd spoken with John Brandon, the Foundation's lawyer. "I told him you fixed the computer and got everything working smoothly again."

"Oh? Mm-hum." Sam replied, not really caring to hear about this other fellow. "And what did your lawyer friend have to say?"

"Well, you know, it was funny. I expected him to be pleased, especially when I told him the grant application was completed and how well written it was, but he was angry about it. I suspect it's possible he may be a bit jealous, perhaps."

"Why so?" Sam asked.

"Well, we were to write it together. But, heavens, he's always too busy to find the time. I'm just glad you came along when you did."

"So, your friend was a bit testy, hey?" Sam asked, feeling a certain satisfaction at having nettled the man.

"Yes. I was really surprised by it…and I told him so. It was really rather out of character for him. He kept questioning your credentials and implying that I acted improperly and risked so much on someone I had so recently met and knew so little about."

"What did you tell him about me?" Sam asked, interested.

"I told him what you told me—about who you've worked for and what you've done." Then she blushed and stammered slightly as she added, "I told him…what a nice man you are…and…and that I trust you completely."

On hearing this—the way she said it and the way she'd looked at him when she'd said it—Sam melted in his chair. He smiled boyishly and looked down at the table, overwhelmed by her compliment. "I, uh, I don't guess he liked hearing that," Sam said.

Kelly chortled, "No. I don't guess he did."

The waitress appeared with a tray to begin serving them, and as Sam and Kelly enjoyed a fine, leisurely meal, they chatted and laughed comfortably, sharing stories, both pleasant and painful, of past incidents in their lives.

When their plates had been removed Kelly raised the wine bottle and refilled both glasses.

"Whoa!" Sam exclaimed as he watched her pour each glass full. "Careful there."

Kelly looked across the table with a mischievous smile as she raised his glass and handed it to him. Then, standing and raising her own glass, she said in a seductive tone, "Follow me."

Sam stood and followed behind her as she led him through the room into a large, adjoining banquet hall. Chairs and tables were stacked high against one wall and the room was dark except for one ceiling-mounted spotlight shining over a baby grand piano in the near corner.

"Oh," Sam uttered, pleasantly surprised as she led him over to the instrument.

Kelly sat on the bench and patted the empty space beside her. "Sit here with me, Sam."

Sam eagerly complied, taking a seat next to her on the bench and watching as her fingers began to glide across the ivory keys to test the tones. "It's a little out of tune," she told him as she played something unfamiliar to him. "I'm not surprised considering the abuse and neglect it must receive."

"I can't tell," Sam said. "It sounds fine to me."

"What would you like to hear, Sam? Anything in particular?"

"Hey. Whatever. I'll be pleased to listen to anything you play."

"Well. All right. Since you're here for a tour of the battlefield, how about some Civil War selections to set you in the spirit of the times?" she said, then began to play "Bonnie Blue Flag." She played a medley of several rousing

selections, including: "Battle Hymn of the Republic," "Tramp! Tramp! Tramp!" "Rally 'Round the Flag" and a few other tunes from that period. Then she slowed the tempo, playing a slow, touching rendition of "All Quiet Along the Potomac Tonight." Playing the piece from the heart, she put so much emotion and feeling into it that her eyes began to well with tears.

Sam was equally moved. He listened to her affecting rendition while staring at her nimble fingers moving so effortlessly across the keys and the effect was trance-like. He so easily imagined soldiers in blue uniforms lounging around their camps in the glow of the evening fires. He began to visualize the movements and the faces of men leaning close to the fire to cook their rations while others sat reading letters from loved ones back home.

It appeared almost a peaceful scene, touching on the romantic—until their uniforms then changed from blue to camouflage—and the fire became extinguished. Sam was back in Vietnam. Nighttime. The barbed wire was strung; the deadly claymore mines set; his men entrenched deep in their foxholes. The waiting. The listening. The praying that "Charlie" would not attack tonight and the hope that the darkness would pass without incident as the hairs on Sam's head stood with every sound of a snapping twig or rustling branch.

All was quiet save for the crackling of voices on the radio as commanders of other units radioed information or requests for orders. Sam sat in the darkness, his stomach twisted into knots—feeling alone and frightened.

Shaking off the flashback, Sam blinked his eyes to focus on the present moment. He glanced at Kelly and saw that she seemed to be playing by rote. She stared into the darkness of the room and appeared lost in thought; daydreaming; oblivious to the present. He noticed, too, that the melody had changed. It was a piece familiar to Sam, but he couldn't quite place this mournful air. He listened awhile, then recognized it as a Strauss waltz.

Though Kelly performed it beautifully, instead of the quick and lively tempo in which it was written, she was rendering it into a sad, almost grieving composition. When she stopped playing suddenly, Sam looked from her fingers, still gracefully poised over the keys, to her tear-filled eyes. Her chin was quivering as she continued to gaze out into the room.

"Kelly?" Sam asked, concerned.

Abruptly, the woman started to weep. Dropping her hands to her sides, tears began to stream down her cheeks. Sam put an arm around her to pull her closer and she began to cry into his shoulder.

"Is something wrong? Are you all right? What is it?" he asked, drawing a handkerchief from his back pocket and offering it to her.

Kelly gained some measure of composure and sat up, dabbing at her moist eyes and sniffling. "I-I don't know. It's nothing. It's just…oh, never mind, Sam."

"No. Tell me. I want to know."

Still dabbing at her eyes and sniffling to clear a stuffy nose, she stammered, "It's just...every time I...play that...that way...it makes me cry."

Sam gave a comforting squeeze of his arm around her waist. "It is beautiful, the way you play it. Sad, but beautiful."

"That's just it! Why do I play it like that? It's a piece meant for dancing and gaiety; to be played lively and spirited. Then I come along and turn it into a funeral march." Then she looked away, mumbling, "I don't know why...I don't know why."

"Well, let's choose another," Sam said. "I know. How about 'Dixie'?"

Kelly looked at him and smiled, appreciating his attempt at lifting her spirits. She started to play and Sam began to sing along, softly, at first, then louder. Kelly joined in and soon the two were putting their heads together and laughing as they harmonized through several verses.

In the middle of the third verse of their second rendition the door pushed open and a rotund, balding man in his late fifties stood filling the doorway. "Just a minute" he said. "You two are entirely too loud in here. I didn't mind the piano playing, but this singing—oh no! We can't have that. You can hear it in the dining room"

Kelly and Sam both gawked at the man. He looked almost comical to them with his pencil thin mustache, protruding belly and huge, fat cigar. They glanced at each other and burst into laughter.

"Were we really that bad?" Sam asked.

The man just stood chomping on the unlit cigar and glaring at Sam.

Sam turned to Kelly and shrugged. "Well, it is our first audition. It's only normal for things not to flow well."

Kelly snickered as she addressed the man, "We'll practice hard and try again. We really need this job." Then she started to play the "Minute Waltz," her fingers flying across the keyboard flawlessly. Sam's eyes widened in amazement as he watched her. The older man's cigar almost dropped from his mouth as he, too, watched and listened, impressed.

Her fingers racing across the keys, Kelly glanced up at the balding fellow. "Just let me play this last piece," she said to him. "I'll only be but a minute. Maybe only half..." Then she laughed and said to Sam in an aside, "I'm just showing off."

"Jeez, Kelly. You are good!" Sam exclaimed.

"Bah. This is an easy piece. Next time I'll play you a really difficult one," she laughed.

When she'd finished playing, she rose from the bench and took a sip of wine from her glass, then gestured for Sam to follow her. As they squeezed past the heavy man who'd moved only enough to allow them room to exit between himself and the doorway, Kelly smirked over the dumbfounded expression on the man's face. "It's a little out of tune," she told him. "You might want to have it looked at."

The man glared at them as they hurriedly settled their tab and departed.

When they were back in the DeLorean and on their way to Sharpsburg, Sam, still awed by Kelly's musical dexterity, said, "Kelly, I can't believe you play like that. You're really good."

"Was good, Sam. Like anything, you have to keep up with it. You know—'use it or lose it.' I don't play much anymore so I've been losing it."

"Well, I'm impressed," he said pointedly. "Tell me, though, why do you play some of the pieces with such sadness? You don't strike me as a depressed person."

"Oh, that," she sighed. "I wish I knew. I didn't always do that. It must be something psychological. I don't know why. It's just a feeling that'll come over me when I play certain numbers. It's as much a mystery to me as this weird dream I've been having lately."

"Oh, yeah. The dream. I'm sorry, but I overheard you tell that lawyer fellow you'd had it." Sam glanced at her. "You had it again last night, didn't you?"

Kelly turned to look at Sam. "How did you know?"

"I heard you. You were mumbling. Unintelligible. But definitely speaking to someone. You were uncomfortable with it."

"You're...you're right. It does make me uncomfortable."

"Tell me about it."

"No, Sam. It's too eerie. Almost...other-worldly, or something."

Sam kept driving. Watching the road. Silent. He flipped on his windshield wipers and fog lights as a light rain had started, mingling with the low-lying ground fog. Though at first, he had thought to drop his inquisitiveness for lack of ideas on how to coax the description from her, now he chuckled and said, "This is great! It's a perfect night for a chilling ghost story. Check it out." Then; lowering the pitch of his voice and taking on a serious tone he announced, "A man and a woman, driving a flashy sports car down a foggy, rain-soaked highway.

Their first date together. He: an unassuming, boring, pale, lurching buffoon, stuck in the dead-end, lifeless world of artificial intelligence. She: an overbearing, bleached blonde, scantily clad bimbo. A frustrated acid rock organist, if you will, recently rejected from her last and final effort to break into the big time..."

"*Bimbo*" she interrupted, as if insulted by that particular description. But she laughed as he went on.

"Two people headed home after a memorable evening of orgy and drugs, unsuspecting that the road they are on is leading them to a fork in the road; a fork that, regardless of which direction they choose to follow, will lead them into a new dimension—a dimension beyond sight and sound, in which reality is distorted and nightmares become real. They're about to share an experience in... the 'Twilight Zone.'"

Kelly shook her head, amused at Sam's monologue. "Talk about "distorted realities." I'm in a car with a nut," she laughed.

"I know. Everyone tells me that. C'mon, now. I've set the stage. Let's hear it."

"Oh, okay. But, it's pretty strange."

"Dreams often are. That's why I'd like to hear it."

"Well...it's dark. I was going to say twilight, but after your introductory oration I'll call it dark. Anyway, I'm seated at a piano—a baby grand—and it's outside, in a field somewhere. I'm all alone on top of this big hill and, suddenly, there's this faint light in the distance below the hill. As it starts to come nearer, I can hear the sound of hooves pounding the turf. Riders are moving with the light—or the light's moving with them. I can't be sure. But they come closer and closer...until they're not but fifty yards away, riding across in front of me. I can't make them out, but they're dressed in some sort of uniforms. There's quite a lot of them, I think, but they're shadowy and their numbers fade into the darkness. They're carrying banners...and I can see the outline of swords and other armaments. The light doesn't shine out onto them to make them recognizable but it's so brilliantly lit ahead of them, like a lighted tunnel. They seem to be riding toward it but it keeps moving ahead of them—leading them, perhaps. Anyway, one of the riders turns his horse from the others and comes a few paces toward me. The others are still cantering, but they're not advancing—just marking time, sort of. So, this one rider pulls his horse up about fifty feet in front of me and I get up from the bench and move to the side of the piano."

"Wow. This is eerie," Sam said. "Then what happens?"

"Well, I stand there and watch him. I can only see his form in the darkness, but there's this odd feeling that I know him—or knew him. I don't know. He just sits on his horse and gazes at me awhile and I watch myself raise my arms out to him. I call out his name, though I haven't a clue what it is; I just see myself doing this. I can tell the rider is really saddened about something and I start to cry. If he is, I can't tell, but I think in the darkness and from the sense of things happening he must be tearful, as well. He doesn't speak. he just sits there a bit, watching me. Then his horse starts to become uneasy and restless. He nods to me and, telepathically, mind you, he relays to me something about missing me...and...and about rejoining me. Then he turns his horse and spurs it back to fade into the gathering and they continue on, following the light tunnel. Weird, huh?"

"Phew! Sure is!" Sam exclaimed. "How often do you have this...dream?"

"It used to be only now and then; maybe a couple times a year in the past. Then, in the last year or so it's become more frequent. Now, sometimes, twice a week, or more. What do you think?"

"Mm...it's got me stumped. I used to have weird dreams when I got back from Nam, but they eventually ended with time. Yours is pretty strange, all right."

"Don't I know," she sighed. "Let's...change the subject. Okay?"

"Fine," Sam replied, aware Kelly was disturbed by the conversation. "Tell me about playing in an orchestra. What was that like?"

As they continued down the road toward Sharpsburg, Kelly told Sam about her years of performing professionally with various orchestras and ensembles from the Philadelphia area; the cities and countries she'd toured, and the notable guest conductors she'd performed under.

Sam found it all quite fascinating, this being an occupation he knew so little of, nor even been given to consider.

When they arrived back at the Foundation headquarters Sam offered to escort Kelly to the door and she readily accepted. He took her hand to help her from the car and, as they walked toward the old house Kelly told him, "Sam, I had a wonderful evening. It was fun. Thank you."

"Hey. Don't thank me. You paid for dinner, and provided the entertainment," he told her. Then, when they stood on the porch of the log house, he turned to her and gazed warmly into her eyes. "I really enjoyed your company, Kelly."

"And I, yours," she replied. "Would you...like to come in? I could make you some coffee."

"Well...no. No. I really should be getting back. I need to sleep."

"Oh. Of course you do. You hardly got any last night."

A quiet moment fell between them as they gazed breathlessly into one another's eyes. Sam wanted to kiss her goodnight but was unsure of just how to make an advance. Drawing his courage, lest the opportunity should pass, he moved closer and placed a hand on the back of her elbow to urge her closer. Kelly relaxed and moved closer to him, excited at the prospect of being taken into the arms of such a handsome man.

"Kelly?" came a voice from out in the street that interrupted the moment.

Both Sam and Kelly stopped and looked as a tall figure approached the steps.

"Kelly. Where the hell have you been?"

It was John Brandon, and he moved deliberately onto the wooden porch where the couple stood. A tall, slender man, he was dressed in an expensive, charcoal grey, pin-striped suit. The white, light-weight dress hat he wore with the brim turned up in back seemed to add several inches to his six feet, two-inch height. His black, horn-rimmed glasses, though stylish in design, made him look just a bit less attractive than he was, but, also, a bit too arrogant to suit Sam.

"John?" Kelly said in surprise. "Who—what are you doing out here? I thought you were busy and couldn't get away."

Totally ignoring Sam's presence, he addressed the woman. "I finished earlier than expected. Where have you been? I've been waiting since eight o'clock."

"Well, I...I told you I was taking Sam, here, out to dinner," she explained, apprehensive over the chastising tone from the usually unconcerned man. "Um...John Brandon; Sam Baker. Sam; John."

The two men managed to grumble a hello to each other, adding a slight nod of recognition. It was performed strictly as a matter of protocol, and no hand was offered by either man.

"Well, where the hell did you go?" John demanded. "I thought you were just going to catch a burger or something."

"We were up in Hagerstown. We had a nice meal."

"Christ, Kelly! Like you have money to go treating everyone who helps the Foundation."

"John! What's with you? Sam, here, did us all a considerable service. Besides, it's my money. I'll spend it as I see fit."

She began to fumble in her purse, searching for her keys. When she found them and began to unlock the door, John Brandon cast a hostile glare toward Sam. "Look, uh, I hope you had a good meal and... yeah, thanks for doing...whatever it was you did to help us. Uh, have a nice evening," he said quickly and in an obviously condescending brush-off.

"Pardon?" Sam asked, hardly believing the impertinence of this man.

"Look, it's been a long day for everyone. Kelly told me you were up quite late and I think you should go and get some sleep."

Sam's brow furled as he stared at the man. Since his divorce he held all lawyers in disesteem, and for that reason alone he already didn't like the fellow. He further didn't care for him because he was a rival suitor for the attentions of Kelly. Now he contemplated decking the man for the way in which he was being addressed by him. Sam felt his fist involuntarily clench.

Then, realizing it would make a rather poor impression on Kelly to see Sam knock her boyfriend into the street, he unclenched his fist and outwardly composed himself. "Well...you're right," he said, nodding in agreement. "I have had a rather long time of it." Then, watching the attorney turn to follow Kelly into the house as she opened the door, Sam drew himself up to full contending height—broad shoulders squared and stiffened, chest puffed, head erect with his chin jutted—"and Kelly, here, was thoughtful enough to invite me in for a cup of coffee to keep me awake on the drive back. I take it black," he said, and pushed ahead in front of the man.

John Brandon, noting the solid physique and the determination of the man barging in front of him, realized he could suffer very serious physical damage should he protest. He followed behind the two.

While Kelly began to set up the coffee maker, Sam casually took a seat on the metal folding chair against the wall opposite the computer station. John appeared anxious and stood by the desk looking over some papers scattered across its top. He finally broke the uneasy silence by asking Kelly where the grant application was.

"It's in the file," she replied. "I'll get you a copy."

"I don't want a copy. I want the original," he demanded as Kelly began to dig through the file drawer.

She paused in her searching and glanced back at the man. "Whatever for? A copy will read just as well."

"I'm sure it will. But I think I should read it over and make the necessary changes."

"There are no necessary changes," she said, then whipped out a packet of papers and handed it to him. "Read it over. You'll see. It's quite remarkable."

John went through the motions of turning the pages but it was obvious he was only glancing them over superficially. "This is a copy. Where's the original?"

"I have it filed away safely. Tomorrow, I'll take it to Dennis for signature and he can present it to his friend on the McPherson board."

"Kelly, as legal counsel for the group I must demand that you wait until I've had time to review it."

"And how long will that take? John, we're already coming up on deadline."

"I'll do it tomorrow. I have a light schedule and can do it right after lunch."

"Fine. I'll wait until three o'clock. Then I take it to Dennis."

"Kelly, what's going on here? What's with you? You're certainly not acting yourself this evening."

"What's that supposed to mean?" she asked, a touch of anger in her voice.

"I mean, I don't understand your actions. First, you let some guy off the street—no offence, friend," he said with a quick glance at Sam. "Mess with the computer, then you want to rush out and turn in our only real hope of saving this whole effort without someone knowledgeable reviewing it. We could get turned down flatly. These things need to be worded in a specific way. One poor sentence, or the omission of some critical data, and those people will kick it. We don't even know this guy, here," he said, pointing a finger at Sam. "Look for all we know he could be working for Marco, coming in here and sabotaging our organization."

"John!" Kelly gasped at his accusations.

"We don't know anything about him. He just shows up and you let him take over. Those people are like that, Kelly. They'll stop at nothing and try anything."

"John, I don't believe I'm hearing you talk like this. Sam's done an excellent job on both the computer and the grant. I think you owe him an apology."

"Do I? We'll see," he said, shaking the papers in the air for emphasis.

"I'll just take it black," Sam said coolly, nodding toward the coffee maker. He'd been sitting back, casually propped against the wall on only two chair legs, and now, as John turned his head and glared at him, he came forward to sit erect. "Counselor, we'd offer you a cup, but your caffeine level's running pretty high already."

John shot Sam an icy stare. He had wanted to provoke the man into an argument that might give Kelly cause to ask him to leave so that John and she could speak privately. Instead, the man calmly sat there as if he hadn't even heard the suspicions and it was he, John, who was left fuming. He stared into Sam's eyes to warn him off with an angry glare, but Sam just stared back with a cool, steady eye. Even as Kelly handed a cup to Sam the two men remained locked in their mental game of staring the other down.

John finally broke under the strain. "Okay," he shrugged, looking at Kelly. "Have it your way. You trust him; so, we'll see. I'll read over the papers and call you tomorrow with the changes." Then he turned and stomped to the door, closing it behind him with a force that emphasized his anger.

Sam took a long sip of coffee, swallowed it with a hard gulp and said, "You date that guy?"

"Oh, please. Not you, too. Marylou's always on me about him. I go out with him. That's all. And after tonight that may be over. He was pretty upset."

"That was 'cause of me, I'd say. Jealousy—and with good reason. Anyway, at least now I've met my competition," he said, quickly taking another long sip and looking over the cup for her reaction.

Kelly's face lit. "Competition? Mr. Baker, are you implying you'd like to see me again?"

"If milady has no objections."

Kelly smiled. "Not at all. In fact, I was going to ask if you'd like to go riding tomorrow. Um...have you ever ridden a horse?"

"Hey, I was practically born in a saddle."

"Yeah? English or western?"

"Um, uh...whatever."

"Great! There's a private stable just down the road. How's eight o'clock sound?"

"Fine," he replied rising from the chair. "I'd better go get some sleep." He handed Kelly the cup and, finding himself standing so near to her, the desire to kiss her goodnight returned—as well as the awkwardness of how to approach it.

Before he could act, though, Kelly drew up and kissed his cheek. "I had a good time tonight, Sam. Thank you."

"So did I. I guess I'll see you at eight, or there about."

"Great! I'm looking forward to it," she said, walking him to the door. "And, Sam, thanks for coming in. John was pretty upset and I really wasn't up for a long confrontation."

"Yeah, well...I couldn't leave without goading him at least a little after what he said about me on the porch."

"You really kept your cool. I was impressed," she told him.

Sam just smiled. He decided not to tell her how close the man had come to becoming hamburger. He just winked at her and said, "Night, Kelly."

****

Cutting his lights to avoid shining them onto the tent where the Coopers were scrunched down into their bags, Sam pulled in to park alongside the van. Flames were dancing high out of the steel ring where Dave had thoughtfully banked the fire for his friend to better see his way through the camp.

Sam judged from the burn of the stacked logs that Carol and Dave could not have turned in more than fifteen minutes or so before his arrival—a permissible period, he figured, for rousing them to come and hear about his evening.

Seated around the fire after Sam awakened them, Carol and Dave were impressed with the glint in Sam's eyes as he spoke of the lovely girl, telling of their evening together. Neither of them had ever before seen that gleam in their friend. Dave could recall a brighter-eyed Sam in Vietnam as the guys all shared photos of sweethearts and wives, and Sam had had his Barbara—so he thought. But that low spark had long since died. Tonight, it was shining brighter than ever in his life.

Carol cuddled close to her husband, hugging his arm as she listened to Sam's endless list of adjectives in describing the girl. "Well, Sam, are you going to see her again?"

"Yeah. Tomorrow. We're going riding."

"Horses?" Dave asked.

"Well, yeah. What else?"

"You ever been on a horse?" Dave asked, grinning, for he knew full well Sam's experiences in life did not extend into the equestrian field.

"Yeah. I have."

"Sam..."

"Well, when I was in Bragg, a bunch of us went out to this stable just off the post and rented horses."

"Trail ponies," Carol smirked. "Oh boy, Sam. Good luck."

"How hard can it be? You get on and the horse goes along. I'll be okay."

"What time are you meeting her?" Carol asked.

"Eight."

"Eight! Oh, jeez," Carol exclaimed. "Go to bed. We'll finish talking in the morning. I'll set the alarm and Dave and I will see you get a good breakfast."

"Last meal for a doomed man," Dave chortled and rose to his feet. Then, he and Carol said goodnight and made their way to their tent. Sam ducked into his own tent, removed his shoes and pants, then lay back on his sleeping bag and fell fast asleep.

****

When the first rays of the morning sun began to filter through the trees and burn off a heavy fog enshrouding the campground, Sam awoke with a start. He sat up quickly, yelling "Huh?" and as his brain began to interpret what his eyes were groggily focusing on, he realized it was Carol tweaking his big toe to stir him.

"Mmh...Carol. Jeez. You gave me a start."

"I did? Well, I'm sorry. Good morning," she smiled pleasantly.

"Mgh...Morning," he mumbled sleepily.

"What time is it?"

"Six-thirty."

"Christ. The sun's barely up."

"You have a date. Remember?"

"Yeah. I better get up."

"Are you okay?" Carol asked, sensing Sam appeared disturbed. "Did I wake you wrong?"

"No. No. It's okay. It'd have been nicer if you'd have reached a little higher to tweak something else," he smiled and watched Carol roll her eyes over the comment. "I was...having that dream again. Whew! Weird."

"That one you had the first night you were here?"

"Yeah. Must be something about this place. Maybe it's the water," he said, collapsing back onto his pillow. "I was right in the middle of it. Weird dream."

"Well, c'mon. Dave's got breakfast about ready. Eggs, bacon, toast; the whole nine yards."

"Yeah? Damn, you two are great."

"Thanks. C'mon out and I'll pour you coffee."

"A tall one!" he hollered after her as she had popped back out from the tent flap.

In a short while Sam stumbled from his tent, buttoning a flannel shirt over his hairy chest. He made his way to the fire where Carol handed him a freshly poured cup of coffee and Dave was crouched tending a skillet of scrambled eggs. Glancing up, Dave chuckled at his friends unkempt, sleepy-eyed appearance. "Oh, it's you! For a minute there I thought we were being attacked by the creature from the deep."

"Mmgh...grumph...," Sam mumbled as he took a swallow of coffee. He ran his fingers through his hair several times to straighten the cowlicks. "Do I look that bad, huh?"

"Not really. I'm just messin' with you. Go sit down. We're just about ready, here."

"Smells great," Sam mumbled as he went to the picnic table and took a seat.

While the trio sat and ate together, Sam continued his story from where he'd left off last night. He told them about the incident with the lawyer, saying there was something about the man he just didn't like.

"Well, it's only natural," Carol said. "You're jealous of another suitor."

"No. It's more than that. There's something not quite right about him. I just picked up these vibes that didn't set right with me. Jealousy is one thing; I can wade through that. There's just something not kosher about him."

"Next time, deck him," Dave said. "At least you'll feel better."

Carol interrupted, changing the subject to one more pleasant while casting her husband an admonishing look for his last comment. "Well, listen, we're going into Harper's Ferry today. Is there anything you want us to get you?"

"Yeah. A mug, if you can find a nice one," Sam answered. Then, glancing at his watch he said, "Damn. I better get a move on or I'll be late." He downed the last of his coffee and hurried off to his tent.

Carol and Dave watched him go and exchanged smiles over their friend's lively step. Carol took her husband's hand and squeezed it gently. "I'd say he's in love."

****

Sam picked Kelly up at eight o'clock. While they drove to the stables, he confessed to knowing little more about horses than which end was the head and which was not the head. Kelly assured him she would pick him out a gentle gelding and that they would go slow and easy.

Sam was surprised to learn Kelly was on a first name basis with the owner of the stables and was familiar with all of the mounts. She chose a stalky, gentle, dun-colored gelding quarter horse named Dreamer, for Sam; a high-spirited, glossy-coated chestnut stallion called Future, for herself. Sam's horse she had saddled with a comfortably worn, western deep-seat while she rode an English jumping deep-seat.

When they had mounted and started out over the fields, Kelly gave instructions to Sam on how to properly guide the horse and relate to the animal through light touches of the heels and gentle pulls on the reins. After an hour, or so, into the ride Sam was feeling at ease and gaining a small measure of confidence. A service road through one of the long, flat fields served the purpose of demonstrating and practicing a trot, then into a canter, both of which Sam mastered beautifully.

The hours seemed to pass quickly, the two covering much of the battlefield unseen by those touring along the paved roads by car. "This is great!" Sam exclaimed at one point in the trail. "It's so thrilling to be seeing this on horseback. I've walked over some other fields, before, but it gives you a whole different perspective to view it on a horse."

Kelly was riding just ahead and smiled back at him. "I knew you'd enjoy it. That's why I suggested it. The first time I rode over these fields I felt a sense of relating to how the men who fought here experienced it. They didn't drive up in Pontiacs. This is how they saw it. I wanted to share this with you."

"Well, thank you. I'm glad you did," he replied, riding up beside her.

She clicked her mount into a trot and Sam did the same, following close behind as they rode up over a little knoll to a long, flat cornfield. Here, Kelly drew rein and Sam halted beside her. "Recognize where we're at?" she asked with a little laugh.

Sam gazed out over the landscape before him, trying to spot a familiar reference point. Then, seeing a white plywood sign on the side of the gently rising hill across the way, he laughed. "Oh, yeah. This is where I first saw you. You were off over there," he said, pointing to the area of the field in which she'd been standing. "That's the Schiels farm across the road."

"Right. We came up on it from a different direction. C'mon. Let's ride over to it. Stay in between the rows. We don't want to anger any farmers by flattening the corn."

Sam kept his horse guided carefully in line behind Kelly's, following her through the corn and down to the macadam road then into the hay field on the opposite side.

"Okay, Sam. This is as good a place as any," Kelly said.

"For what?"

"For a gallop."

"What?"

"C'mon, Sam. Don't be afraid. You've trotted and cantered. In that deep saddle and on ol' Dreamer, there, it'll be like riding in a Caddy," she laughed. "Just relax and let your body flow with the horse."

"Got 'cha. I think."

"We'll head for those two old oaks," she said, nodding to the twin, old trees at the very top of the hill. Then, squeezing her horse's flanks, she began to ride off, trotting, at first, then into a canter. Sam's horse followed stride immediately, instinctively sensing a possible race with the stallion.

Both horses began to pull for more rein as the dun began to stretch its legs and gained a head on the chestnut. Sam found it impossible to control the beast and allowed the horse its lead, hoping it was as sure-footed as Kelly had said. Kelly sensed the competition between the two animals and laughed in delight as she let her mount go, spurring the chestnut's flanks to bolt into a gallop.

The dun, not to be left behind, and finding it had a free rein, dashed after its companion, the two horses now racing up the slope in full contention. With its longer legs the stallion kept a length ahead, but the gelding lunged desperately to catch and overtake it. Turf kicked high from the pounding hooves and their heavy, steaming breath had the quick, steady chugging sound of a fast freight.

Sam was thrilled! His body relaxed and moved with the steady, flowing stride of the animal as they seemed to fly up the hill. He found himself coaxing the horse on, squeezing its flanks and yelling, "Go, boy! Go! You can catch 'em! Hah!" Then, climbing the steeper part of the hill, Sam tried to imagine how it must have felt to be in the midst of a cavalry charge with saber drawn and pistol cocked, the Rebel infantry drawn up on line ahead, with muskets lowered and aimed.

The fright!

The terror!

The excitement!

Sam had been under fire before and knew well the vibrant feeling of aliveness when faced with the possibility of sudden, violent death. To tempt fate by running directly toward it, charging into the blazing fire and smashing lead would be a wholly unique and exhilarating experience—and one in which Sam immediately decided he'd rather not sample directly.

The dash up the slope was electrifying as the wind swept by him and the ground passed dizzily underneath. But strangely, Sam's heart began to beat faster than the excitement of the ride. His cheeks flushed warmly and he began to feel light-headed. Everything began to move in slow motion; the stride of the horses, the loose, flapping reins, Kelly's tousling hair as the wind swept through it; all, curiously, seeming to be like in a dream. Sam winced and blinked his eyes to clear the sensation and, for an instant, found himself standing off on the side of the hill watching his body move on the horse as he rode just a stride behind Kelly.

His mind reeled at this fantastic experience, but the sudden awareness of his psychic detachment jerked him instantly back onto the horse—though now his vision was obscured by a dark, dense mist that seemed to have enveloped the hill. He was aware of the horse and rider in front of him but couldn't focus on them as their forms blended into and became part of the peculiar fog.

Other riders seemed to have joined them—many others—for he could faintly hear the sound of many hooves beating against the ground as they made their way furiously up the steep slope. The sounds of battle filled the air, muted and distant, but audible to Sam's ears. Men were screaming, horses whinnied in panic, and the loud booming of cannons all blended together into a horrible chaos.

"No-o-o-o...!" came a loud, agonizing scream that penetrated the void above all the other sounds from the pandemonium. As instantly as the mist had surrounded and blinded him, it was just as quickly lifted, and Sam found himself drawn up under the shade of the two tall old oaks on the hilltop. His horse was breathing hard, frothing and sweating. Sam, too, breathed rapidly; dazed and confused.

"Sam! Are you all right?" came a voice from nearby. Kelly had halted just a few feet from him and was watching him, concerned. "What's the matter?"

"No...No...I'm fine. I'm okay!"

"I heard you yell. I thought you were in trouble."

"No...Just...just out of breath," he lied as his mind reeled through what had just occurred. "That was...thrilling. Whew! What an... experience."

"You were fantastic," she said to him. "You're a natural in the saddle."

"Thanks...That was...fun," he replied, still breathless and feeling a bit dizzy.

"Oh, I love galloping like that," she said, moving her horse closer to him and reaching out to touch his arm. "Are you sure you're okay? You seem as winded as the horse."

"Yeah...Fine. Just the excitement, I guess."

"Well, okay," Kelly said, accepting his answer with skepticism. "You gave me quite a scare when you yelled out."

"I don't know why I did that. I'm sorry."

"That's okay. C'mon. We need to walk the horses to bring them down. We should be heading back, anyway."

Kelly started to move her horse along, passing under and between the two trees. Sam turned the gelding to follow but as soon as they neared the passage between the oaks the horse spooked, giving a warning snort, then a frightened whinny. It reared up, flailing its front legs at something unseen.

"Whoa, boy! Easy!" Sam yelled and held on in panic.

"Don't let go!" Kelly shrieked when she turned to see the gelding rearing high. "Hang on, Sam! Pull the rein around!"

Sam instinctively clung to the horse and gave a pull on one rein. As the dun came down it followed the rein, dancing in little circles and backing away from the trees.

"What the hell's the matter with him?" Sam yelled as he fought to control the beast.

"I don't know. Something's spooked him," Kelly answered. "Mares'll spook at anything. But it's not often a gelding will, especially one with his disposition. Move him away from the trees."

"I'm trying! I'm trying!" Sam yelled, pulling the rein and spurring the horse. It snorted as it backed away from the trees and finally settled enough to allow Sam to guide it off and down the hill.

"Well, that was certainly odd," Sam said as they walked the horses together down the slope.

"Yes. I've ridden Dreamer before and never knew him to spook like that. You'd think he'd seen a ghost, or something."

"Well, I believe I've had enough excitement for one day. Let's head back. My butt's sore anyway. Ughh!" Sam declared, shifting in the saddle for a more comfortable seat.

Kelly laughed and nodded in agreement and led them to a trail that would see them more directly to the stables than the route by which they'd come. When they arrived at the horse barn and had dismounted, a young stable hand gathered the reins and led the horses off for grooming. Sam walked a bit stiff-legged back to the car, amusing Kelly by exaggerating his saddle-sore, bow-legged movements.

Once they were in the car Sam wheeled the DeLorean out into the highway leading back to Sharpsburg. They discussed how hungry they were and the possibilities of where to have lunch. The car purred along the two-lane road cruising the peaks and valleys of the low rolling hills like a slow, easy roller coaster passing by farms and fields and houses under a hot summer sun.

Sam paid little heed to the tractor trailer parked on the side of the road over the next hill. He'd seen its brake lights as he'd crested several hills before it on the long, straight road, losing sight of it as he'd dip into a valley, then spying it again as he'd top the next hill. As the little car came over the final hill before it, Sam gave a shout. The truck had pulled into the highway and was stopped dead just ahead of them. He jerked the wheel left into the on-coming lane, swerving just in time to avoid colliding into the back of the rig. Kelly gasped as they careened around it.

"Jeez!" Sam yelled as he straightened the wheel and continued on. He slowed the speed of the DeLorean and glanced over at Kelly. "Are you all right?" he asked, seeing she was visibly shaken and breathing hard.

"My God, Sam. We could have been killed," she panted.

"You're telling me. I can't believe that guy just parked there. He must have stalled his engine or something. Damn!" Sam reached over and took Kelly's hand. "It's okay. We're all right," he assured her, feeling her trembling. But even as he said this, his eye caught a glimpse in the rear-view mirror of the large truck dipping into the valley he'd just come out of—and it was coming fast!

"Damn!" he yelled and his hand flew to the gear shift. He jerked the transmission into a down-shift and floored the accelerator, shooting on ahead as the truck came up on their bumper. "What the hell's the matter with that guy?" Sam hollered as he kept an eye on the mirror. He was going faster and faster and the truck stayed right on his bumper as if the driver was trying to roll right over the little car.

Kelly looked back and gave a start as she saw the headlights and grill of the rig all but in the car with them. "Sam!" she shrieked in terror as the truck kept right with them.

"Son-of-a-bitch is trying to kill us!" Sam yelled. He shifted up, gaining on the rig, and a quick glance at the speedometer showed seventy miles per hour—then eighty. "He's nuts!" Sam exclaimed as he looked for any place to pull off to avoid being squashed by the huge truck. Speeding the car on ahead to gain more distance the speedometer jumped to ninety-five. His eye glanced to a hay field up ahead on the left and saw there was no guard rail. He prayed there was no ditch.

"Hold on!" he shouted to Kelly as he cut the wheel sharply, aiming for the field. He hit the brakes and quickly down-shifted as they bumped and jostled through the field. The tractor trailer roared on by, blasting long and loud on its air horn as it disappeared down the highway. The DeLorean finally skidded to a stop in the middle of the field and Sam and Kelly tried to catch their breath and calm themselves. "Sam!" Kelly gasped. "I think he was trying to kill us!"

"I don't know. Jesus, there are a lot of nuts on the highway. A guy like that behind the wheel of a semi-. Damn!" He opened the door and got out, then came around to help Kelly out. She was trembling and Sam put an arm around her to comfort her. "Hey. We're okay. We're all right," he assured her.

Kelly cuddled against the broad-chested Sam and nodded hesitantly in agreement as she tried to calm herself, inhaling deeply several times. When

Sam felt her relax enough to release her, he walked around the car to inspect for damage.

"Shouldn't we report him?" Kelly asked, watching Sam bend down to inspect the exhaust system.

"And say what—'there's this big blue truck that tried to push us off the road'? He'll be miles away by the time the police write up the report. Neither one of us caught the license number. We don't even know what make of truck it was."

In impotent frustration Kelly crossed and uncrossed her arms repeatedly, then stomped her foot angrily. "Damn! That makes me mad! That guy is going to kill somebody driving like that."

"Yeah. I know," Sam replied, standing now, satisfied there was no damage to the car. "We better head back."

When they climbed back into the car and Sam made it back onto the highway, he reached over and squeezed Kelly's hand. "We'll go back to the house and I'll go out and get us something to eat. Will Marylou be there? Is she working today?"

"No. We're closed today since we're open on Saturdays and Sundays."

"Well, I'll get you settled first, then I'll go out."

"Thank you, Sam," Kelly said, returning the press of his hand.

****

Sam parked the DeLorean in front of the Foundation house and popped his gull wing door open to hurry around and help Kelly out. They walked together onto the porch and as Kelly began to search through her purse for the keys, she noticed the door was not closed tightly. "That's funny. I thought I locked the door before we left."

"Maybe Marylou's inside," Sam suggested.

"Oh, yeah. I'm kind of surprised she'd come in on her day off. Maybe she forgot something." Kelly pushed the door open and entered with Sam, expecting to be greeted by her co-worker or one of the board members. But as soon as she entered, she exclaimed, "Oh my God!"

"Oh, jeez! What happened here?" Sam gasped rhetorically, for it was rather obvious.

The room was a shambles. Furniture was toppled, pictures were pulled from the walls, the pamphlets and brochures were strewn all over and the carpet had been cut. As they proceeded through the dishevelment for the back room, Kelly shook her head in disbelief over the destruction of the room.

When they peered through the partition doorway into the office area, they were aghast. The file cabinet drawers were pulled open and the files pitched all over the floor. The desks had been ransacked, the furniture overturned—and the computer was gone.

"Sam, they stole the computer!" Kelly cried out. "What happened here?"

"I don't know," he replied and put a steadying hand on her shoulder as he saw her chin begin to quiver. "Seems pretty destructive for a small town like this. I could see going through some drawers for money, but this is going overboard."

Kelly pulled away from Sam and ran upstairs. "Oh, God!" he heard her exclaim and he quickly bounded the stairs to know the cause of her alarm. Here, as below, everything was in disarray. The mattress was pulled from the bed, the dresser drawers opened and emptied onto the floor, clothing was scattered about from the closet and the pictures torn from the walls. A hurricane could not have done as thorough a job of scattering everything around.

Kelly started to cry. Tears streamed down her face as she walked about the room looking at the stew that had only this morning been her neat, private, secure room, invaded now by faceless intruders. She stopped in the center of the room and surveyed the damage through her tearing eyes, and when the full impact of the violation came upon her she drew her arm to her eyes and began to sob.

"Aw, Kelly," Sam said as he approached her and put his arms around her to comfort her. She sobbed into his shoulder, asking through her tears who might have done this and why. Sam had no explanations but tried, as well as he could, to reassure her that they could clean it up and straighten it all out and that everything would be okay.

Kelly turned her face into his neck and kissed him there. "You're such a good man, Sam," she said through watery eyes. "I just feel so awful."

Sam felt like crying with her. Feeling her tear-drenched cheeks against his jaw and neck brought a sadness gushing over him that he'd not experienced before. He couldn't recall ever having had a woman cry in his arms. Certainly, his ex-wife never had. This was the vulnerable side of women that Sam had never experienced and, as he now had discovered it, he found it upsetting that she should be brought to showing it.

While he felt such deep concern and compassion for Kelly, it angered him that someone had hurt her so greatly by their deeds as to bring her to tears. Sam could feel his anger flare. He wanted to lash out at those responsible for bringing this unhappiness to the beautiful woman he held in his arms. He controlled his rage as well as he could, however, not wanting Kelly to feel his muscles tense nor witness his fighting blood boil. What she was in need of, presently, was a reassuring shoulder and some tender words.

Sam held Kelly warmly and felt her return the embrace. When she relaxed and pulled back from him, wiping the tears on the backs of her hands, she went to the night stand beside the bed and bent down to the pile of jewelry and scarves heaped on the floor. She picked up a locket and chain from the pile and stood to inspect it, seeming to be relieved to have found it. "Well, this is odd," she said as she examined it. "They must have been rather stupid thieves to have not taken this."

"What? What is it?" Sam asked, moving closer to see what Kelly held.

She held it out in her palm for Sam to inspect. It was a small, gold locket, richly engraved in a precise ribbon over oak leaves design.

"It's beautiful," Sam exclaimed. "Looks like pure gold."

"Mm. It is. It's been in my family for generations, though no one knows the story behind it. A distant aunt sent it to me as a graduation present. She wrote no story of its origin and I hardly even knew her. It just came in the mail one day with a note that said "congratulations" and "may you find the happiness you seek." She died before I could even write to thank her and ask her of its history."

"Oh, yeah?"

"Yes. And look, Sam," she said as she gently opened the two halves. On one side, inscribed so finely over more scroll work, was the message:

Our love is time eternal / It spans both sun and moon / Your thoughts when cast upon me / will see us together soon.

The opposite half contained an old, blurred, daguerreotype of a handsome, young, light-haired Union cavalryman.

"Oh, my," Sam exclaimed as he read the inscription and studied the faded picture. His eyes focused sharply on the picture of the young lad and he stared at it, mesmerized.

"I often open it and look at him and just stare at him. It sounds weird, I know, but I try to imagine who he was and what his life was like. Did he…die…in the war…or maybe go on to live a happy life? He might be a cousin, or an uncle. Or, maybe he was the beau of one of my distant relatives. I don't know. It just captivates me, though. It's one of my most prized possessions."

Sam didn't respond.

"Sam?" Kelly said again, expecting a comment from him on what she'd just told him. She looked at him as he stood beside her and he seemed to be almost hypnotized by the picture. "Sam!"

"Oh…Oh, yeah," he responded, forcing his eyes away.

"Are you okay? You look funny."

"No. No. I'm okay," he said, though he felt a certain uneasiness from deep within. "Um, I was thinking. If whoever did this, did it for the money—why didn't they take that, too? It's obviously valuable. Anyone can spot it as gold."

"I know. Look!" she exclaimed, stooping to the pile on the floor. "My pearl necklace, my rings, my broaches. They're all here. Either this guy was real stupid or he was after something else."

Sam chewed on his lip as he stood thinking. Then he asked, "Kelly. Where's the grant proposal?"

Kelly's eyes grew wide in alarm. She draped the gold chain over her neck and turned to hurry down the steps with Sam close behind. She knelt amid the papers that were strewn on the floor and began to search for the folder that held the grant application.

"I'll lay you odds it's not here," Sam said, joining in on the search.

Kelly found the manila folder—empty. A further search could not uncover any of the documents. "Sam. You don't think…"

"…That Marco sent someone out here to rifle your files? I'd say that's a good bet."

"But…But…"

"There's a lot of money riding on this project for them. Maybe their methods are more devious than anyone's suspected."

"Oh, Sam. Surely not," Kelly said in disbelief.

"I hope not. I really do. Maybe the papers will turn up, yet. Right now, we better get this place cleaned up and notify the authorities. Let's just treat this as a theft and say nothing of our suspicions."

"I-I better call Marylou to come help. I better call Dennis, too. As board president he'll need to be notified of the theft."

"Good. And ask Marylou if she'll bring something for lunch. I'm hungry…and it looks like it's going to be a long afternoon."

"Oh. I better call John and tell him to bring his copy of the grant. At least we can still get it in on time to have it considered."

Sam frowned at the mention of the man, but he said nothing.

By late afternoon things downstairs were in pretty good order. Marylou had brought a good lunch and busily helped to restore the files. The police department was finishing its inquiry into what had been stolen and Dennis Woods had been contacted and was on his way from Frederick.

Sam sat on the floor near Marylou and sorted through some papers. He looked over and saw Kelly pressing numbers on the telephone. "Who are you calling?"

"John," she replied.

In a low voice he warned her, "Don't tell him anything of what we talked about. You know…"

"But, Sam..."

"Kelly."

"Oh, okay," she agreed.

Marylou looked at Sam, puzzled. "What's this?"

"Nothing, Lou. I can't say anything, yet. I just don't like that guy."

"Well, welcome to the club," Marylou said as she continued her filing.

Sam eavesdropped on Kelly's conversation, hearing her tell John about the break-in and theft, that the state police were there taking statements, and that Dennis Woods was on his way. He listened as she asked the man to hurry and bring the copy of the grant proposal out so that Dennis could present it to the board for approval, then pass it on to his friend on the McPherson Corporation board of directors. Sam could not hear all that was spoken for Kelly talked in a low voice.

He did hear her mention him by name as she told the fellow where she'd been that morning. The conversation became testy from that point, and Kelly spoke louder as she grew more irritated.

"What do you mean? No! You'll do it now! What? It had all our records...No, he isn't! I...By five o'clock and that's final!" she said and slammed the phone down in its cradle. She glared at the phone, fuming.

"Wow! What was that all about?" Sam asked.

"Oh, that man!" Kelly exclaimed. "After all that's happened, he says he hasn't had a chance to look it over but will do it right away. Then he says he thinks you're working for Marco Development, and our going out this morning was a ploy to get me away so someone could come in and do this. Do you believe that guy?"

Marylou rolled her eyes, saying, "I told you he was a jerk."

"Well, I'm beginning to believe you," Kelly replied, still fuming.

One of the state police investigators entered the room and interrupted them. "Excuse me. We just got a call that there was an accident up the road so we're going to take off. I think we've got enough information for our report. We'll be in touch with you if we have any further questions or learn anything."

"Fine. Thank you," Kelly said to the man.

"It wasn't anything serious, I hope," Marylou said from her seat on the floor.

"Don't know, yet," the trooper replied. "Somebody took a turn too fast and went over an embankment. Thanks for your cooperation. We'll be in touch," he said, then turned and departed.

Sam and Marylou worked for several more hours at straightening the downstairs. Kelly had turned her attention to putting some semblance of order to her living quarters on the second floor, hanging up clothes, straightening out her dresser drawers, making the bed, etc. Around five o'clock the Coopers entered and went back to the office area to find Sam and Marylou sitting on the floor amid the stacks of papers and files.

"Whoa!" Dave exclaimed. "When you get involved in a project you sure throw yourself into it. Did you go riding?"

"We did," Sam replied, standing up to stretch his back. "When we came back the place had been ransacked and the computer stolen."

"Oh, no!" Carol exclaimed. "How terrible!"

"Damn. Too bad," Dave said. "Can we help?"

"Sure," Sam told him. "Carol, maybe you could give Kelly a hand upstairs. They tore her room up pretty bad. She's got a real mess up there."

"Of course," she replied and immediately went to the stairs. Sarah followed along, partly out of curiosity but, too, with an earnest desire to help.

Dave began to rehang pictures torn from the walls and to replace books scattered from their shelves. Even Jeff was put to work carrying reassembled files to the drawers to be placed in their proper order.

Not a half hour after the Coopers arrived and began to 'pitch in' and help, Kelly came down the steps. She seemed in better spirits as the rooms were slowly gaining some semblance of order.

"How's it going?" Sam asked as she came beside him to peer down at his work.

"It's coming along. Your wife is a real help, Dave. She's so pleasant and friendly."

"Yeah. That's my Carol," he replied.

Kelly explained she'd come down to call Dennis Woods, wondering why he hadn't arrived, as yet. She punched in some numbers on the phone and waited. There was no answer. She then tried his home phone, but no one answered there, either. "Hmm. That's odd," she said aloud.

"Can't reach him?" Marylou asked from over by the file cabinets.

"No. I should have thought Dennis would have come right away."

Dave looked at Marylou. "Who's Dennis?"

"He's the president of the Foundation's board of directors. He's also good friends with a key member of the McPherson board. I think the guy is one of the major stockholders or something. Dennis is from up in Frederick. He owns a catering business and banquet hall."

"Oh," Dave replied. "Well, maybe he got delayed at work," he suggested.

Kelly was on the phone again, this time asking the party on the other end for John Brandon. "...Oh, I see. How long will the meeting last? Have him call me as soon as the meeting is over, please...Yes, he has my number," she said and abruptly hung up. "Bitch!" she said to the phone, then looked up at the attentively listening trio as they had paused in their chores.

"That secretary of his!" Kelly exclaimed. "We talk to each other several times a week and she still pretends she doesn't know who I am. Every time, she asks, "Does he have your number, Miss Gracie?" You'd think the stupid bi-, the…the girl would have more sense if she's working in a law office."

Kelly's fuming was interrupted by Carol descending the stairs. With an exaggerated sigh she said to Kelly, "Well, it doesn't look too bad, now. We've got it back to livable, anyway."

"Thank you, Carol. I really appreciate all the help—from all of you," she added.

Dave suggested this as being a good time for a break; that they should all go out for a bite to eat. "My treat," he informed them.

"Whoa!" Sam chuckled and stood from his kneeling position on the floor. "I won't pass that up. Dave's treating. That doesn't happen often."

Dave feigned a sneer at his friend as the others laughed. It had been a long day and they were ready for a break. Before they could comment further, however, the phone rang. Kelly hurried and answered it, believing it must surely be John Brandon.

"Hello," she said to the caller…"Yes, this is Kelly Gracie"…"Wh…what?" she asked, her face turning grave. "My God! No!" she exclaimed, and as she listened further, her eyes traveled to each of the friends in the room, settling on no one, but revealing by her wide, expressive eyes that the news she was listening to was upsetting. "We're…we're on our way," she said and set the phone down. She stood frozen, as if to absorb fully what she'd just heard. Everyone looked at her, anxious for an explanation.

"Kelly?" Marylou asked.

Kelly slowly raised her eyes to them. "It was the state police. Dennis was in…in an accident," she said slowly. "His…his car went over…an embankment."

"Oh, no!" Marylou gasped. "Is he hurt? Is he all right? What'd they say?"

Kelly's eyes met Sam's and lingered there while the two seemed to exchange thoughts. She held his eyes even as she continued. "They…don't know. He's unconscious. They think he might have been…forced off the road by another motorist. He's…in the hospital up in Frederick. His, uh, his wife told them to notify us." The woman's eyes widened in question. "Sam?" she asked, trying to keep from growing alarmed.

Sam bit his lower lip and furrowed his brow as he seemed to be thinking while he and Kelly mentally telegraphed their suspicions. He shrugged to show her he wasn't sure there was a connection between Dennis's accident and their earlier experience with the truck. But his eyes showed he wasn't ready to write it off as coincidence.

"I-I better go see him," Kelly said.

"I'm going with you," Marylou said, closing the file drawer.

"We'll wait here," Sam told them. "Call us and let us know what's going on."

Jeff looked confused and asked to have explained to him just who was hurt, and did he, Jeff, know the person. Before Carol could begin to clarify it for him, though, Sarah came bounding down the steps to complain of being hungry and wondering when they were going to eat. While Dave and Sam saw the two women to the door, Carol briefed the kids on what had happened. When the men returned to the room Dave suggested the two kids go around the block to the diner for "take-out." They wrote a list of "who-wanted-what" and sent Jeff and Sarah on their way.

When the kids were out the door Dave turned to Sam and asked, "Okay. What's going on? There's something more to this than just some guy skidding off the road, isn't there?"

Sam explained about his and Kelly's experience with the tractor trailer, then told of their suspicions over the robbery.

"Wait a minute. Wait a minute," Dave said. "You're thinking this development group is behind this? Causing accidents, breaking in and stealing files and things so they can assure themselves of getting this land, right?"

"I don't know," Sam replied. "It just strikes me there's something peculiar about it all. It's just a feeling I'm getting."

"Jeez, Sam. This is like a bad plot in one of those stupid 'made-for-T.V.' movies. It's a little far-fetched, don't you think? I mean, I don't doubt your sanity, ol' friend, but aren't you reading a bit much into what could just be a set of coincidences? Maybe that trucker is just one of those crazies that likes to torment cars. We've all had our experiences with them on the road."

Sam sat in the padded office chair behind the desk that used to hold the computer. He swiveled slowly back and forth, his eyes lowered as he contemplated Dave's rationale. "Well-l-l...maybe you're right. I don't know. I just have these...feelings," he said. "I guess, maybe, I'm just reading too much into it. Kelly and I both were pretty shaken by..." But whatever Sam was going to say was interrupted by the phone ringing.

Sam reached out and drew the receiver to his ear, clearing his throat to answer formally. "Hello. Historic Antietam Foundation... No, she's not here. She was called away on an emergency," he said, trying to sound business-like and professional. ..."Sam Baker, here. Who's calling, please? Oh, yes. You're the, uh, lawyer," he said, placing a cold emphasis on the last word. He rolled his eyes for the amusement of Carol and Dave. "We met last night...Well, she ran up to the hospital in Frederick. Dennis Woods was in a car accident and was taken there. She and Marylou went up to see how he is and help comfort the family...Yes, it is tragic...I'm here with some friends of mine helping to straighten up some...Yes. I do know what she wanted. She wants your copy of the grant proposal...Pardon? ...Ghee, that's too bad," Sam responded to what John Brandon had said.

Sam's voice now sounded patronizing and dull-witted, and he began to make amusing faces to Carol and Dave as he spoke..."Well, I sure do hope you can locate it. I can just imagine how many papers you must look at during the day. I've been in a lawyer's office a few times and I've seen the stacks of papers and folders and all. Hey! Maybe your secretary misfiled it?...Well, I'll be sure to tell her when she gets back. Boy, is she going to be upset...Sure. Nice talkin' to ya'. Maybe we'll run into each other again, sometime. Good hunting. I sure hope you find it...Mm, yeah. Goodnight to you, too," Sam said. He set the phone to its cradle and shook his head with a wry smile.

"What was all that about?" Dave asked.

"Oh, man. You aren't going to believe this," Sam said. He sat back in the chair and shook his head in disbelief as he turned the corner of his mouth to display a scornful look. "Now I know something's definitely not kosher."

"What? Tell me."

"That was the lawyer friend, John Brandon, that Kelly's been seeing. He's the solicitor for the Foundation...volunteered his services. Hear me—volunteered. So, he takes a copy of the grant proposal back to his office in D.C. to re-write it—like I don't know shit about writing them. Anyway, he claims he lost the copy; misplaced it somewhere. Oh, he's determined to find it, though. Oh, boy, I'll just bet he is. Keep in mind this would be the only copy we'd have. Now what do you think?"

"I think we better stick around a few days to see how this turns out," Dave replied.

Carol looked at her husband. "Dave, you're opening a new store. How are you going to take off? We're supposed to head back tomorrow."

"Alan can handle it. It's all ready. He knows what's going on. I'll keep in touch with him."

"Well, if you're sure. You've worked too hard to get it ready. You really ought to be there for the opening."

"Honey, this is pretty important. Somebody has to help. It'd be different if it were just financial troubles. But you can see something is going on here. Sam may be right about all these incidents being related."

"What about your job, Sam?" Carol asked. "Aren't you supposed to start it pretty soon? You've got to find a place to live, yet."

"Well, fortunately I'm in a position where I can do what I want, when I want. I won't be holding up the project, or anything. They'll just have to wait for me to do my phase of it. The team I'm to work with can mark time till I get there."

Carol shrugged. "Well, if you guys are sure this is what you want."

"Carol," Dave said, moving close to her and putting a hand on her arm. "This is important to us. We study the battles, we read everything we can on it, we feel it in our very bones. Now we have a chance to do something to help preserve a part of it for future generations, for other folks that feel the same pull and obsessive fascination that Sam and I do. We have to do this, Carol. I think it's what we're supposed to do."

Carol signed resignedly and nodded. "I know," she said. "I just want to be sure you two know it, as well. I've always believed that life sometimes singles people out for certain and specific acts. When we're wise enough to have an awareness of it we follow the direction we're led and do what we're supposed to do. Maybe you guys were led here for a reason. Anyway, be careful. I'm feeling danger, here," she added, slipping an arm around her husband's waist.

Sam shrugged. "We've faced danger before. We always survive."

Sarah and Jeff returned with bags of sandwiches and drinks and, as they all sat and ate, they made plans for sending Carol and the kids back north the next day. Dave and Sam would seek lodging in a nearby motel and Carol could rejoin them when she'd made arrangements for the children to stay with friends. When dinner was over and the containers discarded Dave took his family back to the campsite. Sam stayed to await word from Kelly and Marylou.

It was nearing eleven o'clock when the two women returned from the hospital and informed Sam that Dennis Woods was in stable condition with a concussion and some serious cuts and bruises. All that was known was that a white vehicle had tried to pass him on a winding stretch of road and had forced his car over the embankment, then fled the scene. Dennis kept fading in and out of consciousness and could not add any further information, yet. Authorities were looking for a large white car or truck with a wide wheel base and a scrape along the passenger side.

After listening to some details of the doctor's reports and of how Dennis's family was bearing the incident, Sam informed Kelly of his phone conversation with her lawyer friend. When he told her John Brandon claimed to have misplaced the important document, she became outraged. "Sam, I don't believe this! Something is going on here. I'm going to call that son-of-a-bitch and tell him he'd better find it—like right now!"

Kelly went to the phone and grabbed it up but Sam stopped her, putting his hand over the receiver. "No. Leave it be. We don't need him," he said to her. "Let him play his game, if that's what he's doing."

"Why? What do you mean?"

One corner of Sam's mouth rounded upward in a sly grin. "I can retrieve everything. Your mailing list, the grant, all your accounts payable and receivable—everything you had on your discs. I transferred it all into the computer at Carnegie-Mellon. I don't know why. I guess just so it'd be there and I'd have a record of it. Sort of, I don't know, like a souvenir from my, uh, my time spent here."

Kelly looked stunned. Then a smile slowly formed on her lips as she absorbed what Sam had said. Marylou laughed out loud and clapped her hands. "Yeah, Sam!" she cheered gleefully. "Way to go!" Then she said to Kelly, "When you see that John again, tell him to take a flying leap."

"Humph! You know I will," Kelly assured her.

Sam explained both his and Dave's intentions to stay until the land dispute became resolved. "Right now, I want you to get some things together and come stay with us tonight at the campground. I'd just feel better knowing you weren't alone here after what all has happened today."

Marylou looked at him curiously. "Why, Sam? You don't think the robbers might come back?"

"Probably not. I just want to play it safe; at least for tonight."

Harboring suspicions that Marylou was ignorant of, Kelly readily agreed. She said goodnight to her friend and went upstairs to gather some clothes into an overnight bag.

Sam walked Marylou to her car parked just down the street and as they walked, she looked at him and cocked her head. "You two are growing fond of each other, aren't you, Sam?"

Sam's blush was visible even by the dim light of the street lamp and he smiled, amused. "She's a terrific girl," he said. "Intelligent, witty, talented, independent—and very beautiful."

"And available," Lou added with her own amused smile. "Work on her, Sam. She'll make you a wonderful friend and companion. I think you two were made for each other."

Sam opened the car door for Marylou and leaned to kiss her cheek. "Drive safely, Lou. Goodnight."

Marylou stood for a moment and sighed as she touched the cheek Sam had kissed. "Oh, if I weren't married..." Then, as she took her seat behind the wheel and Sam closed the door for her, she looked up at him. "Take care of her, Sam. Don't let her get hurt."

"I won't, Lou. Believe me. I won't," he said. "She'll be okay with me." Then he turned and left to go back inside for Kelly.

Chapter Eight

Tom Charles entered the large, ornate reception room carrying his leather attaché case in hand and several blueprint tubes tucked under his arm. "Morning, Cheryl," he greeted the well-dressed strawberry blonde behind the large, curved desk.

"Morning, Tom," she said cheerfully. "Would you like a cup of coffee?"

"Mm, yes. That'd be wonderful. Thank you," he smiled to the women of about thirty years of age. She rolled her chair back to stand, and, as she headed for the small kitchen just behind and to the left of her desk, Tom admired her curvaceous figure in the clinging, short dress. "You're losing weight. You look good," he said as she went in to pour coffee.

From the small room used for the express purpose of providing refreshments and quick lunches for James Brody, the girl hollered back, "Thank you for noticing. I've been doing an aerobics program." She reappeared with a coffee mug in hand. "Lotta' cream, no sugar," she smiled as she held it out for him.

"You remembered! That's terrific. Ah-h-h...that's what it is when you're good."

"My, aren't you in a chipper mood this morning. Why so?"

"I don't know. Nice day, I guess. Um...I assume he's in," Tom said, nodding toward a large wooden door that led into James Brody's office.

"Oh, he's in, all right. And so is every money man in North America. Lots of dollars behind that door," she smirked.

"I'm not late, am I? At least I didn't think so," Tom said, slightly concerned now that he heard the meeting was already in progress.

"No. No," Cheryl assured him. "In fact, you're a little early. He had them scheduled for an earlier meeting, to brief them, I think. Listen," she snickered, and she held down a button on the intercom. James Brody's voice was distinctly heard replying to a question from one of the visitors.

Tom's eyes widened and his mouth dropped in surprise. "Cheryl! You shouldn't be doing that."

"Oh, I listen all the time," she said with a playfully wicked chortle. "I know most everything that goes on. Hey, when you work for Mr. Brody, you have to stay one step ahead of him or you're out on the street. I have to know what he's thinking, when he's thinking it—and sometimes I have to think it for him.

That's why he pays me better than the insurance firm I was at. I take care of him; pamper him. If it weren't for the pay I'd be out of here in a minute. I sweat every time he comes through the door. He can be a real bastard to people, even when they think he likes them."

"Well, I'm sure you're capable," Tom said as Cheryl clicked off the intercom button.

"Should I tell him you're here?" Cheryl asked, her finger poised over another button.

Tom glanced at his watch. "Yeah. I suppose you'd better. He's probably wondering where I am."

Cheryl pushed a button on the intercom.

"Yes, Cheryl? What is it?" came the voice of James Brody.

"Mr. Charles is here, Mr. Brody."

"Good. Send him in, Cheryl."

"Yes, Mr. Brody," she replied. She depressed the button and watched Tom take a big swallow of coffee.

"Well, wish me luck," he said as he turned to the large office door.

"Hey, Tom," Cheryl hailed him. "You know, he thinks a lot of you."

"Pardon?"

"I heard him say so to one of his bankers on the phone, once. He thinks you're 'creative and imaginative.' Those were his words."

Tom just smiled.

"'Course, he did add that you were weak in structurals, though," she said as he stepped before the electronic eye. As the large wooden door slid open Tom grinned at her, then walked into the adjoining room.

James Marcus Brody's circular office was very large and plush, expensively decorated with contemporary furniture and impressionist period object d'art. The walls were adorned with paintings, sketches and drawings of all the development projects he had constructed since becoming head of the company. In the center of the room there stood a large circular conference table capable of seating no less than twenty people around the outside.

A short break in the table enabled a speaker to walk through to address those seated around it. At the very opposite to the break in the table, the two halves met at a point where the table was raised by one step. The person seated there, of course, was a head higher than those around them. And that, of course, was where James Brody sat. Tom always chuckled at this as being King Arthur's Round Table.

Beyond the conference table the floor was raised several steps and shaped in a curve from wall to wall. A massive, beautiful, antique, highly polished rosewood desk sat as the centerpiece on the carpeted platform. Also included in the office were a computer station, a drafting table, a stock monitor, and a large, expensive pool table.

The several file cabinets were of some rare, exotic wood and were built into the wall so that only the drawer fronts were exposed. Three large, thick, wooden doors led off into different rooms, the doors being constructed of the same material as the file drawers and, like the files, without handles—each being activated by an electronic eye.

Tom made a hurried scan of the suits seated around the table. There were twelve men of varying ages and each was expensively dressed and very well groomed. He recognized several of the men as financial backers from other projects and two lawyers from the firm that always handled Marco Development's legal affairs. There was also Meredan Joynder, the project engineer for the Antietam development project. The other men Tom didn't recognize but assumed they were to be financially involved with the project.

"Ah, Tom. Come in. Come in," James greeted him from his seat at the raised section of the table. "Gentlemen, let me introduce Tom Charles, the architect of the centerpiece of our little project."

Several men nodded in polite greeting, but most just sat straight-faced and without acknowledgement.

"Tom, go ahead and set up. I've a little introductory information to relay while you're getting ready for your display," James told him. He flipped a switch in a control panel before him and two large color monitors began to lower from the ceiling, opposite each other, so that everyone had a view without having to turn his or her head.

Another pressed button began a movie on the monitors, the announcer of which sounded very similar to an often-heard voice on PBS documentaries. Scenes of Washington, D.C., Baltimore and the surrounding megalopolis were displayed, focusing on the crowded streets and sidewalks, the jammed parking lots, rush hour traffic on the beltway and short clips of oppressively hot, summer days outside luxurious homes that were spaced too closely together.

The movie then changed to scenes of the interior of a high-speed commuter train passing out of the city and on into pastoral settings of rolling farmland where well-dressed children, displaying wide smiles, waved to the passing cars. A handsome man in a business suit is seated in air-conditioned comfort, reading the newspaper and sipping a tall, cool drink. He smiles to the children and returns a relaxed wave as the train speeds by. A quick flash to the clock on the wall reveals it is 5:15, leaving the impression that the man has only been riding for fifteen minutes.

A scene change shows the man stepping off the train and strolls over to his shiny, gray BMW parked just at the edge of the lot. The man is whistling cheerfully as he enters his car.

The announcer has been explaining the advantages of living outside the city and of the convenience of commuting by high-speed train to the peace and security of the wide-open spaces and scenic farmland of western Maryland and Virginia, far removed from the crime-ridden streets of the megalopolis. The businessman is followed to his house where his children, playing happily on the well-manicured lawn, run to surround him and greet him with hugs.

Aerial photos are now displayed on the screen showing vast tracts of open areas while the narrator describes the various tracts available and the bargain price tags offered. The movie ends with the announcer reminding the listener that land never depreciates in value and that populations always increase.

James pressed a button before him and the screens projected satellite photographs with overlying grids. "Gentlemen. There is a new westward expansion," he began. "The urban sprawl of the eastern seaboard has created a pressure upon us to seek out new development areas so that the young professionals in our society can live in quiet, safe surroundings. Amtrak has made it possible for us to reach points of the city, from out in the countryside, within minutes. Light, high-speed trains are coming within the next two decades.

Already there is experimentation with high-speed transit rail utilizing super conductivity. Our government, not to be outdistanced by foreign competition, is willing to pump millions into experimentation of this system. The Federal government is proposing to establish a prototype system at three possible sites. The line you see flashing in blue on the screen before you is one of those possible sites. Gentlemen, let me assure you, it is most probable that this is the site that will be selected.

Already a straw poll of the Congressional committee vested with the power of selecting the site for this innovative transportation system shows a strong favoritism toward this section of the country, as well as this particular area. A strong favoritism, I emphasize, due to the receptive and open minds of those Congressmen with the vision to know where the future lies. We at Marco have been working diligently to demonstrate this fact to those committee members, if you know what I mean."

"The flashing green squares along that line, gentleman, are the tracts of acreage already acquired by my corporation."

Voices began to mumble to one another on hearing this.

"My staff has been working diligently and tirelessly, creating a master plan for the entire area. The flashing yellow squares on the screen represent those tracts that we are presently in negotiations for and will soon acquire. Thousands of acres! All prime real estate, located directly along the future rail line. Homes for the wealthy professional. Shopping malls for their wives. Private schools for their children. Country clubs for relaxation.

Long have we sought exclusive communities in which to live and relax among those of our peers who have obtained and enjoy the power and wealth that are the rewards of long hours of toil and study. The over-burgeoning population along the eastern seaboard has caused lower cost dwellings to be constructed too near our beautiful homes. As we drive home in our cars we sit in traffic next to Chevys and Fords. We are forced to wait at counters while some laborer or lower-level bureaucrat receives service ahead of us. It's our right of having obtained power and wealth to afford exclusiveness.

Today, I will unveil to you the master plan I have designed to bring us a step closer to exclusiveness. To start the project along we have chosen a tract of land located in beautiful central Maryland, just off the Antietam battlefield. Estate houses will be erected with care in the design to attract the young professionals. My plan is to start at the outermost tract of the program and work back into the city. This will enable us to avoid the appearance of simply building another housing plan at the already congested urban perimeter.

Gentlemen, inside all of us dwells a little voice that tells each of us we are different from the man next to us; we are exceptional from the masses. We are successful and prosperous; a cut above the rest. At the very least we will concede that a select few are our equal and we will tolerate those others in social proximity. In our advertising, we will appeal to that small voice, providing an exclusive, restricted community secure from the noise and pollution and crime of the urban area; an island of wealth in a beautiful section of the countryside.

At this point, I'm going to turn the meeting over to the architect of the first phase in the master plan. When you've viewed the contemporary design of this community, we'll open the meeting up for comments and questions."

James now looked at the architect and said, "Tom," to indicate he now had the floor.

The architect hurriedly straightened his face, knowing his mouth had been agape at hearing James explain the company's future, grandiose plans. It annoyed him that James had had each team of engineers and architects work simultaneously on designs for the different communities, but kept them all ignorant about each other's project. He wondered who in the company knew of the ultimate strategy. A quick glance at the unsettled expression on Meredan Joynder's face told he'd been taken completely by surprise by this scheme.

Some of the guests were whispering to one another and others were scribbling notes. The only ones sitting calmly and observing the reactions of the guests were James, of course, and the two attorneys on his immediate right. Tom believed that they were privy to the company's plans, for it would be their firm that handled all the legal transactions for the land purchases. Also,

Tom knew that their firm contained both lobbying and consulting divisions and reasoned they had been employed to lobby for the experimental rail system to be located at the site James favored.

Tom was irritated by the unabashed audacity of James Brody to appeal directly to the vainglorious nature of individuals. Washington and the surrounding area were awash with money. It was, also, awash in crime, hate and fear. Plenty enough, there were, of pretentious people believing themselves to be above the common man; people desirous of escape from the inevitable release of the lower classes hostilities as the poor would, soon enough, begin to invade their no longer secure world.

James knew how to feed and nurture this haughtiness; how to free them of any associated guilt for possessing wealth. He could convince them that this was their right and privilege—and he led by example. The master plan for exclusive, secure, self-contained communities for the rich, Tom feared, would probably succeed.

He had a sudden, flashing moment of guilt as he thought about his own position. Though he wasn't in the same financial league with those attending this meeting, he knew his renumeration was considerable when compared to the salaries of other architects. He and Connie were quite well off. Their home was lovely and expensive, though not as pretentious as his salary could permit. He thought to soften the guilt with the fact that he donated generously to causes he deemed important and often lent his services, free of charge, to non-profit organizations such as Habitat for Humanity or special renovation projects by groups wanting to preserve historic buildings.

Now, after listening to James talk of wishing to separate the very wealthy from having to dwell in proximity to other peoples, he felt ashamed of having so much and of not having done more to help those less fortunate. He felt ashamed of even knowing James Brody, and worse—for having helped to develop this scheme.

A realization came upon Tom just as clearly as though someone had turned on a light in a blackened room; he was being made privy to James Brody's plans because he was to be in charge of the master project! He, Tom, as architect and Meredan Joynder as chief engineer. Meredan, Tom believed, would be right at home in that position. He relished the privileges and luxuries of having money. Carrying himself with an assumed dignity, he treated the secretaries and clerks more as servants than as co-workers. He vacationed on private islands and utilized the company limousines and aircraft whenever possible. He was so oddly idiosyncratic about the cleanliness of other people that he opened doors with a white handkerchief and, in less than posh restaurants, wiped the silverware with a napkin before using it, all from fear of catching transmittible germs from "commoners."

As Tom glanced at Meredan he had a sudden fear; was he looking into a mirror? Was he, Tom, perceived in the eyes of others in the same way as he perceived Meredan? Was that why James was singling him out from the senior architects, because he fit the mold of self-indulgence and conceit?

With all of these thoughts racing through his mind he almost stumbled as he entered the circle and began to spread his prints onto the specially designed table in the center of the circle. With a camera projecting his drawings onto the monitors, Tom began his demonstration for the monied audience. He had redesigned the entire concept to James's satisfaction, certain that the dwellings were in full view to all tourists of the battlefield.

The exteriors were brilliantly conceived in contemporary design with polished brass highlights on the doors, plenty of glass to let in sunlight and roof angles to catch the eye and demand a studied stare. The interiors were unusually bold and intriguing with cathedral ceilings revealing alcoves and hallways leading off mysteriously to other wings of the house, transmitting the feeling that one was standing in an abstraction, yet maintaining a warm, friendly, comfortable atmosphere.

Built-ins of every imaginable convenience were available to the owner; the oven, refrigerator, stove,—even the ironing board, washer and dryer—were integrated into the plans to maintain streamlined, sanitary contours in the kitchen and laundry areas. Abounding in electronic wizardry that included a pre-programmed computer controlling everything from door locks and lawn sprinklers to the climate and atmosphere in each separate room, the houses were an inspiring credit to the young architect's already impressive design portfolio.

Tom tried his best to sound enthusiastic, though he had not been in favor of the project since it's conception. Now that his design pleased James Brody so, and after hearing the man explain his plan for the entire corridor, from central Maryland to Washington, D.C., he became even less enthused.

Elated when James had first chosen him for the project, passing over the more senior architects with the firm, Tom began to wish, more and more, he'd been assigned to a less prestigious project such as a shopping mall or middle-income housing project.

The morning passed. Tom finished his presentation, then answered questions posed by the guests. Then James spoke again, further tying this project with the over-all scheme. When the meeting broke for lunch, James hailed Cheryl over the intercom, telling her to notify the caterers the party would soon be adjourning to the dining room.

The large, wooden door soon slid open as Cheryl entered with a pleasant smile and greeted the men who were slowly milling toward her, talking and murmuring to one another. James escorted the group to where Cheryl waited, though the two attorneys remained seated at the conference table. "Cheryl, if you'd be so kind as to show our guests to the dining room," James said to her, loud enough for all to hear. "Gentlemen, I have some other business to attend to before I join you. If you'll excuse me for just a couple minutes... Tom, Meredan. I need to see you for a second," he said, signaling them to remain. The two men turned and followed James back into his office.

James put a hand on each man's shoulder and grinned widely. "Well, fellas, what do you think? It's a rather bold plan, isn't it?"

"I think it's magnificent," Meredan exclaimed. "Brilliantly conceived! Masterfully created!"

"Tom?" James asked, turning to him when he was not forthcoming with his answer.

Tom was still unsettled about the entire scheme and his mind raced for a reply that would sound favorable to his boss. "Well...it's, uh...certainly bold," he finally answered. "I think it'd have been nice if we'd all have been informed earlier of the scope of the project. It might have helped in coordinating our designs, like finding a common theme to...to tie it all together, for instance."

James dropped his hands from the men's shoulders and, showing a sly grin, moved over to where the two attorneys sat straight-faced and serious. "Yes. Exactly," James said. "That's where you two come in. I kept each team in the dark about this, except for a select few. We've been buying acreage under fictitious names to keep the prices from being inflated, of course. The fewer people that know of this, the better. I now own, or soon will own, the key tracts of land along which this experimental train will run. And, trust me, fellas, this is the route that'll be chosen. I've gone to great expense to insure that it will," James said as he looked at the two lawyers. One of the men shifted in his seat and responded with a slight nod.

James now leaned casually against the conference table. "So, uh, look, I don't guess I really have to spell it out for you two. The plan is daring, visionary, and imaginative. It's going to take a couple of guys who themselves are visionaries to lead it. I picked you both because I know you can be trusted with it. You're both conscientious, hard-working, and, like us, you love money. I know I can count on you two to do me a standout job. Incidentally, you'll both find your salaries have been substantially increased to reflect your new responsibilities," James added, watching for the signs of gratitude and enthusiasm on the two men's faces.

Meredan assumed a posture of serious concern, standing erect, as though rising to the occasion of the weighted responsibilities. He was scarcely able to conceal his elation at the news of his promotion, though, and was checked only by his staid personality from jumping for joy. "James," he said with complete sincerity in his voice. "You can count on us to deliver. We'll make this project a showcase for the world to admire. I know Tom's work and abilities and, together, we'll make Chevy Chase seem like a slum. People will give their houses away to move into one of our communities."

James smiled from the corner of his mouth. "That's what I like to hear. I know I made the right choices in you two."

Tom tried to smile and appear pleased. He raised his brow and forced a smile and his mouth was open as if he were speechless, unable to express his feelings to his boss. And, in fact, he was speechless. Never had he imagined anyone would presume he was greedy or arrogant. But James had as much as concluded the fact by appointing him to this new position. He knew he looked stunned and he was relieved that James read it as elation. He needed time to think this over. He wanted to reject the offer outright but knew that to do so would mean losing his job. James did not have it in his nature to be understanding, especially over a decision of character.

James came to the two men and placed his hands on both their shoulders and turned them to walk them to the door. "Congratulations, fellas. I know, together, we'll make this project succeed beyond anyone's imagination. In a few short years this company will be envied by Wall Street...and you two will be right at the top with me."

The door slid silently open as the three stood before the electronic sensor. James patted both men on the back, saying, "Go and help entertain our guests. Talk up the project with them. We'll need their backing, for a while, to get this thing going. I've a few details to discuss with these men, here. We'll be along, presently. We've got a lot of work to do, fellas. A lot of work."

Tom and Meredan stepped into the outer office and the thick wood door slid closed. Meredan gave a look at Tom and, slowly, a smile formed on his lips. He could no longer conceal his elation as he clenched a fist as if in grasping victory and shouted, "Yes! Do you realize what this means? We're on top! We're number one! Numero uno!" he exclaimed in an excitement peculiar to his character.

Tom remained unemotional. He shrugged, saying, "It's going to mean an awful lot of work for the both of us."

"So what? That's what it's all about. We work hard, do a good job; we become tops in the company. We'll answer only to James! We'll make fortunes in the profit sharing. Hell, man, this is what guys like us dream about—making it to the top! Tom, once this project gets rolling, we'll be jumping even deeper into the foreign markets. We'll be global!"

Tom smiled in the best simulated excitement he could muster. "Yeah. That'll be great," he replied. Then he turned and leaned over Cheryl's workstation for her phone. "Listen, go join the others at lunch. I'm going to make a few phone calls."

"Can't wait to tell the little woman, hey?" Meredan chuckled and nudged Tom with his elbow.

"Yeah. Something like that," Tom replied.

"Okay. But don't be long," Meredan said as he started to leave. Then he stopped a moment and mumbled loud enough for Tom to hear, "I've got to start figuring out how I can hide my salary increase from my ex-." Then he moved on, the large office door leading out to the corridor sliding open for him, then silently closing as he left.

Tom moved around behind the large desk and lifted the receiver to his ear with every intention of placing a call. It wasn't to his wife, as Meredan had suggested, but to his secretary on some routine office work he needed her to handle.

As he started to push on the extension button for his office on a lower floor of the building his eye caught sight of the intercom button Cheryl had pressed earlier. He paused from pushing the last number of his office extension and, uncontrollably, he watched his finger move to the button Cheryl had pressed. His heart beat rapidly as he tried to resist the urge to listen in on the conversation in the next room, but it seemed almost compulsive. He gasped as he watched his finger press in the button marked "Listen."

"...Well, it's not enough. We've got to be a little more persuasive with them. Up our contribution to their campaign chest. Do it through the lower pipeline, but make sure they know it was from us—and why." It was James Brody's voice coming through the speaker as he addressed the two attorneys. Tom was embarrassed that he was listening, but his finger refused to release the button.

"Send their wives the presents we talked about. No, wait! Make it their girlfriends. If their girlfriends are happy, it'll make them happy. Tell them we're doing it, but make the address originate from their offices. Now, what about this Antietam thing? Where are we on it?"

"Well, Marc, we're coming closer to the deadline. I've tried stalling it as long as I could, but some guy from up north joined them and wrote the damned thing. I'm afraid it's ready to go," one of the men explained. Tom recognized the voice as one of the two lawyers.

"Who is he? Can it be stopped?" James asked.

"Not without the help of...uh...Rudy White, I'm afraid," the man answered, stammering over the very mention of the man's name. There was a long pause.

"Okay," James finally said. "Contact him. Tell him its got to be done right away. I don't want any delays. Do whatever it is needs done and however it needs to be done. While he's at it, let's get rid of that orchard guy. If he's out of the picture his wife will sell to us. Give her the same numbers as before but tell her we'll buy the damn peaches, too. Offer her the house down the road, or something. She'll collect the insurance and live happily ever after, a rich widow. I need that ground for a depot."

Tom couldn't believe what he was hearing! He hoped he was just interpreting the conversation incorrectly, but he feared he was not.

"Oh, something else," he heard the one lawyer say. "On the Antietam thing, again. We weren't able to get the McPherson people."

"Why not? Did you make them the offers we talked about?"

"Uh…yeah. But they're all a pretty wealthy group of people. I'm afraid they don't need us. We, um…we also found out one of the members is friends with this Dennis Woods fellow, the president of that Antietam group."

"Do what's necessary," James answered. "Get this Woods guy out of the way. Send some of those McPherson people on a cruise, or something. This thing's got to come together!"

Tom shook his head. "This is too much," he thought to himself. He grew angry with not only what he was hearing, but, also, that he was associated with a person as despicable as James Brody.

"One other piece of business has to be settled," came the voice of the other lawyer who had been silent until now. Tom bent his ear to listen more clearly but the large door from the hallway began to slide open. He quickly disengaged the 'listen' button and, still holding the receiver to his ear, began to speak into it as though giving instructions to someone. Cheryl entered the room and waved to him as Tom said goodbye into the receiver and promptly set the phone to its cradle.

"Aren't you joining the money changers for lunch?" she asked him as she moved around to her chair behind the desk.

"Hm? Oh, yes. Right now, as a matter-or-fact. Had to, uh, make a call first. Thanks for the use of your phone. How are they?"

"How do you think?" Cheryl replied. "A bunch of boring suits that can't talk about anything but money and leer at my breasts and behind. They aren't even subtle about it. Next time I'll wear a mini and bend way over. I'd like to hear them try to talk about stocks and bonds with…hey, are you all right? You aren't even listening, are you?" she asked, for Tom had been standing there, staring at the phone with a distracted look about him.

"Hm? Yeah. Okay. I'm fine. Just, um, thinking about something. I better go. See you after lunch," he said, turning to leave.

"Oh, I'll be here. Where else am I going to go? I'm tied to this chair."

Tom entered the plushy carpeted hallway and went to the elevator that would take him to the banquet room on the second floor. He wished he could leave and just find a nice quiet bar in which to have a drink and think things over. His stomach felt queasy and his head began to throb. The last thing he wanted to do was to be around James again, but he knew he would have to pretend to be excited over the project until he could figure out just what he should do about the whole situation. The elevator doors opened and, as Tom entered, he determined he had to try to deal in some way with what he had overheard. He could not sit idly by and ignore the fact that innocent people were going to be harmed because of the greedy aspirations of one maniacal man.

****

Sam pulled the silver sportscar into the shadow of the trees to park beside the blue van. The hour was well past eleven o'clock and, when Sam and Kelly approached the fire where Dave was stooped feeding logs into the licking flames, Carol came from the tent to greet them both and join them by the fire. As they settled into the low camp chairs Kelly looked at Sam. "So, what's our next move? What do we do?"

Sam picked up a stick and began to poke at the fire. "Well, we need to take a trip into D.C. tomorrow to retrieve a copy of the grant. I know a friend there who has a computer that'll get us a copy from the CMU system. You'll have to get the board together to approve it, then get it to Dennis' friend so they can act on it right away."

Dave pitched a few twigs into the fire and looked at Kelly. "Would it do us any good to go see that old lady who owns the farm and plead for more time?"

"I don't think so," Kelly replied. "I've never met her, but they tell me she's strange. She talks in gibberish most of the time. Besides, she has a signed agreement with Marco Development. It's pretty tight."

"Who looked at it?" Sam asked.

"Um...John," Kelly said, a bit meekly and embarrassed.

"Figures," Sam replied. "I'd still like to go talk to her."

"Okay. I'll try to set it up for us."

"Good," Dave said. "I'd like to meet her, too. We'll break camp in the morning." Then, turning to Carol, he told her, "Once we find a motel I'll call Alan and leave all the info with him. You should be back here, say...oh, probably early evening, anyway."

"Yeah. That's what I was figuring," Carol said.

"You guys make a list of what you'll need me to bring back. I'll stop at the house, first, then take the kids over to Cathy's. She'll be delighted to have them stay awhile with her."

"Okay." Sam said, satisfied with their plans. He stood and gave a long stretch and the others followed him up, rising from the low camp chairs. "Let's all get to bed. We've got a busy day tomorrow."

Kelly stretched and yawned, but as everyone started off to their tents, she cleared her throat for their attention. "Ahem..."

They all stopped and turned to look and see her still at the fire. "Oh! Oh, yeah," Dave said for them all as they realized there had been no arrangements made for where Kelly was to sleep.

There was an awkward moment as everyone glanced to each other for an idea. Sam blushed some but finally said, "Um, why don't you sleep in my tent?"

"I've got extra blankets...and a pillow," Carol said. I'll go get them."

"Thank you. That'll be fine," Kelly replied.

Sam smiled and shrugged, "You can have my bag...and the air mattress. I'll take the blankets and Mother Earth."

"Well, thank you, Sam. That's sweet of you," Kelly said, showing a disarming smile in the orange reflections of the leaping flames.

"My pleasure," Sam replied with a courteous bow, and when he rose and glanced at her as she stood behind the fire he was unable to tear his eyes away. With the flames licking and snapping upward between them, her gentle face seemed to have an everchanging, shimmering radiance that served to add a sensuous allure Sam found irresistible. Her eyes further dazzled him as they sparkled in the reflective light as brightly as the stars in the night sky overhead.

Sam, too, appeared to have an aural glow that emanated more from within him than was cast by the flames. Kelly's gaze lingered on him as she appreciatively studied the contrasts in the man across the fire. She saw a gentle, caring man whose heart was admirably overflowing with tenderness and warmth.

But the big hands, brawny chest and muscular arms revealed a harnessed power that, when fully unleashed, could explode with a frightful force upon whomever his anger should be vented. Now, though, she was seeing the mild, unpretentious, handsome gentleman standing across from her, and she very much enjoyed looking at him.

Carol and Dave stood well enough back from the fire to be in the shadow of their tent and watched the two exchange dreamy stares. Carol put an arm around her husband's waist to give him a hug in her excitement over the couple's growing infatuation with each other. Finally, when a wide yawn reminded her how tired she was she interrupted them. "C'mon, Sam. I'll give you those blankets."

"Oh, uh...yeah. Okay," he said, tearing his eyes from the lovely woman to follow Carol. "Uh...Kelly, um, why don't you, uh, go ahead and get settled in. Let me know when you're ready."

"Fine," the woman replied and started for the tent.

"There's a flashlight just inside the flap," he added as she moved to duck into the tent's opening.

Sam followed Carol and Dave to their tent and Carol slipped inside, returning shortly with an armful of sheets and blankets and a pillow. She handed them over to Sam and the three then said goodnight. Sam started to leave with the bedding and, as he moved off toward his tent he mumbled, "Jeez, I hope I don't snore tonight. I'll be real embarrassed." When he stood before his tent he cleared his throat to announce his arrival. "Ahem. I'm...uh...I'm back," he said to Kelly through the thin nylon material of the tent.

"Oh. C'mon in," she answered.

He ran the zipper of the flap and ducked in to find Kelly sitting up in the bag, brushing her hair. "Well, looks like you're settled in," he said as he began to arrange his bedding.

"Mm...and quite comfy, thank you," she smiled in reply.

"Good. Serves you right," he said as she helped him spread the blankets. He stood to remove his pants and, with his hands on his belt buckle he paused. "Um...," he said awkwardly as Kelly watched and began brushing her hair again.

"Oh. Oops," she giggled and turned her head so he could undress to his skivvies. He then wiggled down under the covers but sat up to remove his shirt. Kelly watched him, gazing fancifully at the broad chest and muscular arms. "Do you work out?" she asked, setting her brush down and fluffing her pillow.

Sam pulled on the Cleveland Browns football jersey he'd been wearing as a night shirt. "Yeah. Why?"

"Thought so," Kelly replied as she laid back onto the pillow and drew the bag up over her chin to conceal a secretive, delighted smile.

"Ready?" Sam asked as he reached to turn off the flashlight hanging from the supporting pole.

"Mm hm." she nodded.

Sam clicked off the light and lay back on the mattress of blankets. "Ohhh...," he groaned uneasily. "You forget how hard the earth can be."

"Oh, Sam. I'm sorry," she said in sympathy.

"No. It's okay. I just have to...find a...comfortable... position," he explained as he wriggled on the blankets. "The trick is to...contort your body...to lie between the...larger rocks."

"Aw, now I'm feeling guilty," Kelly said. "Listen, you take the air mattress. I'll sleep on the ground."

"No. No. It's not as bad as I'm making out. I'm just teasing. Hell, this 'ol back has rubbed nature's skin more times than I can remember. From Cub

Scouts to Explorer Scouts, then into the army. Ha! The army," Sam chuckled with a grim reminiscence of the uncounted nights he'd slept on the ground while in the service.

"Oh, yeah. You told me the other night you'd been in the army. Vietnam."

"Mm," he answered as he rolled onto his side and propped himself on one elbow to look at her as she lay facing him. The burning logs from the fire shed a dim light for them to see each other. "That was a whole lifetime and another world past. I try not to dwell much on it. It wasn't the kind of war you came back from and talked over war stories with the guys in the V.F.W."

Sam paused and Kelly could see his thoughts were churning. Then he continued, "You know, this fascination Dave and I have for the Civil War—it's rather strange. Reading about it, studying diaries of the men who fought in it...well, they almost sort of romanticize it. They speak of the horrors and the butchering and death, but it's still with a far more romantic and adventurous reminiscence than guys like Dave and I will ever feel as we grow older."

"Well, wars are getting uglier. The weapons are deadlier," Kelly suggested.

"True. But death is still death. Pain and suffering are still very much a part of it all. You can't separate it out."

"No. You can't," she agreed. "But, then, the romanticism comes from the glory. That's the big factor."

"What?"

"The glory. It has to have glory with it...and glory only comes from fighting for an ideal; a cause. You have to believe completely that what you're fighting for is right and worthy of giving it your life. Many of the men on both sides of the Civil War were committed to their causes."

Sam mulled that over some, then said, "Humph. I've played with that before. The jury's still out." He rolled onto his stomach and was silent awhile. Then he asked, "Do you believe in reincarnation?"

Kelly blinked in surprise as the question caught her off guard. "I...I don't know. I've never really thought of it much. Why?"

"Well, Carol's something of an Earth Mother—that's what I call her, anyway. She dabbles in herbs, holistic medicines and yoga and stuff. You'd never know it to look at her. I guess you'd expect someone like that to have long, straight hair and wear beads and wire-rimmed glasses and the like—and I think she did at one time. Anyway, she's very mystical."

"Carol? Really? You're right. I wouldn't have guessed it."

"Anyway, she has these theories, or ideas, on reincarnation and one of them is; if you've been in a war in a past life, or in this life, too, and you've taken a life or caused pain or suffering to anyone as a result of your actions, you're doomed to have to repeat it again in another life until you do something to change it. You have to alter the act or, if you do the same thing over again, you have to do something to make up for it to break the cycle."

"Karma," Kelly said.

"Yeah. Karma," Sam repeated despondently. "I hope she's wrong. I sure don't ever want to be in a war again. Not in this life, or any other."

Kelly reached out and put a hand tenderly on Sam's back. "It's just an idea, Sam; just a belief. Besides, from the little I've read about it, Karma works in strange ways and there's never really any way of knowing why something happens to a person, good or bad. Sometimes people just seem fated to have things happen to them. I guess all we can do is try not to hurt anybody and hope for the best."

"Mm. I suppose. Carol says that, too."

"Go to sleep, Sam," she said, patting his back to comfort him. "Don't think about that."

"Yeah. You're right. I shouldn't have brought it up. It's just that...I was thinking about that dream you've been having. I, uh...I've been troubled by this weird one of my own and...ah, never mind. I don't think I really want to get into it, now. Goodnight, Kelly," he said, then rolled over to find a comfortable position.

Kelly rolled onto her back but her eyes remained open as she thought of all the events of the day. After a long pause she turned her head on the pillow. "Sam?"

"Mmh?" he asked with his eyes closed as he was starting to drift into sleep.

"Sam, am I in danger? Should I be scared?"

Sam opened one eye and turned his head slightly to look at her and reached over to take her hand. "No. You're not in danger. We're both okay, Kelly. Dave and I aren't going to let any harm come to you. You'll be all right." He squeezed her hand in reassurance and laced his fingers in hers and Kelly rolled onto her side to snuggle closer against him. They both closed their eyes and fell asleep.

Sometime during the night Sam was awakened by thrashing and moaning next to him. The fire had long since died down and the bright moon shone only enough light to faintly see the slender figure lying next to him reaching out into the darkness for something, or someone. Sam watched and listened awhile as Kelly moaned and uttered something incomprehensible. Then she began to sob, crying out, "No-o-o-o...Come back..."

Her plea was heart-wrenching and Sam sighed, "Aw-w...," as he reached over and took her in his arms to comfort her. She rolled into his arms and cuddled to him, crying into his chest. Sam tenderly stroked her hair and listened as a sudden and curious gust of wind blew up, shaking the tent and rustling the leaves and branches throughout the woods. Kelly never woke up, or if she did, she fell back asleep again, spending the remainder of the night pressed against Sam's firm body, held securely in his arms.

****

Dawn broke warm and sunny over the high ridge of South Mountain, filtering through the trees to sweep away a thin ground fog and dry the dew that covered the woods below. Sam was awakened by the muffled clanging of pans and skillets and the occasional low murmur of voices throughout the campground. Kelly was snuggled against him, her head cradled in his arm as she slept soundly.

His arm was numb but he ignored the lack of sensation in favor of the enjoyment of having her warm body against him. He slowly eased his arm out from around her and she stirred only slightly as he sat up and replaced his pillow where his arm had been for her head to rest on. He smiled as he looked at her and began to curl and uncurl his forearm to get the blood flowing through it. When enough feeling had returned, Sam stood and slid his pants on, threw on his flannel shirt, then quietly unzipped the tent flap to step outside. Still groggy, he made his way to the dining fly where Carol and Dave were heating water on the camp stove.

"Hey, guy," Dave greeted him. "How'd you sleep?"

"Ugh..." Sam replied and rolled his back to display its stiffness.

"That bad huh?" Carol smiled.

"Naw. It was okay. Makes a body appreciate a nice mattress." He stretched wide and yawned, looking skyward as he did. "Nice morning, huh?" he commented through his yawn.

"Mm. We've been lucky. No rain," Dave said.

"Is Kelly still asleep?" Carol asked, checking the water for a boil.

"Yeah. I think. She had a hard night," Sam said.

Carol poured the steaming water into the cups. "Oh? I'm sorry to hear that."

"What'd you do," Dave chuckled, "let the air out of her mattress so she'd be miserable with you?"

Sam smiled over Dave's suggestion. "No. She had a bad dream. I think it was the same one she told me she's been having lately."

"Oh, my. Did she tell you what it was about?" Carol asked.

Sam told them of the night at the Foundation headquarters when he'd heard her murmuring in her sleep and had gone up to investigate. He then described the dream as Kelly had told it and explained that it was recurring more frequently. When he'd finished, the three stood around the lighted camp stove, sipping coffee and contemplating the possible interpretations. No one spoke for quite a while until Carol finally said, "There are some obviously classic symbols in it. But the dream as a whole, I can't make sense of."

"That makes two of us," Kelly said, stepping out from under the tent flap. She wore blue jeans and a ragged sweatshirt, her hair pulled back in a ponytail.

"Good morning," the three greeted her as she approached them.

"Coffee?" Carol asked, nodding toward the pot of boiling water.

"Mm, yes. Please."

Carol measured out the instant coffee grains, then poured the water. She motioned toward the milk and sugar on the picnic table as she handed the cup to Kelly. "I'll let you fix it how you like it," she said, and as Kelly thanked her and began to stir in some milk she said, "Sam tells us you didn't sleep well last night."

"No. I slept okay. I was very tired," Kelly replied and took a sip of the coffee.

"You had that dream again, didn't you?" Sam asked.

Kelly sat down on the bench and grimaced. "Mm. I did. I heard Sam tell you guys about it. Pretty weird, huh?"

In an effort to be polite, the three, at first, just shrugged and gave hesitant nods. Then, amused at their own timid courtesies, they all chuckled and nodded more pointedly.

"You want to know something even weirder? I saw the rider's face last night," Kelly told them, and watched their mouths drop open. She nodded slowly to reaffirm what she'd said. Then she looked off into the woods. "They came the way they always do; following the light. When the rider came out from among them, he paused in the shadows as he's always done, just back of where I could see him more clearly.

This time, when I came to him, I heard myself say, 'Is it I that draws you from among them?' and he squeezed his horse forward a few paces, coming closer and...and I saw his face," she choked as a tear ran down her cheek. "He's so young...so handsome. He had blond hair and the sweetest, most friendly eyes. His face looked so drawn and saddened—like he was so alone and scared. Then, the longer we looked at each other, he started to smile—just a little—but like he'd just discovered or realized something pleasant."

Kelly turned her head back to the three listeners and exclaimed, "I knew him! I mean...I recognized his face! I don't know who he is, or was, but I knew right away that we knew each other somehow. That was why he smiled, I think; either because he recognized me, or because I finally recognized him!" she exclaimed.

"Who was he?" Carol asked, intrigued by Kelly's experience.

"I don't know. But I did in the dream," Kelly said. "And deep inside..." she continued, speaking slowly to consider what she was saying, "I have this strange feeling...that I know him, still."

"Meaning?" Dave asked.

"I, I don't know what I mean by that. Just that...I know him."

Sam handed her a napkin on which she wiped her moistened eyes and asked her, "Could you make out the uniform this time?"

Kelly nodded as she dabbed with the napkin. "Yes...it was blue. He was wearing a Union officer's coat. I could tell that much."

"Then what happened?" Dave asked, also intrigued by the unusual story. "After he smiled at you?"

"I, um, I reached out for him. I wanted to hug him. Oh, he looked so handsome and dashing...but those eyes looked so full of want," she explained. "He, he turned his head as if the others were calling to him, beckoning him back and...when he looked down at me again his smile was gone. Then he turned his horse and galloped back to the others. I cried," she said, again the tears welling in her eyes. She searched the faces of each of her three friends for some explanation but received only puzzled shrugs.

Sam sat next to her and put a comforting arm around her shoulders. "Hey," he said. "Look at it this way; it sure beats the heck out of my dream—mine has the feeling about it that I'm dying. You only get visited by a ghost. I'm going to end up being one," he chuckled, trying to ease her concern.

Carol cocked her head curiously at that, then turned the corner of her mouth in a suspecting smile.

"What?" Sam asked as he read the change in her expression.

"Oh-h...nothing. Just had a thought, maybe. An idea to play with," she answered.

"Let's hear it," Dave said.

"No-o. Not yet. Maybe when I get more info on these dreams. It's even too wild a thought for me to actually believe."

Sarah and Jeff wandered out of the tent and came toward the picnic table to join the adults. When everyone had said hello to them, Dave suggested they all eat, break camp, and get Carol and the kids headed home.

By nine o'clock Dave was kissing his family goodbye and Sam and Kelly were busily packing the DeLorean full with luggage. When the van pulled away, Dave stood and waved his family off till they were out of sight, then turned to help Sam and Kelly tie baggage to the trunk lid. "You could use a bigger car, you know," he said to his friend as he tied off a corner of the rope.

"I have a bigger car—back in Cleveland."

"Well, listen," Kelly said as they secured the last of the bags. "When we get to a motel and get settled in, we should take my car into D.C. At least it'll be more comfortable."

Dave opened the door on the passenger's side and chuckled. "Wow. This is going to be like those circus clowns that fit into one of those little wee cars."

"Just shut up and get in, both of you," Sam said, pretending annoyance.

Kelly and Dave laughed as they squeezed into the passenger seat with so many exaggerated grunts and groans. Sam just rolled his eyes over their teasing and took the seat behind the wheel.

They stopped at different motels along the way to inquire about vacancies, and, this being the height of the tourist season, considered themselves fortunate in finding a suite of rooms at a Comfort Rest Inn, a small, independently owned motel near Hagerstown, Maryland. There were two bedrooms, each with its own bathroom, connected by a shared sitting room kitchenette combination.

The car was unpacked with the baggage hauled in and set in the middle of one of the rooms and the three explored the suite, noticing the twin double beds in each room. They glanced at one another, awkwardly, as the thought of sleeping arrangements came to mind.

"Well, you two should be okay in this room," Kelly said. "You've got your own bath and all."

"Hm…" Dave said, cocking an eyebrow. "I guess that decision's been taken care of."

"I suppose we don't get a say in this?" Sam asked.

"Sure, you do. You two can pick which bed you want."

Sam shrugged and sighed in resignation. He had hoped to have Kelly as a roommate instead of Dave.

They unpacked some clothing to settle in and, as they had had little time after a breakfast of cold cereal at the campsite, Kelly spent some time in the bathroom to refreshen herself. When she rejoined the men in the kitchen Sam was already on the phone to his friend in Alexandria, Virginia. He talked at length, catching up on past histories as they hadn't been in contact for several years, and when at last he hung up the phone, he had a clever smile on his face.

"Old friend, huh?" Dave said with a suggestively questioning grin. "You didn't say your friend is female."

"Yeah. Good ol' Pat. She's quite a gal," Sam said. Then, as he now noticed Dave's grin and Kelly's slightly anxious look, his chin dropped. "Whoa! Wait a minute. It's nothing like that. Pat and I go back a ways, but it's just as good friends. We worked together as part of a research team at 'Big Blue' for a time. She's got her own business now, she said; does consulting work and some computerized billing for municipalities, or something. She's a whiz with these things, too. She was married when I knew her but always used her maiden name. Guess she knew she'd end up single again."

"I gather she's divorced, now?" Dave asked.

"Yeah. Pat Marley," Sam pronounced in thoughtful reminiscence. "Cute little thing. Blonde hair, green eyes; about, oh, I don't know, five-five, five-six. Hm...she must be about forty-two or forty-three, now. Still sounds spunky. Has this deep, sexy voice. You guys'll love her."

"Great. Can't wait to meet her," Dave replied. "I've got to make a call, then we can go."

Kelly explained that she, too, needed to make some calls before they could leave. Dave went back to the bedroom to use a separate line, placing a call to his friend and employee, Alan, to inform him of his being detained in Maryland for a while longer. Kelly used the phone in the kitchen to contact various board members to be certain they were still meeting that evening.

The next move was to return to Sharpsburg and check in with Marylou. When they arrived, Lou was just saying goodbye to a family of tourists from Ohio, having received from them a twenty-five-dollar donation and their name and address for the mailing list. Kelly was introduced to the Buckeye state natives and spoke with them awhile. When they had finally departed, she talked with Marylou, asking her to prepare some material for the board meeting as she, Kelly, would be in D.C. for the day. Lou readily agreed to the assignment and wished them success on their trip into the city.

When the trio left and walked across the street to Kelly's car, Sam waited as she unlocked the front passenger door. Dave was standing by the rear door and casually glanced at his friend. "Bet you're excited."

"Oh? Why's that?"

"About riding in this car. You really flipped over it the other day."

Kelly giggled over the comment as Sam grimaced and curled his upper lip at Dave.

****

In a deep blue, cloudless sky the sun was hanging directly overhead when the three travelers turned into the parking lot of the office towers in Alexandria, Virginia. They rode the elevator to the eighth floor and proceeded down the hallway to a glass enclosed suite of offices with the name "Data Resources and Processing" stamped in bold black letters on one of the windows. Inside, a receptionist greeted them and asked their business. Sam gave his name and explained that they had no appointment but that Pat Marley was expecting them.

The receptionist pressed a key on the console in front of her and picked up the phone to announce the presence of the guests in the office. When she received a reply, she smiled to them and said politely, "You may go in. Ms. Marley is expecting you. It's the second door on your right."

Sam thanked the woman, then led the way down the hall toward Pat's office. Dave and Kelly paid scant attention to the office arrangement, but Sam's eyes were busily noting that the larger outer room had been separated into several separate offices by free-standing, metal and glass partitions. The paneled hall they were walking through led them past several doors. Two doors on the left were marked "Men" and "Women," the third had the label "storage" across it. Directly ahead, at the far end of the hall, was a heavy glass door with "Keep Door Closed" stenciled in bold letters. Visible, inside, were two middle-aged men and a younger woman conferring together at a terminal. Sam recognized that as the main computer room.

The first door on the right was opened fully and, as they filed past, a woman seated at the desk inside glanced up to note the passing visitors. A quick look in the cramped office revealed stacks of file folders on every available surface.

The second door on the right was also opened wide and, though half again larger than the preceding office, it, too, was filled with stacks of files and computer printouts piled all over the contemporary furniture. As the three visitors entered the room Sam showed a broad smile to the woman seated behind the desk. She was talking on the phone but returned Sam's smile, adding a wink of one of her green eyes.

When she said goodbye to the party on the other end, she pressed a button on the phone and said, "Hold my calls." Then, setting the phone in its cradle she stood excitedly and moved around the deck. "Sam Baker," she exclaimed, and they hugged one another as old friends will after an absence of too many years. They exchanged pecks on each other's cheeks, then a quick kiss on the lips.

After another hug, Sam pulled back and said, "Ah, Pat. It's good to see you again."

The woman grasped Sam's hands and glanced to Kelly and Dave. "Do you believe this guy? Not a letter; no post card; not even a computer message over the last few years and here he is dropping in out of the blue. Let's take a look at you," she said, smiling wide and scanning him up and down. "Wow! You're still in good shape." she complimented him. "I figured you would be."

"Yeah, well, the years haven't taken their toll on you, either," Sam said as he glanced her over with an appreciative eye.

"Mm. I try to work out as much as I can. It's pretty tough, though, trying to maintain both a business and a figure."

Pat Marley's five-foot six-inch frame did belie her forty-five years. She looked healthy and vibrant with a tanned complexion from jogging under the hot Washington sun. Her blonde hair, worn fashionably in a shoulder length bob with bangs cut just at the eyebrow level, had only the faintest trace of gray blending into it. The only other sign of her nearing middle age was revealed upon close inspection of her green eyes, where crows' feet lines were just beginning their permanent etchings into an otherwise smooth face.

"So, you've got your own business now." Sam said. "This is great! It looks like it's doing well."

"Yeah. We're okay. It's been a hard climb, but we're turning a dollar or two."

"What kind of system are you using?"

Pat started into an explanation of her computer system but was cut short by Dave gesturing with his hands. "Hold it. Hold it. Time out, you two. How about remembering there are illiterates present. Can we just talk English and you two can go over this some other time?"

Sam and Pat both looked at Dave and smiled. "Oh, Sorry," Sam apologized. Remembering he hadn't introduced his friends, yet, he said, "Pat, this is Dave Cooper, my best friend; and Kelly Gracie, my new, other, fast-becoming, best friend. Dave and Kelly: Pat Marley, another, long lost, best friend."

The three exchanged pleasantries, then Pat asked of Sam, "So-o...you're going back with the Pentagon?"

"Aw, for a while. I'm being paid as a consultant. I call the tune and they do the dance, this time, though. Remember Tom Snyder...worked for a while with me there? They offered it to him but he turned it down. Said I was the only one who could go in and put their little puzzle together so they had no choice—they had to come to me. I'm only staying long enough to put a team together and train them on what I design and then I'm out of there."

"Well, you set the whole project up originally. You should be in on the revision, if that's what they're doing."

"Some of its revision and modification of the existing program, but a lot of it is new. You know I can't tell you anything about it, though. But I don't think it'll take more than eighteen months, or so, then I'm gone!"

Pat looked at Dave and Kelly and, shaking her head, said, "That Sam Baker; never in one place long enough to wear out a pair of shoes."

Sam just shrugged.

"Well, c'mon. I'll show you a terminal you can work at," Pat said, leading them out of her office. They followed her to the glass doors of the main computer room and Sam held the door open for them to enter. There were six workstations within the large room, each separated by steel and glass partitions to form small offices. As Pat led the three to one of the spaces, the five employees present glanced up from their stations to watch the small party file through.

"Here, Sam," Pat said to him, "You can work in here. We're a bit cramped for room, I'm afraid. Business is growing faster than we ever imagined it would and we have to keep improvising for space as we add more people. I've got some calls to make but Larry, there, can help if you need anything." The man in the next cubicle, having easily overheard the conversation through the glass window, nodded and waved in greeting and in confirmation of what Pat had said.

Sam returned the nod respectfully, saying, "Thanks. I should be all right, though." Pat started to leave, then paused and asked in afterthought, "Uh, this is legal, right?"

"C'mon, Pat," Sam said as if surprised by her question.

"Just checking. Just checking," she said as she walked off, wiggling her fingers "goodbye."

Sam took a seat at the computer and began to press keys as Dave and Kelly watched over his shoulder. Code numbers began to be displayed on the screen and, as Sam continued typing, others appeared, accompanied by flashing security warnings. Sam continued to type access codes in number series and these would be followed by more numbers and letters with further security warnings.

"Jeez," Dave commented, staring intrigued at the procedure and knowing that what he was viewing was entry into highly classified government information.

Kelly, too, was watching in amazement as Sam negotiated the maze of entry into the classified files. "How do you know all the right numbers and letters to hit?" she asked, for the screen was displaying a scrambled mix of numbers and letters.

Sam looked up at her with a rather clever smile. "I devised it."

"Oh," she said meekly, and she and Dave exchanged facial expressions behind Sam's back to imply that it should have been obvious to them.

"But, of course," Dave said, feigning an attitude of haughtiness.

"Stop that, you two," Sam said. "This is what I do. And I'm not half bad at it, either." Then, typing another series of words and numbers, he said. "Okay. Now all I have to do…is…bring up…your file…Ha! Here we go."

While Sam worked at the keyboard Kelly and Dave grew bored and uninterested and began to gaze around the room. In just a few minutes Sam rolled back in the chair and stood, saying, "Okay. Now all we do is wait for the printer to spit it all out for us. Let's grab a cup of coffee in Pat's office."

"Sounds good," Dave said as he and Kelly followed their friend to the outer offices.

Pat poured them coffee into Styrofoam cups as she asked Sam what he thought of the operations of her business.

"I think it's great. You've done well for yourself. You picked some good hardware for the job and your software seems adaptive to your requirements. You could use some more room, though. You're doing a lot of medical billings?"

"Yeah. That's my mainstay. I do some municipal tax roles and some sewage and garbage billing but they're bid so close it's more just coffee and beans. Medicine is my real steak. I've got a bunch of doctors and one of the big hospitals in Baltimore. I just picked up a hospital in Richmond, so I'll be adding some more staff. It's really fun. A lot of work, but a lot of fun."

Sam was delighted to hear that his old friend was doing so well. They chatted for some while until an inner-office phone call interrupted them to inform Pat that her guests' material had finished running and was being sent forward to her office. When she hung up, she told Sam the data was on its way.

"Great," he replied and took a last sip of his coffee just as the man named Larry appeared in the doorway with a small cardboard box of papers and some discs. He handed the bundle to Sam who politely thanked the man.

"You're Sam Baker, aren't you?" the man asked as he handed the material to Sam.

"Yeah. Why? Do we know each other?"

"No. Not really," the man replied. "I met you at a conference, once, a long time ago. You gave a presentation on a new data base you'd helped develop for IBM. It wasn't too long after that they did an article on you in 'Time' and 'Newsweek', and practically every other major magazine."

Sam blushed at hearing this. "That was a long time ago."

The man extended his hand and Sam grasped it cordially. "Hell, there's hardly a year goes by we don't read something about you in one of the trade journals. I'm very pleased to meet you."

Sam looked over at Pat who had come around the desk to stand near him. "Did you pay him to say this?"

"No," she laughed. "You can run, but you can't hide."

"I guess not," Sam muttered. "Well, don't believe everything you read. It's mostly hype," he said to the man. "They pick on me just to liven up otherwise dull subject matter."

"Well, you do have an ingenious and inventive mind, Sam Baker," Pat told him.

"I'll second that," the man added. "I read your last paper on formulating collective interlibrary networking. Brilliant idea! I believe they've started instituting the plan among some university and public libraries."

Sam started to blush again and thanked the man for the compliment. When the man excused himself and left, Dave drew attention to the time and suggested they begin their trip back to Sharpsburg before rush hour traffic delayed them. Pat saw them to the receptionist's desk, extracting a promise from Sam to stay in touch. He thanked her for her help and took her hand in his. "You're a good woman, Pat. I'm glad we're friends," he said, and kissed her quickly on the lips. "I'm happy that your business is doing so well."

Pat squeezed his hand and again made him promise to stay in touch.

"I will," he said as they began to file through the door into the hallway. He walked backwards a few paces, waving goodbye as the heavy glass door slowly closed between them. When he turned to walk with his two friends down the hall toward the elevator, he noticed Kelly was giving him flattering glances. "What?" he asked as he pressed the 'down' button at the elevator door.

"Well, I had no idea I was in such esteemed company," she told him. "I mean, you did mention you were proficient in your field but, whoa, Sam, articles written about you; publishing papers..."

"Ah, don't listen to them," he said. "It's not that big of a deal. I'm no more knowledgeable than the next guy."

"Ha!" Dave quipped as they stepped into the elevator for the ride down.

Sam shot him a glance. "Don't you start."

"I don't have to. I've known you a long time."

****

Interstate 70 east led them quickly out of the city and by 4:30 P.M. Kelly had parked the car in an available space several houses down from the Foundation's log house in Sharpsburg. Marylou greeted them in the front room with the news that she had signed on, as new members, and received donations from, no less than twenty members of a bus-load of senior citizens.

Their chartered bus had broken down just a few blocks away and, while a mechanic was replacing the water pump belt, a large group of the passengers had wandered the streets and chanced to stop in out of curiosity.

Then she relayed the sadder news that Dennis Woods had slipped into a deeper coma, since the head injuries were more serious than had first been diagnosed. Kelly became disturbed at hearing this. In the few months she'd been working with him she had grown to respect and admire Dennis for his tireless efforts and selfless devotion to the causes of the Foundation.

He had been one of its principal organizers and activists in a desire to maintain the historic integrity of the acreage in proximity to the Antietam battlefield. That his labors may very well have led to an attempt on his life, or, at the least, caused him severe injury, was upsetting to her. Her chin began to quiver as she lowered her eyes to the floor.

"Have you heard anything more from the police?" Dave asked. "Do they have any more information on the accident?"

"No. Not yet," Lou said. "At least they haven't called any of us to let us know."

"Well, we've got to be determined to win this thing," Sam said. "If these developers are in any way responsible, we can't let them get away with it."

Marylou looked puzzled. "Why? What do you mean?"

Remembering that Marylou was not aware of their suspicions Sam quickly brushed over his statement. "Oh, nothing, Lou. Just, uh, if it weren't for them, uh, being after the land, Dennis would be all right. There, um, there wouldn't be a need for this organization and he...he wouldn't have been traveling that road."

Lou cocked her head and showed him a look that indicated she wasn't certain she bought his explanation. For now, though, she dropped her inquiry and moved to her desk to retrieve some papers she'd typed for Kelly. Handing them to her for review Kelly thanked her, then sighed as she commented on having to do some more preparations for the evening's board meeting.

She was grateful when Lou said she'd stay awhile and help her. Kelly did thank, but released Sam and Dave from their offer, telling them it was only some typing and phone calls and that she and Lou could cover it all. She suggested that, as it was really their vacation and their interest, they should go and visit the battlefield again.

Both men consented to the idea, but only after Kelly again assured them their help was not presently needed. Dave first placed some phone calls north to inquire of the safe arrival and departure of Carol, then of any business he need consider at his auto parts stores. When he'd concluded his business the two set off for an early evening visit to the National Cemetery at the Antietam Battlefield.

****

Those who have been under fire are moved to a greater sadness for those of all wars who lie in the ground as casualties of the conflict. Life ends for all reasons and at all ages, and the dying is the same whether young or old, in peace or war, in bed or in the street. But, for those who have sipped the bitter wine that pours from the cup of war and have died so violently as in the clash of two armies, their deaths are grieved more tragically by those who have drunk from the same cup and lived.

So, it was for Dave and Sam as they walked reverently among the thousands of graves, pausing occasionally, to read some of the names on the headstones. Though both men had experienced more than their share of killing, carnage and the useless sacrifice of human life, they stood tearfully, awed and respectfully humbled at the sight of row upon row of brave men who had lain down their lives for the causes in which they so firmly believed.

It was with no little effort that the two men were finally able to turn away from the field of white markers. Neither had spoken a word this entire time. Now, as they left the cemetery walking through the entranceway, Sam looked at his friend and, his voice a mix of anger and frustration, said, "Dave, we can't let that ground fall into the hands of the developers. We can't! That ground was trampled on and fought over by two armies. I just can't believe soil that was once soaked with men's blood is going to have Valvoline and STP seeping down into it from leaky Jaguars and BMWs. It's just not fitting, man. It's not right! We've got to stop them, somehow."

Dave said nothing in reply. Knowing what Sam was feeling—for he, too, shared the same emotions—he patted Sam's shoulder several times in commiseration as the two men walked back to the car.

The drive back to the Foundation house was mopishly slow and the conversation, when there was any, quietly spoken. It wasn't until Sam looked upon Kelly's now serious but still beautiful face that his spirits began to lift. Finding his friend less morose, Dave, too, became a bit less burdened by his gloomy mood.

Kelly was seated behind her desk, a pen held crossways between her lips, typing furiously on an old electric typewriter. She paused when they entered the back-office area. "Well, how was your visit?" she asked with the pen clenched in her teeth and her hands poised over the keys.

"Oh...okay," Sam answered.

"Sad," Dave added.

Kelly ran a line of type across the paper then ripped it from the machine. She took the pen from her lips and wrote something on the bottom of the page, saying, "Stupid question, I guess. If you visit a graveyard, it sure isn't going to bring you up any." She stood from her chair and moved around to the stereo unit. "I'm finished," she said as she searched over the titles of a stack of cassette tapes. "What say we go get something to eat before the board meeting? I'm going to go change and brush my hair."

"Yeah. Sure," Sam said.

Dave nodded in agreement.

Kelly popped in a tape, turned the volume up and waited a minute. The speakers suddenly exploded with the opening guitar riff of *One Way Out* by the Allman Brothers. She turned around to see Dave and Sam both smile at this and begin to nod their heads in time with the music, their glum moods beginning to be displaced by the lively tempo. Dave soon began to play an air guitar, tapping his foot as he played the lead. Sam joined in on his own guitar, shouting, "Oh, yeah! The Allman Brothers!" and played along with Dave in accompaniment.

Kelly beamed at their change in spirits and began to dance her way over to Sam, taking his hand and leading him out from against the wall. They held hands as they danced and smiled widely while the speakers blasted at near full volume. Dave danced a jitterbug beside them, holding the hand of an imaginary partner.

"Oh, yeah!" Sam exclaimed. "Love these guys!"

"Whoa!" Dave hollered excitedly, now stopping to play his guitar while all three sang along with the group.

When the song ended Kelly laughed gaily and said she was going upstairs to change. As she started to leave, Bob Seger's *Feel Like a Number* began to explode into the room.

"Yeah!" Sam exclaimed as he and Dave began again to play their invisible guitars and undulate around the room as they performed. Kelly laughed and bounded up the steps.

Several other selections kept the two fellows rocking downstairs until, after several more songs, they glanced over to see Kelly standing on the stairs watching them. She was dressed in sandals, a long blue cotton skirt and white silk blouse with delicate embroidery. The gold locket hung at her bosom as the gold chain disappeared under her flowing blonde hair, now strategically combed to partially hide one eye, adding a mysteriously alluring appearance to the pretty woman.

Both men gave a slight wave of hello, continuing their singing and playing. Then, together, they suddenly stopped and looked at her again, their eyes widening and their mouths opening. She was stunning. Neither man spoke as the song continued on without them and Kelly stepped down the last few treads and moved past them to the stereo. Turning the volume down low she looked back at them and asked, "Ready to go, gentlemen?"

They both snapped out of their stare as Sam answered, "Uh, yeah. Sure." Then added,"Kelly, you look great!"

"Thank you," she replied to the compliment. Then, popping the tape from the machine she said, "Now that you two are out of your down—let's eat."

****

They had dinner at a small diner but a short drive from the house, returning just before eight o'clock to set up chairs in the front room as the board of directors began to arrive. The first to enter the house was Mitchel Page, a doctor from Frederick, Maryland and vice-president of the board. Kelly introduced him to Dave and Sam and they chatted briefly about Pennsylvania, the doctor informing them of the places he'd visited there. Then, excusing himself, he pulled Kelly aside to discuss the evening's agenda, leaving the two men to linger patiently for the arrival of the other members.

The screen door opened and drew all eyes to the figure that entered—a bespectacled, dark-haired man of about forty, sporting a full, neatly trimmed beard and wearing casual golf clothes and loafers with no socks. He smiled as he nodded hello to everyone, and Sam and Dave were just about to move across the room to introduce themselves when a second figure entered. Sam gave a nudge of his elbow to Dave's arm and whispered in a quick aside, "That's him. That's the lawyer fellow."

"Hm..." Dave said as he quickly studied the figure of the taller, suited man.

John Brandon followed behind the slighter figure and scanned the room to note those already present. He displayed a well-practiced smile and, when he made eye contact with Sam, his smile remained fixed but his eyes narrowed momentarily in a telling sign of displeasure. Sam started toward the two men with Dave following close behind.

"Well, John," Sam beamed and extended his hand in greeting. "It's so good to see you again."

"Yes...yes...eh, how are you?" the lawyer asked, taking Sam's hand to continue the amicable facade.

"Fine. Fine," Sam replied. "Did, uh, did you find the copy of the grant you misplaced?" Sam asked, still shaking the man's hand.

John pulled his hand away, uncomfortable with the extended greeting. "Actually, it was my secretary that had misplaced it when she filed away some other papers. This happens sometimes," he quickly informed Sam. "And, yes, I did find it. I had a chance to read it over and make a few corrections."

"Great! It's so fortunate you're able to lend your expertise to this group...and without monetary renumeration."

"Well, uh, we all feel it's a, uh, worthwhile endeavor, don't we?" John replied awkwardly. Both men were glaring at each other even as they wore beaming smiles.

"Oh, let me introduce my friend, Dave Cooper. Dave, John Brandon. John's the legal talent guiding the Foundation through the various judicial approaches available to stop the developers."

The two men shook hands and exchanged polite smiles.

The bespectacled man had stood silent as the introductions and greetings had been exchanged but, now, he interrupted to extend his hand in greeting. "Hi. Russ Feranto. I'm treasurer of the group."

"Yes. Hello," Sam greeted the man with a friendly handshake.

John Brandon interrupted this exchange by excusing himself to go across the room to where Kelly was reviewing some papers with Mitchel Page. Sam continued his greeting and exchange of pleasantries with the treasurer but glanced to see the attorney steal Kelly off to the partitioned office area.

Other members began to arrive and Dave and Sam introduced themselves to each in turn. There were short discussions on the unfortunate tragedies having occurred both to Dennis Woods and of the ransacking and theft at the Foundation house.

For some of the members they answered inquiries about where they were from or discussed shared concerns for the possible fate of not only the ground around Antietam battlefield, but for all unprotected historic sites whose plight could well fall to the developer's acquisition.

Sam managed to maneuver his way over to the wall that partitioned the two rooms and strained his ear to eavesdrop on the conversation between Kelly and her former suitor. There were now at least fourteen people cramped into the close quarters of the small front room as those who had dared to spill into the rear office area were quickly warded back by a signaled glare from John Brandon as he had words with the young lady.

Everyone on the board was aware of the two as being 'an item' and could sense from the air being transmitted in that back room there was now trouble in the relationship. Sam had difficulty hearing what was being said but could clearly discern there was an argument. Kelly's voice was raised to just above a harsh whisper and, though the others chose to try to avoid listening, Sam bent his ear closer to hear Kelly verbally assaulting the man.

She was scolding him for acting carelessly and irresponsibly in his charge of duties which then hampered her ability to perform her duties effectively for the Foundation. His "flagrant procrastination," she said and "lax attitude concerning work she was responsible for, had come so very close to discrediting her before the board and had been salvaged only through the timely appearance of, and help from, a stranger from the north." She further informed the man that she "no longer desired his company or affections," and that "their relationship would be limited to a professional association only.".

Sam was inwardly relieved to hear that his competition for the attentions of Kelly was now lessened by one. He listened to the harsh whispering in the next room and grinned widely while politely exchanging conversation with those in the room he'd not yet met, but who came forward to introduce themselves to him.

Mitchel Page looked a bit uneasy over what was transpiring in the next room and wiped his brow with a handkerchief as he chatted to different members of the board. He kept glancing over to the doorway of the office area, anxious for the two key members of the organization to finally emerge—as friends. His fear was that one or the other—or both—would resign from the organization at such a critical time. He was a little relieved when the two did appear from the next room.

They carried sullen expressions as they took seats on opposite sides of the room from each other and Mitchel cleared his throat uneasily as he brought the meeting to order.

The board formally approved and accepted the writing and composition of the grant request as originally worded. John Brandon had tried to amend some of the wording, volunteering to re-write it with the changes but, due to the time involved, the board thanked him but turned him down. Other business had filled the remainder of the evening, including an expression of sympathy over Dennis Woods' condition and worry over the possible consequences to the Foundation because of his being incapacitated.

His role was crucial to the success of the grant money and the Historic Antietam Foundation's entire effort because of his association with Buck Morganti of the McPherson Corporation. Dennis and Buck were old friends and Dennis had hoped to call on that friendship in influencing the decision of the McPherson Corporation to grant the necessary financial support. With Dennis too infirmed to lend his weight to the request there stood little chance of even being acknowledged by the McPherson Corporation's grantors as they were more than halfway into their budgeting year.

The evening was chasing eleven o'clock when the members adjourned the meeting and began to slowly depart. Some left rather hurriedly while others lingered to chat with those they came in contact with only at these monthly meetings.

Mitchel looked glum as he said goodbye to Kelly with the promise to send the material by special delivery in the morning. John Brandon had sat talking to some of the members and, as he saw Mitchel preparing to leave, he excused himself and called out, "Mitchel! Mitchel! Hold on. I'll walk out with you." He rose quickly from his chair and strode over to the man, nodding goodnight to Kelly in passing.

Kelly returned the nod but could not bring herself to say anything to the man as he put his arm around Mitchel's shoulder to hurry him out into the street. She stared out the doorway after them even as they disappeared into the night. She could utter only distracted replies to the remainder of the crowd as they filtered past her by twos and threes.

Dave and Sam stood leaning against the far wall watching her; waiting. When the screen door closed behind the last member to leave, Sam stood upright. "Well? Okay. Let's hear it?"

"What?" Kelly asked as she turned from the door to face him.

"What he said to you...in the other room. It was pretty obvious you were reading him the riot act."

"How did you know?"

"I eavesdropped, or tried to, anyway. I couldn't hear much. You guys talked too low. You're supposed to raise your voice when you argue."

"Says you."

"No. It's in some psych book. Really. I read that. It's better for your mental health, I think."

Kelly smiled, amused. "Well, then what's to tell?" she said, throwing her hands up and starting to walk away.

"Stop teasing. I'm interested in knowing how he took it. You were blasting him pretty well back there."

Dave chuckled, commenting, "He's probably going to file suit against you."

Kelly had begun to collapse the extra folding chairs but paused, now, to look at both men. "You know, it's funny. I did chastise him in there for all the delays and procrastinating. Then I said I didn't think we should see each other socially anymore...and he didn't seem to care. He apologized, but then he started in on you, saying I shouldn't trust you, that you could be a 'plant,' working for the developers. That really shook me. He has such hostility toward you."

"Mm...well, probably because you're hanging out with me, or me with you. You know what I mean."

"I do. But, no. That's not why. At least I don't think entirely. He should have wanted to talk more about it. Either he's very good at hiding his emotions or he never cared for my companionship as much as he led me to believe."

"I'd guess the former," Sam said quietly. "I don't know how he could have helped not falling for you."

Kelly smiled at hearing this and blushed as she looked at Sam. He squirmed uneasily and averted his eyes, embarrassed at having blurted that out. She swept her hair back from her face, using the act to break the awkwardness of the moment between them as neither was able to think how to further respond after Sam's comment. Then, continuing the work of folding the chairs to be put away, Kelly said, "You know, it struck me as rather odd the way John left with Mitchel. I hope he doesn't try to persuade him to make any changes in the proposal. The last thing we need is a further delay."

"Mm, yeah," Dave said as he glanced reflectively toward the door. "But it's out of your hands, now. It's up to Mitchel to do his job."

"My hands?" Kelly questioned. "Our hands, you mean. You two have become very involved and important players in this whole situation."

"Hm. Yeah. I guess you're right," Dave replied. "I hadn't really thought about it. We've just been sort of going along with things. It's kind of weird, isn't it? We figured this to be just another vacation to just another battlefield. It's turning out to be rather interesting, actually. Wait till Carol gets back and...Oh, jeez! Carol." Dave exclaimed as the mention of her name brought her back to mind. "She's probably at the motel by now. I'd better call her."

"Yeah," Sam agreed. "Tell her we're on our way. I'll help Kelly close up."

****

Carol had arrived at the motel only an hour before Dave's phone call and was exhausted from the ten hours of driving and all the bustling she'd done beforehand. She had unpacked the car of camping gear, repacked it with some extra clothes for both Dave and Sam and gathered up fresh clothes for the kids stay at their friend's house.

When she dropped Jeff and Sarah off, she stayed only long enough for a cup of herbal tea, over which she flipped her friend the house keys, asking her to stop by and pick up any necessities she might have overlooked for the kids in her haste. Carol gave her friend a hurried explanation about why the rush, thanked her with a big hug and was out the door in a flash. When she'd finally arrived at the motel in Hagerstown and was given a passkey by the night manager, she lay back on the bed and fell asleep, only to be awakened a short time later by Dave's phone call.

When the trio entered the motel room around midnight Carol was sleeping soundly under the covers. She failed to stir even when Dave leaned down to kiss her cheek before he and Sam went off into the other bedroom. As he turned to follow Sam, he said goodnight to Kelly, unwittingly adding, "Pleasant dreams." Then he paused at the doorway in remembrance, saying, "Um...and I do mean pleasant dreams."

Kelly smiled uneasily that he'd brought this to mind. "Thanks, Dave," she replied. "I hope so."

Chapter Nine

Dave Cooper let one eyelid drift open to see a haze of light filtering into the room. The fresh scent of brewing coffee began to permeate his nostrils and serve to awaken him further. As he slowly opened his other eye, he focused on the slender figure of his wife leaning in through the connecting doorway.

"Morning, sleepy heads," she greeted his slowly, widening blue lenses, though the cheerful greeting was meant to awaken both men so sound asleep in the double beds.

"Mmgh…hhgg…," came a murmur from the groggy bundle she recognized as her husband. A slight stirring from under the sheet in the next bed proved to her that Sam was still alive and slowly coming around.

"Rise and shine, boys. It's going to be a beautiful day outside. You don't want to miss it." Dave grumbled something incoherent and forced himself into a sit. He gave a wide yawn and looked over to see Sam slowly rise from his pillow on the other bed.

"We've got the coffee all ready. Do you guys feel like eating?"

Clearing his eyes to adjust to the morning light Sam groggily asked through a yawn, "Your wife's always this chipper in the morning, isn't she?"

Dave nodded and smiled to her.

"I remember…Barbara…just slept all the time," Sam said through another yawn. "I'd get up and go to classes, or work, and she'd still be asleep."

Dave swung his legs out over the side of the bed. "That's why you're not married anymore. It was who she slept with when you left that was your undoing."

"Yeah. I suppose," Sam shrugged.

Carol returned to the kitchen to allow the two men their accustomed morning bathroom rituals and, when each had completed what nature necessitated, they joined the girls at the table. Coffee was poured for the two men and they all chatted awhile, discussing Carol's trip, then filling her in on the board of director's meeting. When a second cup was poured for Sam, he said he wanted to discuss their plans for the day. "I'd like to see if we couldn't pay a visit to the Schiels' farm. Is that possible?" he asked Kelly.

The girl shrugged. "I don't know. Like I said, I don't really know them. Dennis and John, and some of the others, were always the ones who dealt with them. I could make a call and see if we can. Why? You think it'll do any good?"

Sam took a sip of coffee. When he set the cup down, he had a glassy, dreamy look in his eye. "I'm not sure," he said, seeming preoccupied in his thoughts. "Curiosity, maybe." Then he seemed to shake off his distraction to say, "Besides, I'd like to hear from their own lips why they set a deadline for the sale. Maybe see if something can be worked out. Who knows?"

"Well, I'm sure Dennis and John have tried. But, okay. I'll call out there and see. I guess it can't hurt anything, our visiting them."

"Yeah," Dave agreed. "I'd like to visit the farm, too."

"Okay. You make the call, Kelly," Sam told her. "We'll play it by ear from there." Then he looked at Kelly and asked quietly with concern," Did, uh, did you have any dreams last night?"

"No. Thank goodness. If I did, I don't remember it."

"No. Neither did I," Sam said. "I think we were all so tired we dropped off immediately. Too tired for ghostly visitation."

"Well," Carol said. "It was nice of them to let you guys get a good night's sleep."

Dave chuckled some, adding, "At least they're thoughtful ghosts." Then taking a last sip of coffee, he suggested they get ready for the day.

Sam and Carol cleaned up the few dishes that had been dirtied while Dave and Kelly took their turns in the bathrooms. When Dave returned to the kitchen, now fully dressed, he found Kelly ending a conversation with someone on the phone. As she set the receiver to its cradle, she gave Carol a nod of affirmation in answer to the anticipated expression she wore sitting across from her.

"Great!" Carol exclaimed and looked up at her husband as he came to stand beside her.

"What? What's great?" Dave asked.

"Just a minute," Kelly said as she held her finger up in a pausing gesture. She hollered out for Sam to join them and, as he popped his head in the doorway, still buckling his pants, she explained. "Okay. I've set it up. I talked to some woman, or girl, who's staying with the Schiels'. She said it would be all right to come out around eleven. She must be a nurse, or something, from the way she sounded. Anyway, I heard her ask Mrs. Schiels and she said "yes, she was expecting us." I don't know what that meant."

"Maybe she thinks we're someone else," Sam suggested, coming fully into the room, now. "In any case, that's fine, too. We'll jump on it."

"You bet we will," Kelly replied. "The woman warned us that the couple is old and we should have a lot of patience in talking to them. It sounds like the

193

old man is pretty well out of it but that the wife is still coherent most of the time. First, I want to pop into the office before we go. Can we do that?"

"Yeah," Dave said. "We should have plenty of time if we get rolling soon."

****

After leaving the macadam road, the half-mile lane rose gradually for a short distance, hiding from view the Schiels' house and out-buildings that would be visible once the driveway had been crested. Three hundred and ten years—four farming generations—of iron-banded wheels and horse hooves, and later, rubber-tired vehicles of all description had eroded the lane down to the hard bedrock pushed up in the last ice age.

The van moved slowly over the torturous, natural granite washboard, Dave, keeping an eye out for particularly nasty looking rocks that jutted up, here or there, or cavernous holes that would be found lying hidden between the vein-like ripples of stone. The other travelers sat passively taking the bumps as they watched out the side windows, their view limited to the sides of the deep cut through which they were driving.

To the left, the lane was bordered by an old split-rail fence, suffering long for needed repairs and replacement rails. Tightly strung woven wire with a taut, single strand of barbed wire at the top followed along on the right, behind which an occasional Holstein, grazing contentedly, would lift its head to follow the van with a disinterested eyeball.

A massive, reddish-brown rectangle began to appear on the right of the horizon as the van neared the crest of the slope, growing in size with the van's increasing elevation. As they crested the hill it became obvious that this was the rusting roof of a massive dairy barn, the corrugated tin sheets sagging toward the center to indicate sorely needed structural repairs. Dave halted the vehicle to allow everyone to adjust their senses to the dramatic change in the view before them.

Below, the countryside opened into a patchwork of fields and pastures, dotted occasionally by sections of woods. The ground sloped and rolled gently downward for a half mile, or so, then rose gradually again into the distance for another half mile, meeting steeper hills that would eventually border the Antietam battlefield. The view was spectacular and inspiring, intensified for having just emerged from the limited, tunnel-vision effect of the rough, sunken driveway.

At the end of the lane, now but a few hundred yards distant, stood the farm house and out-buildings, their now degenerated appearances belying the once meticulous attention and care shown to them in the past. The tin roofs atop the sheds were brown with rust and many panels had sprung free of their deteriorating fasteners to flap and rattle with the breeze.

Gaps were sorrowfully too common in the vertical hemlock siding, either blown off by the wind or forcibly ejected by the downward pressure of sagging timbers. Across from the barn, a large old coop—once home to as many as five hundred birds on two floors—listed ominously, persevering in the hot summer months for the first serious winter storm to end its crippled misery.

Beside the coop stood a five bay, three-sided tractor shed, empty now but for a few old worthless and worn implements that none but the scrap dealer would give a second look over. A few other pieces had been trailed and unhitched behind the shed. Scavenged for their pulleys, wheels and bearings, they were silently overgrown with weeds and small scrub trees.

Oddly, however, considering the exhausted, deteriorating condition of the buildings, and the questionable lack of the usual abundance of equipment necessary for full-scale agricultural activity, there was a full crop in the fields and black and white cattle milling about in the enclosed pasture.

Then, too, before the large sliding door leading out to the upper pasture from the ground floor of the barn sat a bright green manure spreader hitched to an enormous red marvel that was barely recognizable as a farm tractor. The modern-day mechanical wonder was long and sleek with an enclosed cab of tinted glass. The wheels, alone, eclipsed most passenger vehicles, and they were duals, lagged together, front and rear, to ensure traction, giving the impression that this was simply an engine on wheels. The fiberglass shrouding served solely as a cover for the powerful engine with little regard given for style or appearance.

There was nothing romantic about it, and its looks evidenced it was but another piece of equipment on the inventory of modern, large-scale agribusiness. No farmer could love that machine and tender it the same affection as their old Allis W.D. or Farmall M. This was a mechanical device, and not a second wife or close friend, and its sleekness stood in marked contrast to the surroundings of a homestead that had seen its past glory slide into the inevitable reclamation by time and nature.

The visitors sat quietly and surveyed the crumbling fabric of what once had been the carefully quilted center block in a patchwork of fields and pasture. The barn, coop, tractor shed and other out-buildings had all been erected in strategic proximity to the house, and to each other, with an eye given both to enhance the beauty of the setting and for efficiency of operations. The craggy lane continued down through and between the sheds to complete itself as a circular driveway, skirting the base of the long front porch on the house.

The stone and plank house were still sturdy and comfortable, though in desperate need of numerous minor repairs. It had been a splendid dwelling, not too many years ago, and could be so again were the right person to come along with hammer and paint brush. Expanded and remodeled by each descendant as the farm had prospered, it still displayed the colonial appearance of its original construction. The principal two-story structure was clothed in gray stone, gathered from the surrounding fields and stream beds. Massive chimneys on each end of the house protruded castle-like above the tin roof, their fires long snuffed in favor of a more efficient, less troublesome fuel oil furnace. Single story rooms, covered in six-inch, horizontal sheeting had later been added to each end, their flat, tar paper roofs bordered by a decorative wood railing. Six long, wooden steps led up to an expansive portico of stone and wood that ran the breadth of the original house.

The weathered mortar contrasted just slightly from that used on the house to prove it had been affixed by a later descendent. Flower gardens, losing in their struggling competition with weeds, sadly neglected boxwood hedges and other shrubbery, were abundantly planted in both the front and side yards with pathways of flat, white limestone leading to, and between, them.

As the travelers lamented the waning beauty of what once had been a carefully cultivated scenic splendor, their thoughts were disturbed by the sudden emergence of a small uni-loader carrying a bucket full of manure from below the barn and moving around to dump it into the green spreader. Dave took his foot off the brake and edged the van down the lane, pulling to a stop by the pasture fence near the machinery.

The four visitors exited the van and went over to the fence to hail the operator on his return run. When the uni-loader emerged again and dumped its load, the man seated at the controls caught sight of the waiting party. He turned the machine in their direction and powered it over to where they stood, killing the engine just short of the fence.

"Hi," Dave greeted the man." You, uh, you must be Mr. Schiels?" he asked, hesitantly. He had understood the farmer was a very old man while this fellow appeared to have not yet reached sixty.

The man chuckled, "No. No. I just rent the fields and barn off ol' Milward. I 'spect you'll find him up at the house on the front porch settin' 'n watchin' out. That's all he does these days. Ol' Milward hasn't set a plow in the ground in years; not since a stroke crippled him up pretty badly. It's Varina you'll be wantin' ta talk to. That's his wife. An old woman, but she still has her wits about her."

"Then, those are your cows out there?" Sam asked.

"Yeah. My place is over the hill aways. I run ma' heifers over here. Helps to keep the pasture down; the place lookin' nice. Say, you folks from the development company?" he asked, trying to mask a touch of malice in his voice.

"No. No way, man," Dave answered quickly. "We're, uh, we're with the Antietam Foundation. We're trying to save this place from development. I guess you don't care for the developers, either?"

The man leaned forward and spit a long stream of tobacco juice onto the ground beside the loader bucket, then sat back and eyed the foursome suspiciously. "I don't like you folks any, neither. Bad enough I might lose this ground to houses. Either that, or have to pay you folks some sky-high rent that I'll be lucky to break even on. Hell, you folks are already gittin' local ord'nances passed, tellin' us what we can and can't do with our own farms; where we kin build 'n how they gotta' look. It ain't right!"

Kelly tried to speak in defense of the local land use ordinances, beginning by telling the man that the conservation easements were actually a help to the property owner in the affected areas.

"Yeah, yeah, yeah. I've heard all that crap before," the man interrupted gruffly. "The bottom line is; if you folks get all them laws passed yer still tellin' me what I can and can't do with my land. My land!" And with that said, he fired up the machine, wheeled it quickly around, and drove back into the barn, leaving the four visitors looking at one another in surprise.

Dave finally shrugged. "Well, that's too bad he feels that way. He's only looking at one side of it." Then he turned to start for the house, the others following him up the slight grade of the barn bridge to where it joined the driveway, then walking the two hundred paces or so to the house.

When they reached the house and climbed the stairs to the porch, they were struck silent by the sight of a frail old man seated in a wheelchair off to the right. He sat slumped, with his head bowed, as if asleep, covered to his chest by a brown wool blanket. The visitors gathered on the porch and questioned each other through facial expressions as to whether or not they should disturb the old man who seemed to be sleeping so soundly.

They were relieved of having to decide by the timely appearance of a rather squat, plump woman in her late twenties who emerged from behind the screen door and joined them on the porch. "Are you the folks from that Foundation thingy that was comin' out from town?" she asked as she moved to the old man to check on him. As she adjusted his blanket, he momentarily opened his eyes and rolled his head to look at the girl, then closed them and bowed his head again.

"Why, yes we are," Kelly answered. "You must be the person I spoke to on the phone."

"Yeah. That's me. Wilma," she said, standing by the wheelchair. "I take care of 'em both. This here's Mr. Schiels; Milward. Ain't no good tryin' to talk to him, though. He's out of it. Has been for some time. Ain't 'cha, Pa?" she asked him, patting the man on the shoulder. There came no response from the slouched form in the chair.

"He's your father?" Kelly asked, confused that there had been no reported heirs in the Schiels' lineage.

"Ah-ha-ha! Sakes, no! I jist call 'im Pa cause he's so old. Milward's too hard to say. Can you imagine that; anyone callin' their kid 'Milward'? Sounds like 'mildew,' or somethin'."

"Uh...how old is he?" Dave asked, curious.

"Ninety-two, last month. Ain't worked in prob'ly twenty or more years. You kin see how run-down things is gettin' 'round here. Think he had a stroke, first, or maybe the ticker went first. I don't never remember. Anyway, these last few years the crazies have taken over. He can't do nuttin' on hizzone. I dress 'im 'n feed 'im; clean up after 'im. He's just like a little baby. Ain't 'cha, Pa?" she said, patting his shoulder again. Still no response came from the man.

"Alzheimers?" Kelly asked.

"Ou'nt know. S'pose it's called sumthin' like that. I jist call it the 'crazies'. Every now 'n then he'll come back to life and say some things that make sense. One day, he was in the parlor, 'n sittin' in front a the T.V.—I sit him there, sometimes. I don't think he even knows it's on, but jist in case. So, I goes out to make supper, 'n when I came back he 'uz clutchin' a letter in 'iz hand he'd wrote all by 'imself."

"Really? What'd it say?" Kelly asked.

"Oh, Ou'nt know. Gobbledegook. Somethin' 'bout bein' lost in a maze. Like there were all these doors 'n rooms in his head, 'n he couldn' find the one ta get out. He was sittin' there jist like this, but clutchin' that note. Weird, heh?"

"Aw-w. How sad," Carol replied.

The girl showed no emotional response but shrugged and moved toward the door to enter it. "C'mon in. I'll take yeh back ta Varina. She's in the kitchin. Bin' expectin' yeh."

They filed in behind the woman, entering first into a wide foyer. The rug-covered floor led off into what seemed to be a library or study on the right; a parlor or livingroom on the left. The couches and chairs in both rooms were all old and faded, and there appeared to be no collaboration of fashion or color. What did astonish the eye was the vast array of fine and valuable antiques that filled the rooms.

Tea tables, dropleaf tables, lamp stands, corner cupboards, gun cabinets, and more, were all crammed against the walls or placed throughout the rooms and hallway in no particular order or design.

On each piece sat a clutter of bric-a-brac and trinkets from more than three hundred years of accumulation. Oil lamps, candlestick holders, vases, clocks, figurines, pictures in intricate brass gilt frames, old books, ashtrays; every available surface contained items collected throughout the years, placed on display by the purchaser, and very little, if anything, had been taken away to storage to make room for the new.

The significant redeeming aspect of all this apparent clutter, however, was that, upon closer inspection, the keen eye realized the value of those items. The house was a treasure trove of valuable antiques worth a considerable amount of money.

The heavy-set girl had halted the group in the foyer to afford them an opportunity to gaze around. She did this often with new visitors, watching their faces for the astonished expressions always displayed when entering the house for the first time. She was not disappointed by these four. "Quite a mess, ain't it," she stated as she watched the eyes of the guests sweep the rooms to either side.

"Well...yes, it is," Carol said as she peered around. "But, my gawd, these are all valuable antiques."

"Eh, when yeh gotta' dust all these every week they ain't nothin' but old junk. These folks never threw nothin' out. It's been like this since I was a little girl. I grow'd up on the farm over the hill and nothin' never changed. You should see the attic! Hoo, boy, trunks jist full o' ol' stuff. There's dresses Varina's grandma wore when she was a little girl; all kinds o' stuff. Course, they sold all the stuff from the barn when they had the auction. Did real good on it all, too. Dealers out o' the cities all come with their trucks 'n vans—I still r'member it. Pretty exciting."

"Is that right?" Dave asked from where he stood by a cherry lamp table just inside the study. He was scanning the room through an old, tarnished brass monocular. "Man, this thing is neat!" he said as he came around and focused it on his wife's bosom. Carol bent slightly to bring her face into his scan and give him a telling look. He collapsed the scope and set it down. "When was that?" he asked. "The auction?"

"Eh, ou'nt know. Maybe fifteen years. They bin livin' off it ever since. That, 'n what the gov'rment gives 'em. It ain't much, though. Not enough to put 'em in a home. That's wher' the'r goin', ya' know."

"Oh, no. That's too bad," Kelly replied.

"Yeah, well. Milward's too helpless fer jist me 'n Varina to handle by ourselves. They'll be t'gether in the home. It ain't that far from here," she told them. Then she drew a long sigh, saying, "Yeah. Gonna miss this place. Be kinda sad to see houses 'n such all over here steada' the fields 'n barns. But, that's progress, I suppose."

"Not if we can help it," Kelly said abruptly.

"Well, that'd sure be fine. I remember this place when it was a real looker. Course, that was some time back. Place falls apart pretty fast when no one ain't usin' it."

Then came a frail but stern voice from down the hall. "Wilma! Wilma! What's the trouble?"

"No trouble. We're jist flappin' our gums," the girl hollered back. "Hold yer horses. We're comin'." Wilma harrumphed for the benefit of her audience, but it was done with an affectionate smile. "We better go back 'for Varina gets riled," she chuckled. She turned to lead the way down the hall, passing the staircase that led to the second floor, then through a swinging, solid birch door that accessed the kitchen.

The room they entered was half the size of the original first floor and it, too, served as a chronology of three centuries of accumulation. Against the center wall that divided the kitchen from the living room was a huge stone fireplace, the rusting ironwork attachments, cemented into the mortar, revealing its early use as the main source of cooking. Before it, on the hearthstone, and now blocking the fire box, sat a large iron woodstove that held an assortment of cooking utensils on its cast iron surface. Next to this stove sat a more modern, electric range, though its styling and design showed it to be of an early vintage.

The room was crowded with all manner of food preparation utensils long since abandoned but never retired from sight. A butter churn sat in one corner, half concealed by an old copper boiler which, itself, was filled to overflowing with old gadgets, long unused and, most likely, forgotten. An old wooden ice chest, its brass hardware tarnished to a dull brown, and its top covered with various sized colanders, stood beside an old, white, rounded refrigerator, amazingly still in use after so many years.

In the very center of the room was an immense table of solid red oak measuring six feet wide, twelve feet long and at least six inches thick, supported by six-inch diameter logs of white oak that served as legs. The surface of the table was slightly uneven from so many years of scrubbing and sanding and bore the scars of so many knives preparing countless meals for several generations of family and guests.

On the far side of the table, seated on one of the many mis-matched chairs, sat a frail, old woman. She had sheening white hair, neatly combed and flowing down over her shoulders, its color accented by her deep plum silk blouse. She was hunched over the table, studying an arrangement of cards, and she glanced up only once as the group filed into the kitchen and fanned out across from her. There was a long silence as the visitors gazed at the old woman and waited.

"She's readin' the cards," Wilma explained. "She's always readin' 'em. Sounds crazy, don't it? But she kin tell ya' a lot about yerselfs from them. She kin tell the future and the past...'n it's really true, too."

"How is my husband, Wilma?" the old woman spoke, though with her head still bowed.

"He's okay. I got 'im out on the porch for some sun. He likes that. These here are the folks you was expectin'."

Varina slowly raised her eyes to smile at the girl. "Thank you, Wilma," she said, her soft green eyes revealing a calmness within the aged form. She was alert and attentive and, though she showed many age lines around her eyes and ears, her cheeks and forehead were perceptibly smooth and flush with but few patches of brown pigments. As she turned her eyes upon the four visitors, she began to study each in turn, appraising them with a friendly, though somewhat complete thoroughness that made them feel she was reading their very thoughts and most intimate secrets.

And yet, there was a comfortable, trusting air to the elderly woman that put them at ease in her presence so that they didn't mind her knowing every detail of their beings, their every fear and passion. She was a gentle woman, exuding something of a mystical, almost spiritual aura, invisible to the eye but touched by the soul. Indeed, it was as though she coexisted simultaneously in the physical world and the ethereal; as if, were she to walk across a field under the warming rays of the morning sun her body would melt away with the slightest breeze, her atoms scattering to blend into nature, her spirit becoming part of the whole.

Varina first looked at Carol who stood to the left of her husband, and examined her with curious, penetrating eyes. Then she turned her gaze upon Dave, slowly running her eyes from his head to his toes, then upward again, fixing her gaze upon him in study. Her eyes then traveled to Kelly, standing between the two men.

When their eyes met, a sudden smile came upon the older woman's lips as if she satisfied herself with an important discovery. The smile then melted to one of sympathy, which Kelly thought a bit odd as Varina began to nod her head slightly in an apparent affirmative answer to herself. "Child," she said in greeting to her, and Kelly awkwardly, but politely, returned the greeting with a nod and a hesitant hello.

Varina moved her gaze to Sam, focusing on his eyes and staring long into them. The smile again appeared on the woman's face as she said to him, "What a fine-looking young man you are again."

"Pardon?" Sam asked, confused at the woman's comment.

Varina turned a card over from the deck and placed it in order in the formation before her.

"What's she doing?" Sam asked aloud for anyone to respond.

"It's the Tarot," Carol said and moved closer to the table. The others gathered around for a better look.

"Tarot cards?" Sam asked. Then to Varina; "Are you reading your fortune?"

"Shsh...Quiet, Sam," Carol hushed him. "Just watch and see. It's not her fortune. See the center card? It's a man's she's reading. That last card she laid out, the nine of wands, I believe it represents 'strength in opposition'."

"Meaning?"

"Meaning, whoever it is she's reading for would be a good guy to have on your side."

Varina looked up at Carol and, still with a smile on her thin, pale lips asked, "You know the cards?"

"Mm...some," Carol replied. "I mean, I used to play around with them when I was younger. There's a force there, but I could never tell clearly whether it was for good or evil so I gave it up. You have to be really 'hot' or 'cold' for spiritual dabblings, to feel if it's right or wrong for you. If you can't tell, it's best not to get involved with it."

The old woman flipped the next card over and set it down in its place, looking at Carol to interpret its meaning.

Carol studied the formation of the cards, trying to gather meaning from the cards exposed. "Hm...the two cups is a good sign. I know that one. There's a special woman either coming into this man's life...or she's already there. It's love. Passion."

"My mother taught me to read the cards," Varina told her as she looked at Carol's face. "And my mother learned from her mother."

"It must have been frowned on in the old days," Carol replied as she continued to gaze at the cards. "I wouldn't think folks back then would be too accepting of anything outside of Christianity."

"Oh, we've had our troubles with the neighbors. Mostly, folks just left us alone. We never did it openly, and them that knew usually didn't talk." She set out another card, laying it in position.

"The Oracle!" Carol exclaimed, her eyes brightening. "That's a good sign. It means 'good fortune will prevail. That, which this man deserves, will come to pass'. Am I right?"

"You are, my dear," Varina nodded. "Every time I search this man's future this card turns over."

"Wow. That's pretty amazing," Carol said. "He's a lucky man."

"It has nothing to do with luck, Carol," the woman stated flatly to her.

"You're right. I'm sorry. It's his karma. Whoever this fellow is, he has very good karma," she said, correcting herself. "How did you know my name, and, who's life are we reading?"

Varina didn't reply. She slowly, almost painfully, rose from her padded chair and made a motion with her hand for the visitors to stay and halted Sam as he'd started around the table to help her up. "Wait here," she said to them, more as a command than a request. She slowly made her way to a swinging door that exited into the right-wing addition.

When the door swung closed behind her, Kelly said, "This isn't what I'd expected we'd discuss."

"No. But it's kind of neat," Carol replied.

"Well, it's different. I mean, you don't usually expect to find some eighty-some-year-old woman sitting around reading Tarot cards," Kelly said.

"I don't remember you dabbling in cards," Dave quizzed his wife. "You've been involved with a lot of different things but I don't remember you doing cards."

"Oh, that was way back in college, before I met you. I hardly remember much of it. It's fascinating, really. But not everyone can do it. You have to be, I don't know, how would you say it, tuned to the spiritual frequency, I guess."

"Is it real?" Dave asked. "Does it really work?"

"Well, let's just say it was predicted I would fall in love with an ex-soldier, troubled and confused, who would eventually work in the field of automobiles. You tell me?'

"No kidding. Weird," Dave said.

They fell quickly silent when the door through which the old woman had exited slowly began to open inward. They saw first the boney, wrinkled left hand of Varina as she used it to push upon the door's edge. Clutched carefully between thumb and forefinger was a brownish tinted slip of paper.

As she emerged from behind the door they spied, grasped in her right hand, the hilt of a long saber, the scabbard's end dragging along the floor as though the weight of the weapon was a bit too much for that frail, old arm to carry. Coming to stand directly before Sam, she rested the scabbard tip on the floor and leaned the hilt toward him. Then, raising her eyes to look at him, she said in a matter-of-fact voice, even with a curious hint of relief behind it, "This belongs to you."

Sam was confused, but he reached out to take the sword from her and raised it up to examine it. The others drew close to inspect the beautiful armament. The pommel and hilt were cast in a precise ribbon over oak leaves design. The scabbard, engraved with delicate scrollwork with copper inlay was well preserved, though rather tarnished from the years.

As Sam held it up, grasping the hilt with his right hand and the scabbard in his left, he seemed prepared to ceremoniously unsheathe the instrument. He hesitated, however. His heart began to beat rapidly and his breathing shortened as the odd feeling came over him at once, as though to open the blade was to open Pandora's box—a gesture of opening himself to a knowledge that was better left concealed and forgotten in the very shadows of his mind.

Dave, unaware of his friend's uneasiness, interrupted by asking the woman, "What do you mean 'it belongs to him'? How could it?"

"It's beautiful," Kelly commented as she studied the intricate scrollwork on the scabbard.

Varina gave no reply but turned and moved to a comfortable, padded, bentwood rocker by the old woodstove in front of the hearth. With what seemed like agonizing discomfort she lowered herself into the chair, then glanced up to see the four visitors eyeing her with puzzled expressions.

She closed her eyes and appeared to be either praying or falling asleep as she released a long, deep sigh. No one moved, but they waited patiently to see if the old woman would stir or give some indication of her state of rest. An inquiring glance to Wilma was of no help, for the girl just smiled ignorantly and shrugged, saying, "Ou'nt know."

Varina opened her eyes and gazed out into the room. "There is a veil over the cards," she said. "They don't allow even me to understand all that is involved. I just know that you are the rightful owner. My family has held it for several generations, waiting for the heir to return for it." She closed her eyes again, either in weariness or in meditation, for she turned her right palm open and up, resting it on her right thigh, her left hand open, palm down on her left thigh, still clutching the age-worn, folded paper between her fingers.

The four guests glanced at one another, their eyes revealing the confusion and curiosity Varina had instilled in their minds. When they looked at Sam to elaborate on the old woman's explanation he shrugged and shook his head to show he knew no more than they.

"Kelly," Varina then spoke, though her eyelids remained closed. "Go to the table and turn over the next card. Say, 'This lies before him', and place it above the last card I set down."

Kelly winced and looked startled. Though they had never been introduced, old Varina knew her name and spoke with a voice of familiarity. She moved around the huge table to where Varina had been sitting when they first entered and, with some hesitancy, reached out and lifted the top card from the stack. She moved it over to its position in the arrangement as instructed; then, in a low, timid voice she repeated, "This lies before him." She gasped as she turned the card over. It was death.

Varina, still with her eyes closed, smiled and began too rock steadily and deliberately. "It is death, isn't it?"

"Y-Yes. It is," Kelly answered. Her hand trembled as she laid the card down and quickly drew her hand back.

"Don't be alarmed. That card comes up every time I do the reading," she explained calmly, almost with a satisfaction that the death card had been drawn.

Sam winced and became upset. "Wait a minute. Wait a minute. I'm getting the feeling here that this is my reading. Is this my reading? Is this my reading? What's going on, here? Am I going to die? I want to know why this seems to be my reading and, if it is, am I going to die?"

Dave tried to calm his friend, saying, "Hey, Sam. Cool down. You don't believe all this stuff anyway." Then, looking at Varina, he asked, "Are you reading Sam's future?"

Old Varina continued to rock rhythmically in the chair but now opened her eyes. "We're all going to die someday, Sam. I'm not entirely certain what that card means. Like I said, there's some sort of shroud, a cloudiness, over the reading. From the relationship of that card to the others around it, all I can see is that you're going to visit your death."

"Excuse me?" Sam asked, listening intently but now even more confused.

"I truly don't understand it, myself," Varina continued. "I've drawn that card in readings for people over the years and saw plain as day when they were going to pass on. Saw how it was going to happen. Sometimes, I could even see the day. But this...this has me stumped. I can only interpret that you're going to see how you will die, or that you will be in your grave but not be dead. I truly don't know," she said as she rocked back and forth with a puzzled look on her face. "I truly don't know." Then she closed her eyes to them as she continued her rhythmic rocking.

Kelly considered the group's original intent of this visit and was about to raise a question concerning the sale of the property. Mysteriously, Varina seemed to have anticipated her thoughts as, still with her eyes closed, she spoke again. "Old Milward is getting along in years, poor dear. Too old, too helpless to keep at home anymore. Gonna' put him and me in a home near the city. They can care for us, there. Yes-s...gonna' miss this old farm. All my kin are buried here abouts. Yes-s...gonna' miss this farm, all right."

"Then why sell it?" Kelly asked her. "I mean, why to the developers?"

"Got to, child. Need the money to stay in the home with my husband. They saw the ad and came right out. Didn't even argue price. I said I had to think it over a bit. The cards told me to hold off signing right away."

"The cards told you that? Did they tell you to sign with the developers even after the Foundation came out to talk to you?" Kelly asked.

"Oh, child, the cards show everyone's heart and know everything. I was to wait and talk to you folks, sign that letter I was given, and all. Even was let known the date it was to all end on. The cards know everyone's heart. Don't you worry none. Things always work out. Saw it right there on the table.

Everything has a reason...Everything has a time," she said, gently rocking in the padded chair.

Kelly still looked rather confused at all of this. She was amazed that this old woman relied on the draw of a card for her advice rather than making rational, logical decisions. It did not seem appropriate to her that the fate of this farm should be hinged on the order of a randomly shuffled deck of cards. The future use of this land could well determine the later fate of the remaining, surrounding lands, affecting the scenic beauty of the battlefield forever. Her mind reeled in its search for something pertinent to say that would not be offensive to Varina. She blinked her eyes in disbelief as she tried to accept with understanding the old woman's reliance on the cards.

Dave and Sam looked confused and even a bit irritated. Sam clutched the sword at his waist but, as yet, had not unsheathed it. "This is really weird," he murmured to Dave as they watched the old woman rocking in the chair.

"Everything has a reason," she repeated softly on hearing Sam's words. "Everything has a time."

Only Carol seemed calmly reflective of Varina's words and, from her position by the table, leaning over the cards for closer study, she asked, "Varina? May I call you Varina?"

"Certainly, child. Please do. I've no use for formalities. Those land people, what's their name, Marco, or some such, they were so formal. So polite. Saw right through 'em. Don't really like dealing with them at all."

"Varina," Carol continued. "What else do the cards tell you? I can't read them very well. I see something else here, about a woman, but I don't know what it means."

Varina smiled. "Oh, ho. Yes. The cards show a lot, but they won't tell all just yet. We'll have to wait to see what's meant. It's very unusual. More than that I can't see." Then she opened her eyes and looked at Kelly. Holding out the shaking hand that held the faded paper she said, "This is for you."

Surprised, Kelly came around the table to the outstretched hand. "Me?" she asked, taking the paper from between the two bony fingers. "Is this a gift, or something? What is it?"

Varina didn't explain. She sat back in the rocker and closed her eyes again but, now, Wilma came over to her and leaned down to her ear. "Missy. It's time for your medication," she said loudly, as if to wake the woman from sleep.

Varina opened her eyes in a start and looked crossly at her. "I'm old. But I'm not deaf! Quit sneaking up on me like that."

Wilma turned her head to the visitors and smiled as she helped the old woman up out of the chair. "Huh! D'y'ever see any'un this old with as much spunk? She fights me all 'a time."

The four just smiled politely. Then as Wilma started to walk the old woman toward the hallway door Carol asked, "Should, uh, should we be going?"

Wilma shrugged. "Yeah. Mebbe so. She gets kinda played out after takin' her medicine 'n all this excitement. I'm prob'ly gonna put 'er down for a spell. Ou'nt know, though. S'pose yeh kin hang r'round if yeh want."

"Well, thanks. But we really should be going," Dave replied.

"Suit yerselves," Wilma said as she leaned passed Varina to hold open the swinging door with one hand for the old woman to shuffle out.

Varina stopped in the doorway and looked around at the four. "When you come again...I'll tell you more," she said. Then she left, moving through the door and into the hall.

When the door had swung closed the four just stood and looked at one another with inquisitive faces. Then, slowly, smirks began to form on their lips. "Well, this has to be one of the oddest mornings I've ever spent," Sam said. "Did any of you understand her or is it just me being thick-headed?"

"Heh! You are thick-headed," Dave chortled. "But I have to admit, I'm baffled, too."

Sam raised the sword to inspect it again, holding it out before him. "Did you understand why she gave this to me? Not that I'm complaining, mind. What do you suppose she meant, 'it belongs to me'? I don't know of any ancestors I had in the Civil War."

"It's a cavalry sword," Dave said. "See the shape?"

"Yeah. I know," Sam replied. He grasped it firmly by hilt and scabbard to draw it forth and his eyes gleamed in excitement at having been given such a splendid gift, even if he hadn't a clue as to why. He paused, though, relaxing his grip but still holding in the excited breath he'd drawn in anticipation of unsheathing the blade. His head was cocked curiously.

"Sam?" Dave asked.

"Um...heh! Deja vu. Man! That's been happening a lot, lately."

"What? You holding a sword? Sam, you lived with a machete in your hand in Nam. You're probably putting the two together."

"Yeah...Maybe. I just...feel...Well, never mind," he said, then quickly drew the blade from the scabbard.

"Oh, my!" Carol exclaimed with an excited smile as they looked at the instrument.

"What a beaut!" Dave added.

"Wow. This must have been a general's sword," Sam said. "No officer of the line ever carried anything this fine, especially into battle. Look at the inlay! This is a real piece of art!"

"It's Northern," Dave said.

"Yeah. The channeling shows that. I guess we know my long, lost relative was a Yankee, anyway. I wonder who he was. Now I'm miffed."

Kelly gave a long, deep groan from behind them. The three had been so engrossed in inspecting the sword that they hadn't noticed she wasn't among them. They turned to see her standing on the other side of the table, teary-eyed, holding the fragile, age-worn paper that Varina had handed her. They immediately came up to the table. "What is it?" Carol asked. "Is it a letter?"

"Y...yes. And...such a sad one, too," she managed between sniffles. She held it out for Carol, who took it and began to examine it. Kelly took a seat in the padded, high-backed, cane chair that Varina had been sitting in and listened as Carol read the letter aloud:

*"In Camp, near Frederick
July 16, 1864*

My darling Katie,

We are encamped tonight along the Potomac and in good spirits for having driven the enemy back well away from the Capital. It is rumored we have found their position and shall attack as soon as our forces are gathered. Tomorrow we shall chase the rebels back into the valley—or, perhaps, rout them into surrender, as I believe we have superior forces for the task at hand, and fight for the greater cause.

All is quiet tonight and there have been no encounters with the enemy pickets. Most often in the evenings, they agree not to fire on one another, and the men exchange coffee and sugar, etc. that we have a plenty, for their tobaccos.

As this war drags on, I find it increasingly difficult to understand how we can convene so amicably in the evenings with men whose lives we so savagely try to end on the morrow. I am not apprehensive in performing my duties, and discharge them with unwavering convictions. But, oh, they are becoming arduous now that I have an even greater reason to desire this conflict to end———you.

Katie, there is so much I want to say to you and I tell myself inwardly that we shall have enough time when this war is over. My love for you grows so much stronger with each passing day that I realize I need all eternity to love you in. It's when I think of that—often sitting around the campfires—that I find our separation hardest to bear. Though again, I know it is not time that matters.

I still cannot believe how blessed I was by Providence for the few hours allowed by your side, two nights past. How thrilled I was at the opportunity to spend those stolen hours with you—how saddened we both were at our parting.

As I rode out from Washington next day, our regiment was posted in reserve and, seeing no action, I chanced to enjoy the day's ride, often gazing upward to the sky. It was one of those warm, blue, hazy days in which the sun seems far off and so absorbed in itself, that it neglects its oppressive heat while brightening the world below. Even as the regiment rode, my thoughts were of you and the days we spent riding together in early spring. Those were just such similar days and are easily remembered by me as such a joyous event.

Oh, but that we could be together oftener than we have been able. But again, I remind myself—there is time. There <u>will</u> be time. This war cannot last much longer.

Thomas and I reconnoitered our position today and were caused to ride over ground that had known some previous clash of arms. Thomas confided it disturbs him to fight on ground we've already fought over so desperately, and to see the graves of so many of our comrades and friends. Often, they are dug hastily and shallow, and, when washed out, reveal twisted bones in the ragged chards of blue or gray cloth. It does not bother me, so as I fear, I have grown callous to death and corpses. Should I chance to fall upon the field, I pray my remains are buried deep as not to become exposed to the curious, nor to the wild dogs that carry off and feast upon the rotting flesh and bones. You must promise that, should the final fate befall me, every effort will be made to retrieve my spent form for a proper Christian burial.

Katie, I grow so weary of this war. It seems I have been so long in service that that period I refer to as my youth is but a shaded memory of days more pleasantly lived. More pleasant only because of the absence of the agony and suffering I see so oft' around me; less pleasantly lived, though, as my life was void of the love I feel so desperately for you. Oh, what contrast there exists in my life between knowing the carnage and ravages of war—and the serenity and beauty of you.

My lovely Katie, nothing in this world can stir my spirit more than when, after enduring the monotony of camp, the long marches, the perils of battle and the long ride back to you, I see the comforting gaze of your beautiful blue eyes cast upon me in glimmering excitement as I enter your gate; the sweet melody of your angelic voice as you greet me; the tender embrace of your loving arms as you hold me. I live and yearn for such moments.

We shall not be long in our present task and, in but a few days, I should be with you for leave while the regiments are refitted and resupplied before heading south again.

"It, um, it wasn't signed," Carol said as she cleared her throat.

"It wasn't finished," Kelly added through cloudy eyes and stuffy nose. "For some reason...he never finished it...or sent it."

No one responded further. They stood in silence, thinking thoughts of the author's fate they hoped were not fact.

"We should go," Dave said, breaking their melancholy. "This has been a strange day already. Let's go get a beer and something to eat. We need a pick-me-up.

Sam raised a half-hearted smile and nodded. "I'm with you. Let's go find someplace cheerful."

Kelly refolded the letter and carefully tucked it into her purse. Sam returned the saber to its scabbard and led the way down the hall and out onto the front porch. Each gave a glance at the old man slouched in the wheel chair as he sat staring blankly out into the yard. Out of politeness, or as a matter of courtesy, both Sam and Dave gave a slight wave of goodbye to the catatonic form. The women cheerlessly moved past after a hurried glance and an awkward smile that went wholly unnoticed.

Once off the porch and headed toward the van parked out by the barn, Sam brightened some and moved off a few paces from the others. "I gotta' do this," he said. He raised the sword overhead and drew the blade from its sheath and began to twirl it above his head. "Yeah-h-h!" he yelled as the blade swooshed through the air. "Wow! This is great! I was born a century too late."

"Maybe," Carol remarked as she watched him. "And maybe not."

Sam paused the sword in mid-swirl as Carol's words had a sudden strange, haunting affect on him. With a reflective eye, he cocked his head and looked down at the shorter woman as he briefly tried to summon the feeling of ever having performed this action beyond his conscious memory. His gaze drifted slowly upward to the sword he held positioned overhead. Then he chuckled and drawled, "Naw-w-w," as he lowered the sword. "Now, if this were a cutlass, maybe..." he said and began to lunge and slash at the air before him. "I could see myself as a pirate... Avast, me laddies! Look lively, there! Way anchor!" Then he grabbed Kelly around the waist and pulled her close to him. "A ransom for this beauty or she walks the plank."

Dave shook his head, saying, "Sick. He's sick." Then to Sam, he said, "Sorry, ol' boy, you just won't make it as Errol Flynn."

Sam shrugged, then wiggled his eyebrows. "Okay. I'll take her to my cabin, instead. If we're not out in thirty minutes, way anchor and sail south to Bermuda."

Carol and Dave groaned over Sam's mimicry. "He's hopeless," Carol laughed.

Sam released Kelly, who gave him some rather queried looks as she straightened herself. "What an odd bunch I've taken up with these last few days. I better start getting out more...meeting some sane people."

"Sane people? Sane people?" Sam asked as he began to run his finger along the blade length. "My first wife used to call me insane." He looked at her with wide, bulging eyes and a contorted mouth. "Then I chopped her into little pieces, mwah-ha-ha-hah. She doesn't call me that...anymore."

"Ah!" Kelly shouted and began to run toward the van.

Sam was right behind, chasing her as she laughed and screamed playfully, running across the lawn and driveway to the barn bridge, then down the short slope and over to the van. She reached for the door handle but Sam caught her, grabbing his hand over hers and trapping her against the vehicle as they laughed together, winded and excited. She turned to him and leaned against his chest, laughing gaily as Sam put an arm around her waist to claim capture of her. Then, slowly, their laughter subsided as they both began to realize how close their unmindful frolicking had brought them. Sam's capturing arm relaxed to a caring embrace even as Kelly reached her hands to his shoulders. They exchanged lingering gazes to discern one another's emotions while their eyes telepathed that each enjoyed and desired the situation in which they had so easily and naturally now found themselves. Their gazes met and held, and Sam found himself drawing closer to her inviting lips.

"Well, if you two children are through...," Dave said as he approached the car with Carol.

Sam and Kelly parted quickly; their faces flushed by the momentary passions that had almost overwhelmed them.

"If they'd have seen you chasing her down the street like that in Sharpsburg they'd have arrested you," Dave told him, not having noticed what almost occurred between the two.

Kelly laughed and flashed a blushing glance at Sam. "I think he does belong in jail."

Sam raised an eyebrow to her. "Careful what you say to a man with a sword, me dear."

"Oh, jeez," Carol laughed. "Don't you two start again. C'mon. Let's go. I'm hungry."

Sam opened the sliding door for Kelly, then took a place beside her on the bench seat. As they buckled their seat belts they each stole a glance at the other. When their eyes met, they smiled warmly and allowed their stares to linger awhile before looking away. Neither spoke of it, but both were aware of the amorous feelings beginning to develop between them.

"We must stop at the Foundation house, first," Kelly said as Dave began the journey back over the treacherous lane. "I have to check in with Marylou."

Chapter Ten

Marylou Greggs greeted the four friends with a wide smile as they entered the front room of the Foundation house. She immediately bombarded them with questions, asking, "Well, how was it? Did you learn anything? What are they like? Did you get us any more time?"

Kelly answered as she led the way back to the office area. "Not really. All we seemed to have accomplished was to find out Varina Schiels is a kind old lady who reads Tarot cards and mystifies her guests by giving them odd gifts and speaking in riddles."

"Huh?" Lou asked, returning to her seat behind her desk.

"Oh, never mind. I'll explain it all to you later. We're all famished and are going to go eat. Have we been busy?"

"Ha! I feel like the Maytag repairman."

"Have you heard anything more on Dennis? How's he doing? Any changes?"

"Mm...he's out of coma but he can't talk yet. He's in a lot of pain so he's real heavily sedated."

"Aw-w, the poor guy. I wish there was more we could do. Have the police learned anything more?"

"No. Not yet. Still looking for a big white vehicle with a long scrape on its side. The tire marks proved it to be a car, anyway. They don't think it was a truck, so that narrows it some.

"Oh, by the way, some guy has been trying to get a hold of either you or, as he called him, 'that fellow from up north'! He's called twice now. I told him you probably wouldn't be back until late afternoon."

"Who is he?" Kelly asked.

"I don't know. He won't leave his name. Just said it was extremely important to talk with you."

"Well, we're going down to the Kozy Kitchen for a sandwich. If he calls again tell him we'll be back in an hour, or so."

****

The restaurant to which Kelly directed them was fairly typical of truck stops found all over America. Well lighted by long fluorescent fixtures, it had a tile floor, long counter, and booths lining the front wall looking out into the parking lot. Tables and chairs were available in the larger, carpeted dining room.

A multitude of various Elvis's on velvet paintings adorned the walls for sale at prices ranging from twenty-five dollars to two hundred-fifty. Carol nudged her husband as they passed a particularly large painting of "the King" in white sequined bell-bottoms with matching wide-lapeled shirt, microphone in hand, frozen for posterity under a narrow-beamed spotlight. "That would look good in our bedroom," she kidded.

"Mm, right next to the velvet stag you bought me for my birthday last year," Dave agreed.

To their astonishment—and embarrassment—a waitress, who'd been within hearing, smiled and, in a blend of both southern and hillbilly, drawled, "That is nice. Buht ma' fav'rits' the one ov'eh thahr." She pointed to an early likeness hanging on the opposite wall—a profile of Elvis's head and chest.

"It, uh, it does have its appeal," Carol replied.

Dave slapped her playfully on the rump to get her moving.

They took seats at a table in the dining room. Kelly sat beside Sam, facing the entrance to the room, and Dave and Carol sat across from them. They were not long into their meal when Kelly caught the eye of a man standing at the end of the counter. He had dark hair, was in his early forties, comfortably dressed in a light coat and tie, but sporting a not so neatly trimmed beard. He was eyeing the patrons with a selective gaze, skimming over most of those seated until his eyes contacted Kelly's.

He gave a slight squint through his glasses, as if to study her more closely, then began to approach their table. Kelly nudged Sam's elbow to alert him to the stranger. Sam looked up to see the dark-haired fellow drawing nearer and, seeing the man had a genuinely friendly face and a pleasant expression, smiled as the man paused before them.

"Excuse me," the fellow said, "I'm really sorry to interrupt your meal. Actually, it looks pretty tasty. How is it?"

"Mm. Not so bad," Sam replied. "You know; truck stop food. Institutional."

"Yeah. I travel a good bit. Have to eat out a lot when I'm on the road. You really savor finding a restaurant that does the little things...like make their own gravies, or serve real turkey instead of pre-packaged stuff. You know."

"Sure do," Sam said. "I eat out a lot myself." Then he looked at the man curiously. "Is there...something we can do for you, friend?"

"You can if you're the right people. And I've got you pegged as being them—or is it 'being they'? I never get that right. Anyway, you wouldn't be

Kelly Gracie from the Historic Antietam Foundation, would you?" he asked her.

"I might be. Why?"

"Then you must be that new fellow who just joined the group—the one from up north—Sam...Sam...Sam Somethingorother."

Sam smiled at the man's attempt to recall his last name, then said, "Oh, wait a minute, here. You must be the 'two calls' fellow. I guess you found us. Now what?"

The man beamed and stretched his hand in friendship. "Three calls. Then I stopped in. The young lady at the building—what's her name, Marylou? Charming person. Very cordial. Though she tried her best to have me fill out a membership card and practically picked my pockets clean for a donation. Well, she told me I might find you here. She said to look for the loveliest young woman sitting beside a...well...she called you a 'gorgeous hunk'. She got the woman part right, anyway."

Kelly blushed. Sam laughed and sat back, saying, "That's Marylou." Then, taking the man's hand in greeting he asked, "So, what's this in reference to?"

"I'm Tom Charles. I'm an architect for Marco Development Corporation. Actually, I guess now I'm 'the' architect and project director for the Antietam project Mr. Brody wants to build," Tom said amicably enough.

Sam unclasped and withdrew his hand and four friendly smiles faded to cold glares.

"Aw-w, don't do that," Tom pleaded. "See, I get that reaction all too often from people when I tell them that. Unless, of course, they're on the other side and are going to make a profit in some way. Think I'll start introducing myself as somebody else."

Dave showed a disdainful expression. "What'd you expect? We aren't particularly in the same camp."

"That's not necessarily true," Tom replied. He looked around for a chair and spied one directly behind him at an empty table. Drawing it around he asked, "May I?" as he had started to sit, then hesitated.

"If you must," Sam said.

"Thank you," Tom replied sitting at the end of the table. "Look, uh, I don't know quite where to begin with this except to say I understand your, uh, your wariness of me. But—but, but, let me explain something to you. I'm not as far removed from your concerns as you might expect. I've worked for James Brody for several years and, and, we've turned out some very beneficial enterprises that have helped revitalize communities and areas that were otherwise dead or decaying. Everything runs in cycles and, and, when manufacturing operations abandon entire city blocks there has to be something done to lure people back to a district that otherwise is falling apart."

"So, you build malls and shopping centers," Dave commented. "You buy the place for a song and replace hard industry with soft retail stores or housing."

"You say that with some condescension and—and, and I can see your point. I'm not praising it or defending it. I'm just saying that we do work in some way to provide jobs for people who might otherwise be left unemployed. There is something in that."

"So, what's your point?" Kelly asked coldly, still suspicious of the man.

"I don't know. I guess, maybe, I'm just trying to justify a little of my work. Most often I enjoy what I create. But, but, this Antietam project...well...I'm as much troubled by it as you people."

Sam shrugged. "So? Why don't you quit?"

"Ha!" Tom exclaimed. "Don't think I haven't thought about it. But, that's no solution. Somebody else would just take my place. No. I think I might be in a position to help you on this, though. But I need your help and cooperation as well."

"Okay. We're listening," Kelly said.

"I, uh, I didn't ask for this assignment. In fact, I was hoping not to have any part in it when it first came up. I knew there'd be controversy over it and I just didn't feel right about the whole thing. So, my first design was to have as little impact on the surrounding landscape as possible. He didn't buy it."

"Your boss, James Brody?"

"Right. He wants something prominent, pretentious; what, what I call 'gawdy', in fact. And that's what's going to happen unless we do something to stop it. Oh, this is getting way out of hand. I can't tell you the full scope of his intentions, but I will say this; we've got to check him now...or in ten years you won't recognize the entire valley. And—and, that's not to say the whole thing may not come about anyway. But at least maybe we can preserve one piece of it."

"Why?" Kelly asked. "What are his plans?"

"Well, like I said, I don't think I can reveal everything. But my suspicions are that he's becoming rather resolute in seeing his program realized. I think he's employing extra-legal means to accomplish it."

Sam sat forward. "Dirty tricks? Like rifling the files at our organization...or stealing computers and discs?"

"I heard about that. I'm afraid there may well be a connection," Tom said. He watched their expressions as they seemed to absorb and consider the seriousness of the information. "Um...and that's not all. You know your president of the group—what's his name, Dennis Something? His, uh, his accident may not have been an accident."

Sam squinted an eye suspiciously. "No?"

"No. I, uh, I overheard a conversation that leads me to think it was planned. I'm not certain how, or by whom, but I suspect foul play. There's this fellow that hangs around sometimes. I'm not sure who he is except that he runs some trucks out of Florida. He's kind of creepy-looking, you know; sort of a hard-looking character. If—if, if he were cast in a movie he'd easily fit in as the bad hombre, dressed in black, and all. He just always seems to be around when there's trouble. If there's trouble with the union, or a building James wants to buy, but can't get on his terms—this guy is always showing up. Heads get busted, buildings get burned..."

"People get run off the road," Sam interjected.

"Exactly. It's more than just coincidence. Actually, it's kind of scary."

"Hm. It was a big truck that tried to run over Kelly and me," Sam said.

"Really? I hadn't heard about that. I'm sorry. But, but, you see the seriousness of the situation, now. James Brody can be a vindictive, punishing person if he doesn't get his way. There's a real greedy, evil side to him that I think is growing worse every year."

"So, what are you saying?" Kelly asked angrily. "That we should give in and let him have the land?"

"No. Not at all. I think he should be stopped. I think he should be caught and his, uh, his behind thrown in jail. But! You've got to realize that to go up against him could be dangerous. This guy plays hard ball...and it's winner-take-all."

The four glanced at one another for any signs of reservations. In fact, each showed a determined, almost defiant, expression as they nodded in confirmation of their willingness to continue.

Sam looked at Tom. "Got any ideas?"

"Actually, I do. But I need your help to bring it about. Do any of you know anything about computers? How to run one; search through files and stuff?"

They all smirked and looked toward Sam. "Oh, I've had a little experience in that area."

"I'm, I'm not talking about just a home computer you put your monthly bills on, of course. This is big business. This machine is one of the latest designed. They only came on line with it a year, or so, ago. I mean, this thing does everything—including not burning the toast. If I can get us into it I'll need some help sorting things out."

"I'll, uh, I'll give it a try," Sam replied.

"Okay! Great! Now, here's the plan as I see it. The only way we can stop James Brody is to get something on him. He's so damned powerful—got lawyers up to here," Tom gestured. "He's got politicians falling all over themselves to spend weekends with him at one of his retreats. We can't take him on in court—we'd lose 'hands down'. The only way I see it is to find who he's been paying off; when, how and why."

"We get into his computer," Sam said.

"Exactly."

Sam sat back and began to think aloud. "Hm... If I have some codes, I could always use Pat's machine—she's a friend of mine," he added for Tom's information. "Trouble is, he's probably got a special file and accounts for his under-table funds. It could take too long to crack if he's hidden it well." Then he looked at Tom. "Can you get us into his system?"

"Well. That's what I thought we might need. Yeah. I can get us into the computer room, but I don't really know too many of the codes. The ones I do know probably aren't going to reveal too much."

"You may not need them. I may be able to do something there," Sam replied.

"Really? Are you a hacker?"

"Ha!" Sam laughed. "Of sorts."

Carol's mouth had been open as if to speak, and her eyes widened in astonishment as she kept looking from Tom to Sam. When they paused to let her speak, she blurted, "Can we have a reality check here, please? I feel like I'm in some kind of 'B' movie. You guys are talking about breaking into a building, pilfering somebody's records...and blackmailing him with the information obtained?"

Sam and Tom looked at each other with their heads cocked as they mentally weighed Carol's summarization. Then, simultaneously, they both smiled and nodded to her. "Yeah. That's basically it," Sam answered.

"Well, did it occur to either of you that that's illegal? We're no better than they are if we do this. And what if we get caught? Huh? Do you think they're going to say, 'Oh, that's okay. No harm done', and let us go?"

"No," Sam replied. "They'll probably throw our asses in jail for a while. We'll lose our jobs, our homes. We'll be street people, living out of garbage cans and begging with tin cups. 'Course, we could always hustle you girls for change, too."

Dave chuckled, "Eh...wouldn't get much."

Carol elbowed him at that. "This isn't some kind of joke, you know."

"No. No, it isn't," Tom said to her. "Look, we're not going to be breaking in. This isn't *Mission Impossible*. I can get you in very easily. And, and, if we're caught, I seriously doubt if they'll prosecute. I know too much already about the inner workings of the Man and his plans. The resultant publicity would ruin his whole scheme. At worst, I'd lose my job. But, but, that's okay. I'm going to leave anyway. I'd just like to take him down a notch or two before I do."

Carol studied this, turning it over in her mind.

"They're right, you know," Kelly added. "We've got only one recourse to block this project. I agree with Sam and Tom. I vote we go."

Carol looked at Kelly and blinked her eyes, bewildered. She was listening to her friends decide this as casually as though it were which movie they might like to see.

Tom read her anxiety and attempted to relieve some of her fears. "Trust me. It'll be okay. You won't get into any trouble."

"Trust you?" she remarked with no little indignation. "I don't even know you. You come in here and take a seat with us and start convincing us that the only way we can stop this project is to jeopardize our lives by breaking into a business and rifling computer files! And you say 'trust me'? Mister, for all we know you could be trying to draw us into a trap to discredit us and the Foundation. Have you guys thought of that? Maybe this guy is setting us up?"

Tom's face sagged after this verbal lashing and it was apparent his spirits followed along. He looked at the table and began to fidget with a napkin, folding it in half, pressing the crease with his finger, then folding it again, and so on, while he searched for an answer. There was a long silence between them all. The clanking of dishes and the chattering from the other patrons went unnoticed by Tom as he was aware of their eyes fixed intently on his face.

He raised his head to look at them and opened his mouth to speak, not even knowing what it was he would say. But when he saw their questioning faces and realized there was nothing convincing, he could say, he looked down again, dejected.

"You're right," he finally admitted with a shrug. "I don't have any way of proving to you I'm on your side. I can sit here all day and tell you till I'm blue in the face but I've got no convincing evidence other than my word...and—and, and I don't have the right to ask you to accept it without even knowing me. I guess I just had some wild idea that maybe I could enlist your help in what I know sounds pretty off-the-wall—especially to strangers. Look, uh, I'm really sorry for interrupting your meal and, um, for any inconvenience I might have caused. I'll get out of here and leave you be," he said, his eyes clearly showing regret. He then looked at them directly and purposefully. "Look, um, I've got to ask you one thing, though. A favor...for me, even though you don't know me. Don't tell anyone we had this conversation. You're right in believing there could be spies among you. James Brody is just that kind of man. I know him. You people go on and continue fighting him the way you have been. I've still got to try this my way and, oh, jeez, if he got wind of this before I could move...well...it, it could ruin everything. All I ask is you, please, don't even mention you met me. Not to anyone. I need about twenty-four hours. That's all I ask."

"Fine. You got it," Dave answered, sounding a bit sorrowful they'd turned down what had sounded like so adventurous and hopeful a scheme.

"Not so fast," Carol said. She leaned forward and crossed her forearms on the table. She looked at Tom's face, catching his glance to study his eyes more directly.

Tom was uncomfortable under her scrutiny but allowed her to stare at him. "So, so what do you see?" he asked, interested in her resulting observations. Under her gaze he blushed some, and a slight, embarrassed smile formed on his lips.

Carol cocked her head studiously. "I think..." she began slowly, a smile forming on her own lips, "I see...either one helluva good salesman and liar...or a truly intentioned heart with a concerned soul."

"Which one do you believe?" he asked, a glimmer of hope returning to his eye.

Carol nodded agreeably. "Okay, Mr. Tom. We'll throw in with you. You and your wild scheme to get us a sure ticket into the state pen."

"Great!" Tom exclaimed. "You don't know how ecstatic that makes me feel. Eh-h...besides, I'm sure you girls both look lovely in stripes," he laughed. The two women just frowned at him. "Really, though, I'm the only one who stands to lose anything. I really don't believe anything could happen to you four."

"Mm," Kelly sighed. "I just hope it doesn't reflect back on the Foundation. I mean, should we be caught, it could topple the entire group."

"Maybe," Tom replied. "But, of course, we'll claim we were acting solely on our own and without the knowledge or consent of the Foundation. Besides, I don't look for any trouble. I think we'll be all right."

"So, you've got a plan, Tom?" Dave asked, leaning forward in his chair. He was obviously eager and excited, the passions stirring within him over the prospect of involving himself in a situation otherwise extraordinary to his life. Astronauts, race car drivers, bungee jumpers, parachutists, jewel thieves—anyone about to experience the exhilaration of an event in which they have some measure of control but with which there is an element of danger attached—have felt these same passions. It had been years since Dave was motivated by such emotions. His training at OCS, the plane ride to Vietnam, helicopter rides into hot landing zones—all of it; one long, stimulating, roller coaster of emotional fervor. Civilian life had offered him little opportunity for such hair-raising escapades, especially in the auto parts business. For Sam this held true, as well, as the computer business offers even less dangers or physical excitements. And so, with a measure of bridled enthusiasm, Sam and Dave sat forward to scheme with Tom, the breaking and entering into the Marco Development Corporation office building.

The women, for their part, were outwardly placid, adding their advice, calmly discussing their roles and trusting to the men—who spoke with such bold confidence—that no harm would come to them.

When the basics of the plan had been laid, Kelly interrupted to suggest they needed to return to the Foundation house. Marylou was due to leave and Kelly was to take her place.

"Mm...I don't know," Tom replied. "It wouldn't do for me to be seen going in there."

"There's a back door," she informed him. You could park around the back and enter and leave through the backyards."

Tom consented, agreeing to meet them there to finish the details of the scheme.

****

There was a long silence among them on the drive back to Sharpsburg as their thoughts were centered on the illegal venture in which they had agreed to participate. After a few long, quiet miles Kelly asked, "Are we really going to do this?"

Sam just nodded and murmured, "M-hm."

"You guys aren't worried or scared?"

"Mm...some, maybe," he answered. "But I think it's like Tom says; we're kind of against the wall on this. We really don't have much of an alternative. It'll work out. Even if we do get caught probably the worst that can happen is a slap on the wrist. And if the police say they suspect foul play in Dennis's accident it'll work in our favor. We'll threaten to 'finger-point' and Marco will let us go if we don't tell on them. They couldn't stand the adverse publicity. We'd just trade 'them catching us' for 'us catching them'."

"We hope," Dave muttered under his breath. Carol glanced at him uneasily.

"Well, okay. If you guys aren't scared, then I won't be," Kelly said.

"Oh, I never said I wasn't scared. I'm just not worried," Sam told her.

"Oh, that's comforting," she said, much chagrined.

Sam took her hand and pressed it warmly between his. "Hey. It'll be okay," he assured her. He kept her hand fitted in his for the few miles back to town.

****

Tom entered the back door of the Foundation house and was relieved to find only his four co-conspirators present. Marylou had been shuttled out the door rather hurriedly to avoid an awkward explanation of who Tom was and why he was entering so secretively through the rear entrance.

They quickly went to work finalizing their plans in careful detail as Tom drew some sketches of the interior of the office building to show them where to enter and where to position themselves. They then discussed what equipment would be needed and decided on their disguises.

"You really had this well thought out," Sam said to him. "How long have you been working on this?"

"Thank you. Only a day or so. But, it's so obvious and easy. I mean, no one will suspect anything unusual. People are always working late, there. We're in; we're out. The hardest part will be finding the right files. I don't think that'll be too easy."

"Leave that to me. I'll need to bring a friend along. The woman I spoke of earlier—Pat. She's very good," Sam explained.

"Well, if you're sure we need her. The fewer people involved, the better."

"She'll be a big help. I'll call her and set it up."

Dave then spoke up, asking, "You're sure about there being only one security guard?"

"Positive," Tom assured him. "And he doesn't really do much anyway. I'll have him diverted. There'll be no problem there." Tom pulled a business card from his wallet and scribbled an address on it. "Here. This is a watering hole where you can wait. When I think the time is getting close, I'll call you at that place. I'll ask for...hm...let's see...uh...how about Alexander Mundy?"

"Who?" Kelly asked.

"Alexander Mundy. He was a character Robert Wagner played in a TV series called *It Takes a Thief*. Ran in the sixties."

"I remember that," Dave chuckled. "I used to watch it all the time."

"Sounds appropriate," Sam said.

There was a noise at the front door as someone began to enter. Tom took a quick, careful peek around the corner, then ducked back. His eyes showed alarm as he scrambled to leave, saying, "Quick. Hide my card. I'll call you tomorrow night unless I think of something else we need." Then he shot out the back door leaving the four slightly bewildered.

Kelly rose to see who was entering, moving through the partition doorway to greet the visitor in the front room. "John!" she gasped, stunned at the unexpected appearance of the man with whom she'd so recently broken relations. "Who—what are you..."

"Kelly. I came to see you," he interrupted her. "Look. I know I've been a real jerk to you lately and I'm sorry for that. What with all the pressures at the office and all, well, things just haven't been going well for me. I've been working so hard on some big accounts and I've slighted you because of them. Things will be easing up on me soon and...and I want us to give it another try."

Sam, Dave and Carol, out of sight behind the partition wall and remaining very quiet, began to roll their eyes upon hearing him.

"But...but, John, I..."

"Kelly, I know it'll work between us. You and I have so much in common. Our efforts here at the Foundation are but a small sampling of what you and I can achieve together. Look how far we've come with it. And, though success may ultimately elude us in this instance, there will be other projects you and I can work on together. We can choose some social cause where we will make a difference, where our efforts won't be wasted."

"John, you're talking like we've lost already. You sound so defeatist."

"No, Kelly, realist. Look. We haven't a ghost of a chance against Marco. The grant money will probably not materialize and we haven't a prayer in court."

"Why won't the money come through? The people at the McPherson Corporation are sympathetic with our cause. They'll vote us the money."

"Kelly, half of them are out of the country!" John replied, his voice sounding with impatience.

"How do you know that?" she asked.

"Ne-never mind how I know. Oh, that's not why I came here. I came all the way out from Washington to see you. To win you back."

"To win me back? Win me back from what? From whom?"

"From...from that northern fellow. What's his name—Sam somethingorother."

"Well, you might have saved yourself a trip. Look. I'm not in love with Sam, or anyone else. He's a nice fellow and a concerned person. He has the same desire we all do to save whatever piece of history we can from the greedy clutches of money-grubbing developers. He's fun to be around and he can make me laugh—something, I might add, I did very little of with you. Not that you didn't show me some good times. But, John, there's something drastically lacking between us."

In the next room, Sam's smile and clever, mocking faces of John's appeal, drooped to one of perceived injury on hearing Kelly speak. These last few days with her had brought him a lift of spirits he hadn't felt in years. And now, listening to her explain to John that she viewed him only as a 'nice fellow' sobered him into questioning what he'd surely believed had been the beginnings of requited affections from Kelly—affections he had so purposefully and openly displayed for her.

Carol and Dave ceased their mimicking expressions and looked with sympathy at their friend.

"Well, Kelly," John replied. "If you aren't having a relationship with that man, come and join me for dinner. We'll go to any place you desire and have anything on the menu you wish."

"John, you just don't understand, do you? You don't want a girlfriend; you want a convenience. I look good on your arm. I'm a trappings. It's like your Corvette—it looks good around you. But, John, you can't even drive it properly…and I don't think you can treat me properly.

"Kelly…"

"John, I don't know anyone else that has an aquarium company come in everyday just to feed the fish. You don't even know what kind of fish you have except that they're expensive and it adds atmosphere to your townhouse. You love money, John. Prestige and money. Why or how you ever involved yourself with this organization is beyond my comprehension. I mean, it's great that you did. That's, at least, in your favor. But, John, you and I can never be. It wouldn't work. I'm sorry."

"It is that other guy. Isn't it? I'm telling you, Kelly. Don't trust him."

"It's not him! I told you, we're just friends. Go home, John. Go find some girl who wants the kind of life you can offer her—full of money and big houses and fancy cars. There are other girls out there that want that kind of life. It's not for me…not with you. I'm sorry."

No reply could be heard by the three listeners from behind the thinly paneled partition. There was the sound of the door opening, then closing, and Kelly reappeared through the doorway. "Whew! That guy. What a character. I thought I'd gotten him out of my life."

"Yeah. What a character," Sam repeated quietly. "Listen, I'm, uh, kind of tired and we have a long day ahead of us tomorrow. I think we should just head back, maybe watch some TV and get some sleep."

Sam was acting rather somber, but Kelly took him at his word, that he was just tired.

"Well, it's still a bit early. But, okay. I can close early. I doubt we'll be getting any tourists this late in the day. Let me gather some things and I'll be along," Kelly said. She started for the stairs but stopped abruptly and looked at the three. "Queer, wasn't it, how our friend Tom left so hurriedly."

"Well, Carol replied," he did say he didn't want anyone to see him here."

"Yes. I suppose that was it. Oh, well. You can go cool the car down. I'll be along. It'll be a relief to dive back into air conditioning again," Kelly said as she fanned her face with her hand.

As Kelly disappeared up the steps Sam turned with Carol and Dave to lead them out the door. When he caught their looks of sympathy for him, he just shrugged and continued on.

****

The trip back to the motel was rather quiet. No one spoke much, especially Sam. He sat beside Kelly on the bench seat but kept his eyes mostly downward or out the side window, initiating no conversation and answering only in short sentences when addressed.

Kelly failed to be observant of Sam's change in behavior. She, also, believed Carol and Dave must be as tired as Sam claimed to be, so she commented only occasionally of their plans for tomorrow. In response, she received only short replies from the couple in the front seats.

At the motel, Carol and Kelly stayed mostly in their rooms, taking turns in the shower, then curling up on the beds to read magazines. Sam and Dave, too, settled in, watching a baseball game on the sports channel in their room. Sam placed his call to Pat Marley, asking her to meet them at an appointed time at the address Tom had scribbled on the card. He told her only that he needed her to look at a computer with him and that it was very important. Pat had agreed, giving no real consideration to the lateness of the hour he'd requested. She'd worked with Sam before and knew his eccentricities. With that accomplished, Sam relaxed on the bed and picked up the saber to more thoroughly examine it. "Pretty nice piece of equipment," he said to Dave on the other bed.

Dave pulled himself from the TV and threw his legs over the edge of the bed to sit where he could look at the sword. "Yeah, it is. I still don't understand why she gave it to you."

"She seemed pretty certain I was to have it."

"Yeah. Who can figure? At least you got it. That's neat." Then Dave pointed to the engravings. "Somebody really crafted this sucker with care."

"Yeah," Sam replied, studying the pictures. "I wonder where they were. Here's a mill; this is a house, or something..." and as Sam pointed to the delicate etchings his heart began to flutter. He looked away.

"Sam?"

"Huh? Oh...whew! I'm okay. Just...just another, I don't know, weird feeling that crept up on me."

"Maybe you should join one of those vet groups when you get settled in at Pittsburgh. Talking about and sharing your experiences from over there can help, you know. It's not uncommon to have things surface after a number of years."

"No. No. It's not that. I can't put my finger on it, but I'm sure it's not Nam related. It's...different, somehow. It's not really a flashback. More like a weird kind of déjà vu. You know how, when we walk over a battlefield...and there's this feeling like the, um, the ghosts of all the dead are still around...watching us; like they're trying to communicate with us...to tell us not to forget them?"

"Yeah. Go on..."

"Well, it's sort of that feeling, only magnified considerably. Like...I'm here one minute, then my mind is suddenly tugged back to somewhere in the past."

"Maybe Carol's right," Dave suggested. "Maybe we do live many lives...and through some crack or wrinkle in the cosmos, you're carrying a faint memory of something that happened in one of those other lifetimes."

"Eh-h-h...I don't know if I buy all that reincarnation stuff. I don't reject the idea, but I don't really believe in it."

"Yeah, well, I just throw it out as one possibility."

Sam grinned. "Thank you. It's duly noted and filed." He raised the sword overhead and flailed it several times. Then lowered it and returned it to the scabbard, commenting on its well-designed balance. Then, setting it on the floor beside his bed he told Dave he was going to turn in.

"Aren't you going to say goodnight to the girls?"

"Goodnight to the girls," Sam muttered, pulling his sheet back and stripping to his shorts.

Dave watched his friend climb under the sheet and felt a genuine sympathy for him. "Sam, that cut, what Kelly said today, didn't it?"

Sam didn't respond for a while. He laid there thinking about it, then raised an eyebrow. "I suppose it did. I guess I read the signs wrong. It's been so long since I've really enjoyed the company of a woman—especially one so pretty. I guess I just mixed good friendship with something deeper. I was looking to let it happen; wanting it too much. I just got careless with my emotions."

"Well, she's an easy girl to fall for. She's got looks, talent, and a personality."

"Yeah, well...goodnight, Dave," Sam said, and rolled over to face the wall.

Dave went over to say goodnight to his wife and Kelly. The two women were under their sheets, propped against the headboards with stacked pillows, reading. They smiled up at him when he knocked and entered. "I came in to say goodnight," he said as he moved to the edge of Carol's bed.

"Is Sam in bed already?" Carol asked.

"Yeah. He's pretty tired. He said to say goodnight to you both. We've got a long day ahead of us. Don't stay up too late."

"No," Kelly replied. "I'm just going to finish this article and I'm done."

Carol closed her magazine and set it aside. "How 'bout a kiss, Loverboy?" she purred to her husband.

"Mm..." Dave responded and moved closer to sit now on the edge of the bed beside her. They hugged and exchanged a short kiss, but it was obvious from the momentary lingering in each other's arms that they were both desirous of a really long, wet 'smooch'. They controlled themselves, though, since Kelly was present, and Dave pulled back. He said goodnight, then turned to go.

When he was out of hearing distance Kelly smiled over to Carol. "You two are still really in love, aren't you?"

"M-hm. Why?" Carol asked, blushing slightly that their affection for each other was publicly visible, but proud of the fact nonetheless.

"Well...it's nice to see. So many people today have split up. I know more people that have divorced than have stayed married to their first spouse. It really leaves me with an anxious feeling about marriage. I mean, I've known a lot of men. Nice guys, most of them. Jerks, some of them. But nothing ever stirred within me enough to make me feel like I wanted to spend the rest of my life with any of them. I used to toy with the idea, picturing myself, say, ten years down the road with some guy. Twenty years. Old age—tied to the same fella. And every time I did, the idea was almost revolting. At least until I..." Kelly's voice trailed off, leaving the sentence unfinished. "It must be comforting to have 'Mister Right'?"

"It is," Carol said, smiling reflectively. "Oh, we have our fights. Nothing ever major, though. We work at our relationship. That's half the enjoyment of marriage. If you're not willing to compromise it won't work. It's a little scary, at first. You never really know a person till you've lived with them awhile. Even after so many years you're always learning something new about them. Have you given up on the idea of marriage?"

"Oh, no. I'm open to it. I suppose most everyone is."

"Well...you know, you might want to look a little closer at Sam Baker," Carol said.

Kelly laughed and blushed at this, but gave Carol a wink. She closed her magazine and reached over to turn off her bed lamp, giving no further reply.

****

Sam's breathing was labored, his heart burned and his head throbbed. He tried to focus on anything that would anchor the swirling, rushing, blend of green

and blue colors he knew to be the ground and sky. He was vaguely aware that he was lying on his back in a slight, hollowed depression, but more, he could not discern. As if to test he was not dreaming he willed his left hand to rise from where it rested on his chest. When it feebly came into view he saw that it, and his sleeve, were coated in blood.

He gazed at this curiously awhile, undisturbed by it, until the effort to hold his hand up became too strenuous and he let it drop to his chest, clutching at the burning sensation near his heart. He closed his eyes to clear the confusion in his mind and when he reopened them, he was pleased to find the scenery around him had ceased to swirl. Overhead, the sky was a peaceful, deep blue with two large, puffy clouds lingering lazily and low, unhurried in their passing.

Sam's head no longer throbbed and the pain in his chest was relieved. In fact, he felt no physical sensations at all, experiencing a complete relief for having shed the burden of his body as, oddly, his conscious mind had become detached. He was now floating—in the state of being—just outside of the body that lay on the ground, and was viewing it as if he were now in a hazy, cloudy dream.

Literally beside himself, he watched his right-hand travel to his neck and labor at retrieving something he had tucked away in his shirt. When he drew it forth, he saw it was a gold locket. His thumbnail pried the cover open and, as he raised it into view, he could barely discern the picture of a beautiful young girl in full-length gown with long, flowing hair. He tried to focus more clearly on the still form in the photograph, squinting, then blinking his eyes several times, but could not see her well.

He heard himself mumble something and assumed it was her name, but could not identify what he called her. Then, staring more intently and concentrating deliberately, he drew his mind closer to the locket, hoping to get a clearer view of the girl. As he floated nearer, the locket seemed to grow in size and dimensions until Sam now became a part of the photo, standing just inside the very edge of the oval frame, peering through a dense, gray mist.

He could barely make out the lithe figure of the girl as she seemed silhouetted in the void. "Katie!" he called out to her, though why he'd chosen that name he hadn't a clue. It had just blurted from his lips. "Katie!" he called again.

The girl seemed to respond to his calling, leaning to peer through the eerie mist, then moving to approach him. Coming closer, she halted at a point just beyond where he could see her face. "Sam? Is it you?" she exclaimed, clutching her bosom in excited surprise. "It is you! Sam!"

There was no uncertainty now. Sam knew that voice and the figure to which it belonged. "Kelly!" he hollered. "Kelly! My God! Yes! It's you!" he exclaimed. He tried to move through the gray mist to get to her but his legs felt weighted with lead and refused to cooperate. Every movement was an exertion as he tried, futilely, to gain even a footstep nearer and grasp her reaching hands. Then, in horror, he realized he had no body with which to make the journey to her. It was only through his consciousness that he was able to view her.

"Sam!" she called to him and reached to grasp at that which was not there to hold. "Sam-m-m..." she called again, her voice becoming more frantic, but beginning to fade even as the shadowy vision of her slowly began to pale.

"Katie!" he called out to her in the desperate hope his pleading voice might stop the form from disappearing completely. "Katie...," he called. But he became aware that it was not he that was calling out to the girl. It was his prone form, calling out to her from behind his floating consciousness. His mind slowly began to draw around for a curious look at his body, and the instant his concentration relaxed from the locket he found he was now beside the prostrate form.

Able, now, to better view the form from this position he saw he was dressed in the blue uniform of a federal officer. His left hand clutched at his chest. The hand, and the material beneath it were soaked to a deeper blue as it absorbed the crimson liquid.

Sam looked at the locket in the right hand, held just below the prone figure's chin. Set into the locket was a photograph of a lovely girl. Her light hair was gracefully gathered and braided high and behind on her head. Her gentle smile was sincere and inviting and her eyes gleamed with all the vitality and energy so prevalent in youthful passions that expect so much out of life and love.

Sam stared at the picture for some time, almost expecting the girl to speak to him. In a low murmur, to himself, he whispered, "Katie..." Or, maybe it came from the lips of his prone form lying there in labored breathing. He wasn't certain. With some apprehension his awareness began to travel along the prostrate form, moving over the strong but quivering chin; the dry lips that gasped for breath; the pale nose and cheeks; then to the eyes. They were wide, tearful and pleading—blue eyes that were full of sadness and desperation. In the instant Sam beheld them he gasped "Ah-h!" as he knew he was looking into his own spirit.

Sam wasn't certain if he had fainted or had awakened from a terrible dream. He was only aware of being on his back, straining his eyes to adjust to a confounding darkness. Never could he remember it being so black, nor ever feeling so strange, so chilled, so completely alone. He wasn't fearful of the darkness, but he was bothered by the confusion of not being able to determine where he was, whether he was on the ground or in a bed, inside a dwelling or out in the elements; whether he was even alive...or dead.

Then, strangely, he became aware of the faint, diminishing sounds of gunfire off in the distance and wondered if it had been resounding all along and he'd just not taken notice of it until now. Men were conferring only a few yards distant to him but he could not make out what they were saying. He wondered if the men were Northern soldiers...or perhaps Rebels, searching for prisoners.

In the cold, still air of the disorienting blackness his mind raced with the sudden panicked thought that those men might well be North Vietnamese Regulars, and he cringed in fear from the often-told rumors of their terrible prison camps and their harsh treatment of American officers. The voices were so muffled he could not tell to what army they belonged and he cursed the blinding darkness as, try as he might, he could not see anything.

As quickly as it had begun, the distant crackle of small arms fire ended and the voices fell silent, replaced by the sudden hailing of a familiar voice. Sam strained to hear the voice again, concentrating every effort to discern what the voice was calling.

"Sam! Sam! Are you all right? Wake up! You're dreaming!"

A blinding light painfully seared Sam's eyes as he abruptly opened them. He blinked repeatedly to adjust to the sudden transition from despairing darkness to the intense brilliance and streaming warmth of the light. Taking a moment to gather his senses Sam slowly surveyed the room. Good, he thought, he was back in the motel room. His eyes traveled around the room and he felt comforted in recognizing familiar objects; the television, his clothing bag—opened and disheveled as he had left it—old underwear hanging on the back of a chair...and Dave Cooper, sitting on the edge of the bed, looking worried.

"You okay?" Dave asked as Sam's eyes settled on him.

"Yeah...Yeah...I think so."

"You must have had one hell-of-a dream, man. You were shouting and thrashing all over the bed."

Sam raised to a sit on the bed. "Thank goodness. I dreamed I couldn't even move at all."

"Ha! You were moving, all right. What were you dreaming about?"

Sam thought a moment. He closed his eyes to allow the memories to filter in only long enough to find them uncomfortable. When he looked at Dave again, he said, "I, uh...I don't think I want to talk about it right now."

"Suit yourself," Dave said, swinging his legs back up onto the bed and reaching for the bed lamp. "But try to dream about more pleasant, quieter things. At least, then, the rest of us can get a good night's sleep."

"Yeah. I'll try to bear that in mind," Sam replied. He lay back on his pillow and watched the shadows on the window curtains affected by the occasional passing vehicle. He tried to decipher the strange experiences of the dream, but his mind refused to settle on any particular thought. Then, emotionally drained, and owing to the lateness of the hour, Sam pulled the sheet up over his chest, rolled onto his side and allowed sleep to claim him once more.

Chapter Eleven

May 13, 1863

Katie Wheatly returned from her early morning ride and led her horse to the stable behind the house. When she'd groomed and stalled the animal she entered the house through the rear door into a mud room off the kitchen. Taking a seat on the short bench to remove her boots she glanced in to see Aunt Lin peering into the cookstove to check on several baking loaves of bread.

"Smells almost done, Lin," she said, sniffing the air as though the scent could determine its degree of finish.

"Oh! Gracious, Child. I didn't hear you come in. Back already?"

"Mm, yes," Katie replied, slipping into her black, ankle-high, button shoes. "The army has all returned and the streets are so crowded with troops."

"Think I'll give them just a few minutes longer," Lin mumbled, closing the oven door. "Whew! It sure is hot. Wish I had a summer kitchen. Milrose always promised to build me one," she said as she wiped the perspiration from her brow. She turned around to face Katie who was still buttoning her shoes. "Have you heard any news of your father? With the army returning he should be coming around soon."

"You know Father. He'll have been the last to leave the field and the last out of camp. I chanced to see the latest casualty list. He wasn't on it, thank God. I wish I had news of Sandie, though. It's been weeks with no letter."

Lin showed a wide, clever grin. "Have you looked on the piano, Dear? You may find a surprise on it for you."

Katie stood quickly, her eyes beaming. "A letter? From Sandie?"

Lin nodded, barely able to contain her own excitement at seeing the girl's face alight. "It came just a while ago. The Reeger boy brought it over. It's posted the 9th so it's been only four days getting here. Fairly remarkable what with everyone so occupied with the wounded and with moving supplies."

Katie ran to the drawing room to find, just as Lin had said, a letter addressed to her from her beloved Sandie. She opened it hurriedly, sitting on the bench to read the opening lines. Before reading further she set the letter on the music holder and began to play. She had promised Sandie she would play something lively whenever she read his letters, hoping her cheerfulness of spirit and song would drift on the winds to wherever he might be and brighten his posture as well. Now, feeling exuberant to find he'd come through this last campaign unscathed, she began to play a lively tune by Johann Strauss, as it was to his music that she'd first felt the strong arms of the young captain about her.

May 9, 1863
In camp along the Potomac,

My Dearest Katie,

Please allow that this conflict often draws me to duties not so pleasant and, far too often, prevents me from attending to those I more pleasurably desire. I have been in the saddle for nearly a month and I've found no time in which to take pen to paper to inform you of my condition. Know that I am aware of how it concerns you so when I do not correspond during a particularly large engagement, but trust in the Lord that I am under His protection and am in no danger. When my duties are completed, I go directly to my quarters to write you. Unfortunately, due to the nature of this latest campaign, I could not remain in contact with you. I am sorry.

I fear this last campaign was not as successful as we and the Country might have desired. Weeks of unrelenting rainstorms prevented us from maneuvering as we had planned. When we did move, the enemy was not where we had thought it was. We split our column in the hope of creating greater destruction but managed to accomplish little, save burning a few mills and bridges.

Rations were sufficient, though for a short period our forces were scattered and we experienced some anxiety about the dwindling supplies.

Thomas is fine and sends his greetings to you. We heard from Gen'l. Stoneman himself that your father's brigade made a good showing for themselves at Chancellorsville. I do so hope there is a promotion in line for him. He well deserves it for his bravery and performances.

I've applied for liberty in hopes of coming to the city in a few days. I've been too long from seeing your beauteous smile and glimmering eyes. I've a present for you that I'm sure will please but you must have a small photograph taken of yourself before I present it to you. Promise to have this done by when I see you next.

Oh, Katie! There is not a day passes, nor an hour lapses, in which I do not think of you. Pitiable, it is, to see men in the camps whose names are not called for mail—for they have no loved ones anxious for their return. The emptiness shows on their faces as we others tear open, so eagerly, the notes received from those who await us. Then, it is we who are to be pitied, for we yearn so desperately and pine so longingly for this conflict to end and our obligations to our Country fulfilled that we might return home the sooner. Our longings are evidenced by our postures when the letters are read and our thoughts are turned to those we miss.

Can it be fair, my Darling, that you and I have been led to find one another during such circumstances as prevail at these times, only to be torn apart for such long durations? It is not for me to question the workings of the Almighty, yet, blessed as I am for having you brought into my life, there is the wonder of why the Light could not have chosen a more pleasant and less violent time to draw us together.

I must end, my Katie, as other duties call for my attention. Pray we might soon be together.

Yours,
Sandie

Katie stopped playing when she'd finished the letter. She smiled affectionately and closed her eyes, trying to imagine the handsome young man standing before her as he had done on his last leave three long months ago. He sipped coffee from a large mug while she played for him. His blue uniform was cleaned and pressed and the brass buttons sparkled in the morning sun's rays that streamed through the parlor window. He beamed with enthused appreciation of how fluidly and assuredly her fingers glided along the ivory keys. He was tall and proud...and she missed him so.

Dreamily, Katie opened her eyes. "Oh!" she gasped, startled to see a blue-black coat with brass buttons before her gaze. "Father!" she exclaimed in surprise, and stood to throw her arms around the man and kiss his cheek.

"Well. What a nice greeting," Miles said, embracing his daughter with one arm as his other hand held a leather satchel of papers. "I may go out and come in several more times if I may be greeted in like manner each time," he laughed.

"We were expecting you soon. A letter from Sandie just arrived, and now you're home! Oh, what a pleasant day this is becoming."

"How is the boy? What news does he write?"

Katie chortled, though with fondness. "He's homesick, as I imagine you all are. He says the campaign did not fare as well as they had hoped, but he is fine. He's applied for leave to come see us."

"Us?" Miles chuckled. "I dare say, I don't believe he's coming to visit with me or your aunt. And I'm certain he's not making the trip over a fondness for Milrose."

"Well, Father," Katie said, loosening the top buttons of the man's tunic, "You know he is fond of you. He always inquires of you in his letters."

"Yes. Yes. And I hold him in high regard, also. He's a brave and gallant lad and I enjoy his conversation very much. But it's you he's coming to visit. I'll wager he'd much prefer if none of us were even around so he wouldn't have to share you with us."

"Father! Sandie is much too gentlemanly to even entertain such thoughts and I'm surprised at you for even suggesting he would."

Miles laughed at the rise he'd stirred in his daughter. "Ho! Katie, I'm just teasing with you. You're so like your mother when you're flustered." With those words Miles Wheatly fell silent, as did Katie. The memory of the woman who was once such a vibrant, cheerful force in their lives, and then withered away in such a cruel and agonizing death, remained an open wound for them both. Neither looked at the other as they awkwardly fought to control their emotions. Miles set the leather satchel down and took Katie's hands in his. He looked at her with sensitive, concerned eyes as he'd decided it was time to discuss with her an important matter, he'd been long in delaying because of its very nature. "Katie," he said to her. "There is something we must talk about."

"Yes, Father?"

"Sit down, dear."

Katie sat on the piano bench; her hands still held by her father's as he stood before her.

"Katie, your friend Sandie is a soldier…"

"Of course he is."

"…And, like all soldiers, he's sometimes subject to some rather arduous and difficult situations…situations incomprehensible to those who have never experienced them." As he spoke, Miles could see that his daughter was uncertain of what it was he was trying to explain. But he continued. "Your mother's death was devastating to us both. I buried myself in my work…and you in your studies and music. We lost one another, for a time, when we lost her. You are all I have, now. I couldn't bear to lose you again; to see you fall into that melancholy. It would break my heart to see that happen to you again."

"But why should it, Father? I've conquered that. I know we were both affected by…by Mother's passing. But, I'm all right now. I still feel the pain of her absence, but it no longer overwhelms nor subjugates me."

"Oh, Katie. Don't you see? It's Sandie who has drawn you from that darkness; Sandie who has lifted your spirits and turned your lips to smile."

"I know that…and I thank the Lord every night for having brought him to me and pray He keeps him safe."

"But, Daughter, Sandie is a brave lad with such passion for the cause for which he fights. Passion enough to throw caution to the wind and too often tempt the fates to claim him."

"And you would have me know him otherwise? Could you think I would hold him in favor knowing he would act less than is his nature? Father, that is one of his attractions. It's not out of a childish recklessness that he acts and, quite probably, often places himself in jeopardy. It's his convictions and his resolve to do his absolute best that kindles the determination within him. I see that in him. It separates him from so many other young men whose quest is but promotion or profit. Father, he's not unlike yourself in many respects. Those are some of the very same characteristics that attracted Mother to you."

Miles Wheatly squeezed his daughter's hands in an affectionate gesture and nodded his agreement to all she had said. "You're right, dear. There is no argument to the contrary. I just need to be certain you've thought this through and are prepared for any possibilities…"

"…That Sandie could be…could fall on the field? I…try not to think of that. And even so, can anyone really prepare themselves for something such as that? Should they? Mother's passing taught me it cannot be so. There are no certainties. No one can know how they will react until the event occurs. I haven't a clue how I shall react should some harm befall my handsome captain, nor should like fate befall you. I love you both dearly and would be devastated in either instance. But, Father, what matters is that I love you both and am content with the two men in my life. I have you both, now, and all else shall come as a matter of course."

Miles nodded his understanding as he gazed at the girl. "You're grown so," he said to her. "You've matured into a fine young lady. I know most of your friends don't see and feel life as you do. That's your mother's wisdom coming out in you. It's…important that you realize these things we've talked of. I hope I haven't upset you. It's awkward for me…for us. Your mother was always your confidant."

Katie smiled warmly to her father, then looked away. "I say this all so boldly, now, knowing you both are well. I believe I'd die should anything tragic befall either of you."

Miles wanted to say more. He searched his mind for the appropriate words with which to respond but was presently interrupted by his sister.

"Miles! You're home!" she exclaimed.

The man bent to kiss his daughter's cheek, then turned to Lin. "Yes. I had to see to some things before I could come over. I can stay only a day or so. It did not go well for us down there."

"Yes. I know," Lin said sympathetically. "We've been reading about it in the papers."

"Well, we'll refit and have another go at it. There were too many mistakes made…too many mistakes…" he repeated, more to himself than to the ladies.

"I'll put some coffee on for you. I've just pulled some bread from the oven and the clover honey will taste wonderfully on it. Come and sit. We've so much news to catch up on."

****

Katie helped Aunt Lin finish the breakfast clean-up, then carried a cup of tea onto the porch where Miles sat, writing on a lap desk. The sun shone clear and brightly in a cloudless sky as the girl placed the cup on the railing for him.

"Did you sleep well last night, Father?"

"Mm...wonderfully!" he said continuing to write even as he answered her.

"What are you writing?"

"Hm?...Oh, just some reports. Routine. The army can't move without reports." He set his pen down and arched his back in a wide, long stretch, saying, "I don't know if anyone ever actually reads these things. But I submit them nonetheless."

A rider approached from down the street, his horse at an easy canter, and Miles and Katie watched him draw nearer over the tops of the bordering hedge. When he arrived, he dismounted and came through the gate to present himself to the general, bowing courteously to Katie, then exchanging salutes with the man. He handed over some dispatches he carried, then took his leave.

Miles sighed and began to open the sealed letters to brief them. "See what I mean, dear? More reports. These, from my colonels, which I must compile and report to my superiors. If they would just let us fight as we know how, and to hell with all this paper work."

Katie was about to seat herself on the top step when her eye caught sight of yet another rider coming forth. He, too, cantered his steed at an easy gate and Katie smiled whimsically. "Well, it appears you'll receive little privacy or rest today. Here is another approaching."

Miles again released a long, resigned sigh. Then he noticed his daughter had perked up. She peered attentively down the street with her vision fixed on the approaching horseman. The nearer the rider drew the more aroused Katie seemed to become. Miles glanced out at the blue-clad figure, keeping one eye curiously on his daughter.

"It's him!" she cried out. "It's Sandie!" she joyfully exclaimed as she ran to the gate and out to the street to greet him.

Miles watched the boy raise his hat in a wave of greeting and spur the horse on. Then his view became obstructed by the tall growing boxwoods.

Out in the street Katie waved excitedly until Sandie drew rein before her. He gazed down at her and tipped his hat politely, trying to deter, momentarily, the pressure that was so desperately prying an upward arc on his lips. "Pardon, Ma'am, but is this not the house I'm told gives comfort beyond rival even to the famed Mrs. B's."

Katie blushed at his ribald whimsy but took her cue to play along. "Well, brave Captain, a fine meal, refreshing bath and soft pillow are complimentary of this house. 'Other comforts', shall we say, are negotiable," she said in teasing voice, fluttering her eyes dramatically. Then she broke into a laugh for having played her role.

Barely able to restrain the broad grin he'd so far managed to stifle, Sandie dismounted, saying, "Well then, Ma'am, I'll take my lodgings within for the night."

Katie laced her fingers together in prayer fashion and propped her chin on them for support. She cast a sorrowful expression and sighed, "Alas. I am sorry, gallant Sir, but you see, we're all 'full up'. Haven't a room to spare. Now, we do have a fine barn out back...," she said, pointing toward the rear of the house.

"'Full up'?" Sandie exclaimed. He lunged to grab her hand and Katie gasped in surprise, though she laughed at his playfulness. "I'll give you 'full up', he decried as, laughing with her, he drew her against him.

Their playfulness ceased.

Katie seized him tightly, their embrace an opportunity for her to release so many months of frightful anxiety. "Oh, I've missed you," she said into his chest.

"And I, you," Sandie replied, holding her warmly. He stroked her hair as they stood this way for some while, allowing the silent joy of their reunion to penetrate through to their very souls.

When at last Katie relaxed the pressure of her embrace, she pulled back only slightly, afraid to release him completely. Sandie, likewise, was reluctant to disentangle himself from her arms.

"How long can you stay?" she asked, looking at him with eyes that begged to hear of an extended leave but fearful of knowing better.

"Only three days," he replied. "So, we must make the most of it."

"Oh-h...only three?" she sighed. But she recovered quickly, brightening at once to say, "And so we shall. We shan't waste a moment of it. Oh, but I'm forgetting myself. You must be tired after your journey. Would you like to rest awhile?"

"Perhaps later," the blond youth replied. He gazed at her long, studying her face, as though recalling it from memory while away from her had not served her real beauty judiciously. She was even more enchanting than he remembered. "I would savor a nice bath," he finally said. "I haven't been in a tub since...oh, dear, since last I was here."

"Come," she said, taking his hand and leading him through the gate. "Father's here. He arrived only yesterday."

"He's well, then?"

"Oh, yes. Quite. He'll be overjoyed to see you."

She led him up the pathway and to the porch where Miles stood at the top step to greet him. After an exchange of salutes Miles extended his hand to the boy.

"I see you're looking well, Lad."

"Thank you, Sir. I feel well. Suffered through a bout of dysentery a few weeks back. It made for a rather unpleasant ride through an otherwise beautiful Virginia countryside."

"Ah, yes. Stoneman's a bit uncomfortable himself over that whole affair."

"Will they be replacing him, do you know?" Sandie asked.

"I would suspect. The word is that the weather was against him. But the impression is he just wasn't the man to lead the operation. Hooker himself will go down over this last fiasco, and with good reasons."

Sandie shrugged. Being lower on the chain of command, he understood only that good men had been asked, once again, to go forth without question and be slaughtered for no real gain. Politics of the upper-echelon were not to be questioned by one as he.

Uncomfortable with this talk of soldiering, Katie excused herself to prepare a bath for the weary boy. When she was out of hearing the two men seated themselves on the porch step. Miles sprawled out comfortably, but Sandie, worn though he was from a long day and night ride from his camp far up the Potomac, sat properly, remembering himself. He was after all, in the presence of a man who was both a superior officer and Katie's father.

"Chancellorsville was a real debacle, Captain. Terrible," the general said reflectively. "A lot of good men were wasted because of poor commanding. This is between you and me, understand."

"Of course, Sir. You have my strict confidence."

"I thought so," Miles replied. "There will, of course, be changes made both higher up in command and in the lower ranks. A terrible number of vacancies have been created due to the casualties."

"Yes, as always after a battle. It's unfortunate, but it is a fact."

"As it is, Sandie," the man said, sitting up to look directly at the boy, "there is a vacancy on my staff that has opened. One of my aides was wounded rather severely and I fear his soldiering days are at end. There would be a major's rank accompanying the position."

Not slow in comprehending the suggestion laid before him by the older man, though feeling a bit awkward that his senior had even made the gesture, Sandie feigned a look of contemplation, as if actually considering the post. Then, after a short pause, he hesitantly said, "I, uh, I thank you for the offer. But, um…well…you see, I couldn't leave my men, nor the cavalry. I look for promotion within my own brigade. It can't be too much longer in coming."

Somewhat disappointed, Miles nodded in understanding. "It was just a suggestion. You're an intelligent young man who can be trusted. I need men on my staff who can think for themselves."

"Paper pushing is not my forté, General. I've a fancy for a spirited charge under the gun. I can't see myself shuffling papers while others are out on the line. I do thank you, though, for the offer."

"May I speak to your commanding officer? I could perhaps influence his decision on promotions."

Sandie bristled at this, the idea not auguring well with him. "I would appreciate if you did not, Sir. I'll not supersede the order of seniority because of who I know. I've known that to occur in certain instances and have seen the effect it has on those subordinates passed over. Again, thank you. The offer is quite generous and more than tempting. But I'd rather seek promotion through merit."

"Spoken well, Lad," Miles said. "I had not expected you to accept my offers, but I felt the need to afford you the opportunity, given the circumstances."

"Circumstances?"

Miles nodded back toward the house. "What with you courting my daughter, and all."

"Ah-h-h...I see," Sandie replied. "General Wheatly, Sir, I've been through hail storms of shot and shell. I've clashed with sabers and pistols in many heated contests and have come through them all with not so much as a torn coat sleeve. I could as easily fall from a step and break my neck, or come off a horse that stumbles in a hole. Granted, the possibilities are not as great as stopping a mini-ball, but still..."

"It's enough, my boy," Miles interrupted. "I get the message. I was only offering as a concerned father. I will not bring it up again. Just know that, should you ever change your mind, a position on my staff is available to you."

"Thank you, Sir. That's most generous."

Miles patted Sandie on the shoulder as a friendly gesture, then stood to stretch. "Well, I've been away from my correspondence long enough. If I can clear it away by this evening perhaps, I can spend a pleasant evening on the porch."

"Reports, Sir?"

"Endless."

"Well, I'll leave you, then. I'll help Katie draw my bath, and I've yet to say hello to your dear sister. She is here, isn't she?"

"Oh yes. I believe she's in preparing a goose for noon meal."

"Wonderful!" Sandie exclaimed. "With her chestnut stuffing, I hope?"

"Oh, yes. They are a match, as only Lin can prepare them."

Then, timidly, Sandie asked, "Uh...is, uh..."

"...Milrose at home?" Miles finished for him, guessing at the inquiry. "No. He's at his work. Won't be home until later."

Sandie gave a slight sigh of relief. The few times he'd had leave to visit at the Sheffield home—some of those stays lasting five or seven days—Milrose usually managed not to be present except at meal times. Often, he might spend hours in his study to avoid having to converse with Sandie. His only acknowledgement of the young man was to gesture with a nod, followed by some indistinguishable sound for hello or goodbye. Sandie was uncomfortable in the man's presence and had given up any pretense of friendliness for a reciprocating politeness.

"Milrose is an odd sort of fellow," Miles said to him. "He's a disgruntled person who, unfortunately, knows no other way. I've known him for years and still don't understand him. I don't know what he feels inside, except for his anger, nor what made him the way he is. Don't let him bother you, Sandie."

"Thank you, Sir. I'll try not. If you'll excuse me, then."

Miles was about to give him leave when he seemed abruptly to have a thought. "Ah! Wait," he said, turning to the leather satchel beside his chair. "I have something for you." He began to search through the deep pouch, telling Sandie, "I know that you generally abstain from liquors—but I also know there are times in the mess when a soldier desires a good stiff swallow...eh, for toasts and the like, of course." Miles produced a small silver flask and handed it to Sandie. "It is a gift from both Colonel Selkirk and myself. Colonel Selkirk provided the spirits—a remarkably smooth Scotch whiskey which any in the mess will appreciate. I was going to present this to you later but there may not be another opportunity when one of the ladies is not close by. Not that they would object, mind you. But these things are best kept from their eyes."

Sandie examined the small container and was slightly flushed as the older man awaited his reaction. Finally, Sandie looked at Miles. "Sir, I don't know what to say. It's very thoughtful of you and the Colonel. I'm...I'm a bit embarrassed. I hadn't expected it and am unprepared to return the generosity."

"No need, Lad. It is a gift. When I see my daughter smile and hear her laughter when you are near, my gift is paled next to what you have given me."

"Thank you, Sir. I..."

"Go on, Sandie," Miles interrupted. "See to your bath. There's nothing like relaxing in a tub after so many months on the march."

"Thank you, Sir. If you'll excuse me."

****

Sandie greeted Lin in the kitchen and visited with her awhile. Then, after helping to draw water for the tub he took a long, leisurely bath. Lin gathered his socks and pants and some other of his clothes to wash and mend. Katie saw to stabling his horse, then whisked his tunic and provided him with a fresh shirt of her father's.

When he'd dressed and reappeared at the kitchen doorway, he was shown a seat at the table where tea and biscuits were served him. Katie sat next to him, nibbling on a biscuit as the two talked a long hour. When at last Sandie asked if she'd complied with his request to have a small photograph taken of herself, Katie replied, "Oh, but Sandie, you're letter only just arrived yesterday. I had intended to accomplish that today."

"Good. Then I'll accompany you," he told her as he downed the last of his tea and stood. "Let's see to it now."

"What? Now? Sandie, I look a fright. My hair isn't properly brushed, and, Heavens! I shouldn't want those with whom I'm acquainted to see me out in this dress. I'd have to change."

Sandie smiled to her and took her hands. "Katie, you look beautiful. How could it be possible for you to look any more lovely? Were we to be off for an evening at the Stewart's, I couldn't imagine you looking finer."

"Sandie, I couldn't go like this. Goodness! I probably smell like a field hand. I must be properly attired."

Sandie leaned close to her and inhaled a long, deep breath. "Your fragrance is of lilacs on a spring morn. You need only slip into another dress, if you must. Hurry! I'm anxious for you to receive what I've brought you."

"Oh, very well. Since you're so insistent. I'll do it only because of my fondness for you. But if we meet anyone familiar, I'll expect you to lead us away from them directly."

"I will! I will!" he assured her. "Now, hurry and go. We'll want to be back for noon meal. My delight for your Aunt Lin's roast goose is closely matched to my affection for you."

"So, you compare me to a goose, do you?"

Sandie laughed, "Go on, I'll see to the buggy."

****

The streets of Washington were crowded with soldiers and civilians in all manner of conveyances. Buggies, ambulances, cannons limbered to their caissons, bulky supply wagons, people afoot and on horse or mule all jammed into and slowly filtering their way through the dusty avenues.

Sandie and Katie were driving Milrose's buggy hitched to a fine bay mare the army had exempt from procurement because of the uncle's influence with friends in the Treasury Department. Sandie halted the buggy in front of the Brady Gallery at 627 Pennsylvania Avenue, N.W., and escorted Katie inside.

They waited only an hour for her standing as some fellow officers bowed to courtesy and waived their priority to allow the beautiful young lady to proceed ahead of them. When it was done, and several fine standings were taken of Katie, Sandie paid the camera operator but begged an extra moment of his time. The two men went off into the darkroom for a time. Then, when Sandie rejoined Katie, they thanked the man for his time and departed, heading back to the Sheffield house and roast goose.

"Sandie, what did you say to the man?" Katie asked as they turned off the busy avenues to a quieter side street.

"What man?"

"The photographer. Why did you go off with him?"

"Ah-h. I had him prepare something special for you."

"You did? What is it? I'm dying to know. You were very mysterious in your letter. Won't you tell me about it, now?"

Sandie pulled the rig to the side of the road, and, with a clever smile, turned to the girl. "My last leave home was spent raving about you to everyone I knew. I think I bored the whole town with stories of our times together. Well, just before I returned to camp, the artisan who did the engravings on my sword, Paul Cashdollar, presented me with two of his finest pieces, and..." Sandie left the sentence unfinished as he pulled from his coat pocket two small, oval-shaped, gold pendants. They were identical with raised scrollwork of oakleaf cluster in braided chain bordering. Inside the bordering, thin, faint lines had been delicately etched for texture. A fine gold chain was attached to each for wearing about the neck.

"Oh, they're lovely!" Katie said upon seeing them.

"Ah. But wait," Sandie told her. Then, using his thumbnail, he opened each locket to reveal a portrait of himself in one; the lovely Katie's picture in the other. On the blank side of the cover, across from either likeness, were engraved the words: *Our love is time eternal/It spans both sun and moon/Your thoughts when cast upon me/will see us together soon.*

Katie smiled endearingly to the handsome man beside her and, unable to find the appropriate words to express her feelings, could only sigh. She took the locket with his picture set inside and closed it, then fastened its chain around her neck. "Thank you, Sandie. It's lovely."

Sandie placed the other chain around his neck, but before closing the cover he studied her portrait for a time. He spoke softly, more to himself than to her, "Now I should not be as lonely on the long nights. I shall open the case, gaze upon your loveliness, and feel comforted." Then he closed the lid and tucked it into his shirt.

Katie put her arm through his and snuggled closer on the seat. "I can't think of a better present you could have brought me nor anything else I could have desired more, except for this war to end."

"Nor I, my dear," he said as he gathered the reins. "Except, perhaps, roast goose with chestnut stuffing," he chuckled.

Katie poked him playfully in the ribs.

"Gid 'yup, mare!" he commanded, and steered the buggy back into the street.

Chapter Twelve

Sam opened one eye to see the morning sun slipping in through a narrow crack in the drawn curtains. The bed beside his was empty and he could hear voices speaking softly in the kitchen. He gave a long stretch and opened the other eye in an effort to awaken more completely, then gathered himself to stand and pull on his pants and shirt.

When he left the bedroom, he found his three friends in the kitchen, seated at the table, drinking coffee. Dave and Carol, with their backs to him turned to say good morning. Kelly, facing him as he entered, said hello, but with some hesitation. Sam noticed she looked at him strangely, almost startled, with wide, questioning eyes. He halted briefly when he caught her gaze and the memories of her part in his bizarre dream raced through his mind. Shaking the thoughts away he mumbled, "Morning," and moved on to pour a cup of coffee at the counter. He knew, though, from Kelly's stare, that there was something upsetting her.

Dave watched him pour the coffee and said, "You weren't alone in your dreams last night, Sam."

"Oh?" Sam replied, his back to them.

"Yeah. Apparently Kelly was having one of her own wild, nocturnal hallucinations," Dave chuckled. "You know, maybe you two should try meeting together some night while you're both out there in the twilight zone."

Sam stiffened uneasily at this. He turned partly around to glance at Kelly and found she was already looking at him with a measure of apprehension. He almost asked her if they had, in fact, shared the same dream last night. It had been so vivid; so clear. Then, thinking it might sound foolish and humiliating, he changed his approach. "What, uh, what did you dream?" he asked her.

Kelly pulled her eyes from him and looked down at the floor. "I'm...I'm not ready to talk about it. It was too upsetting."

Sam turned back to stir his coffee, mumbling, "Well, I can relate to that."

"Ah! You guys are killing us," Dave said. He tried to sound jovial but was keenly interested in what his friends were experiencing in their dreams that was cause for such uneasiness. "You're having these wild, extraordinary dreams that have you crying out and groaning, tossing and turning all around...and you're not going to tell what they are? Oh, man!"

Sam turned around and took a sip of his coffee. He appeared to be mulling this over for a bit. Then he looked at Dave, smiled, raised an eyebrow and curtly replied, "Nope!" and took another sip.

Dave grinned and nodded compliantly, knowing not to pursue the subject further. "Fine," he grumbled. "See if I tell you any more of my erotic ones."

Carol gave her husband a sharp glance. "If you have any erotic dreams, they better be about me."

"Oh, they are! They are!" he laughed, raising his hands to protect himself in case she tried to nudge him with a playful elbow.

Sam was unamused. Still at the counter he sipped his coffee and seemed preoccupied. When he spoke, finally, his tone was serious. "We better plan our day. We've got to be ready for tonight. This is going to be some difficult business and it's got to go off smoothly. A lot rides on what we accomplish at that place—our asses included."

The others agreed and turned to developing their strategy and reviewing those plans that were already set. Carol and Kelly were to pose as custodial personnel—the real employees having been diverted to another floor by some ingenious design on Tom's part. Sam, Pat and Dave would steal into the computer room and search the files for whatever incriminating evidence they could find relating to Marco Corporation dealings in the Antietam project. Tom was to roam the floors, keeping in contact with the others through small, two-way radios, alerting them to where the security guard was or any other late-night employees.

When they were satisfied with their plans and had developed and practiced their roles, they discussed their disguises and the hardware needed for that evening's affair. A trip into Hagerstown was necessary to acquire the supplies and it was agreed they would split up. Carol and Kelly would take their list; the two men, a separate one. They would meet back at the motel room no later than five o'clock. Noon had already approached faster than the four had realized and it was time for a break. Their anxiety levels were running high from all of the intensive scheming—the tedious effort of designing every possible detail or situation that might develop—and the amusing diversion of going into town for awhile became appealing.

Adjourning to their separate rooms they weren't long in preparing to leave, though the men outpaced the women in getting ready. Dave strode in to see Carol and Kelly to say goodbye and wish them luck in finding everything on their list. When he'd bid them well and turned to leave, Kelly asked if Sam wasn't coming in, also.

Dave was unsure of what to reply—how to phrase an awkward truth—and he stood for a moment and glanced at his wife, hoping she'd speak for him.

Carol was standing at the mirror applying lipstick. She paused to return her husband's eye, then looked down at the bureau as a signal to Dave that she was deferring comment.

"Well...uh...I guess not," Dave shrugged. "He's busy getting ready...going over the list again, and all. We'll see you girls at five. Bye," he said, and turned to slip out the door.

Kelly was suspicious of his answer as she watched him leave their room. "Hm-m... That's funny," she said aloud. "Carol, have you noticed Sam acting different, lately?"

"Lately? How lately?"

"I don't know. Last night. Today..."

Carol stayed at the mirror, running a brush through her hair. "Oh, you know men. Moody, sometimes. Who can figure them."

Kelly considered that answer for a moment, then shrugged. "Yeah. I suppose," and turned to brush her hair in the twin mirror.

****

Carol placed the last of the packages into the back of the van and closed the door. She dabbed her brow with the back of her hand and glanced up at the digital clock in the bank's parking lot across the street. 3:46...96‘F...3:46...96‘F... flashed continually in yellow lights. "Whew! I'm baking," she said to Kelly standing beside her. "You want to catch a cold drink?"

"Sure. Sounds good to me," Kelly replied.

They started to walk down the block and found a suitable restaurant only a few doors away. It was brightly lit, clean, casual—and air-conditioned. The hostess showed them to a booth and both women ordered iced tea, tall and cold. They had built quite a thirst in their hurried shopping and were glad to be out of the heat and resting tired feet.

"I'm certainly glad you spotted that thrift store," Carol said. "We might still be out looking for appropriate clothing."

"Hmph. I probably should have just looked in my closet. Most of my wardrobe would have sufficed."

"I doubt that. Every time I've seen you you've been fashionably dressed. Actually, I'm rather envious of your clothes."

"You? Ha!" Kelly laughed. "I, uh, I don't believe we shop from the same stores, Carol. Your tailor is a bit over my budget. Quite a bit."

"No. No. It's not that. It's how you wear what you have. Look at me. All my clothes read: comfortable, white, married, children..."

"...Expensive," Kelly added with a chortle.

Carol shrugged and smiled. "Maybe. But you, yours read: chic, young, imaginative..."

"...undesirable"..., Kelly again interjected.

Carol cast her a dubious eye.

"Well, I haven't been able to...," but Kelly cut her sentence short and lowered her eyes. When she raised them to look at Carol her face was a bit flushed. "Carol, you know Sam rather well. How...um...how do you think he feels about me?"

Carol smiled widely as she noted the inquisitive glimmer in Kelly's eyes. "Oh, Kelly!" she laughed. "Can't you tell? Sam's mad about you."

"Do you think so? Really?"

"Listen. I've known Sam for a long time. He's always had these big, sad eyes. I mean, he's so handsome and virile and intelligent...but he has these really empty eyes. You haven't seen them. They disappeared when he met you. It's kind of sad. I had real hopes you and Sam might have been headed for something special. Poor Sam. Love just seems to elude him. He's..."

"What do you mean?" Kelly interrupted. "You're talking as if it's over before it's even really begun. Did he find fault with me? Is there something about me he doesn't like?"

"Sam? Heavens, no. I think he finds you perfect in every way," Carol said. Then, with some hesitancy, she explained, "We...we overheard the conversation with your friend, John, yesterday. Oh, Kelly, if you could have seen Sam's face when he heard you say you two were 'just friends'; that you weren't interested in him... Well, it cut him pretty deep."

"Oh, my. I hadn't thought of that. So, that's why he's being cool and moody. I only said that to John to get rid of him. If I'd said I was interested in Sam I would have had to have this long argument with John and I just wanted him to be gone."

"Then you do care for Sam?"

"Yes. Very much. I don't know what it is, but I feel so comfortable with him; so at ease. It may sound crazy to you but it's like I've known him for years. "Now I feel awful. I hope he's not mad at me."

"You'd better have a talk with him."

"Well, yes. Of course. We were starting to get along so well. I hope he hasn't hardened himself against me."

"Mm...I doubt that," Carol said. "He's pretty enthralled with you. I think, if you find some way of letting him know you're still interested you can easily salvage it. Sam's a very smart man. But, like a lot of men, sometimes you have to hit them over the head to get them to realize things."

Kelly laughed. "Well, I better take inventory of my clubs, then, and choose an appropriate one."

They laughed and clinked their glasses together, then downed the last of their drinks. Requesting refills from the waitress, they sipped these more leisurely while Kelly pumped Carol for more information about the handsome Sam Baker.

****

Sam glanced at his watch and moved to the window to see if the van had pulled into the parking lot. He had been repeating this maneuver continually since the minute hand had touched the hour. "Damn!" he said impatiently. "It's five twenty. Where are they?"

Dave looked up from his comfortable reclining position on the bed. "Relax, Sam. I've got it under control. We don't really have to leave for another hour, or so. I know Carol and shopping. I just said 'five'. She'll roll in in a couple of minutes." He turned his attention back to the TV. "Damn it! If the Pirates blow this lead...," he fumed, and began to rant about the pitcher.

Sam was barely listening. He paced between the kitchen and bedroom, returning to peek into the parking lot through the crack in the curtains. Then, after several more repetitions, the sound of closing car doors brought Sam hurriedly back to the window. "Well. Finally," he said.

"See? What'd I tell you?" Dave grinned, watching as Sam opened the door for the women.

Carol entered ahead of Kelly and immediately began to apologize for being late, explaining that they had started back in plenty of time. "But we came across this neat little dress shop with the most darling silk blouse in the window," she told them.

Dave had risen to greet his wife and, as he gave her a quick kiss, laughed, "...And you just couldn't pass it up."

"Yes. It was marked way down."

"Did you get it?" he asked.

"No. I didn't. It fit Kelly so beautifully, though. Wait'll you see her in it."

"Well, go and get changed. We'll be leaving soon."

"But we're starving," Carol complained.

"We'll eat at the bar, or night club, or whatever it is," Dave said. "We have to meet Pat there so we better get rolling."

"I hope I can hold out that long," Carol frowned as she headed to her room carrying an armload of packages.

Kelly stayed a moment to ask Sam, "How did you guys make out? Did you get everything you need?"

"Yeah. Yeah. We did," he answered. And, though his tone was friendly enough, it lacked that little extra, underlying warmth Kelly had heard in it before last evening. He looked at her only occasionally.

"Wonderful," she remarked, then told him, "We found everything on ours, too." Kelly's eyes remained fixed on Sam in an effort to relay the especial favor in which she held him—but Sam wasn't noticing.

"Good," Dave answered for him. "I guess we're all set, then."

Kelly let her eyes move to Dave. "I guess we are," she said, forcing a smile. She knew she would have to find some way of letting Sam know she did feel an attraction to him and that what he'd overheard her say to John Brandon was simply not true. She hoped she could find some time alone with him soon. As she excused herself and went to join Carol in the other room, only Dave noticed the pensive expression on Kelly's face.

****

The drive to Bethesda was quiet. They were all a bit nervous about the purpose of their journey and, too, Sam was being rather moody. He sat beside Kelly on the bench seat but stayed to one side. Dave put on a classical music tape, hoping to calm everyone.

They had dressed casually, taking their disguises along to change into later. The men wore cotton slacks and sport shirts and the women wore skirts and blouses. Kelly was stunning in the new, embroidered, silk blouse, the white sheen of the material accentuating her golden hair.

The address to which Tom Charles had directed them proved to be a popular night spot called the Journey's End. Nestled between two taller office buildings in a revitalized former manufacturing district, the three-story, brick building that had once served as a police station had been extensively remodeled. The exterior facade was that of an old English pub and the décor was carried throughout the interior, complete with rough-hewn beams, ornamental brass spittoons, wine and ale casks and pewter mugs.

A young, stylishly dressed crowd spilled out onto the street, so filling the barroom that it was necessary to turn sideways to move around. The tables that lined the walls were so occupied, as was the twenty-foot wide aisleway. The bar was packed four or five deep.

Dave halted a passing waitress to ask where the dining area was, hoping Pat would know to seek refuge there. Learning it was through a door on the opposite side of the room, Dave took a deep breath and dove into the crowded pool of bodies to knife a path for the others to follow.

"This is crazy!" Carol called out to her husband above the noise of the crowd and blaring sound system.

"Stay close!" he shouted back with a laugh. "You could be lost for hours if we get separated."

Finally reaching the far wall they found it quieter and much less congested now that they'd slipped through the low archway and wooden door leading into the dining room. A hostess greeted them and, when given the name 'Marley', showed them to the table where Pat was already seated sipping a strawberry daiquiri. She smiled to them as they greeted her and seated themselves around her.

"Sorry we're a little late," Dave said. "We had a bit of trouble finding the place. Have you been waiting long?"

"Two daiquiris," she snickered. "But, that's okay. I was having fun just watching all the people."

Cocktails were soon ordered and delivered and, while they sipped their drinks and studied the menu, Sam controlled the conversation, keeping it light and frivolous. When their dinners were served and the waitress had disappeared, he then allowed Pat to innocently inquire about the help he needed tonight.

Sam took a bite of his steak and chewed on it thoughtfully, wondering how he could explain the party's real intent to Pat. He failed to design any less direct approach that might ease her into the objective of the evening, warming her to the idea so they could easily win her sympathies and her help. Besides which, Sam knew Pat to be a shrewd businesswoman, impatient with, and intolerant of, addressing a proposition with embellishing prefaces. So, swallowing his mouthful after well over chewing it he told Pat what they were going to attempt, and why. Then he explained why he needed her help.

When Sam began to speak, Pat's pleasant smile began to fade. The longer he spoke, the wider her eyes grew as the incredible scheme became revealed. When he began explaining her role in the affair, Pat cocked her head and began to survey the stoic expressions on the others around her. When he was finished and sat back to await her reply Pat was speechless. She blinked repeatedly as she stared at her friend across the table. "My God, Sam. You're serious."

"Never more so. Will you help us?"

Pat tried to utter several responses but failed to even get past her first words. She looked down at the table awhile, deep in thought, and her head would cock first one way, then the other, as she seemed to be mentally arguing every point of consideration. Then, slowly, a smile formed. She raised her head and rolled her eyes in disbelief and nodded expressively. "Gawd! I don't believe I'm saying this. Yes. I'll help you."

Dave, Carol and Kelly gave a low cheer of gratitude. Sam stood, leaned over the table, and took and kissed the back of her hand. "Thank you, Pat. I'd really hoped for that answer."

"Hm-m...I only hope I don't end up regretting it," she said. "This could well be the dumbest thing I've ever agreed to. But I guess everyone's got to take a stand on something, sometime, and lay it all on the line. This may as well be my cause. Let's hear your plan, Sam. I'm sure you've got it all figured out."

The course of the meal stayed focused on relaying every bit of information to Pat. They discussed everyone's role in the plotted break-in and explained the events that culminated in their decision to take these extra-legal means. While Pat listened, she added her suggestions on their actions once they were into the computer. She and Sam planned their search strategies, dividing the labor as not to duplicate where the other was roaming.

When Pat was well briefed and certain of her role, and the waitress had cleared their dishes for coffee, Dave excused himself to visit the lavatory. When he returned and took his seat he was grinning. "Wow! This place is incredible," he said. There's a whole other room back there with video games, pool tables, ping-pong and stuff. No wonder it's so crowded. They're covering all the bases."

"Really?" Sam asked. "Let's go see. Maybe it'll help pass the time."

The check was settled and they all adjourned to the game room. Situated just off the dining room, the noise was insulated by a heavy wooden door. Video games, pinball machines and other electronic games lined the walls. Two ping-pong tables were spaced in the back of the room and four pool tables dominated the front and center. Two young men were just ending a game on one of the tables so Sam chose a cue stick from the wall rack and laid claim to the table by chalking his stick over it. "Who's up for a game?" he asked, blowing the excess chalk from the tip.

"I'll play," Kelly answered and went to the stick rack to select a cue. She held one of the sticks out and sighted its length for straightness, then checked for weight and balance.

Sam racked the balls, saying, "Okay, my dear. How about a game of eight ball? That's when you have to put in either all of the balls with the solid colors or all of balls with—"

"I know the game," she interrupted him. "I've played it before."

"Yeah?" he smiled. "Okay. Great. Would you like to break?"

Kelly chalked her cue and said, "Mm...no. Go ahead. I'll watch you run the table awhile."

While the others stood back to watch, Sam lined up the cue ball, sighted down his stick for aim, then fired hard, sending the white ivory ball slamming into the pack. The tightly packed triangular formation shattered and balls rolled randomly around the table. "Anything go in?" he asked, moving to the far end of the table to check the pocket gutters.

"I don't think so," Dave replied.

"Okay. The table's yours," Sam told Kelly, motioning with a sweep of his hand.

Kelly surveyed the table, moving around it to view different balls and the angles of their approach. "Hmm...I've always favored the high balls. I think I'll go for them."

"Kelly," Sam said. He pointed to the left corner pocket where the two-ball sat directly at the edge. "You've got a dead shot on the two."

"I see that. I'll work around it," she said, her voice almost businesslike. She crouched down and aimed for the fifteen ball—a bank shot into the side pocket. Dead on, the ball banked perfectly and dropped into the pocket with a thump.

Sam's mouth also dropped.

"Thirteen; in the corner," she said...thump! "Twelve in the corner"...thump! "Eleven; bank, far corner"...thump!

Everyone stood and watched in amazement. Sam's look of surprise turned to one of delight as he watched this comely girl play a traditionally male pastime...and play it excellently.

"I've got a feeling I'm being hustled," he laughed as Kelly split the nine and fourteen, sending the fourteen into the side pocket. The cue ball spun backwards and stopped in perfect position for a shot at the nine ball.

"Hah! I'm just getting warmed up," she smiled. "I haven't played in a long time. Nine ball; side," she said and sent it ricocheting against two corner bumpers and back to drop into the side. "Whew! I wasn't sure of that one. That was tough."

Carol and Pat were beaming over Kelly's proficiency. "Where did you learn to play like that?" Pat asked, astounded.

"My father," Kelly said, re-chalking her cue stick. "He loved pool. Since I was his only child, we played every Sunday evening. He was very good at it. He was also very competitive. You had to beat him. He wouldn't let you win. He was one of those guys with a big male ego. Didn't like to lose at anything—especially to a girl." She looked at Sam after saying that to judge his reaction and was pleased to see him smiling with enthusiasm.

"Did you ever beat him?" Sam asked.

"Sometimes. Not too often, though," she answered, hitting at the ten and sending it riding along the rail to squeeze it into the pocket between the still positioned two ball. It hit against the two before dropping in, but did knock that ball from in front of the hole. "Darn! I hit against your ball. I guess it's your shot," she told him.

Sam chalked his stick. "You're a tough act to follow, Kelly. Not only pretty—but a mean pool shooter, too." He leaned over the table, lined up a shot and fired the seven down into the far corner. "Six; in the side"...thump. "Five; down here"...thump. "Bank the two. My free-be shot you so selfishly hit away," he chuckled...thump!

"Oh-h, Sam! Nice shot. You're not too bad, yourself," she grinned.

"Hey. It's my male ego thing," he replied with a wink. "Four," he said, and sent the ball on a double bank into the corner pocket. "Three ball; corner," he said, hitting straight on to where he aimed. Unfortunately, the cue ball came to rest behind the eight, blocking a perfect shot at the one ball.

"Aw-w, too bad," Kelly sighed. "That was a nice run. Not enough English on the ball."

"Hm-m...," Sam said as he studied the table, traveling around it to survey different angles. "I left myself in pretty poor position. I don't know if my male vanity can allow for this. It's pretty unsettling to me, you know. Seems I'm always behind the eight ball with women."

The others smiled at this and watched Sam study several more angles.

"Try banking off the side," Kelly suggested.

"Well, I'm not always confident of my bank shots," he said. He leaned far over the table in an awkward position, lining up a shot through the eight. "No... No...," he continued, concentrating on his shot. "I'm...more of a...straight on...kind of guy..." And he angled his cue stick and hit under the ball with enough force to send the cue ball leaping over the eight. It rolled down the table, hit into the one and sent it into the corner pocket.

Everyone cheered at the shot and Sam smiled and took a deep bow. Kelly came around the table to him and hugged him to her side. "Oh-h, Sam! What a shot!" she beamed. "Now who's being hustled?"

Sam returned her hug, placing his arm around her waist and giving her a light squeeze. "Whew! I was sweating that one."

Kelly laughed and nodded she understood why. Then she told him, "Go ahead. Sink the eight."

Sam looked at it a moment, then said, "Naw-w. Let's leave things equal between us," and he squeezed her side again. With his arm around her and seeing the glow of excitement in her eyes, Sam found it difficult to forget what he'd heard her say to John Brandon. He had been ready to accept their relationship as one of being "good friends", if that was what she wanted, and the hurt was beginning to subside a little, now, too. He just wished she'd stop looking at him so admiringly with those deep blue eyes. It made it all the more difficult to keep from falling for her.

"Well, not only is he handsome, but he plays a pretty darn good game of pool," Kelly laughed, squeezing her arm a bit tighter around him.

They laid their cue sticks on the table and, as a group, exited through a set of heavy wood doors into an adjoining room. When in the game room, they had assumed this was the bar through which they had originally entered. Now they found it was a completely separate room, even larger than the first bar. Though it, too, was dimly lit, there was an illuminated stage with a nine-piece band complete with piano and horns. Glittered lettering on the bass drum and across the backs of black leather jackets of several of the performers showed "Solid Old" as the name of the group. A small dance area in front of the stage was packed with people twisting to the band's rendition of a Chubby Checker tune.

There was a long bar to the right of where they had entered but it was packed deep with bodies. Dave was about to lead them across the room to the exit when a waitress, clearing mugs from one of the tables, caught their eye and flagged them over.

"What do you think?" Carol shouted above the noise of the band and crowd. "Have we got time for a drink?"

"Dave looked at his watch. "Yeah. Why not? I sure could use one." He led the way, weaving through the crowd of tables and chairs to where the waitress was wiping the table with a damp rag. She took their orders, then melted into the darkness of the crowd behind them.

Their table was along one side and at the very edge of the dance floor. Sam took a seat at the back of the table that was exposed to the twisting couples and hoped he wouldn't get clubbed by a wildly flailing arm. He relaxed only when the band finished playing and the floor began to empty.

A host disc jockey from a local radio station came to center stage from his electronic booth on stage left and thanked the band for "their great rendition of an old favorite." A young man in his mid-twenties, he plugged both his station and his name: Cliff Hanger, from WREQ, Bethesda. "Okay. I hope you're all enjoying yourselves 'cause the fun's still happening. We've got another brave soul ready to rock the roof and shake you up. He says he was here several weeks ago, but I don't remember him. Maybe you do. So, let's give a big hand to Larry—the Prince—Moore!" he said, stretching his hand to stage left.

The crowd cheered and whistled as a young man came out across the stage and stood at the microphone. He looked to be in his early twenties with long brown hair and standing about six feet tall. Not too handsome, but not unpleasant looking, either, he was just slightly overweight and wore blue jeans and a black T-shirt with a picture of Elvis printed on the front. As the crowd settled down, save for a small group of several of his friends at the bar who continued their jovial bantering, Cliff Hanger greeted the young man. "Larry, it's good to have you back...and to know you haven't wised up any over the last few weeks. I take it those are your friends in the back of the room?"

The young fellow leaned to the microphone. "Yeah. Some of the guys I work with," he said. Then he hollered, "Quiet down back there, you bums. I'm ready to go to work here." This, of course, only served to intensify their ridiculing comments.

"With friends like that... Well...," the deejay joked. "Okay. Larry's going to do a couple of Elvis numbers for us. He's a great fan of "the King" and says he collects memorabilia. You've been to Graceland how many times?"

"Six."

"Six! Okay! You haven't, uh, seen Elvis or his ghost on any of those visits, have you?"

"No."

"No ghosts! Well-l...you're probably one of the only ones claiming not to have seen him. Okay! Larry's tribute to the late! great! El-vis-s-s...," Cliff Hanger exclaimed, gesturing to the fellow in presentation as he slowly backed away. Larry took the mike from its holder and looked at the band for his cue. They began the introduction of *Jailhouse Rock* and when the young man started to sing, he had such a similar voice to that of "the King's" that the audience listened attentively. When he began to gyrate his pelvis, it so mimicked the song's originator that the crowd began to cheer and applaud.

"What is this?" Dave asked, shouting to be heard above the speakers.

"Karaoke," Kelly hollered to him in reply.

"What?"

"He doesn't get out much," Sam laughed over his shoulder. He'd been sitting backwards in his chair to more easily view the performer. He turned around, now, to explain it to Dave. "Karaoke. It's popular in a lot of night spots. They provide the music, either by tape or band, and you do the lyrics. It's a lot of fun."

"Pretty wild!" Dave shouted. "But you'd never catch me up there."

With their attention turned to the stage neither Sam, nor Dave took notice of Kelly leaning to Carol's ear, then to Pat's. Carol leaned to the men and said, "Excuse us. We'll be back in a bit." She left with Kelly and Pat to wind their way through the crowd.

On stage, Larry was finishing both his lyrics and his gyrations and the audience clapped and cheered. Cliff Hanger walked part way across the stage to stand at a second microphone and applaud as the young man took a bow. "You liked that, did you?" Cliff asked the audience, and the crowd responded enthusiastically. "Well, okay. Larry has another number he'd like to do, I believe."

The young man showed a broad, blushing smile as he nodded and turned to confer with the leader of Solid Old. Cliff Hanger took the opportunity to again plug his radio station and the night club. He gave some information on other events on different nights at the club, then plugged Solid Old, reminding the audience, "If you'd like to perform with them, just come over and tell me what song you'd like to do. Solid Old knows most of the songs from the 50s and 60s. Hey, these guys were performing them back then when they were just released. That's why they're called Solid...Old. They're old...but they're still solid!"

Cliff looked over at the group's leader and was given a nod. "Okay. I think we're about ready. Larry. You're all set?"

The young man stepped up to the mike and took it from the stand and, in an amazing impersonation of Elvis, said, "Yes, Ah' ahm, Mr. Hanger. Ah'd li'hk to do ah little number me'n theh boys sort'a put togetheh theh otheh day. It goes somethin' li'hk this." The young man snapped his fingers three times to cue the band and launched into *A Big Hunk 'O Love*.

The crowd loved it. They cheered and whistled as the fellow twitched his leg several times, then began full pelvic gyrations. He bounded around the stage with such energy that his added weight seemed of little burden. As Cliff Hanger moved off stage for fear of being knocked into by the wildly undulating Larry, people began to move out onto the dance floor. Sam, once more, found himself trying to protect his head from the flailing limbs of the jitter-bugging couples.

"He's really pretty good!" Dave hollered. "He's got Elvis down pat. Too bad he doesn't look like him. He could make a living impersonating him."

Sam just nodded in reply, believing it too much of a strain to try to be heard above all the noise.

As the song drew to a close and the audience clapped and cheered, the young man took his bows. Cliff Hanger walked out across the stage, paused to confer a moment with the band leader, then continued on to join Larry at the microphone. "Okay! Yeah! Terrific!" Cliff exclaimed into the mike as he clapped for the young man. He patted Larry on the back and shook his hand, thanking him for a remarkable performance. As the young man started to walk off stage to the accompaniment of cat-calls and jeers from his friends in the back of the room, Cliff grinned into the mike. "Okay. Right here at the Journey's End. All kinds of hidden talent. We just haven't discovered any of it, yet. Well, maybe our luck is about to change. We've got a special treat for you now. Three lovely young ladies in their first appearance at the Journey's End. Let's give a big 'End' welcome to The Yankee Belles...," he announced, motioning off stage left to applaud their entrance.

Both Dave's and Sam's mouths dropped open in astonishment as, from out of the left wing walked Kelly, Pat and Carol. The two men looked at one another, speechless, then back to the stage. The audience howled and cheered

as Kelly came to stand beside Cliff Hanger at the microphone. Pat and Carol stood together by the second mike just a few feet away.

Cliff set his mike into the stand to share with Kelly and the crowd noise began to diminish. Carol gave a wink to her husband as Pat adjusted the mike stand to their height.

"What-the-hell?" Dave said to his friend. They were both amused at this, but also surprised.

"This ought to be interesting," Sam laughed. "We're with three crazy ladies, tonight."

"'Crazy' isn't the word I was going to use," Dave replied, shaking his head in disbelief.

Cliff Hanger leaned to the microphone. "Okay! Huh...? These girls can really ring your chimes! If their voices ring out as lovely as these girls look, we're in for a 'hum dinger' of a time." These remarks brought many groans from the audience. "Okay. Okay. A stand-up I'm not. What can I say? This job is taking its 'toll' on me." More groans came from the crowd. "Hey! Keep it up. I'll ring out a few more puns," he said to the crowd. Then he turned to Kelly, asking, "So, are you girls vacationing here?"

Kelly leaned close to the microphone to answer. "Sort of, I guess."

"Well, great! Welcome to Bethesda. Have you three sung together before, or is this your first time?"

Kelly laughed. "No. We've just recently become friends so, no, we haven't sung together. This'll be a first for all of us."

"Okay! Well, I'm sure you'll be great. Let's get on with it, then. Right here at the Journey's End! The Yankee Belles-s-s...!" he announced, gesturing with his hand in presentation.

While Cliff Hanger moved off stage Kelly glanced over to Carol and Pat poised at the mike with a copy of the lyrics in hand. When they nodded they were ready; she looked back at the band and signaled them to begin. As they started to play Doris Troy's, *Just One Look*, Kelly snapped her fingers and moved her hips to the rhythm, waiting her cue. Then, leaning close to the mike she sang;

Just one look...and I fell so hard...in
love...with you...
Oh-h oh, oh-h oh.
I found out...how good it feels...to
have...your love...
Oh-h oh, oh-h oh.

She looked only at Sam as she sang, her body swaying and her arms gesturing. The only times she glanced away were to be sure Carol and Pat were set to join in on the back-up vocals. She plucked the mike from its holder and moved down off the stage.

Say you will...will be mine...forever...and
always...
Oh-h oh, oh-h oh.
Just one look...and I knew...that you...were
my only one.

Kelly had moved over close to stand before him and Sam blushed as she sang right to him. She took a light hold on his shirt collar and pulled him to his feet.

I thought I was dreamin'...but I was wrong.
But I'm gonna keep on schemin', till I'm
gonna make you...make you my own.

Then she kissed him quickly on the cheek. As the crowd cheered and whistled, Sam melted and turned a deep crimson. Kelly moved off, singing her way back to the stage and leaving one tall, dark, handsome man standing awestruck and infatuated in her wake. As she climbed onto the stage to join her female back-ups, Carol gave her a wink. Both women knew Sam had received the intended message—perfectly.

Cliff Hanger started across the stage to join them as the number was ending. He started the applause, clapping appreciatively over the sensational performance. The women had sung wonderfully, their voices blending so smoothly that it did sound practiced.

Sam approached the stage, arriving to stand before Kelly just as Cliff approached. She took one deep bow to the crowd's roaring approval, then gazed down at Sam, her eyes glistening. Sam cocked his head and looked up at her with a romantically wondrous smile...and Kelly smiled back. Cliff began to speak into the microphone, complimenting the women, but Kelly wasn't listening. She watched Sam raise his arms to her and, standing at the edge of the stage, she fell into them. While the two held each other in a silent, loving embrace the crowd responded with "oohs" and "aahs" over this display of affection. Dave had approached the embracing couple and, as he stood nearby, he and Carol beamed delightedly.

Cliff Hanger tried to address the women to ask if they cared to do another selection. Pat was unsure of what to reply but she was the only one of the three not wholly distracted. She started to stammer into the microphone but was handily rescued when a deep, rugged voice suddenly boomed over the p.a. system: "Dr. Alex Mundy, your office is on the phone. There's an emergency call for Dr. Alex Mundy in the office."

Dave and the others exchanged glances on hearing the message and their festive mood now turned serious. Pat thanked the audience for their enthusiasm and added a thanks to Cliff Hanger, who had an awkward moment as Carol and Pat both stepped off the stage to join the others. The crowd once again applauded as the party turned to leave. The band took the opportunity of the lull to begin playing a Buddy Holly tune and the dance floor immediately began to swell with bodies. The room once more was drowned in rock 'n roll.

Asking directions from a passing waitress, Sam guided the party to the office in response to the phone call. He was admitted into the office by a short, husky man in blue jeans and T-shirt. "You Dr. Mundy?" the man asked.

"Yeah."

"Over here," the man motioned. Sam followed the man to the phone on the desk. "Ya' know, we only allow emergency calls passed in through this phone."

"Well, it must be one," Sam remarked picking up the phone. "Mundy," Sam said into the receiver.

On the other end of the line Tom said only, "The patient is ready for your exploratory surgery, Sir."

"Fine," Sam said in reply. "I'll be at the hospital as soon as I can." He set the phone down and thanked the man then joined the others outside the office door. "Let's go," he said to them.

As planned, Dave went to the van and retrieved a carrying case for the women. He returned and handed it to Carol and the three women went off to the lavatory to change. Dave and Sam went out to the van and changed into white, button-down dress shirts and non-distinctive blazers. Dave put on a loosely knotted tie and black horn-rimmed glasses. Sam had chosen brown turtle-shell glasses and fitted a white painters cap on his head.

The women soon returned to the van, having traded their stylish apparel for cheaper dress more suitable for cleaning floors and scouring sinks. Kelly wore blue jeans, an old pair of tennis shoes, faded blouse and a blue bandana to conceal her blonde hair. Carol and Pat were dressed similarly, though in pink and turquoise cotton slacks respectively.

Both women wore hair nets to cover their fashionably styled hair and all three had removed their make-up or applied it in such a way as to be less conspicuous or unflattering plain. They filed into the rear seats of the van and Sam handed a small two-way radio to Carol. As they made the short drive of several blocks to the office building of Marco Development Corporation they reviewed their plans again, taking care Pat was thoroughly familiar with them.

****

The lighted parking lot and buildings encompassed about fifteen acres behind a high cyclone fence. This late at night there were only a dozen or so cars sitting around the seven-story brick office. Perhaps six or eight more sat silent near a ten-bay mechanic shop located several hundred yards from the office. Yellow earth-moving equipment, storage and office trailers, cranes, and trucks of all description were lined in neat rows in a back lot between the office and mechanic shop.

Across the dimly-lit street Dave idled the van so they could survey the complex. A large tractor trailer hauling a big yellow dozer came down the street and turned into the compound gate. Proceeding unchallenged past a dark and empty guard shack, the group watched as it roared through the lot and over to the service garage.

"Well, let's do it," Dave said. He wheeled across the street into the compound, passing just beyond the glass side doors. Here, he stopped to let Carol and Kelly out. Both men wished them luck and Carol took her husband's hand as he reached back to her. She squeezed it tightly before leaving.

Kelly slid over on the seat and paused to put a nervous hand on Sam's shoulder. "See you inside," she said to him.

Sam patted her hand, then gave it a reassuring squeeze. "It'll go okay."

"I know." Then to Pat, she said, "Take care of these guys."

"I will," Pat told her. "Good luck to you."

"Thanks," she said, then took a deep breath. "Well, here goes," and she ducked out to join Carol on the asphalt.

Pat had been sitting in the furthest rear seat and now slid over to sit behind and between the two men. She waved to Carol and Kelly as Dave drove away, leaving the compound to park in an alley around the corner. Sam switched on the two-way radio to monitor the progress of the girls as they entered the building. Each floor was fully lighted as the janitorial staff went about their business and a few draftsmen, engineers and other employees worked late to meet deadlines.

"...We're in the elevator," came Carol's voice, soft and low over the speaker. "...You there?"

"Gotcha'," Sam replied.

Kelly and Carol rode the elevator to the fourth floor. When it stopped, and the door opened, they peeked into the hallway. Finding it deserted they proceeded down the hall to a utility closet at the far end. They pulled out the utility cart and pushed it to the middle of the hall, stopping in front of a heavy wooden door. Under the numbers, emblazoned in heavy black letters, was printed "Private: Authorized Personnel Only." Kelly glanced up and down the hall and, seeing no one in sight, tried the door knob. It turned freely. Her heart racing, she gave a slight push on the door and opened it only enough to fit her head through. She could plainly hear the quiet, combined hum of electric motors and transformers and the unmistakable sound of printers rattling and chattering. As she leaned in to look around, she suddenly gasped,

"Ah!" as she was startled by the sight of a bearded fellow sitting at one of the terminals.

"Well, you made it!" Tom smiled cheerfully, looking up from his workstation in the brightly lit room. "Where are the others?"

Recovering quickly from her initial surprise, Kelly slid inside and closed the door. "They're out in the van."

"Are they coming in?"

"Yes. As soon as we contact them. It's okay?"

"As far as I know. If they don't act suspicious no one'll even notice them. People are always coming and going at all hours of the night here."

Kelly opened the door and leaned out to Carol. "Tell them to come in," she said in a low voice. Then she closed the door and turned to Tom. "Tom, why don't we just use one of the terminals in another room? Why are we in here?"

Tom paused his fingers over the keys and looked up at her with his jaw slightly distended and his mouth slacked as it always did when he gathered his thoughts from having been intensely concentrating on something else. "Uh-h-h...cause nobody ever comes in here. Everybody has a terminal at their desk so there's no reason for them to come in here. These are just set up to handle any overflow or for expansion, I guess. Truthfully, I think the company that sold us all this hardware just managed to slip a few extras in on us. This was to sort of be the hub of everything but—but, why leave your desk to come in here?"

Kelly made no reply. She simply shrugged in agreement. "Have you found anything yet?"

"No. Not yet. I'm still trying to get into the records. I just can't gain access, I'm not real good at this stuff."

"Well, hopefully Sam and Pat will get in. Sam's pretty knowledgeable with computers."

"Mm...I hope so," Tom murmured, looking back at the screen to resume searching.

Kelly slipped out the door to join Carol. In a short while the elevator door opened and Pat, Sam and Dave stepped out. They came down the hall to where the women stood and Dave gave a wink at his wife.

"Tom's inside," Kelly informed them. "He said he isn't doing real well."

Sam grinned cleverly and made a motion of pushing up his shirt sleeves. "Step aside, my dear, and let the pros in to do their thing."

Kelly laughed and made a sweep with her arm toward the door. The trio entered and closed the door, leaving Carol and Kelly to stand watch outside. The two women pushed the cart to one end of the hall to take a position by the window.

Kelly opened a pack of cigarettes and took two from the pack, handing one to Carol. When they lit them, they both grimaced at the rank odor of the smoke that floated up from the burning ends. Carol set the radio on the cart so she could easily lean to speak into it without being obvious as they kept a keen eye on the floor indicator of the elevator.

In the room, Dave and Sam exchanged greetings with Tom, then introduced Pat by first names only. Sam and Pat both eyed up the hardware.

"Not bad," Sam remarked.

"I'm jealous," Pat confessed.

"Well, that's what money can buy," Sam said. "Bigger toys. Actually, Pat, it's not all that much more powerful than yours."

"It's a lot faster and bigger," she said. "And I bet it's paid for. I'd swap him even up."

Sam laughed, then said, "Let's get to work."

They both took seats at workstations beside each other and Sam stared at the monitor, thinking. "Okay. Let's see...," he said. "We think Mr. Marco is paying people off—probably in cash, maybe in gifts. Hmm...it'll be easier to track money. It leaves a nice trail." He looked at Pat and asked, "You know any hackers in Florida?"

"I'm not sure. I can always post some inquiries on the bulletin board. Why?"

"Tom. What's the name of a trucking company in Florida this company might use on a regular basis?"

"Humph. Good question. I don't know much about that end of the business."

"Okay. Let's start with banks. Your company pay checks?"

"Uh...First Maryland Bank & Trust."

"Can you get into it?" Pat asked, watching Sam begin to tap on his keyboard.

"Easy. I've got a security clearance for the Pentagon's big one, remember. I've roamed through it, just for the fun of it, and found how to get into Langley's. You wouldn't believe where you can go from there. Check this out. First...we find the keys...to the Fed. Bank...," Sam said, punching up codes and maneuvering through a labyrinth of security blocks. In a few minutes he was searching the Federal Reserve Bank files for the access codes to the Maryland bank."

Watching Sam's handiwork from his own screen, Tom looked up in astonishment. "This is amazing! I don't believe this. We, we could end up in big trouble for doing this, couldn't we?"

"Mm...yeah. I suppose," Sam replied, absorbed in his probing. "There are other routes to get the same info but it would take longer."

"Wouldn't matter," Pat said. "We'd be in big trouble any way we went in."

"True," Sam agreed, sitting back in his chair and folding his arms. He watched numbers on the screen flash by, then glanced up to Dave who was looking over his shoulder.

"What are we doing?" Dave asked as indecipherable letter and number lines automatically appeared on the monitor.

"The computer's searching for the access codes to the Maryland bank's computer. I want to go in and search for any major cash withdrawals on Marco's records. That may prove useful to us if we can cross them with anything significant we stumble on in other records." Sam watched his screen, then said, "Ah. Here we go. It's coming up now." He watched a series of lines appear across the monitor and sighed, "Damn. I did something wrong. I've got all the banks in Maryland. Pat, take this and go through it. I want to see if I can't go into some of the corporate records."

"Sure. Piece of cake," Pat replied, scrolling through the list to find First Maryland Bank & Trust.

While Sam began tapping on the keyboard, Dave stood behind him and looked on. "Jeez," he exclaimed. I've read about this sort of thing but I never knew how it worked. I couldn't even imagine trying it."

Sam smiled and nodded. "Hey. This is C.I.A. They go anywhere they want. They know we're into their system. I'm sure they're monitoring us right now. We'll be long gone before they realize this isn't one of their people calling up info. As far as they know, one of their people is logged on. I haven't done anything to raise suspicions—yet. By the time they trace this back to the Pentagon and find it's my access number invading them, we'll be out of here. I've done this before...when I was bored. There's some pretty scary stuff they have filed away from the public."

"Did you get into trouble?" Dave asked. "Will you get into trouble over this?"

"Naw. They hollered at me; threatened to take away my security clearance, then wanted to hire me to make their system impenetrable. But I turned them down. They'll probably give me some flack over this, too. Fuck 'em if they can't take a joke."

Tom's mouth was hanging open in a mixed expression of both astonishment and delight. "This is amazing," he said, folding his arms square and using them to lean against the desk of his workstation. "Truly unbelievable! I thought, 'yeah, sure, everybody knows something about computers'. I had no idea you were this serious about these things. Boy, did I pick the right guy out of the crowd."

Sam looked over at him and just grinned. "Glad to help."

"Well, listen," Tom shrugged. "You guys are far and above me on this. Why don't Dave and I go up to James's office and see what we can find in his wall files."

"Good. Take a radio with you to keep in touch," Sam suggested. Then he paused. With a curled finger he began to brush at his moustache. "Hm-m. This is interesting."

"What? What have you got?" Tom asked.

"Hm. It's a corporate statement. He has a sizable amount of money in a bank in the Caymen Islands. I wonder if I can get in there," he mused, his fingers beginning to rapidly play on the keyboard.

"You've got a corporate statement?" Tom asked.

"Yeah. I think it's an unofficial posting. There are several banks listed. Christ! He's worth a lot of money. There's a list of stocks and bonds and stuff clear off the screen."

"Can I see?" Tom asked, starting to get up from his chair.

"Later, maybe. I'm going to try to get into that island bank and scroll his records there." Then, to Pat, Sam asked, "Where are you?"

"In First Maryland. I'm pulling transactions of cash deposits and withdrawals and any checks to trucking companies."

"Good. When that's done see if you can pull up any tax records. Maybe they have their returns on computer."

Tom looked at Dave and beamed, "Your friend is pretty amazing."

"Sometimes," Dave chuckled and patted Sam on the back. He grabbed up a radio from the sports bag, saying, "C'mon. Let's go see if we can contribute to this."

While Pat and Sam continued reviewing the records of Brody's organization the two men headed off to climb the stairway to the seventh floor. They moved deliberately down the hall to the door with James Brody's name stenciled on it and Tom used his passkey to open the door to the secretary's office. As he took care to lock the door behind them Dave asked, "You have a key?"

"Sure. A lot of us do. But, only for the front room. It's supposed to be a secret, how to get into Brody's office. Fortunately, his secretary is lax in discreetness," Tom said. He went behind Cheryl's desk and fumbled under the top for the hidden switch that activated the electronic sensors. With that done, Tom moved to stand in front of the hidden eye and the heavy wooden doors silently parted.

"Where is everybody?" Dave asked as they entered the plush, private office of James Brody.

"Down on the second floor. Apparently a five-gallon bucket of paint upset in the utility closet and ran all over the carpet. Uh...besides which, um, one of the toilets in 'real estate's' bathrooms backed up. Oh, it's a real mess down there. They'll be quite a while mopping it all up. It's really too bad," he said sarcastically.

"How about security?"

"He doesn't do much. He's probably down flirting with the girls on second. He'll be making his rounds, but all he does is jiggle door knobs. What's to steal?" Tom held the radio close to his mouth and pushed the talk button. "We're in," he whispered.

Sam's voice came back through the speaker. "Good. We're doing well here. Better than expected."

Kelly's voice came through next. "So far, so good. Elevator's quiet. No signs of life."

Tom led Dave to the wall files, flicked a button, and a long drawer slid silently open.

"Impressive," Dave commented as the drawer slid toward him.

Several floors below, continuous ribbons of paper were accumulating in several neat stacks as the printers responded to Sam's and Pat's requests for copies of data they were uncovering from bank transactions and corporate records.

"Where are you, Pat?" Sam asked without even a pause in his own research.

"I've got a list of trucking companies paid by check within the last two years," she told him, moving the cursor down through her list. "Ha! Sunshine Trucking, out of Florida," she exclaimed.

"Take the whole list. We'll use your machine to go over them later," Sam told her. "We're almost done. I think we've got enough to work with."

"Elevator's moving," Kelly said into the radio. "It's heading down."

Sam and Pat both paused and looked at each other, breathlessly waiting to hear more from the radio.

Upstairs, in James Brody's office, Tom was hurriedly faxing information to his home machine. From the private, wall-mounted file drawers he'd discovered a folder simply labeled "Antietam." They were astonished to find, among other documents in the folder, a handwritten list of local county officials. Several names had dollar amounts beside their names while others had checkmarks or an "X". A second item retrieved from the folder was a short, typed dossier on the members of the McPherson Corporation Board of Directors and a list of those members who made up the grant committee of the McPherson Foundation.

Dave was at the small photo copier, running off another article he'd uncovered in one of the drawers of Brody's desk. It was a four-page list of both Senators and Congressmen and the committees on which they served. Several of the names were circled, and, whether or not it could prove useful, the men chose to take a copy with them. Dave also copied material that seemed to reveal James Brody held interest or ownership in other businesses, some completely unrelated to his construction firm.

Both men continued working but kept a cautious ear tuned to the radio as they heard Kelly say, "Ground floor." There was a pause. Then, "It's moving!"

"Hurry!" Tom said, feeding another sheet into the facsimile machine.

"It's passed the fourth...heading to five. Tom...! Dave...!"

Tom picked up the radio. "Got it," he replied anxiously.

"I'm done," Dave said to him. He gathered the copies, collected the originals and hurriedly replaced them in the desk drawer. Tom pulled his last paper from the machine and returned it to the folder. He ran to the open file drawer, stuffed the folder into its order, then hit the "close" button. Motioning for Dave to follow, he took them to a side door that led into a conference room. The doors parted with the press of a button and, as the men passed through, closed neatly and quietly—just as the doors to Brody's office slid apart to admit two expensively-dressed figures.

Dave stopped and turned to peek through the slight crack between the two doors. He could see the figure of a tall, handsome, shoulder-length blond haired man moving to the liquor cabinet directly opposite the doors.

"Scotch?" the impeccably dressed young man asked the other person who was still out of Dave's view.

"Yes, thanks. With ice."

The young man, Dave guessed, was James Brody. He made himself so at home and carried himself with such a commanding presence that it could be no one but he. The other figure was still out of view.

"What's the latest with our asbestos suit? Can we get E.P.A. off our backs?"

"Uh...well, James, I'm afraid it's not that easy. These guys don't get lost and they don't go away. All we can do is swamp them in paperwork for a few years. I think we can convince them to let us leave it in place and seal it. We're still going to have that expense, though."

"Damn my grandfather! He should have never got the company involved in a situation like this. That kind of thing should have been contracted out. Are you certain we can't lay it all on him and have them sue his estate for expenses?"

"No," the still unseen man answered. "We investigated that possibility. When you took over the assets of the company you also assumed its liabilities. The law's pretty clear on that. We think we stand a good chance of suing the asbestos manufacturer and recouping our losses. We will, of course, bleed all we can from what's left of your grandfather's estate."

James had poured two glasses of scotch and turned, now, to move a few steps and hand one to the other man. Dave could only see the fellow's hand reach for and accept the glass, the rest of his body remaining obscured. Tom was pulling at him to follow but Dave stopped him. "Just a minute," he whispered and peeked in again.

"So, how's that fellow from the Sharpsburg group? Any change?" James asked as he sipped from the tumbler.

"No. The last we heard; he was still in a coma. At any rate, he still can't communicate."

"Good. In a couple of days, the land will be ours. I spoke to Transportation today. The rail line is ours. There's just the formality of procedures. The project is taking shape," James told the man. He held his glass up, as if in toast, then took a sip of the scotch. "Yeah, it was too bad about that car running that fella off the side of that mountain," he said sarcastically. "We owe Rudy a bonus."

Tom and Dave looked at each other on hearing this and now Tom, too, bent his ear to listen closely.

"I'll want to break ground immediately. No waiting. Get the paperwork processed so we can start excavation. Find a place for that old lady and get her husband committed. I want those buildings ashes."

"James, the agreement says she can have six months to vacate."

"Pardon?" James quipped.

"I'll work on it," the man said.

James went to the computer that sat just off to the side of his desk and began to tap on the keys to display some data. "Come here and look at this. I just got the figures back for the first quarter earnings on the Philadelphia Wharf project. It'll impress the hell out of you."

As the man now walked into his line of vision Dave almost gasped when he identified the figure who so intimately held the confidence of James Brody. It was the Historic Antietam Foundation attorney, John Brandon.

"Holy shit!" Dave said in a harsh whisper to Tom. "That son-of-a-bitch is working for Brody! I should go in there and kick his ass!"

"Later. C'mon. Let's get out of here," Tom said, tugging on Dave's arm. Dave paused for one last look at the two figures standing together at the computer.

"Something's wrong here," James said. He took a seat on the chair, now, and began to press the keys that should have displayed the data he requested. "Somebody's in the files. Is someone working late in accounting?"

"I don't think so. The only one who can legitimately access those files is Lewis, and he's out of town."

"Well, what-the-hell...? Call down to fourth floor and see who's there?"

John Brandon picked up the phone on James Brody's desk and pressed an extension number. After waiting a short while, he pressed another. When there was no response, he repeated the procedure several more times. "No one's in accounting. At least no one answers, anyway."

"Did we see anyone on first floor when we came in?" James asked.

"Survey was working late. I saw Scott down there and waved to him. I don't know about the other floors."

"Shit! Somebody is in the files. You go check the fourth floor; I'll go down to third. Call security. Have him check the first floor and don't let anyone out. I want to sweep the floors and find out who the fuck is snooping where they shouldn't."

Dave moved from the door. "Time to go!" he said to Tom, and the two men scurried out the conference room door that accessed the hall. They ran to the stairwell exit and, once on the other side of the heavy steel door, Dave paused only long enough to radio the others. "Close shop!" he said into the speaker. "Trouble's on its way. Go! Go!"

Sam and Pat hurried to shut down. Sam closed out the program while Pat ran to the printers to gather up what material had been compiled.

"We're in the stairwell," Dave reported.

"Elevator's moving," Kelly radioed. She and Carol moved the cart down the hall to position it in front of the elevator doors, blocking the path of anyone wishing to exit if the doors opened.

Sam and Pat hurried out of the room and over to the two women but Carol waved them on. "Go!" she told them. "If it stops here, we'll stall them." Continuing on down the hall the fleeing couple passed through the exit doors as the elevator stopped and the door slid open.

Carol and Kelly were careful not to look up as one of the occupants tried to exit but found the utility cart blocking his path. As though ignorant of the courtesy of allowing passengers to disembark first, Carol attempted to push the cart into the elevator, steering directly into the path of the man. "Oh. Sorry," she said, adding an embarrassed giggle. The man moved back and tried to crowd between the cart and the door but Carol jockeyed it in that direction. Again, she apologized with a foolish titter over the accidental hindering.

The man paid it little heed as he leaned out the door to glance down the hall, waiting for the woman to either pull the cart backward or to push it in around him. "Is there anyone working on this floor?" the man asked, reaching to hold the door from closing.

"We're here," Kelly answered, giving the cart a push in opposition to Carol's pull.

"No! Anyone from the staff!" the man said, his voice beginning to show his impatience.

There was something too familiar in that voice and it caused Kelly to look up at the man who spoke. "John!" she exclaimed, shocked to see it was her former suitor at the other end of the cart.

John Brandon's eyes widened in surprise as he looked at the woman across from him. "Kelly?"

They were both stunned. Holding each other's gaze their minds reeled with the confusion of the other's presence. Time slipped its dimension for Kelly as, in the quickness of a breath, the shallowness of the relationship she had once had with this man now became obvious and, too, the revelation of the reason for that superficiality. There had always been a distance between them that Kelly could never fully explain nor understand. Try as she might she could not bring herself to become affectionately involved with him. Though they had dated often, there was always something too rote about their affair; something thin. She overlooked the fact that he'd never taken her to his offices—she wasn't even sure what building they were in—nor that he ever spoke much of his clients or work. He had seemed so professionally inept while working on Foundation business—something Kelly was also willing to make allowances for—and yet, he afforded and enjoyed all of the trappings of a powerful and successful attorney.

She had tried to convince herself that time might change all of this; that they might grow closer as they became more familiar. But there was never the magic in their affair; no mysterious magnetic attraction—not like that which she had experienced on her first sight of Sam Baker. John had whispered the "sweet nothings" in her ear but it had all sounded too practiced. She had tried to appreciate what he said though his gentle words had never fascinated her—not in the way she found herself hanging on every syllable when Sam spoke and longing to hear his voice when he was silent.

Now it became all too clear to her. John Brandon was a plant.

A spy!

All this time he had really been working for the developers! She blinked several times, as if not trusting her vision, but there was no altering the fact that it was the same man—the man in whom she had placed so much trust these last months. Her anger heated instantly, then exploded in a fury. "You bastard!" she shouted and lunged the cart forcefully into the bewildered lawyer, knocking him against the back wall of the elevator.

Carol jumped out of the way as Kelly pulled the cart back into the hall. She would have attacked him savagely but, before she could move around the cart, the door slid silently closed. Her last glimpse of the man was of him sprawled on the floor, dumbfounded, trying to collect himself. The other passenger, a blond, younger man, was standing with an equally startled expression, so aghast at what occurred he couldn't move to help. Kelly threw herself at the door, clawing to reopen it. Failing that, she pressed repeatedly on the lighted hailing button to halt the elevator's descent. "Come back here, you bastard!" she hollered, pounding her fist on the metal door.

Carol was just as astonished at this sudden, vehement behavior that seemed so foreign to Kelly's character. She could only stand there and blink repeatedly as the woman pounded on the door. Then, realizing the gravity of having been recognized she grabbed Kelly's hand, yelling, "C'mon. We better get out of here."

Together they hurried to the stairwell, bounded through the exit door and ran, almost leaping, down the many stairs to the ground floor. The guard had not yet returned to that floor and, finding their way unhindered, the women ran out the glass side exit door. As they reached the end of the walk to the asphalt parking lot Dave pulled up with the van. The door was flung open and the two women jumped inside, barely seating themselves as Dave sped off, rounding the building and out the gate.

Breathless and frightened, they all watched out the rear windows of the van for signs of pursuit. When they were several blocks away Carol finally gasped, "Where's Tom?" fearing they had left one of their party behind.

"It's okay," Dave said quickly. He, too, was showing signs of uneasiness. "He'd already been seen tonight by too many people. He thought it best just to return to his office and act like he'd been working all along. He said he works late all the time. He'll be okay."

Kelly had been sitting quietly in the dark of the van's interior. Now, she suddenly burst into tears, sobbing into her hands.

"Uh-oh. What's wrong?" Sam asked, twisting in his seat to look back at her.

Carol put her arm around her and pulled the woman close to cry on her shoulder. "We were made," Carol explained to the men.

"What?" Dave asked. "By who?"

"John Brandon. He and some other guy were about to get off on that floor and he recognized Kelly—or she recognized him. Anyway, we were made."

"That other guy was James Brody," Dave told them. "You're sure he recognized you?"

"Oh yeah. No doubt about that," Carol said with an amused smile. "Kelly knocked him back against the wall of the elevator. I mean, she really flattened him!"

Kelly raised her head from Carol's shoulder and cried, "I trusted him, that son-of-a-bitch." Then she returned to weeping in the nestled crook of Carol's sympathetic arm.

"So, I guess he was a plant all along," Carol suggested.

"Yeah," Dave replied. "Tom told me Brandon's firm is on retainer to Marco Development. That was why Tom left the house so hurriedly when Brandon stopped in to see Kelly. He thought the guy was there on legal business. I guess no one at the company knew the guy was doing the legal work for the Foundation. What a creep, huh?"

Dave drove for a few minutes more, then pulled up in front of a brightly-lit diner, suggesting they grab a cup of coffee for a needed and deserved break. They waited until Kelly had composed herself, wiping the tears from her red and swollen eyes to finally nod she was able to accompany them.

Inside the diner they gathered around a large, black formica-topped table. Except for placing an order for coffee, no one felt like speaking just yet. The adrenalin was still coursing through their veins, causing their hearts to beat rapidly as they exchanged nervous glances with one another. The sound of a distant siren made them wince as butterflies flitted in their stomachs. They looked out the window, half expecting to see flashing lights whirling out in the street, the police having come for them. When the waitress returned and served them coffee and tea, they could barely summon the words to mumble a thank you.

Sam shook his head to clear the anxiety inside him, as well as to try to relieve the worries of the others. "This is nuts. We're all shaking scared here, and we really don't have anything to worry about. We're tensed up and frightened over nothing. Even if they do discover it was us, they can't do anything about it. We hold all the aces. I think we've uncovered enough dirt to bury this James Brody and his whole company. He's the one who should be worrying about us...and he probably is right now."

"How did they know we were there?" Carol asked clutching her abdomen with her folded arms. Below the table her knees were causing her heels to tap the floor in nervous trembling.

Dave put an arm around her to try to calm her. "Brody went into the program to pull some records to show Brandon," he explained. "Either Sam or Pat was already in those records and Brody could see that they were being accessed."

"Mm...Unfortunate," Sam shrugged. "But, history. It doesn't matter. Tomorrow Pat and I will run this all together and see what we've got. If I'm not mistaken, by tomorrow night we're going to have some very interesting reading material."

"I hope so," Kelly said. "We've only got two days left to win this and then the land becomes condos or houses."

"Well, don't fret, Kelly," Sam said to her. "I think we'll turn things around here. I only hope we can bring down that son-of-a-bitch attorney, too."

"Don't start, Sam," Carol shushed him. She motioned with her eyes toward Kelly as a reminder. Sam let it drop.

"No. It's okay," Kelly said, having intercepted Carol's glance. "I'm okay about it. Look. We only ever dated. I'm not upset about betrayed love or anything like that. I'm just really mad that a person can be so despicable. He betrayed not only my trust, but everybody else's who belongs to the Foundation."

"The guy's a real Benedict Arnold," Pat quipped resentfully. "If you think about it, he kind of sold out the American heritage."

Dave put his hands on his knees and looked at everyone. "Well. It's late. We've had quite a day of it. We better get Pat back to her car and head for home." He released a wide yawn, saying, "I've got some serious sleeping to do tonight."

As they stood to leave, Dave stayed behind to put some cash on the table for the waitress. Sam put his arm around Kelly and the woman snuggled closer to his side as they headed for the door. Pat followed along behind them with Carol and raised a curious eyebrow as she cast an inquiring glance at the woman beside her. Carol answered her with an expressive and purposeful wink.

Chapter Thirteen

A light rain was falling to offer some relief from the hot, muggy days of the past week. Sam lay in his bed and listened to the splashing sounds made by the passing cars on the road in front of the motel. From the dim light peeking in around the curtains, as well as the increased amount of traffic, he guessed it to be around eight o'clock. People were on their way to work or, at any rate, up and going about their business as usual. He stared at the ceiling and smiled as he thought over the interesting though unusual events of the last week.

No ordinary vacation this, he mused. Not by any stretch of the imagination. And certainly not business as usual. What an amazing and bewildering turn his life had taken. The causes and effects that seemed to direct him without his even having a decision in it were curious in themselves, he thought. Circumstances just seemed to be moving him as needed. He felt like a pawn in some spiritual, cosmic chess game. But it was so exciting, and the winnings so rewarding, he felt impatient on awaiting the next move.

Most of his life it had been he making the decisions, and always after carefully considering the risks and rewards. He had decided where he would go to college, what he would study. He had decided who he would work for and how long. He had made the decision to enter R.O.T.C. and go to war. He had passed on an offer to serve in military intelligence, favoring, instead, to serve in the infantry. Now, this week, he was just rolling with the tides, doing that which he seemed directed to do. He longed to know the finish; what would happen next.

His thoughts were interrupted by the telephone ringing on the shelf between the two beds. He quickly rolled over, glancing to see the sleepy form of his friend stirring in the bed next to his. As he reached for the phone he saw the digital clock beside it. It was 8:20. "M'yeah...," he answered groggily.

"...Sam? It's me."

"Tom?" he asked, becoming alert and swinging his legs off the bed to come to a sit. "What's going on?"

"I'm at home. I wanted to reach you before I went to the office. I called the Foundation and got your number from Marylou. Quite an arm-twister, that girl. You know, I had to pledge a fifty-dollar donation before she'd give it to me? How are you guys doing?"

"I don't know, yet. We're only just getting up."

"Oh? Should I be sorry I woke you?"

"No, no. We should be getting up. We've got a lot to do. How'd it go after we left? Are you okay?"

"Oh, yeah. Fine. I'm not suspected at all. At least, I don't think so. I was back in my office working when they came in. I made it pretty believable that I was ignorant of the whole thing. They told me what happened. I asked if they were going to call in the police."

"And?"

"No way. You must have uncovered something James is afraid to have go public. What I'm worried about is his telling me he'll handle it his own way. You, you better be on guard. He can be really nasty."

"Yeah. I guess so if he can arrange to have people run off the road."

"My point exactly," Tom said. "Watch your back. It could be dangerous for you."

"Thanks for the worry. We're going to go over what we've gathered. Is there a way to get a hold of you and fill you in on what we find?"

"No. It's probably better that I call you. Are you going to stay there for the next few days? You're not changing motels or anything?"

"No. Not unless we have to," Sam told him. "We'll keep you posted through Marylou."

"Good idea. I just hope I don't go broke trying to get any information out of her," Tom laughed. "Listen. I better cut this short. I've got to get going."

The two men said their goodbyes and hung up. Dave, now sitting on his bed and leaning against the headboard, asked of the conversation. Carol and Kelly, awakened by the phone, had entered the room and waited, also, to be briefed.

Sam told what he'd learned from Tom and it relieved everyone to hear they weren't in trouble with the authorities. Not wanting to upset the women, he didn't tell them they could possibly face a reprisal from James Brody. He wanted to wait until Dave and he were alone and could talk about how to avoid any unpleasant surprises.

****

The rain was falling heavier when Sam left the motel room and made a dash for his car. He had taken time only for a quick cup of coffee and a phone call to Pat Marley to tell her he was leaving promptly for her office. Carol had telephoned her children as she'd done every morning, then she, Dave and Kelly dressed and prepared to go into Sharpsburg. Kelly knew an enormous amount of paperwork had piled up on her desk these last few days and she was anxious to clear much of it.

They arrived at the Foundation house around ten o'clock and were greeted by Marylou. Kelly confided in the woman all that they had done last night and Marylou's eyes grew wide in amazement as she listened to the tale. When she learned of John Brandon's deceit she was outraged. "I always suspected there was something not credible about that man," she said. She and Kelly talked about how they might repair the damage the man had wrought. They concluded that the board must be made aware of the situation and make those decisions on what actions should be implemented.

When Kelly asked for an update on activities at the Foundation, Marylou smiled. "Oh...things have been buzzing around here. Of course, it all pales next to what you guys have been involved in. We've had some inquiries into our organization...and have received a few sizable donations. A couple of reporters from different newspapers have called and asked for updates; some guy from the A.P. service wants to run a story on tomorrow's outcome and, let's see...; oh, yeah, a fellow from *Civil War Times* magazine is supposed to stop in later today. I have a feeling we're going to be a very busy place tomorrow."

"Well, that wouldn't surprise me," Kelly said. "There'll be a flock of reporters from all over the country, I'm sure."

"Mitchel Page was on the phone all last evening calling members of the McPherson Foundation. They're supposed to fly back to their corporate office for a special meeting to act on our request. Hopefully, enough of them can gather to decide on it."

Kelly was delighted to hear this. "Oh! This is wonderful news! I only hope they can reach a decision before tomorrow. Nothing like bringing it down to the last minute."

"We have that jerk face John Brandon to thank for that," Marylou said. "Anyway, some other really good news is; Dennis has improved remarkably. He's able to talk some, though he says his memory is groggy about what happened."

"Was he able to tell who ran him off the road?"

"No," Lou told her. "Only that it was a big white car. He said it happened too quickly."

"Hm... Well, Sam's working on it from another angle. If he has the right material, he's hoping to use bank records to put something together. He's guessing there'll be some paper trail he can connect. It's a long shot, if you ask me, but Sam thinks there might be a lead in it to follow. He and Pat are working on that and some other stuff."

"Wow! This is all kind of exciting," Marylou said from behind her desk.

Over by the filing cabinets Carol rolled her eyes. "Yeah. But excitement like this I'd rather just read about and not be a part of."

Kelly laughed and said she agreed with that. She began wading through the paperwork on her desk and soon had both Carol and Dave employed, helping with typing and stuffing envelopes. Kelly spent much of her time on the phone contacting board members.

Without going into the particulars of how she learned of it, she explained the situation involving their attorney's association with the developers and discussed what actions might be taken both in correcting the damage and any legal recourse against him. Marylou fielded calls from both concerned individuals and a string of reporters from the media around the country.

Having anticipated the certain flood of inquiries, Lou informed each caller that there would be a press conference at the Foundation house at 7:30 the next evening. She and Kelly had planned this to give the board time to prepare a statement on whichever way the decision went on the ownership of the land.

It was around 3:30 in the afternoon with a heavy rain pelting loudly on the old tin roof above that Carol took a turn answering the phone. "Historic Antietam Foundation," she said, answering in the manner she'd heard Marylou.

"...May I speak to Kelly, please," the voice on the other end asked.

Carol recognized the voice...and that his tone was more of a demand than a request. "Just a minute," she replied. She pressed the hold button and looked at Kelly. "I believe you'll want to handle this call. It's John Brandon."

Kelly sat fixed, momentarily, with a hostile, angry glare growing in her eyes. She reached out for the receiver on her desk.

"Be cool," Dave cautioned. "Firm. But cool."

Kelly placed the receiver to her ear but paused her finger over the blinking light. She drew a deep breath to calm the storm that had immediately grown within her. Then, releasing it, she pressed the buttons for both her extension and the external speaker. "This is Kelly Gracie."

"Kelly. It's John."

"Well, this is a surprise. I didn't expect to hear from you again. At least, not out of court."

"Kelly, just what the hell do you and your friends think you were trying to accomplish last night?"

"I believe it's called 'tit for tat'," she replied.

"You know I could bring criminal charges against you and that whole organization? I could carve you up in a courtroom till there's nothing left of any of you."

"Oh-h, I don't think so," she said, winking at Dave and Carol. "I mean, I suppose you could take us to court. But in the process, there would be some very interesting reading material on Marco Development Corporation. It could be very embarrassing to some very influential people."

"I don't know what you think you've got there, and I doubt if it could be used in court. It doesn't matter anyway."

"No? And why not?"

"Listen, Kelly. I've got one mad as hell boss upstairs who doesn't appreciate having his files rifled. Now, I've managed to talk him into dropping any legal action against the Foundation. All you have to do is return everything you copied."

"Oh-h-h..." Kelly said. "So, you admit you do work for him. Well, fancy that. And here I was willing to give you the benefit of the doubt. I thought maybe you were just trying to talk James Brody into dropping the development plans and let us have the ground. Well, well, well. Imagine that."

Kelly had been speaking tongue-in-cheek. But she changed her tone now, allowing her anger to vent. "Look, you son-of-a-bitch. I'll never forgive you for this. You betrayed a trust and there's nothing more despicable than that. Judas may have been forgiven by God but they'll serve ice water in Hell before I ever forget what you've done to me and the Foundation! We're going over the material from your company right now, and believe me, when we're finished with Marco Development, they won't be able to get a permit to build an outhouse! And if I have to dance naked on the judge's bench to get you disbarred along the way it'll be well worth it!"

There was a silence on the other end. And whether the lawyer was thinking this over or, perhaps, conferring with someone, no one at the Foundation knew. They waited for a reply.

"Kelly," John said at last, his voice calm but with a trace of urgency. "I don't know what else to tell you. Forget about me and what hurt I may have caused you. Listen. We need those papers back. You've got to get rid of them. We're talking about millions of dollars here. These guys play rough for that kind of money. Do you think they're just going to throw up their hands and walk away from it? C'mon, Kelly! There's too much at stake here. Get rid of those papers. Burn them. Trash them. Anything! Just don't even contemplate using them."

"Oh, you creep, you! And to think I went out with you. The only thing you care about is money. I sure hope he's paying you well."

"Kelly. Kelly. Mr. Brody is going to send some people around to pick up those papers. When they get there...just hand them over to them. Don't try to be a heroine. It's not worth it. This project is going to happen and nothing you or anyone can do will stop it. It's called progress, Kelly. People have to have homes and schools and churches and the past can't stand in the way of the future. There's already a national park where people can go to visit. You can't preserve all the land. It's happened at other battlefields and it'll happen here, too. It's inevitable."

"I've seen what your progress has done at Manasses and South Mountain and a host of other historic places around the country. You build right up to and even over the ground that others fought and died on just so someone can live in an overpriced, overbuilt house and think they're just a little bit superior than the guy down the street. You destroy our country's history so you can make a couple extra dollars. Well, times are changing, Mister! People aren't going to allow their heritage to be sold off that easily anymore. At least, not without a fight. And I'm proud to be one of those people directly in the front lines against money-grubbing leeches like you and that...that James Brody of yours."

"Oh, spare me the citizenship course. I had that in twelfth grade high school, taught by a World War II vet who was well intentioned but lived in a dream world. This is reality; contracts and deals are made and money turns the wheels. Just give those people what they're after, Kelly. You're a music teacher. Go back to teaching. It's safer for you there."

"You go to Hell!" Kelly spat and slammed the receiver down. She sat there awhile, fuming.

Dave gave a low whistle, saying, "Whew... Glad my ear wasn't against that receiver. You sure toasted his."

Kelly looked up at Dave and blushed a little as she recalled what all she'd said. "Hm. Guess I kind of lost it a little, huh?"

"No. No," Dave smiled. "We're all looking forward to seeing you 'dance naked on the judge's bench'."

Kelly laughed, "I don't know where that came from. It just slipped out."

Carol was a bit more sedate as she sat considering what John Brandon had said. "You know, he is right," she said to them. "This is the real world. And money does grease the wheel, unfortunately. The good have to keep fighting the bad. It never ends...and it never will." She looked at her husband. "What do we do? Those guys probably do play rough."

"Not to worry," Dave told her. "We'll be all right. He's just trying to scare us. They aren't going to do anything stupid. They're more worried about what dirt we may have on them and what we'll do with it."

"We should give Sam and Pat a call," Kelly suggested. "We should tell them about John's phone call."

Dave nodded in agreement. "Good idea. I'm interested in how far along they are."

Kelly dialed up Pat's office and asked to speak with Sam. Lou went out to the front room to greet a young couple on tour of the battlefield so Kelly kept her conversation off the external speaker. Dave and Carol could tell from the upbeat tone in Kelly's voice and her constant use of the word "great" that Sam and Pat must surely be relaying good news to her.

They listened as Kelly discussed John's phone call with Sam and, just as Dave had said, he, too, assured her they would all be okay; not to worry over empty threats. When they were finished talking and Kelly set the receiver down, she was showing a smug grin.

"What'd he say?" Dave asked eagerly.

"Well. Heh, heh...," Kelly chortled. "It would appear Marco Development has pretty well nailed their own coffin."

"Why?" Dave asked excitedly.

"Well, for starters, James Brody has made some sizeable cash withdrawals from his personal account this last year."

"Proving?"

"Well, nothing on its own. But it just happens that Sunshine Trucking Company in Florida made some rather substantial bank payments, in cash, close enough to the dates of Brody's withdrawals to raise an eyebrow. Sunshine does a lot of hauling for Marco Development."

"How did he find all this out?" Dave asked.

"He said he just called Sunshine's bookkeeper for references. One of the names she gave him was the truck dealer where they buy all their trucks. When he called them, the dealer's accounts receivable gave him a whole history. It seems they were even eager to give the dates of payments and whether it was by check or cash."

"What else? What else?" Dave asked, his enthusiasm overflowing.

"It gets better," Kelly chuckled in delight. "You know the list of senators and representatives you found in Brody's desk? Pat took a few of the names that had checkmarks beside them and made some inquiries to find out what committees they served on. Then, just on a hunch, she called their offices to find out the last time they'd been out of the country, where they went, and what hotel they stayed in."

"They gave out that information?" Carol asked, surprised.

"Sure. It's a matter of public record. Especially if you make it sound like you're one of their constituents back home. They'll tell you everything, especially which ones they paid for out of pocket. All Pat had to do was dial up the hotel computers for the guest registry and find out who really paid for it. Guess who picked up the tabs for our representatives' jaunts to a certain resort on St. Thomas?"

Carol was amazed, "Really? Marco?"

"Correct, for $500.00," Kelly chortled. "Now for the daily double. Carol, for $1,000.00, can you name two local, county officials on the zoning board who, after returning from respective trips to St. Thomas, changed their votes to grant a variance to Marco Development?"

"Whoa!" Dave remarked.

"Mm-hm," Kelly nodded. "The trips were given through a promotional company. And who is the owner of Skyway Promotions? None other than James Brody."

"Oh, man! This is great!" Dave beamed.

"Isn't it? There's more, too. But Sam didn't want to elaborate on the phone. He wants to wrap up as much as he can and be back here around five o'clock. We're all going out for dinner so we're to wait here for him."

Marylou had returned to hear most of what Kelly had said and she frowned, now, from behind her desk. "Shoot. I wish I could go with you guys. It sounds like maybe we'll have something to celebrate."

"Why can't you?" Carol asked her.

"Oh, my husband invited some friends over we haven't seen for a while. I've got to go home and cook dinner."

"Well," Kelly said, trying to cheer her some. "If things go right, and Sam can somehow use what he's found, we'll have a real celebration tomorrow night."

"Wouldn't that be great?" Lou smiled.

The phone interrupted them and Lou cheerfully answered it. Dave, Carol and Kelly returned to their work, passing the next few hours rather routinely. The drizzling rain had ended and, though the sky remained overcast with dark, threatening clouds, it was with a lighter step and a rekindled optimism that the four went about their duties inside. They watched the clock and waited impatiently for Sam to return with the material he was assembling.

Along about 6:15 Sam finally did return. Marylou had left for home and, too, wasn't there to greet the tall handsome man wearing a subtle smirk as he swaggered onto the porch. "Hi, y'all," he said from the partition doorway. He was holding a cardboard box with Crown Royal imprinted across it. He leaned against the partition and breathed a long, satisfied, but tired sigh.

The three looked up at him warmly—Carol, from her seat at Marylou's desk; Kelly, from her desk, and Dave, from a kneeling position at a lower file drawer.

"Hey, friend," Dave greeted him pleasantly, noting the exhaustion behind the man's contented expression. "What'd you bring us? Booze to drown our sorrows in?"

Sam held his subtle smirk and looked at his friend, then at Kelly and Carol in turn, watching their eyes glimmer in bridled excitement to hear his reply. "No," he said. Then slowly he stood erect and held out the box to them. "I brought you one hundred and fifty acres of prime farmland adjoining the Antietam battlefield."

"Yeah, Sam!" Kelly exclaimed and clapped her hands together. She got up from her chair and came around to him, arriving at his side as Carol approached him from the other. Kelly relieved him of the weighty box and Sam put an arm around each woman, sharing a joyful hug. When they relaxed their embrace Carol asked to hear about everything he'd uncovered in the records.

"Oh, man," Sam sighed. "It's a long story. And one better told over a juicy steak and a tall draft."

Kelly squeezed his side once more. "I'll bet you're exhausted. It'll take us only a minute to close up and we can go eat."

"That sounds good to me," Sam told her.

In but ten minutes time, Kelly was locking the door to the Foundation house. Sam stepped off the porch and went to his car, parked about five spaces behind Dave's van. Dave carried the box of papers to his van and, as he unlocked the side doors, hollered over to question Sam why they were not taking only one vehicle.

"Kelly will ride with me," Sam replied. "You follow us. That'll save having to come back to get my car. We can just head back to the motel after dinner."

Dave helped his wife into the van then saw Sam approaching with the sword in hand. "Hey. Hey," he said. "We're just going to dinner. You planning on a cavalry charge or something?"

Sam chuckled and, opening the rear door of the van, explained, "You don't think I'd leave this in the motel, do you? It goes with me. It'll be easier to hide in here." He placed the sword on the floor along the near side panel. Then he turned and took the box of papers from Dave, placing it beside the sword. He covered both with some throw pillows from the seats and an old blanket, trying to make it all look like just an inconspicuous pile of bedding.

A short drive from Sharpsburg found the four seated in a quiet corner booth in the back of an Italian restaurant. Once their order had been placed with the waitress Sam began his story, explaining how he and Pat had accessed various bank records and several businesses to match deposits, withdrawals, wire transfers and other money movements that could be construed as payoffs or kickbacks.

"Much of the money goes through two dummy corporations," Sam said. "One, I told Kelly about earlier, is the Contiguous Information and Education Awards, Incorporated. Sounds pretty distinctive enough, doesn't it? I mean, if you were to be awarded an all-expenses paid trip from a company with a title like that, a person might believe you earned it through some diligent act of merit. Turns out the company is on the government's lobby register. Sole stock owner; James Marcus Brody, of course."

"Oh, this is good," Dave said.

Sam nodded and continued. "The other company is some sort of off-shore, export-import, holding company. It's supposed to be chartered to trade in antiques and collectibles but its accounts receivables, oddly, don't match its accounts payables. All its banking is done in the Cayman Islands so it was all but impossible to track the money any further in just a few hours."

Carol looked amazed as she listened to him. "Sam, how do you do all this? How can it be that easy to get into other people's records?"

Sam blushed a little and shrugged. "It's easy if you know how. I've been at it so long it comes second nature to me. Once you learn how to move through the networks and trade codes and passwords with hackers it's rather simple."

"Trade codes and passwords?" Carol asked.

"Yeah. You send out the word that you're looking for a particular code and somebody's sure to have it. Then you trade them a code or password of equal value. Hell, since I have access to a lot of places that are forbidden entry to others, I've got a lot of value to trade."

Kelly looked unsettled at hearing this and Sam was quick to pick up on her disapproval. "Oh! Don't worry, Kelly. I didn't give away any classified info. I only shared stuff for accessing private facilities; places where I helped develop the software. I always design in some critical window that can't be opened. They'll roam around and have some fun and think they're really into something exciting. Then they'll find the locked window and that'll be that."

"I'm relieved," Kelly sighed. "You made it sound like you were giving away the store."

"No. I really don't condone hacking, even if it's just for a curious look around. But I don't condemn it, either. I've, uh, I've done my share of it. Anyway, the point being, Pat and I were able to match records of trips made by people on that list we have with where the tab was picked up by one of Brody's bogus companies. It all fits together so nicely to smack of political influence peddling. If those records were to be released, I'd wager there would be quite a few red faces and stammering explanations both in Washington and in the county courthouse."

Sam paused and looked around the table at each of them while, as was his habit when he searched for the words to form a conclusive statement, he sucked on his lower lip. Then he nodded in agreement with his own thought, saying, "Well, ladies and gentlemen, I believe the game is moving to check."

"Well done," Dave said. He refilled everyone's beer from the pitcher, then raised his glass over the center of the table in toast. "To Sam and Pat...and the wonders they have performed."

The others joined his glass with theirs but Sam stopped them. "No, no. Here's to all of us, and to everyone associated with the Foundation," he said. They clinked glasses, then downed some hefty swallows.

When she set her glass down Kelly looked at Sam, puzzled. "So, Sam, why do you suppose someone with James Brody's business savvy left such an easily followed trail?"

Sam set his glass down after another large swallow and shook his head. "Actually, it isn't that easy to follow. If he were audited his books would be in order. Nothing shows up as illegal. It only coincides with other events. He's allowed to move money between his companies as long as a proper invoice is written. Show me a public official that won't brag to the people back home of having won a trip for outstanding service. I'm sure they've got it set up as an educational conference, complete with speakers and pamphlets. Of course, if anyone bothered to check attendance, they'd probably find the meetings held around the pools and golf courses. He's a clever man, Brody."

"Ah-h...but not as clever as our Sam Baker," Kelly said, tilting her glass toward him.

Sam smiled and took the compliment with a bow. "But, let's not be forgetting Pat Marley," he added. "She's been most helpful."

"Speaking of which—where is she?" Dave asked.

"Mm, she had to work late in order to take tomorrow off. She wants to be here to see what happens. Too bad, too. She'd have enjoyed our little party."

Kelly frowned on learning the reason for their new friend's absence, then turned it to a smile, saying, "Well, maybe she'll be able to make our victory celebration tomorrow night."

"Here's hoping we have one," Sam said with a tip of his glass.

During the meal Sam told more of what he and Pat had discovered about the shadier dealings of Marco Development and how they had uncovered them. He assured his friends he had enough information on the Sunshine Trucking Company to warrant an investigation of that company's log books and shipping manifests. Also, since it was a company involved in interstate commerce, the F.B.I. could be enlisted with all their investigative resources.

Then, in the spirit of their new-found optimism, the group turned to discussions livelier. Kelly was coaxed to talk about performing with professional orchestras and world-renowned conductors. Sam and Dave entertained with stories of wild partying in late night Saigon and the many odd characters they'd met in the service. Fascinated, as this was so foreign to her, Kelly listened attentively and begged for more stories.

When Dave took a turn, he told of their adventure of being ambushed along a muddied, desolate road in the jungle. Careful to omit any mention of killing or violence he relayed, instead, how hilarious Sam looked flailing a machete overhead and yelling so fiercely as to frighten the enemy back into the brush. Except for Sam, everyone had a good laugh when Dave so vividly described how the ruptured flask first startled the three companions to think Sam was wounded, then amused them in believing he'd wet his pants.

Sam shrugged and blushed. "Yeah. Go ahead and laugh. I can't believe that story still cracks you up. Anyway, that flask probably saved my life," he told the others.

"Heh. Saved your family jewels is closer to it...too closer to it," Dave chortled.

"My point exactly," Sam smiled.

"Do you still have it?" Kelly asked.

"What? The flask? Yeah. Both it and the machete are hanging on my bedroom wall. It's a reminder to me of how precariously life is balanced."

"Tell her about the flask, Sam," Dave urged him. "Listen to this. This is strange in itself. Go ahead. Tell it," he urged again.

"Well, there's not much to tell, really. It's a silver flask my brother picked up for me in a little antique shop in Jersey. He was in Trenton on business and his car ran out of gas in front of this little shop. He phoned for a tow truck and, while he was waiting, he browsed around the store. When he picked up the flask and inquired about it the store owner said he'd had a lot of offers for it over the years but wasn't inclined to ever sell it. When my brother mentioned it would make a great gift to send me overseas the guy changed his mind and sold it to him. I'm glad he did," Sam added.

"So am I," Kelly said. Then, embarrassed at how that came out, she blushed and lowered her eyes.

Dave, along with the others, smiled endearingly at her for the comment. But, to rescue her from an awkward moment, he said, "Well, I've had a good meal and a fun time. It's ten o'clock. I'm starting to wind down."

"You're gettin' old, Buddy," Sam teased.

Carol sighed. "He's always pushing himself too much. He's at work from sun up to supper. Then four nights a week at the gym either working out or instructing. You need to slow down," she told him.

"I will. I will," Dave said. "Just as soon as the new store gets rolling."

"You said that about the other one," Carol reminded him.

"Well, who knew it was going to be so successful?" Dave said with a shrug. He pushed his chair back to stand and, once erect, he stroked Carol's cheek with the back of his hand. "I'll go take care of the bill. You guys meet me out front."

"The man's treating," Sam exclaimed as though he was surprised.

"Well," Kelly said, playing along. "Had I known that I'd have ordered the lobster."

"Heh! Doesn't matter," Dave replied. "It's Carol's card. Comes out of her house money. You don't think I'd use mine? That's my poker money. You guys aren't that good of friends."

Carol rolled her eyes. "Have sympathy for me. I have to live with this man."

When the four stepped from the restaurant into the evening air they were pleasantly greeted by the fresh, invigorating scent attendant when countless days of oppressive heat are finally terminated by a full day of cool, gentle rain. Sam led them around the corner of the building and through the gravel parking lot, carefully avoiding the puddles formed in the slight depressions.

The lot had been full when they arrived late for the dinner hour. Now, with most of the patrons having departed, their two vehicles sat alone at the far end of the lot. Eight or ten other cars, most of which belonged to the employees, were parked under the lone pole light near the building. Dave walked in rear of the others and became aware of a figure approaching deliberately from the shadows behind. His first thought was to divert the group to the better lighted area so he and Sam could confront the stranger should a situation arise.

Too late! The man stepped up close to Dave's back and instantly he felt uneasy. He turned around quickly to face the man.

"Got a light?" the man asked as he held up an unlit cigarette between thumb and forefinger. The others stopped and turned to look, only now becoming aware of his presence. He was a shorter man, about five feet, six inches, in his mid-forties. Though he had a solid, stocky build he also had a rather large paunch.

"No. We don't smoke," Dave answered for them all. He instinctively sized the man up. He sensed danger, but he thought perhaps he was just over-reacting.

"Those your cars over there," the man said. It was a statement with an obvious conclusion since that was the direction they were headed and there was no other reason to walk to that end of the lot.

Dave remained uncertain about the man. "Yeah. They're ours."

"Nice cars, DeLoreans," the man said. "Very sporty. Maybe you got a light in one of them cars."

"No. I don't think so," Dave replied, not liking the feeling of this man or the situation. Even by the dim glow of the mercury vapor light Dave could see the man had a rough, unfriendly face and his mannerisms suggested hostility.

The "swish-click" that sounded from the opening switchblade confirmed Dave's impressions as the man flashed a seven-inch knife blade before him. "Let's go see...," he sneered.

"Whoa! Now, wait a minute, Buddy!" Dave said as he and Sam threw up their hands to shield their bodies. "Easy there. No trouble."

"Trouble you got, Mister," the man said harshly. "Get goin'." He waved the blade at Dave's face in emphasis.

"Dave...?" Carol cried, cowering behind him for protection.

"It's okay, Honey. He isn't going to hurt us. We're going to cooperate with him and he'll be on his way." Dave backed up a pace, then turned to get the others moving. When they turned around, they saw four other men appear from hiding from behind the van. One held a length of pipe, one had some sort of blackjack, and the other two held guns. The figures fanned out to surround the helpless four.

"Oh, shit," Sam murmured. "I think we're in trouble, Buddy."

"Yeah. Could be," Dave replied. As they were herded over to the cars Dave looked back at the knife-wielding man. "Look. What do you guys want? We don't want any trouble. We'll give you whatever you want. Just don't hurt us. Please?"

"You took something that doesn't belong to you. Some papers. Now, we want them back. Hand them over and we might not hurt you—too badly."

"What papers?" Dave asked, halting momentarily. He waited for the man to draw closer, hoping to feel the knifepoint against him so he'd know precisely where it was.

"Funny man," the stranger said, performing exactly as Dave had wanted by stepping up and poking the knife to his back. "Don't fuck with me, asshole. You know fuckin' well what papers."

"Jesus Christ, Dave!" Carol screamed. "Give him the damned papers!"

"Now there's a smart lady. This your husband, Lady?"

Carol seemed almost hysteric. "Y-yes. Please don't hurt him," she begged. "He's not well. He's...he's sick. Please!"

"Okay. Okay," Dave said. "They're in the van. Sam. Get them for them. They're in the sheath. Give it to 'em."

"Dave?" Sam said, puzzled at his friend's request.

Dave tossed him the keys, repeating, "They're in the sheath. Give it to 'em, Sam. They mean business. We've been ambushed."

"Fine! All right! I'll give it to them. Damn! This is the last time I get involved in something like this with you," Sam muttered. He moved to the side door of the van and fumbled with the keys. Two of the men gathered in close. The other three stayed close to Dave.

"Look. You promise you won't hurt us, right?" Dave said, his voice trembling almost to the point of tears. "We give you what you want and you'll let us be. Please?"

"Take it easy, ya' fuckin' jerk. Gawd, Lady, did you ever marry a wimp," the knife-wielder said.

"You're telling me," Carol replied. "Look. Just take what you came for and leave. Okay? Just leave us be."

"I...I didn't have anything to do with this," Dave whimpered. "He, he did it all. I didn't even know he was doing it till he told me about it. He's the guy you want. Not me!"

"Shut up! Asshole," the man commanded, pressing the knife a bit firmer into Dave's back.

Sam inserted the key into the lock but stopped to glance at Dave. "Thanks a lot, 'Buddy'. You mastermind the whole thing and try to put the blame on me! You aren't weaseling out of it this easy. Don't let him fool you. He's the one that set the whole thing up."

"Would you two shut up and just give them the damn papers," Carol shouted.

"That fucking boyfriend of yours has really got us into trouble this time," Dave spat at her.

"Boyfriend! What do you mean?" Carol asked angrily.

"Think I don't know about you two? Always sneaking around behind my back. Having affairs while I'm at work..."

"You bastard, you! That's it! I'm divorcing you as soon as we get home. I'll take you for everything you've got!"

The five intruders relaxed a bit, amused over listening to the banter raging between the three. Kelly was trembling, confused. She looked from one complaining figure to the other, not able to make sense of them venting their long-held frustrations.

"Fat chance of you getting even a penny," Dave said to his wife. "Not once the judge sees those photos of you two."

"What photos?" Sam asked. "You've got photographs?"

"You bet I do. I had your asses followed by a private detective."

"You son-of-a-bitch," Sam shouted. He turned and whipped open the van door and bent way in as if to search around in the dark. He pretended to fumble in the van until one of the men leaned over him to peer in. Then, when the man was close enough, in one swift motion Sam exploded backwards, drawing the sword from its scabbard as he knocked the surprised man to the ground. The other man near him, holding a pistol, hadn't reacted yet to seeing his companion sprawl onto the wet gravel. As Sam burst from the van, he released a blood-curdling yell that sent a shiver through everyone, stunning them momentarily. The long blade flailed and, with one fell swoop, Sam brought it down onto the man's gun arm. As it cut to the bone it pushed the arm downward and continued across the man's stomach and side. Blood squirted from the wounds as the man dropped to his knees and cried out in agony.

The blade glinted in the scattered light of the distant pole lamp as Sam raised it overhead and turned to the figure still sprawled on the ground. The man caught sight of the sharpened steel now being directed toward him and cried out in terror, instinctively raising the length of pipe for protection. The sword clanged against the metal pipe and deflected away, saving the man's skull from being cleaved. The very force of Sam's blow drove the pipe onto the fellow's head and temporarily laid him flat.

Sam acted as a man possessed. He shrieked again that savage howl and raised the sword for a fatal blow.

"Sam! No! You'll kill him!" Kelly screamed, causing him to pause with the sword held high in position to strike.

The dazed figure on the ground looked up and cried in horror. With the gash from the pipe swelling one eye closed immediately, the man rolled along the gravel several turns in an effort to get away, scrambling and stumbling to his feet. Sam let him go, turning to give what aid he might to Dave.

Dave had watched his friend strike at the first man and knock him backwards. Knowing he had the instant in which his adversary would be startled he turned and knocked the knife away with his forearm, then grasped the man's wrist to hold it away. With his free hand he struck with the heel of his palm, shattering the man's nose and drawing blood immediately. He drew back quickly, and, in a blink, he slammed a forceful front punch into the chest area, shattering several ribs.

The man with the second gun was frightened and stunned but raised the weapon in a threatening manner. Dave moved with such speed and agility that all the world seemed to move in slower motion to his as he swept his leg around to brush the gun aside. Then, drawing back, he threw a side kick to the assailant's nose, knocking him unconscious.

Still with a hold on the knife-wielding wrist Dave turned back to the fellow. "Wimp, did I hear?" he shouted. He grasped the arm at the elbow and brought his knee swiftly upward. The man groaned and fell to the ground, clutching the compound fracture.

Without hesitating an instant Dave threw a jump-spinning round kick to the head of the last man as he attacked from behind, blackjack raised for a crushing blow. The man halted, dazed and stunned. Before he could recover to think to try attacking again, Dave threw a spinning whirl kick to the man's temple, toppling him to the ground. He stood in fighting position, ready for another onslaught, but none came. The men all lay groaning and choking on the rain-soaked gravel, writhing in pain.

Sam, too, stood ready for all challengers. With sword overhead, he waited to be sure no one rose from the ground.

"C'mon. Let's get out of here," Dave said.

They scrambled into their vehicles, gunned their engines and sped off, racing feverishly in the direction of the motel.

****

Carol sat quiet for a long while, listening to her husband's excited, heavy breathing as he raced the van to equal measure of his rapidly pounding heart. When they were a few miles down the road Dave began to recover, slowing the speed of the van as his heart, too, began to slow to a more normal beat. He glanced in the mirror to see the DeLorean was no longer behind him. "Hm. I wonder where Sam's gone off to."

Carol looked at her husband, studying him, then asked, "Are you okay?"

"I will be in a little bit," he answered. "My adrenalin is still pumping wildly."

"I know. I can tell," she remarked. She put a hand to his thigh to squeeze and stroke it in an effort to soothe him.

"Are you all right?" he asked, reaching down to squeeze her hand. He found she was still trembling some. "Did that scare you back there?"

"A little. Not too badly, though. If I'd been with anyone else, I think I'd have been terrified. I knew you had a plan when you first started to act cowardly."

"Yeah...well, we had to distract them. You played your part well."

"Mm, Dave, you were really pretty wonderful back there."

"Heh. I guess all those years of karate lessons paid for themselves tonight."

"I'd say," Carol smiled. "I won't ever complain again over how much time you spend at the club."

"Yeah? Where's the tape recorder?" he laughed. "I want those words recorded."

Carol ran her hand along his thigh and squeezed it tenderly. She gasped in delight when she felt a certain hardness protruding down along his inner thigh and she squeezed this warmly. "Ooh...And what's this?" she cooed.

Dave just glanced at her, his smile widening.

"Are you horny?" she asked him.

"Heh! It's, um...it's kind of a psychological side effect, I guess."

Carol twisted around to look back and confirm that the DeLorean was not following, then gave her husband another playful squeeze. "Well...hm... Maybe you should find a back road to pull off on and we'll break in the back seat. No sense letting this excitement go to waste," she purred.

Dave raised an eyebrow in excitement, then cut the wheel sharply at the first divergent road.

* * * *

Sam quickly wiped the blade clean with a handful of Kleenex, then tossed the sword behind the seat. As he and Kelly raced behind the van, matching its speed, neither said a word. They breathed heavily and their hearts pounded wildly in frightened stimulation. A safe distance from the restaurant Sam cut the wheel onto a side road and drove another quarter mile, stopping, finally, along the side of the dark macadam lane. He popped the door open, jumped out, and walked restlessly ahead of the car, then stood to peer down the dark stretch of road. He turned around and leaned over the hood and pounded on it several times. "Damn!" he shouted as he smacked the hood. "Damn!" he yelled again, his voice furious, almost to the point of sobbing.

Kelly opened her door and stood up to look over the car at him. "Sam?" she called both in confusion and sympathy.

He glanced at her only briefly, pounded the hood again in frustration, then turned to walk several paces up the roadway. He stood with arms akimbo and gazed out into the darkened field on the right.

Kelly approached him, coming up to his side. She put an arm around his waist, asking, "Sam? What's wrong? What is it?"

He glanced at her, then looked off into the field, shaking his head. "They shouldn't have pressed it! They shouldn't have made me hurt them. I hate violence like that. They should have backed off!"

Kelly could see the anger and worry in his eyes. His body was tense, straining. She squeezed her arm tighter around him. "Sam, it's not your fault. You were forced into it. You had to do it. You were defending yourself," she told him. "You were defending...me."

He looked at her when she added that last comment and he seemed to calm some. The fire in his eye began to die down as he let her words penetrate. Kelly could feel his muscles begin to relax, his breathing start to shallow.

"I think those men would have hurt us even if we had given them the material," she continued. "You were courageous. Thank you." Then she leaned up to his taller form and kissed his cheek.

Sam closed his eyes and took a deep breath, collecting himself. Kelly turned fully to him, still at his side, and wrapped her other arm about him, waiting for him to regain his composure. When he released the long breath and opened his eyes, they met hers shining warm and bright as they reflected the light of the DeLorean's headlamps. She smiled up at him when she knew the calmer, gentler Sam had returned and she squeezed him tightly.

Sam smiled down at her and for a long while they gazed dreamily into each other's eyes. He could no longer resist the urge to kiss her. He swallowed nervously, then turned to put his arms around her. The sounds of something big and wet began suddenly to splatter on the road beside them, then they were quickly surrounded by it. Faster and more frequently the heavy wetness splattered and they both looked about to determine for certain what the noise was. Then the heavens opened up, sending torrents of thick, heavy rain drops splashing all around.

"Ah-h!" Kelly screamed in a laugh and tore away from him. Sam followed her, both of them dashing for the shelter of the DeLorean. They laughed as they closed the doors, the two of them dripping wet in the short time they'd been exposed to the downpour. Sam pulled the car into gear and turned it around to head back to the main road and their two friends who must surely be fraught with worry back at the motel.

****

Sam turned on the lights in the motel bedroom and went through to the kitchen with Kelly. He was curious why the van hadn't returned but reasoned Dave and Carol had probably stopped for groceries.

"Shall I make some coffee?" Kelly asked him, opening a cabinet door.

"No. I think I'd rather have a scotch," he replied. He reached into another cupboard and pulled out a bottle of Chivas.

Kelly drew out two glasses, saying, "I believe I'll join you. I could use one myself." She watched Sam drop in several ice cubes, then pour several fingers in each glass. She took a seat at the table and watched Sam take a rather large swallow. He closed his eyes to concentrate on the burning sensation that spread throughout his body, trying to speed it to every nerve ending. When he opened his eyes, he saw Kelly sipping from her own glass but with her gaze fixed on him.

"So, Rambo...have a seat," she smiled up to him.

Sam blushed and sat across from her. "Rambo...," he muttered, shaking his head.

"Well, my God, Sam. You guys reacted so swiftly. I didn't know what was going on. I thought you were going to give them the papers. Did you see Dave fight? My goodness! I thought I was in some Kung Fu movie," she laughed.

"Yeah. Dave really looked impressive. He's been taking karate for quite a few years. A pretty tough hombré."

"I'll say," Kelly agreed. "And all that stuff about pretending you and Carol were having an affair... You picked right up on it; played right along. I mean, I was almost convinced it was true."

Sam took a smaller sip of his drink, leaned back in the chair and smiled. "Yeah. That worked out pretty well, didn't it? Threw those guys right off guard." Then, with an anxious look he stood and moved to the window to peer through the curtain to the parking spaces out front. "I wonder what's keeping them? They should have been back long ago."

"They probably had to stop for something," Kelly suggested. "Groceries, maybe?"

"Maybe. I hope nothing's happened to them."

Kelly stood and came next to him. She took his hand and gave it a tug, saying, "C'mon, Sam. Let's go in and turn on the news. Maybe a good movie is playing. It'll take your mind off everything and help you relax."

"Mm..., maybe," he replied. "You go on in and find something. I better call Tom and tell him what's happened."

"Okay." Kelly said. "I'll turn on the set in my room. You can join me there." She poured herself another drink and turned to enter the bedroom.

Sam called Tom's home phone and talked with him for at least twenty minutes. They agreed to meet at the Foundation house in the morning to review the material taken from Marco Development's records and discuss how best to utilize it in blocking the efforts of the developers.

When he set the phone down Sam returned to the window for another peek. There was still no sign of the van. He downed the last of his second drink and headed into Kelly's room, mumbling, "Now I am worried. There's still no sign of them." But just as these last words left his lips he stopped and all but gasped when he saw Kelly lying on the bed. She was reclining on two pillows propped against the headboard. The sheet was drawn up to cover the lower portion of her ample bosom which pushed to overflow the shimmering, white, silk nightgown she wore. With her flowing blonde hair combed to sweep over and cover one shoulder she was the perfect portrait of a man's desire. Sam felt his knees start to weaken and his heartbeat quicken.

Kelly looked over at him and smiled. "I'm sorry. What did you say?"

"Nothing," he replied, musing over her form where the sheet dipped and tucked so strategically and appealingly. "Not a thing." He looked toward the ceiling and fancifully offered up a low, "thank you..."

"What?" Kelly asked, seeing him stand there with a wide grin.

"Nothing. Just thinking how nice it is to know you...and what a wonderfully beautiful person you are."

"Yeah?" she beamed on hearing this. "Thank you, Sam Baker. And I feel the same about you." She patted beside her on the bed. "Come over here and rest those weary bones. There's a good movie on. I've seen it before and it quickly became one of my favorites."

"Yeah? What is it?" he asked, moving around to stretch out beside her.

"*Breakfast at Tiffany's*. You may not care for it. It's kind of a tear-jerker."

"No. No. I love this movie. I haven't seen it in years."

"Really? I wouldn't have thought you'd like movies like this."

"Why not?" Sam asked.

"I don't know... You know...," she stammered blushing, but flashing her blue eyes at him. "...you're tall...and handsome...and strong...," she started.

Sam pushed up to a sit, leaned against the headboard and puffed his chest out, "I like this," he said. "Go on."

Kelly laughed and pushed at him good naturedly. "I should have added weird, too." Then she blushed again, saying, "Well...I don't know. I guess I figured you more as the volleyball on the beach type. You know, the guy all the girls swoon over and all the guys want to hang around with. You're smart and successful...and secure...and sexy and...I...I guess maybe I figured you were...too busy being Mr. Perfect to...well...be sensitive...and...jeez, I've had too much to drink and don't know at all what I'm saying...," she said.

Sam's amused expression turned to one of admiring infatuation. He slid down beside her and put a hand tenderly on her far shoulder to turn her toward him. "Wow. Have you got me wrong," he said quietly. "I don't worry about money or job security, if you call that being successful." He flushed and looked away from her. "I, uh, I wasn't very handsome in high school. My features never caught up with each other till I graduated...and I guess I wore my hair in a way that sure wasn't flattering. I didn't hang out with the cool kids. I was just me," he said. "I was so madly enthralled with this one girl who wouldn't give me the time of day. I made it my crusade to catch her eye and it wasn't till college that I finally won her heart and married her. Well...I guess I really never won her heart. I was just 'convenient' for her."

"That was Barbara?"

"Yeah," Sam replied, rolling onto his back and releasing a sigh. He cradled the back of his head in his hands and shrugged. "I was a bookworm. Not so much a nerd—at least I don't think so—I was just always studying and helping out around the house. I wasn't much interested in girls. I was always playing with electronics, taking things apart to see how they worked. You know, when I was fourteen, I built my own TV set."

"Really?"

"Mm. I collected parts from old sets in junk yards and built a color set. We used it for years in the family room. Then, when computers came into vogue, I got hooked on them and, well, guess that's where I'm at now.

Anyway, it wasn't till I went to college that I changed my hair style, started to work out regularly and took more notice of my appearance. By the time I realized girls were interested in me I was already dating Barbara so I didn't notice them back."

"Why did your marriage break up?" Kelly asked. Then quickly, "Oh! I'm sorry. I maybe shouldn't ask that."

"No. No. It's okay. I don't mind talking about it," Sam assured her. "I don't know, really. I guess she never really loved me. She probably still saw the old Sam Baker whenever she looked at me. It's pretty flattering, but girls actually started to swoon over me and it caught me off guard. I didn't know how to handle it. Barbara, being Barbara, took up with me just because the other girls on campus wanted me.

She wanted to flatter herself by being the one who landed me. Once she had me, she really didn't want me. Of course, I was blind to all that—I had the girl I always wanted, or thought I did. When I was in Nam she took up with another guy. It's okay, I guess. It taught me a good lesson about how to look for the sincerity in other people.

See, people give off certain...vibrations. You learn to read people by what your heart tells you about them. You see inside of them and ignore their outward appearance and mannerisms. Some people are real good at putting on a facade, and they're not even aware they're doing it—like my 'ex-'. They become so practiced at it that it becomes a part of them and even they can't tell that they're doing it. Then there are others that are just frauds—like that lawyer fella', John Brandon. I could tell right away there was something deceptive about him...and it went deeper than my, um...my jealousy over you."

Kelly perked at hearing this. "Yeah? You were jealous of John?"

Sam glanced at her and allowed his smile to suffice as an answer. Then he looked back to the ceiling and continued. "Anyway, the hurt cut deep for a long time. I guess I've sort of been, well, keeping myself distanced from women ever since. Oh, I've dated a few. But it's been a long time since I've felt...um...feelings toward...any...one...woman."

Sam had difficulty uttering his last sentence for Kelly had reached over and begun brushing her hand up and down the rough stubble of his cheek. She turned his face toward her and the two gazed at one another.

"I'm not Barbara," she said reassuringly.

Sam nodded. "I know that." He watched Kelly raise herself from the pillows and lean toward him, her lips parted and relaxed to join against his...

There was a rattle at the door as the handle moved with the sound of a key being inserted into the lock. Kelly and Sam just looked at each other and smiled and Sam sat upright as Carol swung the door open. "Hi," she said cheerfully as she entered with Dave close behind.

"Where have you two been?" Sam asked. "I was worried about you."

Dave shrugged and with a mischievous smirk replied, "We, uh, we kind of got sidetracked."

"Sidetracked? You should have been back more than an hour ago. Christ, Dave, after what we just went through tonight, I was about ready to call out the militia to go look for you," Sam told him.

"No. We were okay."

"Where have you been?" Sam asked, pressing for a reply.

Dave and Carol exchanged impish smiles. "We went parking," he said.

"Parking?" Sam exclaimed. "Parking? I'm worried sick about you and you're out necking on some back road. I've been pacing the floor wearing a hole in the rug."

Dave cast his eyes downward and sheepishly rubbed his foot back and forth along the carpet. "Sorry, Mr. Baker. It ain't a school night...and Carol n' me have been goin' steady for some time, now. She has my ring..."

"See, Daddy," Carol said, holding out and wiggling her wedding ringed finger. "I wrapped it in angora. Isn't it 'cool'?"

Sam just shook his head, saying, "You two are hopeless. I'm never going to give either of you another thought. Ever."

Kelly laughed at Carol and Dave's repartee. "Don't believe him. He was worried, but not as much as he said. We've been lying here having a nice chat together."

"Oh?" Carol asked. "What about?"

"Forget it," Sam replied. "Speaking about 'stuff', though, where's the box of printouts?"

"Still in the van," Dave told him. "I'd better go get it. Don't want to take a chance on leaving it outside."

Dave retrieved the documents and returned to take a seat in one of the two chairs that accompanied a small round table in the corner of the room. Carol was seated on the edge of her bed, opposite Sam, and Kelly sat upright, propped against the headboard with the sheet drawn high.

They listened as Sam informed them of his conversation with Tom and that they were to meet him at the Foundation house in the morning. The four played with some ideas on how to approach James Brody with the possibly incriminating evidence, hoping it might cause him to reconsider his plans for the valuable Schiels' property. They decided to defer any definite course of action until they had spoken with the young architect and listened to his opinions.

The day had been long and fatigue was evidenced on the four drawn faces. Wide yawns and lengthy stretches continually interrupted the conversation till Dave, finally succumbing to the urgings of his muscles and joints, excused himself for want of sleep. With a rather wide yawn of his own, Sam agreed on the need for rest and, after saying goodnight to the ladies, the two men departed for their own bedroom.

****

Late into the night and far too deeply into her own exhausted nocturnal slumber from which to be easily aroused, Carol never heard the troubled groans from her friend in the next bed.

Kelly was dreaming again. Totally disarmed and so easily malleable from the day's excitement, her subconscious was unguarded to the supernatural forces that had been visiting her so frequently of late. In her dream her eyes were wide in fear as all that surrounded her swirled so quickly, she could discern no one particular object. She was freefalling—spiraling downward through a circular, cone-like funnel of void. She grasped desperately for the blurred, just-out-of-reach side to halt her dizzying descent. Though she tried to cry out in terror, her voice could produce no sounds.

Plummeting uncontrollably deeper into the shadowy abyss Kelly saw that in her right hand she clutched a folded, time-worn slip of paper. She became vaguely cognizant of having seen the fragile, faded sheet previously and her curiosity now became completely focused upon it. Instantly, her fear of the fall passed as she resigned herself to whatever fate awaited her at the bottom of the mysterious, esoteric chasm. She could think only of the paper she clutched so tightly.

She brought the paper into view and carefully, her hands trembling, unfolded the ragged edges. Holding the note only inches from her eyes she could see the writing across its surface but could not decipher the words. She became frustrated, then angry at her mind for not allowing her thoughts to concentrate on the penned script.

Kelly looked away from the page to chastise her mind and refocus her concentration for another attempt at understanding the written words—and found she was no longer falling. She was now standing on that same familiar hillside she had found herself on so many previous nightly visits and, as always before, it was a darkened, fog shrouded, chilly evening.

Her hand, though still clutching the letter, rested on the dew-glistened piano that was ever present in this scene. She listened for the accompanying sound of thundering horse hooves from below the knoll and knew well, by now, what to expect.

She watched in breathless anticipation as the shadowy figures drew nearer with the extraordinary tunnel of light just before them, neither enveloping the riders nor illuminating them, but always at its continued distance. She observed them patiently, waiting for the solitary outrider to depart and present himself from the others.

Kelly felt less timid on this occasion and determined not to allow her emotions to interfere as they had on so many past encounters with the ghost. With her new resolve came the immediate realization that this was all only a dream. Her mind floated away to become separate from her body by the piano and she began to observe the scene from just behind her upright form. A calm reassurance came to her now, knowing that she needn't fear the dream and could comfortably observe and even explore within it.

Believing herself in control, Kelly watched the rider, as always, come forth from among his thundering company. She delighted in willing her form at the piano to stand firm and unfaltering as the rider drew nearer. She determined to will him closer—then to unhorse him to stand before her in explanation. As his distance closed, the dark horse at a canter, he drew rein suddenly. The animal whinnied and locked its powerful legs, sliding in the moist, soft turf. Confused by this irregular action, Kelly watched as the shadowy figure, still some distance from her, sat his horse as the steed nervously trampled the ground below.

The rider sat silent a moment, playing the reins to constrain and settle the jittery beast. Then, raising slightly in the stirrups, he peered forward in queried scrutiny. He looked first at the form standing patient and unmoving beside the piano. Then his gaze lifted over her to look into the observing mind's eye that was behind her, as if her dreaming subconscious had a form or solidity that was visible to him. Though his eyes were shrouded by the darkness Kelly had the feeling they were staring right at her very spirit, now bare of its burden of flesh.

Alarmed momentarily, she then relaxed as she knew his gaze to be sincere and familiar. She found herself drawn back into her body and watched the gray form lower his head to look down at her as he settled back into the saddle. He nodded in recognition and greeting.

Kelly was unsure of herself at this point but raised the hand in which she grasped the note and waved to him in salutation. The figure again rose in the stirrups and leaned forward to better view what it was she held so firm. The horse began to prance nervously and to turn about in a circle. As the rider moved with the beast, he ended the turn and drew forth a long, glimmering saber which he began to flail triumphantly overhead.

Kelly glanced at her hand, still in the air in greeting, and knew that the letter it held was the cause of his sudden, excited maneuver. He reared the steed onto its hind legs and turned it about quickly. Then, setting spurs to its flanks, he rode headlong back toward the riding column of horsemen just as they were about to descend over the other side of the hill.

This time, however, he did not rejoin and melt into the multitude of ghostly figures. With horse steaming at full gallop and sword flailing wildly he rode to the very head of the column. Then, without hesitation, he entered and vanished into the brilliant incandescence.

Kelly gasped at the mysterious action of the ghostly young soldier. His complete disappearance both disturbed and frightened her. "Sandie!" she called after him, her voice shrill with alarm for his fate. Why that particular name had escaped her lips she had no idea. It had just seemed to spring from her larynx in her effort to hail him back from the esoteric brightness. "Sandie!" she hollered again, pleading and desperate as the confounding light and the ever-pursuing ghoulish horde began slowly to fade down the fog-enshrouded hillside. "Sandie!" she cried in vain, her voice now choking, drowned by the tumultuous clamor of a thousand and more horse hooves thundering over the dew moistened turf.

Then came a voice calling in answer to her. "Kelly!" it sounded. "Kelly! It's okay. It's all right." The voice seemed to be answering from the direction of the fading column. Indeed! from within the dimming tunnel of light. "Kelly! Kelly!" it called again, becoming louder and clearer with each cry, though the light and the ghostly pursuers grew continually more obscured.

Kelly almost wept with joy as she recognized the familiar, deep-based resonance of Sam Baker. She would have called out to him, and was about to do so, when she felt her body being shaken and disturbed. She opened her eyes to see Sam sitting on the edge of her bed, his hands on her shoulders as he gently prodded her from sleep. "Kelly...it's okay. You were dreaming," he said to her, his face leaning close and fraught with concern.

Kelly blinked several times, trying to adjust her eyes to the dim light from the nightstand. Carol and Dave stood over her, their faces also masked with worry. "S-Sam?" she quivered, not certain within which world she was yet fully a part of.

"Yes, Kelly. It's me. I'm right here," he told her with a comforting voice. He helped her to a sit, taking her hands in his to squeeze lightly. "You were dreaming again."

Kelly sat and collected herself awhile. Carol went to the kitchen, returning with a glass of water for the woman. While she took some sips her friends stayed gathered to watch her slowly regain her awareness. "That must have been quite a nightmare," Dave said. "You even woke Sam and me back in our room."

Kelly blushed some at this. "Sorry. Was I shouting, huh?"

"Were you ever," Carol smiled, taking a seat on the edge of her bed now that she saw Kelly was all right. "You were yelling out a name; calling to someone named Sandie."

Kelly thought for a moment. "Yes. That's right. I remember," she replied. "Oh, this is getting more and more strange. It was the soldier on the horse," she explained. "He came out of the crowd again, only this time he stopped way back from me." She stared off as she pieced together her remembrance of the dream. "I…waved my hand to him and…oh my! I had that letter in my hand—the one the old lady gave me. He saw it and must have known what it was."

"What'd he do?" Carol asked.

"He pulled out a long sword and…" she paused to look reflectively at Sam. "…and then he waved it over his head. Then he turned and galloped back to the rest of the riders. They were all still in motion, riding after the light tunnel, but everything remained stationary—like they were waiting for him to catch up to them."

"Uh, huh. Sure. Go on," Carol urged her.

"Well, this time, instead of going to the group, he…he dashed right into the light. It was like he was supposed to do it; like it had waited for him and it was his turn to be allowed in, or something. That was when I started to call to him."

"How did you know his name?" Sam asked.

Kelly looked at him, puzzled. "I don't know. It just came out. But I know that was it. I'm certain of it."

"Hm…," Carol mused, as she pondered this. "I wish I had my dream books here to look up what all the interpretations are. The light tunnel has to be about passing through to the other side. The rest I'm not sure about. It could be, with the delivery of the letter, you freed the soldier's spirit to pass over from being locked in between worlds."

"Whoa!" Sam interrupted. "We're getting kind of deep here, aren't we? It could be her subconscious telling her it was now allowing the shrimp scampi to pass through her digestive system," he grinned. "The sword could have signified indigestion. Some Tums before going to bed might have kept the sword in its scabbard."

Carol rolled her eyes—amused, but exasperated. "Sam, you've done the world a great service by not entering the field of psychology."

"Thank you," he chuckled. Then, looking at Kelly he asked, "You going to be all right?"

"Mm. I think so. I'm just a bit unsettled yet. I…have this odd feeling, I don't know why, but…I think that's the last…I'll see of that dream. At least, I hope so. I think Carol's right; for some reason, the soldier's gone and…and it's ended. I only wish I could have known more about him and why I was involved."

Sam patted her shoulder. "Well, if it is over, just be glad. Maybe you'll be able to sleep a full night without waking up startled. I know all the neighbors will be happier."

They laughed at Sam's comment. Then, being assured Kelly was all right, the men said goodnight and returned to their room. When they had gone, and Carol was settling back into her own bed, Kelly asked, "Carol. What do you make of all of this? These dreams are far too vivid and real to be caused by something like stomach upset. It's like I'm really there; like the dreams are alive.

Then there are all the other weird things that have happened, like old Mrs. Schiels giving me that letter; Sam's tarot, the sword she gave him, saying it belonged to him; Sam's dreams... It's really strange."

Carol leaned against the headboard of her bed. She thought for a moment before replying, reviewing the events as Kelly had listed them. "Hmm...I'm not really sure. You are right about it all being so strange, though. I suppose it could all be just an eccentric, confused old woman and a bunch of circumstances just happening to coincide. Now, me, I always look for deeper, mystical meanings in things. Not that I'm always right, mind you. In fact, often, what I perceive can't be verified. It's just a feeling I get inside. But if you want my opinion, I'd say you and Sam, maybe even all of us, have been brought together for more than just to try to save an old farm from developers."

"Meaning?"

"I don't know. It just seems there's a connection here. Sam, having his weird dreams as soon as he got here; us, stopping in at the Foundation house when we did; the odd things Varina said to Sam... There's a connection here, but I haven't been able to figure it out. Maybe, if we go back and talk to old Varina we can find out more."

"I'd like that," Kelly replied. "Isn't she an odd one, though."

"Odd? Perhaps," Carol agreed. "But she's very mystical. She's very close to the spiritual world. There's a word for it and I can't think what it is. But, if you believe in that sort of thing, you'll know she's very receptive to things most people can't see or understand."

"Like a medium?"

"Of sorts. I don't know about contacting spirits and such. More like, she's very in tune to supernatural forces. She can look at things differently; with more insight."

"You can do that, too?" Kelly asked.

Carol chuckled some. "We all can, Kelly. Ever hear of 'woman's intuition'? That's sort of what it is—at least, a small part of it. Women don't have the ego men do so we're a bit more receptive than men. There are ways to increase your abilities, too. I used to be a lot more intuitive than I am now. Children are a great distraction and tend to pull you away."

Kelly listened intently, sitting with the sheet over her waist and her arms hugging her hunched knees. She didn't notice the big yawn Carol released nor see her glance at the clock on the nightstand. Afraid Kelly was going to pursue her inquiry, Carol finally asked, "Kelly. Can we continue this over breakfast?"

"Oh. I'm sorry," the woman replied. "I guess I lost track of time. Sure, we can. I just find this stuff so fascinating. I've never had a chance to talk to anyone about it before."

Carol reached over for the lamp switch, saying, "Well, tomorrow we can talk all you want on it. Right now, I'm going to try to dream my own dreams." She fluffed her pillows in the dark of the room and snuggled down on the mattress. "Good night, Kelly."

"Night, Carol," she replied and lay back on her pillow. It was a long while before sleep overcame Kelly again. With her eyes open her mind swirled with thoughts of all that had happened since meeting her three new friends. Never, in her life, had such extraordinary events occurred so closely to one another as in this past week. She had been party to a raid on an office building, involved in a violent scuffle, almost became a vehicular murder victim—and had fallen in love with a handsome stranger from Chicago...or Cleveland...or Pittsburgh, or wherever he was currently living. She closed her eyes to remember the feeling of Sam holding her close on that dark, deserted highway. In the glow of the car's headlamps, just before the thundershower interrupted, she had seen the love in Sam's eyes. She regretted having reacted to the heavy droplets falling and wished she had stayed to taste his lips. It would have been romantic, she thought, to be held tenderly and kissed lovingly in a downpour. Perhaps it would be even sweeter when the next opportunity presented itself, she hoped. For now, she tried to imagine having enjoyed that kiss—feeling his muscular arms wrapped about her, the rain drenching them, and Sam leaning closer as she parted her lips in tingling anticipation...

Sleep claimed her tired, prostrate form.

Chapter Fourteen

Carol finished tying her satin robe as she entered the kitchen from her bedroom. She looked sleepy and bedraggled and was surprised to see her husband standing there dressed and ready for the day. He was gazing out the window, coffee cup in hand, but he turned to notice her as she reached for the coffee pot. She paused for a wide yawn before she poured.

"Good morning," Dave said to her. "You look fine."

"Mruf grumph rrmph," Carol barely managed to mumble. She glanced at him as she poured to see if he'd understood her reply.

"Ah-h-h... Up late last night, were we?" he teased, watching her blindly pour. "Out with the girls, playing poker? Drinking and chasing loose men, perhaps?"

Carol slurped a sip of the hot coffee and made a grotesque face. "Blah! You made the coffee," she commented.

"Yeah. Why? Too strong again, huh?"

"Slightly. I've had weaker espresso."

"Sorry. I'm used to drinking it at work like that. It sure wakes you up, though. And fast."

Carol took another sip and sat at the table. "Is it raining again?"

"Mm. Yeah. Looks like an all day one," Dave replied, glancing dreamily out at the drizzling scene in the parking lot. "It's a nice rain, though. Slow and steady."

"Good. It'll help the flowers grow," Carol said. She was slowly waking up, contentedly watching her husband stare out the window.

Sam came in and, like Dave, was dressed and seemed eager and energetic. He moved directly to the coffee and poured into the cup he carried from the bedroom. "Morning, Carol," he greeted her cheerfully.

Carol just glanced at him. "Gawd. What's with you two? You're both showered and dressed. Did I miss something here? Is it daylight-savings time, or something?"

Sam chuckled as he turned to her. "I don't know. I woke up early. Couldn't sleep. Guess I'm excited to get the day underway and see what develops."

Dave turned from the window and leaned against the sink top. "And since he couldn't sleep, he decided I didn't need to, either. Made me get up to make coffee."

Carol shot a playfully disdainful look at Sam. "Big mistake."

"I found that out," Sam replied. "He makes it so well over a campfire, though."

"Yeah," Carol sighed. That's the only place he's good at cooking—campfires and barbecues. I think he fakes it every other time so he can get out of helping at home."

Dave raised an eyebrow as he looked at Sam. "She's catching on to me."

The phone in the women's bedroom rang several times, diverting their attention. From out in the kitchen, they could hear Kelly talking to someone and, though they couldn't make out the words clearly, her voice sounded dispirited as she replied to the caller. She entered the kitchen shortly afterwards and her expression was as sullen as her voice had just been. "Morning," she said, sounding rather glum.

"Morning, Kelly," Sam greeted her. "Who was that?"

Kelly reached for a cup from the shelf. "Tttt!...Oh, that was Marylou's husband. She's got a terribly upset stomach and won't be in today. Guess I'll have to work the store alone." She poured her coffee, adding, "Darn. What lousy timing, too. This is going to be a really eventful day."

Carol watched her slowly stir in some milk. In an effort to cheer the girl some, she smirked, "Hmph! Must have been her husband's cooking. One of my husband's fellow conspirators, no doubt."

"Well, hey," Sam told her in his own bid at raising her spirits, "We'll help you. We'll be hanging around."

Kelly raised her cup and turned to face her friends. They saw their efforts were rewarded by a slightly upward curl of the woman's lip. "Thanks," she said. "But aren't you going to meet and confront Brody this morning? I was really hoping to be with you for that. Especially if that low-life worm of an attorney is with him."

"Careful with the coffee," Carol warned, seeing Kelly about to take her first sip. "Dave made it. It'll take the hair off a gorilla."

Kelly took a careful, sampling taste and scrunched her nose over it. "Whew! This'll wake the dead," she joked. But her smile was not long in remaining.

Sam watched her mouth again turn slightly in a pout over her resigned acceptance of having to miss the all-important meeting with James Brody. He felt an overwhelming urge to move to her and comfort her with a tender hug and a hotly pressed kiss. He wasn't sure if it would really relieve her fallen spirits any, but she looked so darned pretty standing there with a sulking expression he knew he'd at least feel the better for it.

"Hey," he said to her. "We're not sure when we're going to meet with Brody. Tom's going to discuss that with us this morning. Maybe we can get Brody to come to the Foundation for a pow-wow. After all, we hold all the aces."

Kelly perked up only a little at hearing this. She took another carefully measured sip and nodded hopefully. "Well, we'll see," she sighed. "I'm going to be so busy anyway, even if Lou were coming in. I've got to prepare press releases for either outcome. I suppose the phones will be flooded all day with inquiries. I couldn't have dumped all that on Lou."

"Let's just play it by ear," Sam suggested. "You never know what'll develop."

Carol stood to leave for the bedroom, explaining, "Kelly and I should go get dressed. We'll want to get a good breakfast if this is going to be such a busy day."

"Mm. You're right," Kelly said, standing to follow her. "I've got a bunch of phone calls to make once we get there. We should be getting along."

The two women were dressed and ready to leave well before Dave or Sam would have suspected. They breakfasted at a diner just outside of Hagerstown, along the interstate. By nine o'clock they had arrived at the Foundation house and found the telephone already ringing. Carol assumed the task of fielding the calls, which were mostly interested parties concerned with developments of the disputed acreage. The conversations were congenial and sympathetic, and there were a few small donations pledged by some of the callers. As there was little information Carol could supply regarding any settlement of the ground, she contented the callers with discussions, in general, of the problems and need for preserving historic sites.

Carol's assistance in handling the main line callers, coupled with Dave and Sam's help in other jobs, freed Kelly to begin work on the press releases. Her efforts in this were hampered by both that she had to type on an antiquated, manual typewriter (the stolen computer not having been replaced yet) and that she had no information with which to continue the body of her statements.

She tried calling Mitchel Page to determine if the McPherson Foundation members had gathered to discuss the grant application but could get no answer at his home. A call to his office revealed that he had not arrived yet, and was now an hour overdue. Calls to other board members availed her nothing as they were as ignorant of the situation as she. The only positive and greatly pleasing information Kelly was able to obtain from her numerous inquiries was that Dennis Woods' condition had been upgraded to "guarded". He was much more alert and attentive and the doctors had concluded there was no brain damage. Time, rest and months of therapy were the prescriptions now.

Kelly was able to write only the introductions and endings of the reports. The body content of the letters would be determined as the day's events unfolded—the first of which occurred with the timely appearance of Tom Charles.

****

Just past ten o'clock there was much clamoring and banging at the screen door of the Foundation house. With a degree of awkwardness, someone was trying to enter the front door. Four faces in the back office looked up to see the cause of the commotion and were pleasantly surprised to see Tom Charles at the partition. His face was beaming as he stood holding a computer monitor in his arms. His black trench coat was dripping wet, as were his thickly combed hair and beard, and his glasses were splotched with droplets.

"Hey, Tom!" They greeted him cheerfully. "Good morning."

"Whew! Whoa!" he exclaimed as Sam came over to relieve him of the monitor. "It's really coming down out there."

"Kelly, get some towels, please," Sam asked. He carried the monitor over to the desk and set it where the Foundation's computer had once been positioned.

Kelly hurriedly climbed the steps and soon returned with two bath towels, handing one to each fellow. Sam began to wipe the screen while Tom dabbed at his hair and face, chuckling as he toweled off. "You'd know the rain would hold off until I started down the street with that thing. It just let loose and dumped on me."

Carol helped him off with his raincoat, commenting that she had heard there would be thundershowers off and on all day.

"Maybe we'll wait till this one passes before we bring in the rest of this stuff," Tom said as he held his glasses and wiped them dry.

Kelly had gone over to watch Sam dry the monitor and was puzzled about its appearance. "What's this, Sam? What's going on? Where did this come from?"

Leaning over the white plastic machine Sam looked up cleverly and winked. "It's a little surprise for you."

"Yeah?" she asked, smiling curiously.

"Pat and I sort of put this together for you yesterday. She knew a friend wanting to unload it so we talked her into donating it. It's worth more as a write off then what she could get for it on the market. It's kind of dated by our standards, but it's on par with what you had before."

"Sam, I hardly know what to say," Kelly replied. "Thank you. And thank Pat for me."

"Our pleasure," Sam said, pleased with her reaction. "I also have all your software to go with it. I had all your data stored in Carnegie-Mellon's computer the first night I was here, remember. I retrieved it all and made you copies. Now you have something to work with."

"Oh, Sam. You're a wonder," she said, then flushed slightly as she realized she'd said this so eagerly.

Sam enjoyed the fuss she made over his efforts. "Thank you," he smiled to her.

Tom noted the rain had slackened to a light drizzle and suggested they take advantage of the lull to retrieve the remaining components. Everyone traipsed down the block to Tom's car to help carry in the equipment. In short order, Sam had the unit together and running and stood back with an appreciative and admiring Kelly to watch the system warm up. The color screen glowed in brilliant blue. In the center of the screen a tiny red dot appeared and began to grow, holding the viewer's attention as it pulsed and throbbed while increasing in size. Now, distinguishable as a heart with an arrow through it, it continued swelling, much as a balloon, expanding larger and larger until—it exploded! Like a sky rocket it fragmented into many tiny hearts, each floating gently downward. Each of these burst open randomly and released clusters of tiny red, puckered lips that then floated aimlessly like so many bubbles.

Kelly eyed the screen, amused. "What's this? I'd guess it has all of the markings of a Sam Baker creation."

"Oh, just something I dreamed up to add a little life to the screen. It beats watching a boring picture," Sam told her. He patted her lightly on the shoulder. "Okay, kid. Go to work. It's all yours."

Kelly took her seat at the keyboard and began to hurriedly run through some of the functions. She brought up the membership list, then the spreadsheet, the current pledges, and so on, glancing at each only long enough for an elated confirmation that the data was indeed present and available. "This is wonderful! Oh, I don't believe it! It's all here!" she exclaimed as she viewed the items requested. "Marylou and I have quite a job ahead of us entering all the data that's accumulated lately."

Dave spoke up, telling her, "I can help out with that. I may not be a whiz like Sam, but I can do data entry, anyway."

"You're on!" Kelly said quickly with a little laugh. "Any and all help is appreciated around here."

Tom then interrupted, his voice sounding with a more serious note. "Listen, uh, we should discuss what we're going to do here. Can we go over the data you've collected on my employer?"

"Yeah. Good idea," Sam said in answer.

The three men seated themselves around the coffee table in the front room and began pouring over the computer printouts Sam had collected and organized. Kelly and Carol worked at other business, the constant interruption by the two phone lines also occupying much of their time.

After working awhile reviewing the material and coming up with several suggestions on presenting it to James Brody, Dave pushed back in his chair. "Well, fellas. We better narrow this down and polish it up pretty quickly. We're running out of time. It's already pushing noon."

Sam and Tom both glanced at the clock to confirm what Dave had just told them. They both sat upright and nodded in agreement.

Kelly saw the men stir and asked them, "Are you ready?"

Sam looked back into the room at her and shrugged. "Close. We've got to iron it out some to be prepared for anything he may counter with. We need to sound convincing, almost short of threatening."

"Well, what are you going to say?" she asked. "When are you going to meet with him?"

Tom turned now to look in at her. "I set up a meeting with James for four o'clock. We're supposed to go over some design specs. That way, we'll be sure to…"

Tom's explanation was cut short by the phone ringing on Kelly's desk. She held up a finger to silence him as she raised the phone to her ear. "…Hello. Historic Antietam Foundation. Kelly Gracie speaking," she chimed. "…Where have you been? We've been trying to get in touch with you," she told the caller. As Kelly listened to the caller her brow furrowed in concern. From the front room the men were watching and now stood to gather in the doorway. "What?" she exclaimed. "Oh, my heavens? No! He can't do that." "…I can't get over there. Marylou called in sick. Sam Baker and Dave Cooper are here; the party from up North. They'll come." "…I don't know. We haven't secured new legal counsel, yet." "…I'll have her taken there. She ought to be there, of course."

The four observers glanced at one another, wondering who the caller might be, knowing only that the information being relayed was unsettling. They came in to gather closer to Kelly's desk. When she finished her conversation and set the phone to its cradle she was visibly shaken.

"What?" Sam asked. "What is it?"

She looked up at him, her face clearly masked with worry. "That was Mitchel. He said they've moved a bulldozer onto the site. They're going to start excavating."

"What?" Sam exclaimed. "How can they do that?"

"They, uh, they have all the building permits and apparently are going ahead with some preliminary work," Kelly replied.

Tom nodded thoughtfully as he mumbled aloud, "Well, that son-of-a-bitch." When the others looked at him, he explained, "See, we got approval for the first set of plans that I drafted. The second set needs to be re-submitted for further approval since he had me change everything. I'd hoped to buy us some time by dragging my feet. I guess James is going ahead to shove some dirt around and worry about the approvals later. It's more of a symbolic gesture—like a dog marking its territory. This is James Brody's way of peeing on a tree. Oh, I don't like this. It's much harder to get an injunction to halt construction once a project is started…even if we could find a sympathetic judge."

"We better get out there," Dave said.

"Right," Sam agreed.

"Wait!" Kelly halted them as they moved to pack the material into the cardboard box. "Mitchel wants us to get Mrs. Schiels out there. She's the only one who can maybe stop them."

Dave looked at his wife, asking, "Carol, can you go get her?"

"I, I guess so. Leave me the van," she said.

"Fine. We'll take Tom's car."

Tom, Sam and Dave threw on their raincoats and picked up the box of papers. Promising Kelly they would keep her posted on events, they hurried out the door. Kelly phoned and talked to Wilma at the Schiels house. After explaining to the girl that the situation might require Varina's presence at the site they made arrangements for Carol to swing by and escort the old woman to the hilltop.

When Carol had gone, Kelly found herself alone in the house for the first time in several days. She poured herself a cup of tea and sat back in her chair at the computer terminal. It was quiet. The phones had stopped ringing and all that could be heard was the muffled patter of rain on the tin roof. It was a comforting sound and Kelly gave it an ear for a while, resting.

As she sipped her tea, she let her mind drift aimlessly until it came to settle on the one greatest influence on her life this summer—Sam Baker. She smiled affectionately as she reminisced over their first meeting—seeing Sam tumble over the trunk of her car. She thought of the evening she'd played for him in the empty room of the Wayside Inn, and how they had been yelled at by the owner. Her smile broadened as she dreamily remembered their horseback ride over the battlefield and their race up the hilltop to where the two, tall, old oaks stood. That had been fun, though Sam's horse had mysteriously reared, all but dumping him from the saddle. She found it curious for so gentle an animal as Dreamer to spook for no obvious reason.

Kelly tried to visualize that scene again to consider why the horse had reacted in such a strange manner. She took a sip of tea and set her cup on the desk and a sudden shiver coursed through her body. She blinked to clear her thoughts as an odd light-headedness came quickly upon her.

She had had a substantial breakfast and, since she felt no immediate hunger, so eliminated that as a reason for the queasy sensations beginning to attack her. She hoped she wasn't falling ill with whatever may have afflicted Marylou, for she certainly didn't want to be ailing with all that was happening today. She reached for her purse and dug through it to retrieve several aspirins which she chased down with the tea. Then, trying to will away the dizziness, she drew a deep breath and pulled herself up to the computer to resume working.

****

Tom pulled in line behind the two dozen or so cars parked on either side of the narrow macadam road. The rain had subsided but the gray sky still threatened as Sam, Dave and Tom walked along the string of cars to join a small crowd of spectators gathered around a long low-boy trailer. Several men were lowering the detachable gooseneck in preparation for unloading a big D-8 dozer from the trailer.

Chains were being loosened as taut binders were released and one fellow sat on the big yellow machine cranking over the reluctant diesel engine. Sam overheard one of the onlookers comment, "This better not take long. I'm heading back if it starts raining again." He turned to see that the fellow making the comment wore an oversized lapel pin from a T.V. station. The other man held a camera. Only now did Sam realize many in the crowd were representatives from the different news media. "Oh, great," he moaned as he nudged Tom and Dave. "The press is here."

"Yeah. I noticed," Tom replied. "They wasted no time. That's not good for us, I don't think."

A service truck sitting beside the equipment was opened and one of the workmen in red coveralls and hard hat produced a can of ether to aid in starting the dozer. Far up on the hill a survey crew was busily setting their transit while a group of men in fluorescent orange raincoats and white hard hats poured over a set of papers. Just to the left of the white-hatted men a wide blue ceremonial ribbon had been strung between the two lone oaks at the hill's crest.

Tom walked off a few feet from the others and gazed at the hilltop and the decorated trees. He stood silent for a few moments, then looked back at his two fellows, motioning them to join him. "Looks like we won't have to travel to Bethesda this afternoon."

"Why's that?" Dave asked him.

"Unless I'm wrong about this, James Brody will be coming here. See that tie?" he asked, pointing up the hill. "That ribbon is for an official opening ceremony. He very rarely does that, and when he does, he always attends to it personally. It means it's special. It's the start of something extraordinary. His blue-ribbon project. He's even notified the press to be present. This isn't good."

The sudden roar of the big diesel droned out any further conversation and the three men turned to watch the operator begin to back the machine down off the steel carrier. Cameras began rolling and flashbulbs snapped as newspeople took the opportunity to record the moment on film.

The yellow earthmover was cautiously crawled down the ramps to the ground. A track was locked to swing the machine to face the hill. Then, with throttle pulled back, it roared forward, clanking its way up the slope. The ground trembled under the weight of the iron monster as the cleat tracks violently marked its path, biting into the sod and crushing the green growing timothy and alfalfa. The newspeople and other spectators filed in line to walk in the defined scars left by the crawlers. Tom, Sam, and Dave could only stand and watch, mesmerized by the incredible destruction of the serene field.

"Pardon me," came a voice from directly behind them, startling them from their absorbed viewing of the transgression before them. "You're the two Pittsburgh fellows. Right?"

They turned to see the voice belonged to Mitchel Page. He was in the company of another man much older than they. The fellow was about five feet, six-inches tall, slightly rounded, and had a friendly, grandfatherly appearance with his bushy, gray mustache and wire-rimmed spectacles. He had on soiled hiking boots and, over unpretentiously casual clothes, he wore a black waist-length riding duster. His head was protected by a well-worn black fedora with the brim curled down.

"Yes. Hello, Mitchel," Sam replied, extending his hand. "Sam Baker...and Dave Cooper. Good to see you again."

"Yes. I thought it was you two. Kelly told me to look for you," Mitchel said, shaking hands with both men. He nodded toward the older man, saying, "Let me introduce someone to you. This is Buck Morganti." While the men exchanged handshakes Mitchel explained, "Buck is chairman of the board of McPherson Corporation. He sits on the board of the McPherson Foundation."

"Oh, yes," Sam said. "You're the friend of Dennis Woods."

"Yes, I am. I was in France when I got word of what happened to him. Flew back as soon as I could. We had a fire at one of our plants over there. Dennis had convinced me about the importance of this project to you all. We don't usually get involved in this type of thing, but, since Dennis is a friend of mine,

I told him I'd have a look at it. I had every intention of convening the board to consider your grant when this trouble at the factory came up. I'm sorry things didn't work out as they might have."

"I'll lay odds on knowing who was behind your fire," Dave commented under his breath.

"Oh? Who?" Buck asked, having heard him clear enough.

A bit embarrassed for having said it, Dave decided to speak his mind anyway. "Well, we just know James Brody was trying to get most of your members dispersed so you couldn't meet. Apparently, the man is prone toward any action necessary to achieve his goals."

Buck reached into his back pocket and produced a pouch of chewing tobacco. He took a big plug and stuffed it into the side of his mouth. "Those are serious accusations. Can you prove it?" he asked, passing the pouch in front of the others in offering. They all declined.

"Not immediately," Sam replied to him. "I think, given enough time it could be shown, but only circumstantially. Brody's too smart to be directly involved. He'd only be implicated by innuendo. Think about this: didn't many of the board members take leave at about the same time? Did they get called away on business or personal matters that arose rather abruptly?"

Buck cocked his head and his eyes narrowed as he looked at Sam while he considered that.

Tom interrupted. "Well, that's all rather irrelevant at the moment. We've reached the deadline and it's pretty apparent the McPherson board isn't going to be able to convene. You're here...and the others are who knows where. All we can hope is to use what we have now."

Buck leaned slightly to his side and spit a long brown stream of tobacco juice. "Why? What have you got?" he asked, looking curiously at Tom.

"I'm, uh, I'm not really at liberty to say. Just that...we might have available certain information that could persuade James Brody to change his plans somewhat."

Mitchel looked puzzled over Tom's statement and glanced at Buck to see if he knew what Tom meant. Buck's jaw was moving rapidly, working on the tobacco. One side of his lip curled upward in a tell-tale sign that he understood. "You boys have been doing your homework, huh?"

The three fellows exchanged looks with one another, then back to Buck. "I guess you could say that," Tom mused. Then he held out his hand to introduce himself. "Tom Charles. I'm an architect for Marco Development Corporation."

Buck smiled and shook the hand. Mitchel looked a bit stunned and a lot confused.

Buck shook the hand and leaned over to spit another stream of tobacco juice. "Having misgivings about this project, huh?"

"All along, Sir. All along," Tom replied.

"Well-l...," Buck drawled. "It's not very pleasant to watch good farmland taken out of productivity. Especially to build houses on. Once it's gone you never get it back again. And you folks are right; it's not going to be very pleasant to walk over the battlefield and see buildings all over the place. I just wish there could have been something my people could've done to help prevent this. I know I could have persuaded the rest of the board to help fund you. Too bad things worked out against you. Mitchel, here, told me about the troubles you had, what with the break-in and about your lawyer, and all. You know, you could have him disbarred for that."

Tom shrugged. "Yeah, well. Water over the dam. We might want to take some action against him later." He nodded ahead of him, saying, "Right now we ought to get up that hill and see if there isn't some way of influencing events here."

The others agreed and slowly began their ascent. As the five men slowly gained the hill, trudging over the sodden earth now so conspicuously disturbed by the giant machine, they drew increasingly despondent. Each footfall seemed weighted more with discouragement and futility than with the mud clinging to their shoes. Ahead of them, high up at the hill's crest, shone the massive silver blade of the earthmover. It was now turned and positioned a little back from and directly between the two old towering oaks. Once the ribbon had been cut the blade would be lowered to make a ceremonial swath of the ground.

Another cause of disconsolation to the small group was the seeming indifference of the newspeople now gathered around the base of the oaks. They talked and laughed, exchanging stories and jokes as they awaited the arrival of James Brody while hoping the rain would hold off until they had their pictures and stories.

They weren't kept waiting. The whirling blades of the Bell Ranger helicopter beat a quick and steady rhythm as it roared in low with "Marco Development Corporation" clearly emblazoned on its sides and belly. It came from behind the hill, swooping just over the tops of the two oaks to cause everyone below to duck in an instinctive reaction. Circling the field once to survey the ground and the gathered spectators, it returned and hovered above the trees. The branches swayed and flailed, releasing the rain droplets cupped in their leaves and showering the many unfortunates below. Then, roaring off to the flats beyond the hill it slowly lighted down.

Tom Charles, nearing the crest in lead of the small party, refused to bow under the looming presence of the whirring beaters. His smile was sardonic as he watched the reporters bend their knees and lower their heads. "Well-l-l..., and guess who that is," he said to the four men behind him.

Through reflex the men had at first started to cringe from the nearness of so awesome and powerful a machine. But, taking their cue from Tom, they stood erect, almost defiant, as they watched the craft rotate slowly above them.

"Well, I'm pretty certain it's not Bruce Catton," Dave replied. "So, I'm going to guess it's your boss...or, ex-boss."

"Yep! It's 'His Majesty', himself," Tom snorted. "He does like to make an entrance."

They moved over near the crowd but stayed a little apart from it. In short order a shiny, new, red Chevy Suburban approached from the direction of the helicopter landing. When it pulled to a stop near the bulldozer the tall, blond-haired James Marcus Brody stepped out from behind the wheel. Exiting from the opposite door and moving around to join James as he surveyed the crowd was Senator Russell J. Coggins. He was accompanied by Patrice Bennett, the sensationally lovely young starlet and latest in the line of enraptured escorts of James Brody. Exiting the rear doors and also gathering around James were several state and county officials. Flashbulbs snapped and film footage advanced as the small group of dignitaries moved to the blue ribbon strung between the trees.

"Wow! He's pulled out all the stops on this one," Tom commented. "He's got, like, half the politicians in Maryland with him. I keep expecting to see a brass band come marching up the hill with his name on a banner."

"So, that's your boss, is he?" Buck inquired, amused over the spectacle being played out before him. "I've seen some about him in the medias. Never thought I'd run into him in person. Never wanted to."

"Well, he was my boss 'till today," Tom replied. "I suspect when he learns my sympathies are with his opposition my position with the company will be terminated."

Buck spit a stream of tobacco and looked at Tom. "I'm awfully sorry to hear that, son. It may sound a bit cliché, but it is true that a man's got to live with himself. You do what you know is right. Goddamn trouble with business people today is we got too many folks concerned with only the bottom line—profits. I know. I've got a whole damn office full of M.B.A.s and accountants, keep pressing to cut people here, cut people there. Hell, they don't think of the workers as having families—only as numbers. I sometimes wish I could get rid of the whole lot of 'em." Buck reached out and patted Tom's shoulder. "You tender what your heart tells you. You'll do all right."

"Oh, I'm not worried about it," Tom said. "I can get work anywhere. I've even been toying with the idea of setting up my own shop."

"Good for you," Buck told him. "When Sammy McPherson and I started our business, it was on an idea and borrowed money. Hell, we were both young and scared shitless. Now we've got fifteen factories and ten different businesses on three continents." Buck spit a stream of brown juice for emphasis. "And that ain't including the subsidiaries we acquired along the way.

Hell. Your boss; he isn't anybody. Just flash and dash. He'll come down a peg or two in time. His kind always does."

Tom shrugged indifferently, "I don't know about that. He's got a lot of charisma that's worked pretty well for him so far. I'd be content to see him just stumble a little over this project. Like, maybe into the next county."

The men now quieted themselves and turned their attention in the direction of the two oaks and listened as first the senator, then the lesser officials, each spoke in turn. They praised the virtues of the project for being a boon to the economies of the county and state. Countless jobs would be created in construction, service, support and recreation. Everyone would prosper. They spoke of their indebtedness to James Brody and his company for their aid in revitalizing an otherwise stagnated economy; for bringing progress and development to a section of the state too long neglected in favor of its eastern half. The rolling hills and gentle valleys would thrive and be envied as a most desirable setting in which to raise a family. People would flock to the region in want of settlement. They claimed it would be "a new beginning for western Maryland. A rebirth, of which all the citizens of the area should boast of pridefully."

When the politicians were finally winded, James Brody stepped to the forefront. He thanked the gatherers for attending and the other speakers for their kind and generous praise of himself and his company. "It is all of you will make this project work and become a reality," he told the small crowd before him. "I am but the dreamer. I plan for a better tomorrow—an organized, safe and comfortable community from which we can all realize the benefits. It is you, the people of this county, that make all the difference with your aid and cooperation."

"Who's he talking to?" Tom asked in an aside to Sam. "Those are mostly all reporters, there. I doubt if too many of them even live anywhere near here."

"There has been some minor dissent toward this project," James continued. "Backwards, radical elements—opposed to modernization of any sort—have attempted to stymie our dream...our vision. Given their way we would all return to bark huts, oil lamps, horses and buggies, and outhouses...which our forefathers so long endured, and did emerge from, to progress and cling to the modern conveniences we now take so for granted. Fine houses, good automobiles, clean and safe schools and playgrounds...and jobs! These have become our birthright!

The American dream is a reality in which we can all share. It must be made available to everyone. Unproductive ground—be it an abandoned strip mine, an idled, useless hillside or marginal farmland like that upon which we stand here today—must be utilized for the benefit of all Americans. We cannot allow a handful of self-appointed 'do-gooders' to thwart our efforts of fulfilling our destiny for no better reason than they are familiar with the landscape in its present contour and cannot envision it any other way.

I am no stranger to historic preservation. But! I view it through the eye of objectivity. One must have the wisdom to discern when to cherish the relics of our past and the knowledge to sort through the clutter to determine what is treasure...and what is just so much trash. When my company undertook the job of refurbishing the harbor area, I initiated a declaration that no less than sixty percent of the buildings be registered as historic landmarks.

They were of value, there. They could easily have been torn down and replaced with modern buildings. But I saw our heritage, there. I saw America's past in those old, dilapidated structures. American fathers gave their sweat and blood to earn a living and to raise their families in those buildings and factories. They had to be preserved...no matter what the cost."

"Oh, brother," Tom smirked to the fellows around him. "I worked on that project, some. The government underwrote the cost difference to save those structures. That was purely a financial decision."

"To those of you who would thwart our efforts on this ground below us; who would conspire to keep western Maryland in the dark depths of high unemployment and languishing in decay; to those of you who would have us watch as the rest of the nation marches on in progress and growth, I say to you: stand aside! We are going to prosper. We are going to be the showplace and the envy of the nation!

Gentlemen...and Ladies...I give you—western Maryland's future."

James motioned with a sweep of his hand and two workmen, clad in new red coveralls, carried forward a five feet square watercolor painting depicting what the site would eventually become: large, expensive houses on well-landscaped lots with a centrally located community playground. The entire complex was completely surrounded by a tall, artistically designed security wall, accessed only through a large, ornate, electronically operated steel gate.

Flashbulbs popped as the workmen mounted the artist's rendering onto an easel for all to study and admire.

Tom shook his head in disgust. "Looks more like a modern-day feudal fortress, doesn't it? Walls all around; iron gates to keep out the riff-raff like us. They'll even have their own police force, eventually. He plans on running a corridor of these communities the whole way to D.C. with this as the anchor."

"It sure is impressive," Buck commented, leaning forward and squinting to better see the painting. "Did you do that?"

"Shamefully, I confess. I'm almost embarrassed. My original design was quiet. I had everything set over the hill, there," he pointed. "This would have been the gardens area and the playground would be just there. You could barely see the roof lines from most of the battlefield views. Of course, James didn't go for it. So, I thought I'd go the opposite extreme. I made it all what I thought was gaudy so he'd take me off the assignment. Damned! if he didn't love it."

James Brody spoke further of his plans to draw the eastern populous out to the western districts. He informed the crowd of his efforts in working closely with both the state and federal departments of transportation to upgrade existing roadways and conveyances. He explained his desire and efforts to lure the government funded, high-speed rail system into the area to make commuting to the city a pleasant, comfortable adventure. This would serve as the catalyst for this new prosperity, drawing the people out to the peace and serenity of the countryside.

Dave glanced back and spied his wife far down the hill. Beside her, moving slowly and carefully and helped along by Carol, was old Mrs. Schiels. Nudging for Sam's attention and nodding in the direction of the two women, he said, "I better go help her."

The other men had overheard Dave and glanced back down the hill. Mitchel Page gave mention of recognizing Varina and, as Dave started down to them, Sam explained who the women were.

The ribbon cutting ceremony had ended by the time the women finally joined the small group. Greetings and introductions were made by the men, all of whom the older woman eyed approvingly, her smile never changing as she shook each hand. Varina Schiels looked up at the big, yellow earthmover and watched James Brody climb onto it to make the first official scrape of dirt. "Pity to waste so much of a fine second cutting of hay," she said. "It'll cause the baler to pick up these rocks that's exposed. Probably some clumps of sod, besides."

"I don't suppose they'll be making any hay off this field after today," Buck said to her.

Varina smiled secretively and replied, "We'll see... We'll see..."

Chapter Fifteen

The big diesel failed to start. For all its shine and polish for the special occasion, several attempts by James Brody revealed the batteries were too low to turn the crank fast enough. Trying to put on a good front, James came out and stood on the track and, with a red face, explained to the crowd that it would be only a few minutes until the batteries were recharged. Already, workmen were scurrying to carry up booster cables from the heavy service truck that was bogged in the mud from its attempt to run the hill. The new four-wheel-drive Suburban had to be brought over closer to serve as the booster.

Tom nudged Sam to follow him and the two men headed up toward the machine. James had climbed down off the track and was talking to a few gathered reporters. He smiled broadly when he spied Tom and excused himself to go and greet the man. "Hey, Tom. This is a surprise. I didn't know you were coming out."

"Yeah. Uh, it came as a surprise to me, too. I hadn't heard you were going to do this. I wish I'd have been informed of it."

"Spur of the moment thing," James answered. "I decided to celebrate the land becoming ours. I didn't tell too many people. Didn't want to give that opposition group time to organize a protest." James took Tom's arm and tugged lightly, saying, "Hey. Come. Let me introduce you to some very influential people. Senator Coggins is here. You ought to get to know him."

Tom pulled back, resisting the man's efforts to lead him toward the senator. "Uh, maybe later," he said, his breath a bit short. He was nervous, but tried not to let it show. "Listen. Uh...we, we have to talk. Real quick like."

James tisked it off. "Tom...Tom... Not now. We'll talk later, at my office. Don't worry about anything. It'll wait. Christ, man! I'm right in the middle of this."

Tom looked at James with a certain boldness. "It's about this that we need to talk. I really think we need to do this now."

"All right. Quick, though. What is it?" James asked impatiently.

"Let's walk over here where we won't be disturbed," Tom said. He led James out of hearing from the crowd, Sam following beside and a little behind them.

James began to show greater impatience. "So, what's so goddamned important that it can't wait till later this afternoon? I should be entertaining Senator Coggins. You don't realize how important his vote is going to be to me. You got sixty seconds."

Tom halted and faced his boss. The condescending manner in which James had addressed him now turned Tom's nervousness to resentment. With no definite plans on how he was going to approach the subject he glanced at Sam standing in close and extemporaneously said, "Oh. I'm sorry. You two haven't met. Sam, this is James Brody. James...Sam Baker."

Since there was no sign of acknowledgement of him from Brody, Sam, likewise, ignored the introduction.

Tom smiled wryly when Sam's name failed to make any impression on James. "Sam's from up north," he continued. "He sort of got involved with that Antietam Foundation."

"So?"

"An, an amazing fellow, Sam," Tom said. He was anticipating a reaction from James when just the right amount of information was delivered. "He works with computers, you know."

"Yeah. And...?" James asked, glancing to see how the work on the dozer was progressing.

Sam wore no expression. He stared directly at James, also waiting for a response.

"He's a real whiz. He, he not only writes programs for computers, he's actually led teams that have designed and built them. Isn't that amazing? I'm still working on programming my VCR to record when I'm not home. There's not much Sam doesn't know about computers."

James was curt. "Look. What's going on?" he demanded. "I can't keep these people waiting, you know."

"No. No. I understand that," Tom said. "Let me finish. See, Mr. Baker, here, is sort of a hacker." He winked at Sam. "Oh-h...I shouldn't have used that word. He's touchy about it. Let's say 'he's very adept at accessing other people's systems'...uh, retrieving and interpreting data—data that could be rather compromising."

James now looked at Sam and, though his expression remained unchanged, his eyes widened slightly, responding in reflex until he managed to control them. Sam grinned overbroadly.

"So, you're him?" James said matter-of-factly. "I was told about you. You like my office? Nice, isn't it?"

Sam shrugged. "I didn't get to see it. I was on a lower floor. I like your system, though. First class."

"Yes. I always like to go with the best."

"You know, you really should hire me as a consultant. For all its expense your system's too easy to access. I could fix that."

"Are you the best, Mr. Baker?"

"Mm...beyond doubt," Sam nodded with his reply. "Take, for instance, your little enterprise that awards educational grants. Now, most hackers would find that rather dull to peruse; would have glossed right over it—especially when the award money is wired in from a coded account in a Cayman Island bank. Not me. No sir. I found it fascinating to spend a little time retracing electronic trails all over the place. I'd be willing to bet the I.R.S. would find it just as interesting. Hell, I found material in your data banks that could keep a team of investigators from the Attorney General's office busy for months. You're a very clever businessman, Mr. Brody. But your computer people left you open to scandal. That's unfortunate."

"So, it's blackmail," James said coldly. "You want to add that to your list of breaking and entering, theft, trespass and whatever else I can level against that shitty little group you're with."

Tom interrupted, saying, "Look, James. All they want you to do is give up this piece of ground. The project can be just as successful starting down at the orchard ground. All you need do is..."

"Bullshit!" James said angrily. "I picked this ground and this is where it starts! You know, you really surprised me, Tom. I took you under my wing. I gave you everything. You get a respectable salary, fringes; everything! And this is how you repay me."

"It's wrong, James," Tom said to him. "These people are right. I tried to live with the situation, but; but, you've crossed the line. You should have..."

"Oh, bullshit! I don't have to listen to this shit. If you've got anything on me you best try and use it. Put up or shut up! I'll sue you people until none of you have a dime left to your names. This is going through to finish!"

James stormed off. The workmen had been motioning that the batteries were sufficiently charged and the machine could be started. He climbed over the track to the seat and hit the start button. The engine roared loudly at full throttle, attracting everyone's attention. The crowd gathered and lined itself on either side of the machine and waited as the work crew now hurried to secure the battery covers and collect tools.

Dave brought the two women over to where Sam and Tom stood behind the machine. "Well?" Dave asked, curious about the conversation between the three men.

"I don't know," Sam replied. "We talked to him. But he sure doesn't seem concerned. He's sure one arrogant son-of-a-bitch. I think he believes he's above the law."

"Damn!" Dave said. "Then we're sunk."

Tom stood silent beside the others. He seemed to be deep in thought; his stare, focused on someone in the gathering. Varina stepped away from the small group and came to stand directly in front of him. She put a frail hand on his chest and, nodding in affirmation of her words, told him, "Go on, young man. You must do it."

"Mmhh?" Tom startled, drawn from his distraction to look down at the old woman.

"Go on, if it pulls so strongly," she said. Then she moved to stand beside him, as if to watch him go.

With no word of explanation to the others, Tom walked over to stand next to the Senator. He leaned over close to the man and said something in his ear as the diesel engine roared.

The shining blade was lowered to the wet sod and pressed deep by the force of the hydraulic cylinders. James pulled the drive lever to engage the clutch and the metal cleat tracks began to turn. The powerful machine crawled slowly along the ground as dirt piled up and was pushed in front of the blade. An eight-foot-wide swath was scalped from the field, leaving a trench several feet deep.

Sam shivered with a sudden chill shooting up through his spine. Though it was a warm, almost hot day, large goose pimples erupted over his skin. He wrapped his arms tightly across his chest.

"You okay?" Dave asked him, causing the other to turn and look.

"I'm...I'm not sure. I just got this...weird chill...that came over me. Jeez! Look at my arms."

"I know. I can see," Dave said. "Put your raincoat on. It's starting to rain, anyway."

As Sam slipped into his rain jacket, umbrellas sprouted open among the crowd. Carol opened and shared her's with Varina. A light rain had begun falling but the dark clouds threatened and heavier showers were certain to follow.

The blade of the bulldozer had filled with a mound of earth as wide and as high as itself. James had pushed between the two oaks and a little beyond, halting at the crest of the hill. He switched the engine off and posed for the cameras with a triumphant "thumbs up" and a broad grin. As the cameras clicked and whirred, Sam clutched at his chest and, unconsciously, massaged his ribs near his heart.

"Sam, old buddy. What's wrong?" Dave asked him. "You look pale."

Sam shook his head. "I don't know," he replied, his voice distant and preoccupied. He began to move with tremulous footsteps toward the excavated strip, stopping now and then to turn an ear, as though listening to some silent beckoning from the trees. He halted at the edge of the cut, just behind the oaks.

Dave watched him a moment, then headed over. When he came beside him, he asked, "Sam? What's going on? Are you hearing something I'm not? You're acting awful strange."

Sam didn't answer directly. He moved his head in perturbed, irregular motions to better receive some muted signal perceptible only to him. "Dave. This is really strange," he finally said. "I'm feeling, like…, the ultimate…déjà vu. My hair feels like it's…standing on end. I feel like…I'm floating. Like, I'm on drugs, or something. Phew!"

Dave became really worried, now, and he put a hand on Sam's shoulder. "Sam. Is it your heart? Are you having a heart attack?"

Sam only now realized his hand was massaging his chest. "No. I don't think so. I don't have any chest pains. I just…feel so…" His voice trailed off as he again became distracted. Cocking his head curiously, his eyes swept along the plowed strip of ground. As he stared down into the cut his face suddenly tightened in a stunned, frightened expression. A shiver coursed through his body.

"Sam?" Dave hollered in alarm as he watched his friend turn pale. Sam groaned and turned away. Moving to one of the tall oaks he leaned against it and cloaked his eyes in his forearm. Dave glanced down to where Sam had been looking and gasped at what he saw. There, exposed and disturbed now that their blanket of earth had been stripped away, lay various bone fragments, the remains of some long-forgotten individual.

"Holy jeez!" Dave gasped. He jumped into the cut for a better look, careful to avoid getting too close. "Jesus! I think it's a grave?" He leaned over closer to examine the bones and was tempted to stick his foot out to flip a few over. He decided better of it, not wanting to disturb the site any further. A closer stare at one dirt-encrusted formation showed it to be a jaw bone and teeth—definitely human.

Something other than bone fragments lay partially exposed in the loosened soil—a small, round metallic object. Dave wrestled with the urge to reach for it but watched his hand uncontrollably snatch it up. His thumb quickly brushed the dirt away as he palmed the small object. Frightened of being seen by anyone and accused of grave robbing he hurriedly slipped it into the pocket of his raincoat. He felt ashamed and humiliated for having taken the item as a souvenir but was unable to force himself to replace it. His hand refused to pull it from his pocket.

"Dave. What are you looking at?" It was Carol, standing behind him on the grass.

"Uh-h...I'm not sure," he replied, hoping she hadn't noticed his blatant thievery. "I think it's a grave," he said, turning his head to her. He saw, now, that the others in his party had come up to look.

"Well, sure enough," Buck said loudly. "Those are human bones, all right."

"Yeah," Dave agreed. "Look. There's part of a jaw bone; still got some teeth attached. That looks like part of a hip or something."

"My God!" Carol gasped. "We better notify somebody."

One of the reporters wandered over, curious why a small group had gathered off from the crowd and was examining the cut. When he learned from Carol what had been discovered he immediately hailed his photographer who approached and began to snap pictures of the unearthed remains. Other news people began to respond. One by one they filtered away from James Brody as he stood upon the track of the dozer and answered their questions.

Then, a mass exodus ensued as the entire gathering rushed to the edges of the cut to peer down at the discovery. James then pushed through the crowd to see what had drawn everyone's attention away from him. "What have you got?" he asked, jumping down into the now tacky soil. A steadier drizzle began to wet the newly exposed dirt as well as to affect a crude washing of some of the scattered bones.

"It's a grave," a reporter informed him.

James stared down at the dirt encrusted skeletal fragments and determined to hide his contempt of the discovered curiosity. He feared the possible adverse publicity, added to an already controversial project, might result in lower property values. If more graves were discovered during the excavation people might be reluctant to invest in the project. "It's probably just a horse or a cow," he said. "Farmers always buried dead animals on the back side of their farms."

"That's no animal," someone commented. "Those are human teeth."

Another spectator pointed out an object that clearly wasn't bone fragment. "What's that, there?" she asked.

A workman jumped into the cut and, pulling on a pair of gloves, bent to carefully pick up the object. He examined it for fragility, then, finding it solid enough, he brushed the mud away and held it out to show the crowd. The man grinned widely for becoming the focal point of the camera lens, if only for a fleeting moment. "It's a buckle," he announced. "Got 'U.S.' stamped right on it. Probably brass metal. Might be a belt buckle."

"Humph," was the only reply James gave, and that was low, not to be clearly heard. People stood around the sides of the cut talking. As they speculated about the grave, film footage was shot and camera flashes popped endlessly. James stood silent, scheming inwardly for how to downplay this unforeseen situation. Someone touched his arm for attention and James snapped a look over his shoulder. Senator Coggins tugged on his arm and motioned with a twitch of his head for James to follow him off from the crowd.

Dave climbed up out of the now mudding dirt in the strip to go to where his friends had clustered around to console Sam. Buck and Mitchel stood back from them, watching Sam try to regain his composure.

"Your friend has a rather weak stomach," Buck said, following his statement with a spit of brown juice. "Hell, it isn't any more than a pile of old bones."

"No. It's something more than that. I've seen him stuff pieces of men into body bags. It's not that."

"Maybe it was something he ate," Mitchel volunteered politely.

"I don't think so," Dave said. Worried, he moved in closer to where Carol stood over Sam. She glanced at her husband, showing an expression of concern, but helplessness. Dave put a hand on Sam's shoulder. "You okay?" he asked.

Sam looked up at him, glassy eyed and dazed. "No, man. I feel really weird. Not sick... But not well. I gotta' get outta' here."

"Yeah. Come on. I'll take you down," Dave said. He helped Sam to his feet from where he was squatting slumped against the tree. When they started off, moving down the hill, Carol rejoined the patiently observing Varina Schiels under the shelter of the umbrella.

James Brody again drew everyone's attention. He had climbed back onto the dozer track and, standing under a large green and white striped golf umbrella with his company logo printed on it, began to address the crowd. "As you know, I've spent countless hours of work and an extreme amount of money preparing for this project. It means more to me than any project I've ever undertaken. I've gone to great lengths, with much personal sacrifice, to assure this project's success—for the betterment of western Maryland; for a better life for its citizenry. However! because of what we have discovered here...I can only, in my heart, believe that a complete change of plan is necessitated. Senator Coggins and I have discussed the situation...and we believe that, though we have uncovered only one grave, which may well be that of a Civil War soldier, there may be others scattered about in these fields. In my heart, I know that I cannot disturb the resting place of brave men who fought and died here—men who helped to make this country what it is today. Therefore, I am exercising my option not to purchase this acreage so that it will remain undisturbed forever. I know that there are groups interested in this ground with intentions other than the economic recovery of the region. I will tell you that Marco Development Corporation will work closely with these groups to ensure that this ground is preserved in its natural state...for the benefit of future generations...and as a token of our thanks to the men who lay sleeping in these fields."

While James continued his blustery remarks Tom rejoined the little circle of friends. He wore a sly grin as he asked, "Did you hear? Are you listening?"

"Wow!" Dave said in answer, unable to restrain his elation. "This is remarkable!"

"Isn't it?" Tom said, still smiling secretively. "I thought you'd all be pleased."

"Did you say something?" Dave asked. "I saw you talking to Senator Coggins."

"Not, not really. I simply introduced myself to the man. James said I should get to know him. We talked some and I casually informed him how ugly this whole affair had become—Marco raiding your files; the Antietam Foundation raiding Marco's. I really thought he ought to know that a certain "gift" list was among the many documents discovered in James's files and that the Senator's name appeared on it rather often." Tom smiled broadly, now. "I think Senator Coggins had a convincing chat with James."

"Well, you son-of-a-gun, you," Dave smiled to him in praise.

"Thank you," Tom said, taking a slight bow.

"Wait a minute," Sam interrupted. "I don't remember his name on the list very often. And I didn't think you even got to see the list."

"I didn't. You told me about it. I took a chance. It paid off."

"Wonderfully, too," Carol added.

"Isn't this terrific?" Mitchel said, though he wasn't entirely certain what Tom meant by these lists. But, to Varina he asked, "You will allow us a few more days to raise the money, won't you?"

Buck chimed in, saying, "I'll get the board to convene in a couple days. I believe I can talk them into approving the grant."

Varina Schiels had a satisfied smile on her face. "Yes. I'll give you your few days—and you will raise the money." Then to Carol she said, "Come, dear. Take me home. My legs are playing out. You folks, come to my house and we'll talk. I'll make tea."

"Thank you. We'd enjoy that," Dave replied.

Mitchel begged off for both Buck and himself. He thanked her for the offer but explained he wanted to stay and be certain the proper authorities were notified of the remains. "They'll have to be exhumed and examined," he said. "I want to speak to the press, too. Not that they seem to care, but I'd like to get a plug in for the Foundation. It'll help bring in donations."

Tom smiled and shook his head, being both irked and amazed. "Isn't this ironic? Brody really seems to have stolen the show. He's coming out of this smelling pretty sweet—as usual."

"How much do you think he'll work with the 'other interested parties'?" Dave asked.

Tom chortled, "About as much as he has all along." Then he grinned. "You know what you should do? Call him for a donation. I'd love to see his face when he takes that call."

The others laughed, agreeing to pass the suggestion on to Marylou as she could be cleverly verbose in her approach and would enjoy placing the taunting call to James Brody.

The small party again expressed their excitement over the turn of events and congratulated themselves on their success. Dave, Sam, Carol and Varina then turned to leave, saying goodbye to the other three men. As they made their descent, the further Sam distanced himself from the hilltop, the more composed he became. When they reached the van, he felt much better, though still a bit disturbed from the queer ordeal. He spoke little on the way to the Schiels house which, though only over several hills and across some sloping fields by tractor, was a good three miles around winding roads by car.

Dave stopped the van in front of the old farm house and Carol stepped out to hold an umbrella for Varina. Dave and Sam followed behind them, their raincoat hoods flipped up on their heads to protect against the steady downpour. Wilma was standing on the porch to greet them as they approached the house and she showed a wide grin as they came onto the porch and under the shelter of its roof. "Eh. How'd it go?" she asked them, though her cheery demeanor seemed to reveal she already knew the answer.

"Oh! Wonderfully!" Carol told her as she set the umbrella aside. "You can't imagine what happened up there."

"I think I can. But tell me anyway."

"My God, they found the remains of a person," Carol said. "They had this big bulldozer up there and when they pushed a big pile of dirt away there were these bones lying there. They think it was a Civil War soldier. Somebody found a buckle with 'U.S.' stamped on it."

"Eh-heh!" Wilma chuckled. "Was it between them two big trees up in the top hay field?"

"Why...yes. It was. How did you know?"

Wilma didn't answer her. Instead, she looked at Varina Schiels and said, "Eh-heh! That's just where you said he was, huh?"

"Who?" Carol asked.

"What happened then?" Wilma asked, ignoring Carol's question and everyone's curious stares. "Did that developer fella' back down and give up the ground to yous guys?"

"Well...yes. But..."

"Eh-h-h heh-heh. Well, you were right," Wilma chuckled to the old woman. "That's ten dollars I owe you."

"'Course I was right," Varina grumbled to the younger, plump girl. "You won't pay me anyway so I don't see what difference it makes."

Wilma smiled to the three visitors as she held the door for Varina to enter. "We never pay each other. We just make these bets for fun to see how we'd do if we really did bet fer real. You folks comin' in?"

"Uh, yeah. We are," Dave said. "Mrs. Schiels invited us for tea."

"Good. C'mon in," Wilma said, leading the way. "Comp'ny's always nice ta' have." She halted them in the hallway and looked into the cluttered room on the left. There, she had positioned the old man in front of the T.V. Varina went in to stand beside him and check on his comfort. "He's all right," Wilma told her from the hall. "I just emptied his pee bag a little bit ago. He doesn't need changed, yet. He'll be okay fer awhile. We played cards while we was waitin' fer ya'. He cheats at solitaire, ya' know."

Varina adjusted the collar of her husband's shirt as an excuse to touch him, then lightly brushed his cheek with the back of her hand. There was no response. "He always did cheat at cards," she said, remembering. "He'd let you catch him, though. Thought it was funny; a big joke. He was a good card player, though." She patted his shoulder fondly, then turned from him to join the others.

Wilma led them down the hall to the kitchen, asking, "youn's want coffee or tea?"

"I'd like coffee if it's not too much trouble," Sam replied.

"Nope. Got a pot on already," Wilma told him. "I drink tons of it durin' the day. Varina, she drinks chamomile. Prob'ly why she's as old as she is. I'll prob'ly never live as long as her. She could tell you, but she don't tell nobody when they're gonna' croak."

"Can you, really?" Dave asked Varina as she shuffled ahead of him.

When the old woman didn't reply, Wilma spoke up as she held the swinging door for Varina. "Sure, she can. She learns all kinds 'a things in them cards. Don't 'cha?"

"Fix my tea, dear," Varina said to her.

"'Dear'. Heh-heh-heh. She always calls me that when she wants me to shut up."

As they seated themselves around the big wooden table—Varina easing herself into the rocker by the hearth—Wilma poured everyone coffee or tea as requested. She took a seat at the far end of the table. "So, youn's gonna head up north soon?" she asked.

"Yes," Carol replied. "We've stayed longer than anticipated. Dave's work is piling up and Sam has to find an apartment in Pittsburgh."

"Yeah. You prob'ly miss yer kids, huh?"

"Yes. I do. I call them every day," Carol said. Then, hesitantly, she asked, "How, uh...how did you know I had children?"

"Eh. Varina told me. She told me all kinds 'a stuff about youn's. There ain't a whole lot t' do around here. Mostly, we just sit around 'n read the cards, findin' out stuff. Jist curious. You know." Then Wilma looked at Sam. "Ain't 'cha gonna ask 'er?" she said, nodding toward Varina, sitting quietly, sipping her tea.

Sam looked a bit surprised. "Ask her? Ask her what?"

"'bout the grave, up there on the hill. Ain't 'cha curious about it? I would be—'cept I already know about it."

Sam looked at the plump brunette suspiciously. Then, turning his head slowly around to the silently rocking Varina, he asked, "Do you know about it? Do you know who it is?"

"Yes. I know who it is," she replied, quiet and slow. "Don't know his name. Nobody does. He's been in my family for years.

My daddy used to plow up souvenirs every spring. Belt buckles, canteens, bullets. Ho-o-o, got a lot of bullets. Mini balls, they call them. All kinds of things from the battle fought here."

"Was that how you found the bones?" Sam asked. "From plowing?"

"No. No. Heavens, no," Varina said, chuckling at the thought. "We left them two trees there as a marker—my grandaddy, leastways."

"My grandmother was a little girl on the farm when the big battle was fought. They didn't bother our place much. Just had troops camping all over it. There was another battle fought sometime later. Oh, just a little one compared to the real big one. Some of General Early's men and some of the Yankee General Sigel's men. I know. I looked it up, once."

Varina rocked slowly for a while. She seemed to be assembling events in her mind before she continued. "After the battle was fought, and the Yankees had skedaddled, my grandmother went over the fields giving water to the wounded boys lying about moaning and crying. She came across this one fella' lying right there between them two trees. "Course, they were just little saplings back then. She knew he was dying, she said, 'cause he had a hole in his chest—caught a ball right near his heart. So, my grandmother bent over to give him a drink, and she said he was holding a locket. Said the girl whose picture was in it was beautiful. He showed it to her. Then he handed her the letter and made her promise to see it got delivered to the girl. Made her swear to it, he did. Poor boy died before he could tell her the girl's name. Pity, too. She said he was a very handsome young man. Wars are such a waste of youth," Varina sighed.

Sam was listening attentively. His heart raced as he visualized the face of the young boy that haunted his dreams. "And the sword?" he asked. "That was this fellow's, too?"

Varina closed her eyes and nodded as she rocked. "Oh-h, yes. That was his, too. Confederate soldiers came to dig a hole to bury him in. They stripped his boots and pants; took his guns. When they weren't looking, grandmother snatched up his sword and stole away. A long time we waited... A long time..."

"But, why did you give me the sword?" Sam asked. "Why the letter to Kelly?"

Varina opened her eyes and turned her head to look at Carol. She smiled gently and said, "You know. Don't you, child?"

Carol blinked, bewildered, as she returned the older woman's gaze. She knew what Varina was implying but she couldn't bring herself to verbalize it. The very thought was almost too incredible to consider. She searched for a reply to the gray-haired lady but was unable to formulate one.

Instead, it was Wilma who answered for her. Looking at Sam she said, "Don't 'cha get it? It was you was that young fella' up there. Them's yer bones."

"Wha-what?" Sam asked, astounded at her answer.

"Sure. From yer past life. Don't 'cha believe in reincarnation?"

"No. Not... I don't know. I never thought much on it," Sam replied, thoroughly confused and flabbergasted.

"Well, ya' should. "'Course, it don't make no difference, anyhow. What the heck, when yer dead, yer dead. Neat thing is; yer prob'ly the only guy in the world ever got to' know where his old bones is buried. That's somethin', ain't it?"

"Y-yeah... Sure," Sam replied. He was skeptical though something inside him reasoned that he was listening to an answer for the strange and fantastic dreams that haunted both his and Kelly's nights. Not that he found any of this so difficult to believe—just totally surreal! He'd never really given the idea of past life any consideration. Now, to be bombarded with the suggestion as to the actual location of his grave—and to have viewed his own remains—was a bit too much for him to absorb at one sitting.

"Okay. Okay," Sam said. "Let's assume there is such a thing as reincarnation. But, how do you know those are my bo-, uh, remains up there? They could be anybody's."

"Naw-w-w... Them's yers. Ol' Varina knows. She read it in the cards. Her ma' read it before her, 'n she learn't it from her ma'. They even knew, sort o', when you was gonna' show up. They're psychic. They know these things. Missy learns all kinds a' things from the cards."

With his head cocked in a continued portrayal of skepticism, Sam asked, "Well, if that's so, why did she sign the agreement with Marco Development? She must have known the Foundation would come up with the money."

"Ou'nt know," Wilma shrugged. "Why'nt 'cha ask 'er?"

Sam turned his eyes to Varina. She was gazing ahead and continuing her slow, rhythmic rocking, but knew his eyes were on her. "You can't change what is to be," Varina answered. "You can only learn what's to happen. You can't change it."

"See?" Wilma said. "Ya' learn all kinds a' things 'round here. Some of it makes sense; some don't."

Dave had draped his rainjacket over the back of his chair and now reached down to retrieve the souvenir from the pocket. With his other hand he fumbled in the opposite pocket for some tissue. He brought both items out over the table and began to wipe the dirt from the small, round trinket.

"What's that?" Carol asked as everyone watched him.

"I'm...not...sure," he said, lightly rubbing off the soil. "I, uh...I found it in the grave. I know it was wrong to take it, but I couldn't stop myself."

"You took it?" Sam asked, somewhat shocked.

"I'm telling you; I couldn't help it. I tried not to. You know I don't do those kinds of things. Something made me do it. I couldn't stop myself. I feel guilty as hell."

"Is it a watch?" Carol asked. "It looks like a little pocket watch."

"I don't know. It's gold, though. I'm sure of that. That's why it didn't deteriorate." He carefully opened the cover, the fragile hinge, stiff and reluctant, loosening as he delicately worked at it. A thin layer of clay had seeped in to mold onto both sides and he gently rubbed it away from the back of the cover. "There's something written on it, but it'll take a good cleaning to read it clearly," he informed them. He started to work on the opposite disk, cleaning the soil impacted over it. As he worked, his eyes widened in surprise and he paused, stared at what he was uncovering, then worked quickly to uncover more. He looked up at Carol and Sam sitting across from him, blinked in astonishment at what he'd discovered, then gaped again at the gold oval in his hand. There, amazingly preserved after more than a century underground, was a photograph of a lovely young lady.

"What?" Sam asked, curious of Dave's reaction. "What is it?"

"It's a...it's a photo. A daguerreotype, maybe—I don't know. Depends on when it was taken and by whom. But...It's a photo of a ...very beautiful...girl. Here. Have a look," he said, passing the locket across the table to him.

Sam looked down at the photo and almost gasped. His heart pounded as he gazed at the portrait in the locket. Though he said nothing to the others, he immediately recognized the young lady as the same one he'd seen in his dream the other night.

Carol leaned in for a look. "My. She's very pretty...or was. I wonder who she was?"

Sam still could not bring himself to speak. He stared at the photograph, his face flushing and his mind reeling as he tried to remember the name he'd called out to her. He turned the locket cover to examine the scrollwork and was shocked to find that, of what he could remember of hers from examining it closely only once, it appeared a match to the one Kelly often wore around her neck. "This is too much," he mumbled, turning it again to gaze at the picture. "This is crazy."

"What is, Sam?" Carol asked, not having noticed he was emotionally distraught.

"Nothing. Never mind," he said. He couldn't think how to begin to discuss what Varina—and even his own mind—was suggesting: that he, indeed, was the reincarnated life of that dead Civil War soldier up on the hill.

Dave did pick up on his friend's state of mind. He could tell Sam was strangely upset but seemed reluctant to talk about it openly. He decided to try to make light of it, saying, "Uh, hey, Sam. Why don't you keep the locket as a souvenir. Heh, if Varina's right, it's yours anyway."

Instead of a slight chuckle Dave had hoped to draw from his friend, Sam glanced up at him and, though his gaze was direct, his eyes revealed that his thoughts were elsewhere. After several seconds of blank stare, Sam finally responded. "Uh...yeah. Um...thanks." He looked over at Varina and saw the woman gazing ahead, rocking rhythmically, a knowing smile on her face.

Varina didn't look at Sam, but she knew of his confusion. "You don't have to believe it, Sam. You can just take the gifts and enjoy having them. Makes no difference one way or the other. My job is done, leastways. Long time we waited for you to come back. My grandmother kept her promise to you."

Sam was stunned. He blinked several times. "What d'ya mean 'it makes no difference'? Why wouldn't it make a difference? If that really was me up there, I'd say it makes a really big difference."

Varina stopped rocking and turned her head to look at Sam as though surprised by his ignorance. "Why on earth should it?" she asked. "Dear Boy, that life is over and here you are again." She turned back and started rocking, though a bit faster than before. As she began to speak again, she nodded her head to affirm what she told him, "Never mind what was. You concern yourself with doing what's proper in this one."

Sam cocked his head and squinted one eye as he studied the gently rocking form of the older woman. He sucked on his lower lip while considering what she'd said and found it all too fantastic. Not wishing to take issue with her, but being so involved already anyway, he decided to pursue her last statement. "Yeah? And how do I know what's proper? Who determines what's proper?"

Varina displayed her patience with him by slowing the chair to an easy, rhythmic rock again, "Oh-h-h...we all know. It's inside us," she said slowly. "We all know. Most of the time we don't give listen to it. Like a little voice, way deep down, it tells us. But we mostly don't listen. Think we're too important," she continued, smiling and nodding her head in agreement with what she was saying. "So the circle keeps goin' round, unbroken. We keep coming back to learn the lessons all over again...on and on...'till finally, someday, we get it right."

"And I'm back again, huh?" Sam asked, though he said it more as a concluding statement.

"We're all back again, Sam," Varina sighed. "We're all back again..."

Carol was intrigued. She rested an arm on the chair back and turned to better look at the older woman on the broad hearthstone. "Why did he have to die so young?" she asked.

Varina had paused to take a sip of tea. When she replaced her cup onto the iron stove beside her and began to rock again, she shook her head, "Who can tell, child. Perhaps to keep him from living a long life wrongly. The more wrong we do in one life... the more we pay for it in the next. 'Course, the better we do, the more rewards, too. But only He can know why anyone dies."

"So, you believe everything is pre-destined?" Carol asked.

"That's right, dear. We create our own future by the things we've done in the past; the things we do in the present. It all comes back around to us. That's why I never tell anyone when anything painful is going to happen to them. No sense having them fret about it beforehand. It's going to happen anyway."

Varina spoke with such conviction that Sam was unsure of what to make of it all. He believed he understood what she was saying, and some of it even made sense to him. But, being told his old body—or what was left of it anyway—was lying up there in a hay field was just preposterous. He hadn't been at all prepared to listen to such talk—not while on vacation. Still, fascinated, he had to learn more. "Let me ask you this, then. Out of curiosity, if Kelly and I knew each other and were lovers in a past life, obviously our relationship was cut short—I'd guess my being killed would have pretty well ended that. Are we going to be together in this life? Is this where I finally get the girl and go riding off into the sunset and live happily ever after? What do the cards tell about that?"

Varina leaned forward, took up her tea cup for a last sip and set it down again. With some effort she lifted herself out of the rocker and turned toward the door. "Won't that be interesting to see," she mumbled as she shuffled along. "All this activity has played me out. I need to lie down awhile." She moved on through the kitchen door with no other words to her visitors.

"I'll be up ta' help you in a bit," Wilma called after her.

Carol started to rise from the table. "Well, we should go."

"Eh, you don't have to. You kin stay awhile. I'll help ol' Missy get comft'erble 'n come back."

"No. No. We really should be heading back ourselves," Dave told her. "It's getting late and we've still got loose ends to tie up."

"Eh. Suit yerselves," Wilma shrugged as she started to lead them down the hall. "It was nice havin' the company fer awhile. Missy, she don't get many folks visitin' her. Me, I go home after I get things tidied up 'n get them two in bed. Stop around 'fore you head back up north 'n say g'bye to the old folks."

"We'll sure try," Dave told her as they followed her onto the porch. "Thanks for the tea and coffee."

"Oh, yer welcome for that. It was Varina's stuff, though. Not mine."

"Well, thank her for us," he said.

They stood on the porch and gazed out at the surrounding barnyard and fields. The rain had slackened to a slight drizzle but a thick low fog had set in, so enshrouding that the huge barn was barely even visible.

"Whew!" Wilma said. "Check this out. Ya' better drive caref'lly."

"Does this happen often?" Carol asked her.

"Eh. Sometimes. D'pends on the weather. Usually, it's in the mornin'...or late at night. Ain't gonna' be much fun fer the t'erists. All this rain. Now this."

"Excuse me, Wilma," Sam blurted, his voice displaying an uneasiness he'd hoped to try and mask. "Why wouldn't Varina answer my question?"

"Which one?"

"About me and Kelly. Why'd she leave and not answer me?"

"Beats me. I guess she was tired."

"No. Come on. What's up? Is something going to happen to one of us?"

"Eh, she don't always tell me everything. Maybe she's leavin' it as a surprise."

"She said she never tells people when some calamity is going to happen."

"Yeah. So?"

"So-o-o..."

"Ou'nt know. She's weird sometimes. Don't figure, her leavin' ya' wunderin' like that, though. Maybe she don't know. Maybe the cards never told 'er. I wouldn't worry 'bout it. What's gonna' happen's gonna' happen."

"Don't worry about it? How am I not going to worry about it?"

"Eh! Who knows? Ol' Missy's got 'er ways. Old people: ya' just can't always figure 'em. Well, gotta' go. You all take care, now," Wilma told them.

Sam watched the heavy-set girl turn and go back inside. He was dissatisfied with her reply and frustrated at being left with so many unanswered questions. He braced an outstretched hand against a support column and humphed, "Well, ain't that just great."

Carol moved close to him and put an arm about his waist. "Aw, Sam. I don't know what to say."

"There isn't much to say, is there? I'm probably a dead man—again! Hey! Maybe in another hundred some years I'll dig up these bones. Then I can die all over again. Maybe you guys should have me cremated. Wouldn't that throw a wrench into the karma or whatever?"

"Come on, Sam. Stop it," Carol said. "You don't know what Varina meant by her silence. She must have had a reason for it. She seems too wise to have just left you hanging like this. I know she didn't mean to have you so anxious and crazy over it. Let's just calm down and give it some time. Maybe it'll come to us."

"What'll come to us?"

"Her reasoning."

"Right!" he snorted. "You calm down. You're not the one some calamity is about to have happen to them."

"Well, maybe you aren't either. Did you ever think maybe it's Kelly she was referring to. Why you? If it is a calamity, it might be Kelly who's going to get hurt."

Sam stiffened. "My God, you're right! We forgot about her! She must be wondering what happened to us. I'll bet no one's even told her what's happened up there. We better get over to the Foundation."

Dave glanced at his watch. "Jeez. It's way past four. We've been here longer than I realized. Let's get going."

They climbed into the van and Dave started off up the long lane, his speed hampered by both the treacherous roadbed and the heavy fog. As they jostled along, Sam's mind was unwaveringly chained to thoughts of Kelly. He sat on the edge of the seat and gazed steadily out the window, wishing he could part the fog and will the lane smooth to return to her more speedily. Much he had been given to consider, should he choose to give Varina's words credence. But for now, he could think only of returning to the lovely woman and to know of her safety.

Chapter Sixteen

Mitchel and Tom stumbled through the front door of the Foundation house with all the finesse of two men who have celebrated just short of their tolerance levels—which, in fact, they had. Tom was singing the chorus of *Battle Hymn of the Republic* while Mitchel provided the music by way of a seriously off-key hum. They marched with triumphant spirits through the front room and into the office area.

Kelly raised her groggy head from the desk and tried to focus on the two as they continued to march around the tight confines of the room. "Who—what's going on?" she asked, massaging her temples.

"Ha! Ha!" Tom laughed merrily. "We're celebrating."

"C-celebrating? Celebrating what?" she asked, still in somewhat of a daze. "What time is it?"

The two men halted their march and song and looked at Kelly ambiguously. "Come on," Tom said. "You mean you don't know? Nobody told you?"

"Told me what?" she asked through a stretch and yawn. She glanced at the clock and was stunned to see it was just past five o'clock. "My gawd. I must have dozed off."

"Oh. You are out of it aren't you?" Tom chuckled. "I figured for sure Sam would have called to inform you."

"I don't know. Maybe the phone rang and I slept right through it. Tell me what, for crying out loud? What are you talking about?"

"We won! Tom exclaimed. "The land is ours!"

"What? You're kidding!" she said, interrupting her massage as she'd again tried to rub her temples of the throbbing sensations.

"We're not!" Mitchel said.

"Well, how? Tell me about it. Who talked to Brody? Where's Sam and the Coopers?"

"Oh, they'll be along," Tom explained. "They took Mrs. Schiels home. She moves a little slow. I suspect they'll show up any time." Tom picked the phone from the receiver. "I gotta' call my wife and tell her. Isn't this exciting, though! We took on 'James the Omnipotent'—and won! This is great!" He sat on the edge of the desk and punched in the numbers for his home phone.

"Wait! Wait!" Kelly said. "Tell me what Brody said. Tell me about it."

"Well," Mitchel began, "actually it was a combination of several things. See, Tom, here—. Are you all right? You don't look well."

"I don't know. I must be coming down with something," Kelly said. "I feel a little dizzy and...I don't know. Go on. Tom what?"

"Well, Tom went over and spoke with Senator Coggins, telling him of the importance of preserving the area's scenic beauty and, well, you know the spiel. So, he's talking—."

"But wait!" Kelly interrupted. "Tom, didn't you and Sam talk to Brody about—."

Tom shushed her. He moved behind Mitchel while waiting for his wife to answer and quickly put a finger to his lips for Kelly not to pursue it.

"Uh-h..., never mind," she said to Mitchel. "Go on."

"Well, James Brody hopped up on the bulldozer and made a pass, digging up a wide swath right smack in between those two big trees. And, damned! if he didn't uncover the grave of a Civil War soldier."

"Who—what?" Kelly gasped, shaking the dizziness from her head.

"That's right," Mitchel nodded, smiling broadly. "There were these bones and some teeth...and somebody found a U.S. buckle from a belt or something. Imagine!

So, Brody tried to make light of it at first...," he continued. Mitchel went on explaining the events as they had played out that afternoon.

Kelly wasn't listening. She clutched at her temples and closed her eyes, unable to hear what the man was saying. All external sound was drowned out by a softly whispered hum in her mind. She tried to identify the sound and thought it possibly was the low gentle pitch of a French horn or trumpet—perhaps both, together. As she followed the drone it increased intensity to become an entire orchestra of every wind, brass and string instrument—all playing the same, soft tuning note, over again, in unison. She covered her ears only to find that a chorus of soft voices now blended coincidentally. It was not at all an unpleasant sound, but was one she'd never experienced. For a quick moment her heart beat rapidly in panic as the sound "o-o-h-h-m-m-m..." continually echoed in a low whisper through her mind. She opened her eyes and looked up to see Mitchel was still talking to her. As she rose to her feet his words began to again reach her ears, the gentle hum fading slowly away.

"Where—where is the soldier?" she asked him.

"...Up between the two tall oaks," Mitchel replied, interrupting his story. "Up on the hill. You know where I mean. ...So, the county coroner came and..."

"You're—you're certain...there were...remains there...and that it was a Union soldier? A captain?" she asked, her voice almost frantic. Kelly's eyes had glazed and her face flushed with the blood of excitedly pumping arteries.

"Well, yes. There are bones there. Everybody saw them. Haven't you been listening? Nobody knows what rank he was. I doubt we'll ever know," Mitchel said.

"Oh, God!" Kelly cried out. She moved quickly from behind her desk, grabbing up the keys to the DeLorean Sam had left her.

"Kelly?" Mitchel called to her as she hurried from the room. "Kelly!"

Tom had been talking to his wife and hadn't noticed the girl's peculiar behavior. But as she hurried from the room, he looked at Mitchel for an explanation.

"I don't know," Mitchel said with a shrug. "I was just telling her what happened and she got up and took off. She doesn't look well, you know."

Telling his wife he'd call her back Tom set the phone down and hurried to the door with Mitchel. They were in time to look out into the drizzling rain and see Kelly wheel the DeLorean out of its parking space and speed off down the road.

****

Kelly hadn't the slightest inkling why she was driving so frantically to reach the excavation site. She knew she was acting on impulse. Some subconscious, emotional possession was bending her helplessly to its will, conducting her movements while creating a void in that area of her mind from which rational thought stems. And still she drove on, her heart pounding wildly.

The windshield wipers served to swish away the raindrops but had little effect increasing visibility through the dense fog. Kelly slowed the car to a crawl as she rounded the curve before the back side of the Schiels farm and found a county sheriff's car was positioned along the road with its parking lights on. A deputy glanced idly from his newspaper and admired the sporty little car as she cruised by him.

Kelly drove well down the road to where her taillights would be shrouded from him by the thick fog and pulled the driver's side tires onto what little strip of berm was available. When the gull-wing door popped open Kelly sprang from under it and dashed through the rain, scurrying up the steeply sloped sides of the hill. She slipped and fell several times in the wet grasses only to flail and scratch at the ground in a frantic effort to scramble to her feet again, sobbing hysterically as she neared the crest.

Soaked from the rain and the sweat of her own exertions, and blinded by the veil of some unfathomable, yet irresistible urgings from her soul, Kelly raced to the area where the tall trees stood. Out of breath—but more, out of mind—she rested against one of the old oaks for support, hugging its trunk as though it was the final goal in some long—journeyed, arduous search. Her emotions were of a mix to cause her to both weep and laugh as she looked out over the fog-covered fields below. She could see the faint outline of a uniformed figure running toward her. His arms were waving and he appeared to be shouting something at her as he slipped and slid while trying to gain the hill.

Ignoring the man, for in her dazed state her ears were again filled with a chorus of softly humming vibrations, Kelly ended her sobbing and composed herself a little. She slowly turned her head to gaze down into the open furrow and released a lamented sigh as her eyes fell to where the remains lay. A yellow police tape had been strung around the perimeter to warn off unauthorized intruders and a dark canvas tarpaulin was stretched and staked over the remains to protect them until the coroner could inspect the site more thoroughly.

Kelly viewed the tarp as a funeral shroud covering the body of a dear friend or loved one awaiting the hearse for its final ride. She envisioned a form to those remains, picturing a young, light-haired boy finely dressed in the dashing uniform of a Union cavalry officer. The face was paled from the lack of its life force; the form was stiff and cold.

She released her hug on the oak and turned to the silent grave, her tears flowing anew. She stretched her arms out in wanting to the imaginary form under the canvas and wept in frustration as the desire to throw herself upon the boy for a final farewell was overpowered only slightly by the knowledge that there really was no form under that cold, wet cloth. She crossed her arms over her body and closed her eyes to imagine the boy as clearly as if he lived and was standing before her. She knew his every detail: the brightness of his eyes, the bent of his nose, the thinness of his innocent smile, his broad shoulders and solid build. It was all there; all in view to her. He was the boy who came to her in her dreams—the ghostly rider; the boy whose likeness was in the locket she wore around her neck.

Kelly imagined holding him, their arms about each other tenderly, gazing into one another's eyes with an intensity of love that knew no boundaries of time. She leaned closer to kiss his lips and, opening her eyes to better know the blissful moment...he was gone. She was standing alone—fervent and wet. Her heart pounded and her mind reeled in confusion. She gazed down at the canvas that covered the spot where the boy had waited so many years for her to find him and she wavered, trembling and weak. A shadowy curtain seemed to draw across her vision, closing out all light and Kelly covered her ears to silence the now increasing volume of humming. Through the mysterious blackness that engulfed her mind she screamed out, "Sandie!"

****

Behind tightly closed eyes Kelly observed not the usual glimpses of unpatterned, indiscernible colored light flashes, but a darkness so complete and so material as to be chilling. She was not frightened or panicked, but felt disoriented and vexed. Her whole being ached with an unusual weariness that seemed to drag her toward an unconsciousness different than sleep, and her mind rebelled against the mysterious pull, sensing it was derived from the supernatural.

She tried, feebly, to open her eyes to confirm it was still daylight but released a low groan in finding her efforts too exhausting, the lids weighted too heavily. No longer able to endure the nauseating sensations tugging at the very life force within her, Kelly resigned herself to its pull. If she was to die, she thought, so be it. She could not alter the experience. Death's beckoning was too powerful to battle. She succumbed.

The very moment her will ceased its futile resistance a calm settled through her. The darkness was still overwhelming, but she no longer cared about it nor noticed any coldness in it. It was there and she was within it. Then appeared a pin-point of light—so tiny and distant, yet so obvious as to radiate a certain warmth and hope. Slowly, it began to grow in size, either expanding or drawing nearer. The darkness was edged away, not in increasing shades of lighter grays, but with the sharp, definable border between black and white. Kelly believed she was passing through some dark, dank tunnel which ended directly into the shining sunlight, except that the tunnel appeared to be moving around her while she remained motionless.

When the light came upon, then surrounded her, she became blinded by its brilliance; so encompassed and deluged by it that she believed she had become a part of it.

The light flickered, allowing her the glimpse of an interruption of shadow and demonstrating that she was still separate from the light. It flickered again, the lapse lasting just a bit longer now. When it again occurred, Kelly tried to concentrate on discerning what could be seen in those contrasting, darker intervals. The next flickerings were again of longer duration and came more often. With her consciousness aimed increasingly toward the distinctive gaps there developed a strobe effect, the light and not-light becoming equal. It disturbed Kelly and caused her to concentrate further on what appeared to be shadowy forms between the light flickers. She blinked; then blinked again.

Slowly the realization came to her that she was able to move her eyelids. A subtle joy crept over her as she became aware she was not dead but, in fact, very much alive—if not wholly awake. A moment of panic then arose as she thought to struggle free from death's grasp as quickly as possible lest it decide to draw her back again. She slowly lifted her eyelids and saw the familiar brush swirl design on the white plastered ceiling. Moving her eyes along, she spied the leaves and vine border stenciling along the top of the wall. As her eyes lowered further, she recognized the soft glow of burning gas lamps reflected in the large mirror of the cherry wardrobe.

Her breathing was difficult—raspy and short—as her lungs were quite congested with fluid. She felt the cool compress across her brow; a warm, damp dressing over her chest, under a pile of thick quilts that covered her. When she swallowed, the mucous went down with difficulty.

She glanced to her right where Aunt Lin was seated in a wooden chair and held her hand. The woman was smiling affectionately but was obviously grieving as the tears welled behind swollen, red eyes. Uncle Milrose stood at the foot of her bed, the unlit stub of a cigar tightly clamped between his lips and his eyes cast downwards in sorrowed expression. She squeezed Lin's hand weakly and looked to her left. There, her father knelt by the bed, his uniform ruffled, the empty sleeve pinned back, and his hair unkempt from days of neglect as he remained faithfully by his daughter's side. She met his eyes and tried to smile to him but was barely able to turn the corner of one lip. The handsome, kind face smiled and said her name in a soft voice.

She closed her eyes and her mind swirled with thoughts of Sandie, picturing his glowing, youthful face as she'd last seen him. He'd stood with her at the gate, pledging to return as directly as events would allow. Confederate General Jubal Early was being pushed back from the outskirts of Washington and it would take but a few days to make his route complete. Then, a ten-day leave would be granted to the handsome captain; ten blissful, idle, romantic days in which the young lovers would be inseparable.

When Thomas had returned alone from the sortie with the tragic news of her Sandie's death, and explained how the body had to be abandoned to the enemy, she had become hysterical. She had ridden out to the battlefield to search for the grave of her lover, inquiring to all the townsfolk if they might know where the young boy had been buried. There were so many graves; so many lives tragically ended. Bodies had been dumped down wells, stuffed in hollow tree trunks or thrown into mass pits and mounded with only a thin layer of earth. It was impossible to know who lay where or for which side they had given their lives. Her search had been futile and in vain, and in the end, it had worn her down to complete exhaustion, leaving her body too weak to fight the pneumonia, her will too broken to try. Her only thoughts were of seeing her beloved Sandie, and if death was the door that would lead her to him, she determined to open it.

She looked into her father's sadly drawn face and closed her eyes. The strobe effect of brilliant light flashes instantly returned and she felt her body sinking into paralysis. No longer could she feel the soft touch of Aunt Lin's comforting hand, nor the burning pain in her chest. As the light became stronger and of greater duration than the darker intervals, she became disoriented. Again, the intensity of the light flashes increased, slowing the rate and duration of the shadowy grays until she found herself once more within the light; absorbed by it; at one with it. She floated timelessly and peacefully within it, yet she retained her awareness of it.

As she realized she was not the light, she began to separate from it. It began to move away, slowly retreating until she could again see a black border of void replacing the fading brilliance. When the light was but a speck, and all but disappeared, she saddened at being alone in the dark once more. A slight chill came over her. It was not the coldness of despair, but of regret for not having savored and appreciated the loving warmth of the light. Still, she felt no remorse for having withdrawn from it for she felt there was something left untended; something yet to finish before she could remain a part of that brilliance.

Abstractions of vague light colors began to move across her vision, pronouncedly changing the pitch of the black void to one of simple darkness—a familiar darkness. She opened her eyes.

"Kelly! Kelly! You're okay!" Sam exclaimed. He was leaning over her with a relieved expression.

"Sam...?" Kelly said, looking up at him, uncertain of her surroundings just yet. It took several moments for her to realize she was on her bed in the upstairs of the Foundation house. Dave, Carol and Tom were also fanned out around the bed and looking relieved. "Wh—where...? How...?"

"You passed out," Sam told her. "A deputy sheriff at the excavation site found you. What were you doing there? You didn't have a raincoat, umbrella, or anything. We've been worried about you."

"Never mind that," Carol said. "How do you feel, honey?"

"I'm...a bit fuzzy, yet. But I...think okay."

Carol reached down and took Kelly's hand to give it a little squeeze. "The doctor said you'd be a little groggy when you woke. It's from the injection he gave you."

"Doctor...? Injection...? How long...have I...been out?"

"About five hours," Carol replied. "Listen, I'm going down to tell Marylou and the others."

"Others?"

"Yeah. A bunch of people from the group. They're downstairs. We've all been worried. I'll be right back," Carol assured her.

340

Kelly glanced around the room to reacquaint herself with her present surroundings. She felt as if she had been on an extended journey and had forgotten so much of what was significant in her life. When her eyes landed on Sam, she smiled up to him and reached for his hand, her mind swirling in emotions as she gazed at the man.

She began to wonder if she could believe what she had experienced while she had been unconscious or if it had been just a dream—the resultant side-affects of whatever drug the doctor had given her. It had seemed so real! All the memories of another lifetime had come rushing back for those few minutes just as long-forgotten childhood memories will sometimes, suddenly and unexpectedly, unlatch themselves from some anchor in the mind's basement and come floating to the surface for reminiscence.

So it was with Kelly's experience. The memories were as real as any she could recall in this lifetime. And though the sight of the saddened faces she had viewed gathered around her bed was fading from mind as quickly as their names had, the experience was nonetheless genuine.

The one memory that did not fade, however; the one that was as clear and as strong as she was alive…was the memory of her love for a certain soldier. A boy. A young, blond, cavalry captain named Sandie. That memory had transcended time…and death…and life, again, to present itself to both her and him.

"Sam," Kelly exclaimed passionately as she gazed up at him. "There are some things we need to talk about! Things that won't really make any sense to you. But I need to tell them to you!"

"Shsh… Sure, Kelly," he calmed her. "We'll talk. Right now you need to rest. We'll talk in the morning. You need to try to sleep."

"But, Sam! I…"

"Kelly, the doctor said you need a lot of rest. He may want to run some test on you. I think we'd all better go down and let you sleep," Sam said. He promised to stay the night with her, then kissed her hand and pressed it to his cheek. "I'll be right downstairs if you need anything."

The men departed to join the others below. They had intended to have a celebration, rejoicing in the unexpected turn of events in their quest to save the Schiels farm. Instead, they sat or stood in the cramped rooms of the Foundation house, drank coffee from paper cups and talked softly. Though they were elated at their victory over the developers they felt to reserve their glee to share it with the one member who had given so much of her time and energy and now lay exhausted in the room above.

Now, they made plans for a formal celebration to be held in the next several weeks, or as soon as a reception hall could be secured. They would withdraw a small amount of reserve cash and hold an event to be opened to all members and supporters. Tasks were then divided among them—some, to arrange for a social hall; some, the refreshments; others, the entertainment, and so forth. Dave, Sam and Carol apologized for not being able to stay and help organize the event. They were long overdue in returning home but promised to return and attend the festivities.

When the evening was at an end the visitors began to depart. They each, in turn, thanked their northern friends for the help they provided and wished them well, expressing their desire to see them again at the celebration. Tom Charles was the last to leave. Sam, Dave and Carol saw him to the door, chatting about, and chortling over their covert operation of the other night. Tom particularly reveled in having thwarted his former employer's efforts.

Dave looked at him with some concern. "But what will you do now, Tom? It's a safe bet you're unemployed."

"Hm. That bet would be a winner if you could find somebody to take the other side," Tom laughed. "Well, he hasn't officially fired me, yet. But I wouldn't go back there for any money. I think I'll go home and type up my letter of resignation, just to beat him to it."

"Can you get another job?" Carol asked. "Are there many openings for architects?"

"Doesn't matter," Tom said, shaking his head. "I'm done working for other people. I've always wanted to start my own shop. Think I'll look around for a quiet little town that's showing some growth potential and 'do my own thing,' as they say. My wife has been after me for years to take the step. What the hell, now's the time."

They shook hands and said their goodbyes, looking forward to meeting again at the festival. Then, with Tom gone, Carol and Dave said goodnight to Sam, telling him they'd stop by in the morning after checking out of the motel, bringing the rest of both his and Kelly's luggage. Sam saw them off, watching until the van drove off down the street and made its turn.

****

Sam was in good spirits. Using the trade in which he was so genuinely gifted, and employing it for a purpose for which he had such strong emotions, he'd helped accomplish something that would be of benefit to so many others. He felt really good about that.

Then, there was Kelly. He felt even better thinking about her. Never had he known such a girl. There was the gloriously exquisite infatuation, yet it was coupled with a respect and consideration for one another's dignity and self-worth. Perhaps, he pondered, there was a grain of truth in what old Varina had alluded. Perhaps he and Kelly had loved each other in a different life. It made for fascinating musings, if nothing else. And, it went a long way in serving to explain a lot of curious experiences that had befallen him these last weeks. But it was all rather irrelevant. What he cared about was the present—this life; this woman.

Sam pushed the two easy chairs together to form the less-than-comfortable bed he'd slept on only several nights ago and bemoaned the thought of another restless night spent in back-wrenching agony. He flicked off the lights to the front room, but before climbing onto his makeshift bed he crept quietly up the stairs to check on the sleeping girl. Trying to be as quiet as possible, the creaky wooden steps failed to cooperate and announced the set of each carefully placed foot. He peered from the landing and saw Kelly was asleep on her side, the sheet pulled only to her waist. The day's rain had cooled the night air to a more comfortable temperature so Sam moved across the floor to pull the sheet up over the sleeping woman's shoulder. When he leaned over her, she surprised him by opening her eyes.

"Sam," she mumbled. "Is everyone gone?"

"Yeah. They just left," he said quietly.

"Are you staying the night?"

"Yeah. I'll be right downstairs if you need anything."

"Not on those two chairs again?"

"I'll be okay," he assured her.

Kelly reached over and grasped the cover on the far side of the bed and pulled it back. Still half asleep she murmured, "Here. Crawl in with me."

The man needed no further urging. Hurriedly, he shucked his clothes, undressing down to his skivvies, then slipped in beside her. Kelly drew the cover up over them both and nestled against him. She purred softly and kissed his shoulder, then closed her eyes and fell asleep.

****

The clouds were beginning to disperse, allowing the early morning sun to peek through every so often to cast its warming rays onto the two joggers. As Sam and Kelly rounded the corner to the street in front of the old house Sam immediately spotted the blue van parked out in front. When they reached it, he and Kelly halted and began walking in little circles to cool down from their run. Neither said a word as they caught their breaths, but they exchanged glances as both realized their time together was drawing to a close. With reluctant steps they turned and entered the house.

"Hi, guys," Sam said, forcing a warm smile as he greeted his two friends in the back office.

"Hey, two," Carol grinned. "We figured you'd gone for a walk or jog. Nice morning for it."

"Beautiful," Kelly replied, moving to the coffee pot to pour for both her and Sam.

"We brought all your gear," Dave told Sam as he watched him stir in some cream. "Thought we'd travel together awhile until you split off for Cleveland."

"Yeah. Sure. Fine," Sam said, his voice sounding a bit glum. He took a long time on one sip of coffee, then asked Kelly if he could shower and change before leaving. He retrieved a bag from his car and, not a half hour later, came down the steps with duffel in hand and wearing a fresh change of clothes. "Well, I'm ready," he said with a resigned shrug, making no attempt to hide his sadness.

Dave and Carol said a long goodbye to Kelly, then hugged her affectionately. Dave told Sam they would meet him outside and he and Carol went to the van, leaving Sam alone with the woman.

Sam stood in the doorway that separated the two rooms. He was leaning against the wooden framework and staring down at the floor. He smiled, reminiscing, and looked up at Kelly who stood with her arms folded. "It's been a hell-of-a vacation," he mused.

"Certainly not one's usual," Kelly added, returning his smile with her own.

"Different," he said. "A lot of interesting things happened. A lot of nice things."

Kelly nodded and rolled her eyes. "Yeah. Well. Who says things are slow and easy in the south?"

"Yeah," he grinned. Then he lost the smile for a more serious face. "The nicest thing to happen on this trip...was meeting you."

Kelly blushed and averted her eyes momentarily. "I...I know. Me, too," she said. She struggled for something appropriate to say but no words would settle long enough to allow her to speak them. She finally just looked at him and smiled.

Sam stood straight and shouldered his duffel. "Well. Guess I better go," he said. He turned and they slowly headed toward the door. "I've got to start looking for an apartment and get moved in this week."

"Good luck," she said to him. "I hate moving. Packing; moving boxes; then unpacking."

"Mm. Yeah. I know. You end up living without a lot of accumulated junk so you don't have to move it all the time."

They halted simultaneously at the door and turned to face each other. "Sam," Kelly said to him, "You'll call me when you get settled in?"

"First thing," he quickly assured her. But he then rolled his eyes, displeased with his answer, knowing it was spoken from nervousness. "I'll call you from Cleveland and let you know I made it safely," he corrected himself.

Kelly delighted in the reply. "Good...Good," she nodded happily.

"You keep things rolling here. We've got the momentum. Keep it going."

"I will," she promised.

Sam fidgeted uneasily with his duffel, his eyes glancing everywhere but into her's. "Well. That's it then. I, uh, I guess I'm off. Guess I'll see you in a week or two for the celebration."

"I...guess so," Kelly replied, her eyes flitting over his chest.

There was an awkward moment between them, standing just inside the front door, as both anticipated a long, final, farewell kiss. Sam believed it was his responsibility to initiate the move and Kelly assumed to have deferred to his lead, not wanting to appear overeager herself. His heart pounded as he reeled from the desire to gather her into his arms, certain she would respond favorably. Her eyes and her demeanor all seemed to display that she was as desirous of it as he. Now, believing the time was right, Sam reached an arm for her waist, wrapping it around her back to draw her close. He began to lean toward her and Kelly gazed dreamily up into his eyes, readying herself for the gentle press of his lips.

"Well, hello, you two," came a voice just on the other side of the door.

Sam drew back instantly and saw Mitchel Page on the porch. Mitchel opened the screen door and Sam and Kelly parted to allow the man room to enter.

"Oh. I see you're off," he said, eyeing the bag slung from Sam's shoulder. He extended his hand in friendship, saying, "Thanks, again, for all your help. It's people like yourself, getting involved and staying committed under pressure and against the odds, that can get mountains moved. Of course, heh-heh, in this case it was keeping the mountain from getting moved."

"Yes sir. Thank you," Sam replied. "It's been a real pleasure meeting and working with all of you. It's been quite an experience."

"It has, hasn't it?" Mitchel said. He grasped Sam's shoulder lightly. "You take care of yourself. We'll see you at the celebration." Then, to Kelly, he said, "Kelly. There are some things we need to go over this morning. Buck, uh, Mr. Morganti, is stopping by to pick up some information for the McPherson board. I want to have everything ready for him when he gets here."

"Oh. Sure. Okay. I'll be right there," Kelly answered. But Mitchel stood with them, taking no clue that they might wish for a moment alone.

Resigned to having the other man unwittingly present and watching them, Sam put an arm around the girl's waist and kissed her cheek. "See you soon," he said to her.

Kelly nodded. "Bye, Sam. Take care of yourself." She followed him out onto the porch, Mitchel right behind her, and both of them watched as Sam crossed the street to his car, tossed his duffel into the seat, then climbed in. As the van pulled away, tooting its horn several times, Sam followed behind it. He watched in his rear-view mirror as Kelly stepped out into the street, still waving goodbye.

Chapter Seventeen

July 12, 1864

Dawn broke over the horizon to find an anxious and frenzied Washington. Confederate General Jubal Early had made his way up the Shenandoah Valley to Harpers Ferry, brushing aside only scant resistance. He now stood with 10,000 troops not seven miles from the Nation's capital. Grant had taken the Army south in an effort to flank Lee, and all that remained to man the Washington defenses were militia and clerks—and those, nowhere near enough in numbers to fight off battle-hardened Rebel troops bent on sacking the city.

Early had drawn up in front of Fort Stevens the day before and reconnoitered the rather formidable earthworks that lay between his army and the Northern Capital. His men, played-out from long marches on little food and parched from a beating sun, had been given the day to rest. Early's plan was to attack at dawn on the 12th, hoping Grant had not been able to send sufficient reinforcements in time to bolster the entrenchments.

Awakened by the faint popping of musketry heard in the distance, as well as the noise and commotion of the panic that was occurring in the streets, Katie rose at first light and hurried down to the kitchen. There, she found both her Aunt Lin and Uncle Milrose sitting at the table in a nervous and worried state.

"Couldn't sleep either, dear?" Lin asked, watching as the girl poured herself a cup of tea.

Before Katie could reply, Milrose snorted, "Who could, in the face of all this? Where the hell's our army? Grant's got them far off in Virginia, that's where!" he harrumphed. "Lot of good it does. I hear Lee's given Mead the slip and is right now crossing the Potomac with more than 100,000. They'll burn us out, you know. They'll torch the whole city, mind you!"

"Uncle Milrose," Katie said frightfully. "Surely that won't happen?"

"Mind my words. We're surrounded! Telegraph's down. Railroad's down. They'll be attacking in a while—and we've nothing but a handful of clerks and pea-brained militia."

"But I've heard Sheridan has sent some men. They've come down from Baltimore," Katie said, trying to sound hopeful.

"What good are they? A few dismounted cavalry. They'll probably join in the foray—plundering and looting."

"I wonder if Sandie is among them," she said thoughtfully into the air.

"Humph!"

"Sandie's not a plunderer or looter and you know that!"

Milrose said nothing, but raised his mug and took a big swallow of coffee.

Someone knocked loudly at the door and the three looked at one another nervously. Milrose stood to answer it and, while he passed through the hallway, Katie hollered to him in a bid for some levity. "Well, I doubt if it's the Rebels. They'd hardly knock if they were going to plunder the house."

"I'm coming! I'm coming!" Milrose shouted to the repeated pounding. When he opened the door and saw the so early morning caller his expression was one of relief and delight—but only momentarily. He soon dropped his face, saying, "It's you. Well, come on in. We're all up, anyway."

"I'm delighted to see you, too, Mr. Sheffield," came the reply, though delivered more cheerfully. The figure entered and followed Milrose back to the kitchen.

"Who could sleep anyway with all the noise going on outside?" Milrose grumbled over his shoulder.

"Who is it, Dear?" Lin asked, hearing the sound of a second set of footsteps on the wood flooring.

"Sandie!" Katie cried out at seeing him enter behind her uncle. She rose from the chair and rushed into his arms, the two greeting with a warm embrace.

Sandie pulled back from her, finally. "I can only stay but a moment. We've just disembarked and are on our way to Fort Stevens."

Milrose took his seat at the table, grumping, "Well, did you bring any men with you, or are you all they sent? Lee's got his whole army coming. Where's ours?"

Sandie put his arm around Katie's shoulder and pulled her closer, feeling the need to hug her once again. He reached with his other hand to grasp a warm mug of coffee Lin had poured for him. "Lee? Lee's still in Virginia. We've several divisions with us. More than enough to give Early his due. I don't expect he'll attack anyway. First light's come up and he's missed his chance. It would be suicide to try against these fortifications now. I suspect he'll withdraw."

"But what's all that firing going on then if he's not attacking?" Katie asked. "We've been hearing it for quite a while."

"Oh, those are just the skirmishers. They come forward to remind us to keep our heads down and try to make us jittery."

Katie tightened her arm more securely around the young captain's waist, comforted and more at ease now that he was near at hand.

Sandie took a few long gulps of the coffee and set the mug on the table. "I must go," he told her. "I received permission to steal but a moment from my command. Walk me to the door." Begging leave from both Lin and Milrose, he turned and went with Katie out to the front porch. "I don't know how long we'll be out," he said as he turned to her. "They may send us directly south to rejoin Grant, but my commander believes we'll have at least ten days while our mounts are refreshed. Wouldn't that be nice?'

"Oh, don't tease me like that," Katie answered. "Just the thought of you being here so unexpectedly stirs my heart so."

"And mine," Sandie told her. "We'd better not dwell on such thoughts. Let us hold to our plan of looking forward to my next leave. All else will be bonus." He leaned down and kissed her cheek as he held her hand. "Dream of me, my Love. My spirit cannot be distant when your thoughts are of me."

"Oh, Sandie," she sighed deeply and reached to embrace him one last time.

When they released their hold on each other he turned and left, moving hurriedly down the path and through the gate to his steed. Katie pulled the locket from her blouse and clutched it tightly. She bit her lip to fight back the tears as she waved to him, watching him mount. When in the saddle, Sandie reined his horse about and waved goodbye. Then, setting spurs to the animal's flanks, he galloped off down the lane.

****

Sandie's words about General Early's tactics had been prophetic. Information had been relayed through spies that several divisions of the XIX Corp had landed and were filling the trenches and fortifications of the city. Deciding the risk of attacking was too great, Early withdrew, leaving a small force as a rear-guard, should the Yankees brave leaving the forts to take the offensive.

It was not until six o'clock, the evening of the 12th, that a Union brigade set out to chase away the Rebel skirmishers. Finding several Confederate divisions drawn up in battle formation behind the skirmishers, a full-scale battle ensued, lasting well into the darkness when the Confederate forces finally pulled back. Overnight, the Rebel column proceeded unmolested across the Potomac and made camp around Leesburg. After a two-day rest, Early began to move his troops back to the valley.

With things in good order back in Washington, and all danger real or imagined had passed, Major General Augur ordered a brigade of infantry and several companies of cavalry to pursue and harass Early in the hope of pushing him far down the Shenandoah Valley and thus give up any further ideas of returning for another attack on the Capital.

Captain Theodore Sandfeld Duncan's company was in lead of the advance, marching through Rockville, then Poolsville, where several citizens of the town reported that at least several brigades of rebel infantry, and perhaps an entire division, had headed back north toward Frederick or Sharpsburg. General Wheatly, commanding the brigade, believed it wise to salvage and protect what stores might be left in Harpers Ferry from Early's previous raid on his way to Washington.

Ordering most of the brigade on toward Leesburg under Colonel Selkirk, he led several of the regiments and two companies of cavalry on the road toward Frederick. His plan was to link up with the garrison at Harpers Ferry, containing about 2,000 men, then, perhaps, to be joined by General Sigel who had 5,000 over near Martinsburg. This combined force, he believed, would be sufficient to thwart any attempts by Early's detached brigades bent on raiding Harpers Ferry.

About daybreak on the 17th, a messenger came galloping up to the cavalry encampment near Frederick to report that General Wheatly had received word that the roving enemy brigades were in fact at or near Sharpsburg, scene of the great battle fought not two years ago around Antietam Creek. He would draw up in battle formation for an attack at dawn. Word had been sent for Sigel to join him by a forced march, their combined weight surely enough to dislodge and scatter the Confederate invaders. Sandie was to come at once.

"Damn him!" Sandie remarked as he showed the dispatch to Thomas. When it was handed back to him, he crumpled it up and threw it into the fire around which the two captains and several other men were brewing coffee. "Sigel will never make the march in time and Wheatly will attack anyway."

"Think so?" Thomas asked, turning the pointed stick on which he was cooking a morning's ration of beef.

"Yes. Damn it! I know him—and Sigel. Sigel will take all of last night and part of today preparing to make the march—then not make it. General Wheatly will get it into his head that a well-planned attack, even with fewer numbers, will frighten the Rebels out of their positions. He'll attack, all right. We'd better make plans to go."

Sergeant Rome looked up from his stooped position on the other side of the fire. "Does this mean we aren't going to get to finish this fine meal we're cookin' up, Sir?"

"'Fraid so, Sergeant," Sandie replied. Then he looked to a man at another fire nearby. "Corporal Resh," he hollered to him. "Have the bugler come up."

Sergeant Rome mumbled something about favoring his meat "not still moving," then took the piece from the end of his stick and began to bite at it as he stood to leave and prepare his mount.

Thomas took the pot of not-yet-brewed coffee and poured both him and Sandie a cup. "We'll have to ride hard to get there," he commented, handing Sandie a cup.

"I know. We'd better get mounted," Sandie replied.

Both men took but a sip or two of the warm, brown liquid, then poured it over the fire.

****

The ride took several hours, the booming of cannon being heard from several miles off, telling them in which direction to ride. As the two cavalry companies drew closer the constant rattle of musketry provided evidence that a general assault was underway.

A rider galloped up to the approaching columns and Sandie halted the troops behind him. When they had exchanged salutes the courier said, "General Wheatly sends his compliments on your timely arrival, Captain. He sent me to instruct you in the disposition of your men."

"How goes it up there, Lieutenant?"

"Not very well, Sir," the man replied. He paused when he saw another captain approaching.

Thomas pulled rein and returned the courier's salute. "What is it?" he asked Sandie.

"I don't know, yet."

"General Wheatly attacked just awhile ago, Sirs. There's probably three brigades up on the hill. We came at them from the other side; had quite a climb to get up it, too. We made a good showing of ourselves but there's just too damn many of them. We had to fall back."

"Did Sigel make it up?" Thomas asked.

"No, Sir. Not a word from him. The Rebs are driving us back over the hill. Best come quick, Captain, before they over-run us."

Sandie turned to Thomas. "I'll go ahead and reconnoiter with the lieutenant. You bring up the column."

"Right," Thomas replied.

Sandie galloped off with the junior officer and came up on the far flank of the scene of battle. To their left, high on a hill that sloped gradually upward for several hundred yards, then rose more steeply, Confederate infantry were drawn up in line of battle preparing to make a counter-attack on the outnumbered and retreating Union forces.

"Looks like the 'old man' tried another attack," the lieutenant said.

"Yes. And we'd better help quick or they'll run right over him," Sandie replied. He could see to his right some half mile from the higher hill upon which the Confederates stood, the less elevated knoll from which point the Union regiments had started their attack, and to which they were now frantically scurrying for safety. A large number of blue-uniformed men lay scattered prone across the fields, either wounded or simply lying flat to avoid being hit in the back by a zinging mini-ball. To Sandie's alarm, there, in the very center of the conflict, down in the dusty wagon ruts that served as the lane and ran between the two hills, lay Miles Wheatly. Several of his aides were around him, raising him, to a sit and tending to him while ignoring their own safety.

"We'll form the companies here!" Sandie shouted.

"Excuse me, Sir," the lieutenant said, "But General Wheatly suggests you form up on the ridge, dismounted, to cover our withdrawal."

"Do you see down there!" Sandie exclaimed, pointing with his arm extended in full aim toward the general. "The plans must be changed! I take full responsibility!"

"Yes, Sir. I'm with you," he nodded. Then, touching the tip of his hat he said, "If you'll excuse me, Sir. I must join my men."

"Good luck, Lieutenant," Sandie answered, then watched the man gallop off to join his command.

Companies "A" and "B" soon arrived and Sandie explained to Thomas what he thought might be their best course of action. His plan was to form a line of charge in back of the field on the extreme flank of where they now stood. Obscured from the enemy's view by a small patch of woods between their position and the Rebel's, they would swoop down in a surprise charge and disrupt the Confederate counter-attack. Then, wheeling left, they could charge the hill to silence the four Rebel cannon that were pounding the Union forces and preventing them from mustering on the opposite slope.

The two Captains hurriedly drew their companies into an attack formation and took their places ahead of their men. The order was given to move forward and, with pistols and sabers drawn, two hundred started forward at the trot, colors unfurled and snapping smartly in the steady breeze. When they were just in sight of the fury and tumult occurring on the field ahead of them, the bugler sounded "charge." The two companies of cavalry broke into a gallop just as they came into the enemy's view from the small patch of trees. A cheer arose from the blue-shirted soldiers who had been retreating so desperately. Now, inspired by the sight of the many flashing sabers advancing to their aid, they turned, bold and defiant, to renew their advance.

The Rebel attackers halted, watching the band of horsemen advance upon them from their unguarded flank. With not a moment to react, the blue-mounted soldiers were among them, slashing and hacking, creating unexpected havoc within the gray ranks. Sandie maneuvered his way over to the wounded General Wheatly, drew aim with his revolver, and shot down a Confederate who had taken a bead on the wounded man. Confused and surprised, the gray-clad ranks at once turned in retreat, fleeing back up the hill from whence they'd come, hoping to find safety behind the crude earthworks they'd hastily thrown up earlier that morning.

Commands were shouted down the line to which the horsemen responded, reassembling in charge formation along the crude buggy path at the bottom of the hill. Sandie and Thomas took positions ahead of the lines and, with a wave of their swords, motioned the ranks onward. "Charge!" blasted from the bugle as a wave of blue cavalry rushed the hill, supported by infantry close behind. Those Confederates that made it to the entrenchments turned to stalwartly meet the attack, laying down a terribly effective cover fire for their comrades. The cannon switched to deadly canister, felling horse as well as rider.

Fire burned in his eyes as Sandie rode madly in lead of his troops, angling toward the cannon that were lined on the crest of the hill. Ignoring the mini-balls whistling past he reached the summit and leapt the earthworks to a cannon placed between two small oak saplings. Even as his horse touched down, he fired at and dropped the cannoneer, then raised his saber to slash at a rifleman nearby. Instantly, he felt himself jolted up out of the saddle and saw his horse race on from underneath him.

****

Captain Sandfeld Duncan was awakened by the sound of footsteps approaching near where he lay. His first thought was to grab his revolver in case the footfalls were those of the Rebels, but he found he was too tired to bother. His arms were as lead weights and the energy required for such a series of movements seemed drained from his body. In any case, he reasoned, it was pitch dark. They were likely to pass by and not even notice him lying there, unless they stumbled over him.

He could hear the sounds of wagons rolling by some ways off—the jingle of harness and the rumble of steel-bonded wheels; some men chatting. He wondered who they were and where they were headed. He thought it odd that it was so quiet in the camps—if indeed that was where he was; he couldn't remember. There were no fires lit to reveal any friendly faces huddled around boiling coffee, as was the habit. All was quiet on the picket line.

Someone came close to him. Very close. They raised his arm and held his wrist a moment, then dropped it. "This 'un ain't dead yet. Will be soon, though," he heard the person shout.

"Drag 'im over to the pit," came a voice in reply. "We'll throw 'im in when he is."

"No!" sounded a third voice. "Bury him here, where he fell. Such a gallant lad deserves his own grave. Besides, he's an officer."

"Aw, but Major, he's a blue-belly."

"Do it! And leave him his sword. It isn't but dead weight to a foot soldier anyway."

On hearing this, Sandie tried desperately to clear his mind. If it wasn't night, as these men seemed to prove by their assured movements, then he must have his eyes closed and must fight to open them and see the light. Groaning from the effort, for it was as if he were awakening from a long-needed sleep, he raised his eyelids to find there was still a bright sun shining just west of overhead—though, for all its radiance, there was so little warmth. His eyes lowered to his hand clutched at his chest and he raised his thumb and forefinger. There was a crimson wetness coating the two digits and he knew, now, it was he those men were talking about. He was the officer soon to die. He closed his eyes a moment, wanting to cry, but found no tears would flow.

"You go on, now! Git outa' heah," one of the men said. "This 'un's beyond need'n your help. We're diggin' his grave. Go on now. Git!"

Sandie opened his eyes and saw a young girl staring down at him. No more than 13 or 14 years old she was clothed in the simple sack dress of a farm girl. She carried a wooden bucket in one hand and a tin cup in the other. Slowly, arduously, Sandie forced his hand into his coat pocket and grasped a letter he'd been penning. He pulled it forth and, barely able to raise the two fingers between which it was trapped, he gasped, "P...please... Promise me..."

The girl reached down and plucked it tentatively from him. "You want me to see someone gets it?" she asked, and Sandie could only blink as a gesture of reply. Then, moving his hand down to the saber lying across his body, placed there by the burial crew, he tapped the hilt with a bloody index finger.

The girl glanced at the two men who were preoccupied with their digging and reached down to grasp the sheathed instrument. She picked it up, then turned and started to run away.

"Hey! Hey! You little brat!" one of the men hollered after her.

"Aw, let 'er go," the other man replied. "It's his guns and boots is all we afta'."

While the one man grumbled but returned to his digging, Sandie moved his hand up to his collar and began to fish out the pendant from around his neck. Taking it in palm, he wedged a thumbnail under the cover to pry it open.

Then, gazing at the picture of his beautiful Katie, his eyes welled from the sadness of knowing he was leaving her forever.

He swallowed hard and the thick, bitter-sweet taste of blood mingled saliva caused him to cough, then shudder at knowing his death was imminent. He'd seen other men die—countless others—and he resigned himself to his own, placing his soul in the hands of the Almighty with the comforting belief he was dying for a noble and worthwhile cause.

Lying there, looking skyward, Sandie's mind turned to thoughts of home and family. Regretting not having tried to see them more often, he wondered how they would take the news of his passing.

The landscape slowly began to swirl around him but Sandie gave it no concern. Incidents from his life began to weave through his vision, intermingling with the present as his thoughts now floated freely, anchorless, unweighted by any concerns of this world. He slowly closed his eyes and, while doing so, became aware of a shadow passing over him. He considered it was perhaps the shadow of death come to claim him, but he fought for another moment of consciousness to more clearly discern who the figure might be. Opening his eyes, Sandie beheld a peculiarly dressed man bending down beside him, peering intently at the photograph of Katie. The stranger seemed confused and troubled over the picture and Sandie heard him call out to her, but it was not any name by which Sandie had known her.

The man slowly turned his head and Sandie watched his eyes linger at the wound, studying the steady absorption of the crimson color that tainted the blue wool. The fellow's eyes traveled further and, when they met Sandie's, he gasped aloud. Sandie, too, released a startled groan, though his response was much weaker. What astounded both men was the sense that they were looking into, or through, some strange, mystical mirror in which they could simultaneously view their own reflection and that of the other.

For but a breath Sandie viewed himself through the eyes of the visitor, looking down at his own face as he lay prone on the tall, green clover. A flush of panic brought all that surrounded him to begin a dizzying swirl. Colors and objects blended together until Sandie found himself in an eerie, chilling darkness. How long he remained in this black void he could not determine, but when he opened his eyes, he found himself again looking skyward, the curious figure gone.

Sandie glanced a last time at the beautiful, smiling face of the girl in the locket, then closed the cover. He labored to work it back into his shirt, hoping the Rebels would overlook it for its prized value as precious metal. From far away he heard a faint voice say, "This hole's plenty deep. Think he's dead yet?"

Sandie never heard the reply.

Chapter Eighteen

August 14, 1988 Pittsburgh, Pennsylvania

"Jeez, Sam. I still can't believe you bought the damn thing. It's huge!" Dave exclaimed as he stood back in the driveway for another look at the two story, red brick structure. "Carol's going to flip when she sees it."

"Yeah...Well... I've lived in apartments for so long I thought I'd try a real house. The deal was there so I couldn't pass it up. It'll be a good investment...'case I move again," he laughed.

"When was the last time you mowed a lawn?"

"Heh," Sam chuckled as he thought about it. "Not since I was a kid. I'll go buy a lawn mower next week. Hedge clippers, tree pruners, all that stuff. It'll be fun. I'm an official homeowner, now."

Built in the 1930s, it was a large house of red brick with black mortar, and capped with a gray slate roof. Sam had purchased it from a young doctor who had left to join an established practice in another city. The man wished to quickly divest himself of the house and was willing to absorb a substantial loss, believing he could easily make the difference good in a few short years.

Though spacious and well maintained, the house was rather ordinary for the older, quiet, affluent neighborhood. Most all of the original inhabitants of that section of the city had either died off or were in retirement homes south of the Mason-Dixon.

A handful of the hardy, conservative, older generation did remain and were quick to greet their new, young, professional neighbors with stories of the old neighborhood, then to brief them on protocol and conduct—especially concerning children. Most often, the lectures went unheeded, however, for this was the generation of their grandchildren and their friends' grandchildren, returning from the suburbs where they were raised to buy and refurbish the homes that their parents grew up in. They had their own ideas about childrearing, parties and how high their hedges should be. Still a relatively quiet and friendly place, the neighborhood was taking on a fresher, rejuvenated appearance. Sam was already explaining to Dave about his plans for a small garden, which trees were going to be pruned or felled, where the sun deck would go, and on and on.

Following a tour and inspection of the outside, Sam led his friend into the house to show him through the many rooms. When they'd finally arrived at the master bedroom, the fourth and largest of the spacious sleeping quarters, Sam turned to Dave and, with a wide grin, asked, "Well? You think she'll like it?"

"Who?"

"Kelly, you dumb ass. Who else?"

"What do you mean, 'do I think she'll like it'?"

"Do you think she'll like it? That's what I mean."

"Yeah. Probably. What difference does it make?"

"What do you mean, 'what difference does it make?' It makes all the difference. She's got to be happy here. She's got to like it."

"Wait. Wait. Back up a minute, buddy. What are you saying? Kelly's going to live here?"

"Well, yeah! Of course!" Sam said as though it was an obvious conclusion. "I'm going to marry her."

Dave looked at his friend, cocked his head as if he hadn't, perhaps, heard the man correctly, then blinked slowly under a raised brow. "Want to run that by me again?"

Sam shrugged matter-of-factly. "I'm going to marry her," he said again. "I've thought about it over and over and I know it's the right thing. Dave, I'm crazy about her. I love her, and I know she loves me. I can't think of anything but her. I go to bed at night and I see her face when I close my eyes. I wake up in the morning and the first thing I think about is calling her. As soon as the phone service was connected yesterday, I called her; talked to her for an hour or better. Dave, I want to live with her. I want to spend my life with her…and all my future lives," he added with a grin.

Dave smiled. He was happy for his friend. The gleam in Sam's eyes that hadn't shown for many years had returned to full brilliance. "Have you asked her yet?"

"No. How could I? I haven't seen her yet. You don't call someone up and say, 'hello. How are you? Just got my phone turned on. By the way, will you marry me?' These things take time. You have to work into them slowly."

"Well, when are you going to ask her?"

"This Saturday night. At the party."

"That's certainly giving yourself some time. Why the long courtship?"

"You're laughing, aren't you?"

Dave dropped his amused smile to put on a more serious face. "No. No, I'm not, Sam. We've been friends for a long time. We've come through a lot together, you and I. You're my best friend and I care about you every bit as much as I care for Carol and my kids. You're family. I want only the best for you. I think Kelly's the perfect woman for you. She's bright, witty, brave, accomplished...and damn, is she ever pretty!" Dave put his hand affectionately on Sam's shoulder. "I want to ask you just one question, though, about your relationship with Kelly."

"Shoot, man. What?"

"Do you plan on ever kissing her?" he asked, his straight face breaking into a mask of wrinkled laughter.

Sam good-naturedly pushed him over the footboard of the bed, sending Dave sprawling onto the mattress. "Fuck you," he said, trying to keep a straight face, though a smile kept returning.

Dave was chortling as he lay back on the bed. "But, it's true. Right? You're going to ask a woman to marry you...and you haven't even kissed her yet."

"I've kissed her," Sam muttered low.

"Not on the lips."

"So what? Hell, in a lot of countries the bride and groom don't even meet each other till their wedding day."

"Good point! Good point!" Dave nodded in agreement. "You two could fly to, say, Waziristan or wherever, and get hitched. You'd be right at home there."

"Hey!... Hey! Listen. I plan on doing a whole lot of kissing."
"Heh! I hope so. And who knows, someday you might even have sex. Wouldn't that be something?" Dave sniggered.

"Oh-h...fuck you, again. You know, the first thing I'm going to do when I get settled in here is call 1-900-SPORT and find me a new best friend. I knew I shouldn't have given you my address. I may not even invite you to my wedding."

"Doesn't matter. I'm golfing that weekend. Besides, I'm just getting you in shape for the abuse you'll be getting from any woman you marry."

"Yeah. I suppose," Sam laughed. "C'mon. Help me stack books in the study."

The two men spent the day arranging Sam's meager collection of furniture—so crowded in the apartments he'd always rented, but now so scant in relation to the huge, multi-roomed house. They hung pictures and other memorabilia, unpacked dishes and so much else associated with trying to establish oneself into a new residence.

Sam had wanted to keep the house a secret from Kelly. He told her only that he'd found a place in the Squirrel Hill section of Pittsburgh and that it was larger, though more expensive, than he'd been accustomed. Now, with his enthusiasm for the house exuding from every pore, he knew he could wait no longer. He had to call her and tell her about it.

While he and Dave sat in the kitchen eating Japanese take-out and sharing a bottle of warmed Saki, Sam reached at his collar and pulled on a gold chain. Lifting it over his head, he held it out for Dave's inspection.

"Well, I'll be...," Dave said as he reached out and took it in hand. For there, dangling at the end of the chain, was the gold locket he had given Sam, buffed and polished to reveal every detail of its quality craftsmanship. He examined the cover, then flipped it open. "You had it professionally restored?"

"Yep!" Sam said, as he reached for the phone. "A jeweler in Cleveland did a rush job for me. He offered to buy it, but I just laughed and told him 'no thanks'; that, 'I'd had it for years...and years'," he laughed. "See. I put Kelly's picture in it over that other girl's."

"It's a nice inscription," Dave commented after having read the words on the inside cover.

"Yeah. It is," Sam nodded. He lowered his eyes to the table and his face took on a more serious expression as he fidgeted with the phone. "Can, uh, can I tell you something?" he asked uneasily, almost to the point of an embarrassed blush.

"Sure, man. Go ahead."

Sam struggled a minute, uncertain if he should say what it was he wanted to tell Dave. Finally, he stammered, "Well... That inscription, there?"

"Yeah?"

"It, uh...it's the same verse as is in Kelly's."

Dave looked at his friend in disbelief. "No-o-o. Get out of here."

"It is," Sam said, watching the expression of amazement grow on Dave's face. "And...and that's not all."

"There's more?"

"Yeah," Sam replied with a slow nod. "The girl there...whose picture you originally saw in it; I've seen her. She was in my dreams...when we were in Antietam. The lockets are identical. They were crafted by the same person."

"You're sure?"

"Yeah. When I showered and changed at Kelly's before we left that day, I examined it. She had it lying out on her dresser."

Dave blinked as he looked at Sam and tried to comprehend what he'd just heard. "This is pretty weird, Sam. Even if it were simply coincidence, it's pretty weird."

"Isn't it?"

"Does Kelly know all this?"

"No. I haven't told her yet. I'm still trying to understand it myself. I don't know what it all means, but I'm sure of one thing; Kelly and I are meant for each other. I'm starting to believe it's all more than coincidence. I'm not letting her get away. I'm not going to lose her again."

"Again?" Dave asked, raising an eyebrow.

Sam bridled at this, his eyes widening momentarily. He looked quizzically at Dave, surprised at what he'd said. Then he shrugged and shook his head. "I don't know what I meant by that."

"Neither do I. But it sure was Freudian."

"Hm-m... Maybe," Sam muttered, more to himself than to Dave. He paused, as if in thought, then shrugged, saying, "You read about a lot of strange stuff that happens. But you never think it's going to happen to you." Then he sighed. "Well. At least I'm not being abducted by aliens. Ghosts and such I can handle."

"Yeah. Especially since it's your own that's haunting you."

They laughed, and Sam then explained that he wanted to call Kelly and tell her about the house. He pressed the numbers and waited, but it was Marylou that answered. They conversed for awhile, but when he asked to speak with Kelly, he was informed she had left rather hurriedly and without explanation earlier in the day. Marylou knew Kelly had called and talked to Carol Cooper around mid-morning, and that she had planned on visiting Varina Schiels sometime during the afternoon.

Of what Carol and Kelly had talked about Marylou was uninformed. Too, whether Kelly was to see the older woman on business or for other reasons, Marylou was not aware. Only of the fact that the woman seemed unusually distracted and distant this morning could the woman comment with any certainty. Kelly had been so vibrant and vivacious these last few days—full of talk about Sam and seeing him this Saturday; how much she missed him, and so forth. Today, she seemed distraught, silent and withdrawn. Introspective, maybe. Marylou wasn't sure. In any event, she promised to have Kelly call him just as soon as she returned.

When he had hung up, Sam was unsettled. He told Dave about the conversation and that he felt an odd but keen sense that Kelly was disturbed about something. At his urgings, Dave called his wife. He'd planned on doing so anyway to tell her he was starting for home, soon. Now, he asked also about the conversation Carol had had with Kelly.

Carol told him that the woman had called to inform her of the progress for this Saturday evening's gala event, and that she'd taken the liberty of securing them two rooms at a motel in Harpers Ferry. Carol said that she did notice a certain distraction in Kelly's voice and that it was attributed to an upsetting dream the woman had had last night. She wouldn't relay it to Carol, but it apparently troubled her.

When he hung up, promising Carol he'd leave directly, Dave told his friend what Carol had said. Sam mulled it over awhile, finally saying, "Damn! I wish she'd have told Carol the dream. They're pretty fantastic but they always seem to relate to something. I hope she's all right."

"What's to worry about?" Dave asked, for he could see Sam was disturbed now.

"I'm...I'm a little afraid something's going to happen. Remember our talk with Varina Schiels? She said something calamitous is going to occur. What if Kelly's dream is a portent?"

"Varina never said that," Dave argued. "She just didn't answer the question about your future. That didn't mean impending disaster was looming over anyone. She never told us we were going to get the land, either, and that was something positive. Maybe she doesn't tell anyone their future, good or bad. Listen. Don't fret about this. Nothing terrible is going to happen. They've probably just laid too much work on her and she's a little stressed."

"What about her dream? You know her dreams."

"Look. If she's troubled about a dream she'd have called you and talked about it. Just relax and wait for her to call you. I'm sure everything's okay." Dave stood and stretched. "I've got to be going," he said to Sam. "Carol wants me home. I've got to be at work early tomorrow. The new store is an outrageous success."

"No kidding? Doing okay, huh?"

"Yeah. I'm drowning my competition. It's kind of sweet tasting."

"Good for you." Sam told him. "You deserve it. Come on. I'll walk you to your car."

The two men went out to the driveway where Dave's '67 GTO sat glimmering in the reflected light of the street lamps. Sam gave the meticulously restored auto an admiring inspection on the driver's side. "Well, thanks for coming down and lending a hand," he said, opening the car door for Dave.

"Hey. Anytime. I'm glad you're nearby. I always hoped you'd move closer again some day. There's a whole lot we've got to explore and expand on. Welcome to the neighborhood," he said, extending his hand.

Sam took it, then the two men fell into a hug over the car door. When Sam pulled back he chuckled. "Ha! All the neighbors are going to think I'm gay, now. Unmarried and hugging another man out in public." He nodded toward the street. "Somebody is in there."

"What?" Dave asked, turning his head to look. At the end of the driveway, parked just across the street, was a shiny white luxury edition Cadillac. "Neighbor?" he asked.

"I don't know. Probably. I think some doctor lives over there. I haven't met them yet. Everybody on the block drives a big car, as near as I can tell. Yuppies, or old farts who've retired wealthy enough."

361

"Eh! How do you know anyone's even in it?"

"I saw them light a cigarette."

"Well, I doubt it's the doctor, then," Dave said. He whimsically blew Sam a kiss and jumped in his car. "There. That'll really give them something to talk about."

"Thanks. I needed that," Sam said in sarcasm. "That'll really help me make a good impression on the folks around here."

"Well, when Kelly moves in with you tell everyone she's a lesbian."

Sam shook his head, feigning irritation. Dave chuckled, then hit his ignition, roaring the big engine.

"Hey! Hey! Easy on that," Sam said. "This is supposed to be a quiet neighborhood."

Dave grinned and gunned the engine to let the four-barrel carburetor kick in for an even louder roar. "What'd you say? I can't hear you."

"Yeah...yeah," Sam chuckled, waving his friend to leave. "Get out of here." He watched Dave back the car down the driveway and into the street, gunning the engine until the chrome blower screamed powerfully. Then, aimed down the street, he raced the engine and popped the clutch, squealing the tires half way down the block. Sam rolled his eyes but smiled fondly over his friend's predictable behavior while he listened to the car being power-shifted several blocks away. He turned and went back inside.

In the kitchen, cleaning up the boxes of take-out, Sam again tried Kelly's number. The phone rang only three times when Sam's front doorbell chimed. "Damn," he grumbled, setting the portable phone on the counter. "It's probably the police come to get Dave's address for disturbing the peace." He walked to the front door, hollering, "Coming! Coming!" in answer to the impatiently repeated chimes.

He slid the deadbolt and turned the knob, but as he began to open the door it was suddenly kicked aside, hitting him full front and sending him sprawling back onto the tile floor of the foyer. Two men entered and stood on either side of him. Sam nursed his forehead with his hand and tried to react to what was happening, focusing enough to see they both held guns. "If you came to rob me you won't get much. I do everything with credit cards," he said, rubbing his forehead.

"Shut up! Asshole," one of the men commanded in a deep, graveled voice. Sam had heard that voice before. He glanced up in the direction from which it was spoken to see a third man closing the door. His nose, hugely swollen, had a large white bandage over it, and both eyes were blackened. His right arm was in a cast and sling. The man stood over Sam with a leering grin. "Hello, asshole. Bet you didn't think you'd see me again."

Sam propped himself up on one arm, his other still holding his forehead where the door slammed into it. "I hope you're not my neighbors," he said, unable to think of any other response.

"Fuck you!" the man on his right spat and kicked him in the ribs. Sam groaned and clutched his side. He made a move to go after the man but stopped when he heard the hammer of the pistol being cocked. "Go ahead," the man sniggered, pressing the barrel to Sam's head. "I'd love to be the one to do you. You cut my brother so I figure I owe you. Too bad we couldn't have your karate kicking friend join our little party. I'd like to see him try to use that shit against a bullet."

The shorter, bandaged man spoke again. "All right. Let's stop fuckin' around. You know what we're here for. Where is it?"

"Hell, I don't know," Sam said. "It's all packed away in one of the boxes upstairs."

"Well, what do you say we go have a look," the man sneered, waving his gun for Sam to get up.

Sam led the men upstairs to what had been a bedroom, but which Sam had chosen to use as his study. His computer was set up on a large desk and many of his books were stacked on the movable shelves. But many boxes, both full and empty, still cluttered the room. One of the men went to the boxes and began to dump the contents onto the floor.

"Hey! Hey! Come on!" Sam shouted. "There's no need for that. I'll find them for you."

"I don't mind," the man snorted. "I'm havin' fun." He continued to turn boxes over and scatter the contents.

When he picked up a Crown Royal box Sam halted him, saying. "You may not want to scatter that one. That's the one you're after."

"Bring it here," the shorter, ugly man with the ruddy complexion and broken nose and arm commanded. It was set down on the desk before him and, with his good arm, he reached in and began to leaf through the stack of papers. "Yeah. This is it. Good. Let's go," he said to the others. The man who had discovered the box gathered it up to carry out.

"Well, listen. Don't make yourselves strangers. Always glad to entertain guests," Sam said with a sarcastic grin as he waved goodbye to them.

The shorter man looked at him and, in an equally backhanded tone, remarked, "Thanks. But we enjoy your company so much we thought you might take a little ride with us."

"What for? You got what you wanted. Take it and get out!"

"Hey, Rudy! Check out these blades," the third man interrupted.

Along one wall in the study Sam had begun arranging a collection of memorabilia—a collage of framed photographs surrounding various souvenirs he'd wanted to keep in view. The sword he'd brought back from Antietam was carefully placed above the machete he'd carried in the war. Below this were some lesser knives and various Civil War relics he'd acquired.

The man stuffed one of the knives into his belt, then took down the sword. "Hey, I'm takin' this with me," he said.

"Yeah. Give it to your brother," Sam snorted. "I did."

"Fuck you!" the man said. He pulled the sword from its sheath and pressed it to Sam's stomach. "I was gonna enjoy puttin' a bullet in your head. But maybe I'll run you through with your own blade...after I cut your balls off with it."

Sam spat in the man's face. The fellow flinched and became enraged.

"Billy Ray!" the man named Rudy shouted at him, halting him from running Sam through with the blade. "Not here! Bring him along, now. You can have your fun with him later."

Rudy turned to lead the way out. Sam and the leaner fellow called Billy Ray glared at one another. "Know what, mister? I'm gonna leave your spit on my face. I ain't even gonna wipe it off, 'cause the longer it's on there the madder I'm gonna get. When we get to where we're goin,' I'm gonna have some real fun carvin' you up," he sneered angrily. He lowered the sword point to Sam's groin and pressed it with some force. "Now get goin'."

When they had moved downstairs and near the front door Rudy stopped them. "Billy Ray, find some rope or something and tie this fucker's hands. I don't want any tricks on the way." He turned to the other man, saying, "Simple. Go out to the garage. See if you can find a shovel or something."

"For what, Rudy?"

"To dig with. What else do you do with a shovel?"

While Simple went out to the garage Billy Ray went over to the draperies in the dining room. "Need some cords?" he chortled wickedly. "Comin' right up." With one swoosh of the keen-edged blade the curtains crumpled in a pile on the floor. Billy Ray bent and picked up the pull cords and leered at Sam.

"That's okay," Sam shrugged, pretending to be unconcerned. "They were left here by the folks that moved out. I didn't much like them anyway."

Billy Ray stalked over to Sam, pulled his wrists behind his back and wound the cords tightly. When the job was finished the two men led Sam out to the white 'Caddy' parked across the street.

Simple returned from the garage with an army entrenching tool. He slid into the back seat to sandwich Sam between himself and Billy Ray. "This is all he got," he said, showing them the tool.

"It'll do," Rudy said from behind the wheel. He pulled the selector into forward and drove off into the night.

****

On such a warm summer's night Dave had his windows rolled down to enjoy the refreshing breeze that rushed past as he cruised along the four-lane. Creedence Clearwater Revival blasted from the built-in 8-track cassette player and he drummed the steering wheel as he sang along.

Though he was not inclined to hold material objects in particular adoration beyond their legitimate due as functionally utilitarian, Dave loved this car! He'd bought it as a rusting hulk, discovered quite by accident on a Sunday cruise in the countryside as it sat in some farmer's fence row. Countless hours and plenty of money had been spent reworking every detail of the engine and body until it was restored to showroom perfection. He drove it only about six times a year, and only when the weather conditions were perfect—not too humid, not too dry, not too sunny, and never! never! in the rain.

Today had been one of those perfect days. Taking the day off work to help Sam move into the new house, he'd chosen the occasion to celebrate his friend's arrival with a spin in the GTO. Now, as he sang the lyrics to *Bad Moon on the Rise* he down-shifted and tromped the accelerator, moving into the passing lane as he began to climb a long hill. He listened with juvenile delight as the carburetor opened and the blower kicked in.

The car roared in a burst of fury and reached ninety-five miles per hour in just seconds. He raced up the hill at this speed, weaving in and out of traffic until deciding he'd fed his immaturity sufficiently to last until the next time he drove the car. The other reason he backed off on his speed was due to a quick glance at the gauges. The oil pressure read "good;" the water temperature read "good;" the gas gauge read "empty." Dave had forgotten to fill the tank before leaving the city. Maintaining a speed of 55 mph, and letting the car coast down the hills and grades, he breathed a sigh of relief when he saw an exit sign and knew fuel was only a mile or so away.

Dave breezed into the station and pulled under the canopy to one of the pumps. While he began to fill the tank, his head turned to watch the dollar numbers roll over on the pump, he didn't notice the cute, blonde owner of the little white car in front of his return from having paid the cashier. As the woman tucked her wallet into her purse and set it on her seat her eyes caught the glint of the shiny chrome on the black GTO. She paused a moment to admire the car. "Nice car," she hollered to the fellow with his back to her as he finished topping off his tank.

Dave closed the tank lid and turned to replace the pump nozzle. "Thanks," he said in response. "It's a classic. I...Kelly!" he exclaimed as he had glanced to address the voice and was stunned to see it was Kelly Gracie.

"Dave?" she gasped, equally surprised to see him there.

"My gawd! Kelly! What are you doing here?" he asked as he moved to meet her between the cars for a hug. "Sam was trying to call you. What are you doing here?"

"Well, I...I wanted to see Sam," Kelly explained, blushing slightly. "Partly to surprise him...and...partly to be sure he was all right. I was worried about him."

"Surprise him, you will! Actually, he was worried about you. You never returned his call—obviously."

When Kelly asked if Sam was all right, Dave assured her that he was and told of having just left him moments ago. "He's got a real surprise for you," Dave told her.

"He does? What is it?" she asked, her voice much calmer now that she'd learned Sam was fine.

Dave refused to tell but offered to lead her back to Sam's so she could avoid having to hunt for his place in the dark. Kelly gratefully accepted the offer and followed the GTO into Pittsburgh. She pulled into Sam's driveway and parked beside Dave. When she got out of her car, she looked at Dave quizzically. "What is this?" she asked, starting to survey the house and grounds from where she stood in the driveway. "This is a house. There's a sold sticker over the realtor's sign."

"It's Sam's surprise," Dave smiled. "He bought it! Do you believe that guy? On a whim he decides to buy the place." He looked at Kelly with glee on his face and an obvious suggestion in his voice as he said, "I think he wants to settle down."

Kelly blushed and quickly looked away, her eyes sweeping over the red brick structure. "My. It certainly is big," she replied in a bid to not discuss his last comment.

"Isn't it? Wait till you see the inside. He's going to have to buy a lot of furniture. It looks pretty empty, with all the more he has. C'mon. Let's go in." Dave urged. "He'll be thrilled to see you."

Dave led the way into the side entrance that accessed the kitchen. "Hello!" he hollered. "Yo! Sam! I'm back!"

Kelly gazed around the room, commenting, "Wow! It's a roomy kitchen. The cabinets are lovely."

"Aren't they? They're walnut. They look handmade," Dave said, then called out again for Sam. When no reply was delivered, he started down the hall but stopped when his eye caught sight of the pile of draperies below the dining room window. It puzzled him. "I wonder what that's about?" he muttered loud enough for Kelly to hear. Then he explained, "That wasn't like that when

I left." He led the way to the stairs and as they climbed them Kelly called out to Sam.

Still there was no reply.

"Maybe he ran down to the store," Dave suggested, shooting for any reasonable explanation why Sam did not appear to be home. But when they passed the room that was to serve as the study and saw the papers strewn about, Kelly gasped. Dave was bewildered. "Well, what-the-hell," he said, surveying the littered papers and boxes.

"Something's happened to Sam!" Kelly said, her voice trembling in alarm.

"Now, just wait," Dave told her. "Don't jump to conclusions. Give me a minute. I'll be right back."

Dave hurried down the stairs and out the front door. While he was gone, Kelly did a search of the remaining rooms, including a look into the attic and basement. When Dave returned, finding her waiting in the living room, he moved directly to her and grasped her shoulders in his hands. His eyes revealed a frightened concern. "You had a dream last night. What was it? Quick!" he demanded.

"Dave, what is it? What's going on?"

"Your dream! Tell me what it was!" he asked impatiently and excited.

"Oh, God!" she cried. "Oh, my God!" she started to panic, tears welling in her eyes.

Dave shook her. "The dream! Tell me! Now!"

Kelly was trembling but she managed to stammer, "S-Sam was...in a woods. There were some...shadowy figures around him. I—I think they were soldiers; I couldn't tell. They were all gray...and—and it was dark."

"Why soldiers? Did you see their uniforms?"

"N—no. But there was a fort in the distance. A log fort. I couldn't see it clearly...but it was there. Sam...Sam was lying in a hole," she quivered. "A grave! Oh, God! We better call the police!"

"No time! Anything else?"

Kelly wiped her eyes on the backs of her hands, saying, "No...No... That's all... Um, he...he was clutching the locket from...from Antietam. The one you found. Only, it...had my picture in it."

Still holding her shoulders in his hands Dave's eyes widened as he looked at her with astonishment. "Your picture? You saw that?"

"Well, I...I just knew it. You know how dreams are. It was a picture I'd given him before you all came back north. He cut it down and...and put it in over the girl that was there. I saw it clearly, or at least knew it was done. Why?"

"Because that's exactly what he did!" Dave told her. "He showed it to me today. He was wearing it! Anything else about the fort? Did you see a name? Anything distinguishing? Kelly! I need to know!"

Her voice fraught with worry, Kelly tried to continue. "Dave, I...," she managed, but then broke down, sobbing.

Dave squeezed her shoulders tightly. "Kelly! Not now! Get a grip! Anything else?"

Kelly tried to compose herself. She sniffled and wiped her eyes again, brushing the tears from her cheeks. "The fort...was...on a hill..."

"On a hill. You're sure?" he asked. "Not on a plane, by a river or anything?"

"No. I'm sure."

"Think, Kelly!" Dave demanded. "Were there any houses nearby, old or new? Any particular trees? Roads; were there any roads near it that you saw?"

"I...I don't know," Kelly cried. "Dave, it was just a dream."

"Yeah! But a telling one. Your dreams don't seem to be like everybody else's. When you have a dream that disturbs you there's usually something significant behind it; something too real."

Dave left her and bounded the stairs. He hurried to the study and pulled the machete down off the wall, his eye quick to note the empty pegs that had held the valued saber. When he returned to Kelly, he grabbed her hand. "C'mon," he said. "We've got to hurry!"

Dave pulled her along, hustling her to the car. Kelly stumbled after him, barely able to contain her tears. "Shouldn't we go to the police?" she asked as they hurriedly slid into the car.

"There's no time," Dave told her, hitting the ignition and roaring the engine. "It would take so long to convince them of anything. And what are we going to say; you had a dream about your friend being in danger so they ought to check out the forts in the area? They'd give you a drug test. I'm not sure even I believe it all...and I know you."

Dave raced through the suburban streets, slowing at the intersections, but then racing through when they were clear of traffic. "Where are we going?" Kelly asked, clutching to hold on to the arm rest on the door.

"There's only two places they could go that would head them back south," Dave said, shifting the transmission and flooring the accelerator through a red light.

"Who?" Kelly asked, frightened and confused.

"I think this is the work of James Brody. There was a white Caddy sitting across the street tonight. We thought it was the neighbors, but I checked. It wasn't. The guy across the street thought it was one of Sam's friends. There were cigarette butts all over the ground where it was parked, so they'd been sitting there quite awhile. There's only two possibilities. One: these were just regular thieves, checking out the place to rob later—but that doesn't fit. Only the study was messed up.

They didn't even search the bedroom, which is where most people hide cash. Or, two: it's Brody. Sam never turned over the documents to him and he probably wanted them back. I'm sure he'd want them back! They're too incriminating to have out. Damn! We should have taken care of that. Nobody thought," he said, disgusted even with himself. "We just walked away and forgot about it. Too much was happening—me, with my new store; Sam, with his moving."

"Well, if you're right, Brody didn't forget about it. You still didn't answer me. Where are we going?"

Now, out on the four-lane highway, Dave raced the car along, weaving in and out of traffic in a desperate attempt to overtake the white Cadillac. "There's something...paranormal, I'd guess you'd say, about your dreams," Dave said to her. "I'm not even going to begin to try to understand it, but there is. If you dreamed you saw Sam at a fort, then that's where we're going. There's only two I can think of that they could pass on their way back south. One is in Bedford, but it's on a wide plane. Fort Ligonier is not that far from here. It sits up on a hill and could be the place they'll go. It's a less direct route for them to take, but conceivable. I only hope..."

"What?"

"Nothing. Never mind," Dave said. But in a low aside he muttered, "I sure hope I chose right."

Beside him, Kelly was becoming even more upset. By the lights of the oncoming vehicles Dave could see an occasional tear stream down the woman's cheek and knew she was straining to hold back a welling torrent. In an effort to keep her distracted from thinking about the end of their journey he said, "You went to see Varina Schiels. Was it about the dream?"

Kelly bit her lower lip and looked down, embarrassed. "Yes."

"Why didn't you tell me?"

"I don't know. I guess, maybe, I thought you'd think I was nuts, or something."

Dave reached over and took her hand and gave it a comforting squeeze. "Never," he told her. "What'd she say? Did she read the cards?"

"No. She refused to see me. She stayed in her room and sent word with that girl, Wilma. She said the cards wouldn't speak to her. I think she was lying. I took it as a bad omen. That's why I came up. I wanted to be with Sam in case something happened. And...and now I...might be too late...," she cried.

"No! Don't say that," Dave said. "Think positive. He's okay."

****

"How far are we gonna go before we do this guy?" Billy Ray asked from the back seat of the plush Cadillac.

"I don't know," Rudy answered from behind the wheel. "I don't even know where we are. Look at the map and see where in the fuck we're at."

Billy Ray reached over the front seat for the map and flipped on the little courtesy light by which to study it. He examined it awhile, then stated, "Shit, Rudy. How'd you get us onto this road? We ain't nowhere we're supposed to be."

"How the fuck should I know? I must'a turned off the wrong exit. We're headin' south, though. Right?"

"Yeah. But, hell, it's gonna' take all night to get back. I'm s'posed to take a load of steel out tomorrow afternoon. I'll be in great shape to drive. You should'a taken the turnpike."

"Yeah. Right. That'd'a looked good pull'n into the toll booth with asshole back there all tied up. Just relax. We'll get back," Rudy said to him.

Simple wriggled in the seat and glared at Sam. "Look. I'm gettin nervous about havin' this guy back here. Can we just fuckin' get rid'a him and get the fuck back home?"

"Yeah. Yeah. In a bit," Rudy answered. "We'll find a place somewhere. Shit, as dark as it is we could end up plantin' him in somebody's front yard and not even know it."

Billy Ray switched off the courtesy light, refolded the map, and tossed it into the front seat. "Just keep takin' this road. It's runnin' in the right direction. It's just gonna be a bit longer. It'll still hit the interstate at Breezewood. We'll have to dump him before that, though."

Sam could see no way out of this predicament. It bothered him that his end seemed near, and that it would be at the hands of such unsavory characters. He knew well that pleading for his life before these men would avail him nothing, and the idea was revolting to him. Still, he tried out of desperation. "Look," he said. "You guys don't have to do this. You've got the material. Just let me go. I won't tell anyone."

His plea brought an angry, "Shut up!" from Simple, who drew the knife Billy Ray had taken from Sam's house, and he pressed the point to Sam's neck. "You make me nervous enough! Just shut up or I'll cut you right now!"

"Hey! Hey!" Rudy yelled over his shoulder. "Back off! You get blood on my upholstery I'll fuckin' do you! Just put the blade down, Simple."

"Tell 'im to shut up, then!" Simple hollered. "I don't wanna hear him!"

"Hey. Mister. Don't talk. It makes Simple nervous," Rudy said.

Sam swallowed hard, feeling some relief when the knifepoint was drawn away. Sweat flowed from every pore of his body as he knew these hard men could not be deterred from their mission. They were sent to kill him and they would fulfill their task with no remorse.

They rode in silence for a long time. Simple and Billy Ray stared out the windows, occasionally turning to glance at Sam, then back to the windows. Sam stared straight ahead, trying not to draw their attention as he worked at the ropes that bound his wrists. The cords were too tight—they wouldn't slacken—and Sam's heart began to sink. He knew he was running out of time. His only consolation would be to not go down without a fight. At the very least he determined to hurt one of these men before they ended his life.

Rudy stopped for a traffic light about an hour out of Pittsburgh along Route 30. They had arrived at Ligonier a quaint town of several thousand inhabitants. It had neat homes along tree-lined streets and a bandstand in the center of the town square. As Rudy waited for the light to change, he stared at the log fort on the hill across the street. "What's that? Some kind of fort?" he asked.

"It's Fort Ligonier," Sam volunteered, then quickly glanced at Simple for a reaction to his having spoken. But Simple leaned forward to gaze at the log compound. "It's an old French and Indian War fort," Sam added, then wondered why he'd bothered to inform them.

"You don't say," Rudy murmured. "Hmm..."

When the light changed, instead of continuing along Route 30, Rudy turned right, driving down the street a few hundred yards, then turning left into a long flat field.

Billy Ray leaned forward to watch out the front window as the Cadillac drove over the broad, mowed field, aiming for a patch of woods on the far side. "What are we doin', Rudy?"

"It's perfect," Rudy answered. "Ain't nobody gonna do no diggin' down here. This is government ground. They'll never find him." He pulled the car to a stop under a grove of trees that shielded them from the roads.

"Rudy, there's houses all around," Simple remarked, noticing the house lights in the distance as they twinkled through the swaying leaves and limbs of the trees.

"Don't worry about it. They can't see us. And if they did, they'd probably think it's a car full o' kids havin' a party. Let's get out."

The men exited the car and Billy Ray reached in to grab Sam by his collar, pulling him out. Rudy reached in and retrieved the small shovel from the floor where Simple had mindlessly left it. Switching on a fluorescent lantern, he said, "C'mon," and led the way, taking them deeper into the grove of trees. When they had walked about twenty yards Rudy halted them and turned to the others. "Okay. Cut 'im loose," he ordered.

"Huh?" Simple asked, a dumbfounded look showing on his face.

"Unless you feel like digging, stupid!" Rudy said.

"Oh... Oh-h-h! I get it. Yeah. Right! He digs his own grave," Simple chuckled, amused at the idea. He cut the cords with Sam's own knife, then pressed the blade into his back. "No fuckin' around, Shithead. I wanna get home tonight."

Sam massaged his wrists, working to get the circulation returned. He said nothing in reply, but took the shovel from Rudy when handed it.

Rudy raked the ground with his foot to mark a spot for Sam. "Okay. Right here. Dig!" he commanded. He set the lantern on the ground and reached into his pocket for a small revolver. Waving it at Sam, he said, "No funny stuff. This ain't the movies. You even look at me wrong, I blow your fuckin' brains out."

Sam glared at the man, then around at the others. He set the shovel point to the ground and started to dig.

****

The GTO sped down the highway, weaving in and out of traffic and slowing only enough at traffic lights to be sure it was clear to roar on through. Dave was hoping a police cruiser might sight him and give chase, acting as reinforcements when they arrived at the fort. Traffic had thinned considerably when he left the town of Greensburg behind with its outlying shopping district that sprawled for several miles along Route 30. The road narrowed from a wide, modern highway to a narrower, older, four-lane that ran through dense woods on either side.

Aware that he was only minutes away from saving his friend, Dave tramped the accelerator, racing the car to incredibly reckless speeds. Rounding a blind curve on an unlit section of the road, they glimpsed two eyes instantly appearing in front of them, reflected by the headlights of the car.

Dave hit the brakes and tried to swerve around it, but a loud "thump" and flying fur indicated they'd hit the deer that was innocently making its crossing. A loud fluttering began to resound from the engine as Dave fought to bring the car under control and steer the right-side tires back onto the roadway. He cut the wheels left, but an erosion break in the berm tore the steering from his hands and sent the car careening over to scrape along the medial barrier guard rails.

Kelly was white. Frozen in her seat, she clutched the dashboard to brace herself for the worst as Dave struggled to ease the wheels away from the continuous ribbon of gray steel that divided the two oncoming lanes. As he pulled the car back onto the road, ending the long stream of red sparks emitted from the friction of the grinding metals, he breathed a quick sigh of relief.

Kelly still clutched tightly to the dash, but her concern, now, was for the car, lest it break down and leave them short of their destination. "What is that?" she asked of the frapping noise under the hood.

"It's nothing. Don't worry about it," Dave said. "The radiator got pushed into the fan. I think it'll be okay. We can still go," he assured her. But Dave could smell the leaking antifreeze burning on the hot engine. He kept an eye on the heat sensor, wondering how long he could keep running until the engine overheated and seized up. He knew he was only a few miles from the fort, and the choices were to either nurse the engine and stretch the mileage, or go for maximum speed and coast along when the engine blew.

Believing time was the critical factor, he tramped the accelerator, pushing the car to speeds he had never dreamed of reaching before. Several miles were gained in a breath and Dave believed that if he could maintain control of the vehicle at these speeds, they would reach Ligonier in minutes. The adrenalin was coursing through his body, keeping his reactions swift and instinctive and his psyche encouraged. But the red indicator lights flicked on and he felt his foot pressing uselessly on the gas pedal. He looked at Kelly, his face displaying his fear and worry.

"What's wrong?" she asked, turning her head to him as she now noticed their decreasing speed. "What's the matter with the car?"

"The engine blew. We'll coast as far as we can, then we'll have to run."

"Oh, God! How much further is it?" Kelly asked, her voice desperate.

"I think only a couple miles or so," Dave answered, coaxing the car around the bends and praying for a long, sloping grade he knew did not exist on this stretch of road.

Their speed was decreasing more rapidly than Dave had anticipated and he began to believe he had made the wrong choice. Perhaps, he thought, he could have gained a few miles further if he'd chosen to pamper the engine instead of racing it. He began to feel the remorse already, blaming himself if they should arrive too late to save their friend. But an intersection sign just up ahead encouraged him. Route 711 crosses Route 30 directly beside the fort in Ligonier.

Dave knew they would be close enough to it when their glide ended. As they drifted by the sign he said, "Keep your fingers crossed. We're close!" Then he pulled the car to the berm with just enough momentum to clear it off the highway. He yelled for Kelly to, "C'mon!," grabbed the machete, and they sprang from the car. They could see the traffic light not a half mile distant and their feet tried torturously to match the cadence set by their pounding hearts as they ran for the lighted intersection.

Time seemed in slow motion for Dave as he ached to reach the crossroads. Though he was in good physical shape, he cursed his aging body, remembering a time in his youth when he could have sprinted the distance in a fraction of the time it seemed to take him now. When he did arrive, he breathed deeply to catch his wind and his eyes hastily surveyed where he should run next. Kelly came along beside him, panting heavily, and Dave asked her, "Where to?" for it was her dream that had brought them this route.

"The field!" she gasped, nodding to the long expanse to her right. "Try the field!"

Dave took off running and Kelly now matched his step as she gathered the energy for what she prayed would be the last leg of a life-saving sprint. When they reached the edge of the field, they again stopped to hurriedly study the area, straining to peer through the darkness. The field lay empty, and were Dave to have directed his scan onto Kelly's face instead of the surrounding landscape, he would have seen the anguish and despair that showed upon it.

"Do you see anything?" he asked, breathless and frantic. His eyes were fixed on and sweeping the graveyard on the hill across the road. It seemed to him the most logical place to search next.

Kelly, too, began to look across at the neat rows of numerous headstones that faded into the night far back over the hill. She felt as if she and Dave were on a stage below some ghostly amphitheater from which the dead were viewing the poignant efforts of two of the alive daring to rescue their friend from too soon joining the audience. A shiver ran through her as she envisioned Sam's spirit standing by a granite marker, silently watching them.

Dave nodded toward the graveyard. He put a hand on Kelly's arm, intending to start them both moving that way when she glanced a last, hurried look over her shoulder to the woods at the far end of the field. The lights from a passing car making a turn at the intersection swept across the broad field and chanced to flash against a small red reflector just inside the tree line. "There!" Kelly cried, knowing the momentary illumination could only have been from a vehicle.

They hurried across the field, moving through the darkness in the direction Kelly had spotted the small glint of red. When they neared the woods they slowed their approach, cautiously stealing up to the white car parked just in the trees to determine if it was abandoned. Finding it empty, they peered over the roof and only then spied the glow of the fluorescent lamp, further in the woods.

They heard some grumbling from those around the light and Dave put a finger to his lips as a warning to Kelly to be silent and move quietly. He led her toward the light, carefully placing each step so not to be given up by a snapping twig or crinkling leaf. When they were near enough to view the figures gathered around the light they halted to watch and were aghast at what they saw.

Dave immediately recognized the shorter, stalky man holding the light. The arm in the cast and sling was proof enough that it was the same fellow with whom he'd fought in the parking lot in Antietam. The other two men he could not place, and if they had been party to the attack that night he could not determine. It had been dark and Dave had moved swiftly to disarm and disable the assailants.

Now, as he and Kelly peered through the limbs and leaves of the dense woods, they watched the three men surrounding Sam as he stood in a shallow pit. One of the men—a tall, lean, younger fellow with a nasty sneer on his lips—held Sam's hair tightly in his grasp, pulling his head back. The arm he held Sam with was cut deeply and dripped blood profusely. He held Sam's saber in the other hand, raised high in a threatening manner. "Fucker!" he hollered at Sam. "You want to cut? I'll show you cutting!" He released his hold on Sam's hair and drew back the sword to strike a blow.

"No!" the third figure shouted to stop the man before he could deliver the blade to Sam's head. "It's my turn, Simple. I owe him for my brother." The man then held a silencer equipped gun to Sam's temple. "It's bye, bye time..."

Kelly shrieked a deafening, "No-o-o...!" as she watched in horror when the man had placed the gun barrel to Sam's head.

Dave was already moving. He leapt through the tangled tree limbs in a desperate effort to reach the gun, flailing the machete and raising so frightful a yell as he'd only heard once before in his life—and that, by the very friend he was now trying to save. But on his way through the brush a muffled shot was heard, and Sam slumped to the ground.

****

Sam kept trying to steal glimpses of the men who stood over him. He was looking for any break in their guard, hoping for an opportunity to strike and attempt an escape. Rudy held the light by those fingers exposed from the cast, but held a small pistol in his good hand. Billy Ray, too, held a gun.

But he stood back too far from Sam's swinging radius. The third man, the one they called "Simple," held only the sword, and was not so mindful of his guard. He drank whiskey from a pint bottle and leaned against the hilt of the sword having jabbed the point into the ground.

The men talked in lowered voices as Sam dug. Billy Ray and Simple were truckers working for a firm in northern Florida that seemed to have close ties to Marco Development Corporation. They kept talking about enjoying the regular hauls of building materials as opposed to the long, hard hours spent over-the-road trucking. Sam believed Rudy was some lesser Teamster official who no longer drove and picked up extra cash to support heavy gambling debts by doing this sort of extra-legal work. All three were hardened men who portrayed a willingness to perform these tasks for hire with no misgivings. Sam knew he must try to get away.

"That's about deep enough," Billy Ray said when Sam had dug to about 18 inches. Simple took a long swig from the bottle and handed it over to Billy Ray. Sam now saw his chance and reacted swiftly. He swung the shovel at Rudy's hand, knocking the gun away, then whirled to slam the shovel into Simple's arm, the edge cutting flesh and dropping the man to the ground. Moving quickly, he turned to scramble out of the hole but his foot caught a root and he stumbled, falling flat. Billy Ray pounced on Sam's back, pinning him to the ground and holding the gun to his head. "You son-of-a-bitch!" he spat at Sam, then grabbed his hair and pulled him to his feet.

Simple recovered and gained his feet. He clutched his arm at the wound and came at Sam with a vengeance, drawing the knife from his belt. "Pull his pants down! Hold him down! I'm gonna' cut his nuts off for that," he sneered viciously.

Rudy stepped forward and held the light close to Sam as he stared directly into his face. He seemed to be thinking about whether to allow the two men their fun, or to just finish the job and move on. His stare was cold; evil. But Sam flinched not at all, returning the icy glare in kind. "Just do 'im and let's get the fuck outta here," Rudy finally said.

With a flick of his wrist Simple flung the knife downward, sticking the point into the ground. He grabbed the sword and moved in to crowd Billy Ray aside. "Let me do it!" he said, taking Sam's hair and jerking his head back forcefully so he could snort into his face. "Fucker! You want to cut? I'll show you cutting!" He released his hold and drew back the saber to strike a blow.

"No!" Billy Ray shouted to halt his companion before he could deliver the blade to Sam's head. "It's my turn, Simple. I owe him for my brother." Billy Ray took a step toward Sam and held the gun to his head. "It's bye, bye time...," he hissed, grinning malevolently.

A loud scream pierced the night and caused the men to look in the direction from where it came. Someone was crashing through the woods, emitting such a horrible wail that, for a moment, it gave them cause to consider fleeing. But the attack was coming from the direction of their car, blocking their escape. Then, too, they held guns and were quite ready and willing to use them. Simple held the saber high, aiming it to strike once the intruder showed himself. Rudy cocked the hammer of his gun and made ready.

Billy Ray paused and glanced into the trees. Like his companions, he, too, had a moment of panic as he heard the terrible approaching war cry, and his reaction was to fight. Believing there to be only one or two assailants, he determined to dispatch Sam promptly and then turn to this coming interruption.

Sam's heart beat wildly. In the instant of hearing the scream, followed by the fierce, banshee wail, he turned his head to see, knowing that cry could only be from Dave Cooper. With but a precious fraction of a second in which to react he instinctively dropped to the ground, hearing the muffled crack of a gun as he fell.

Sam lay in the trench and tried to ascertain the extent of the damage to his body. He was aware of the sounds of more shots being fired and recognized the unmistakable clash of steel swords above him. He blinked repeatedly as he accounted for his limbs and torso. His head was still intact and he felt no pain anywhere on his body.

He wasn't dead. He wasn't even injured! Relieved, but spending no time rejoicing, he made his way to his feet to discern events above, lest Dave should need his help. When he stood, he looked around, confused and shaken, but ready to fight or flee. He saw Dave standing poised with the machete cocked, aimed at a now empty-handed Simple. Rudy had dropped his gun and held his one good hand up in a sign of surrender. Billy Ray lay dead on the ground, a bullet through his forehead. Sam surveyed the scene around him and looked to Dave for an explanation.

Kelly now sprang from the thick branches where she had been hiding. She ran to Sam, sobbing in jubilation at seeing him unhurt, but also at having witnessed the violent confrontation that had occurred. She threw herself against him, crying, "Sam! You're all right!" as she clasped her arms about him.

Sam put an arm around her, returning her embrace. But seeing her only compounded his confusion. He saw Dave keeping a vigilant eye on Simple and Rudy, but continually looking at the trees on his left as if expecting someone to step out into view. The two other men were also watching in that direction, though they cowered nervously.

Sam pulled the light from a stunned and trembling Rudy and aimed it in the direction in which all eyes were turned. A lone figure stepped from behind a thickly branched pine tree and moved closer to the group. A handsome fellow in his early thirties, he had a round, clean-shaven, boyish face with neatly combed, thick, black hair. Of average build, and just shy of six-feet tall, he wore a blue blazer, khaki slacks, and held a silencer-equipped automatic.

He moved casually but carefully around the group, keeping Rudy and Simple under the gun, and all eyes followed him as he went to the body lying on the ground. "Well, this is sure going to complicate things," he harrumphed as he nudged the body to be certain no life remained within it.

Sam cocked his head and squinted suspiciously. As the fellow bent down to pick up Billy Ray's gun he asked, "Who are you?"

Disarming the weapon and stuffing it into his belt the man looked at Sam with a boyish grin. "Well, tonight I'd guess I'm your guardian angel."

"Cutting it pretty close, don't you think?" Sam said as the man moved and snatched up Rudy's gun from the ground. This, too, he cleared of ammunition, then slid it into his coat pocket. He stood behind Rudy and frisked him with one hand, searching for other weapons. "Well, it was my call," the man explained. "I had to weigh the decision to get involved or not."

Sam gave a sarcastic grin as some understanding came to him from the last comment. "Spoken like a true government employee. C.I.A.?"

"Mm—mh," the man shook his head. "N.S.A... C.I.A. isn't allowed this type of work in the country. They passed it on to us. Seems they were concerned about a security breach. They were curious why you were snooping through their computer without proper authorization. I was assigned to the investigation. You've got some pretty impressive credentials, Mr. Baker. I decided it would serve the national interest if you were kept around awhile longer. I wasn't supposed to get involved, but it was my call. I could play it as needed." The agent gave a resigned sigh and looked down at the lifeless form on the ground. "Now I've got a real mess to deal with."

Sam could feel Kelly quiver against him, trying to keep her eyes from the lifeless form on the ground. He tried to calm her by holding her tight while he talked to the agent. "Are they going to investigate Marco Development?" he asked. "You guys must know about James Brody and his dealings."

"We went over what you were delving into, certainly. We had to learn why you were snooping into that company's records. You weren't all that discreet about using Langley's gear. We figured you left a trail on purpose. We followed it and had a look. Whether it'll be pursued on our part is up to my supervisors. They may turn it over to Justice; they may not. It touches some pretty high offices in Washington." The agent sighed again as he looked at the corpse. "In any event, I've got to come up with a cover story why this guy is dead in case they don't want to get any more involved. I've got to clean this up quick. You three can help by clearing out and going on home. It'd be best if you weren't around in case the local cops show up." The man looked at Dave and asked, "Where'd you park?"

"Park?" Dave echoed, a frown turning down one corner of his mouth. "I didn't. I blew the engine back about a half mile or so down the road. I hit a deer and banged the car up pretty badly."

"That GTO?" the agent exclaimed. "What a shame! That was a great car."

"You saw it?"

"Sure I did. I had the house under surveillance. Man! That's too bad. Can you get a ride?"

"Yeah. I can call my wife. She'll come for us," Dave told him.

"Good. You can call her from my van. It's parked around the corner by that log fort. My partner's in it. He'll take care of you." The young man pulled a small radio transmitter from his coat pocket and began to speak into it, informing his partner of the situation, then relaying instructions. When he closed the set, he again told Sam they were all free to go.

"That's it?" Sam asked, hardly able to believe he would not be needed to hang around for an investigation.

"Yeah. That's it," the agent replied. "I told you; I've got to handle this discreetly. I'd really prefer none of you were here. There'll be someone from the agency stop by to talk to you in a few days. Don't speak to any law officers and, please, not a word to any news people. We'd just deny everything."

"Who'd believe me, anyway?" Sam shrugged. He made a move to leave, then stopped and looked at the younger man. "Listen. Thanks for taking him down. That was almost me lying there."

The man just nodded to Sam. "No problem. Glad I was around to help."

They turned and walked across the field toward the road in silence, their thoughts reflecting on an evening so full of violence and a score of days that had proven so bewildering. The further they distanced themselves from the brutal place that was plotted to serve as Sam's murder and burial site, the more their spirits were consoled that this whole incredible episode was finally concluding. They perceived themselves as having been like marionettes these last few weeks, led through a series of motions that were directed from the supernatural. Sam and Dave had hoped for a few restful days of escape from the hectic pace of their busy lives—a quiet interlude during which they could pursue their favored interest in the Civil War.

Instead, they had found themselves embroiled in a confrontation with a dangerous and powerful company. Too, they had conjuncted with mystical forces that continued to hold them in fascination and awe, enhanced by a curious old lady in Maryland.

Kelly had wanted to pass the summer quietly, performing some worthwhile charitable pursuit that would occupy her time until the fall semester took her north. A score of days in that lazy, southern, mid-summer's heat had, instead, brought her mystery, intrigue—and Sam Baker. As she walked toward the road and felt his arm slip around her shoulders, there welled from the very depths of her being a certain awareness—a subliminal signal—that allowed her to feel a peaceful relief.

For all her brushes with jeopardy these last two weeks there now came a tranquility that seemed to touch her spirit like a warm wind blowing the chill from her body. She remembered Carol's remarks about "woman's intuition" and believed she must now be realizing such an occurrence, as there seemed no other way to account for this peculiar sense of certainty. Glad to believe the dangers were at end—and so, perhaps, the odd, chilling dreams, as well—she rejoiced in having met and fallen in love with the man whose arm was now tenderly comforting her. In a sudden rush of emotions, tears began to flow down her cheeks.

Dave noticed Kelly's tears and reached to put a sympathetic arm around her waist. She sniffled and wrapped her arms around both men and hugged them closer.

They found the van cloaked in the shadow of a large maple tree in the parking lot of the fort, just off the highway. The side door opened as they neared it and a shorter, round, bespectacled man leaned out. He looked to be in his mid-fifties, wearing a white shirt with brown suspenders. Clean shaven, he had thinning brown hair, neatly combed to the side. He had no facial expressions except for looking tired, and his demeanor was businesslike.

The van was crammed full of electronic surveillance and communication equipment, and as the agent remained seated in a captain's chair, he motioned for them to be patient while he spoke into the mouthpiece of a radio headset. Dave and Sam recognized that the man was relaying landing coordinates and believed he was summoning a helicopter to aid in the clean up operations. When his message and instructions were transmitted, he moved the mouthpiece down out of the way. "You must be Cooper," he said correctly to Dave.

"Yeah," Dave answered.

The agent reached to a wall on his left and lifted one of several telephone receivers from its hook. He handed it to Dave and promptly spun the chair around to a computer keyboard. "What's the number?" he asked, his fingers poised over the keys in readiness. As Dave repeated the numbers the man typed it into the computer.

Carol answered after several rings and Dave told her simply that he'd hit a deer with the car and that she must make arrangements to come and get him. In answer to her queries about how he ended up in Ligonier, he explained he went for a drive after leaving Sam's and was taking a circuitous route home.

He thought it too complicated to try to explain over the phone that he had coincidently ran into Kelly at a gas station; that, heeding a fantastic dream the woman had had, they raced at incredible speeds in pursuit of anonymous people they believed had kidnapped Sam, and arrived just in time to see one of the men shot dead. Dave decided to wait until he saw his wife in person to tell her the whole story.

He made one other call, this to a towing company, making arrangements to have the car taken to his house. Then, while they waited for Carol, the three walked to a nearby convenience store for a cup of coffee. They sat on the curb outside the well-lighted store and talked little but for some trivial comments that filled the void between personal thoughts.

When they returned to the fort parking lot, they found the van was gone, the agent probably having driven into the woods to join his partner. They moved to a wooden park bench along the perimeter of the lot and, there, sat to await Carol's arrival.

Not an hour after he'd called her, Carol pulled up in her two-year-old Buick and stopped beside the bench. The three stood to greet her, and, when Carol got out of the car, the widest look of surprise was across her face. She hurried to Dave and hugged him, exclaiming, "Oh! Thank God you're all right!"

Dave reassured her he was fine. Then, for the bewildered and quizzical look she wore at seeing Kelly and Sam with him, he let her stutter through her questions of how and why the two were present. He told her the entire story, finishing only a moment before they heard the storming whirl of a large helicopter roar in overhead. It circled in a wide arc only once, then hovered directly over the center of the field. A large spotlight was switched on under it to scan the perimeters of the field as the machine then quickly descended.

Dave and Sam hurried with the two women to the edge of the field and looked on as the searchlight was aimed at the edge of the woods where the Cadillac had entered. The taillights and reflectors of the car were illuminated and they could see a handful of men moving about quickly in the woods. The long, churning blades of the helicopter remained at an increased throttle, indicating it did not plan to remain on the ground long. Cars were already beginning to slow or stop as passing motorists sought an inquisitive look.

"I'll have to ask you people to stay back," came a voice from near them in the darkness. It took them some time to adjust their eyes from the light to the darkness off to their left, but they focused on the figure of a young man not fifteen feet from them. He stood as a perimeter guard, dressed in black military fatigues. They said nothing in reply to the man, but looked again at the activity under the light. Rudy and Simple were being hurried, under guard, to the helicopter, and two men carried a litter with the body of Billy Ray on it, stuffed into a black body bag.

The soldier on guard was speaking to someone through a small radio, his voice too soft for them to hear what was said. But one of the figures left the escort and began moving toward them. As he drew close they recognized him as the agent they'd first encountered and saw he now carried Sam's sword and machete. "Baker," he said when he got directly in front of Sam. "I believe these are yours."

"Thank you," Sam answered, taking them from the man.

"Did they take anything else from you? Any money, rings, watches?"

When Sam replied that they hadn't the agent nodded to the soldier who promptly hurried back to board the waiting machine. Several other figures who had fanned out to guard the area also retreated to now appear at the doorway and jump on. The agent held up his radio and spoke only, "Andrews; clear." The blades immediately increased rotation and, as quickly as it had lighted, the unmarked machine lifted off, roaring away into the night.

"Well," the agent shrugged, "guess now I wait for the tow truck. Damn! I've got a mountain of paperwork to do over this." He looked at Sam and grinned. "Don't go getting into any trouble tomorrow. You won't be so lucky as to have me trailing you around."

Sam made no reply to the man but to tighten his lips and nod slowly in a silent gesture of thanks.

The agent said goodnight to them, then moved off to cross the field. As they watched him disappear into the darkness, Dave put an arm around Carol's shoulder and hugged her nearer. "Well. Let's go home," he said, feeling her return his hug by wrapping her arm around his waist. In a voice that sounded with as much relief as they were all feeling, he added, "I think it's over." Then he turned with Carol to lead them back to the parking lot.

Sam and Kelly lingered behind, letting the two go on without them. They faced and gazed at one another for a long moment and, though neither spoke the words, their eyes mirrored similar thoughts. They were considering all they had been through in the short time they had known each other, but more, they were pondering the mysterious enchantment and powerful attraction between them. Then, as though prompted to move on some mentally telegraphed cue, they drew together in a loving embrace and kissed passionately.

****

Dressed only in a pair of blue satin boxers, Sam leaned against the doorframe of his study and took a long swallow of coffee. He surveyed the mess of papers and books strewn across the floor from the incident last night and sighed as he thought of all the time that would be required to sort and rearrange his files and notes. Then he shrugged, determining to put it all behind and not let it bother him. It would be a nuisance chore and would certainly consume time better spent in so many other areas, but he would get it done and move on. It was of small concern, he reasoned, considering what he'd been through.

He entered the room, moving to the desk and workstation, and glanced at the stack of facsimile papers gathered in the receiving tray, then at the computer messages sent him from the job he had only recently reported to. He grimaced at the thought of the amount of work ahead of him later in the day. Normally, he would have plunged right into it, not taking time even to shower or dress, ordering delivery meals to avoid interruption as he'd spend hours pouring over data. Sundays, holidays, morning and night all blended together to Sam. No one particular day was special from another. As long as he could lose himself in his work he was fine. He enjoyed what he did and received a satisfaction at being on the cutting edge of an industry that advanced in leaps and bounds—for he knew he was one of those creating the leaps, developing the new technologies and finding practical applications for them.

Not this morning, he mused. This morning was for himself, and the rest of the world would have to wait awhile for anything more he would give it. He was feeling relaxed and contented—alive! He was viewing the world with a fresh and rejuvenated attitude and he wanted to dwell on the feeling, to relish it.

Sam set his coffee cup down on the desk and picked up the sword and machete he'd set down when Carol and Dave had dropped him off last night. When he replaced them on their hangers, he stood back a few paces to study them, contemplating how close in proximity to his own death both instruments had been associated. Having faced it so often, Sam knew he had no fear of actually dying. In the past, as he could remember from back in his war years, he had accepted it as inevitable since it was all around him. Then, he feared only that he might be struck down before he had had a chance to really experience life—for, to live with death every day, he believed, given the chance, he would enjoy and appreciate life all the more when he returned home.

Now, his care was only of not having enough time in which to love Kelly—a frivolous concern since the intrigues of the Antietam affairs were now ended.

As Sam stared at the magnificent saber—the fine inlay, the delicately worked etchings of a home, a mill, and some other buildings—he wondered what significance they held for whomever it had been fashioned. Truly, he believed, it was an honor to have acquired the piece, regardless of how it had come to him.

The longer he gazed at the etched stills, the further his mind floated, until, incredible as the thoughts might seem to him, Sam felt he had to consider if he, indeed, couldn't lay rightful claim to the sword's ownership. It felt as much a part of belonging to him as anything else he owned. He began to wonder if all that Varina Schiels had alluded to might be true after all. Perhaps, he thought, he had little fear of death because it had, in fact, allowed him the comfort of at least the slightest glimpse of its mystery—that we do live again. Had he carried this knowledge deep in his subconscious all his life, he wondered, brought to the light of mind only recently? If some mystical door had been left ajar to him, why not try to push it open just a bit more?

Sam closed his eyes and tried to quiet his mind of all present, distracting thoughts, concentrating on his mind's eye in the middle of his forehead. He brought forward visions of events in his past, continually regressing to his earliest childhood memories, hoping he might be able to think back even further—just one small memory from past life. When he became stuck on a memory from age three, he tried to contain his frustration, knowing it would interfere with the regression process.

But instantly and uncontrollably, a vision drifted by—the horrific dream he'd had in the motel in Hagerstown. He could see the prone form of that young, Union officer, dying on the field of battle. Sam's heart fluttered as he recalled the instant of having traded places with the boy—of looking into those red, swollen, frightened eyes and then, suddenly, momentarily, being that boy!

Standing there with his eyes closed and his mind focused intensely on that thought, he tried to recreate the feeling that caused him to gasp when he'd looked up to see himself leaning over the prostrate form. His hope was for some long-forgotten memory to be stirred that would permit him to peer into another age—another lifetime. He needed only again to be a moment in that young boy's mind—his own long forgotten memory.

His thoughts were interrupted abruptly by a pair of arms encircling his chest. They were soft and gentle arms, and they squeezed him tenderly.

"What are you doing?" Kelly asked him, planting several warm kisses across his broad shoulders.

"Just standing here, looking at my memories. How you doin'?" he asked, enjoying the feel of her warm body pressed against him.

"Me? Oh, I'm fine," she purred. "Feeling wonderful."

"Me, too," Sam said, turning to face her. She had slipped on his blue satin robe and Sam enjoyed how cuddly erotic it hung on her. He thought of opening the loosely-tied belt and attempting to fit into it with her as he gathered her close and their lips met for a long, warm, romantic moment. When the kiss ended, Sam smiled down to her. "Good morning."

"Good morning," Kelly replied, returning his pleasantry with her own endearing smile. "How long have you been up?"

"Oh-h...I don't know. Not long," Sam answered as Kelly disentangled herself from him and reached for his coffee mug. "I made coffee and stared out the window awhile. I've just been, sort of, wandering around the house, looking into different rooms, having little fantasies of what life could be like here...with you in it," he added.

Kelly was in mid-sip on the coffee and swallowed hard with his added sentiment. Flustered a little, she hid her smile behind the coffee mug. "Why...Sam...What are you talking about?"

Now it was Sam whose face flushed as he realized he'd mentioned it. He hadn't wanted to bring up the idea just yet, but he had thought to soon warm her to it; to "test the waters," at any rate. So, now that the subject was out, nervously he pushed ahead. "Um. I mean. Uh...I think you ought to, um, live here this winter...with me," he stammered. Then he spoke rapidly, trying to express it all at once. "I mean, why should you pay for an apartment somewhere? This is a big house with plenty of room and, after all, we have grown fond of each other and I'd really be thrilled having you here and sharing it with me."

He lowered his head to hide his deepening blush and paused to both gather his thoughts and to allow Kelly a moment to consider his rambling request. He raised an eye from under his brow and spoke in a gentle, boyish innocence. "I'd, uh...I'd really miss you if you weren't here."

Kelly's heart fluttered. She lowered the cup and her eyes followed it. "Oh-h...," she gasped as the only verbal response she could summon—and this, involuntarily.

"Kelly?" Sam asked, puzzled by her reaction. "Did I suggest something you're uncomfortable with?"

Kelly found it hard to look directly at him. She was red with embarrassment as she bit her lower lip and wrestled with her explanation. "Well, I...I've often thought of...what it'd be like to...live with a man. I mean, I've fantasized about it, of course. But none of the men I've ever known were...well, I've never done that. They weren't suitable candidates for me to... Until you," she said, looking at him through tender, caring eyes. "I'll...I'll have to think about it, Sam. That would be a big step for me. I, um, I know my parents would be uncomfortable with it."

Sam could see Kelly was upset. He reached and took her hand and squeezed it, saying, "Fine. Just think about it. And if you decide not to, I'll help you look for a place of your own. But, mind! It'll be nearby; within walking distance."

Kelly drew close to Sam to hug him, then leaned up to kiss his cheek.

Sam was a little angry with himself. He regretted having asked her to move in with him in such a bungling manner. Being the 80s, it had seemed a natural next step before marriage. How could he have known that it would disturb her so. He was impressed that she was so obviously embarrassed at the idea and, too, that she considered her parents' feelings.

It served to underscore that Kelly was someone special, with principles that seemed to shame his own. He feared now that if she did agree to move in with him it would be out of her love for him, and a compromise of those principles.

He wished he'd proposed marriage, or at least an engagement, but knew the timing had passed. Now he would have to wait until the opportunity again presented itself.

Kelly read the awkwardness clearly revealed on Sam's face and turned her head for a glance at the desk clock. She looked up at Sam with a scintillating smile and wrapped her hands to cradle the back of his neck. "You know, I don't have to be heading back for several hours, yet," she purred, pulling him down to plant a warm kiss on his neck. She took one of his hands in her own and moved it to the tie of the robe.

Chapter Nineteen

Saturday, August 20

Though we may all aspire to some greatness the larger number of us are never led to such prominence that we are heralded by our fellows. We are not marked in time or memory for having directed some event that impacts our civilization. We are but the commoners, living ordinary lives in a not so particularly romantic era (the present never is to those within it; only the past). For many of us it is intrinsic to our nature to reflect upon periods of history and romanticize having lived in some other time.

We are brought closer to those imaginings when we visit historic sites that have been restored and preserved. Like windows into the past, they serve to lend a perspective by which we might gain an appreciation of life in a bygone era. They provide the scenery—the mind supplies the drama. For but a fleeting moment we are a cannoneer on the deck of a wooden frigate, pulling the lanyard to give a broadside to an English man-o'-war. We are a '49er panning for gold in a cold mountain stream in California. We are a friend to George Washington, visiting his home to consult on the problems of forming the new government. We are any Private Smith, hunkered down behind a stone wall by a small grove of trees at Gettysburg, watching the Confederate troops approach in a spectacular wide front not a mile distant.

Not often are we so affected by a historic site. Usually we tour the attraction, and though we are left with a stronger sympathy for what occurred there, we are not given to the passions with which another person might regard that place.

But there is sometimes a particular site that intrigues us. It seems almost to beckon us, summoning to us for repeated visits and drawing us to it with a fascination we cannot explain even to ourselves. We are abstractly reverenced by it, pausing often as if prayerfully absorbing its quintessence—as though we are unconsciously waiting to view—or relive—an experience that has long slipped from memory, leaving only the dust of emotions—and that, felt so powerfully.

****

Dave Cooper hurried home from work to change and pack for the overnight stay in Harpers Ferry. Though he'd had to work the morning, he wheeled into his driveway around noon, his spirits high for the opportunity to be returning to western Maryland. He had a certain fondness for Harpers Ferry.

The steep commanding mountains that overlook the little settlement never change from year to year. Nor does the inspiring scenic confluence of the Shenandoah with the Potomac. Lingering idly by the side of one of the town's restored streets Dave could envision the ghost of "Stonewall" Jackson passing by to take occupation of the town, or see the ranks of blue uniforms parading in step to the music and cadence of their regimental bands. It drew him back often, and he deemed it fortunate to live in proximity to a place so preserved when so many others had fallen to the developer's wrecking ball and excavator.

Jeff and Sarah were having lunch when Dave entered the side door leading into the kitchen. He greeted them cheerfully and talked awhile to catch up on their morning. When he left them and went back to the bedroom he found Carol under the blanket, slumped against the headboard on two stacked pillows. A box of tissues was on the bed beside her and a bottle of cough syrup sat on the nightstand.

"Hi, Honey," Dave said in sympathy as he looked down at her. "Feeling any better?"

Carol made an attempt at a smile for him but dropped it as the effort was too great and not necessary anyway. "Not really," she answered. "It's a full-fledged cold, now."

"Aw-w. Too bad. Summer colds are the worst. You're not going with me then, I'd guess."

Carol pulled a tissue from the box and blew her nose. She looked up at him with such a sickly expression that the answer was obvious.

"Too bad. Would you rather I stayed home and took care of you?"

"No. No. You should go. Sarah and Jeff can look after me. You're only going for one night. I'll be okay," she assured him. "Besides, Sam called a little while ago. He's stuck at work and can't get off until four. So, you really don't have to rush off right away."

"Fine," Dave replied to this news with a shrug. He was glad he could stay awhile longer to help tend to Carol, but saddened a little, too, that the journey he'd been so excitedly anticipating would be delayed. "I'll make you some chicken soup," he told her. "Good for what ails thee."

****

Sam Baker picked out a fast-moving trailer-truck on the interstate and drew up behind it. Keeping a distance of several car lengths he matched its speed of 75 mph, figuring the trucker would have word of any speed traps up ahead by way of his CB radio. Sam was as desirous of arriving in Harpers Ferry as his friend beside him in the DeLorean. "Damn! You know we're going to be late, don't you?" he remarked, glancing at the clock in the dashboard.

"Yeah. I know," Dave replied. "We'll check into the motel, dump our bags and be gone. I'm not changing. I'm just wearing this," he said in reference to how he was dressed. He wore a fashionable, cocoa brown, cotton twill sports coat and white dress shirt—collar open and minus the tie—slacks to match the coat, and loafers—minus the socks.

Sam, dressed similar in style but in charcoal gray with a black shirt, nodded in agreement. "Me, too. I couldn't figure for the life of me what you're supposed to wear to something like this. I guess this is appropriate enough."

They checked into the motel rooms in Harpers Ferry around 9:00 P.M. Anticipating Carol was to have accompanied them, two rooms had been reserved and would be charged against their accounts. So, they chose separate keys, tossed their bags on the beds and were quickly off again.

Their destination was the Schiels farm. The reason for their hurry was the party to celebrate having saved the old farm from development. On such short notice there were no social halls in the area that could be secured for accommodating the several hundred guests that were anticipated. Nor, either, were there funds enough in the budget to afford such a place if they could have located one. Someone on the ad hoc social committee made the suggestion that it would be fitting to investigate using the huge barn on the Schiels farm if it could be determined to be sound enough to hold everyone.

Tom Charles examined the structure and found that, though the roof was wanting for repairs and many sheeting boards were missing, the structural integrity of the timbers proved quite adequate to hold the crowd. "Just pray it doesn't rain," he joked to everyone. "Barring that, we should be pretty cozy."

A group of volunteers worked long evenings to sweep and patch the floors, pull down cobwebs and put up lights and decorations. Long tables were borrowed and set up in one of the large, empty haymows for refreshments. Fresh bales of hay were brought in and positioned around the barn for seating.

The Historic Antietam Foundation was fortunate to count as members and contributors several Civil War re-enactment companies. One such group was a regimental band, formed by a handful of fellows from eastern Pennsylvania. They wore the uniforms and played instruments and music authentic to the

Civil War period. When they received their invitations to the affair they asked if they could provide the entertainment for the evening, waving their normal fees for such an engagement as a form of donation. Their request was gratefully accepted and another haymow, this one above the large grain bin and just inside to the right of the barn entrance, was cleaned and prepared for use by the band.

****

It was dark when the little silver DeLorean bounced and jostled over the rough and rocky surface of the long driveway that led down to the old Schiels farm. When they crested the hill that would begin their descent to the farm buildings, Dave and Sam could see the bright yellow light escaping through the gaps and holes in the tin roof on the huge old barn, then the long, uniform strips as the light diffused between the spacings of the vertical sheeting boards.

Luminary candles were lined on both sides of the drive, adding a festive spirit to the old place as they lit a cheerful path down to and around the broad circular driveway. In the center of the wide circle, a fire was burning. People stood around it sipping soft drinks or punch from plastic cups, and others could be seen milling around outside the barn or passing over the earthen barn bridge to enter or exit through the wide-spaced doors.

Cars were parked first around the circular driveway, then over into an old hayfield where they formed neat rows. As Sam steered into the hayfield Dave remarked that there seemed to be a good turn-out for the event.

Sam nodded in agreement. "Yeah, Kelly said they received over two hundred replies, some as far away as Michigan and Florida. That's great. You need something like this to bring the members closer together. They'll be more inclined to dig deeper into their pockets," he said, pulling into a space beside a sleek, black Mercedes at the end of one row.

When the two men got out of the car they stretched and looked around at the dark, low hills shadowed against a slightly brighter sky. Stars filled the heavens as plentiful as handfuls of confetti and the moon shone so brilliant as to send its beams as a faint spotlight onto the Earth.

"I like this area," Sam declared with a deep breath of the scent of new mown hay. "The low hills, the scenic pastures and fields. There's so much history here. It's rich with stories of people's lives spent clearing the rocks and trees from the fields, scratching out a living from the soil; armies trampling over it on their way to battle…yeah-h. I could live here."

Dave groaned and shot his friend a look of aggravation. "Shut up, Sam. I just got you living closer to me. You aren't moving."

"I meant, some day," Sam explained, smiling over how Dave had taken the wistful comment. "Down the road. Not immediately."

"Hm-m-m...," Dave responded, pretending to keep a suspicious eye on Sam.

The lively melody that the band began to play drew their attention back to the barn. They headed over toward it, glancing at the people who were milling around the fire but failed to recognize anyone familiar. They moved only a few more paces and Dave pulled at Sam's arm, halting him. He pointed through the flames at two figures moving slowly toward the house. "Look. There's Varina Schiels and that girl. What's her name? Cleo, or Betty, or something."

"Wilma," Sam corrected him.

"Yeah. Wilma. That's it. We should go say hello," Dave said, though Sam was already taking a step in that direction.

Wilma was dressed in a faded, white cotton blouse with ruffles down the front. Her overweight form in a black, too tight skirt that stopped several inches above her knees, was a striking contrast to the more slender, petite form of the older woman wearing an ankle-length, emerald voile dress. Varina's white hair was thickly braided and twisted in a neat bun well above the high collar. A shawl covered her shoulders, and relying on a cane to help in her shuffle back to the house, she looked handsome, but older and more delicate than when they'd seen her before.

When they caught up with the older woman and the plump, young girl Sam hailed them. "Varina...! Wilma...! Hello!" he hollered, coming up to them as they halted their steps and waited.

Wilma looked back and smiled to them. "It's them Yankee fellers. The ones who came vizit'n."

"I know who it is," Varina answered. "I can tell by their voices."

When the two men came around in front of them, they greeted Wilma and Varina cordially. "Good evening, ladies," Sam said with a slight bow. "Nice to see you again."

Varina responded with only the slightest upward turn of one corner of her mouth.

"Are you okay?" Dave asked her. "You're using a cane."

Varina nodded slowly, answering, "Yes. Just feeling my years tonight, is all."

Standing before her, Sam proudly announced with a slight chuckle, "Well...as you can see, I'm still alive. Almost wasn't though. That was too close, I must say. I wish you'd have warned me a little better."

"About what?" Varina asked him. "You don't look dead to me. What's the trouble?"

Sam startled at her sharp reply. "Well...none, really. I'm just saying I wish I'd have been more prepared for what happened to me."

"And you'd have done what?" Varina snapped. "You couldn't have avoided it. My telling you about it wouldn't have prevented it from happening. You'd have just worried and plotted needlessly. Death was watching, but that's all it was doing. You've seen its face before, Sam. Nobody ever told you about it before."

"No. That's true," Sam replied quietly. He felt a bit embarrassed and awkward at the rough handling by this older woman.

Wilma shrugged and gave a little laugh. "Eh! Don't mind her none. She's feelin' 'orn'ry t'nite. She's just played out from all tha' 'citment. She aint used t' it."

Varina gave a slow, deliberate blink and cast a sidelong glance of irritation at the girl over her attempt at an excuse. "Dear, go and see how my husband is. It's been a while since we've looked in on him."

Wilma chuckled loudly and said goodnight to Sam and Dave, telling them, "It was nice t' see ya'll a'gin." She started for the house and over her shoulder she reminded Varina not to stay out too late.

The older woman harrumphed and shook her head has she watched Wilma go. "Who wouldn't be 'orn'ry cooped up all day with her as company?" she mumbled. But as if in afterthought a gentle smile came to the woman's face and she spoke more to the wind than to the two men before her. "Oh-h...she means well enough, though." When she shifted her gaze to Sam and Dave the usually clear, piercing green eyes were now blissless and misty. She readjusted her uneasy lean on the cane and swallowed hard, then spoke apologetically, offering both an explanation of her behavior and a confession. "The world I've known all my life is coming to an end," she told them. "Milward and I will be leaving soon...for one of those rest homes. Rest homes, indeed! It's where you go to wait for death. You're herded about like so much sick cattle. Folks soon enough forget about you and quit visiting, not that I've got anyone left to come visiting me anyway."

Varina swallowed again and turned slightly to scan the old buildings, now fallen to disrepair. "I was born and raised on this farm. Milward, on a farm just over two hills. It used to really be something. Horses, cows, chickens, pigs; everything. The buildings were always kept painted fresh; the gardens were lush. Oh, the gardens," she sighed, pausing a moment to remember. "They're still back there," she continued. "Overgrown and needing tended, but still blooming every year."

Varina's moistening, green eyes were fixed on the house and she nodded toward it. "My husband was strong and handsome, you know," she said proudly.

"I'm sure he was," Sam replied, watching her move in a slight, straining twist for a glance back at the barn from where *Aura Lea* could be heard filtering so softly and emotionally.

"Oh, he liked to dance. So full of life and laughter, he was. Swept me right off my feet!" she declared. "It was a harvest fest we had in those days, right after corn was picked. Haymows were full, corn cribs were bursting... I was naught but sixteen. Milward had the eye of every girl around, each wondering if he'd ask them to dance. But I knew. My mother had shown me how to read the cards by then. They never lie. I just had to learn to be patient. Not easy for a sixteen-year-old who was blossoming out. He came right up to me and asked for a dance. Oh-h..., and we never stopped—till he had the accident, least ways. Hasn't been any music on this old farm since," she sighed, lowering her eyes to the ground.

"That's too bad," Sam said to her. "But it's good you had it while you did. What's that expression: 'to appreciate life you have to appreciate music and dance. It's the outward expression of the soul giving thanks to God'."

Varina turned an ear to the music behind her and nodded to affirm what Sam said. "It's good to hear it again; to watch the young folks dance. Saddens me, though. I'm past my time for it."

Now it was both Sam and Dave's turn to swallow hard as they listened to the older woman and tried to think of an appropriate response. Dave finally cleared his throat and inflected his voice to sound optimistic. "Well, now, maybe things will work out for you in your move. Who knows? Things might not be as bad as you think. They'll have activities for you; trips you can go on; people you can socialize with..."

Varina glanced at him from under her brow, showing the slightest trace of a secretive disposition. "I know," she told him pointedly. She looked past the two men to the house. "My husband will die soon. It doesn't take a fortune teller to know that. Then it will be my turn," she sighed, leaning more heavily on the cane.

There was a long, uncomfortable moment in which both men exchanged awkward glances meant to prompt the other into filling the uneasy silence with a response. But, again, neither man could think of anything to reply to the woman's statements.

Varina was drifting in memories as she stared at the house for a long while. When she stood straight and looked at both men the snap returned to her voice. "Oh, don't be so cheerless," she said to them. "I'm just one other old woman among so many. You should live so long." She raised her cane and tapped the knob against Sam's chest. "Don't you concern yourself about me, young man. Your life is soon to take a marvelous turn."

"It is?" Sam asked, impatient to hear more. "How so?"

Varina just smiled mysteriously and turned her head toward Dave, though her eyes lingered on Sam as if to purposely tease him with her secrets. When she drew them away and set them on Dave she said, "Your wife, Carol, is very gracious. I look forward to her visits when I've moved. She'll be feeling better by tomorrow...and her cold will be gone in a few days. She just needed to rest awhile."

Dave nodded in thanks to the old woman for the information. He knew not to ask for any more, nor to show surprise that Varina was aware of Carol's health.

Sam was almost panged and he seethed for wanting her to elaborate on her prophecy. But, taking his cue from Dave's example, he restrained himself, grimacing slightly while trying to hide his frustration. "You're not going to tell me anymore, are you?" he asked, compelled to at least a gentle inquiry.

Before Varina could reply, a voice from over at the house called out, "C'mon, missy! You best be comin' in now." Wilma had come out onto the porch for the older woman.

Varina took a step to move off to the house and patted Sam's arm as she went by him. "Take care of yourselves, boys. We'll most likely all meet again sometime."

Sam and Dave watched her slow shuffle to the house where Wilma waited to help her up the steps. "I hate when she does that to me," Sam remarked. "I think I'd rather not be told anything than to be left dangling like this."

Dave put an arm on Sam's shoulder and chuckled over his friend's uneasiness. "C'mon," he said, giving a tug toward the barn.

The barn bridge was decorated on either side with colored lights strung along waist-high wooden stakes. Red, white and blue bunting was draped over this, as well as tacked overhead to the barn entrance. People were crowded just inside the broad doorways, talking, and watching in admiration those few couples who were brave enough to dance a lively two-step.

As Dave and Sam approached the wide-opened barn doors they saw Pat Morley emerge from the crowd leading a handsome fellow by the hand. They spied one another immediately and came together on the sloping earthen bridge. "Hey, Pat," Sam greeted her with a quick hug. "You're not leaving?"

"Mm...sorry," she said with a nod. "Heading back to the city. We're getting up early. Will and I are going biking." She then introduced her companion, a man prematurely gray in his early forties, of average build at five feet, seven inches.

Before further conversation could ensue, however, Tom Charles squeezed through the crowd to guide his wife out for a breath of air. When he saw his two northern friends talking to Pat Morley he steered his wife toward them. The genuine smile behind his beard broadened further. "Well, you made it!"

he exclaimed, his breathing labored just a bit. "We were beginning to wonder." Tom took a deep breath to catch his wind, chuckling through a gasp. "I haven't danced like that in years. It's refreshing."

"I keep telling him he doesn't get enough exercise," Tom's wife volunteered as he shed his tie and opened his top collar button. She was a pretty brunette, only an inch or so shorter than he. The stunning, pastel, knee-length dress she wore screamed "designer expensive." But the accompaniments—a simple beaded necklace with matching earrings, and her wedding ring—spoke of moderate humility. Little make-up could be noticed on her face as her healthy complexion required no added highlighting.

Dave explained that Sam's work had been the cause of their delay. Then he made apologies and regrets on Carol's behalf, telling of her suddenly coming down with a summer cold.

Tom expressed his sympathies for Carol, adding that he hoped she'd be feeling better soon. Then he laughed good-naturedly, saying, "as far as being held up at work, I don't really have that problem right now." The remark brought a humorous response of nods and smiles from the others. But Tom then said, "Actually, I'm kind of enjoying the time off. It's been a long time since the family has been able to sit down and eat meals together for more than three days in a row. I'm usually getting home long after my boys are in bed. By the way, you two don't know my wife, do you?" Tom added, only now realizing introductions were in order.

"Tom's just awful when it comes to remembering his social courtesies," his wife laughed. She extended her hand to the two men. "I'm Connie Charles."

Dave and Sam each shook hands with the lovely woman and exchanged greetings, learning that Pat and her friend had already become acquainted with her earlier in the evening.

"So. Now we have all the conspirators in one place," Connie joked, though there was a slight, underlying tone of concern in her voice. "I still don't believe you guys did that. I keep expecting the police to pull in the driveway to drag Tom away."

Sam tried to hide a mischievous grin at her alluding to the night of their illegal exploit. "It won't happen, Connie," he assured her. "There's no need to worry about that."

"I know. Tom keeps telling me that. But you guys could have gotten into really big trouble."

A few blushing grins were exchanged between them, but Tom caught the quizzical look on Will's face as the man seemed to wonder what was being discussed. In a bid to divert the conversation lest anyone should have to stretch an awkward truth in explanation, he looked at Sam. "So, I understand you had some sort of weird occult experience with this whole affair?"

"Pardon?" Sam asked, knowing full well what Tom meant but wishing he hadn't brought it up.

"I don't know, really. I only got it secondhand from Marylou. But wasn't there some stuff about Tarot cards and reincarnation or something? She said Kelly was telling her something about it?"

Sam furrowed his brow to feign a confused expression. He shook his head slowly in a display of uncertainty. "I don't know. I can't imagine what she might have been talking about." Then, as if suddenly remembering some trivial matter he added, "Oh, unless she's referring to Varina Schiels reading my fortune with the Tarot cards. It was amusing. Nothing much to it, really," he shrugged.

Now Tom looked confused. "Oh? I'm sorry. She made it sound all so mysterious; so fascinating. Something about you getting a sword and Kelly getting a letter delivered a hundred years after it was mailed. Something about you being related to the soldier they found up on the hill?"

Sam's face flushed as he realized Kelly had confided more in Marylou than he'd have wished, and the story was now being repeated by others. "Oh, people are reading more into this than they really ought to be. You know how the mind works. I'll tell you about it someday. It isn't that fascinating."

Pat was listening closely, her head cocked as her interest mounted. "Well, I hadn't heard any of this. Do tell, Sam."

Sam rolled his eyes. "It's not that big of a deal. But, yes, I'll tell you about it, too—someday."

Pat took that as enough not to pursue it any further and she made a humored, skeptical face to show him she didn't believe he ever would. She gave her excuses for having to leave and along with her date, exchanged farewells with the group. To Sam, she gave a warm hug and a peck on the cheek, extracting his promise to stay in touch with her. Sam assured her he would make every effort, then thanked her again for all her help. With a little wave of goodbye, Pat and Will turned to follow the candle-lighted path out to the hayfield.

"A wonderful girl," Sam said as they watched the two figures move into the darkness.

"Yes. So she is," Tom agreed. "We were fortunate to have her help."

Sam then looked toward the barn, saying, "Speaking of wonderful girls; is Kelly inside?"

Tom chortled with his reply, "Yeah. The last I saw her she was cornered by a group of older ladies. She asked about you earlier, but no one knew why you weren't here."

"Oh, yeah," Connie said as a smile lit her face. "Tom introduced me to her this evening. We heard you two were an item. She's a charming girl."

"She is that," Sam mused, turning one corner of his lips in smile. "You'll excuse me, then?" he asked, bowing slightly to Connie in a polite, formal gesture. He took his leave from the three and turned to enter the barn, squeezing through the guests congregated at the entranceway and found himself at the very edge of the dance perimeter.

The barn was divided into three large and separate bays, each measuring thirty feet wide and sixty feet deep. The center bay, where the wagons were once pulled in for unloading, was walled tonight by members and guests who stood socializing and watching the few couples who were dancing.

The open expanse to the left, separated by large, hand-hewn support columns and a three-foot-high plank wall, had served as hay storage. The floor was weaker there and had been roped off from use this evening to prevent anyone from injury. Buck Morganti sat on one of several hay bales in this section, just on the other side of the low wall. He was surrounded by a small handful of men, several of whom Sam recognized as county officials who had been in James Brody's escort the morning the grave had been discovered up on the hill.

The large bay on the right contained the granary. Made of tongue-and-groove boards, it measured twenty feet wide and was as deep as the thirty feet section. Once bursting full with wheat, oats and other grains, it stood empty now, its door slightly ajar with a rusted and broken hinge. In years past the flat roof of the granary had held hay stacked high to the barn roof. Tonight it scaffolded only the band, seated on metal folding chairs that were borrowed from Dennis Woods' catering company.

A corncrib had been built beside the granary, occupying another fifteen feet of the bay. The remainder of the room was allotted for straw storage and could not be seen well from where Sam was standing. Tables had been erected in the far corner for punch and desserts, and hay bales were arranged to serve as seating for the guests.

Sam could recognize only a few faces as he scanned the room in search of Kelly. Marylou was dancing with her husband, a dark-haired man her own height who sported a moustache and goatee. Too, he noticed a couple members of the Foundation's board of directors scattered around the circle of guests, but he could not see Kelly. He started to move around the crowded circle opposite where Buck Morganti was seated, hoping to avoid having Buck motion him over to talk when he so desired finding the one person who was his main reason for attending.

While Sam wove his way through the crowded room, he became focused only on finding Kelly. The music from the band and the talk and laughter from the crowd all blended into a background blur that he ignored as he looked around for her. He was conscious of seeing an occasional face turn toward him, and the person's lips moving in speech. But what they said, and what his reply might have been as he shook their hand in greeting, he was completely unaware. He could hear and feel his heart pounding; could feel the perspiration on his face; and could recognize the aching worry in his gut.

When he found himself arrived at the old corncrib, he took a moment to compose himself. The hurry to get his work completed that day, then the rushing drive south, the stagnant air in the barn on this hot August night—the overwhelming longing to see and be with Kelly—had all coalesced to affect on him a vertiginous sensation. He pulled a handkerchief from his back pocket and wiped his brow.

Then glancing through the wire screen of the crib he spied her. She was standing in front of the refreshment tables in that part of the bay that was obscured by the crib and granary. A group of older, well-heeled women had surrounded her, and though she smiled pleasantly as she spoke in answer to whatever they were discussing, Sam noticed her eyes were constantly looking over to that part of the room to where her vision had access.

Sam's heart leapt into his throat and he almost gasped when he spied her. On any other night she was beautiful. But this night she looked particularly enchanting to him. Perhaps, he reasoned, it was the way her eyes sparkled in the reflected light of the bare incandescent bulbs, or the way her golden hair was neatly pinned high to reveal a gentle, slender neck, adding an air of sophistication that served to enhance her attractiveness.

The long, print dress with matching belt and accessories seemed tailor-made to fit, and was cause for any man to give a second look and catch his breath. But mostly, Sam believed, her beauty was especial tonight because he knew it was for him that those eyes so fervently scanned the room, watching for the moment he'd step from the crowd of guests and come to her.

So completely intrigued by her charms, Sam propped an arm against the corncrib and watched her. As her eyes wondered again to the center bay, he could see her inviting lips move in speech to one of the women before her. But as her gaze swept past the corncrib it immediately returned again, focusing on the familiar form that was looking at her through the close-mesh wire. She paused in mid-sentence and her eyes widened in joy. Her friendly smile broadened considerably, and when Sam nodded in greeting, she returned it with a wink and a slight nod of her own.

Sam moved from the crib and followed a few paces along the low dividing wall to the gap that allowed entry to the strawmow. He pulled his eyes from her only for an occasional glance to be certain of his path.

The older woman Kelly had been chatting with was now looking at her curiously, wondering why she had cut her sentence short. When she glanced over to see what had distracted the younger woman and noticed the handsome fellow heading toward them with a light, intended step, she became flushed. "Oh!" she exclaimed, and looked again at Kelly. But on discovering the dreamy-eyed stare with which the woman was heartily anticipating the approach of the man, she exclaimed again, "Oh! Oh, my!"

This now drew the attention of the other ladies and they, too, now quieted their chatter to discern the cause of their friend's fluster. But, on observing what the first lady had noticed about the way the two younger people were eyeing each other, a few more "ohhs" were exclaimed by a few more blushing faces. They gathered back a few steps to allow the couple some space, yet huddled close enough to eavesdrop and observe what might later fuel their gossip.

"Hello," Sam said softly to Kelly when he'd come directly before her.

"Hello," she greeted him warmly, then added, "You're awfully late," as she blinked her eyes and pouted for the worry he'd caused her. But her face still beamed with the joy of his presence.

"I know. I'm sorry for that," Sam answered, reaching to take her hands in his. "Can we go outside? It's stuffy in here. I'd like to talk more privately."

"Well...um," Kelly stammered, glancing back uneasily to the older ladies.

The first gray-haired woman patted Kelly's arm, and with an endearing smile, insisted, "You go on, dear. We'll help ourselves to some of these lovely desserts." She stepped between her friends and Kelly to herd the ladies toward the tables, saying, "My. Everything looks so delicious."

Kelly showed a bit of hesitancy, believing courtesy required her to continue her visit with these guests. She began to stammer again, but on seeing the woman pick up a plate and smile amicably to demonstrate that she pardoned her leave, Kelly excused herself to lead Sam off. They had not taken a few steps away when the silver-haired ladies crowded together in a buzz of comments, approving nods and blushing smiles.

When they entered the crowded center bay and began to wind their way to the entrance, Kelly leaned back to Sam to be heard above the noise. "I feel just a touch inhospitable."

"Why so?" he asked, turning an ear to better hear her.

"That woman back there; the one I was talking to? That was Mrs. Morganti."

"'The' Mrs. Morganti? Buck Morganti's wife?"

"The same," Kelly answered. "We were discussing how difficult it is for organizations to raise money. I was softening her up for the big hit."

"But I expected Buck would make a sizeable contribution even aside from what the McPherson Foundation contributes."

"I'm sure he will. But I was hoping his wife might convince him to be even more generous. I'll have to make it a point to speak to her before she leaves tonight."

Sam assured Kelly that he would help her entertain the woman and her friends, and to help tactfully broach the subject of increased financial support. But that would come later, he told her; after he'd had some time alone with the woman he'd come to see.

They stepped out of the barn and walked to the edge of the driveway, stopping a moment to gaze up at the starry sky.

"It's lovely out here tonight," Kelly commented, giving Sam's hand a gentle squeeze. "So many stars."

"It is. Isn't it?" he agreed as his eyes swept the heavens with an awed appreciation for the brilliance and clarity of the celestial formations. "You people did a fantastic job in putting this whole thing together, and on such short notice. The refreshments look great. The decorations are super; and I especially like what you did with the sky—marvelous!"

Kelly laughed, but thanked Sam for the compliment.

The fire in the grassy center of the driveway circle was not needed for its warmth, but its aesthetic and sensory value contributed to the rustic characterization of the evening. People would come to stand and watch it for a while, and others, who had been there long enough, might soon drift away. Most always there was a small handful gathered around at any time.

Kelly steered both Sam and herself to within a few feet of the fire's heat, taking a position beside an older gentleman who looked to be in his early sixties. His hair was graying but he looked healthy and robust. A handsome, distinguished looking six-footer, the man had powerful arms that bulged the short sleeves of his white golf shirt.

He was aware that Kelly came beside him, but he continued to stare dreamily into the flames. Sam had only taken a casual notice of the fellow, and only because of the man's build—unusually solid for one of his age. He gave the man no further consideration but glanced at the faces of the few others around the fire, should he recognize anyone and have to exchange greetings.

Kelly, too, surveyed the members of the small group and dutifully smiled to each, saying a quick hello as her eyes travelled the circle. Then, surprisingly, she nudged for the man's attention beside her, asking, "How you doing?"

The man flinched from his mesmeric stare. "Hm? Oh. I'm okay," he answered, continuing to watch the flames while he replied. "A little tired, tonight. I had a hard week. Listen, though. You did a really terrific job of getting everything together here. The evening's a real success. I'm proud of you," he told her. He slipped an arm around her waist and hugged her to his side.

Sam bristled at this. A twinge of jealousy stirred within him and it did not auger well, especially when he saw her return the man's hug as she thanked him for the compliments. He hadn't known that Kelly was so familiar with any of the other Foundation members. He became even more discomforted when the fellow turned his head and gave her a quick kiss on the cheek, continuing to hold his arm around her waist.

Sam was now beginning to feel a little indignant at Kelly's actions though he was trying to remain calm, knowing there must be a perfectly reasonable explanation. To find it, he decided his best approach was to introduce himself to the man, then tactfully pursue what the fellow's sentiments were concerning the woman he, Sam, was in love with. He was about to initiate his plan when the man then sighed and raised his head, saying, "Listen to that." He swayed his upper-torso in rhythm to the music and hummed a few bars of the tune. "I wish your mother hadn't had to go to Boston this weekend. She'd have enjoyed this band."

"But, Dad," Kelly answered him, "Mom had planned the trip weeks ago. Aunt Paula would have never understood if she'd have canceled out. She'd have been grumpy and upset and would never have forgiven Mom. You know how she is. She's your sister-in-law. What Uncle Mat ever saw in her is beyond me."

Coiled in preparation of asserting himself to learn the meaning of such friendliness between the two, Sam now shrank back. He slowly unwound and his tension turned to simple nervousness as he breathed deep and prepared to meet Kelly's father. He began to perspire immediately, and as if on cue, Kelly put an arm around Sam's waist and drew him close and around to face the man.

"Dad. I want you to meet someone special. This is Sam. Sam Baker—the guy I've been telling you about all month. Sam, my father, Edward."

The man had turned to face Sam and now extended his hand. "Oh, yes. Kelly's told me so much about you. I'm glad to finally meet you."

"Same here," Sam replied, taking to the man instantly as he shook the fellow's hand.

"I hear you're a hell of a pool player," the man said, giving Sam thorough inspection with his eyes.

Sam laughed as he remembered the evening he and Kelly played at the night club. "She told you about that, huh?"

"M-hm. Kelly's told me quite a lot about you. She's rather fond of you."

"And I, of her, Mr. Gracie," Sam replied as the man finally released his hand. "She's a remarkable person. You're to be complimented on raising such a fine woman."

"Yeah," the man agreed. "She's much like her mother. But, please. Call me Ed. I don't much see the sense in formalities between us."

"Fine. I will then—Ed," Sam replied.

They talked for a while and at Ed's request Sam explained a little of what he did with computers. He tried to sound modest and irrelevant, but he knew Kelly had obviously bragged of his notoriety and accomplishments in that field. He learned that Ed was a mechanical engineer for a firm that designed and built bridges and highways, and that he liked to golf and shoot pool.

There was an immediate and remarkable air of congeniality between the two men. They spoke comfortably, interested more in listening to the other than in talking about themselves. They laughed freely when the occasion befitted and sympathized genuinely when that sentiment was warranted.

Ed mentioned he understood Sam had been in the service and had fought in Vietnam. He volunteered that he, too, had been in the army, having served as an officer in the Korean conflict.

Until this point, Kelly had listened with enthusiasm as the men spoke and became acquainted. She had had to volunteer little information about either man to help the conversation along, for it flowed so easily and steadily between them. She was delighted to have her two favorite men meet and respond to each other so affably. But when the subject turned to reminiscing over old army days, Kelly determined to change the course of discussion. "Excuse me, Father," she interrupted them. "It's awfully warm tonight and my throat is terribly parched. Would you be so kind as to get me a glass of punch? Sam might like one, also."

Sam immediately spoke up, saying, "Please. I'll go get it, Kelly."

But Ed saw the clever look on his daughter's face and knew well what that affected, sweet tone in her voice implied. He grinned wide, almost to the point of an open laugh. "No. No, Sam," he said to halt the younger man. "Her mother uses that same tone when she says one thing but means something else. What Kelly's saying is, 'get lost for a while, Dad. I want to be alone with Sam.' I'll go get you both something, honey," he said to the girl, "And I'll try to be real slow doing it."

Kelly leaned and kissed Ed's cheek. He showed his fatherly blush but held out his hand to Sam. "It was good meeting you, Sam. I'll catch up with you two later."

"Likewise," Sam replied, shaking Ed's hand. "The pleasure was mine."

While Sam watched Ed walk toward the barn, he was a little relieved their meeting had ended when it did. He had enjoyed their talk immensely—enough so that it had worried him to wonder when Ed might bring up the embarrassing subject of his daughter moving in to live with Sam. He wondered if Kelly had even spoken of this to Ed, and if so, whether Ed had purposely avoided the subject to spare them from an awkward moment upon their first meeting.

Sam turned back around and realized only now that everyone else had drifted away, leaving Kelly and him quite alone out by the fire. She slid her arm in his and gave it an affectionate squeeze while they watched the logs slowly melt to coals. After a long silence Kelly breathed deep and released a long, reflective sigh. "It's sure been an interesting summer."

Sam smiled thoughtfully as he continued to stare at the flames that licked upward. He nodded slowly several times in agreement and answered, "Yeah. It has been that, all right. Full of serendipity."

Kelly cocked her head in question as she looked at him. "Yeah? Are you thinking about the remains of the soldier up on the hill?"

"Not really. That wasn't a very pleasant experience for me. Actually, it was rather unsettling—as were a lot of other things we both shared. Most of them were more from out of the '*Twilight Zone*' than from the real world."

"Hmph! Tell me about it," she said. "That dream I had after I fainted up there was all too real. Sam, it was as if I woke up in a whole other world—a whole other life! But I was as at home there, in that life, every bit as much as I am in this one, now. You know how dreams have a certain 'way' about them— they feel different from being awake; you know when you're dreaming. That one sure didn't have it. I was alive, there, Sam."

They both fell silent again and watched the fire, letting their thoughts drift over the many mystical experiences they had encountered in the several weeks they had known each other. When Kelly finally spoke again she stammered, as if feeling a little foolish in even mentioning what she was about to say. "Sam. I'm, uh...I'm almost inclined to start believing what everybody else keeps seeming to imply."

"What's that?"

"That...that we're reincarnated lovers."

"Oh. That," Sam said in a tone that did not flatly reject the idea, but didn't accept it with any enthusiasm, either. "You've been talking to Carol, haven't you?"

"Maybe. Some," Kelly confessed. "But I've been doing some reading on it, too. Sam, everything falls into place if you go on that assumption. The weird dreams we both had, Varina Schiels giving us the sword and letter and saying all that about waiting all these years to deliver them. I mean, who could make up a story like that? Right? And we both thought as soon as we met each other that we'd met sometime before. I know it all sounds far-fetched. But, Sam, it is a conceivable theory."

Sam bent and picked up a small branch that was at his feet. As he snapped off small pieces and pitched them into the fire he mused over Kelly's ideas. "Oh-h, I don't know, Kelly. I suppose anything is possible. Maybe it could all be explained away rationally. 'Course, I'd love to hear any theories about the lockets being identical in every detail. That still has me stumped."

"See. That's exactly what I mean. There are too many weird coincidences."

Sam tossed the remainder of the stick into the flames and waited to watch it ignite. "It's kind of fun to play with the idea," he continued. "But it doesn't really matter. It makes no difference what may have happened in a past life. At least, that's what Varina keeps saying." Sam put his arm around her waist and hugged her close. He looked at her and said, "She's right, you know. All that matters is that we're here, together, now. You, Kelly—you're the serendipity. You're the pleasant discovery I stumbled on this summer."

Kelly turned and put her arms around Sam. She snuggled close, burying her face in his chest with a few tears of joy welling in her eyes. "Sam, I'm...I'm in love with you," she stammered. Her voice trembled and she felt her whole body become weak.

Sam became excited at those words. He believed she could probably hear his heart now palpitate wildly as he moved a hand to her chin and directed her to look at him. He gazed down into her eyes with a pleased, gentle smile on his strong face. "I'm glad you said that," he told her tenderly. "I've waited so long to hear that from a woman and know she really meant it. Kelly, I don't believe how quickly its happened, or the circumstances by which it did. But, Kelly, I'm in love with you, too. I know it isn't just some deep infatuation with your beauty, or that I'm intrigued by your character and talents. And it's more than being brought close to you because of the shared dangers we went through together. I love you, Kelly. I can feel it from deep in my soul."

Kelly threw her arms around his neck and they kissed long and passionately. It was some while before they slowly disentangled—and then only to catch their senses from having become breathless and light-headed. Kelly smiled and looked up at Sam, and he watched as she gave an ear to the music that filtered from the barn. Her smile grew broad across her face as she asked, "Do you hear it? Do you recognize that? It's Strauss. '*The Artists' Life Waltz*'."

Sam listened a moment, then he, too, smiled. "It's my favorite piece."

"Mine, too," Kelly replied.

Sam took her hand and held it in his own. They listened and waited as the introduction was played, then stepped off into a waltz. They danced with such grace, turning and twirling with so much elegance as their bodies moved in rhythm with the music—and with each other.

"Oh, Sam. You're a wonderful dancer!" Kelly exclaimed as her light, flowing steps were in perfect synchronization to his.

"Ah, but, Kelly," Sam replied. "It's my partner that draws out the best of my abilities. I feel like I'm floating on air in the arms of an angel."

Kelly glowed from the compliment. "Well. Thank you, kind sir. Such words of flattery may just bring forth further serendipities—quite desirable and very pleasurable, but not discovered by accident."

Sam knew to what she was alluding and he winked at her. "That's what I'm hoping for," he laughed. He danced her a few bars more but his beaming smile then faded and his face became more sober. "Kelly?" he asked, his steps still fluid but his face now showing a certain weightiness. "Did you have a chance to speak to your folks about moving in with me?"

Kelly averted her eyes and her flushing face gave proof of an obvious answer. "Sam, I...I meant to. And I will!" she quickly added. "It's...not an easy thing for me to bring up to them. They have certain ideals and—."

But Sam interrupted her. He breathed a deep sigh of relief and his smile returned as quickly as it had faded. "Thank God, Kelly. I'm relieved to hear that."

"Why, Sam? Have you changed your mind? Don't you want me to room with you this fall?"

"No. No, I don't," he answered her, tightening his arm even a bit more around her waist, and his hand squeezed hers more sincerely. "Not as my roommate. When I dig up these old bones in my next life, I want yours to be beside them—and the headstone to read 'husband and wife.' Kelly, I want you to be my wife. I want to marry you."

Kelly almost fainted with the thrill of his proposal. She closed her eyes to savor her contentment and felt Sam hold her close while awaiting her reply.

The re-enactment band played on, and it was a bold attempt on their part for so few and simple instruments to ever perform a piece written for a broader and more diverse assemblage. But, just as the Civil War veterans were unusually brave in facing the rigors of campaigns and battles, their regimental bands were equally so brave in their efforts to comfort the spirits of the men by playing those tunes the soldiers most wanted to hear around evening campfires.

To those who stood nearby, the music that was heard in the barn was perhaps a bit shallow and brassy. But it escaped through the gaps in the planking and rose up through the missing sheet tin on the roof. It filtered out the widespread doorway and drifted serenely on the warm and gentle breeze that had begun to blow.

The music that reached the ears of the lone couple dancing out on the lawn was an orchestra of harmonious sounds as it blended with their deep enchantment of each other. Their minds swirled in a blissful intoxication as their bodies swayed more sensuously. And through that aura of love that surrounded and engulfed them, they were but vaguely aware of hearing Kelly's reply. "Of course I'll marry you. I couldn't bear to lose you, again."

About the Author

Dennis Roumm was born and raised in the small college town of Indiana, Pennsylvania. After a stint in the Army, he returned to finish college and was offered a job to teach History and American Government in a wealthy suburban school.

He declined that job in favor of the challenge of growing the small, three generation family business into a larger company. Along the way, he bought a small farm to raise his children in the country, teaching them animal husbandry, gardening, and to be both self-sufficient and self-actualized individuals.

Dennis has studied various religions, occults, reincarnation and meditations. As a life-long student of the Civil War, he has led groups to various battlefields, and is a member of organizations working to preserve Civil War battlefields for future generations.

Dennis sold the profitable family business to pursue a quieter life of writing and gardening. He now lives with his wife in a quiet neighborhood in his hometown.

Printed in the USA
CPSIA information can be obtained
at www.ICGtesting.com
CBHW032013061124
16987CB00002B/8